HOMICIDE FOR THE HOLIDAYS

JANE RUBINO
KATHLEEN ANNE BARRETT
FRED HUNTER

WORLDWIDE.

TORONTO • NEW YORK • LONDON
AMSTERDAM • PARIS • SYDNEY • HAMBURG
STOCKHOLM • ATHENS • TOKYO • MILAN
MADRID • WARSAW • BUDAPEST • AUCKLAND

HOMICIDE FOR THE HOLIDAYS

A Worldwide Mystery/October 2000

ISBN 0-373-26362-7

Fruitcake Copyright © 1997 by Jane Rubino.
First published by Write Way Publishing, Inc. For information contact: Write Way Publishing, Inc., P.O. Box 441278, Aurora, CO 80044 U.S.A.

Milwaukee Winters Can Be Murder Copyright © 1996 by Kathleen Anne Barrett.
First published by Thomas Bouregy & Company, Inc. For information, contact: Thomas Bouregy & Company, Inc., 401 Lafayette Street, New York, NY 10003 U.S.A.

A Perfect Time for Murder Copyright © 2000 by Fred Hunter.

Printed in U.S.A.

CONTENTS

FRUITCAKE
by Jane Rubino

For Nancy

"Life is strange. Stories hardly make it more so."
—Eudora Welty, *Place in Fiction*

A young man with an earring dangling from his left ear, a

PROLOGUE

CAT SAW herself running.

The image excited her neurons, infiltrated the paralysis of sleep. Her nostrils flared with panicked inhalations, parted lips gasped for air, calves, thighs convulsed as the Cat in the dream fled, stumbled, recovered, ran.

Distant chimes were barely audible over the drumming of her pulse; the dream Cat homed on the sound, sprinted toward the bells, pain jabbing at her ribs, the thing pursuing her a breath behind. She stumbled. Her arms shot forward and she was falling...falling...

Bells. Cat Austen opened her eyes. She lay on her stomach, one hand beneath her right side, wedged against the bullet wound that was doggedly healing. Cat had lain down for a nap after her mother had picked up the kids and taken them to her place in Atlantic City. Later (or sooner—what time was it?) Victor would come and the four of them—she, Victor, Freddy and Ellice—would drive over to her mother's to celebrate their Thanksgiving four days late. Cat had been in the hospital on Thanksgiving, last Thursday. This was Sunday, November twenty...something. Cat assembled these facts in her consciousness as she willed a dead, numb arm to the phone, watched it flop toward the receiver. "'Lo?"

"Hey,'s this Cat? Cat Fortunati?" The voice was male, familiar.

"Austen," she yawned, rolling off the nagging wound.

"I think of you, I still think Alley Cat Fortunati."

Alley Cat. They had called her that since seventh grade; her brothers had started it. Later (and still) she was simply called Cat. "Who's this?"

"Danny. Danny Furina. How soon they forget."

Cat squinted, tried to call up a recent image of Danny Furina. Her sluggish brain produced a yearbook picture, the in-

scription "Betcha won't forget bio lab. Next frog you kiss,
think of me. Love ya, Danny" scribbled under a winking,
roguishly handsome face. One in every school, the boy from
whom all good Catholic girls were ordered to keep their distance and to whom all were impossibly attracted, determined
to reform.

Danny Furina had stuffed a mound of smoldering pot in the
heating duct that serviced the teachers' lounge. Danny had
released four hundred ninety-seven crickets at the spring con-
cert. (He'd rounded up an even five, but had tossed two to the
neighborhood cat just for kicks and stashed the third in Kevin
Keller's tuna sandwich.) Danny had donned a kilt, mono-
grammed sweater and wig, invaded the girls' gym locker,
nearly made it to the showers before he was caught. Danny
had beaten the odds and made graduation, swaggered up for
his diploma, made a beeline for the dour vice-principal, Sister
Mary Xavier, kissed her full on the lips.

The Furinas' yard had backed up to the Fortunatis' and
Danny had hung out with Freddy Fortunati, the youngest of
Cat's six older brothers, followed Freddy to community college, even into the State Police Academy, but washed out after
a few weeks, did some more college, some law enforcement,
some sales, drifted. He had come to Chris Austen's funeral
two and a half years before, but Cat had been numb with grief
and couldn't remember if they had spoken. Cat's widowed
mother still corresponded with Danny's widowed mother who
had moved, or fled, to Florida. From her, they had heard that
Young Danny (at thirty-eight, he was still "Young Danny")
was a private investigator now, had put out his shingle somewhere in Atlantic City.

"How are you, Danny?" Cat warily contemplated motives
for the call. Maybe he'd heard about Tom Hopper's arrest,
how she'd been shot. Maybe he'd heard that *CopWatch* had
latched onto the Hopper/Dudek story, that they were feeling
out the principals and he wanted in on the fun.

"I'm okay. Look, Freddy around? I called your mom's to
get his number, she said he was over your place."

"Hmmm." Cat saw the square of paper propped against the

phone: Freddy and I went out for a walk in Ellice's elegant script. "He went out with his"—was it any of Danny Furina's business?—"girlfriend."

"He's got a girl?"

"Yes."

"It wouldn't be—I mean—you wouldn't happen to know if he's running with Fawn Caprio, would you?"

Irritation cut through the fog. "What kind of question is that?" Cat demanded. "Why would Freddy have anything to do with *her* after the way she dumped him?"

"Rumor is the Sterling marriage is worse off than Blaine Sterling's balance sheet, thought maybe she'd be on the prowl for a shoulder to cry on, bed to lie on, you know what I mean?"

"I know that Freddy's shoulder isn't on loan to Fawn Sterling. He hasn't seen her since she dumped him for Sterling and that was what? Eight years ago? Try another bed, she'll turn up." *Catty.* "Why are you asking?"

"Oh, no big deal. Don't bug Freddy about it. So's he gonna tie the knot this time?"

"You'd have to ask Freddy that," Cat hedged.

"None of my business, right? Aw well, see you around, Alley Cat." He hung up.

Cat doubted it, doubted in fact that the conversation had even taken place, so swiftly did she relinquish consciousness once more. An hour later, Ellice was gently tapping her shoulder, and Cat woke with a vague sensation that there was something she ought to tell Freddy, couldn't remember what it was and decided, finally, that it really didn't matter.

ONE

"CHRISTMAS, everything goes nuts."

Victor recalled how Stan Rice had muttered the phrase, laughing, as he headed out to execute the warrant on Lowell

Jeffries. Now Victor echoed the sentiment as he drove stop-and-go along Atlantic Avenue, muttered, "Christmas" wearily as he surveyed the shabby tinsel garlands slung across the thoroughfare's four lanes.

And what was this one, his fortieth? No, forty-first. Forty-one Christmases, forty-one buoys marking the course changes in his life: the subdued family Christmases followed by the Three Kings' Day festivities which Victor's parents had observed even after moving to Atlantic City from San Juan; the *Yanqui* Christmases his sisters had coaxed out of their mother after their father's death; the married Christmases, Marisol locking herself in their tiny bedroom to wrap presents, fretting over the sparseness of the tree; and the Christmases after her death when December twenty-fifth had been just another day. Very lately, Victor had begun to consider the prospect of Christmases with Cat. And Jane and Mats. And that family of hers.

Victor was Lieutenant Victor Cardenas, homicide investigator assigned to the Atlantic County prosecutor's office, Major Crimes Bureau. A wretched day had capped a miserable week, and here he was late for his rendezvous with Cat. Victor grimaced at the exhaust streaming from a caravan of casino tour buses making a lumbering exodus to Philly or North Jersey, let his gaze slide past the hodgepodge of enterprises along the route: social service agencies, uninviting storefronts, glaring newsstands, prim florists, grimy pawnshops, palm readers, fast food, elephantine churches of dirty stone, nightclubs that catered to twenty-somethings who were short on cash and had nothing to go home to. Open space, some converted to parking lots, some left choked with scrub and litter, awaiting their shot at the city's promised Renaissance. On the side streets, simple sentences—"Cash For Gold," "We Take Personal Checks"—shrank to monosyllables: "Bar," "Food," "Rooms." Inland, these narrow passages slunk into darkness; a block east, the casino entrances on Pacific Avenue threw down harsh and unwelcome illumination on the one-way streets, parking lots where ten-and eleven-year-olds on inlines muled the perennial favorite, meth, or the comeback kid, heroin. One of them shot into an intersection where Victor's Jag idled impatiently at a red light, rapped on the window. Victor looked at the skinny kid, shivering in his threadbare sweats, saw in the lively dark eyes, the brown complexion, himself at eleven and thought *There but for the grace of God and my parents,* and shoved his shield against the glass. *"Vayate,"* he mouthed and the kid sailed off. *"Madre de Dios,"* Victor muttered. Christmas.

New York Avenue, Tennessee Avenue, South Carolina. Heading toward the Inlet, enterprise thinned out and the expanses of rubble-strewn acreage where something or other was to be erected opened up the sight lines and Victor could see, ahead and to the right, the peaked blue roof of Resorts, the crimson scimitar lettering of the Taj, the green and gold wings of the debutante: the Sterling Phoenix. Cat had said Freddy would drop her there for her interview with Sterling's administrative assistant, then hang out at Resorts while Ellice took a qualifying test for *Jeopardy!* After that, the four of them would go somewhere for a drink, maybe run over to the Showboat to hear some Dixieland.

"I thought when you turned in the Dudek story, you were going to take a break," Victor had reminded Cat. "You're supposed to be taking it easy, remember?"

"It's just a fluff piece," Cat had assured him. "Atlantic City's Three Hundred."

"Three hundred what?"

"You know, the social register."

"I didn't know. We have one?"

"Humble police lieutenants hardly qualify," Cat had replied, archly. "Neither do struggling freelancers, for that matter. I think Carlo and Annie made the cut when he was Chief. Ritchie wants a piece on the major shore parties and the people behind them, and I needed the money."

Victor frowned. Freddy told him once that Cat had considered selling her house about a year after Chris died. He wondered if the writing, supplemented by Chris Austen's benefits, was enough to get by on. "And what are the major shore parties?"

"That restaurant thing in March and the college benefit in the spring and any Night in Venice party on a private deck, the Heart Fund Ball and the Gambol. This year, the Phoenix is hosting that one, and Blaine Sterling's secretary—excuse me, administrative assistant—has condescended to give me some of her valuable time."

"What about an audience with King Midas?"

"No way, not even if he were in town. Anyway, she's the Gambol's engineer."

"Along with Sterling's wife."

"I wouldn't know."

Victor had detected a coolness in her reply.

"Anyway, we're all to meet inside the Boardwalk entrance of Resorts. Around eight?"

"I don't like that. I don't want you walking up the boards alone at night."

"I've done it plenty of times. You worry too much. I heard about what happened today. How's Stan?"

"Pretty low. He blames himself."

"And how are you?"

"I've been better."

"Well, maybe I can take your mind off today. Something amusing came up. At least, I think it's amusing. I haven't made up my mind about it yet."

"All right. Resorts at eight, prepared to be amused. I can do that. But you take care. I don't like you going back to work before you're completely recovered and I definitely don't like your running around at night alone."

"Victor," Cat had replied, gently, "it's Christmas. The season of peace and good will. What on earth could happen?"

AND VICTOR WONDERED what, indeed, in these final afternoon hours, could happen that would surpass the events of a chaotic week. An unemployed mechanic had tried to piggyback his cable and the live-in companion found him in the backyard, self-barbecued; a nineteen-year-old DUI broke his neck running his four wheel drive through—entirely through—the liquor store that had refused him service; a fisherman had hooked a decomposing corpse in the Absecon Channel, female, young, and Adane began a methodical review of the missing persons files; the Margate department sent over a sheet on some woman who claimed she had been attacked in a friend's vacant home, even insisted she had killed the attacker; the cops checked it out and found a baffled owner at home and no corpse. And it had been confirmed that Lowell Jeffries had been sighted in the North Maryland Avenue apartment of a young waitress who was a distant relation and/or former lover.

Jeffries had been sought for the bludgeoning of Alameda "Granma Al" Thurman, whose remains had been discovered three days after the Dudek shooting. Three days after I met Cat, Victor reflected afterward, realizing that the encounter had become a line of demarcation, his recent life suddenly defined as "before Cat" and "since Cat." Pulling Sergeant Rice off Dudek, putting him on the Thurman killing had been a penance exacted for Stan's fumble on the disk jockey's murder. Let him work on something that had gone cold, see to it he hung in until he produced, teach him the virtue of resolve. Stan hung in, stuck to the investigation with an enthusiasm that frankly surprised Victor. But then, Stan had a tender spot for people as gentle and helpless as Mrs. Thurman had been, as her lady friends were. And this dear Stanley Rice, with his easy courtesy, his dimpled charm, captivated the victim's frail cronies.

Stan knew that in these ladies' rambling anecdotes lay vital insights to both the victim and the suspect for anyone with the patience to hear them out. They were of a gentle class who had clung to childhood homes, in neighborhoods eroded by a flood tide of casino development. They took Stan into their kitchens and filled him with cocoa and homemade cookies, told him who was whose cousin and who had married whom, and whose kids got in trouble with the law, and whose had moved on, and sent him back to his desk laden with notes and observations and tins of homemade shortbread (real butter) labeled "For Lieutenant Stanley Rice." Stan would hunker down behind his notebooks and phone and cookies and mutter,

"I don't finger Jeffries soon, I won't get past my next physical. I put on five pounds already!" But the adulation tickled him, as did the promotion.

The bureaus in the Northfield complex ridiculed Stan's proposed stakeout of the Royce girl's apartment because only in dumb movies did the suspect return to the scene. Wagers floated, odds heavily against Rice; money changed hands covertly. In the end, those who had backed Rice collected.

Stan had reasoned that for Jeffries, who had flown the coop possessing no more than six years of public school education and the thirty-seven dollars and ninety-one cents for which he had dispatched Mrs. Thurman, the allure of a familiar nest would become irresistible.

As soon as the kids living in the complex got off to school, Stan, a couple detectives from the Fugitive Apprehension Unit and a ten-man TAC team from the Atlantic City force began to methodically evacuate the adjacent properties and secure the area. Jeffries, however, had made some use of his limited schooling, for he'd ID'd the drunk slumped against the curb, the truants criss-crossing the paved walkway on inlines, the suit pacing anxiously beside his stalled Volvo and the mechanic trying to jump start it. When a florist approached the Royce girl's apartment with an oblong box under his arm, Jeffries fired a couple rounds through the window and informed the cops they should've gone with Domino's, nobody on North Maryland got money for flowers, they were lousy actors and if they wanted to be like that, he would just take his companion hostage.

The officers, never disposed to exercise restraint in the matter of expletives, expressed their dismay with this turn of events in creative, if anatomically inaccurate, scatology. Two hours to secure the area, and now they had to hold off while some hostage mediator called up Jeffries and tried to make friends.

But Jeffries didn't want friends, he wanted safe passage and some cash, and he wanted it in two hours or he'd shoot the hostage. Then he sat back and told the girl—Martita Royce was her name—to fix him something to eat. Martita phoned her boss at the coffee shop and informed him she would probably be late for work as she was being held hostage at gunpoint, and she knew Earlene was bummed because her man split but would Jim ask anyway if Earlene would trade shifts, and maybe Earlene should even count on working a double if Lowell flipped out. Also, Jim was to tell Earlene to be glad Al took off because men were nothing but a pain in the you-know-where. Then she hung up and fried some eggs and sausages for Jeffries and grabbed the remote because as long as she wasn't going anywhere she might as well catch up on her stories and a couple of the talks.

Outside, the cops began to sweat. Another hour or so and the kindergarten bus would drop off the morning kids. A couple reporters had sniffed out the scene. Stan put in a nervous call to Victor, who dropped the year-end performance evaluations he'd been postponing and headed into Atlantic City, but too late. Because, no sooner had Stan shut off the cellular than a hysterical "NooOOO!" emerged from the Royce girl's apartment, cut off on the high end by a gunshot.

Stan gave the green light and five men took the front while Stan circled around back with a couple rookies, tackled Jeffries as he wriggled through the kitchen window, disarmed him and began to recite Miranda, got messed up halfway through and was set right by the offender himself. "No, Jack, now you s'posed to say do I got a lawyer, 'cause I don't got one, I can get one free from the courts. Ain't you never seen *CopWatch*, Jack?"

Stan cuffed Jeffries and handed him over to a pair of rookies, entered the apartment, radioing for the medics, muttering, "I'm homicide, I'm the primary, I'm homicide, I'm the primary." To his profound relief, Miss Royce was unharmed, though furious. She stood sobbing, pointing toward her new Sony twenty-seven-inch with the scratched-out serial number, shrieking, "He shot Geraldo! He shot my man, Geraldo!"

Stan withdrew; the rookies flanking Jeffries were twenty paces ahead of him, moving toward the black-and-white parked at the curb, and Stan gave the thumbs-up to the team remaining on the sidewalk. He blamed himself for what happened next, for the gesture signaled a release of tension, and with it, diminished awareness.

Because Jeffries was double-jointed. Reconfiguring limbs, extremities, digits was his only noteworthy accomplishment, one which had been the source of considerable entertainment to his fellow classmates in those six years of public education. In nine seconds—though Stan's mind would forever replay the moment in slow motion—Jeffries disengaged shoulders from sockets, whipped his cuffed hands from aft to fore, shouldered aside the first rookie, yanked the weapon from the holster of the second, fired, fired again.

The first bullet penetrated the clavicle of Officer MacBride, the second shattered an upper story window in a unit across the walkway from the Royce apartment. Stan drew as Jeffries readied to fire a third round, fired and hit Jeffries' right forearm, sending the weapon into a flat spin on the pavement. Jeffries was seized by the Fugitive Unit guys while Rice ran for the cop who had been hit, and that's when he heard the wail.

At first, he thought it was a siren, but the wail was human, an inarticulate keening that emerged from the doorway of the opposite apartment. Stan's gaze dropped to the doorway as the door creaked open; a young woman staggered across the threshold, her white caftan oozing red at the breast, her arms outstretched, the full sleeves spread like angel's wings.

Stan leaped, caught her as she fell to the pavement, pressed his palm to the wound that seemed too small to be discharging so much blood, worked the CPR as he felt the pulsing beneath his hands grow languid, cease. "No God, no God, no God, no God..."

The paramedics had to pry the dying woman out of his grasp, left him slumped on the curb while they tended to her, to the injured rookie.

Victor arrived then, pushed past the throng of onlookers, got to Stan, but not before a press photographer had ducked under the police tape and snapped a shot of Stan slumped in front of the apartment step, his clothes soaked in the woman's blood, his face a mask of despair.

One of the detectives helped Victor shove Stan into the car before the *NewsLine90* cameras could move in for the *coup de grâce*. Victor drove him over to Northfield, got the county DA on the phone.

An hour later, Jeffries, properly Mirandized and in the presence of his court-appointed attorney, confessed to the Thurman killing.

"Yeah, well, it won't bring'er back, will it, Lieutenant?" Stan muttered.

"It wasn't your fault, Sergeant."

"We rang the bell, knocked, she didn't come to the door, we thought she was working. One of the neighbors said she was at work."

Victor hesitated. "She called in. Her son was sick."

Stan looked up, dazed. "There was a kid in the house?"

"It wasn't your fault, Stan."

Stan rose, ran his fingers through his graying curls. "What was she, twenty-six? Twenty-seven?" He tugged his nine millimeter from his waistband, dropped it on Victor's desk, did the same with his shield. "Give my regards to IA. Tell'em if they wanna chat, they can find me at Bud an' Lou's."

"I'll contact IA. And Adane will take you home."

Serene, no-nonsense Jean Adane had been the imperturbable object of Stan's levity from the day she had joined the bureau. Some time later, he would recall as opportunity blown, the way she had taken him home, helped him change his bloody clothes, washed his hands and face, made him a cup of tea, and then took the phone off the hook and put him to bed.

At the bureau, there was no such thing as off the hook. Victor told the switchboard he'd talk to the DA, Internal Affairs, Mrs. Austen, if she called, no one else. When he left his office, he had to break from two reporters who were lurking in the parking area. He growled a terse, "No comment," and locked himself in his car, took off, snapping on the radio as he headed into Atlantic City.

"...where a hostage situation turned to tragedy this afternoon when a policeman lost control of a murder suspect who grabbed his weapon and introvertedly shot a woman as he was being led away in handcuffs during a stakeout which had been set up at the scene before any of this took place.''

Victor smacked off the button, wondered if Cat was listening to that, imagined the wicked spark the reporter's mangled syntax would ignite, a spark that would mellow into grave compassion as she contemplated Stan's plight. "Cat." He realized that he had whispered her name aloud. He accelerated, as if speed would distance him from this wretched day. "Cat."

At least the worst that could happen had happened, right? Cat had said they were entering the season of peace and good will, right?

Christmas, everything goes nuts.

TWO

ILL FARES the land, to hastening ills a prey, Where wealth accumulates, and men decay.

The lines rambled through Cat Austen's consciousness as she waited for Mrs. Carlton Amis to conclude her eleventh phone call in fifteen minutes. Mrs. Carlton Amis—she had not offered a first name and it was "Mrs. Carlton Amis" on the office door, the plaque on the desk, the creamy stationery with the Phoenix crest—was Cat's sixth socialite in five days; sixth and last, Cat resolved inwardly. The seashore party circuit and who was what and what was hot wasn't Cat's idea of an assignment, not even in her latest incarnation as *South Jersey* magazine's "entertainment girl." But Ritchie Landis wanted some glitz to counteract the gravity of the Dudek piece and the season made Cat acutely aware that except for the Dudek story (for which she had yet to be paid) and a couple of twenty-dollar film blurbs, nothing had come her way to fortify an eroding budget.

Cat checked her watch: 7:55 p.m. She had promised to meet Freddy and Ellice by eight, had set aside the forty-five minutes Mrs. Amis had allotted, arrived fifteen minutes early and was promptly handed over to an oppressively cheerful "hospitality girl" and sent off on the Gambol tour: the shadowy, street-level dressing rooms where Cat was shown racks of Santa costumes, angel costumes, elf costumes rented for the Gambol's serving staff; the third floor kitchens, where Cat was presented with a copy of the Gambol's menu (cucumber vichyssoise with star anise, passion fruit sorbet, scallops of veal with hazelnut sauce and violets (!), puree of butternut squash, couscous with currants and pignoli, hearts of palm with strawberry vinaigrette, white chocolate/coconut sorbet, dessert medley with international coffee bar); the fourth floor storage area where the centerpieces—artwork to be offered for sale, rather than the traditional floral arrangements—were being tagged with prices that Cat could not believe were accurate. Cat scribbled. Every time the perky hospitality girl inquired, "Is there anything more I can tell you, Mrs. Austen?," Cat scribbled. When she discovered that the duration of the pit stops was in an inverse proportion to the extent of her notetaking, Cat scribbled so relentlessly that the girl cut short the excursion and deposited her once again in Mrs. Amis' office.

Mrs. Amis asked, "And how did you find your tour, Mrs. Austen?"

Cat opened her mouth to lie, when the phone rang again.

Cat suppressed an impatient sigh and turned her gaze to the window. The Phoenix had risen on an oblong stretch that extended in length from the Boardwalk to Oriental Avenue, in width from New Jersey to New Bedford, a few blocks before the island swung into the Inlet and headed bayward. The neon glow from the *porte cochere* adjacent to the Boardwalk illuminated the strand of boarded-up row houses slung between two trash-infested lots. In the patch across from the *porte cochere* were a few hunks of rusting equipment that suggested it had been, perhaps was, a playground. The other lot, at the intersection of New Bedford and Oriental was the site of quick, occasionally lethal drug transactions; catty-corner was a decrepit structure, coffee shop on the street and a couple apartments above. Cat recalled something about that building, that the owner had refused a buyout offer from Sterling, who wanted to raze the structure in order to expand his parking facilities. A drug exchange, a greasy spoon and the Sterling Phoenix, Cat ruminated. What a hotbed of enterprise the intersection of Oriental and New Bedford had become.

Princes or lords may flourish or may fade. A breath can make them...

The Phoenix, the portrait of Blaine Sterling in the fifth floor reception area, had touched off the verse in Cat's mind. Blaine G. Sterling. It had been twenty-five years since he had acquired (seized, some had whispered, in a transaction that would not bear close scrutiny) the handful of well-placed hotels owned by his father, had embarked on an aggressive course of renovation, expansion and self-promotion. The Sterling hotels became Sterling Resort Hotels, Inc., operated on the premise that ostentation was elegance, that gaud and refinement were synonyms. Soon, it was Sterling this and Sterling that; the name became an adjective, a verb, a gerund, strayed from the financial pages to LifeStyle and Entertainment, from *Fortune* to *People*. Fame addicted him; he came to have contempt for the anonymity his father had coveted, for accomplishment without celebrity. Soon, cultivating the latter became more absorbing than tending to the former. Blaine Sterling showed up on the talks and talked about everything except business; Blaine Sterling appeared on a soap, doing a walk-on in a party scene; Blaine Sterling turned out a novel (with a ghostwriter) called *King Midas,* a fictionalized bio/fable with a triumphant finale, which had been optioned by Hollywood, then stalled in pre-production.

Favor faltered; the limelight shifted to Sterling's second wife, Fawn Caprio-Sterling. As an aspiring designer, she had snagged the attention and pocketbooks of buyers who could spare five, six figures for an evening dress. CapriOH! she called her budding enterprise. Sterling staked her, made jokes about his excursion into the rag trade, but he wasn't laughing when financial pages dropped him altogether and named Fawn one of "America's Top Five Hundred Entrepreneurs." Some interpreted his descent upon Atlantic City as retaliation for the snub and whispered how appropriate it was that he had chosen to revive an abandoned wreck, wondered how the cash had been raised. The city did not concern itself with that last; how Sterling had come up with the bonds, how he would manage the interest were irrelevant. The city was only too happy to have someone take over the abandoned Poseidon project (a half-completed fiasco that had become a decaying haven for vagrants), to have the project completed, producing.

Sterling expected the project to renew his fading luster, but the local media was not as amiable as he had hoped. The grueling construction schedule he had imposed to make a Memorial Day opening, the disputes with contractors, the speculation whether he would be able to make the first interest payment on the bonds if the casino was not operating by Memorial Day, took their toll on the Sterling persona. His contempt for the general public, camouflaged previously by his carefully orchestrated public appearances, began to emerge. He shunned them now, or appeared among a quartet of bodyguards, sulked openly at the Phoenix ribbon-cutting (in mid-June) when his wife was the one the public turned out to see, the one the photographers angled for.

Cat's musing on this history would have eventually led to its connection with her own family had not Mrs. Amis hung up and asked again "Now where were we?" She detected the object of Cat's glance, rose and shut the drapes, cutting off the view of New Bedford. Cat observed the decisive athleticism in her movement, noticed the absence of padding in the imposing shoulders of the silk shirtwaist. Mrs. Amis had a dark, artfully frosted coif and no-nonsense eyes, cobalt blue. There was something in her aspect that did not conform to the socialite profile, a current of nervous ambition that the others had lacked. Cat wondered if the Sterling salary paid for the Chanel suit, the Italian pumps, the rope of luminescent pearls knotted at the breast, or if they were owed to Mr. Carlton Amis. Cat suspected the latter.

Mrs. Amis resettled behind her desk, adjusting the angle of a framed photograph as she sat. Cat saw that it was a shot of Mr. and Mrs. Amis, tuxed and gowned, arm in arm; she pushed a strand of hair behind her ear, fumbled with her notebook. "Uh, let me see. Two hundred mailings went out for this year's Holiday Gambol."

"Correct."

"And the recipients can get up to four tickets."

"May invite a maximum of three additional guests. And we prefer 'invitations' to 'tickets.'"

"And fifty ti—invitations held back for the high rollers."

"Offered to our preferred clientele, yes."

"Traditionally, the casino host has had the Gambol committee hold back a few invitations for their high ro—clientele, and the rest have been made available to the general public. The way they do with the Restaurant Gala. The Phoenix is the first to restrict the guest list to what has been called the Three Hundred."

The cobalt eyes darkened. "I'm not sure I'm familiar with the term."

Entertainment girl. Cat heard the epithet in the woman's tone; it nettled her. "Actually the term was coined by Bob Sonnenfeld when he was a freelancer. I believe he works for the Phoenix public relations department now."

"Is this 'woman of the masses' angle an appropriate slant for your story, Mrs. Austen? And a bit hypocritical, too. I believe the Fortunatis are no strangers to the Three Hundred."

So she was familiar with the term. And she had done her homework, too. There had been a time when Fortunati's had been *the* place to dine in Atlantic City and the Fortunatis had been one of the first families. But the restaurant was gone, the site was part of a casino parking lot. Cat's oldest brother, Carlo, who had been named New Jersey's Top Cop for the five consecutive years before his retirement, remained one of the Three Hundred, though well into the bottom third, and only there because no one had had the temerity to depose him. "I guess I'm the black sheep," Cat replied.

"Would you like an invitation, Mrs. Austen?"

"I think they're a bit beyond *South Jersey*'s expense account. I wouldn't know anyone there."

"Nonsense. Didn't you say we were neighbors?"

It had been Cat's clumsy icebreaker. The truth was the

Amises Ocean City waterfront, with its one-hundred-twenty feet overlooking the merger of inlet with the Atlantic was nine blocks and light years from the assemblage of three-story upgrades on Morningside Drive.

"Actually, now that I think of it, 'Austen' sounds familiar. Where have I seen you?"

Woolworth's. Cat pressed her lips together, tried to recall if her picture, her name, had been in the papers after the Dudek business.

Mrs. Amis settled back in her chair. "Mrs. Austen, last year the Gambol was attended by four hundred eighty people out of an anticipated eight hundred. That's poor marketing. Poor fundraising, too, because the proceeds go to the medical center. Mr. Sterling would like that donation to come in at a quarter of a million, which means the Gambol committee must direct its efforts to attracting the five-hundred-dollar-a-plate patron."

Now I know I'm not on the list, Cat decided. "And of course, there's the profit to the Phoenix."

"I beg your pardon?"

"Well, in the past the host casino has reported that at least half the guests take a room or a suite for the night of the Gambol. No one wants to trek down from Philly or wherever in full regalia and then trek back at two a.m. The Phoenix Hotel occupancy has yet to meet the projections and another couple hundred guests would give the next quarterly report a boost, wouldn't they? And then, the committee wasn't exactly given a break on the Phoenix's facilities. The ballroom and the"—Cat shuffled through her notes—"the mezzanine? The shopping mezzanine? The Phoenix is charging for the use of public space?" Before Mrs. Amis could respond, Cat pressed on. "I'm only asking because the former hosts usually donated the ballrooms and the service. Of course, they probably got some kind of tax break."

"What makes you think the Phoenix isn't doing likewise?" Mrs. Amis asked.

Entertainment girl. "Mrs. Micki Cortez—she's on the raffle committee, I spoke with her yesterday—showed me the in-

voices. And I thought perhaps revenue was an additional in-
centive for the Phoenix to take on the Gambol only six months
after its opening, since the quarterly earnings will be posted
next month and, as I recall, the first quarter wasn't quite up
to"—*Don't say it, don't say it, don't say it*—"the Sterling
standard."

And that did it.

Mrs. Amis flicked a silken cuff, glanced at the jeweled
watch on her left wrist. Cat noticed the darkened area beneath
the band. A bruise, or just a shadow? "For the party, the
mezzanine is going to be closed to the public and used for the
cocktail reception, which will make an easy transition to the
Phoenix Pavilion Ballroom, which is on the mezzanine level.
Why don't I walk you down there and run you through our
plans before you leave? I'm sure that's more in line with the
focus of your story anyway, isn't it?" She snatched her jacket
from the back of her chair, strode to the door and threw it
open.

Cat rose. "Actually, I have a few more—"

"We can take them on the way down."

Cat followed her through the outer office, past computer
terminals shrouded in plastic, past the reception area where
the trademark Phoenix was worked into the carpet, into the
gilt-edged china beside the coffee urn, into the corners of the
white linen napkins, mentally reciting *mea culpas* along the
route. *You can't blow something as trifling as Party of the
Year, Entertainment Girl,* Cat chided herself. Another slip
could cost Mats those Swordfighting Samurai Sea Serpents
and the Citadel of the Deep with its four catapults and retract-
able drawbridges.

A green-jacketed security guard stood in the corridor outside the Sterling business suite. For a moment, Cat thought he
was waiting for Sterling himself, noticed, with some surprise,
that he followed at a discreet distance as Mrs. Amis walked
toward the elevators. The corridor was flanked on both sides
by glass doors with gold lettering: Accounting, Hotel Operations, Personnel, Human Resources, Legal Affairs, Promo-
tions/Public Relations, DGE (Division of Gaming Enforce-

ment). At the elevators, the corridor split, right toward Security, left toward the exit to the executive level of the parking garage.

Cat noted that the elevator light signaled a descent from above; it stopped on five. The door opened and a man stepped out, started at the sight of Mrs. Amis and Cat. "I thought you'd gone," he said to the former. "I was just dropping off some papers for Blaine."

"I don't expect him to arrive for another hour or so. Shall I unlock his office?"

"No, I just left them upstairs."

"With Fawn?"

The man shrugged. "Consolación said she'd just gone out."

The exchange was trivial enough. Cat wondered why it gave her a chill.

"Mrs. Austen, my husband, Carlton Amis."

Cat had recognized him, of course. Amis, lured by Sterling from a prosperous law firm, had steered the Phoenix project through a swift, unchallenged licensure. It had been a temporary alliance, but now there was talk that Amis wouldn't return to his firm, had locked in the presidency of the Sterling Phoenix. Too handsome for his own good, that's how Cat's mother would have put it; Amis was tall and athletic, with burnished gold hair, eyes that matched his sapphire cuff links, a square jaw marred somewhat by a mouth that was small and soft, a child's mouth, tending toward petulance. He didn't release Cat's hand after he shook it and Cat was forced to wriggle it free.

"Mrs. Austen is doing a little story on the Gambol for … oh dear…"

"*South Jersey* magazine," Cat offered.

"We were going down to the mezzanine. Come along?"

"I need a few things off my desk. You go ahead."

"I'll come back and we can ride home together," Mrs. Amis said.

"Don't you have your car here?"

"I'll leave it."

Amis shrugged. "Nice to have met you, Mrs. Austen."

Did he *wink?* Cat stepped into the elevator beside Mrs.
Amis; the security guard followed. Did Sterling assign body-
guards to all of his aides? Cat wondered. Perhaps because Mrs.
Amis was a woman, working alone late into the night. Though,
Cat decided, she looked well able to take care of herself.

The elevator deposited them on the mezzanine level. Cat
had bypassed it on her way up and so was getting her first
glance of the shopping area, The Sterling Way.

The floor was configured as a long-armed U, The Sterling
Way at the base, two corridors lined with conference rooms
projecting toward the oceanfront ballrooms. The Sterling Way
had a wide ellipse cut into the center of the floor which created
a balcony effect overlooking the slot area twenty-five feet below. The shops lined the walls on both sides. Sterling had
aimed for Madison Avenue/Rodeo Drive ambience, but the
vendors he had initially approached did not choose to share
space with the purveyors of rhinestone-studded sweats, Phoenix logo T-shirts, costume jewelry, tacky Hollywood memo-
rabilia and souvenir photographs that were the standard casino
hotel merchandise. Only when Fawn Sterling agreed to open
a CapriOH! showroom in the mezzanine did more elite enterprises fall into line.

The floor of Sterling Way was carpeted in some intricate
pattern, writhing phoenixes rising from billows of ash green
on a darker green bordered in gold. Between the shops, the
rug climbed halfway up the wall and gave out; the phoenix
motif transferred to pale gold brocade that took over to the
ceiling. A railing of polished brass bordered the ellipse cut
into the center of the floor; a chandelier was suspended over
the aperture, not quite low enough to block the patrician clientele from the sight of the plebeian slot addicts below. Few
enough of both, Cat observed; she estimated only one slot
machine in five was occupied, and no more than two or three
people trolled Sterling Way. Mrs. Amis was explaining the
Gambol theme, Sterling Victorian. ''Green and gold awn-
ings…wrought iron street lamps…carolers…hors d'oeuvres
served on pushcarts…faux snow…''

Cat couldn't quite believe she had heard that last, but didn't

have the nerve to ask Mrs. Sterling to repeat it. She glanced
in the window of CapriOH!; headless mannequins, one in red
beaded silk, one in emerald green taffeta, vamped each other.
There was a framed cover from a New York magazine of a
few years back: "Look Who's Haute!" above Fawn Caprio
Sterling in white satin and rubies. Cat saw how aptly the photographer had caught the restlessness in the gray eyes, the
rapacity that her brother Freddy had mistaken for ardor.

Mrs. Amis was reciting the party line: "Mr. Sterling is confident that this year's Gambol will be an unforgettable occasion..." Cat wrote dutifully, shielding her notepad from Mrs.
Amis as she scribbled, How true the reverse of a popular
maxim may be. Less may be more, but more can be infinitely
less, an observation never more apparent than when one is
strolling along Sterling Way in the Sterling Phoenix Hotel and
Casino. Not bad, Cat thought; said, "Mr. Landis wanted to
know if you and Micki Cortez and Patsy Raab and Dilly Fein-
gold and Bibi Detweiler and Fawn Sterling would be available
for a group photograph."

"I couldn't answer for Fawn. You'd have to check her
schedule with her assistant, and that would be...let me see,
she just picked up another one, Finch. Ronnie or Donnie. Call
Mr. Sterling's press office, ask Ed Bennett if he can set up a
shoot." She offered her hand to Cat. This time Cat saw that
the wrist was indeed bruised. "You can find your way out,
I'm sure. I have to get back to Carl." She nodded, turned
away, began to stride toward the elevators, the silent bodyguard at her heel. Abruptly, she turned. "Austen...I've got it.
Weren't you in some sort of mishap not too long ago?"

Cat hesitated. "Last month. Someone got into my house...a
gun went off."

The blue eyes surveyed her for a moment, not unkindly.
"You survived it, I see."

"Yes, I survived it."

"Well, that's all that counts, isn't it? That and making sure
it doesn't happen again."

OF COURSE, the exchange threw her. Cat had been telling herself she was coping with the aftermath, but often, in that half

second of consciousness before sleep, the horror would sweep over her. *I could have died. What would have happened to Jane and Mats if I died?*

She ambled along the dizzying corridor, shaking off the chill that the memory invariably produced. She hugged the wall a bit, fearing the crazy optic of knotted phoenixes and lights and gleaming brass would blind her, send her staggering over the railing, pitching into the slot players below. It took Cat a few minutes to realize that she might be going in the wrong direction, wasn't sure. Casinos were designed to disorient, encase and siphon into the gaming area. Cat checked her watch: 8:30! She should have met Freddy and Ellice a half hour ago. She sighted a familiar green blazer, asked the guard for directions to the nearest exit. After about a hundred yards she realized that she was headed for the parking garage on the Oriental Avenue side of the building, not toward the Boardwalk exit. Obviously, the guard had assumed she meant to go to her car. Now she would have to find her way through the mezzanine to the Boardwalk and get down to the street level or take the garage elevator to the sidewalk and make the long trek down New Jersey (bad) or New Bedford (worse) to the Boardwalk ramp.

Cat mentally compared the dismal tramp down New Jersey or New Bedford with the optical nightmare of Sterling Way, opted for the former. She slid her coat off one shoulder, slipped the strap of her purse over her arm, pulled the sleeve over it, buttoned her coat and took off, doing the high-headed, take-no-prisoners stride Marco taught in his Self Defense for Women class. He called it the BOSS, acronym for the Back Off Scumbucket Strut, provoked a few giggles when he demonstrated.

So Cat BOSSed herself into the concrete cavern of the Phoenix Self-Park, Level Two, looked for the nearest stairwell, crossed the width of the parking level to a poorly lit alcove where the single elevator's metal door was shut, an OUT OF ORDER sign taped to its surface.

Cat saw a red neon EXIT sign above a door twenty feet to her left, turned.

And that's when she heard the sound, a faint, methodical thun...thun...thun...

VICTOR ENTERED Resorts from the Boardwalk, saw Ellice immediately. Even in her simple ribbed turtleneck and velveteen slacks, she was impossible to overlook, Nefertiti with a glossy china doll bob, a dark red coat thrown over her slim, tall figure. Her lips curved, unconsciously sensual as she leaned close to Freddy, smiled at something he whispered in her ear. The mirrored ceiling reflected them, exaggerated the current of activity to which they were so oblivious, the appraisals, cool and often unkind, that Ellice serenely ignored and Freddy never saw. Ellice spotted Victor first.

"Honey, you look like something out of a George Romero flick," she greeted in her Circe's voice.

"I heard about the woman." Freddy shook Victor's hand. He had a pleasant face, a notch below handsome, dark, long-lashed eyes like Cat's. "How's Stan holding up?"

Victor shrugged, shook his head.

"Never figured a guy like Stan for Homicide."

"Where's Cat?" Victor asked.

Freddy blinked. "She's not with you?"

Victor glanced at his watch: 8:45 "I haven't spoken to her since this afternoon."

"Maybe I shoulda walked her to her interview. We dropped her off almost two hours ago."

"Freddy, don't get that look. Cat's a big girl. Her interview ran over, that's all," Ellice assured him.

Victor saw her slip her hand into Freddy's, saw a passer-by frown.

"Look, let me try calling over there," Ellice offered. "If she's not around, maybe someone knows when she left."

Victor was about to respond when his beeper went off. He yanked it from his belt, impatiently. "Let me take this, then I'll call the Phoenix." He crossed the lobby, found a pay phone, dialed his office. He was not surprised that Adane picked up. It would never have occurred to her that once she had tended to Stan, she could leave her unfinished work for Monday.

"I'm sorry to trouble you, sir."

"No trouble. Is it Rice?"

"No, sir. A dispatcher just sent ACPD to check on a report that a body was discovered in a parking garage at the corner of Oriental and New Bedford. I knew you were in the area."

Victor felt a tightening in his gut. "That's the Phoenix public parking area, isn't it?"

"Yes, sir. I took the liberty of contacting the DA."

"The body—was it a man or woman?"

"They didn't say. But it was called in by a woman, just minutes ago."

"Get Long over here right away." He sensed a slight hesitation in her "Yes, sir," dismissed it, slammed down the phone and took off, running.

THREE

CAT WAVERED a moment, holding her coat close around her, felt the chill updraft that swept through the concrete canyon, looked at the broad, dimly lit ramps dissolving into darkness, heard hollow street noises rising from below. She turned toward the stairwell exit, stopped; the faint thun-thun-thunning echoing from somewhere within the elevator shaft probed an inquisitive vein. *It's nothing but a stuck elevator door upstairs,* her sensible voice told her, the voice that bickered with the imps of intuition. *Go find the stairwell and walk down to the street before Victor and Ellice and Freddy send out a search party.*

A peek at her watch supported the whisper of sense, but her feet turned toward the center of the parking level and began ascending the driveway ramp that spiraled upward. She walked slowly between rows of diagonally parked cars, following the

UP arrows painted onto the low concrete beams overhead. On Three, a couple approached the elevator recess, contemplated an OUT OF ORDER sign irritably. As she headed up to Four Cat heard the squeal of worn tread against concrete, saw a small, light-colored hatchback swerve around a pillar, headlights dark, veering straight for her. She leaped instinctively, hit the floor between two cars, raised her head to get a glimpse of the rogue vehicle. She saw the hatchback door rebounding on its hinges, muddied license plate, cracked tail light. A second engine followed after; Cat ducked back between the cars, shivering. *See?* gloated the voice of reason.

Cat counted ten, pulled herself upright. She took a deep breath; the intake of air sent a stiletto of pain between her ribs, in the vicinity of the healing bullet wound. Cat pressed her palm to the pain, rubbed at it shakily. *Just a couple of drunks,* she told herself. *It's not like they were aiming at you or anything.* Cat hesitated, then continued upward, moving away from the center of the ramp, checking the low ceiling for security cameras, seeing none.

As she approached Five, the thunning became louder, more distinct, a slow, persistent drumming, like an obstinate shutter blowing in the wind.

Cat could see the glass door marked CORPORATE ENTRANCE: NO PUBLIC ACCESS, the center parking ramp reserved for the executive vehicles. Angling around a pillar, she saw the elevator recess, the top half of the elevator door. The door was in motion; it slid open, closed halfway, rebounded, closed halfway, opened, closed…

A few more steps brought the entire alcove into view and Cat saw a blanketed bundle on the floor, half in, half out of the elevator, the automated door rebounding against it.

See? Cat stopped. No. It wasn't. It was just someone who had passed out, some vagrant who had come in from the cold and fallen asleep. Because, Cat reasoned, *nobody* comes upon two dead bodies in two months. At least, not in two *consecutive* months. Her staggered brain began to calculate. Thirty-six days since Jerry Dudek had been shot dead in front of her, so it couldn't be a dead body, because unless you were a cop or a mortician, you just didn't happen upon corpses that close together. They would *space* themselves, wouldn't they? So there was no reason she shouldn't just walk over to that elevator and pick up the security phone inside and tell whoever responded that there was somebo-some*thing*—blocking the fifth floor garage elevator and perhaps they would like to have a look.

Cat approached, skirted the thing on the floor, not looking down, groped for the receiver, peeked and saw two feet covered with stained white socks protruding from the corner of the blanket, gingerly picked up the corner with two fingers and got a whiff of human decay.

I'm not going to faint, I'm not going to faint, I'm not going to faint. Cat whispered it over and over as she backed toward the executive entrance, tugged on the door handle. Locked. She began to pound on the door, saw a small bell next to the card slot used by the privileged, pushed it, heard a sharp ring echo somewhere inside, peered down the long corridor.

A burly man in a green blazer jogged down the hall, one hand at his waist, reaching for his walkie-talkie. A cold draft of air drove the scent of death into her nostrils and her legs buckled. Cat recalled how Carlo had barreled into the ER the night Dudek had been shot, threatening to take the place apart until someone told her where Cat was. *I am not going to faint.*

The security guard pushed open the door, poked his head out. "There a problem, ma'am? This isn't a public entrance."

"Yes, I know. But, well, you see, there's a— Over by that elevator? It's, well, it's Santa Claus. He's dead."

VICTOR SHOUTED SOMETHING to Freddy and Ellice, shot out of the lobby and sprinted down the Boardwalk, his tan overcoat whipping behind him like a cape. He skidded down the ramp at New Jersey, saw red lights flashing at the far corner, made out two black-and-whites, a pair of uniforms standing at the parking garage entrance. *Cat! Where was Cat?*

He snatched his shield from his belt, held it aloft as he rounded the corner of New Jersey and Oriental, saw a pair of uniforms stationed at the entrance of the Phoenix Self-Park, gray wooden barricades blocking access. "Who's in charge?" he demanded.

"You guys got here quick. Broad found a cold one, in a Kris Kringle suit, yet. Party's up on Five. There's us, DGE, hotel security, so get ready to rumble. You're gonna have to take the stairs, Lieutenant. I think Ballard's the primary."

Victor found the stairwell, took the five flights three stairs at a clip, burst through the door. He saw a patrol car parked catty-corner, blocking off the recessed elevator, crime scene tape across the alcove. Half a dozen men, some in uniform, some not, stood in a huddle.

He saw her at last, sitting in the back seat of the patrol car, her hands clasped around her knees. He approached the car, opened the door, leaned down. "You all right?"

Cat looked up; his expression was disciplined, immobile, but there was a flicker of apprehension in the dark gaze. "Under the circumstances, I'm doing rather well. Of course, the circumstances have been better."

He heard the quiver in her voice. "You found the body?"

Cat nodded.

"You're not going to make a career of this, are you, *querida?* Falling over corpses?"

"Well, we all ought to do what we do best. But this time, I didn't fall; I kept a very firm footing, I'll have you know."

"Stay here. I'm going to see who's in charge."

Victor made his way to the cordoned-off elevator. Four uniforms, two plainclothes and one wearing the green blazer of Sterling security. Victor identified himself to one of the detectives, who introduced himself as Sergeant Ballard, casino investigation unit.

"The gal you were talking to, one found the stiff?" Ballard confided. "She's some kinda reporter *and* a Fortunati, so watch what you say to her."

Victor said nothing.

The sergeant flipped open his notepad. "She's on Two, gonna take the elevator to the street, it's outta order, she sees the light looks to be stuck on Five, she hears this noise, like it's coming from inside the elevator shaft. Like a thumping noise, that's what she said, thumping?''

"I think it was more like a thoon, a thooning sound," offered the youngest officer, a rookie.

"Thun," corrected his immediate senior. "Thun, thun, thun, that's what she said. Thun."

"So like I was sayin'," Ballard continued, "she's like a reporter, she gets a little nosy, comes walkin' up here, sees the elevator door's stuck, sees the stiff, gets hold of security, they call us."

Something in Victor's cool nod suggested that the men be particularly circumspect in their references to Mrs. Austen.

"So what's the deal? You guys gonna take over from here?"

"I'd like Detective Long to work with your people. The DA's been called."

Ballard scratched his head with the tip of his ballpoint. "Roger here"—he nodded to the other plainclothes—"he's DGE, so technically, since it didn't happen on the gaming floor, he's on the sidelines, and Scott—that your name, Scott?"

The burly security guard who had answered Cat's distress call nodded. "Scott Seltzer."

"The Austen bro—that is, Mrs. Austen over there, rang the bell, Seltzer's assigned to the corporate wing. The execs got access cards, they park there in the center ramp."

"Who's on the floor now?" Victor asked.

"Security shift. Couple people in DGE. Maybe a couple in Accounting, clerical people. The Amises were here, left maybe ten minutes before the lady over there rang the bell. Took his car."

"What about Mr. and Mrs. Sterling?"

"He's up in the city, due in tonight. Her, she comes and goes, she doesn't have an office on Five."

"She have her own car?" Victor asked.

"Yeah. Little Jag convertible. Blue."

Victor glanced over his shoulder at the central parking ramp located directly in front of the executive entrance, saw a couple cars, no blue Jag. "Where does she park it?"

Seltzer gave him a flat smile. "Wherever she wants."

Victor nodded, turned back to Ballard. "Okay, let's see what you've got."

Ballard stepped up to the elevator. A wooden wedge had been jammed into the door to hold it open. Victor leaned into the four-by-four compartment, saw a security camera mounted above the door, facing the rear wall.

"Angle of the camera, it woulda picked up the doer if he was inside the elevator—"

"And if the cameras are monitored consistently," Victor added. "What about the surveillance in the garage?" He looked around the concrete cavern, noted the dim lighting.

Seltzer spoke up. "Just cameras over the entrances, inside the elevators. Sterling's gonna add more elevators, install monitors all over once he buys out the guy across the street and expands in here."

Victor nodded silently, signaled to Ballard. Ballard gestured for one of the uniforms to expose the corpse. The older uniform bent over, flipped the blanket aside. Victor clutched his overcoat around his thighs, squatted beside the body, waved for a flashlight to be lowered.

Much of the face was concealed, the lower portion covered with false whiskers and tucked into the padded chest at an unnatural angle, the forehead hidden by the fur-lined, peaked cap that was pulled almost to the eyes. Victor ran his gloved finger under a fold of the cap, lifted it a couple inches. The flashlight's beam illuminated dark hair matted along an irregular line of hard, brown blood. "Anything in his pockets?"

"*Nada*. Great, here comes the doc."

"Comin' through, comin' through, comin' through!" sang a cheerful voice. "Hey, Cardenas, I just got through scrapin' the last piece of the guy ran into the liquor store." A third of a Snickers bar protruded from his mouth; he gulped it in, dropped his medical bag outside the tape and donned a pair of Latex gloves. "So what's the deal? He's ripe, I caught a whiff four floors down. Jeez, not old Saint Nick!" He eased himself under the tape. "I always said Santy Claus himself could drop in the middle of the gaming floor, slot jockeys wouldn't miss a beat." He pulled on a pair of paper booties. "Place like this, you'd be dead a week before anyone knows you're cold."

"Does it appear he's been dead a week?" Victor asked.

The ME glanced down at the corpse, sniffed the air, critically. "I'm gonna say five days, maybe more. I mean, he ain't popped yet. Then again, he's probably been lyin' around in the cold."

The younger uniform gagged audibly.

The ME eased the blanket from the figure to expose an adult male, curled into a fetal position, suited, capped and gloved like Santa Claus, wearing nothing but stained socks on his feet.

"Can you take a set of prints?" Victor asked.

"Wait'til I get him on the table. Just in case someone Superglued on the gloves. Hey, don't laugh, happened once. Keith goes to prep the corpse and—" The ME sheared his palms together. "Whips the epidermis clean off right to the nail beds."

The young cop's face turned a faint green.

"You ask Raab, does he want this guy bumped to the front of the line, or take a number behind the floater and the Bolton woman got shot this morning. How's Rice doin'?"

"Rice will be taken care of."

"Yeah, well don't let him get screwed by the media. Stan's the man. One time, DA needed prints ASAP, guy's still in rigor and the DA don't wanna wait, so Keith gets out the old meat cleaver and..." he smacked the edge of his left hand onto his right palm. "Whup, there it is. That's what I get for hirin' a kid's second job is in the kitchen over Nick's Soups, Salads and Subs over Adriatic. Y'ever eat there?"

The young cop fled.

"Rookies," grinned the ME. "I love 'em."

CAT SAW THE YOUNG uniform sprint past the car. What was taking the cops so long? What were they talking about? And what was she doing just sitting here when twenty feet away there was a real story? Not some gala-of-the-year fluff, either, but a real, live corpse. No, she wasn't going to get involved in another murder. (*Was* it murder?) Cat concentrated. KRIS KRINGLE'S CORPSE STUNS STERLING SECURITY. So-so. What about Korpse? No, too flippant. Cat wondered if the media were gathering, trying to penetrate the police lock-out, tried to recall the *Press*' deadline. If there was a phone around, she could call the copy editor, see if he'd like a couple hundred words. Ritchie would blow his stack, but it's not like *South Jersey* owned her, she was a gun—that is, pen—for hire, wasn't she?

Quietly, Cat slipped out of the patrol car, crept up to the crime scene tape, tried to look over the shoulders of the group huddled with their backs to her.

"When Detective Long arrives, split up the garage," Victor was saying. "We'll have to expand the scene beyond the elevator. If he wasn't brought here by way of the elevator, he had to be brought up the stairs or in by car. What about the garb? You recognize it, Seltzer? Something used in one of the revues, private party, promotion?"

"Nah, none of our people wear anything like that."

"Yes, they do," Cat blurted.

Victor turned, his mouth compressed in irritation. "I told you to wait in the car."

"I know what you told me," Cat replied, serenely. "And there are racks of costumes just like that one downstairs in the costume storage area next to the dressing rooms. They're for the Gambol. The waiters are supposed to wear them. They were ordered quite a while ago and they arrived yesterday and there are one hundred of them." Cat repeated the facts that had been relayed by the hospitality girl. Brandi. Or Candi. Mandi.

"Just like this one?" Victor asked, sensing a ripple of irritation from Seltzer's direction.

Cat peeked at the figure on the floor. "Identical."

"But you know," Ballard offered, "the big guy, his wardrobe doesn't have a lotta variety. You seen one, you seen 'em all."

Cat shook her head, called up more of Brandi, Candi or Mandi's data. "That's real velvet, not plush or some cheap velveteen, and the belts are notched leather with genuine brass buckles. They were expensive rentals from It's Costumary in Philly. Whoever put him into that suit—"

"Whoa, whaddaya mean, *put* him into it?" Ballard cried.

Cat took another squeamish glimpse at the portion of exposed scalp, turned her gaze on the detective. "Did you ever get a cut on your scalp, Sergeant? I did, when I was eleven. Right here." She slipped her index finger under her bangs. "And it bled all over my face and down the front of my shirt. That costume's clean, everything's fresh except for the socks, and if those stains are blood, I bet they're his type. After he was hurt or"—she swallowed—"someone pulled him across the area where he bled."

Victor cocked an eyebrow at the cops.

"So didn't those Santa suits come with booties?" the ME challenged.

"It's easy to get someone in a one-size-fits-most costume," Cat replied. "But footwear's trickier."

"Goddamn *Quincy* reruns," muttered the ME. "Me, I say the hell with cable, read a book f'cryin' out loud. Where's the camera jockey?"

"When were you in this storage room?" Victor asked her.

"Oh, around seven-fifteen, seven-thirty."

"Alone?"

"No, Mrs. Amis gave me an escort. The Sterling Tour."

"What about access?"

"We took an elevator down to the dressing rooms. They're on the street level. I noticed a door that opens onto New Jersey, stage door, deliveries."

"Guarded?"

"Not that I could see."

Another ripple of hostility emanated from Seltzer.

Cat turned back to Ballard. "So what's the theory, Sergeant? Is this officially a homicide investigation?"

"Gimme a break, Mrs. Austen."

A young man with an earring dangling from his left ear, a

camera bag slung over his shoulder maneuvered past Cat. "Jeez!" reverberated down the ramp as he got a glimpse of the corpse. "All year, I been keepin' to the straight and narrow and ten days before the payoff, the Big Man kicks." He fiddled with his lenses. "Lousy light. Gotta use a flash, there's gonna be shadows."

"This ain't for *Playgirl,*" snapped Ballard.

The photographer blocked Cat's view, leaned over the body; the camera flashed several times in succession.

Victor eased himself in front of Cat, his back to her. "I want a set of photographs and so will the DA. When you get him to the morgue, see if you can get some good close-ups of the face in better light."

"We don't call it the morgue anymore," the ME informed him. "It's the Office of Decedent Observation and Review."

Victor sensed the aura of hysterical mirth. He turned; Cat was studying her shoes, her shoulders quivering. "Sergeant Ballard, are you finished with Mrs. Austen?" he asked.

"Uh-huh. 'Less she can remember the plate on the car almost ran her down."

Cat winced. She had hoped that wouldn't come up just yet. Her gaze ascended Victor's necktie, got to his scowl, backed down.

"What car?" The two syllables sent a chill through the group, though his tone had been perfectly calm, his expression impassive.

"She's walkin' up the ramp from Two, this car comes speedin' down, almost plows into her. What'd you say, light hatchback, was it? Older model?"

Cat nodded. "The plate was crusted with mud, but it was a Jersey plate. I wouldn't be surprised if the driver was involved in this."

"Why not?" Victor asked.

"Because," Cat explained, patiently. "It hasn't rained anywhere in the mid-Atlantic region for almost three weeks."

"So the only mud you would come across is the mud you manufacture," Victor interpreted.

"Precisely."

"Ingenious."

"Elementary."

Victor pressed down a smile, turned back to Ballard. "You're going to have to start with the vacant parking spaces—"

"*Madon'*—"

"Scrap paper, blood, footprints, drag marks—"

"And don't forget to pick up those Out-of-Order signs," Cat suggested. "Well, the elevators aren't out of order, are they?"

"Pick up the signs," Victor ordered. "They don't charge a parking fee here, do they?"

"Not for Self-Park," Seltzer replied.

"All right. Until the area's been checked out, nobody drives in. I want the exits manned, I want a list of every plate that's in here now, anyone who leaves."

"*Madonna mi'.*"

"Lieutenant," Seltzer interrupted, "you can't prevent Sterling customers from entering the garage, or harass them if they're trying to leave—"

"Well, I would dispute the verb, but yes, I absolutely can."

"I'm gonna have to put a call in to Mr. Amis—"

"Report it to whomever you wish. Until the entire area's been checked out, it's off limits." He turned back to Ballard. "I'm going to arrange for Mrs. Austen's ride, then check on Detective Long." He took Cat's elbow and ushered her toward the stairwell.

"Any other small details you've neglected to mention?"

"I would have told you about the cars." Cat could hear the murmur of a crowd from the street.

"I beg your pardon? Was that 'cars'? Plural?"

Cat flushed defensively. "When I did my duck and cover, I got a glimpse of the one that almost hit me. Another one came up behind, but it may just have been someone headed out. It is a garage, after all. I suppose it could have been a coincidence. But then again … Ellice quoted something once, about how we talk a lot about coincidence, but we don't really believe in it."

"I don't, as a rule. At least, I think it's more uncommon than we give it credit. What were you doing wandering around here anyway? I thought you were coming by way of the Boardwalk."

"I got lost trying to escape Sterling Way."

"And just happened to bump into a corpse?"

"Uncommon coincidence."

FOUR

POLICE HAD cordoned off the Self-Park entrance/exit on Oriental. About a hundred people had gathered by the time Victor and Cat emerged. Victor shouldered past a photographer as he lifted the yellow tape for Cat to pass, sensed rather than saw the flash. He saw Freddy and Ellice on the opposite curb, steered Cat toward them.

"There's a body up there, honest to God!" Ellice gasped. "Can't we let you out for half an hour?"

"Guess not."

Victor saw the white crime lab van being waved through the barricade. "Fred, can you take Cat home?"

"No problem."

"Yes, there is," Cat protested. "I'm not going home yet."

"Cat, I'd rather we didn't argue about this—"

"Then don't."

One of the crime scene investigators signaled to Victor, began to cross the street. "Wait here," Victor said, and drew the woman away from the crowd, glanced around to assure that they wouldn't be overheard before he spoke.

"He doesn't want her to come over here, so I won't hear what they're saying," Cat pouted. "What was it … something with a D. D'Allessandro. That's it, Frank D'Allessandro."

"Who is a copy editor for *The Press?*" Ellice countered, still in the *Jeopardy!* mode.

"How did you know that?"

"'Cause he was in the test group before me."

"No kidding. How'd he do?"

"Seven outta ten. That puts him in the running, but I got him beat."

Cat glanced around the dismal block. "Telephone…" she murmured.

"What is a—"

"I meant, is there a pay phone around here?"

"I don't see one. Let's try that coffee shop on the corner; I'm freezing out here."

Cat looked toward the corner. On Oriental and New Bedford, across from the Phoenix Self-Park, was an aging brick structure, a coffee shop at the base and what appeared to be a couple of apartment units above. J m's C ff Sh p, in hot pink neon, was suspended over the door. Cat recalled that the proprietor of the shop owned the entire building, that he had refused a buyout offer from the Poseidon and was currently battling with the Sterling Phoenix, which had planned to expand its parking facilities, snapped up the rest of the dumps along the block, hit a wall when J m refused to sell. There was talk that Sterling was looking into eminent domain as a means of extracting the property from its stubborn owner.

"Freddy, tell Victor we're going in there to get warmed up." Cat linked her arm through Ellice's. "I wonder how they got the neon to circumvent the vowels," she mused. Maybe she could turn out a short humor piece, a hundred words or so, maybe she could get her sister-in-law Nancy to shoot it. *Atlantic City* magazine might take something like that.

J m's had a scarred counter of varnished wood, stools and booths of cracked, taped and recracked vinyl, a floor of so indeterminate a shade that on one occasion fists and ultimately knives had been brandished in dispute over its exact hue. Ashtrays, salvaged from various hotel and club demolitions, were filled to the brim while sugar bowls lay empty and milk ripened in not-so-stainless creamers.

"Lovely," Ellice murmured, as she slid into a booth. "Looks like that urban renaissance thing circumvented this place, too."

Cat checked the phone booth, emerged with a frown, sat. "Out of order. Who said that thing about coincidence, that we talk about it, but don't believe in it?"

"Priestley."

"So, you think you really got a shot?" Cat lifted a sticky menu gingerly.

Ellice propped her chin on her hand. "Shelley's elegy on the death of John Keats."

"Oooh. I know that one. It starts with an A."

"*Adonais,*" Ellice grinned. "No one else in the test group got that one. I'm a shoo-in."

Freddy and Victor entered. Freddy slid next to Ellice, Victor beside Cat.

A waitress shuffled up to the booth. Her silver-white hair had been buzzed to a half inch; her bony form was attired in washed-out jeans split at the knee, she wore black Converse high-tops; and a pin that identified her as "Earlene" was affixed to a T-shirt that proclaimed MEN OF MOST RENOWNED VIRTUE HAVE SOMETIMES BY TRANSGRESSING MOST TRULY KEPT THE LAW.

"Who was Milton?" Ellice nodded toward the shirt.

"Huh?" The girl's eyes were red-rimmed, weary. She plucked the shirt from her chest, looked down at the print. "My boyfriend gimme this, made it up Yardville. But his name's not Milton, it's Al."

"Well, that's two hundred off my score," Ellice murmured, her eyes glossy with amusement.

Cat concluded from the reddened eyes, the air of dejection, that Earlene and Al were on the outs.

Victor ordered four coffees; Earlene wrote copiously before she departed.

"So what's the deal?" Freddy asked. "Who's the vic?"

"Santa Claus," Cat told him.

"He hasn't been identified," Victor said, shortly. "Could very well be someone off the streets."

"Who just happens to suffer a major head trauma, make his way to the fifth floor of the garage, get himself stuffed into a Santa Claus suit and—"

"Cat."

Cat sighed impatiently. "Fine. Just don't everyone get on my case like I was out looking for trouble. I was just trying to escape from that mezzanine—"

"Sterling Way?" Ellice asked. "What're the shops like?"

Cat looked around the garish coffee shop. "What this would look like if it were executed with even less taste and too much money."

"Let's change the subject," Freddy snapped.

Victor saw Cat and Ellice exchange a glance, wondered what it was about the Phoenix that got under Freddy's skin so. "I agree. Cat, you're on. There was something amusing on the agenda, as I recall."

Cat bit her lip. "Well, there was. I'm not sure you're in the mood to hear it."

"Try me."

"Well…have you ever heard of a TV show called *Cop-Watch?*"

"No." Victor watched even less TV than Cat and Ellice.

"Neither had I. But apparently it's been getting terrific ratings for the past year. It's a two-hour show, a ninety-minute docudrama based on an actual crime and then they have this round-table discussion with the real people involved and the actors who portrayed them; one of the cops involved usually acts as moderator."

"What does this have to do with you? Landis got you doing television reviews now?"

"Not exactly." She took a deep breath. "Ritchie sent them proofs of my Dudek story and their staff has decided to use it as the treatment for one of their shows. One of the production assistants called me this morning. They've gone into pre-production, whatever that means, and they want me to sign over the rights to my story and would I be willing to meet with the actress who's playing me sometime before the shoot, so that she can get a—I believe the term was 'fix'—get a fix on my personality."

Victor stroked his mustache. "Are you serious?"

"The production girl told me Barry Fried over at KRZI and his secretary have already signed releases."

The waitress brought their coffees.

"What did you tell this person?" Victor took a sip of his coffee, grimaced.

"I told her I'd have to think about it, which I believe she interpreted as the small-town freelancer holding out for more money, because she got sort of uppity and told me she really didn't need to use my article because they could develop a script from what's in the public record and they were only contacting me as a courtesy."

"What kind of money did they offer you?" Freddy asked.

Cat hesitated. "Seventy-five hundred."

"And you have to think about it?"

"It just seems a bit...sordid...that's all."

"For seventy-five hundred, you fake sordid. What's the difference between writing the story for *South Jersey* and selling it to these people? I'll bet Landis didn't give you a tenth of what they're offering."

Cat declined to tell her brother that Ritchie hadn't paid over dime one yet, even though the deal had been for money on acceptance, not on publication. "You're not smiling," she said to Victor.

"When would this thing air?"

"I think she said something about May sweeps."

"I hope Raab has a jury empanelled before then." Victor shoved his coffee aside. "I'd hate to see Hopper's trial hung up because twelve people saw his TV alter ego play like the persecuted victim."

Cat said nothing. She agreed with Victor on principle; no one, not even Jerry Dudek, deserved to be gunned down in the street, of course. But she had this nagging sympathy for Tom Hopper that she couldn't quite reason away.

The cowbell on the door clanged. Victor looked up and nodded. Cat turned in her seat and saw a slender black male wrapped in a calf-length overcoat, sporting a drooping mustache.

"Excuse me." Victor rose, walked over to the man.

"You see," Cat muttered. "He doesn't want to let me in on what they're saying."

"That one of his detectives?" Ellice asked.

Freddy grinned. "It's Phil Long."

"So what's so funny about a Phil Long?"

"He used to be ACPD," Cat whispered. "He worked vice with Joey. They had this sting operation, Joey played a pimp and Detective Long was a hooker. They'd work the lounges, bust guys for soliciting."

"He worked in drag? Not with the mustache?"

"After a few drinks, some guys aren't real particular," Freddy told her.

"Shhh!" Cat slapped his hand. "They're coming over."

"Guy's head's busted," Long was saying. "ME says it looks like multiple fractures; they just hauled him over to the morgue."

"It's not the morgue anymore," Cat informed him. "It's the Office of Decedent Observation and Review."

Long looked from Cat to Victor. "ODOR?"

"Cross my heart."

Long grinned, turned back to Victor. "ACPD sent one of theirs down the storage room, the order was for a hundred of those Santa costumes, already they ran the count six times—"

Victor shook his head, cutting Long off in midsentence.

But Cat finished it. "And can't get past ninety-nine."

Victor told Long to liaison with Sergeant Ballard and dismissed him. The waitress with the buzzed pate shuffled up, slapped the check on the table. "One a you guys named Cardenas?" The latter emerged "Card-nass," close enough for Victor to reply, "I am."

"Yeah, well there's a guy outside in a black car wearin' a beanie says he wants to talk to you. Jim says you guys got a beef you can take it down the street, he don't want no trouble."

Victor thanked the girl with characteristic gravity; only Cat could detect the note of amusement in his measured syllables. When the girl ambled off, Ellice murmured, "I've never seen a black car wearing a beanie."

Victor stepped outside, saw a modest Oldsmobile idling well out of range of the growing crowd on the corner of Oriental and New Jersey. The front passenger window slid down and the driver leaned over. "Victor!"

Victor approached. Kurt Raab, the county DA, was wearing a black coat, a dark yarmulke pinned to the thinning hair at his crown. Raab was the youngest county prosecutor in the state, probably the brightest, and notoriously camera shy. In the courtroom, he had always been coolly articulate, even witty, until they brought in the cameras, and then his blood pressure went into overdrive. "Please tell me this guy died of natural causes," he pleaded, casting a nervous glance toward the *NewsLine90* van winnowing through the crowd on the corner.

Victor shrugged. "Scalp lacerations, multiple fractures. And he was wearing a costume taken from the dressing rooms in the Phoenix."

Raab groaned. "Oh no, oh no, oh no. I hear Phoenix, I hear Sterling, I hear Sterling, I hear that gal over *NewsLineNinety* tell us how we should tune in at six and eleven, I hear Lizette sayin' she's got the governor on line one, I hear that jerk Landis runs *South Jersey*—oh, hey there, Mrs. Austen, what've you been up to?"

"This and that. Found a corpse dressed in a Santa suit in the garage over there."

Raab glanced at Victor. "Ah, tell me she didn't..."

"I don't suppose you'd like to make a brief statement?" Cat inquired.

"I'm stating for the record that Cardenas is to get you away from the scene. Phil Long report?"

Victor nodded.

"Take off. I'll call you in the morning." Raab rolled down the car window and coasted reluctantly toward the crowd.

"Freddy took care of the check," Cat said. "I think he and Ellice wanted to be alone. Why don't you go chaperone the DA? He needs a knight errant and I need to hunt up a working phone."

"No way. You heard Raab, you're out of here. You can use my car phone."

"It's a personal call."

"I won't eavesdrop." He took her elbow, guided her around the corner away from the scene, the cameras. "Or we could stop at my place, you want privacy, you can use the phone in the bedroom."

"That's not subtle."

"I'm not feeling particularly subtle." He rounded the corner, approached his car.

Cat took the key ring from his hand. "Then I'm driving."

"Can you drive a five speed?"

"I drove Joey's car once."

Victor gave her a wary look, but opened the driver's side door, helped her behind the wheel.

"Sherrie said once she knew Joey was in love with her when he let her drive the 'Vette and didn't wince when she ground the gears." Cat slipped the key into the ignition, pulled away from the curb, swung left, shoved the car in reverse, pivoted ninety degrees on the right rear wheel, shifted into first and shot forward. "Defensive Driving One Oh One. Marco calls that turn the 'Special K.'"

"For the record, I didn't wince."

Cat made a left onto Atlantic, glanced at Victor's profile. The mustache curved downward in a somber crescent, the expression unreadable, except for the shade of tension that hadn't quite receded. "Well, I wouldn't be much of a reporter if I didn't at least *ask* Mr. Raab to comment when I had him right there," she said, defensively.

"You're not being much of a reporter if you abandon an assignment. What happened to Party of the Year?" Damn it! But the words were out, and his immediate "I'm sorry, I shouldn't have said that," didn't smooth the angry pucker forming at the corners of her mouth.

"Better yet, why bother with any assignment at all? Why don't I just sit home and collect Chris' pension and take money from my family instead of trying to earn it and cook and shop and take the kids to the playground whether they want to go or not? Why—"

"Cat, love, I'm tired, that's all."

"I'm tired, too. I'm tired of cops-come-first." She had reached Delancy, made a swift left onto the quiet, dead-end street, slammed on the brakes in front of a three-story structure. "And I'm tired of being told how to manage my life!" She got out, slammed the door. "I'll call a cab to take me home," she yelled over her shoulder as she stormed up the steps to Victor's second-floor apartment.

He heard the tearful undertone in her voice, hurried up the steps after her. "Cat—"

She pushed her bangs away from her face, jabbed one of the keys into the lock.

"Here, let me." The note of amusement in the conciliatory tone angered her more.

"I can *do* it." She got the door unlocked and flung it open, stalked to the phone on the desk in the dining area. Victor took her wrist and gently pried the receiver out of her hand.

"Let go."

He pressed a fingertip to her lips. "In a minute. First, there are four things I need to say. One: I'm sorry our evening was disrupted. Two: I'm sorry if I implied that your work was less important than mine. Three: I'm sorry for everything else I've ever done or may do in the future."

Cat's eyes narrowed warily. "And four?"

"Ah yes, four. Four is that I absolutely adore you."

Her lips pressed together, fighting down an urge to smile. "Well, in keeping with the spirit of this benevolent season, I suppose I ought to forgive you."

"Ah, Cat, beware. Who was it said if you forgive people enough, you belong to them? The man who wrote *Lost Horizon,* I believe. He called it 'squatter's rights of the heart.'"

Cat smiled, lay her hand against his cheek. The dark shadow of beard, the downward curve of his mustache gave his countenance a feral cast; alien. He had looked like that the night they met. She had passed out at the site of the Dudek murder, been rushed to the emergency room; he came in to interview her and both of their lives began to change. Just like that.

Victor could feel the wariness in her touch, a caution palpable in her overtures of intimacy. He turned his head aside, kissed her palm, leaned down to kiss her mouth.

Cat wriggled away. "Hold that thought."

"I have been."

She pressed her palms together in mock supplication. "Does the prisoner of your heart get one phone call?"

He grinned. "Help yourself."

She retreated to the bedroom, closed the door, reached for the phone and dialed *The Press*. She was told that Frank D'Allessandro was not in, did she want to leave a message?

Cat checked her watch, gave the woman her name. "Tell Mr. D'Allessandro I was the only member of the press" (sort of) "who was inside the Phoenix parking garage tonight when a man's body was discovered, and if he wants the—"*don't say it*—"scoop, tell him to get back to me as soon as possible." She gave the woman Victor's number and her home phone number and then hung up.

Victor had thrown off his coat, was sitting on the couch, shuffling through his mail. He tossed it aside, rose. "The kids okay?"

"What? Oh, yes, they're fine."

"Who's babysitting?"

"They're staying overnight at Mama's. She'll bring them back tomorrow for the annual Fortunati Christmas cookie bake." Cat made a face, unbuttoned her coat. "Twelve kinds of cookies. It's one of those ethnic traditions that's charmingly quaint in theory and downright masochistic in practice."

"So, no curfew then?" Victor sat beside her, helped her slip out of her coat. A thin gold chain pulsed at the hollow of her throat. Impulsively, he pressed his lips against the spot, murmured, "Let's neck."

He felt Cat's rippling laughter with his mouth. "I haven't heard that expression in ages. Do people still do that?"

"We could bring it back in style." He noticed that one hand

crept to her ribs as she laughed. He slid his hand over hers, felt her flinch. "You hurt yourself tonight?"

"It's nothing. I just bumped it." When she dove to avoid the cars that almost plowed into her. No, car. One car, and then another.

Cat replayed the incident in her head, then replayed the soundtrack only. The second car had sounded different, the acceleration had sounded different. Like Victor's car.

"Weren't you supposed to see your doctor this week?"

Cat shook herself. "What? Oh, that. I'm fine. He said I could go back to a mild exercise program, but marathons are out for now."

"Define 'mild exercise.'"

Cat edged away from him, gave him a droll look. "Low impact necking."

Victor laughed briefly, stretched out on the couch, drew her beside him. "Stay like this awhile, then I'll drive you home."

Cat kicked off her pumps, nestled her head in the crook of his shoulder. "They say that being a homicide cop makes you morbid. Crazy, even." Though she had never met anyone saner, more in control than Victor.

"Maybe we're all morbid and crazy to begin with and find our niche in homicide."

"'There is, I believe, in every disposition, a tendency to some particular evil, a natural defect, which not even the best of education can overcome.'"

"Beg pardon?"

"Jane Austen. Not my Jane, the original. *Pride and Prejudice.*"

"Never read it. What's it about?"

"Pride. And prejudice. Falling in love with the last person on earth you're supposed to fall in love with and then finding out that you're perfect for each other."

"Like Freddy and Ellice?" *Like us,* he thought.

"Yes, I suppose."

"What is it with Freddy, anyway? He won't park at the Phoenix, he won't walk you to the entrance, what's he got against King Medusa?"

"Midas. King Midas."

"Hearing his name sure turns your brother to stone."

"Clever, clever."

"What's Freddy got against him, Cat?"

"Not him. Her. Freddy was engaged to Fawn Sterling."

Victor's head jerked up. "To Sterling's wife? When was this?"

Cat sighed, traced the pattern of his tie with her fingertip. "It must have been, oh, eight years now? Fawn's from Margate. You know, local-girl-makes-good. Went to Parsons for a while, then to some French fashion academy, apprenticed with a *couturier* in Paris for a year, then came back and started her own operation. She rented a cubbyhole in Soho, hired a couple pattern cutters and seamstresses. Now, the established route would be to put together a few pieces, do the trunk shows, trek around Seventh Avenue, work the back room for one of the name designers, but Fawn wanted to start at the top, reel in those couple hundred women in the world who can drop fifty, a hundred thousand for a dress and not blink."

"You didn't say a hundred thousand, did you?"

"I did. The saga is that she bribed the waiters at Deuxieme to tell her when Madame So-and-So was lunching, then Fawn would get the next table and just happen to drop a couple sketches that just happened to be a design customized for Madame So-and-So. Drop the bait, nurse the Evian, which was all she could afford at a restaurant like that, and reel in the buyer."

"How could she afford to bribe the waiters?"

"It wasn't exactly a cash transaction."

"Oh. Please continue."

"She's only about twenty-four at this time. Her reputation's starting to make the rounds but home base is her parents' place in Margate. She's running back and forth between there and Manhattan, one weekend Freddy picks her up doing ninety-five on the Expressway. She was Caprio, then. Fawn Caprio. Smart, attractive, a career that's starting to take off. Freddy doesn't have Joey's looks, but he's always been a guy women like and he likes bright women, always has. They started seeing each other, which was only half the week. The other half, she's dressing millionaire matrons, still working out of the cubbyhole. She did all the designs, picked the fabrics, everything else she jobbed out, the patterns and sewing, which kept her operation small, which in turn gave it a sort of cachet.''

"Playing hard to get paid off, in other words.''

"Well, in her work.'' Cat paused. "I never liked her.''

"Why not?''

"She'd just come off another relationship when she met Freddy, one of the waiters for all I know, mentioned it in conversation once. Talked about some guy she dumped. Her verb, 'dumped.' It sounded so cold-hearted the way she said it, I was afraid she'd turn around one day and dump Freddy. And once, a bunch of us were watching the guys play ball and she sort of, I don't know, flirted with Stan Rice. It was a little more predatory than flirting, really, though Stan was too much of a gentleman to reciprocate. I mean, she was Freddy's girl.''

"Freddy didn't pick up on any of this?''

"Freddy was smitten, there was no talking to him. And then, she actually did agree to marry him, it was even in the papers and everything. And then it all fell apart.''

"What happened?''

"Sterling. One of the big fish she hooked was his wife. Marlena, I think her name was. She talked Sterling into providing some financial backing for Fawn, Fawn reciprocated by appropriating Marlena's husband. Freddy got back the ring, Marlena got the estates in Long Island and Palm Beach and a nice chunk of Sterling's net worth, and Sterling and Fawn got married. Of course, he really was King Midas back then, everything he touched turned to gold.''

"And now?''

Cat shrugged. "The story is that he started spending too much time cultivating the persona and not enough tending to the purse.''

"Nurturing fame rather than fortune.''

"Fame can get addictive.''

"Still, he took on the Phoenix, which means someone came up with cash, bonds, something.''

"Well, nobody in Atlantic City wanted that skeleton of the Poseidon rotting there on the boards, and for Sterling, a casino was a smart move. A resort chain can have one hotel with a casino and ninety-nine without and the one with gaming will produce over half the gross revenue. I don't know much about the bonds, but I know they didn't come cheap, and the renovation went over schedule, he missed half a lucrative summer season and he's got an interest payment due some time in January that's going to run into eight figures."

"That's a lot of background for someone who's only working the Party of the Year."

"Well, I heard his aide was formidable and I didn't want to go in there unprepared. I didn't do so hot as it was."

"So what's her spin? The Phoenix holding its own?"

"I'm sure she would tell me they were, even if they weren't. He signs the checks. But he can't just break even. Losers break even. That's a quote from *King Midas,* that book he wrote, or co-wrote, or conned the public into believing he wrote. Sterling needs to be Number One."

"And if he doesn't make it?"

"Well, the collateral on the bonds is the first mortgage on the Phoenix, unless he's got something else in his pocket that's worth a few hundred million dollars. You know, I think he named it the Phoenix as some kind of metaphor, Sterling on the upswing when everyone's written him off."

"And then everyone's attention turned to his wife. You ever see her?"

"Heavens no. *South Jersey* did a piece on her a few years back, before I came on board, but that was mostly fluff and photos. She was in New York earlier this fall, showing her first collection. Only fifteen pieces and every one a keeper, according to *Women's Wear Daily.* She spent Thanksgiving alone in Margate, supposedly working up another line. He's been in New York and AC, and that's fueled the rumors they're separating. Then this week, she moved into the Phoenix penthouse."

"Maybe they've worked things out and they're reconciling."

"Fawn doesn't work things out, she works you over and moves on." Cat sounded bitter. Freddy was her favorite brother.

"That sounds rather…voracious."

Cat looked at him gravely. "I think she's one of those women, you know? No matter what they do, how much they accomplish, getting a man is the ultimate triumph. Especially if the man is unattainable."

Victor thought about his sister Remy, bright, creative, but without a man, sullen, bordering on self-destruction.

"Victor…you don't think the Sterlings are involved in any of this, do you? I mean, the dead guy?"

"No comment."

Cat pushed away from him, hopped to her feet, raking her fingers through her shoulder-length hair. "A guy who was dead in the garage but probably not killed in the garage. Wearing a Santa suit—"

"But probably not Santa."

Cat's angular brows lowered. "You know, someone got rid of his shoes, his clothes. Now, that could mean they were getting rid of trace evidence or they don't want him identified through his clothing labels or monograms."

Victor crossed his arms behind his head, cocked an eyebrow. "Should I be writing this down?"

"Don't be smug. You know what else bothers me? Why not leave him stark naked or dump him in the ocean if they want to erase evidence or don't want him found? Why go to the trouble of stealing a costume from inside the Phoenix and then leaving him right there, where someone would have to find him?"

Victor imagined Cat's family circle, the brothers sitting around, talking cop talk, little Cat taking it all in. "I have no idea."

"It's obvious they wanted him found. And not just found by anyone, because the person most likely to come by first would be someone arriving or leaving the corporate wing. Someone like Sterling. He's due in tonight."

"Interesting you keep saying 'they.'"

Cat's mouth puckered thoughtfully. "I suppose it's just that I can't see one person getting a dead body undressed and into another set of clothes. And another thing—"

"My love, this speculation isn't going to get the Party of the Year written, is it?"

"Bills are not paid by the Party of the Year alone."

Victor's gaze softened. "Is that worrying you? Things go overboard during the holidays?"

"Overboard? Italians go crazy at Christmas. We do a pollyanna now, so I don't have to buy a lot of family presents, but there are the kids, and the odd friend. What would you like?"

"You wouldn't be changing the subject as a diversion, so that I won't caution you against following up on this John Doe?"

"Well, I wouldn't mind at least knowing who he is and how he got there."

"I'd mind if you spent Christmas where you spent Thanksgiving." Victor frowned.

"You wouldn't think so if you'd ever spent a Christmas Eve at the Fortunati household. Stop frowning and tell me what you'd like."

"Promise I'll get it?"

"Are you a good boy?"

"Want to find out?"

"Not...yet." He saw the wariness steal over her features once more, her grave gaze introspective, trying to figure him out, figure out how sensations she believed had died when Chris had died could be revived.

"Cat, I know what it's like to lose someone—"

"It's not the same. You don't know what it's like to get absorbed by someone else's life. You lost your wife. You never lost yourself."

Victor looked up at her, soberly. "You haven't lost yourself, Cat."

"But I came close." Cat knelt, cupped his face in her hands. "Victor, I grew up in a family that protected me with a vengeance and I was married for fourteen years to someone I thought I would be with forever. Now when I've figured out how to get by on my own, everything starts to change again. I'm just trying to keep up.'' She kissed his cheek with genuine tenderness. ''I'm sorry, don't pay attention to me. It's Christmas, that's all. I'm always a little strung out this time of year. Give me a few weeks and I'll be back to normal.''

''No need to go that far.''

''All right. I promise not to go that far. And I promise to get you what you want if it's within reason and purse.''

''Fair enough. I haven't had a vacation leave in over fourteen months. I want you to come away with me for a nice long weekend, somewhere where there's sun, sea, no phones, no falling over corpses.''

Cat tilted her chin. ''And how do you want that wrapped?''

''Cellophane.''

Cat's lips puckered, wrestling down a laugh. ''I'll think about it. But I warn you, as Shakespeare said: 'Oft expectation fails and most oft there where most it promises.''

'''And oft it hits where hope is coldest,''' Victor counterquoted neatly.

When he pulled her back onto the couch, she was laughing.

FIVE

SATURDAY MORNING, Cat rose at seven, donned a T-shirt, sweats, Wigwams, battered gray Nikes, nylon jacket. She tried a few cautious stretches, testing the tautness over her ribs, slipped down the stairs, circumnavigated the seven-foot blue spruce the kids had begged her to buy even though she thought fifty-five dollars was way too much (yet adamantly refusing Freddy's offer to pay half), pulled down a wool hat, gloves, from the closet, padded into the kitchen, set up the coffee pot, let herself out the back door, locked it behind her.

She safety-pinned her key to her sweat pants and descended the narrow back stairs to the yard, circled to the front of the house, took Morningside Drive at a brisk walk, hit the curve where Morningside merged with Beach Road and broke into a trot. She tracked the dunes that bordered the east side of Beach Road to the boardwalk ramp at St. James Place, said, "Here goes," the two syllables emerging from her lips in white puffs.

She tested the boards. When the temperature hovered around freezing, the wooden planks were often coated with slick white frost that made running tricky. Today, they were dry. Cat cantered past the snack bars, the amusement pier, the food court, all boarded for the winter, fell into a steady trot and let her mind slide into a review of the previous night. The ghastliness, the bewilderment mingled with satisfaction; Frank D'Allessandro had offered Cat one fifty for a couple hundred words he could use to pad a staffer's story, asked her how Ellice had done on the *Jeopardy!* test ("She got all ten! Even the one on Shelley?"), told Cat she wouldn't get a byline. Cat didn't object to that last; she would rather her brothers didn't see "Slain Santa Found At Phoenix" with her name beneath the header.

The sea had receded to a flat winter calm, a few gulls gliding over the unbroken surface. Familiar forms passed; a loose confederation of runners had consolidated into a club, called themselves the Running Board, many of whom ran in pairs, threesomes, daily. Cat knew one or two by name, others by the voices that emerged from ski masks and mufflers, calling out, "Haven't seen you in a while!" or "Take it easy, Austen!" or "You gonna make the Santa Sprint this year?"

A pulling sensation over her ribs began to wear at her concentration, jabbed insistently when she tried to ignore it. She cut back to a slow jog, turned toward home. Three and a half miles. Be back to six in no time, Cat told herself.

Her home was a three-story house with a ground-floor apartment on the first level. Aunt Caterina had picked it up as a handyman's special, begun a thorough renovation. Cat, newly married, with nothing to fill her days, pitched in. She had always enjoyed the company of her mother's younger sister. Caterina was fiercely independent, funny, unafraid: everything

Cat admired, believed she herself was not. Caterina never married, worked from age thirteen to age fifty-eight, died prematurely, leaving the Morningside Drive house to her favorite niece.

The apartment needed work. Paint the shutters, check out the heating system, replace the kitchen floor, all those things she and Chris had meant to get around to and never did because they had all the time in the world. Rent out the apartment, use the income for the kids' college fund. The senseless, random shooting had put an end to the plans, an end to everything, until another shocking murder, the killing of Jerry Dudek, had changed the course of Cat's life once more.

Cat bounded up the back stairs, let herself in. Ellice was sitting at the kitchen table, glancing over the *Press*.

Cat regarded Ellice as proof that sometimes one had to listen to one's impulses. They had come together by chance. Ellice, recovering from illness and fleeing from a harrowing relationship, had accepted Cat's impulsive offer of safe haven. The impulse had set Cat at odds with her brothers and only Freddy had capitulated completely.

"Did it make the papers?" Cat tugged off her hat and yanked the sweatshirt over her head.

Ellice shrugged. "Not page one." She held up the front page to display the headline STRAY BULLET KILLS AC MOM.

Cat pried off her shoes, kicked them next to the door of the pantry that she had converted to an office. "Maybe Frank D'Allessandro couldn't make the deadline."

"Well, it made the grapevine," Ellice countered. "Carlo called while you were out; he heard all about it."

Cat winced.

"He wanted to know what the expletive deleted you were doing out running?"

"Was that all?"

"No, he also wanted to know what the—"

"Ed."

"Huh?"

"E comma d. Expletive deleted."

"What the ed you were doing running around alone at night, don't you have any edding sense, for ed's sake?"

"Sense doesn't pay the bills. Frank D'Allessandro's giving me one fifty, he said it might not make today's edition, though. Just as well. Freddy rat me out to Carlo?"

"I don't know." Ellice dropped the paper on the table, a troubled look stealing over her face.

"Ellice, what's the matter?"

"Nothing." She raked her fingers through her glossy bob.

"Where did you two go last night?"

"Just walked awhile. I think, you know, when the Sterling name came up, it sort of put him out."

"Of course it did. Why would he want to hear her name, after the way she treated him? Thank God he didn't marry her."

"Does he?"

"Does he what?"

"Thank God they didn't get married."

"Ellice, are you nuts? Freddy's in love with you."

"Yeah, well, I'm sure *famiglia* Fortunati would rather he'd hooked up with someone his own shade. Some, at least, would."

"As shady as Fawn Caprio? No way." Cat felt a sudden chill, heard *You wouldn't happen to know if he's running with Fawn Caprio, would you?*, tried to remember who had said that to her. Or maybe it had been a dream. Cat put her arms around Ellice's shoulder, gave her a brief hug. "Ellice, you're not the one stalling because of *famiglia* Fortunati, are you? They'll come around. You should have heard them when I decided to marry a Protestant. It wasn't until Joey and Sherrie eloped that some of the heat cooled down. They still give her a rough time because she was divorced. Joey's counting on you and Freddy to draw fire away from them."

"Yeah, and who'll take the bullet for us, then?"

"Maybe Dominic will leave the priesthood or hook up with Kevin Keller."

"The deacon?" Ellice laughed. "He's pretty enough. Oh well, I guess you guys are no worse than the Watsons. My brother hears I'm with another white boy, and this time I may actually tie the knot, he's gonna hire some of those deprogrammers. I don't come home one afternoon, you'll know I've been carted off to some motel, they're takin' turns reading me Malcolm X.''

"Don't be silly. People don't read anymore. They'll take the public school approach and show you the movie.''

"You got that right.'' Ellice had been earning her keep as a highly overqualified substitute teacher.

Cat sprinted up to her bedroom, yanked open the drapes. The bay window faced northeast, high enough to offer a view of the ocean and, if she perched on the window seat and craned her neck, a glimpse of the Atlantic City skyline.

She hurried through her shower, wrapped a towel around her wet hair, wiped the fog from the mirror above the twin sinks. Then she tilted her chin and scrutinized her reflection judiciously, trying to see herself as Victor saw her, as someone he had taken it into his head to pursue. Five-seven. The figure didn't jeopardize traffic, but it was well-proportioned, the contours of her belly softened by the two pregnancies. (Three, Cat reminded herself; the miscarriage, a week after Chris' death, was still a painful memory.) The eyes were dark, under slanting brows, the expression fluctuating between mischief and introspective dreaminess. The face was quicker to show irritation and fatigue these days and faint parentheses bracketed the mouth. "A widow with two kids and six meddling brothers,'' Cat reminded the reflection. Not to mention the purpling depression indenting her ribs that the surgeon had said would fade "a bit.'' And nearer forty than thirty.

And Victor was a widower. Did anyone really rebound from that sort of anguish? Would she ever really be over the life she had shared with Chris? And what about Freddy? He hadn't really gotten over Fawn, not completely, until he'd met Ellice. Or had he? Could there be some residual longing? Cat wondered. *Running with Fawn Caprio.* Cat shook her head. No. He had told Cat he wanted to marry Ellice, planned to ask her as soon as the time was right. That other, the notion that he even thought about Fawn anymore, had to have been a dream.

Cat walked into the bedroom and snapped on the radio, began rooting around for clothes. "…unidentified man in the parking garage of the Sterling Phoenix Casino Hotel, wearing a Santa Claus costume. A spokesperson for the medical examiner's office indicated that foul play cannot be ruled out and stated that a preliminary autopsy is scheduled for this morning. Captain Gale Loeper of the county prosecutor's Major Crimes Bureau, contacted at a law enforcement conference in Baltimore, stated that his unit will work with the local police on the investigation. In an unrelated matter, Captain Loeper confirmed that Detective Sergeant Stanley Rice has been suspended with pay, pending an internal affairs inquiry into his supervision of the Lowell Jeffries arrest, during which Mrs. Khamilla Bolton was shot and killed. Captain Vincenzo Fortunati, of the city department, has likewise confirmed the investigation of Officer Malcolm 'Mac' MacBride, who suffered a gunshot wound during the arrest."

The phone rang. Cat snapped off the radio and reached for the receiver. It was Victor.

"I didn't wake you, did I?"

"I was just lying around listening to the radio," Cat commented. "They were talking about Stan. I didn't know it was that serious." Cat had known Stan Rice for some time; her brother Joey had tried his hand at matchmaking a year or so after Chris' death, efforts which Cat had amiably rebuffed.

"The hearing's just a formality."

"Then why do you sound so worried?"

"Do I?"

"Yes. You're afraid if it comes off looking too cut and dried, the media will call it a whitewash. Afraid they'll play up a racial angle because the woman who was killed was black."

"Did I really imply all of that?"

"If you mean 'no comment' you ought to just say it."

"No comment."

"Fine." Cat ran a comb through her wet hair. "Victor ..?"

"Yes?"

"Were you...had you been seeing anyone? When we met, I mean. And don't say 'no comment.'"

"What brings this up?"

"I was just wondering."

"Not when we met, no. Some time before that there had been one or two, nothing serious."

"What were they like?"

"I beg your pardon?"

"You know what I mean. What did they look like? Did they have interesting lives, did you like being with them?"

"They were quite pleasant. One had a couple of ex-husbands and went back to one of them, I forget which. One was just into casual relationships." (He hoped Cat didn't translate "casual relationships" as "just sex," though that had pretty much been the case.) "And one—"

"I thought you said 'one or two'?"

"Or three. No more than three."

"And?" Cat asked, primly.

"Actually, she was the first. A nurse. We had some fun, but she was looking for someone with at least six figures on the balance sheet. Heard she found one, too, more power to her."

"He had more money than you were fun, you mean?"

"Ouch."

"Sorry." At least he didn't sound brokenhearted about it. "I heard on the radio that your unit's been assigned to the John Doe."

"No comment."

"You'll be short-handed without Stan. Of course, it'll speed things up once you find out who he is. Was."

"You're fishing for information, Lois Lane, you'll need a better lure. Landis put you on the story?"

"No." Not yet.

"He tries, you tell him to get lost, you hear me?"

"Must be a bad connection. That sounded like one of those bullying ultimatums I usually get from Carlo or Vinnie."

"You need a keeper, Cat."

"Pay's low and the hours are lousy."

"But how are the fringe benefits?"

"Depreciating."

"I'll be the judge of that. I have to run, love, but don't knock yourself out baking cookies. If I can tie up a few loose ends at the office, I'll come by and take you to lunch."

Cat ambled back to the kitchen, wondering what "loose ends" Victor had to attend to on a Saturday morning. The phone rang again. Ellice lifted the receiver from the wall unit and a shrill "Cat! Cat!" emerged as she handed it across the table.

"Ritchie, take it down a few decibels." She slid into the booth opposite Ellice.

Ritchie Landis was the editor of *South Jersey* magazine. He had picked up a few short pieces of Cat's, offered her the post of "entertainment girl," stuck her with the profile of shock jocks Tom Hopper and Jerry Dudek. When Dudek was shot, Cat became the unofficial "investigative girl," at least for the duration of the police inquiry.

"Who was it they found in the Phoenix last night? Frankie D'Allessandro says you were trollin' around the parking garage, trip over the stiff and *he* gets the story?"

"You gave me the party scene, you're getting the party scene."

"They didn't give you no byline."

"Double negative. How do you know whether or not I'm getting a byline? The story didn't make the deadline."

"Did so. Nice pic, too, you bein' hustled off by the guy, that cop. He slug the photographer?"

"What?"

"Page six."

Cat snatched *The Press* from Ellice, shuffled rapidly. There it was: CORPSE DISCOVERED IN CASINO GARAGE. No mention of the Phoenix until paragraph three and the name Sterling never appeared at all. The photographer had snapped Victor and Cat as they emerged from the Phoenix Self-Park, the caption read MAJOR CRIMES LIEUTENANT VICTOR CARDENAS ESCORTS WITNESS FROM THE SCENE.

"Damn-edding-nation!" Cat exploded. She shoved the paper in front of Ellice.

"So let's not play games," the phone demanded. "Your boyfriend know anything? *NewsLineNinety* says they didn't ID the guy, he's not talkin'."

"The dead guy?"

"Guy over Major Crimes. Somebody's gotta know him."

"The guy from Major Crimes?"

"The dead guy! Jeez, whaddamy talkin' about?"

"I haven't the faintest idea."

"Bet Loverboy's hopin' this'll take somma the heat off the cop got suspended for the Jeffries thing. All's I could find out is he was layin' there maybe five, six days."

"Sergeant Rice?"

"No, John Doe Claus!"

"Was not."

"Was not what? What's the deal?"

"You tell me."

"Tell you what? I don't know nothin'."

"Finally we agree on something. You tell me what the deal is. I'm already working on the Gambol thing."

"Shelve the Gambol. Here some homeless guy comes in outta the rain, drops—"

"Not 'drops.' *Was* dropped."

"What? *What?* Someone stashes a stiff right under Sterling's nose?"

"Not exactly. Sterling's nose is some twenty floors up in the penthouse. And according to his people, he was in transit when whoever made the drop."

"What people?"

"The Amises mentioned it. So did one of his security people."

"I'm lovin' this, Austen. Picture it. Sterling's limo picks him up at the airport, drops him off on Five, which it always does, so King Midas doesn't hafta cut through the public areas to get to the penthouse, mingle with the plebes. Swings past the elevator and there's the little bundle." Ritchie broke off, chortling. "Jeez, Austen, I almost wish you hadn't found the guy first."

"Yeah. Pity I was the only reporter on the scene."

"Don't go bitchy on me, Austen."

"I still have the Gambol piece, I'll maybe look into the dead guy, but you have to come across with the money you owe me for *Deadly Enmity*."

"Huh?"

"*Deadly Enmity?* The Dudek story?"

"Oh, yeah. I'll get you a check first of the week. But we may have to re-think that title."

Cat felt her heart slump. "This half of 'we' likes the title."

"I'm thinkin' something catchier. Somethin' like *Death of a DJ*, whaddaya think?"

Cat swallowed, counted ten, took a deep breath. "I think 'Striving to better, oft we mar what's well.' King Lear."

"Y'see, there you go again with the Shakespeare. Deadly enmity and marrin' what's in the well and stuff, no one picks up *South Jersey* 'cause it reads like the Barge."

"Bard," Cat sighed. "Fine. But re-thinking costs. Whether or not I come up with anything in the next couple days, this does not get passed on to Ron Spivak or any of your other hotshots. It's mine for the duration."

"Look, just don't screw up. Piece like this ain't for the faint of heart."

Cat felt an adrenaline heat. She had taken up the Dudek story reluctantly, but she'd stuck it out, every bizarre and dangerous twist and turn, put together a decent account of the episode. If she passed on this one, she would always wonder whether the Dudek piece had been a flash in the pan. "I'm not faint of heart," Cat returned and named her price. The echo of Victor's "Landis put you on this story? He tries, you tell him to get lost" was drowned by Ritchie's howl.

ELLICE WENT FOR a walk, which worried Cat a little, since Freddy had planned to invade the ladies-only gathering and coax Ellice out for a romantic tête-à-tête. Why had she tripped over that stupid corpse last night, dragging the Sterling name, the image of Fawn, into the picture?

The doorbell startled Cat; she hurried to answer it, expecting Freddy, or perhaps her mother arriving early with the kids. She had gotten a head start on a batch of shortbread, so she rubbed her dough-encrusted hands against the flannel shirt, opened the foyer door and peered through the block glass that bordered the front entrance. The male figure wasn't Freddy or Victor or any of Cat's brothers. She wrestled with the lock, stumbled against the jamb and beheld Carlton Amis.

"Good morning, Mrs. Austen."

"I, uh, Mr. Amis. Sorry, I thought you'd be someone else."

"You're expecting company?"

"Some family."

"I won't take up much of your time then. May I come in?"

"Yes, of course."

Cat caught a glimpse of herself in the foyer mirror, her hair pulled into a barrette, a few wisps falling over her ears, her faded flannel shirt dusted with flour. She rubbed a smear of butter from her nose and ushered Amis through the inner door to the center hallway. "May I take your coat?"

"No, I'll just throw it here." He tossed it over a living room chair. It was cashmere. With the accent on *cash,* Cat thought, resolving to store the observation for future use. Cat noticed his glance taking in her living room decorated for the holidays, taking in the nutcrackers on the mantle, the wall of bookshelves, the undecorated tree at the foot of the stairs, an appraisal that was swift, yet comprehensive, sizing her up. He turned to her with a smooth, intimate smile. "Mrs. Austen, I came to express personally the deep distress Mr. Sterling feels regarding your unpleasant experience last night. Mr. Sterling would like me to assure you that the Sterling Phoenix is committed to the security of its patrons and that the hotel is prepared to compensate—"

"Mr. Amis," Cat interrupted, startled. "I don't think I suffered anything for which a sensible person would ask compensation. It never occurred to me. You don't think I'd file a lawsuit, do you? We have enough of those as it is."

"And more than enough lawyers, too?" He flashed a confident smile. Cat recalled that in his pre-Sterling era, he had been dubbed the Casanova of Criminal Court.

No, she wouldn't dream of suing, especially not when it was more to her advantage to remain on cordial terms with anyone connected to last night's incident. "Did Mr. Sterling get in last night, then?"

"Pardon?"

"You said he was upset by the incident. I was just wondering if he heard about it when he got in or if someone called him in New York."

"That sounds like a reporter's inquiry, Mrs. Austen."

"Does it?"

"Yes. And I'm sure you understand that Mr. Sterling is anxious to avoid any unpleasantness from the media that could affect the outcome of the Gambol."

Or affect the revenue, Cat thought. "I don't doubt it."

"And naturally I couldn't help observing that the article on page six in this morning's *Press* contained a few details that could only have been supplied by someone who had been at the scene. The police have declined to make a statement and the scene was restricted to reporters."

"And you were wondering if I contributed to the piece? Just as I'm wondering when Mr. Sterling got in last night."

Amis hesitated. "When Cookie came back upstairs, she and I left together. I believe Mr. Sterling got in some time after."

"And I contributed to the story in the paper, Mr. Amis."

"Please, call me Carl." There was a liquid intimacy in his tone, a worldliness that a professor might employ on a naive coed. It unnerved Cat a little. "It was my understanding that your *métier* was something in a lighter vein. Entertainment and that sort of thing."

"I don't think I've found my *métier* yet," Cat replied. "I think I'm a late bloomer."

He smiled again, drew up a briefcase constructed of the velvety hide of something that Cat decided probably ought not to have been killed, skinned. "At any rate, I'm sure you really need more than interviews to complete your current piece," he said as he thumbed the tumblers on the combination. "The Sterling Phoenix would like to offer you an invitation to the Gambol."

"I can't take that, Mr. Amis."

"Carl." The smile became sunnier. "It's a gift, Mrs. Austen, not a bribe."

"It never occurred to me that it was a bribe, Mr. Amis. A bribe is what you give someone when there's something you want them to do. Or to forget. My people are Sicilians, Mr. Amis, very well versed in *quid pro quo* and everything that it implies. And since I have nothing to give you in return, and have this inconvenient habit of doing and saying what I choose, I'm sure you understand that it would be useless to attempt to bribe me. So of course it isn't a bribe."

"You're quite old-fashioned, Mrs. Austen. That's delightful."

"Really? Most people find it a nuisance."

Amis laid down the envelope to throw on his coat, turned up the collar with the grace of an Errol Flynn. "Well, please let me know if you change your mind." He slipped his card on the end table next to the phone. "Oh, my wife mentioned that she saw you on the boardwalk this morning. Are you a runner, Mrs. Austen?"

"I try." Cat handed him the envelope.

"I try, too," Amis smiled. "Cookie's the athlete, though. Perhaps we'll link up some morning on the boards."

Cat didn't know what to say, opened the door and followed him into the tiny foyer.

Amis pocketed the envelope. "Oh, and Cookie told me about that little mishap of yours last month. Dudek business, right? I don't suppose you'd like to get involved in something like that again any time soon. Wound up in the hospital, didn't you? It must have been rough on your children. Two children, correct? Boy and a girl?"

Cat decided that the chill in his blue-eyed gaze was all her imagination.

SIX

THERE HAD BEEN something not quite decent in Blaine G. Sterling's acquisition of his father's enterprise. That something—a pact coaxed from the elder that was greatly to his disadvantage, that had relegated him to uselessness, a premature demise...had never been scrutinized by a media captivated with this rising corporate star. The attraction was mutual; Sterling found fame headier, more satisfying than success. Soon fame was no longer a byproduct of the work...it was the work.

The first current of media antagonism came when he jettisoned a twenty-year marriage for a twentysomething up-and-coming designer. The accounts of the crushing settlement wrought from King Midas by his discarded spouse, revealed with lascivious relish, were his first indication that what had been given could be withdrawn. Or worse, it could be bestowed elsewhere; upon his new wife, for example.

The bonding of two such volatile temperaments might have disintegrated under any circumstances; perhaps the media's fickleness only accelerated hostilities as Sterling and Fawn spun in separate orbits. The Phoenix project retrieved some of the limelight, but it was harsher now and the blemishes emerged: the Sterling surliness, the Sterling temper, the Sterling contempt for the general public. When Fawn ignored her husband's project to concentrate on her debut line, the media declared their separation. When Fawn consented to open a showroom in the Phoenix, it was announced they had made amends. When she slighted AC to concentrate on Fashion Week, they were estranged; when he accompanied her to the CapriOH! showing, they were reunited. When Fawn opened her Margate house, spent Thanksgiving there alone, divorce was imminent; when she abruptly shut up her bayfront home and moved into the Phoenix, they were reconciling once more.

All of this was documented in a folder containing a series

of photocopied articles, newspaper photos, a copy of *King Midas*. In a second, slimmer folder lay a summary from ACPD and a half dozen black-and-white photos from the Medical Examiner's office. No prints, no ID. Of course, matters tended to downshift over the weekend, but Adane would have considered completing the file a matter of personal pride.

Victor poked his head out of his office, noted that her desk was in its usual state of near military precision, the chair only slightly askew. She had logged in early, which was routine, left her desk abruptly, which was not. Victor went back to his desk, put in a call to the medical examiner's office, was told the ME was at the hospital, called the hospital, asked for the morgue, was reminded that the site formerly known as "morgue" was now the Office of Decedent Observation and Review. Patiently, he asked for the Office of Decedent Observation and Review, was put through to someone who answered the phone with "Morgue!" Victor asked to speak with the medical examiner, was told "I don't know if I know where he's at," put on hold, where he remained for ten minutes before the connection was broken and he was back to a dial tone. He sighed, considered a second foray through the hospital's phone system, flipped through the file, thought the matter over, pocketed the lab photos, left a note for Adane and headed for the Phoenix.

The Self-Park entrance on Oriental was still cordoned off. Victor parked on New Bedford, adjacent to J m's, walked the long block to the hotel entrance next to the Boardwalk. A perimeter of green, black-veined marble surrounded the gaming floor. It glistened like a wary sea, reflecting the lighting fixtures on the ceiling, the black inverted domes of the eye-in-the-sky. The hotel reception area was to the right, a strip mall—souvenir shop, newsstand, deli, coffee bar—to the left.

Victor observed a few people listlessly pumping change into the machines, heard the jangle of coins, bells, buzzers, a thread of piped-in holiday music punctuated by cries of elation or, more often, dismay. Cocktail waitresses in sequined skullcaps and green-and-gold feathered skirts tottered through the aisles offering coffee, juice and soft drinks with Sterling poise.

Victor found an information booth at the rim of the gaming floor, approached a young woman wearing the regulation green blazer with the Phoenix crest. She flashed the Sterling smile, asked, "May I help you, sir?"

Victor presented his identification and asked if either Mr. or Mrs. Sterling were on the premises.

The smile congealed. "Sir, I can direct you to our head of security or the DGE office."

"Thank you, but I know how to find them."

"I can call up on Five. If Mr. Amis is in his office, perhaps he can arrange to see you."

"Are the Sterlings on the premises?" he repeated, politely.

The girl hesitated. "Sir, I think it would be better if I directed you to security."

Victor paused. Poor kid, it was a tough call, might mean her job. "You know why I'm here," he said, quietly. "I'm sure the matter is being addressed to all personnel at the beginning of each shift. Hotel security and the DGE were on the scene last night and they're aware that my unit has been given responsibility for the investigation. If you feel the need to contact Mr. Sterling's attorney or hotel security, I would be happy to meet them at Mr. Sterling's quarters."

A few people behind Victor were listening covertly to the discussion. A couple began to whisper. The girl glanced at them, nervously. "Take the escalator up to the mezzanine level, turn right toward the north wing conference area, you'll see the tower elevators. Show your identification to the guard there and he'll let you on the elevator to the penthouse."

Victor thanked her and saw, reflected in the polished metal of the escalator, a green-sleeved arm reaching for the house phone.

The security guard at the tower elevator wore the same green blazer, the sleeves straining over biceps that flexed defensively at Victor's approach. "Help you, sir?"

Victor produced ID. "I'm going to the penthouse."

The man studied the ID a few seconds too long, his lips moving as he logged the data on the placard and shield. He picked up a house phone on the wall beside the elevator,

pushed a button, never taking his eyes off Victor. "Yes," he
said, "there's a Lieutenant Cardenas"—he mispronounced the
surname—"here, says he wantsta come up. No, county. Major
Crimes." A longer pause, and something like surprise registered on the man's features. He hung up. "Okay, you can go
up. Get in, push PE, that's Penthouse East, the Orchid Suite.
There'll be a guy up there to check you in."

The elevator made a swift, soundless ascent and the door
opened on a marble foyer, gilt mirrors on brocade walls. Another security guard, same biceps, same slow-witted aggres-
sion. "Cardenas?"

Victor produced his identification again.

"Like to check your weapon, sir?"

"Absolutely not," Victor replied, nonplussed by such a request of a police officer.

Before the guard could reply, a man emerged from the Orchid Suite. "Lieutenant Cardenas?" he asked in a liquid tenor.
"Hi, I'm Donnie Finch, Mrs. Sterling's back office boy." He
extended a hand, gave Victor's a flaccid shake. "This month's
boy," he added, covertly. "The rumor is we don't have much
of a shelf life. Now sugar," he admonished the glowering
guard, "stop working on those frown lines." He ushered Victor into the suite, closed the door.

Donnie Finch was tall, the supple, athletic figure garbed in
too-snug jeans and a yellow silk shirt. He had blond hair gathered into a neat ponytail and wire-rimmed glasses slightly
magnifying his dark brown eyes. A middle-aged woman in a
black dress stepped forward to take Victor's coat; Finch called
her "Consolación" and instructed her, in excellent Spanish,
to tell Mrs. Sterling that Lieutenant Cardenas had arrived and
that Mr. Amis' secretary just called up to say that Mr. Amis
was not in his office, she would try the cellular.

Donnie led Victor down a long corridor. "Mrs. S. agreed
to see you, but don't take up too much of her time, because
she's got a fitting at ten and then a photo shoot with the Gambol committee and a meet with the artwork people and the
linens." He gave Victor a droll stare, lowered his voice.
"Shipped from the Sterling Marquesa in Acapulco. Of course,

we could do with the hotel stock, but it's the Phoenix's debut and, dear, King Midas is determined this *rara avis* will fly.''

''Is Mr. Sterling here?''

''Well, not *here* here. In conference. He got in late last night.''

''He's been informed of the incident at the hotel?''

''Well, it wasn't exactly the hotel now, was it? Not inside, I mean. And anybody can drive into the parking lot, *verdad?*''

Victor looked at the man, decided that the hair color was not natural, that Mrs. Sterling's ''back office boy'' was nearer to forty than thirty, worked at appearing younger. *''Verdad,''* he replied.

''You'll have to excuse me, Lieutenant, I have to get Mrs. Sterling's ginseng. You take milk or sugar? Honey?''

Victor decided that the man was asking if he took milk or sugar *or* honey, replied, ''Nothing for me, thank you.''

Donnie left him in an intimate salon, a curving marble staircase at its center, swept through an archway into the dining room and disappeared.

Victor surveyed the apartment. Orchid, and they weren't kidding. The two inches of costly Berber, the weighty raw silk drapes, the brocade upholstery and matching wall coverings, the moire frames on the photographs, even the stalks of narcissi in the Lalique vase, were all an identical shade of orchid. Pastel nudes, too languid to be erotic, no bookcases. The library table against one wall was piled with stacks of folders, a heap of fabric scraps, a fax machine; a bolt of something diaphanous was tossed underneath.

A trio of twenty-foot windows, bare except for a gauzy valance at the rim, overlooked the Atlantic. The Sterling horizon, Victor observed, no pedestrian Boardwalk detail, just a gray-green sweep of sea and sky. The view from the center window was obscured by a Christmas tree, a tapering mountain of some plush orchid synthetic, its sole ornamentation daggerlike purple prisms that sprayed the walls and carpet with sparks of deflected light.

He heard a faint silken whisper, saw bright turquoise skirts descend the curved oak staircase, pass behind the twelve-tiered chandelier that broke the moving form into a cluster of polygons; it reassembled as a petite, supple form in a kimono.

Fawn Caprio-Sterling was not beautiful by Madison Avenue standards, Hollywood standards. The jaw was too square and resolute, the light gray eyes narrow and feline, slanting above high, flat cheekbones. The arched blond eyebrows were barely visible against the pale complexion, the smooth forehead indented with a deep, narrow widow's peak. But there was a febrile energy that emanated from the small form, a sexual heat that even Victor sensed and that must have been irresistible to a heart as warm and susceptible as Freddy Fortunati's. Victor registered the sensuality with detachment, noted, too, that the expertise with which the makeup had been applied had not entirely camouflaged the tension, the want of rest and composure.

"Lieutenant Cardenas?" The voice was flat, with a husky edge that could wax sexual. "Where did Donnie disappear to?"

Donnie materialized with a silver tray holding a silver pot with an elaborate S engraved on the surface, translucent cups, and a china filigree platter bearing a pyramid of butter wafers.

"Donnie, go down to Five and tell them when Mrs. Amis comes in for the photo shoot, she can talk to the food and beverage people, and let her take care of those damned linens, too. She's the Gambol chair, not me."

"I'll call—"

"Go."

"You sure you wouldn't rather I hung around?"

"Yes, Donnie." Pointed.

Donnie seemed to hesitate; after a moment, he offered a pallid "Hope to see you again, Lieutenant," and departed.

"Now, Lieutenant, how may I help you?" She arranged herself behind the teapot, patted the soft cushion on her right. "Cardenas," she said, thoughtfully. "There's a Remedios Cardenas, a jewelry designer. Any relation?"

Victor hesitated. "My sister." He took a seat opposite her.

"Really? Talented girl."

"Will there be someone from legal coming up, Mrs. Sterling?"

"This is about that dreadful thing that happened last night, isn't it?" The phrase "dreadful thing" had an edge of lurid fascination. She dropped a slice of lemon in her cup, poured. "Tea, Lieutenant?"

"No, thank you. Yes, it is about the incident that occurred last night."

"Forgive me, Lieutenant, I don't quite understand the law enforcement hierarchy around here. I thought the DGE office was handling this. Major Crimes does what?"

"We're assigned to the county prosecutor's office. We investigate any suspicious death."

"I see. Then perhaps I should call in an attorney."

"I'd be happy to wait, if you'd like to place a call to your legal office, but I really came to ask for your help, Mrs. Sterling. Or your husband's, if he's available."

"Blaine's in some conference or other, I believe." She sipped her tea.

"He came down from the city last night?"

"Yes."

"May I ask what time?"

Fawn shrugged. "Hard to say."

"Could you approximate? Was it, for example, nearer to ten than midnight?"

"Oh, not nearly so late as midnight. Is that all you wanted to ask, Lieutenant? My husband's whereabouts?"

"No. The deceased was wearing a costume that was apparently one of those rented for the Christmas party's serving staff."

"Yes, I heard that. A Santa Claus costume, wasn't it? One of the ones Cookie—Mrs. Amis—rented. Personally, I would have gone with something less conventional."

Not a syllable expressing compassion or curiosity regarding the dead man, Victor observed. "It suggests he had access to the hotel, an employee perhaps."

A ripple of something like impatience passed over her attentive features. "A Phoenix employee? You don't know who he is?" She scrutinized him as she would a length of yard goods, looking for defects, imperfection. "Or you know and you're not saying. You want to know if *I* know, is that it?"

"It's possible that you may know him," Victor replied, noncommittally. "I have some photos taken by the lab photographer. Would you be willing to look at them and tell me if the face looks familiar to you?"

"Certainly. But the Phoenix employs a couple thousand people, Lieutenant. I doubt that I know more than a handful of them. Have you spoken to Mrs. Amis? She's Blaine's majordomo—or would that be majordama? Or you could try the personnel files."

"Thank you for the suggestion."

"I suppose those photographs are rather sordid."

"They're not pleasant, no."

She laid down her cup. "Then by all means, let's have a peek." She arranged the skirts of her gown with one hand, extended the other to Victor.

Victor drew the photos from his breast pocket. Fawn's fingers stroked the back of his hand as she accepted them. Victor could not decide if the touch was deliberate.

Fawn's gray eyes darted over the photographs, scanning one picture after the other, never blinking or averting her gaze. The lab had exposed the man's crushed and discolored face for the lens and the photographer had moved in close. Victor wondered what this woman was who could look so calmly on such a face. He tried to put Freddy and Fawn Sterling together in his mind, found it impossible.

There was a pause, then she handed them back and said, "No, I don't know this man," with a resolution that seemed a bit too premeditated, rehearsed. Absurd to think he could take the Sterlings by surprise, Victor thought. She had been well prepared, ready to be questioned, revealing only what she intended him to see.

"Has anything unusual occurred recently, Mrs. Sterling? Problems with staff, disgruntled employees?"

"I'm not aware of anything like that. I've got my own crew; most of them are in the city."

"And the liaison?"

"Who? Oh, Donnie? Well, yes, he is new and I have run through quite a few of them, I suppose."

"Any of his predecessors harbor ill feelings toward you?"

"Not that I'm aware." Again, the question triggered an impatient shrug.

Victor took back the pictures, was pocketing them when he heard the door open, slam, an angry step cross the long corridor and Blaine Sterling himself walked into the room.

Sterling was in his early fifties, tall and angular, but the figure was neither so tall, nor the sagging jawline and abbreviated chin so formidable as they appeared in the carefully posed photographs released to the press. The thinning gold hair had gone half white, the lips were scant, the eyes a milky blue that gave his stare an eerie, faintly malignant cast. The figure was a bit above average height, with narrow shoulders and a budding paunch camouflaged by artful tailoring.

"Fawn?" he inquired, not pleasantly, as he looked from his wife to Victor. For a moment, Victor thought Sterling believed he had surprised his wife in a rendezvous.

"Blaine, this is Lieutenant Cardenas from the county prosecutor's office. Lieutenant, my husband, Blaine Sterling."

Sterling, too, seemed prepared. "We have no statement regarding the vagrant who was found in the parking garage. Call legal and speak to Carlton Amis if there's anything you need to ask."

"What makes you think he was a vagrant, Blaine?"

The question had been on Victor's tongue; he was amazed that Mrs. Sterling would challenge her husband in front of the police. Perhaps they hadn't had time to get their stories straight.

"Who else could it have been?"

"It could have been an employee, Mr. Sterling," Victor replied. "As a matter of fact, I was just asking Mrs. Sterling if she could recognize him from the medical examiner's photographs."

"That's not Fawn's place, Lieutenant. Go down and check with Human Resources or Personnel."

"I've already invited the lieutenant to do that, Blaine."

"Then why is the lieutenant still here? And why the hell didn't you call Carl in? You're not being particularly smart this morning, Fawn."

"Nonsense. I've never been smarter. Why don't you have a look at the photographs the lieutenant showed me? Perhaps you'll recognize the man."

"I'm not looking at any pictures. Lieutenant, I'm going to have to ask you to leave and you may be assured that your supervisor will be getting a call from my attorney today." Sterling shouted the maid's name querulously, snapped "Show this man to the elevator," when she scuttled into the room.

Fawn reached for her teacup, patiently repeated her husband's order in passable Spanish.

Victor heard Sterling grumble, "...can damn well afford to hire help who can speak the language..." as he was hustled into his coat, into the hallway.

In the corridor, he turned to her, asked in a low voice, *"Señora, por favor, la señora de Sterling, estaba aqui ayer?"*

The opaque eyes flicked nervously toward the guard at the elevator. *"Si."*

"Y anoche?"

"No se. Yo no se."

"Y el Señor Sterling—"

"Por favor, señor. No se, no se."

Victor nodded, said, *"Muchas gracias,"* politely and stepped into the elevator.

Passing through the ostentatious mezzanine, Victor replayed the scene in his mind. The night and morning that the Sterlings had to adjust to the unpleasant news hardly accounted for the undercurrent of suspicion and hostility. There had been more than fear of bad publicity in Sterling's attitude, more than the sniping of an estranged wife in Mrs. Sterling's. *The hell with both of them,* Victor thought. He'd put Long on Personnel and Human Resources, put Adane on the morgue—office of whatever. She never got stuck on hold.

His eyes took in the mezzanine; he thought of Cat's description, the interior of the coffee shop executed with a great deal of money and no taste. He was thinking of her as he glanced up at the window of Bon Soie, where an anorexic mannequin was draped in a kimono of shimmering peach, lined with burgundy silk, a matching burgundy gown underneath. He imagined Cat's chestnut hair against the bright silk, the burgundy slip taking on the configurations of a real woman's figure.

Inside the shop, a distractingly pretty salesgirl was folding something in layers of pastel tissue as gently as if it were fine china. Her figure was coated with fuschia knit, a topaz reindeer pinned over one ample breast. ("When a woman is dressed like that," Victor's father had said once, "look her straight in the eyes.")

"That," Victor inquired, pointing to the kimono and looking straight into the woman's eyes. "How much?"

The price named was, within pennies, two weeks' salary.

What the hell, he thought. He made decent money and had no one to spend it on. "Wrap it up," he said.

As the woman lay the peignoir in a box, Victor saw a smear of yellow appear in the mirrored wall behind the counter, the reflection of a figure in the opposite doorway. Victor turned and the figure vanished into the shop across the way; he looked up and saw CapriOH! in gold letters above the door.

So Mrs. Sterling had sent her "back office boy" to spy on him. Interesting.

SEVEN

VICTOR WAS DRIVING through Longport, headed into Ocean City, when his car phone rang.

"Victor, we got some trouble." It was Kurt Raab. "I get a message on my machine, Carlton Amis. I call him back, he reams me out, claims you were over the Phoenix harassing the Sterlings."

Victor checked the clock on the dash. Twenty minutes since he'd left the Phoenix. "There was no harassment."

"Don't get defensive. I'm impressed you made it to the penthouse. Never woulda happened if Amis had been in the building. So what'd you all chat about?"

"The John Doe was wearing a costume taken from the hotel's dressing room. I thought the deceased might be an employee."

"Yeah, well, if that's all you were thinking, you woulda headed for Personnel. You wanted to shake the tree, see what hit the ground."

"I asked Mrs. Sterling if she could identify the man from the lab photos. Sterling came in, told me to leave."

"So did you?"

"Leave? Of course."

"Shake them up."

"Mrs. Sterling was very cool. The only thing that nettled her was when I suggested the man might have been a former employee of hers. Sterling wasn't so cool, but both of them had been prepped. I asked the maid if she could tell me their whereabouts last night, she's not talking. Afraid it'll cost her her job."

"Look, I'll tell you what. Try Amis' wife, Cookie. Patsy says she and Sterling and the first wife go way back. He brought her on board after Amis got him licensed. If you're in Ocean City, drop by their place, it's up North Castle Drive, quite a spread."

"Carlton Amis' wife won't talk to me without her husband's counsel and Amis wouldn't let me in the door."

"*Quien sabe?* She's wired to what goes on in the hotel and she's got Sterling's ear. It's worth a shot. The ME's doin' a prelim on the guy, his lab boy faxed the prints, you get 'em?"

"No." They hadn't been in the folder Adane had prepared. "I've been out of the office. I'm sure Adane's taken care of it by now."

"Adane's on it, she prob'ly got the ID right down to the guy's kindergarten teacher. Now listen, I gotta bring up a touchy subject. Marty Bevilacqua's heading Tom Hopper's defense team and we had a little chat. Hopper'll plead to voluntary manslaughter.''

''Martin Bevilacqua can go to hell.''

''Victor, listen. I know you got a personal stake in the Hopper business, but let me be straight: murder two is weak. Gotta prove malice. Prove, mind you, to the kinda juries they're diggin' up these days. Think about it: I send one of my ladies to the plate, I'm thinkin' of givin' it to The Swan, she's not afraid of Marty B., but still, these juries, Victor, they're bleedin' hearts. I put him up for *numero dos* and Hopper walks, it's all over. It's a mis, we decide to retry, the taxpayers go nuts.''

''I'll testify to what Dudek's sister told me in the hospital. So will the father. A dying declaration—''

''Still might not get admitted. And if it doesn't, we can't tie the murder weapon to Hopper. So basically, all we got is what Hopper confessed to Mrs. Austen and that's hearsay. Plus, that jerk runs *South Jersey* magazine? Landis? He sent me proofs of Mrs. Austen's story. It's a little too damned sympathetic to Hopper to suit me.''

''Can you block publication until after the preliminary hearings?''

''Yeah, right. You know the First Amendment?''

''We've met.''

''Already, I got *Tomorrow Now* and *Front Cover* trying to get me on the phone, not to mention some damned associate producer from *CopWatch* wantsta know do I wanna be on TV! Me! They tug the heartstrings, there go my jurors; they smear Hopper, I gotta deal with—''

''The Sixth Amendment—''

''And you haven't lived 'til you've seen Marty B. work that one for all it's worth, plus I heard the bail hearing's in front of Harkness, so don't be surprised if he's turned loose, 'cause Poppa Hopper'll pay.''

''Don't tell me. The Eighth Amendment.''

''Harkness, that one's her favorite. Hopper, he's in counseling. He's expressing remorse, the son of a bitch. He wantsta thank Mrs. Austen for saving his life, he asked if she'd be allowed to visit—"

"Out of the question. Hopper wants to set himself up as the victim in this, he's not going to have Mrs. Austen's collaboration."

"Thanks. Now, for the *pièce de résistance*. Guess who's coming to dinner?"

"I don't guess."

"The Reverend Marlon d'Esperance." Raab pronounced it as the Reverend did: Dee-esper-ants. "I heard he plans to horn in on the Bolton woman's funeral, stir up the pot. So my goal here is to keep Stan under wraps until the Rev blows town."

"When's Stan's hearing?"

"Monday. We're gonna bring him over to Mays Landing. The rookie, too. I don't foresee a problem with Stan; Mac-Bride might get a reprimand. Everything's gonna go by the book, so d'Esperance can't yell whitewash."

"I don't think he's read the book. My text says it was Jeffries who fired MacBride's weapon and shot the woman."

"Your text doesn't accommodate the agenda."

"It's the truth."

"The truth!" Raab snorted. "Victor, the truth don't mean squat. I been a lawyer long enough to know that."

THERE WERE SIX CARS clustered along the curb in front of 1043 Morningside Drive. As Victor ascended the porch steps, he could hear Carlo's bellow rising above strata of bickering and mirth.

"Season's greetings!" Nancy Fortunati opened the door, waved him into the center hall. Victor saw that an impromptu buffet lunch had been assembled on the dining table, a couple of Cat's brothers making sandwiches, a couple in the living room. "I thought this was ladies only," he said to Nancy as she took his coat.

"It was." Nancy glanced over her shoulder, lowered her voice. "Law enforcement grapevine. The Fortunatis are wired to it. They heard Cat got in a scrape last night, they draw the wagons into a circle. Cat really found this dead guy?"

Victor nodded gravely. "Is Cat around?"

"She went upstairs to dig up cookie tins. Come get a look at what she did with the house. Cat always does a nice job at Christmas."

It was pretty. Garlands had been draped over the archways on either side of the center hall. Stockings had been fastened to the mantle over the living room fireplace, a collection of nutcrackers had replaced the family photographs. Evergreens lay over the banister of the L-shaped stair, a tall blue spruce, undecorated, at the foot, nearly obstructing the small passage to the den behind.

The brothers greeted Victor with varying shades of cordiality. Carlo, a retired chief of police, called out, "C'mon in here, make yourself something to eat." He was piling layers of meat and cheese on a submarine roll.

Victor shook his head, followed Nancy into the kitchen. The room had become a bakery: Annamarie (Carlo's wife) and Lorraine (Vinnie's wife) were rolling and slicing ribbons of pale dough. Jane and one of her cousins were twisting them into knots and passing them off to Cat's mother, Jennie, who presided over a vat of simmering oil. She extended her cheek to Victor, her eyes on the pot.

Victor kissed her cheek.

"Hi," Annamarie greeted. "Wanna roll up your sleeves?"

"I'm not much of a chef."

"That's not what I heard."

Victor wondered what they had heard, whether, on the distaff side of the Fortunati grapevine, he had been the subject of gossip.

"Keep neat," Nancy reminded everyone. "I want to get some family photos later on."

"I hate having my picture taken." Cat appeared in the doorway with an armload of cookie tins.

"So how come it's you shows up in the paper this morning, page six." Vinnie had come up behind her, his expression dour, the dark eyes darting from her to Victor.

Cat caught Vinnie's eye, jerked her head toward Jane, who went on yellow alert at her uncle's remark.

"When the hell you gonna decorate that tree?" Carlo bellowed from the dining room. "You want, I'll go up the attic, bring your stuff down after I eat."

"I'll do it when I do it. I have to get the rest of the tins." She leaned toward Victor, whispered, "Get me out of here," before she left.

Carlo chuckled as his kid sister stalked up the stairs, but Victor saw his dark eyes were sober, concerned.

Annamarie drifted to the table where Sherrie was rolling out shortbread, cutting it in the shape of stars. She helped herself to a nugget of dough. "Cat's is always better than mine. She should've been a pastry chef."

"Nah, Cat shoulda been a cop." Marco wedged himself into the kitchen, shook hands with Victor, opened the refrigerator. "How come all she keeps is Pepsi around here? Second best shot in the family, next to yours truly." Marco helped himself to a Diet Pepsi. "So how's Stan holdin' up?"

"He's holding up," Victor replied.

"I heard, over the range, she outscored you," Carlo called from the dining room.

"Shut up."

"Five cops in the family are enough," Lorraine muttered. "Cat's got the kids and this house, that's plenty to keep her busy."

"Well, I think Cat should have been an interior decorator," Nancy offered. "I mean, Aunt Catti renovated this place, but it was really Cat who pulled it all together."

"Yeah, well, since we're at it, I think she shoulda—"

The sentence was cut short by a clatter of aluminum tins on the kitchen linoleum. "Cat should have been left alone today, that's what Cat should have been!" Cat stood in the doorway. "Has it ever occurred to anyone around here that there's already something I am!" She gave one of the tins a vengeful kick, cut across the room and slammed out the back door before anyone could speak.

Four-year-old Mats had toddled onto the scene, processed what had occurred and went up to his Uncle Carlo, who had been the last to speak, and punched him on the arm. "You stop talking bad to my mom!"

Freddy had been assembling sandwiches for himself and Ellice; he put down his plate. Ellice laid a hand over his sleeve. "Let her have a minute to cool down."

His brothers waited to see what Freddy would do. Freddy shrugged, picked up his plate.

Carlo put down his sandwich and hauled Mats into his arms. "That was a nice shot, Matteo."

Mats flexed a bicep. "I'm gettin' muscles."

"You're gettin' your mom's attitude, is what you're gettin'."

"Good for him," Freddy shot back. "What're you always putting her down for?"

"Shut up. We do not."

"Don't tell me to shut up—"

"Shut up is a bad word," Mats informed them.

"You all be quiet and let your sister manage her own affairs," Jennie said, brandishing a slotted spoon with authority.

"She's just a little strung out, that's all," Annie said. "I mean, she's only been out of the hospital three weeks. It's probably starting to hit her, you know, that she could have been…" Annamarie glanced toward Jane.

"It's this big house," Lorraine cut in. "It's too much for her. I don't know what Aunt Caterina, rest in peace, was thinking, leaving it to her—"

"Cat deserved it," Freddy shot back.

"But it is a lot of house," Nancy interjected. "And what with the kids and the upkeep, not to mention her writing, she's burning herself out."

Mats' eyes went wide with panic. "Is Mom on *fire?*"

Freddy took Mats from Carlo, kissed the top of his head. "No, hon, 'burned out' means 'tired.'"

"Maybe you should make it easier for Cat to do what she wants instead of trying to run her life all the time," Sherrie suggested. She shifted around in the booth to accommodate her belly.

"You don't know what you're talkin' about," Vinnie shot back. "She's our sister, not yours."

"But she's not your baby sister anymore and I do so know what I'm talking about!" Sherrie looked up from her work, her rosebud mouth pursed defiantly.

Victor suppressed a smile. Sherrie had been beaten down once; she wasn't going to take anything from anyone, not even from Joey's older brothers. He liked her.

"And Nancy shouldn't say 'not to mention her writing' like it's some frivolous hobby Cat's taken up for kicks. She's trying to make a career out of it, so maybe you should try to figure some way to help her out."

"Whatever happened to those movie reviews and stuff?" Carlo demanded. "They were okay. All of a sudden, every stiff turns up this side of the Atlantic, she's gotta be right there?"

"What's a stiff?" Mats asked.

"It's what your Uncle Carlo's gonna be he doesn't keep his mouth shut," Jennie replied.

"Excuse me," Victor said, abruptly.

"You leaving?" Vinnie asked.

"Temporarily. It's around forty degrees outside and Cat forgot to grab a coat." Victor cut through the knot of Fortunatis, maneuvered past the Christmas tree and retrieved Cat's leather jacket from the stair closet.

He found her sitting on a jetty, her arms wrapped around her shins, chin propped on her knees. He sat beside her, dropped the jacket over her shoulders.

"Are they signing the commitment papers?"

"No, they can do that after they take you in. They're still rummaging around for the straitjacket."

Cat's mouth curved, mischievously. "I hid it." She pulled the jacket close, gazed at the lazy winter surf.

"Wanna talk?" Victor asked.

"Not really."

"Walk?"

"No."

"Listen?"

"Do I have a choice?"

"No. I got a call from Kurt Raab a short while ago. He thinks that getting Hopper convicted's going to be rough."

"Why?"

"Juries seem to be somewhat less fact-oriented these days. And Landis sent Raab proofs of your piece. Raab said it was sympathetic to Hopper's situation."

"Everything I wrote is fact-oriented."

"The problem is that those facts can be assembled to present Hopper in a exculpatory light."

"So Mr. Raab's saying if he doesn't get a conviction, *I'm* responsible?"

"Cat, no one is saying that—"

"You are too."

"He's simply saying that it's going to be a long haul and asked me to request that you not communicate with Hopper—"

"Order me, you mean. Why would I communicate with Tom, anyway? My story's written."

"So I can have your word that whether or not he makes bail, you'll have no contact?"

"He's made bail!"

"He could."

"Wait a minute—does Tom want to talk to me? Is that what this is about?" Cat contemplated an exclusive with Tom Hopper.

Victor looked at her. "Cat, it's out of the question. I want your word that you won't communicate with him."

"What you want is blind obedience."

"I could live with that."

"Then get a Labrador retriever."

"Cat, do you think about how close you came to getting yourself killed—"

Cat sprang to her feet. "I know how close you are to getting *your*self killed, Lieutenant. If you're looking for a fight, fair warning, in my present mood, I could take you down like *that*." She leaned down and snapped her fingers under his nose.

Victor got to his feet, looked down at her. Cat felt a shudder of trepidation, shook it off and squared her shoulders determinedly; she was not going to be bullied.

"Promises, promises," Victor said lightly, leaned down and kissed her. "I hate a wishy-washy woman. Come on, let's go back. We've let *famiglia* Fortunati stew in it long enough and the kids might start to worry."

Cat slipped her hand into his, her grip tightening as they made their way over the slick, uneven sand. Victor slowed his pace to match hers, noticed that she looked pale. Her family may have a point. She was throwing herself into work too soon, recovering too slowly.

"I suppose I ought to tell you," Cat said after a moment. "Carlton Amis came to see me this morning."

"Amis?" *So that's why he hadn't been at the Phoenix.*

"He said the Sterling Phoenix wanted to compensate me for my distress, tried to give me tickets—excuse me, invitations—to the Gambol. I told him I wasn't going to sue or anything."

"He tried to bribe you?"

"He said it was so I could have the material I needed for my story. But it sure felt like a bribe."

They approached the house; Cat hesitated on the bottom step. "He made me uncomfortable."

"How so?"

His parting remarks couldn't have been a threat. Carlton Amis wasn't that stupid. "Just…you know. They used to call him the Casanova of Criminal Court."

"Flirting with you, you mean?"

He said it calmly enough, but Cat saw the line of his jaw tighten. "It was nothing."

The front door was wrenched open and Ellice stepped onto the porch. "Cat?"

"Yeah?"

"Someone on the phone for you. I was gonna tell her to call back, Freddy saw you guys coming up the street. You want me to take a message?"

"Who is it?"

"Some gal named Veach."

Cat looked at Victor, shrugged.

When they entered the house, the family was picking at the food laid out in the dining room. Cat looked at the dozen pairs of eyes, some contrite, some baffled or irritated. "Look, let's just chalk this one up to PMS and forget it, okay?"

A wake of laughter trailed her to the kitchen. She could hear Mats ask someone, "What's PMS?" as she picked up the receiver, said, "Hello?"

"Is this Mrs. Austen?"

"Yes."

"I'm Linda Veach?" She said it like Cat ought to recognize the name.

"Yes?" Cat repeated.

"Gee, I thought Danny mighta mentioned me. I don't know what to do about him, Mrs. Austen, and I thought maybe you talked to him or something because I found your number on his desk. Danny Furina? He's a private investigator? You know him or something?"

"I used to. We went to school together. Is there something the matter with him?" She could see Victor in the dining room, listening to something Freddy was saying, one eye on her.

"I don't know. I mean, he went outta the office around one Monday afternoon and he hasn't been back since. He's not picking up at home and his landlady says she hasn't seen him and the mail's been backing up at the office? I was wondering if maybe you spoke to him or know where he's at or anything?"

"No…" Cat heard an echo: *I think of you, I still think Alley Cat Fortunati.* But that had been a dream, hadn't it? "I haven't seen him for a couple years," she said.

"Gee. Well, if he does get in touch with you, would you tell him to call Linny and tell me what he wants to do about all his mail and stuff around the office? I'm at my wits' end."

"Of course. But I don't expect to hear from him. Sorry I can't be more help."

"Oh, that's okay. It might just be one of his things he does. Danny can be kinda flaky, you know?"

Do I ever, Cat thought. "Let me know if he turns up," she told the girl, hung up, slid into the booth encrusted with short-bread dough.

It had been a dream, hadn't it? It wasn't important, was it? Danny would probably turn up tomorrow. And anyway, it had nothing to do with her.

But intuition whispered that it hadn't and it was and he wouldn't and it did.

EIGHT

THE REVEREND Marlon d'Esperance had thwarted all inquiries as to whether and when he had been ordained by pronouncing any such speculation to be blatantly racist. And so, while no congregation or sect had stepped forth to claim him, neither would any risk repudiating the Minister of the Minority, the Disciple of the Downtrodden and the Oracle of the Oppressed.

The composition alone was daunting. Protruding eyes flashed like obsidian fire; the glossy pompadour rose from an oversized head, adding three inches to his five feet four. No visible neck; the head was planted directly on the three hundred pound torso and the dimension of his waist, in inches, exceeded the height of his youngest daughter.

Yet corpulence had not rendered him stationary, or silent. He could hustle across a platform like a Rockette, while verbally yanking a single syllable up two octaves, letting it hover like an impending storm, then unleash a torrent of galvanizing oratory.

His arrival caught Atlantic City unaware, for a couple undercover cops had been caught on video roughing up a pair of teenage carjackers in Newark and there was every reason to believe the Reverend would head north. But d'Esperance had heard that the two suspended cops in the Atlantic City

incident were white and the Newark cops were otherwise, and
the Jeffries matter presented too tempting a mix of police mismanagement and racial bigotry to pass up.

He had intended to commence with a carefully staged impromptu shot of himself consoling the bereaved Mr. Bolton,
but Father Fortunati and his deacon barred cameras from the
requiem Mass and personally escorted Mr. Bolton and his
young son to the interment. Plan B was an indignant confrontation with the rookie; sources had informed d'Esperance that
MacBride was attending Methodist services at a Pacific Avenue church. D'Esperance rounded up the camera crew and
headed for St. Andrews, struck a confrontational pose at the
entrance, and prepared to engage the hapless rookie.

The congregation emerged; d'Esperance made his move;
stopped. Who were those two people flanking the young officer? If similarities of face and form did not lie, they had to
be MacBride's parents, one quite light, one rather dark and
MacBride somewhere in mid-spectrum. The press photo had
been overexposed, rendering him lighter in print than in person, but in person, the truth could not be disputed: Malcolm
MacBride was the descendant of African forebears.

Quick-thinking Methodists whisked the three MacBrides
into their church van; the *NewsLine90* crew swooped down on
d'Esperance, who began to improvise resourcefully. It was not
MacBride, for MacBride had been led by his superiors; it was
not Jeffries, for Jeffries had been driven to desperation by
police mismanagement. And who was to blame for that mismanagement? It was the white cop, the Jewish cop, Stanley
Rice. Yes, Rice, *Rice* was responsible for Khamilla Bolton's
death!

VICTOR SPENT Sunday at his mother's home in Vineland. She
gave him a real Puerto Rican meal, told him he was working
too hard, hinted again that he ought to think about settling
down. Remy, the youngest, picked at her food, sullenly silent.
Her latest affair on the wane, she was not in the humor to
advance her brother's love life. But Milly giggled covertly,
said, ''I think Victor's seeing someone downshore.'' Victor

shot her a look, but Milly only tossed her head defiantly and giggled again when the doorbell rang and his flustered mother ushered in a young woman who was the editor and publisher of a local Spanish-language newspaper.

The *editora* made polite conversation—she was quite pretty, thirty or so, never married, Puerto Rican-born—and Victor was unfailingly courteous. But when she left, he ordered Milly into the kitchen and told her to mind her own business and to stop encouraging *mami*, he didn't need his mother and sisters to find him a wife.

Maybe it was time to introduce Cat to his mother and sisters, Victor mused, headed for the phone as soon as he entered his apartment, saw the message light flashing. He pushed the PLAY button. Message one: Raab. "Victor, look, I don't know if Adane's called you yet, but tell her these things happen, it'll get straightened out." Message two: Adane. "Lieutenant, I'm sorry to bother you at home, please don't bother to call me back, I'll straighten out the business with the medical examiner's office by tomorrow morning."

Victor dialed Raab's number. "What's up?"

"Look, Victor, I don't blame Adane, the poor kid takes everything on herself, it wasn't her fault."

"What wasn't her fault?"

"You didn't talk to her yet? Okay, well there was some screw up with the prints, the ME's assistant said he faxed them over yesterday, Adane says you guys never got them. So she says, maybe he faxed them to one of the other bureaus by mistake, so she checks with Burglary and Arson and Narc, she calls Keith back, he's the kid does the prep for the ME, he's left for the day, she calls him at his other job. He does prep in the kitchen over Nick's Subs. So come to find out, he's faxed the prints to the wrong number, you're two one one three, he faxed 'em to two one one five. You following this?"

"So far."

"So Jeannie's tellin' this to Phil, he says he'll take care of it, he'll have Keith run off another set of prints and swing by to pick them up himself. So there's a little delay…these things happen, right?"

"All too often. It hardly seems something Adane would get worked up over."

"I didn't get to the good part. Like I said, Keith faxed the prints to the wrong number. Hit five when he shoulda hit three. And it goes through. To Chooch and Sonny's Pizzaria on the White Horse Pike. Seems they got a real up-to-date operation, you can fax your lunch orders. They're two one one five. I seems that Mr., um, Chooch hasn't exactly been keeping to the straight and narrow and he sees these prints coming outta the machine, he thinks it's somebody's way of tellin' him he's been...you know..."

"Fingered." Victor tugged at the knot in his tie.

"Cardiac arrest. He's in CCU over Shore Memorial, they got him stablized, but Sonny's havin' a fit and I been all day tryin' to convince him not to sue. Adane's ready to fall on her sword, so go easy on her, it really wasn't her fault. My plate's full, what with the Hopper thing and the Rev hangin' around. I turn on one of those TV cop shows, you got your vic, you got your ID, you got your suspect, you put him on the stand, you grill him, he spills his guts, roll the credits. How come it never works out like that?"

"This is real life," Victor replied.

MONDAY MORNING, Victor pulled into his parking space and saw a *NewsLine90* van stationed at the corner of Shore Road, a crowd gathering at the intersection. He strode into the rambling brick building that quartered an assortment of agencies, his "Good-mornings" always polite if somewhat aloof, barely civil today. The denizens of Northfield understood, they had all heard about the fax screw-up, all seen the morning headline: D'ESPERANCE D'NOUNCES DA'S D'VISION, figured Major Crimes would be catching some heat.

Jean Adane, always the first to report, was working at the unit's lone computer terminal.

"Adane, come in here."

Jean Adane had been snatched from the Academy before her graduation, vanished so abruptly and decisively that several weeks had passed before her classmates learned she had not washed out, had been grabbed by the prosecutor's office and assigned to Major Crimes. Her girlfriends from the Academy assured her they always knew she would be the first to make detective and Jean Adane didn't have the courage to tell them that she was no more than a secretary, a taker of notes, a programmer of computers, a filer of reports. Head of her Academy class, now a clerical aide. She had hoped that when Cardenas was assigned, her status might change; Cardenas had a reputation as a patient, fair-minded investigator. But nothing changed except for the extraordinary decorum with which Cardenas ran his unit, and by looks and courtesies, Jean was not beguiled. Appearances lie, she told her envious girlfriends, and a cop who was so downright chivalrous was not entirely to be trusted.

"Please sit down," he said as he hung his coat on the rack, waited until she sat before taking his chair.

For example: Cops did not say "please" all the time or care one way or another who sat first or if she sat at all. Jean sat.

"I spoke with Mr. Raab. There is no reason for you to feel responsible for the error. Has Detective Long straightened it out yet?"

"He's going over to the Phoenix to talk to Personnel and he'll pick up the prints on his way in."

"There was a preliminary on the John Doe?"

As always, Adane spoke from memory. "Yes. A complete autopsy was held up because the DA asked him to give priority to the post mortem on the girl who was recovered from the channel."

"Young girl." Victor swung his chair from side to side, absently. The chair was leather, high-backed, the one indulgence in his Spartan office.

"Yes sir, quite young, and there's a missing person's report on a girl named Van Wyck who fits her description. The young man who ran his car into the liquor store was DUI. Phil's still got a file open on Miss Harris, the prostitute, and he wants to know if he should talk to the children who found her, again."

Ugly business, that one. Victor shook his head. "Not yet. What's going on outside?"

"The *NewsLineNinety* Morning Update said that the Reverend Marlon d'Esperance is planning a demonstration in front of our building to protest the whitewash of the facts in the matter concerning Sergeant Rice."

"Sergeant Rice's hearing doesn't start for another hour. It seems a bit presumptuous to conclude that the facts will be washed white or washed at all."

"Yes, sir."

"And the hearing is being held in Mays Landing. I'm not a politician, Adane, but if I were planning a protest against a miscarriage of justice, I would stage it at the site where justice was being carried amiss."

"But the prosecutor's office is somewhat off the beaten path, sir, and not nearly as likely to attract an audience as a Shore Road intersection."

Victor's mouth curved slightly. "I suppose not."

"And a Miss Veach called right before you came in, sir. She said she wanted to talk to someone in charge."

"About what?" Why did that name sound familiar?

"She said it was something about a missing person."

"Tell her to go to the locals?"

"Yes, sir, but she insisted on talking to someone here."

Philip Long shuffled in, his lithe form swaddled in a calf-length leather coat. "Lieutenant, you heard about that d'Esperance bullsh— 'Scuse me, Jeannie, didn't see you there." He jerked a chair next to Adane's, sat. "Talked to Personnel over the Phoenix, the housekeeping guys clean the dressing rooms, one of Sterling's green jackets doggin' me the whole time. Swear they don't recognize our man, but they're not gonna say anything get themselves canned. Ran through some of the video with Security, didn't see anyone looked like our St. Nick." He reached into the folds of his coat, handed a manila envelope to Jean. "There's your prints, Jeannie."

"The car that Mrs. Austen saw coming down the ramp right before she discovered the body?"

"Hatchback? Light color? Makes it every third low-rent car in the city."

"How accessible are the dressing rooms from the street?"

"Very. There's a stage door on New Jersey about twenty feet from the intersection. Not real conspicuous, but it's there and it's not locked. Show people and the stage crew, they're supposed to clock in, there's a guard on duty most of the time. There's a lounge, couple lavs, two main dressing rooms, two VIPs, workstation for the seamstresses, storage for the costumes."

"So anyone could have walked in from the street and taken a costume off the rack?"

For his answer, Long stood and whipped off his coat. Underneath, he was wearing a fur-trimmed red velvet jacket, loose red trousers rolled up to the knee. "I wanted to see if I could infiltrate the place. I walk right in the New Jersey entrance, no one's down there, I do a quick change, go up to Five, ID myself to Security. I gotta return it."

Kurt Raab scuttled in, closed the door, dashed to the window and peered out, shut the blinds. His thinning hair was disheveled, tie unknotted, coat thrown over one arm. His sleeve was rolled to the elbow, a broad BandAid taped in the crook of his arm. "Jesus, I saw the *NewsLineNinety* guys parked two blocks off, I come in the north side, they got the blood bank set up, I hadda drop a pint before they'd let me through."

Jean Adane quietly yielded her chair, left and returned with a cup of orange juice for Raab. She would have been content to remain standing by the door, but Victor had risen as well, and she knew he wouldn't sit until she did, so she wheeled in the chair from the computer station, wedged it next to Phil's.

"Thanks, Adane." Raab sipped the orange juice. "I saw Rice. He's still shook up, but he'll be okay. He's got PBA counsel, but there's not gonna be a problem as long as he steers clear of—" he nodded toward the streetside window. "Hear about yesterday? He didn't know MacBride was black."

"All that means is Stan's the cheese that stands alone," Long grumbled.

"Cheer up. We get lucky, some video hack'll catch a couple

uniforms working over a DUI in someone else's back yard, d'Esperance'll take off. Long, you changin' jobs?''

"Beats wearin' a dress."

"Oh yeah, reminds me, ACPD vice sends their love. Victor, I told the ME to give the floater priority; I got some real scared parents calling up, okay? You got a preliminary report, right?"

Adane recited, "Approximately thirty-five to forty years of age, dead five to seven days. Cervical fractures, fractures of the clavicle and ribs, skull fracture and contrecoup contusions."

"That means the skull fracture resulted from a fall?" Victor asked.

"Yes, sir."

"You know," Long mused, "I was thinkin' this guy might've been some kinda stalker. 'Member 'bout five months back, this guy walked right onto the casino floor shot his ex six times in the head? Folks standin' around never stopped placing their bets."

"Or someone doing surveillance for a burglary," Adane suggested. "The Gambol is expected to draw a very wealthy crowd."

Raab got to his feet. "For all we know, coulda been some fruitcake practical joke went sour. Meantime, think about what I said, Victor, have a chat with Cookie Amis. I'll give her a ring if you want." He peeked out the window. "Adane, you know a way outta here'll get me past the press?"

"Yes, sir." She took his elbow and guided him out.

"ACPD's still checkin' out the garage levels, they're not gonna turn up anything. I can keep goin' back over the security videos, but that's gonna take some time. I hope Stan gets cleared to come back soon."

"Use Adane if you need an extra hand."

"I may have to hit the streets, check out the neighborhood."

"Use Adane on the streets."

"Right." Long snickered as if Victor had said something amusing, strolled out to show his Santa suit to the guys in Arson.

Victor shrugged, picked up the preliminary report on the

John Doe. There was a rap on the door frame. A young woman stood in the doorway. Victor rose immediately, said, "May I help you?"

"I called? Linda Veach?"

"Yes, come in, please." Victor closed the door, held out a chair.

Linda Veach looked about twenty. Lank brown hair hung around a pale face reddened at the cheekbones, the tip of the nose. She had a pert, fragile prettiness that would peak early, probably already had, and sink into a careworn plainness before thirty.

"I went to the Atlantic City cops and they said I may just be jumpin' the gun, 'cause of the way Danny is."

"I don't follow. May I offer you some coffee, Miss Veach?"

"Oh gee, no thanks. I'm usually the one gets coffee."

"You're a secretary?"

She nodded. "For a PI. Danny Furina? He's got an office in town, upstairs from Giovanazzi's Tailor Shop?" The inflection lifted at the tail end of each sentence; "upspeak" Cat had called it once. "I've been working for him about nine months, started as a temp. He really didn't need anybody full time, he ran the place himself, you know? He didn't even have a place for me to work, just put a little table in the corner and I worked there. Most of the time, we weren't in there at the same time anyway, so it didn't matter, you know?"

Victor nodded patiently, waited for the girl's rambling to take root.

"He does jobs for lawyers mostly, and some insurance stuff, sometimes divorce, you know? But nothing that takes him away from the office for more than a day or two at the most without him checking in. I mean, he at least calls for his messages."

"You're saying that Mr. Furina is missing?"

"I think so. Unless he's pulling some kind of thing like he does sometimes. Danny can be weird, you know? But I have the feeling that something's not right, so I went to the police, but they told me they really couldn't do anything and meanwhile a couple clients are trying to get a hold of him and I don't know what to tell them. And if he's like, dead—" she swallowed and her eyes began to water. "You guys would be the ones to take care of that, wouldn't you?"

"Do you have any reason to think he might have met with foul play? Had he been working on anything unusual or dangerous?"

"I don't know. The only thing that happened weird was about the time that crazy deejay got shot, remember that?"

"Mid-November."

"Around there. Well, Danny tells me, 'Linny,' he says, 'I think we may have hit the jackpot.' And then he tells me to leave off what I was doing and I thought that was weird, you know? Because I was catching up on the bills and Danny always says to get out those bills even if I have to leave off something else. Anyway, he tells me to leave off the bills and take the rest of the day off and practically shoves me outta the place."

Victor propped his elbows on his desk, pressed his fingertips together. "What happened right before that?

She smiled. "You're sharp. He got this phone call. He picks up, so I didn't hear who it was and he didn't say a name, just says, 'Uh-huh, uh-huh, I remember you, I get it' and hangs up, says we hit the jackpot and hustles me out."

Victor studied the ingenuous face, the childish mouth drawn into a pout. The boss had cut her out of the action and she was miffed. "What happened the next day?" he asked.

"It was business as usual. Except he didn't open a file on whoever called, 'cause I checked. He never mentioned it. But he started spending most of his time out of the office, even turned down some insurance work, even though he's taking his camera out with him, like maybe it's an insurance job, and he takes the film to the lab himself."

"And that was usually your job?"

"Uh-huh. Snappier Shots, over on Tilton Road."

"Go on, please."

"So this goes on a couple weeks, and then one day he comes in acting kinda bummed out, like maybe he got fired offa a job. Except he gives me a bonus. Five hundred dollars. Then last Monday, he goes out around one and never comes back. Tuesday, he doesn't show, so Wednesday, I start callin' around and no one's heard from him, not his landlady or Mr. Giovanazzi downstairs or the doughnut shop on the corner, none of his clients. I found this woman's number on his blotter, I even called her. A Mrs. Austen.''

"Austen?"

"Yeah. Lives over Ocean City. She said she useta know Danny, they were old friends or something, but she said she hasn't seen him. 'Course, if she and Danny were up to something, she might be lyin'.''

Victor stood. "Miss Veach, let me have a day or two to look into this. I'll get back to you."

She rose resignedly. She had been told that before.

"Please leave your number at the desk, I'll call you if I come up with anything."

She had been told that before, too; but she said, "Thanks for your time, Lieutenant," allowed him to help her on with her coat and walked out.

Victor sat slowly. On Saturday, Cat had shrugged it of when he asked her about the woman named Veach who had called her. She'd said it wasn't important. A corpse turns up five days after a PI disappears; the hell it's not important! *She knows it, too, damn it.*

His mind flashed back to the image of Cat lying on her kitchen floor, blood soaking through her clothes, to her limp hand pressed between his palms as the ambulance sped toward the hospital.

Cat was not going to wind up in the middle of a dangerous situation a second time. Not if he could help it.

Victor picked up the phone and started to dial.

NINE

CAT UPTURNED a bag of plum tomatoes on the counter, lifted a large cast iron skillet from a hook on the wall. It had the merest trace of a nick where the bullet had struck before ricocheting into her, and the police had taken it as evidence, but Cat had become so distressed by the loss of such a fine piece of cookware that the DA had instructed them to simply photograph it and give it back.

The doorbell rang. Cat put down the skillet and jogged to the front door, yanked it open to find Steve Delareto on her doorstep, hands in the pockets of his gray overcoat, his expression tense, troubled.

Delareto had been another one of the boys from the neighborhood, less rambunctious than Danny Furina, less prim than the Keller boys, never picked fights like the Colucci twins, just a nice, studious boy who had taken Cat to the prom and never quite outgrew his crush. In the yearbook, he had been voted Most Likely To Succeed; he had a small prosperous law practice in Linwood, an upscale community in Atlantic County.

"Steve, what's up?" Cat waved him through the foyer.

"You alone, Cat?"

"Steven."

Delareto actually blushed.

"Jane's in school, Ellice is subbing, Freddy took Mats out to buy him a suit for Christmas. You're invited for Christmas Eve dinner, you know."

"Thanks." Delareto checked his watch nervously. "Look, Cat, can you leave a note for Freddy? I got a call from Lieutenant Cardenas. He wants you for questioning over at Major Crimes, asked me to bring you in."

"What for? Not another deposition for the Hopper thing? They said they were done with me until it goes to court."

"No, it's not that, but I'll be damned if I know what's up. Cardenas says I don't bring you in, he'll have you picked up."

Picked *up?* Homicide cops, Cat fumed, silently. They *were* crazy. "He could do that, just have me picked up like a common criminal?"

"Nothing about you is common, Cat. You haven't done anything criminal, have you?"

"Not yet." She stalked to the stair closet, yanked out her leather jacket, snatched a pair of gloves, a scarf.

"You got a copy of our high school yearbook?"

"What?"

"Cardenas asked us to bring it in. I can't find mine."

Cat threw up her hands in bewilderment, rummaged along the wall of bookcases in the living room, drew out a narrow, plastic-covered volume. She dashed off a note to Freddy, stuck it to the wreath on the front door. "Let's go."

WHEN THEY WALKED INTO Victor's office, he was standing at the window, staring at the expanding crowd at the Shore Road intersection. Cat saw only his profile, read anger in the tense posture, the downward crescent of mustache, felt her own temper simmering.

"All right, what're we doing here?" Delareto demanded, closing the door.

"I have to question Mrs. Austen about a matter under investigation and I need to impress upon her the fact that the matter is a very serious one."

"I'm impressed," Cat returned, coolly.

Victor looked at her. She was wearing a white, cowl-neck sweater, snug jeans, battered brown suede boots. Her hair was swept into a ponytail and she wore no makeup, looked pale except for the spots of angry color settling over her cheekbones.

Delareto had heard from Freddy that Cat and the lieutenant were "seeing each other," wondered what the hell Cat saw in this humorless cop. "I want this interview on the record," he said.

"Fine." Victor stepped out of the office, spoke a few words to Adane. Delareto seated Cat in one of the two chairs, pulled the second beside her and sat. Victor pushed in a third chair for Adane, positioned it at the corner of his desk, facing Cat and her attorney. "Of course, Mrs. Austen understands that she doesn't have to answer—''

"I know Miranda."

"I just want to be sure Mrs. Austen understands—''

"Stop talking about me in the third person."

"Is she taking notes or what?'' Delareto nodded to Adane, who was sitting on Victor's right, hands folded on her lap.

"Adane," prompted Victor.

"Lieutenant Cardenas: 'Of course Mrs. Austen understands that she doesn't have to answer'; Mr. Delareto, D-e-l-a-r-e-t-o: 'I know Miranda'; Lieutenant Cardenas: 'I just want to be sure Mrs. Austen understands'; Mrs. Austen: 'Stop talking about me in the third person'; Mr. Delareto: 'Is she taking notes or what?'''

Victor cocked an eyebrow at Delareto. "You'll be issued a written transcript, of course."

Delareto, on his fourth office manager in eighteen months, asked Adane, "You ever think about changing jobs?"

"Can we get on with this?" Cat demanded.

"Mrs. Austen," Victor inquired, his voice impersonal, "are you acquainted with a private investigator named Daniel Furina?"

"Furina!" Delareto exclaimed. "Okay, I get it now. It's some practical joke Danny put you up to."

"This is no joke, counselor.''

"Danny," Delareto chuckled, shaking his head. "I remember bio lab, Cat, me, Freddy, one of the Keller kids, somehow Danny gets to the specimens before class. To this day, I don't know how he stuffed all those condoms in that frog. Sister Angelica was the lab instructor, remember? You go to dissect and boing! You guys would've died laughing." He looked at Victor's cool frown, Adane's bland attentiveness. "Okay, maybe not you two, but the guys we grew up with, it was a riot."

Cat was holding her head in her hands. "Can we please get on with this?"

Victor tried to imagine Cat at, what, fourteen? Fifteen? "You went to school with Furina?"

"Yeah." Again Delareto responded. "Like I said, we were all in the same grade."

"When was the last time you saw him?"

"It must have been…" Delareto hesitated.

Cat raised her head. "At my husband's funeral."

Victor paused. "And there's been no contact since?"

Cat's recollection went into free-fall; no, that had been a dream, hadn't it?

"Cat?" Delareto prodded, gently.

"I think he called me."

Victor leaned forward. "Furina called you? Recently?"

Even now, it was the dream, the sense of running that seemed real, the phone call an illusion. "I think it was a couple days after I got out of the hospital. The Sunday we went to my mother's for Thanksgiving."

"What did he want?"

Cat shook her head. "It's all so vague. I'd been asleep; the phone woke me. It was Danny. He called me 'Alley Cat' like they used to do in school."

Victor waited.

"He asked about Freddy. Something about…" Cat pressed her fingertips to her lips. *You wouldn't happen to know if he's running with Fawn Caprio, would you?*

"Cat, maybe you and I should go over this alone first," Delareto suggested.

Victor observed Delareto's arm circle the back of Cat's chair. "Do you need a moment to consult with your attorney, Mrs. Austen?"

His tone nettled her. And why was everyone asking about Danny Furina all of a sudden, first that girl who called Saturday, now Major Crimes? What had Danny done? "He said something about rumors that the Sterlings were separating, wanted to know if Freddy had heard from Fawn Sterling. Like if she was running out on Sterling, would she go back to Freddy."

"What did Freddy have to say about this?"

"I never told him about the call. But I don't think he's had any contact with Fawn; he would have told me."

"That was late November. Have you spoken to him since?"

Cat shook her head.

"Anyone else been asking about him?"

Cat bit her lip, looked at Victor. "His secretary called Saturday. She said she had found my number on his desk, wanted to know if I had heard from him."

"That fruitcake," Delareto snorted. "What'd he do, pull a disappearing act?"

"He hasn't shown up for work for a few days."

Delareto turned to Adane. "Honest to God, you getting all this?"

"Mr. Delareto: 'You ever think about changing jobs?' Mrs. Austen: 'Can we get on with this?' Lieutenant Cardenas: 'Mrs. Austen, are you acquainted with a private investigator named Daniel Furina?' Mr. Delareto: 'Furina? Okay, I get it now, it's some practical joke Danny put you up to'; Lieutenant Cardenas: 'This is no joke, counselor'; Mr. Del—''

"I believe! Look, omit the part about the rubbers, okay?"

Adane looked at Victor; he nodded.

"I'm not kidding about the job," Delareto insisted. "Start you at twenty-nine five, medical, dental, paid sick days, three weeks' vacation, Monday holidays—"

Jean's blue eyes widened.

"Where were we?" Victor intervened. His impatient gaze darted to the protective arm still circling Cat's chair.

"My conversation with Danny's secretary. Veach was her name, Linda Veach. She said she hadn't heard from Danny in several days, wanted to know if I had."

Victor stroked his chin absently. "Miss Veach contacted me this morning. She told me Furina did mostly insurance work, small-time legal assignments. Then last month, he took on a case, kept the documentation from Miss Veach. At the end of the month, he calls you asking about Mrs. Sterling, whether she's leaving her husband, and would she go back to a former boyfriend. Apparently, some time after that, he was dismissed from his confidential assignment. And a week ago, he steps out for lunch and hasn't been seen since." Victor leaned back in his chair, hesitated a moment. "And Friday night, a body turns up in Sterling's casino. A body that's been dead several days. You see where I'm leading."

"Whoa, Lieutenant, you don't think Danny knocked off that guy turned up in the parking lot?"

Cat felt her heartbeat stumble, regain its rhythm. "No, Steve, the lieutenant thinks Danny *is* the guy in the parking lot." Her voice sounded hollow to her ears, distant.

Victor reached into the pocket of his jacket, drew out an envelope. He removed several photos, slid them across his desk. "These were shot at the morgue. Could it be Furina?"

In the garage, at night, the lighting dim, the crumpled posture shielding the face of the corpse, Cat had not clearly seen the mottled, ruptured face. Had Chris looked like that, she wondered? So broken? They had never let her see. Carlo had taken care of everything and the casket had been closed. Her last memory was of him bounding down the porch steps, the sun shining on his sandy hair; she had stood in her robe, holding Mats on her hip, waving.

Cat lurched to her feet, dashed out of the room. Delareto jumped from his chair. "Cat—!"

"Wait," Victor ordered. "Adane, see to Mrs. Austen."

Adane rose immediately, exited. Victor turned to Delareto. "You tell me, counselor. Is this Furina?"

Delareto bit back an obscenity. "What the hell would Furina be doing dead in a parking lot?"

"Good question." Victor jutted his chin toward the photos.

Delareto examined the photographs. "Been a while since I saw Danny. Hair's right, general build. This guy's pretty ripe. Furina would be thirty-eight now. Six, six-one. Good shape."

Corresponds with the ME's stats, Victor reflected, grimly. "All right." He slipped the pictures back into the envelope. "Maybe you ought to have a little talk with Mrs. Austen about obstruction, interfering with a police investigation. I wouldn't want her to get herself involved in something that could wind up like the Dudek business."

"Landis hands her this, you want her to take a pass?"

"Absolutely."

"And what about what Cat wants?"

Victor looked up from his chair. "Mrs. Austen's priority is to recover from her injuries and take care of herself. I would hope that's also the priority of her friends. Leave the yearbook; I'll get it back to her. Thanks for coming down. Take her home.''

Delareto slammed the yearbook on Victor's desk. ''One more word, Lieutenant.''

''Yes?''

''Look, I don't know what's really going on here—''

''A criminal investigation.''

''—between you and Cat, but what you did just now was completely uncalled for. Cruel, too. My advice to you would be to treat that lady like she's made of gold because I personally know three or four guys would be happy to step into your shoes. Me included.''

''Really?'' Victor's face was a mask, but he was calculating silently. *Delareto, maybe Stan Rice, who else, damn it?*

''I kid you not. Some free advice, something I don't give out very often. You got something real special there. Don't screw it up.''

''Noted. Can you get her home?''

''My pleasure.''

Damn again, Victor thought.

OUTSIDE, THE CROWD had swelled at the southeast corner of the Northfield complex. Cat tugged Steve's sleeve, dragged him to the intersection to see what was going on.

Planted in the southbound lane of Shore Road, a busy thoroughfare that ran the extent of Atlantic County, sat the Reverend Marlon d'Esperance. He was smartly attired in a capacious overcoat, charcoal gray with a black fur collar; pleated trousers; polished wingtips. The coat formed a gray dome beneath the immense head; his slick pompadour was motionless in the brisk wind.

''Is he hurt?'' Cat looked around for paramedics, saw only a few profoundly distressed cops on the sidelines.

As if on cue, the Reverend's fiery eyes opened, rolled dramatically and the voice bellowed forth. ''I will set me DOWN for the cause of *jus*tice! Any *time!* Any*where!* Set DOWN with me, brothers and sisters! Set DOWN for *jus*tice!''

The brothers and sisters seemed to prefer the curbside to setting themselves down on the frozen asphalt.

"*Justice* for Khamilla Bolton! The police department may want to befog the facts with the fabric of fa-bri-ca-tion! With the mantle of mendacity! With the raiment of—"

"Repression," said Cat.

"—repression!"

"Ha."

"But I say, *justice* must be blind! *Justice* must be deaf!"

"Justice must be dumb," Cat muttered.

Steve nudged her.

"If Lowell Jeffries had not been driven to desperation, this entire tragedy could have been avoided! If the police had used the restraint"—he squeezed three syllables out of that—"they would have used in a white neighborhood, Khamilla Bolton would be alive today! White and black are like oil and water—"

"Let's go," Steve said, laying a hand on Cat's arm.

"Separately, they have their place—"

"*Each* has *its* place," Cat amended.

"But they cannot mix! The safety, the integrity of our neighborhoods can only be entrusted to—"

"Our! He lives in Lawrenceville, for heaven's sake! Why don't the police put a stop to this? Don't you need a permit to demonstrate?"

"—and whoOOO is to blame? Make Rice pay the price!"

"Poetry," Steve muttered. "That's low."

A few of the brothers and sisters had taken up the chant. "Make Rice pay the price! Make RICE pay the price!"

The cops had been taking turns sprinting into the road to wave the occasional car around d'Esperance, but none made a move to confront the reverend as he sat expostulating in the street. A patrol sergeant recognized Delareto, approached. "How ya doin', counselor?"

"That's a misdemeanor," Steve remarked.

"Yeah. But we haul his carcass off in fronta *NewsLine-Ninety* it's yours truly turns up as poster boy for the Sons of Hitler. Mayor says we gotta act with discretion, says he don't wanna see any of us on *Front Cover* in your eight millimeter format.''

"He gets run over, you're in for one hell of a litigation.''

"They put him outta commission, I'll kick in my share,'' the cop muttered. "And you did not hear that from me.''

"Maybe there's a solution you haven't considered,'' Cat offered.

"Cat, the lieutenant said I was to get you home.''

"I don't take orders from the lieutenant. Now Sergeant, what if you detoured traffic at Ridgewood Avenue about a quarter of a mile north? Then do the same around Country Club Road. Re-route everything off Shore Road. Like turning off a tap. That would solve the problem of his getting run over.''

"Yeah, and then what?''

"Let him sit there and remonstrate.''

"In the road?''

"You eliminate the traffic and you've ensured his personal safety, which is what the mayor wants. You let him sit in the road and d'Esperance gets what he wants. Now, it's about thirty-three, thirty-four degrees outside. I think the reverend's considerable *avoirdupois* will prevent him from an immediate threat of hypothermia, but it may put the devoted audience to the test.''

"Mrs. Austen is Carlo Fortunati's sister,'' Steve commented.

The sergeant guffawed. "King Carlo! That figures! He woulda thought of something like that!'' He walked off to relay Cat's inspiration to his superiors.

"Why is it every time I get a really good idea, my genealogy gets the credit?''

"*Mea culpa.* Look at the *NewsLineNinety* crew firing up. Can't wait to see this one on the six o'clock news. There's a wicked brain behind that Mona Lisa smile, Alley Cat.''

VICTOR WAS WATCHING from his window, saw Cat tuck her arm through Delareto's, laugh at something he said, the winter sun raising a coppery aura from her hair. He had crossed the line, he knew it now, too late. But she had nearly gotten herself killed following up on Dudek's murder, he reminded himself. Three or four happy to be in his shoes, were there? Damn them all.

Victor heard a soft knock on his door, turned.

Adane stood in the doorway. "Here's a rough transcription of your interview with Mrs. Austen."

"Was she okay?"

"She seemed a bit shaken up. I gather the head trauma in those photographs reminded her of her husband's death."

Victor raised an eyebrow. He hadn't thought of that. "You send out the prints?"

"It should take no more than twenty minutes." She hesitated. "Sir, I hope I haven't overstepped myself..."

"Adane, that mix-up with the lab wasn't your fault—"

"No, it's not that. It's, well, I heard Mr. Raab mention the name of Mrs. Carlton Amis when he was here."

"She's Sterling's aide. I believe he hired her after he brought her husband into the Phoenix organization."

"Yes, I know that. And it doesn't concern the Phoenix directly, it may be no more than a coincidence, though I'm not sure I believe in coincidence. And of course, we were backed up last week, Friday was particularly hectic, so it's understandable that it might not have made an impression."

"What didn't?"

She produced a folder, slid it onto his desk. "This report. There's not much to it, the matter's been shelved, it seems. It came over from Margate last week."

Victor tried to recall what had come in from Margate recently. An upscale downbeach community with little crime, Margate rarely had occasion to contact Major Crimes. "All I recall is something about a woman—was she a real estate agent?—claimed she was attacked in a vacant home."

"No, sir, the story was that she went to the home to pick up some papers for her employer, she had a key, was attacked inside the house, struggled with her attacker and fled, leaving him critically injured. She summoned the police and returned to the house with them, but the man wasn't there. The owner had returned, and there were no signs of a break-in or a struggle.''

"And this has something to do with Mrs. Carlton Amis?"

"Yes, sir. You see, Mrs. Amis was the woman who filed the report. And the house was Ten Oh One Bay Landing Court, which is owned by Mrs. Blaine Sterling. It had been her family's house, she renovated it some years back, and she's been in the habit of staying there whenever she's in the area.''

Victor flipped open the folder, ran his eyes over the report. "Check with Margate to see if—"

"There have been no other reports of vandalism or burglary filed in that area recently. Bay Landing Court is a cul-de-sac and Mrs. Sterling's home is at the base, the back overlooks the lagoon. They're all very expensive homes, summer properties. The owners all live out of state.''

"Who—"

"An Officer Klass responded to the call. Mrs. Amis had fled the scene and parked on Atlantic Avenue, because it was less secluded, I imagine. She phoned the police from her car. Officer Klass met her and asked her to follow him back to the house.''

"Why—"

"Officer Klass said Mrs. Amis was to pick up some papers Mrs. Sterling wanted delivered to the Phoenix, let herself in if Mrs. Sterling wasn't there. It seems she had her own key and often checked up on the house when Mrs. Sterling was out of town.''

"Where inside—"

"The struggle took place on a second floor landing off the living area. Mrs. Amis claimed the attacker fell over the railing onto the floor below.''

A fall, Victor thought.

"A fall," Adane continued. "The floor below is marble. She panicked, ran and called for help, returned with the officer and the man was gone.''

"Was—"

"There was no sign of forced entry.''

"Adane, you're not—"

"Operating one of those psychic one-nine-hundred services? No, sir."

Victor stared at her.

"Everyone asks me that," she said.

VICTOR DIALED the Phoenix, began a slow advance through the gatekeepers, got as far as the office boy, Donnie, and stalled out.

"Sorry, Lieutenant, Mrs. Sterling's having her face done for another shoot. Something I can do you for?"

Victor paused. "It's come to my attention that you came into Mrs. Sterling's employ quite recently."

"A week ago. How my résumé made it through the slush, I don't ask, don't tell."

"Were you in her employ last week when there was a break-in at her downbeach residence?"

"Say what?"

Victor explained briefly.

"First I've heard of that. I got the royal summons Monday afternoon, told to report Tuesday. I interviewed so long ago, I thought I was out of the running. Someone broke into Mrs. Sterling's place?"

"Yes, and I have a few questions for Mrs. Sterling regarding the police report that was filed."

"I'll give her the message, Lieutenant. Anything else?"

"Perhaps you could tell me if Mrs. Sterling ever mentioned a Mr. Furina? Daniel Furina. Or a Linda Veach."

"Doesn't ring a bell. Could you spell it, please?"

Victor spelled the surnames. "So, to your knowledge, neither of them have attempted to contact Mrs. Sterling in the past week?"

"Not that I know of, but I'll ask."

Victor thanked the man and hung up, certain that the back office boy was stonewalling.

Corpse shoved under Blaine Sterling's nose. Furina?

Back up. Furina vanishes.

Back up. Break in at Fawn Sterling's place, Mrs. Amis is attacked. Shoved the guy off the landing. A fall.

John Doe had died in a fall.

But the police report said the attacker had disappeared.

What the hell.

TEN

MANY SEASHORE TOWNS in southern New Jersey had winked at the real estate explosion of the 'seventies and 'eighties, taken a horrified peek at last and attempted too late to retrench. Campaigns for historical districts and zones of structural uniformity could not alter the architectural muddle that Ocean City had become. Modest split-levels and shoulder-to-shoulder condos covered the island's marshy south end; mid-island, the oceanside was lined with costly singles and duplexes, their lawns backing up to the sand, while bayside, houses rimmed the cul-de-sacs that abutted the network of lagoons and waterways. The extreme north was The Gardens, restricted to single family homes. Here, even a modest house went for high six figures; grander ones, ones that had staked a claim on the Atlantic, commanded seven.

The Amis home was one of the latter. Set upon the pinnacle of North Castle Drive, it overlooked the merger of the Atlantic with the bay. The home was the only one on the narrow, curving street, which was walled-in. Dried vines threaded over the stucco barricade. The wrought-iron gate opening onto the gravel driveway was locked, but a smaller one separating the sidewalk from the slate walkway was ajar. Victor hesitated at the open gate, was considering pressing the intercom button mounted on the wall when he heard a quick step behind him. A tall, slim figure in nylon all-weather running gear, white Nikes, mittens and a ski mask sprinted along the street, cut back to a stride as the person approached the walk. For a moment, Victor thought he had miscalculated, that Amis was not in his Atlantic City office, but when the ski mask was yanked back, a woman's face emerged. She had strong features; deep blue eyes confronted him with suspicion but without apprehension. A woman who could look out for herself, Victor concluded. The face was pink with perspiration, but the breathing was controlled, even, that of a trained athlete. The "Hello" was pronounced in an assured contralto, neither welcoming nor curt.

"Mrs. Amis?"

"Yes."

Victor produced his shield. "Could I have a few minutes of your time?"

She sighed patiently. "Mr. Sterling's office has issued a statement and my husband made it clear to Kurt Raab that we weren't to be approached again without notice."

"It's about another matter entirely, Mrs. Amis. I'd like to discuss the report you filed in Margate last week."

She blinked. "I thought that had been swept under the rug."

"Not quite."

She raked her short hair away from her face, hesitated. "All right. Come in."

She fished a key from her pocket, punched a code into the keypad above the doorbell, waited for the red beam to go green, slipped her key into the lock. A uniformed maid came forward to take Victor's coat. Mrs. Amis told her she wasn't needed. "Take a seat in the living room, Lieutenant, I'll be with you in ten." The marble foyer was larger than Victor's living room. She crossed it in four strides, sprinted up the staircase that spiraled above a low-hanging chandelier. Victor reflected that he had seen more chandeliers in the past three days than he had in the first thirty years of his life.

He passed through an archway into a twenty-by-thirty living room that was a calculated marriage of warm peach and cool ice blue. Raw silk wall coverings threw down a gauntlet to a climate that invited moisture and mildew; costly Oriental carpets were arranged over even costlier oak parquet. A walk-in fireplace framed in white marble, the mantle laden with framed photographs, all of the Amises and all the same pose: he confronting the lens with unabashed confidence, she clinging to his arm with wifely pride. A wall of glass opened onto the deck, the tarped swimming pool, then more deck fanning toward the Atlantic, two boatslips backing into the water. The view was blocked by a fifteen-foot silver tree, decorated in satin balls of pale blue and peach, wreathed with wrapped presents. Christmas cards were crammed onto a library table behind the six-foot sofa. Victor flicked a few of them open, recognized the names of two state senators, two mayors, a superior court judge, a former lieutenant governor, even a nondenominational greeting from Kurt and Patsy Raab.

He heard a light tread descending the stairs, turned.

"Can I get you something, Lieutenant? I'm making myself a toddy." She had showered, changed into Spandex leggings, a tunic sweater, white shot through with silver and gold thread. She wore a heavy gold bangle on one wrist, a broad gold band on the third finger of her left hand, above a sizable diamond.

"Nothing for me thanks." Cat had called her "formidable," but something had undermined that self-command if she was drinking before noon. But then, maybe that was normal for her. He watched as she slipped behind the wet bar, brewed her drink over a small burner, poured it into a mug, stirred it with a stick of cinnamon. Was she stalling, he wondered? Steeling herself, or maybe she'd put in a quick call to her husband. He waited until she was seated before he took a chair.

"How far do you run?" he asked, thinking of Cat.

"Six, eight miles a day. Keeps me in fighting trim."

Obviously, Victor thought. Spandex didn't leave much to the imagination.

"Lieutenant, I didn't mean to sound short, but you have to know something right off. What happened last week, that was the most bizarre thing that ever happened to me. When the police seemed to pass me off as some hysterical woman with an overactive imagination, I resented it, frankly. But now I'm inclined to think they may have been right."

"Mrs. Amis—"

"Please call me Cookie. It's silly, I know, but my real name's Cornelia."

She didn't look like a Cookie, Victor thought. She looked like Sheila, the sex-without-commitment bartender he had dated a while back. And she didn't look like a woman given to hysteria, either.

"This happened a week ago yesterday."

She nodded.

"Mr. Sterling was in the city last Monday?"

"All last week, actually."

"You don't accompany him to New York?"

"Not often. I'm with the Sterling Phoenix. The Phoenix is separate from the Sterling Hotel organization."

"I understand you haven't held your position long."

"It must be about six months, now. Blaine and I are old friends, you see. He wanted Carl to handle his licensure and asked me to persuade Carl to take leave from Bevilacqua, Macklin."

"So the job with the Phoenix was…?"

"Compensation? Well, I had been an office administrator for some time, I know the corporate ropes and I'm a quick study."

"Do you mind if I ask what you do for Mr. Sterling?"

"A little of everything. Look after his appointment schedule, oversee the press office, check the PR copy before it goes out, headhunter when he needed to fill a few key spots, manage the Job Fair, handle in-house grievances, make sure the high-end clients are happy." She sipped her toddy. "And then this year there's the Gambol."

"Quite a step up from office manager."

"Perhaps. But I worked for Bevilacqua, Macklin, De-Angelo, they're major league. I'm used to working with the upper echelon. Marlena Sterling got me the job; her father was Marshall Macklin. That's where I met Carl."

"So you were acquainted with the first Mrs. Sterling?"

"We all went to college together, Blaine, Marlena and I. Blaine and Marlena got married after school, I worked part-time at BMD, went to grad school part time. Carl interned with the firm, we got married, I quit school, worked full-time to make ends meet until his career took off.''

"Ever go back?" Marking time, waiting for the toddy to kick in.

"To school?" She shook her head. "Carl got a spot at the firm, then the partnership, and marriage to a comer became a full-time job. Things got a little strained, of course, after Blaine's divorce. They don't exactly tell you who gets custody of the friends." Her smile hardened.

"I'm surprised Sterling didn't use the legal team with the Sterling organization when he took over the Phoenix."

"Well, Carl's licensed in New Jersey. And then, with the hearing, what they're looking for, what'll get you turned down nine times out of ten, is criminal affiliation. Nothing like a smart criminal attorney to research your organization, get you in shape for the hearing and move you through."

"I imagine so. You like your job, Mrs. Amis?"

She shook a finger at him. "Lieutenant, are you asking why I took the job when I obviously don't need to work?"

"I apologize. I imagine it gives you some common ground with the second Mrs. Sterling, though."

The cobalt eyes flashed, and the "I don't follow" had a raw edge.

"I just meant that she's her own woman, too."

Cookie Amis reached for a cocktail napkin on the table. There were a stack of them, downy white with gold interlocking C's stamped on the corner. "You wanted to know what happened in Margate last week?"

Clearly, he had said something to put her back up. "If you wouldn't mind going over it. The report that came by my desk was very brief. You told the police you injured the man who attacked you."

"I thought I killed him."

Victor nodded, took a notebook out of his breast pocket. "Let's start at the beginning, shall we? You went to Mrs. Sterling's home on an errand. I understand you had a key?"

"Yes. Fawn had closed the place up at the end of the summer. I didn't mind checking on it for her."

"Was that part of your job as Sterling's assistant?"

"Not really, but it wasn't any trouble. You always need someone to make sure the landscapers are keeping up and the pipes haven't frozen and the pool's been treated. None of her right hand boys seem to be around long enough to be shown the ropes, and shore homes can be tricky to manage."

Victor wrote, nodding to show he was listening. "So your reason for going to the house was a maintenance check?"

"No. Programs. I'm sorry, I'm beginning to ramble. Is that typical?"

Victor smiled, faintly. "Perfectly understandable, Mrs. Amis. Just take your time."

"The programs for the Gambol. She jobbed them out to some printer in New York. Personally, I think we could have done as well with the Phoenix print shop, and it surprised me that Fawn was interested in participating in the Gambol at all. Anyway, she'd been in New York, brought them down, called me Sunday night and told me I could pick them up the next day. I told her I'd drop by around one."

"Mrs. Sterling say why she didn't run them over to the Phoenix herself? Or have her assistant do it?"

Cookie shrugged. "Fawn never does what she can get someone to do for her. And I think she was still between boys last Monday. Donnie's quite new."

That jibed with what Finch had told him. "And you didn't know whether or not Mrs. Sterling would be home?"

"She said something about running up to Philly for some yard goods. I was to let myself in if she wasn't there."

"You arrived at one?"

"Yes."

"Is the lock similar to yours, with a coded keypad?"

"Yes. The driveway gate operates on a remote. There are sensors on the sliding glass panels facing the water."

"Was the gate left open for you?"

"Yes. I parked on the curb, though, so I wouldn't be blocking the drive if Fawn came in after me."

"Is there a garage?"

"A detached garage. There's a breezeway that connects to the house."

"You didn't look to see if a car was in the garage?"

Cookie shrugged, shook her head.

"Please continue."

"I rang the bell and there was no answer, so I let myself in. Fawn had said she would leave the boxes on the dining table. I went upstairs—"

"Upstairs?"

"The house is an upside down. There are maid's quarters and guest bedrooms, kitchen and living areas downstairs; upstairs is the more formal living and dining area, the master suite, a gym, Fawn's workroom."

"I think I understand. What happened then?"

"I reached the upstairs landing. The corridor forms a quadrangle, a sort of gallery, the living room is directly ahead, the dining room is off to the right. I had turned toward the dining room—" she broke off, crossed her arms over her chest.

Victor waited.

"It all happened so fast. That's what they all say, isn't it? 'It all happened so fast'? Well, he just came at me; he had a knife. I grabbed this pedestal near the railing and swung it, threw him off balance. We struggled."

"Excuse me—what sort of knife?"

"I— A large knife, I don't know."

"A household knife? Something he may have taken from the kitchen?"

"Does it matter?"

"Well, of course, I'd like to know if he brought a weapon into the house or if he simply took one when he realized he was cornered and might have to fight his way out."

Her head dropped against a cushion, her expression reflective, as if she were considering his theory very carefully. "Why would he have brought a knife?"

"In my experience, Mrs. Amis, people don't carry weapons unless they contemplate the possibility of using them. And I find it suggestive that you say he came straight for you, without hesitation."

"Yes...yes...you may be right." She was guarded now. "I don't know what kind of knife it was."

"When you struggled, was the knife dropped, or did it go over the railing with him?"

"I...I really don't know. I was so afraid he would get up and come after me, I ran down the stairs. He wasn't moving. His head was bleeding. I panicked; I just ran."

"So you don't know whether he was breathing?"

"No. I'm ashamed to say it, I just ran to my car and drove down to Atlantic Avenue. I don't know where the police station is in Margate; I just wanted to get someplace where there were people around. I pulled over to collect my wits. Then I called nine-one-one from my car."

"About what time did you place the call?"

"I don't know. I'm afraid the time frame's a complete muddle. The dispatcher told me to stay in my car and that an officer would come by. A car came up right away, the officer asked if I was all right and if I needed medical attention, I said no, and he asked me if I would follow him back to the house."

"And when you went back to Bay Landing Court, Mrs. Sterling was home?"

Cookie Amis nodded, finished off her toddy.

"Did she say where she'd been? Obviously not in Philadelphia."

"She said she ran out to the post office."

"Did she say what time she left the house?"

"Not that I recall."

"Did she notice anything amiss when she got home?"

"She said she had just walked in a few minutes before we arrived."

Victor stroked his chin thoughtfully. "Then there would have been signs of the struggle."

"Well, maybe she hadn't gone upstairs."

"But you said there was blood on the floor below."

Mrs. Amis ran her slender fingers along her throat, glanced toward the bar as if contemplating a second toddy. "I thought there was."

"Are you saying there was no sign of blood when you returned with the officer?"

"I didn't go in. But it was obvious he didn't see anything suspicious. I'm wondering if I was mistaken."

"Clearly you weren't mistaken about the struggle."

"Yes—I mean, no. Not about that."

"Did the knife turn up?"

"It was…I don't know. I imagine it was gone, too."

"Could you describe the man for me, Mrs. Amis?"

She hesitated. "I think I told this to the policeman. He was tall. Dark hair, dark clothing."

"Eye color?"

"I don't recall."

"Age?"

"Forty, perhaps." Very reluctant now.

Victor changed course. "How did he get inside, have you thought about that?"

She swallowed audibly, shook her head.

"You needed a key, needed to know the code. Break in through the sliding glass doors, it'll trigger the alarms. So how did he get in without setting off an alarm?"

"You seem to have given this more thought in a weekend than I have in a week, Lieutenant."

"It's what I do."

"Of course. I wish I could help you, but I don't know how he got in. He was there. But that's the only thing I'm certain of, now. The police seem to think I miscalculated, that he may not have been injured and fled after I ran off."

"Mrs. Sterling obviously didn't think you overreacted. She moved from her isolated house to a well-guarded suite."

"Well, she closed it up prematurely. She wouldn't have stayed much longer in any case, just for the Gambol, and then I think she intended to go to Florida for a few weeks."

"What I meant was, her return to the penthouse was prompted by the attack and wasn't a reconciliation."

"I really couldn't comment on that, Lieutenant."

"Of course not. Mrs. Amis, can you tell me if the name Danny, or Daniel, Furina means anything to you?"

"No, I've never heard the name."

"What about Linda Veach?"

She shook her head. "Should I know these people?"

Victor slipped his notebook into his pocket. "Mrs. Amis," he said slowly, "the body that was discovered in the parking garage Friday night—"

"You said you wouldn't discuss that, Lieutenant."

"Hear me out. The man was a white male, brunette, late thirties or early forties, suffered injuries that resulted from a fall. He had been dead at least five days before he was found."

Her lips parted and she inhaled sharply. "You don't think the man who attacked me..."

Victor tried to analyze her expression. There was amazement but something else, something akin to relief. Cat had told him how Mrs. Amis had been attended by a security guard in the Phoenix. Had she been afraid the man had survived the attack, might come looking for her?

"Would you be willing to look at a couple pictures from the medical examiner's office? I warn you, they're rather graphic and there may not be much of a resemblance to the man's former physical appearance."

"I think I would know if it's the same man."

Victor offered her the photos. She examined one after another with the same avid fascination as Fawn Sterling, but with considerably less detachment.

"It's him." The words escaped involuntarily in an astonished whisper. "It's him..."

"Is there a possibility you're mistaken?"

She shook her head.

"You're certain?"

"It's him."

ADANE AND LONG were huddled over the computer when Victor entered. "Adane, would you get Margate on the phone, please, have them put me through to Officer Klass."

He walked into his office, slung his coat on the battered coat stand.

"Line one!" Long called.

Victor sat behind his desk, picked up the phone. "Victor Cardenas, Major Crimes."

"I know who you are, Lieutenant," Officer Klass commented.

"You investigated a break-in at Ten Oh One Bay Landing Court a week ago."

"Yeah. Place belongs to Blaine Sterling's wife. Weird situation. The woman, Amis? Her husband's a lawyer with the Sterling organization. She goes over there to pick up some paperwork, lets herself in with her key, says this guy jumps her, she tosses him over the railing and takes off. So I meet up with her, she's real shook up, right? I follow her over to the place, I ring the bell all ready to call for backup, Mrs. Blaine Sterling herself comes to the door. Totally cool 'I just walked in, Officer,' she says, 'What seems to be the trouble?' she asks. I tell her I got Mrs. Amis sitting in her car sayin' she got attacked inside the house just a short time ago. I say, can I have a look around. She says, sure. So I go in, I don't see any signs of a struggle, no blood, no stiff on the Italian marble, no sign of forced entry. Check around back, nothin'. I ask Mrs. Sterling if she made the first call, she says no. I'm ready to chalk this one up as some hysterical society dame—"

"What was that about the first call?"

"The first nine-one-one. Anonymous woman calls a break-in over the lagoon, so shook up she gave us the wrong street at first. I was cruisin' near Atlantic, so I responded to the Amis woman's nine-one-one."

"What time was this, can you recall?"

"The first one, one-fifteen, one-twenty, I guess."

"So who made the first call?" *Don't guess.*

"Beats me. Those places on Bay Landing, they're all shut up for the winter, so it wasn't a neighbor," said Klass. "Want a copy of the dispatcher's log?"

"Please. And, Officer, Mrs. Amis reported that the assailant had a knife. Did one turn up?"

"Nope. Mrs. Sterling didn't find one, neither did I, and all the kitchen knives were accounted for."

Victor thanked Klass, said he'd be in touch, hung up and called Adane and Long into the office. "Any word on Rice?"

"Nope."

Victor scowled. Dragging this into a second day.

"Don't sweat it, Lieutenant. They just don't wanna have the Rev say it was a rush job." Long began to chuckle. "See what they did with the demonstration yesterday? Cut off traffic and just let him sit in the road. Guy didn't last an hour. Someone oughtta get a medal for that one."

Victor wondered suddenly just what Cat and Delareto had been whispering about. "What's the word on the Phoenix?"

"Mimi Maldonado from the crime lab called, said the garage is clean, lab's goin' over the Santa suit."

"Adane, contact Raab, ask if he plans to release the man's identity, see who's going to handle notification."

Adane and Long exchanged an uneasy glance.

"You did send the prints out?"

"Yes, sir."

"What's the matter, his prints weren't on file?" It couldn't be Furina, then; a PI would have been fingerprinted.

"Wait a minute, Jeannie, this one's my fault," Long interjected. "When I called the lab, told that kid Keith I wanted prints on the trauma case came in Friday. So he sends the prints and Jeannie runs them and it wasn't too hard matchin' him up because the guy had a record. So you went out to Mays Landing and I hadda run into AC, so I left the fax on Jeannie's desk so she could put it in the file. So we could keep the file up to date."

"Commendable."

Jean spoke up. "And when I glanced over the sheet this morning, I knew there was something about the name—"

"Which was?"

"Craig Unsworth."

Victor tapped his finger against his lip, thoughtfully. "Why does that name sound familiar?"

"'Cause he was the DUI ran his car into the liquor store. I mean it was my fault, callin' him the trauma case, but who woulda thought he'd still be chillin' over ODOR? No one's staked a claim. I just called them back and told them I didn't want a set on the drive-thru, I wanted a set on the John Doe. I'll run by an' pick 'em up again if you want.''

"That might be best.''

Adane spoke up. "Lieutenant, I hope you don't mind, but I took the liberty of checking with the DMV. I gave them a description of the vehicle Mrs. Austen reported speeding out of the Phoenix Friday night. I thought perhaps it might match one registered to Mr. Furina.''

"And?''

"No luck, I'm afraid. Mr. Furina owns an old Vega with the plates PRIVIT I and a dark green Chevy van, an 'eighty-eight, most likely a surveillance vehicle.''

"What color's the Vega?''

"Red.''

Victor shrugged it off, filled them in on his conversations with Mrs. Amis, Officer Klass.

"She ID'd the stone as the same guy jumped her?'' Long asked. "She sure?''

"She saw the assailant's face clearly. Unfortunately, it doesn't give us a name, a motive, tell us how he got in.''

"I'll call downbeach, check the B and E sheets,'' Long offered.

"Perhaps it wasn't a burglary,'' Adane speculated.

Victor gestured for her to complete her thought.

"Well, if I were a burglar, concealed in a house, and someone walked in, I'd wait until I was threatened with discovery to attack. You said that Mrs. Amis stated he came at her, she didn't see him coming.''

Victor nodded.

"And remember what Phil said before? Wondering whether the John Doe was a stalker, had taken the costume to disguise himself and infiltrate the Phoenix? What if he was after Mrs. Sterling? I mean, it was her house he broke into, he had no idea Mrs. Amis would walk in on him, she said Mrs. Sterling's call was spur-of-the-moment.''

Long leaned forward. "Grabs the wrong gal, splits. He comes to and realizes he blew it, takes off, lays low, finds out the Sterling woman packed up and headed for the Phoenix, so he starts stakin' her out there.''

"But the ME's estimation of the time and manner of his death concur with Mrs. Amis' account. If he didn't die on the scene, he must have died shortly afterward.'' Victor's eyes settled on the slender yearbook lying atop a row of canvas binders. He leaned over and grabbed it, flipped through it to the senior class, to the F's. "Take a look at this picture,'' he said, turning the volume around.

Adane and Long leaned over his desk.

"Daniel John Furina.'' Victor tapped the picture. He drew out the ME's snapshots, lined them up under Furina's photo. "Our man?''

"Aw, Lieutenant, the guy in the book's a kid. That Mrs. Austen?''

Victor looked at the page. Cat and Freddy were side by side, separated from Furina only by Philip Anthony Fosco. "She went to school with him.'' She wore her hair parted in the center, had the La Gioconda smile even then.

"Does Mr. Furina have immediate family in the area?'' Adane asked.

Victor shook his head. "No family… Adane, see if you can get Linda Veach on the phone, ask her if she can meet me at the morgue. If she needs a ride, I'll pick her up. I'll grab the prints while I'm there,'' he added.

Adane didn't have to place the call, though, because at that instant, Victor's phone rang and Linda Veach was on the line. "Lieutenant Cardenas? I been thinking? You know, there was this dead guy they found in a parking garage wearing a Santa suit? And well, I—I been thinking? Wearing a Santa suit, you know? If Danny was ever to turn up dead? That's the kind of thing he'd do.''

VICTOR PICKED UP Linda Veach at her nondescript apartment building in Ventnor. In her simple red coat, her straight, shiny hair pulled back into barrettes, she looked more than ever like a child of twelve. Victor felt a twinge of discomfort. "You haven't heard from Mr. Furina?''

She wrung her small hands, shook her head.

"Miss Veach," he said, gently, "I'd like to thank you for agreeing to come in. I know this can't be very pleasant."

"I figured I might as well find out if it's Danny. And there's really no one else you could call, except for his mom, and she's in Florida."

They waited outside ODOR for the ME, who hustled up with a sweet roll projecting from his mouth. "Lemme sign you in. I got ten parents come in today tryin' to ID the kid got fished up Friday. No takers."

"The drowning victim?"

"Wasn't drowned." The ME nicked his thumb under his neck. "One inch diameter, straight to the carotid, bled out before she knew she'd been cut. Time comes, I wouldn't mind goin' that way myself."

He sneered at the NO FOOD OR DRINK BEYOND THIS POINT sign, poked the remainder of the sweet roll into his mouth. He signed the two in, ushered them into a dim, cool chamber. Three steel tables, three plastic-sheeted figures. He approached the first.

Linda Veach showed her first sign of reluctance. "He's not going to be, well, naked, is he?"

"Kid, we're all naked," the ME told her.

"Just uncover the face," Victor suggested.

"Suit yourself. Ready or not—"

Victor instinctively cupped his hand under Linda Veach's elbow. The ME unzipped the translucent plastic about twenty inches, yanked it apart.

Miss Veach absorbed it in little glances, took a deep breath, clenched her fists and allowed herself a more prolonged examination of the crumpled and discolored face.

At last, she whispered, "It's Danny. Yes, it's Danny."

ELEVEN

CAT STOOD AT the sink rinsing dinner dishes, her movements absent, weary. Since Chris' death, the holidays seemed like a hollow ceremony. Dominic had hinted that perhaps it was a loss of spirituality, that Christmas had become too secular, that she ought to start going to Mass again. Cat rejected his well-meant counsel; she was convinced that they had done her in at last, all those heady, Sicilian festivities, a manic ordeal of shopping, baking, decorating, the extravagant Christmas Eve meal, the pilgrimage to midnight Mass, the family dinner on Christmas Day, the marathon of visiting for days after, had worn her down at last, sapped all the joy from the season and left Christmas a tiresome ritual to be stoically endured for the sake of her children.

The phone rang. *Victor.* They hadn't spoken since she ran out of his office the day before. Cat dried her hands and picked up the receiver, pronounced her most aloof, "Hello?" But instead of Victor's repentant baritone, she heard Ritchie Landis' porcine squeal. "So what'd you get hauled into Major Crimes for yesterday, they come across with anything or you a suspect?"

Cat slid into the kitchen booth. "Suspected of what?"

"You went in with your mouthpiece, you tell me. They ID'd the stiff, right? It's some low-rent PI named Furina."

Cat felt her heart slam against her sternum. "It's been confirmed?"

"I guess. Cherry's brother dates a gal whose cousin knows a woman works in the morgue. Says a detective went in an hour ago with some young gal she thinks is this Furina's office gal in there to ID him. And what's the deal with the DMV?"

Cat found that she had to force the words from her lips. "What about the DMV?"

Danny. Danny Furina. How soon they forget.

"I got a mole over the DMV, says Major Crimes was checkin' up on this Furina, wantin' a description of his car, askin' if maybe it was a light-colored hatchback, old junker.

But Furina's just got a green van and a beat-up Vega. What's with that?''

"The car that almost ran me down Friday night, right before the body was found? It was an old hatchback.''

"The getaway car! I'm lovin' this! You know what I'm thinkin'? I'm thinkin' this Furina—sounds like some kinda cereal, don't he?—I'm thinkin' he got involved with somethin' shady, maybe even the mob, gets himself whacked, they cart him over the Phoenix and drop him.''

"Self-respecting Mafiosi don't transport bodies in a hatchback.''

"Yeah, well, you would know better than me.''

"I.''

"This ain't no time for grammar.''

Cat sighed. "You know, we have to remember something," she said, slipping into the collaborative "we" without realizing it. "This John Doe"—It *wasn't* Danny. It *couldn't* be!—"had been dead for some time. Someone went to a lot of trouble to leave him right in Blaine Sterling's path.''

"I wanted Sterling's attention, I woulda dropped him on the gaming floor.''

"No, the Gambler's Anonymous dropouts would walk right over him. The garage was a good pick. Sterling was due in within hours and he always enters through the executive suite, you said so yourself. I almost wish I hadn't turned down those Gambol invitations Carlton Amis offered me. I'd love to be a phoenix on that wallpaper.''

"When'd you talk to Amis?''

"None of your business.''

"And he's givin' you comps? My dad hadda fork over two grand for his four. I get to bring a guest. I'm askin' Vicky Cloughey.''

"Vicky Cloughey can't stand you.''

"You'd be surprised who'd stand me to get into the Party of the Year.''

"So would you," Cat replied. "Did you ask Vicky yet?''

"Nope.''

"Then forget it. You're taking me.''

"In your dreams, Austen.''

"Nightmares, maybe. Besides, I've never met your parents. I'd like to see who spawned you."

"Hey, watch it. First place, it's formal. You need to wear a dress."

"I'll get one with the check you owe me for *Deadly Enmity*."

"Austen, I told you, it's *Death of a DJ*. The *CopWatch* gal, Steinmetz? She loved the title. They may use it for the show. Second place, with Vicky, there's an outside chance I could score."

"In *your* dreams, Landis. You want some titillation, just gopher through the newspaper files, the Sunday lifestyle sections, eight years ago, April or May. Then you bring me my check and my invitation."

She hung up, finished rinsing the silverware, wedged past the Christmas tree. She checked on the kids. Jane's long braid was coiled around her throat, her face motionless, warm spots of color on the cheeks. Mats had thrown off his covers, one small fist clung to a ragged plush bunny's ears. In repose, there was something of Chris in his face, in the untroubled forehead, the contour of the chin, that provoked a swift, hot pressure behind her eyes. Cat blinked away the sensation, kissed Mats' forehead, backed into the hall.

The light was on in Ellice's room. Cat knocked.

"Yeah?"

Cat entered. Ellice was sitting on the bed, thumbing through a paperback. "Anouilh. *The Rehearsal*. I was working on some translation for senior French. You think it's too advanced?"

"Ellice, you eternal optimist. Didn't the French teacher leave lesson plans?"

"Couple kids took his lesson plans, curriculum notes, threw them in his car, added a dash of lighter fluid and..." Ellice threw up her hands. "*Joyeux Noel*. He's on extended mental health leave, so I got a gig until Christmas vacation. That won't screw things up for you, will it? I mean, I won't be around to babysit or anything."

"Ellice, you're not here because I wanted a—expected you to be their—" Cat was seized with a fit of giddiness.

"Don't you say it—!"

"Mammy!" Cat fell over on the bedspread, laughing. Ellice whacked her on the head with Anouilh. "Ouch. Sorry. I couldn't resist. What about your agenda? I mean, you're in school all day and Freddy's on four to midnight until right before Christmas."

"Maybe Freddy and I need a breather."

Cat bit her lip. Sherrie and Joey had the right idea. Elope and get it over with.

"So," Ellice took up her book, "I guess we're just a couple of bachelor girls again, Lucy, unless that was Victor on the phone."

"It wasn't." Cat sat up, pushed her hair away from her eyes. "Not bachelor girls, Ethel. Criminals."

"Say what?"

"Ellice, say we wanted to commit a crime—"

"Honey, we're just on the outs with our men, feelin' a little down. Let's not go overboard."

"Bear with me here."

"Fine." Ellice tossed aside Anouilh. "Felony or mis?"

"Let's make it a felony."

"Think big, I always say."

"And we need a getaway car and we don't want to use our own car or any car that could be traced to us."

"And we absolutely need this car?"

Cat nodded.

Ellice leaned back against her headboard. It had been a spare room and Ellice had added little to the bone white walls and drapes, the rose carpeting, except for a pair of pine bookshelves and the texts that filled them. "A kid in history class I subbed last month used this expression, I kid you not, 'I need to be gettin' me a jacked-up hoopty.'"

"Interesting grammatical structure."

"You ain't heard nothin'."

"And a—what you said—that would be?"

"Something old, beat-up and inconspicuous. No wild colors, but a lot of horsepower."

"To facilitate the getaway."

"My kids don't use words like 'facilitate,' but yeah."

"So where does one acquire a jacked-on—"

"Up."

"—up hoopty?"

"Steal it, borrow it, rent it if you don't have the cash to buy. Of course, you steal it, you run the risk of getting picked up. Borrow it, you're dragging accomplices into the situation."

"And they could rat you out."

"There you go."

"And rent?" Cat frowned. "I don't imagine there's a Rent-A-Hoopty in the Yellow Pages."

"No," Ellice replied, thoughtfully. "But there are those wreck rentals. You know, they take the cash up front and if it runs, it runs, and if it doesn't, the hell with it. Not much in the way of a credit check, I imagine. Cars probably have no book value. You put up a little cash and your fake ID and you've got wheels. What're we gonna do after the job, make tracks, bail, split up?"

"Ellice, I'm impressed beyond words."

"Hang with a cop, you start to pick up the argot."

Cat thought for a moment. "Bail. Ditch the…hoopty."

"Okay, here's what let's do. Down here in Jersey, you got your pine barrens, you got your marshes, you can shoot right off the Longport Bridge into the bay, though the marine cops take a dim view of that. Or hey, why not just pull into the driveway of some house shut up for the winter? Freddy said once that a lot of people pick up a junker just to park it in the drive over the winter when they close up the house and head down to Florida. Make the place look occupied."

"Like a two-million-dollar house with a two-hundred-dollar wreck in the driveway isn't a dead giveaway. But…you could park it in a big casino garage."

"We're in business."

"That's the upside to being with a cop, you know."

"What is?"

Cat smiled. "You begin to develop the criminal mentality."

CAT CRAWLED into bed, wondering if Victor had even thought about calling to apologize. Probably not. Trying to scare her off the Phoenix story, and going about it in such a coldhearted manner! Well, just for that, she wasn't going to back off. She had her fill of intimidation, knuckling under to overprotective cops. No, that wasn't entirely fair. After all, Chris had been the one who had pushed her to go back to college, get her degree, get on with her writing, made a big deal of every little ten-dollar, fifty-word filler she had turned out. Chris had thought she was capable of better, even when Cat herself had doubted. Then the Dudek murder was thrown in her path and there was no one to push her and every reason to retreat, but she hadn't backed off. And she wasn't backing off now.

Cat hung over the side of the bed, rummaged for the two-year-old Atlantic County phone directory and came up with three possible suppliers: Shot Rods, Lemon Aides and Tyrannosaurus Wrecks. The latter's number had been disconnected, Lemon Aides' line was busy and Shot Rods had a recording that stated their business hours were seven AM to seven PM and that Cat should try calling tomorrow, or leave a message at the beep.

Cat hung up and tried Lemon Aides a second time.

"Lemon Aides, Miss Salamanca speaking, we're available twenty-four hours a day and pick-ups are welcome."

Which reminded Cat of one of Joey's anecdotes about an escort service that had pretty much the same greeting, a recollection that provoked a laugh Cat stifled at the lips, but the effort caused her to blow her rehearsed intro, so she plowed in with, "This is Miss, uh, Victor"—dear God—"from"— where?—"the television show *CopWatch*—"

"Oh God, oh God, oh God I love that show!"

"Thank you. We're always pleased to hear from a fan. The fact is, I'm an assistant to the, uh, production designer and we're looking for a few older-model cars for a shoot we're doing in the area—"

"Oh God, oh God, oh God, is it the Jerry Dudek murder?"

Cat coughed, crossed her fingers. "Uh, yes."

"Well, didja like wanna speak to the manager, 'cause he's not here right now."

"No, I think you'll do just fine. I—we're—looking for something in the way of a small hatchback, light color would work best. You know, the lighting and … all that. It has to be at least twelve to fifteen years old."

"We got two on the lot, but one's brown and one's green."

"Nothing in a white, or say, ecru?"

"Huh?"

"Light…brownish…beige…"

"Lemme think." The process took a minute fifty-seven seconds; Cat clocked it. "We did have one like that, but the guy ha'n't brought it back yet and we may have to take a write-off. It happens."

"People just make off with the cars?"

"Or total 'em."

"Did you rent it locally?"

"I got the paperwork somewhere. Lemme think." She got it down to one forty-five this time. "We tried callin' this guy, but I musta wrote the number down wrong, 'cause alls I got is a pay phone in some coffee shop down Oriental in AC. Here it is. The guy's name is Jones. Allan Jones. Took it out November fifth, he puts down five-fifty cash. That was for three weeks, plus deposit."

"Then it's about four weeks overdue. Why haven't you repossessed it?"

"It was a 'seventy-three Hornet, the book's not even five-fifty. If it's gone, it's gone. Write-off's cheaper than keepin' a repo man on the payroll."

"I see. I don't suppose you could give me this Mr. Jones' address?"

"Well, I don't think I'm s'posed to…"

"It would help if I could track down this car, Miss Salamanca. And while I have you on the phone, I was wondering if you've ever done any, uh, extra work? We'll be shooting most of the show right here in the area and we'll need several local people for the…crowd scenes…"

"Oh God, oh God, oh God, I got on *CopWatch*, I'd die!"

Cat didn't trust herself to respond.

"Look, here's the address. Three Fifty-three New Bedford Avenue. I think it's near the corner of Oriental. Isn't that near where the Phoenix is? Gee, did you hear they found a dead guy in an elevator wearing a Santa suit over there?"

"Something about it."

"Look, you get the car offa him, just lemme know so's I can close the file."

Cat promised, endured the girl's recounting of her favorite *CopWatch* episode—"the two sisters from Wisconsin and the guy who had a thing for stiletto heels"—eased herself off the phone.

Near the corner of New Bedford and Oriental. The tear-downs on New Bedford, J m's on the corner, stubborn J m who had refused to sell out to Sterling. Two apartments above the coffee shop. One of them would be a great lair for someone who wanted to slip in and out of the Phoenix inconspicuously.

Cat looked up the number, dialed, asked for Jim, gave him her Miss Salamanca voice. "I saw you got a couple apartments over your coffee shop, you got one for rent?"

"Guy in B ain't comin' back," barked a gruff voice. "I'll get it cleaned out, call me end of the week. Earlene can fill you in, you wanna talk to her?"

Cat had no idea why she would want to talk to Earlene; Jim took her hesitation for refusal and hung up.

So Danny had rented a disposable car, used an alias, staked out the Phoenix. What on earth had he been up to?

TWELVE

LINDA VEACH HAD turned her back while the ME had yanked the plastic apart, lifted one flaccid brown paw after the other, pressed the ink-covered fingers onto a card, ran over it with a blow dryer on a cool setting and slipped it into an envelope, handed it to Victor.

Victor helped Linda Veach into his car. She sat stiffly, hugging her coat to her chest. He asked her to come to Major Crimes on the following day to give a written statement concerning Furina's disappearance. When he pulled up to her apartment building, she hustled out of the car before he could make a move to assist her, ran to her door and let herself in hastily.

Victor called Raab from his car, was instructed not to discuss the John Doe with the press and told that Stan had been exonerated of any responsibility for Mrs. Bolton's death. Victor headed home, tried to call Cat from his car, got a busy signal, tried again from home, got another, another.

He threw together a sandwich, sifted through his mail, then closed his eyes and tried to make some sense of the Furina matter. Why the hell would a small-time PI break into Fawn Sterling's home? Why would he attack a women who just happened to drop by? And if he had been killed in his struggle with Mrs. Amis, what had been done with the body between Monday and Friday and who had dumped his body in the Phoenix Friday night?

Back up. Before he turns up dead, Furina attacks Mrs. Amis. Remote house on an isolated street, good place for a hit, if that's what it was. But this guy Furina, a hit man? Was that possible? Well, he was a loose cannon, apparently. Linda Veach and Cat and Delareto had all implied as much, so perhaps it was possible, or at least not improbable and Sherlock Holmes had said that once you eliminate the impossible, whatever remained, however improbable, had to be the truth.

Victor tried Cat once more, got another busy signal, slammed the phone down with a curse, mulled over the Furina matter some more until he fell asleep. He woke on the couch, roused by the preset alarm wailing in his bedroom, stumbled to his feet, lurched down the hall, shut off the alarm. Six forty-five. He snapped on the small TV on top of his dresser. A booming exclamation shocked him into complete conscious-

ness. "Is no one then to be held accOUNTABLLLLE!" The
latter four syllables timed out at ten seconds. Victor saw the
Reverend Marlon d'Esperance urging a group of followers to
protest the exoneration of Sergeant Stanley Rice, to insist Rice
be called to account for the death of Mrs. Bolton. This time
he had launched his demonstration from Mrs. Bolton's North
Maryland Avenue apartment complex, was headed toward Atlantic Avenue, marching his ranks down the middle of the
street.

Victor took a quick shower, rummaged through his closet,
yanked out a pale blue shirt, a dark suit, made himself a cup
of instant. It was when he picked up the overcoat he had
thrown on the couch that he realized he didn't recall what he
had done with the envelope the ME had handed him. The one
with Furina's prints. He had it when he walked into the parking lot with Linda Veach, had opened the car door for her,
thrown the envelope into the back seat. Linda Veach. He dialed her number to remind her to give her deposition that
morning, got her machine. Seven-thirty. She ought to be home,
Victor thought; perhaps she had Adane's initiative and was
already on her way over.

A whisper of icy precipitation, too transparent and brittle to
be called snow, had glazed the coastal communities overnight.
Victor's landlady, who had trisected her three-story house into
apartments and lived in the unit below Victor's, was mincing
along the slippery walk in vinyl boots, whipping two one-
pound boxes of Morton's salt over the sidewalk and steps.

"I'll do that, Mrs. DiLorenzo." Victor took the salt and
drizzled an even layer on the ground, heard the crust begin to
crackle underfoot. Mrs. DiLorenzo smiled, hoped the neighbors were watching, the ones who had looked down on her
for taking in a tenant. "They say you pour it on snails, they
frizz up, you ever hear that?"

"I wouldn't know," Victor replied, solemnly, as he escorted her to her door. It was a lie. In fact, there had been
youthful experiments executed with a zeal that did not befit a
future law enforcement officer. But Victor was not about to
undermine Mrs. DiLorenzo's excellent opinion of him by ad-

mitting that, at the age of seven or eight, he had indeed "frizzed up" a snail or two.

He scraped the windshield on the Jaguar, reached for the car phone as soon as he made the turn onto Atlantic; it trilled before his hand touched the receiver.

"Lieutenant?" Adane, already at her desk.

"I'm on my way in."

"I know, but I wanted to let you know right away. The hatchback? A car fitting that description was spotted in the channel at low tide, off Somers Point Boulevard. A nineteen seventy-three Hornet."

"They bring it up?"

"They're doing it now. It'll go to the impound. Apparently, it's a rental from an agency in Northfield called Lemon Aides. That's A-i-d-e-s. You know, those places that rent old cars cheaply? It seems that a man named Allan Jones, that's A-l-l-a-n, rented it on November fifth and never returned it."

"There's an address on the rental agreement?"

"Yes. Three fifty-three New Bedford. It's right around the corner from Oriental, if my geography serves. He gave the number of a coffee shop downstairs for his phone. Lemon Aides never checked it out. I suspect they aren't too particular."

"Who'd—"

"A Miss Salamanca. I described Mr. Furina and she said the man who rented the car fit that description, but it's been about seven weeks, and she only saw him that one time."

"If Linda Veach comes in to give her statement this morning, detain her until I get there. And try to dig up a recent photo of Furina and take it over to this Lemon Aides, show it to the woman, see if she can make him as the guy who leased the hatchback."

"You don't want Phil to do that?"

"You backed up over there?"

"Not really."

"Then you do it. Send Long over to the apartment, have him check the place out, talk to the people in the coffee shop; maybe Furina'd been hanging around there."

"Yes, sir."

"Heard anything from Rice?"

"He's not picking up at home, but we've gotten several calls this morning, all supportive. And the Seniors Organized on Behalf of Stanley are planning a rally this morning to demonstrate their support."

"I beg your pardon?"

"Some of the senior citizens in Mrs. Thurman's neighborhood. They've formed a support group, the Seniors Organized on Behalf of Stanley."

"And would I be correct in assuming that their acronym is—"

"Yes, sir. But as a general rule, one ought not assume." She could not believe she had heard her boss laugh. "And one more thing, sir. When I was speaking to Miss Salamanca, she mentioned that someone had called her last night, inquiring about a light-colored hatchback. The person claimed to be a production assistant from a show called *CopWatch*."

"What did he—"

"It was a woman, sir. A Miss Victor."

"Dios mio," Victor muttered. *She just doesn't give up.*

IT HAD BEEN seven weeks since Lowell Jeffries had bludgeoned the elderly Alameda "Granma Al" Thurman, five since Granma's friend, Mrs. Malba Shallett had made the gruesome discovery. After that six-block sprint in quest of aid, Mrs. Shallett had made two resolutions: first, she was going to yell "Fire" instead of "Help" next time, just like that dear Stanley Rice had advised; and, as it was not right that a woman of but seventy-seven years, not an ounce over one-fifteen, cholesterol one forty-two, not a shred of tobacco ever, nor a drop of alcohol (except for those nice Irish fruitcakes her niece sent her at Christmas and those two Coca-Colas with rum in high school before she had found the Lord), should get herself so winded after six measly blocks, resolution number two was: spend less time with Oprah and get herself some of those Nikes.

She was wearing them now, leading thirty-seven Seniors

Organized on Behalf of Stanley down Atlantic Avenue on a collision course with the followers of the Reverend Marlon d'Esperance. No parade permits had been issued, but the Reverend's demonstration had been anticipated, the department instructed to "exhibit a heightened professionalism and present a non-confrontational posture" which whispered down the lane and emerged on the street as: "Long's he doesn't got weapons, hang back and keep a lookout for the camcord jockeys."

The Seniors Organized on Behalf of Stanley had taken everyone by surprise: the city, the police and d'Esperance, who spied the oncoming rally and assumed, on the basis of hue, if not cry, that they were fellows in the cause. He cranked up the imprecations directed against Sergeant Rice and, despite its less than impressive impact on previous occasions, set himself down for justice once again.

Mrs. Shallet was having none of his shenanigans. She stomped up to the corpulent figure and cried, "Get out of the road, you wart hog of a troublemaker!" Blasphemy had been prohibited in Malba's household; "wart hog" was the most emphatic denunciation she could muster.

"Now see here, Mommy—" d'Esperance began, but got no further. Though he had indeed said "Mommy," his affectionate address for all senior females, Mrs. Shallett's slightly impaired hearing rendered it as "Mammy," an epithet she was in no humor to condone with the same wry humor as, say, Ellice.

"I am nobody's Mammy, leastways yours, you wart hog parading as a human being!" A riposte she punctuated by knocking the reverend flat and planting her one hundred fifteen pounds, Nikes first, on his pneumatic belly.

"OOooouuuUUFF!"

At this juncture the first sacrificial ranks arrived, two patrol cars, four more officers on bikes. They attempted to remove Mrs. Shallett from the Reverend's abdomen and were whacked with placards bearing the logo, "We're for Stan, He's our Man."

What one patrol officer, engaged in dislodging a pair of

eighty-year-old hands from his collar, attempted to communicate to a dispatcher nearing the end of her shift was not meant to emerge as "riot." But the dispatcher was taking no chances. Six months before, a Korean merchant had been beaten by six truants and despite two dozen 911s, it had taken twenty minutes for the police to arrive on the scene. *News-Line90* got a teary interview with the merchant's wife and *Front Cover* had paid twenty-five thousand for the tape. Two dispatchers had been suspended indefinitely.

So within five minutes, twenty cops in full riot gear were on the scene. Marco Fortunati jumped out of the van, did a slow pan that took in the SOBS belting cops and antagonists with handmade placards while an elderly woman was being forcibly restrained from trampolining on the Reverend, and told himself he had put in twenty-five years come spring, time to collect the pension, get an RV, round up Nancy and the kids and get the hell out of Dodge. Once Cat and his brothers got wind of this, his life would be a living hell.

"Wart hog!" echoed along Atlantic Avenue. It took four officers to extract Mrs. Shallett from the Reverend, but not before she aimed one last kick at what she believed were the private areas of the Reverend's writhing form. Fifty-six years of marriage had failed to correct her inexact understanding of male anatomy and she was some inches from a direct hit. "Wart hog!"

CAT TOOK HER morning run, glanced around for one or both of the Amises, could not distinguish among the muffled figures that sprinted past as either the attorney or his wife. She had awakened that morning with a residual discomfort and a sense of sadness, remembering, as she dressed for her run, that Danny Furina was dead. Her mind resisted the thought, resisted the disquieting notion that if she had only said something to Freddy about Danny's phone call, followed up at the time, Danny might still be alive.

She rushed through her shower while Ellice helped Jane comb her hair, sipped a Diet Pepsi while she fixed Mats' breakfast, packed school lunches, salted the porch steps. She

walked a cranky Jane to the corner bus stop, bundled up Mats
and piled him into the car to give Ellice a ride to the high
school, wished Ellice luck with Anouilh, ran back home to
rinse the breakfast dishes, helped Mats brush his teeth and ran
into her room to make the bed before she took Mats to the
nursery school he attended a few days a week. On impulse,
she dug up Linda Veach's number, got her machine—"This
is Linda Veach? I'm not here right now?"—tried Danny's
office—"You have reached Furina Investigative Services..."
They weren't there right now. Cat snapped on the TV to catch
some of the morning news while she made the bed.

Mats crept in as Cat was smoothing the spread. "Do I got
to go to school today?" he asked.

"What's the matter, baby?" Cat sat on the bed, lifted Mats
onto her lap. "I thought Santa was coming to school this
morning."

"Only a helper. My throat itches inside."

Cat stroked his forehead and cheeks. They felt warm. "Lie
here and Mommy will get you some baby aspirin."

"Ty'nol," Mats said, knowingly. "They said on TV not to
give aspring to us kids."

Cat rummaged through her medicine cabinet, found a two-
thirds-empty bottle of liquid Tylenol, tacked *Buy Liquid Tylenol* onto her mental bulletin board as she poured out a dose,
filled a paper cup with water.

"Mom! Uncle Marco's on TV!"

Cat slipped onto the bed beside Mats, gave him the dose of
medicine. On television, a *NewsLine90* reporter was covering
what appeared to be a demonstration prompted by what the
reporter referred to as "the complete clearance of Sergeant
Stanley Rice."

"Why is Uncle Marco grabbing at that nonna?" Mats
wanted to know. "Is she under arrested?"

Cat groped the bedspread for the remote, was about to check
out another channel's coverage when the harried reporter said,
"And this just in: a car was recovered from the channel off
Somers Point Boulevard this morning where it was low tide
and discovered by a passing motorist partially submerged and

apparently abandoned.'' Cat's laugh was cut short by the visual, a car hauled up by its rear axle, a light-colored hatchback, the car that had almost run her down.

"Mats," Cat said slowly, "I'm on assignment and I need a partner, what do you say?"

"What's assignment?"

"Like a secret mission. Kind of like hide and seek."

"Are there gonna be bad guys?" It had been a bad guy who had shot Mom, Jane had told him so.

Cat shook her head. "Just us. But you have to keep it a secret. You can't tell anyone."

"Not even Jane?" Sometimes Jane told him neat stuff.

"Especially not Jane."

"I DON'T KNOW where she is, sir." Adane's cool equanimity was ruffled by what she considered another failure. "I have been trying to get Miss Veach on the phone, but all I get is her answering machine. She never came in to make a statement. I thought perhaps she misunderstood and went downtown or over to Mays Landing, but she hasn't shown up there, either. And I haven't come up with a photograph of Mr. Furina yet, so I took Mrs. Austen's yearbook to Lemon Aides. The woman said the picture of Mr. Furina did resemble the man who leased the car, but of course, Mr. Furina is twenty years younger in the yearbook. I was able to recover the application form that Mr. Jones filled out; I sent it to the state print lab."

"Excellent. If Veach doesn't show soon, I want you to go over to her place and check it out."

"Yes, sir."

Victor turned to Phil Long, who sat with his legs stretched in front of Victor's desk, frowning in unconscious emulation of his boss. "Furina's office phone's on the machine. I ran by there on my way in, place is shut up. Tailor shop downstairs, Don's Dough Nutz on the corner, they say they haven't seen him in over a week."

Victor was pacing, his mouth turned down in a deep scowl. "See if Raab can subpoena Furina's bank statements. I'd like to look at the canceled checks, see who paid the jackpot. What about the flat on New Bedford?''

"This is where it gets spooky. Guess where it is?"

"Tell me."

"Y'know that old coffee shop across from the Phoenix, guy whose property Sterling's tryin' to buy? Place we hooked up Friday night?''

"Jim's," Victor nodded.

"That's it. Jimmy Donato. He owns the building on the corner, been in his family for seventy, eighty years. There's a couple apartments above the coffee shop, entrance to them is on New Bedford. Three Fifty-three New Bedford. One of Jim's waitresses lives in one, seems she hooked up with a dude name a Jones, talked Jim into rentin' the other place out to him by the week. Jones skipped out; Jim figures he's gone for good, already got a couple calls is the place for rent?''

"You get a look at the place?''

"Yeah, Jim let me in. Okay carpet, new paint, those old plaster walls, cheap furniture. Living room, kitchenette, bedroom, john. There's a couple blankets on the bed, no linens. Nylon gym tote, packed. Jeans, skivvies, socks, like he's ready to split. Couple TV dinners in the fridge, some Campbell's chicken noodle in the cupboard. No papers, no keys, no money. Jim said the gal, the waitress? Said something about how this guy Jones ran out on her.''

"You talk to her?''

"I knocked, she didn't answer. Works four to midnight. Name's Earlene Adkins.''

"Check back when she clocks in.''

"Another thing. Furina's got a mom, down Florida.''

Victor dropped into his chair, a troubled gaze stealing over his immobile features. Those three years undercover, he had thought about it a lot, some cop, hat in hand, standing on his mother's doorstep. "Don't do anything about that yet, let Raab decide who's handling notification. But, Adane—''

"I'd already sent a copy of a preliminary report and a description of Mr. Furina to Delray Beach, to a Sergeant Garcia.

He said he would be willing to check whether Mr. Furina had contacted his mother or visited her recently.''

"So Stan comin' in today?" Long asked. "He's cleared, we could use an extra body."

"I called him this morning, his phone's been off the hook," Adane said. "I'm a bit worried about him, sir."

"He's fine. I took a ride out there before I came in," Victor told them. He did not add that he had been admitted by a leggy blond with a mass of curls and a wan, sleep-deprived face. Stan had introduced her as "Judy, my ex." Victor hadn't been sure if Judy was Stan's ex-wife or ex-something else. "He comes back when Raab clears him to come back." Victor leaned his head back, gestured to the pair sitting before him. "Okay, I'm willing to listen to theories if they don't deviate too far from our available and contradictory facts."

Long shrugged. "Furina hits the jackpot, doesn't let the kid, Veach, in on it. Why? Too risky, maybe, and he doesn't wanna get her hurt, or too profitable and he doesn't wanna share. Monday he walks out, acts like he's gonna grab some lunch, but he's really gonna run out take care of business. Only he screws up, hits the wrong woman, winds up dead."

Adane spoke more reluctantly. She was not entirely comfortable with Victor's practice of encouraging his unit to theorize freely and had concluded, from conversations with her girlfriends in the city department, that this was not typical of the morning muster. "Miss Veach said that Mr. Furina didn't open a file on his anonymous client, the one who was, presumably, the provider of the jackpot. Perhaps the client was well-known and didn't want his or her name on the record and could afford to pay for secrecy."

"Private investigators generally respect a client's confidentiality in any case," Victor interjected.

"True. But perhaps the client suspected that Mr. Furina might be tempted to disregard professionalism unless he were given financial inducement. And as it happens, the two names that have come up in connection with Mr. Furina have been the names of very prominent people: Mrs. Carlton Amis, who was attacked by Mr. Furina, and Mrs. Blaine Sterling, in whose home the attack took place. It was also Mrs. Sterling that Mr. Furina mentioned in his conversation with Mrs. Austen.''

Victor hesitated. "Mrs. Sterling was engaged to Mrs. Austen's brother some years ago. Furina was asking if the two of them might have gotten together recently."

"Sounds like Furina was maybe doggin' Mrs. Sterling, caught her hookin' up with some guy—not Mrs. Austen's brother, mind you," Long hastened to add. "But, hey, talk is she plays the field. Maybe it was Sterling hired Furina to tail the missus, lookin' for grounds for divorce."

"Does he need to establish adultery?" Adane queried. "Why not simply claim irreconcilable differences? Unless..."
Victor gestured for her to complete the thought.

"I just meant, well, the Phoenix has placed a considerable financial burden on Mr. Sterling; he may not be able to extricate himself without a fresh source of cash. His first divorce was rather costly; perhaps his finances won't sustain a second divorce when his situation is so unstable. Now, Mr. Furina could have no idea Mrs. Amis was going to walk in on him that day. Ordinarily, the only person who could be expected to walk in would be Mrs. Sterling." Adane took a deep breath. "And, well, it does make one wonder—I don't mean to sound melodramatic, sir—but I wonder if perhaps Mrs. Sterling is worth more to her husband dead than alive."

THIRTEEN

THE RECOVERED CAR had been removed and the roadblock on the Longport Bridge cleared by the time Cat drove into Atlantic City. She took Ventnor Avenue, a broad thoroughfare of fickle traffic signals and thriving businesses: real estate offices, ice cream parlors, delis, and a few nice-looking boutiques, crossed the border between Ventnor and Atlantic City. She slowed when she saw a doughnut shop and Giovanazzi's

Custom Tailoring and Alterations, made a left onto a narrow side street. She saw a wrought-iron staircase ascending the side of Giovanazzi's building, saw DANIEL FURINA INVESTIGATIVE SERVICES painted onto the concrete exterior, an arrow pointing diagonally upward toward a second-story landing.

As Cat surveyed the street, a mail carrier lumbered around the corner, stuffed a manila envelope into the mailbox secured to the bottom of the railing, crossed the street and continued down Ventnor Avenue. "All right, Deputy Agent Austen, let's see what we can see." Cat unbuckled Mats' seat belt and lifted him out of the car, walked him across the street.

"I don't like this place."

"We won't be here long."

Cat strolled around the corner, past Giovanazzi's storefront. The owner sat at a window, basting a pair of trousers, his glasses perched on his forehead, his work held an inch from his eyes. She did a casual one-eighty and approached the side staircase, contemplated the mailbox, decided that simply taking something from someone's mailbox and bringing it up to his office was not interfering with the US Post Office or whatever any more than when the mail carrier put Mrs. Liebener's mail in Cat's box at least three times a month and Cat took possession of it and personally delivered it to Mrs. Liebener, who lived at Ten Forty-three Pinnacle. Right? Conscience abated, Cat removed the manila envelope, casually noted that it was addressed to Danny, marked "Personal and Confidential," and that it had a North Jersey postmark, but no return address.

Cat gripped Mats' hand. "Let's go upstairs."

"I'm tired of being secret agents."

"There'll probably be a chair inside where you can sit down, baby."

The stairs were wrought-iron grill, lightly glazed with ice. Cat thought she saw the indentations of a shoeprint, wasn't sure. The door at the top of the landing had a placard with DANIEL FURINA INVESTIGATIVE SERVICES: PLEASE WALK IN fixed above the knob. Cat turned the knob, entered a small cubicle of a waiting room: cheap linoleum floor; a pine church pew and a couple vinyl chairs; a basket of out-dated magazines. A doorless closet had a couple of metal hooks on the back wall, a mounted pole with a few dozen wire hangers cadged from T. Giovanazzi. The door leading to Danny's office was a demolition sale pickup, a large square of rippled translucent glass filled in the top half. DANIEL FURINA, LICENSED PRIVATE INVESTIGATOR: PLEASE RING was painted on the glass in gold block letters. There was a brass mail slot under the window, a buzzer on the jamb.

Cat sat Mats on the pew and began to think.

If she rang the buzzer, she might alert Giovanazzi. If she broke the glass— *If you broke the glass?* Cat hollered inwardly. *Are you crazy?*

Yes. But she was here now, so she may as well have a look around, right? She knelt beside the door and pushed open the mail slot with one finger, saw a remarkably uncluttered desk, nothing but a coffee mug full of pencils and a phone on its surface, which put Cat on alert, because all through school, Danny's desk had been a monument to disarray.

At Annamarie's last birthday party, Marco Junior had locked himself into Carlo and Annie's utility shed and Marco (who could extricate himself from handcuffs in fifty-five seconds, no key) had picked the lock with an unbent paper clip and the mini-scissors on his penknife and now Cat wished that she had paid more attention. She rummaged in the pockets of her battered bomber jacket—it had been Chris'; the sleeves were too long and the leather had taken a beating, but it had eight pockets—and came up with a Kleenex, a Bic pen, a parkway token, forty-seven cents and her missing Chapstick. She rubbed the latter over her lips, muttering "When the going gets tough, the tough get going."

"Can we get goin' now, then?"

Cat's brows lowered in a motherly frown. Her gaze stalled on the rack of wire hangers. She rose, yanked one free, untwisted the neck and bent one end on an angle, crouched beside the doorknob and inserted it into the keyhole. If this is a deadbolt, I'm sunk, she told herself as she probed and rotated the wire rod.

"Mom, are secret agents 'llowed to do this?"

Cat thought for a moment. "'Society with no other scale but the legal one is not quite worthy of man,'" she quoted.

"Huh?"

"A writer said that. A man named Solzhenitzen. He spent a lot of time in"—she heard a faint click—"jail." She reached up and tried the knob. The door opened. "Okay now, remember, Deputy Agent Austen, not a word. And keep your mittens on."

"So we don't leave no fingerprints," Mats said, wisely.

Cat grinned. Jane had once sprinkled a fine mist of talcum powder over her bureau to prove to her mother that Mats *had so* gone into her room and touched her stuff. "And whisper. And tiptoe. Enemy agents below."

"Okay," Mats whispered.

Executive desk and chair, worktable with a secondhand dinette chair for Linda Veach, computer, printer on a card table, paper shredder underneath, file cabinets in the corner. All clean, down to the wastebasket.

Cat felt the first trickle of genuine dread. Her mind had resisted the idea of Danny's death. If she had heard that one of the Keller kids had died, one of the Colucci's got himself bumped off, that she would have believed, but not Danny. Not Danny. Yet, Ritchie had said someone ID'd the body. And someone had taken every scrap of paper from his office.

The phone rang, startling her. Rang again. Again. Again. And then it struck her: Cat had called that morning and the phone had rung three times before the tape had kicked in. It rang a fifth time. Gingerly, Cat lifted the receiver. "Hello? I, uh, mean, Furina Investigative Services?"

She pushed the EJECT button on the answering machine. The tape was gone. Whoever had cleaned out the office had done it within the last couple hours.

"That you, Linny? It's Linny, isn't it?"

"Oh…yeah."

"Where the hell's the boss been?"

"He's…out on assignment. May I ask who's calling?"

"It's me, Mitch Falcone, 'member?"

"Oh yes, Mr. Falcone, I beg your pardon. I didn't recognize your voice."

"Same here. You sound different."

Cat thought. "I've been taking elocution lessons."

"Yeah, well, keep it up. So I haven't heard from the boss for over a week, I finally turned up that photo. He get it?"

Cat looked at the envelope she still clutched in one hand. "A manila envelope marked 'Personal and Confidential'?"

"That's it. Puts our boy face to face with all parties involved. My guess is it's his way of givin' King Midas his résumé, showin' him how close he can get to the mark. Tell your boss get a fax. Me, I don't trust the US postal."

"I think that's a reasonable— I mean, me neither."

"When can he give me a buzz, do you think?"

"I don't know. Would you like to leave a message?"

"Nah."

Darn.

"Oh hell, why not? Got a pen?"

Delete darn. Cat rummaged for the Bic. "Uh-huh."

"He's gonna love this. I don't got the whole deal yet, but our boy Pritchard—got that?"

"P-r-i-t-c-h-a-r-d?"

"You got it. Textbook sociopath, spent most of his life in the joint. But get this: beat a manslaughter rap a while back, lucked out. Hotshot firms, they like to do a freebie here and there, buff the image, you follow?"

"A well-regarded law firm took on this Pritchard's manslaughter case on a *pro bono* basis," Cat interpreted, wrote Pritchard on the back of the envelope, underlined it.

"You're gettin' sharper, Linny. Carves up the arrest report at the prelim, case gets thrown out, Pritchard walks. Don't stay on the street for long, picked up for some weapons something or other, tried to get the manslaughter mouthpiece to take him on again, but the guy'd taken leave from the firm, so Pritchard hadda make do with legal aid, wound up with two and a half, played nice and got out in ten months. Paroled over the summer; end of October, he skips.''

Cat scribbled furiously.

"But get this: guess who's the mouthpiece beat the man-slaughter rap for Pritchard?"

"I don't gu—know."

"Carlton Amis. Right before he hooks up with Sterling."

"Amis," Cat repeated, flatly.

"So there's the connection. You make sure you tell the boss."

"Yes." *Connection to what?* she wondered.

"I'm gonna try to have a sit-down with Pritchard's parole officer, I hear anything more, I'll give Danny Boy a ring. Better yet, tell him to get on line, we'll go e-mail. I'm gettin' to where I don't even trust Ma Bell."

"I don't blame you," Cat said.

CAT AND MATS faced each other across a booth at Mc-Donald's. "What do you think?" Cat asked, nodding toward the fast-food Santa holding court in the center of the room.

Mats dropped the chicken nugget he had been picking at listlessly. "Helper," he decided.

"How can you tell?"

"His suit doesn't got enough fuzz and he's not so fat."

"Go talk to him anyway. He looks lonely."

Mats' mouth set in a cautious line. Cat's throat thickened. Mats had been six months old when she and Chris had first set him on Santa's lap, cooed and danced like idiots when Mats' lower lip began to pucker.

"Okay." Mats slid out of the booth, approached the Santa tentatively.

"I know you're just a helper," Mats informed him.

Cat checked her watch. She'd give Ritchie a few more minutes to show, then she had to get Mats home. He needed a nap. His fever had risen again and his lethargy worried her. Why did kids always get sick at Christmas?

She glanced out the broad window, saw Ritchie hustling up the ramp, the buttons of his overcoat straining on his short, stocky figure. "Lemme get some food!" he yelled to her, returned in a minute with two Big Macs, fries and a strawberry shake. "She was engaged to your brother!" he hissed, leaning across the table.

"Shhh! That's right."

"I'm not believin' this! Why 'n't you ever tell me your brother was engaged to Mrs. Blaine Sterling, f'Chrissakes?"

"Ritchie, watch your language." Cat nodded toward Mats, who had finished up with Santa's helper and returned, clutching two red lollipops.

"That yours? I love kids. What's your name, kid?"

"I'm not asposed to tell it to strange people."

"It's okay, Mats, mommy knows this strange person."

"Matthew Christopher Austen. What's yours?"

"Ritchie. Cute kid. Well, you win, Austen, we're on for the Gambol. Buy yourself a dress." Ritchie jammed half a Big Mac into his mouth, reached into his breast pocket, tossed an envelope across the table, sucked down half of his shake.

Cat tore open the envelope, suppressed an urge to kiss the check. "Okay. I'll need an extension on the Party of the Year, if you want me to work the Phoenix thing." She told him about Danny Furina's phone call the Sunday after Thanksgiving, the call from Linda Veach the day after the body had turned up in the Phoenix, the Lemon Aides rental that had turned up in the bay. She omitted the break-in of Danny's office, the manila envelope scribbled over with notes, secreted in an inner pocket of her jacket, but Ritchie was hooked nonetheless.

He punctuated each revelation with "This is great! I'm lovin' this!"

Several people glanced toward their booth.

"You're not asposed to talk with your mouth full," Mats informed Ritchie.

"Why'n't you suck one of those lollipops?"

"I'm saving them."

"Ritchie," Cat interrupted. "Let's stick with the program. We've got to figure out a strategy for finding out what Danny was up to that got him"—she glanced at Mats—"in trouble."

Ritchie stuffed the rest of the sandwich into his mouth. "Even before he calls you las' month, he's settin' himself up with the car, the stakeout, sounds like a surveillance gig. And right across from the Phoenix, too. Sterling, he's a real sport, not chargin' the two bucks for parking, so he don't have to hire attendants, which means you can slip in and outta the garage without bein' spotted." Ritchie grabbed a handful of fries. "I say he's doggin' one of the Sterlings, something went sour, King Midas had him whacked."

"Why would Sterling, uh, whack Danny Furina?"

"Furina's blackmailin' him, maybe. Sterling's got cash troubles, doesn't need some low-rent PI bleedin' him when he don't know how he's gonna make the interest on the bonds even. Means there's gotta be a money trail. Con the secretary into lettin' you look at his books."

"I can't get her on the phone," Cat frowned. "And..."

"What? What!"

"I went over to Danny's office this morning. Someone cleaned it out, recently and thoroughly."

"This is great!"

"Shhh!"

"Hey, wanna keep it down over there?" Santa called out.

"Aw, ho ho ho," Ritchie yelled back.

"You'll get coal," Mats warned him.

"Kid, I eat coal for breakfast." He turned his attention back to Cat. "Austen, you keep this up, I'll put you on the beat, get another entertainment gal."

"There's one more thing," Cat added, cautiously. "And don't ask me how I found out. Danny had been talking to a guy named Falcone, Mitch Falcone. I think he's a PI, too, from somewhere up north. Anyway, this Falcone was helping him get a line on someone named Pritchard. Pritchard's a repeat offender, apparently, who skipped parole some time around the end of October."

"So what's the tie-in?"

"Well, I gather this Pritchard is a pretty cold-blooded character. He was arrested for manslaughter a while back and beat the rap, thanks to a first-class lawyer who took the case on a *pro bono* basis."

"And?"

"And if I were this guy Pritchard, I'd be pretty indebted to the guy who saved me some jail time. And that guy would have someone on tap if he needed a gun for hire."

Ritchie peeled the paper off the second Big Mac, took a bite. "Okay, so who's the shyster?"

"Blaine Sterling's number one counsel. Carlton Amis."

Cat could have Heimliched Ritchie competently enough, but Santa beat her to it.

LATER, Cat went through her paces, her mind preoccupied with the events of the morning. Mats padded around after her forlornly as she folded the heaps of clothes in the laundry baskets, vacuumed the bedrooms and the upstairs hall, checked the water in the Christmas tree, emptied the dishwasher, made out her grocery list for Christmas Eve dinner, threw the bathroom rugs in the washer. She took a break to read to Mats, his warm forehead resting on her shoulder. If only she could get him down for a nap, maybe she could dash into her study and put together a draft of the Party of the Year, sketch out a rough chronology of the Phoenix thing.

But what she was not going to do, Cat told herself, was call her mother or go crying to Annie or Sherrie or Nancy; Mats and the house were her jobs, and if she had taken on another job, writing, well, she'd just have to figure out how to squeeze it into her other responsibilities.

Mats fell asleep at last. Cat glanced at the clock, quickly threw some cut-up chicken in a cast-iron pot, added water, broth, covered it, adjusted the heat, chopped onions, garlic, carrots, zucchini, eased them into the pot, then assembled her notes in the pantry-slash-office, worked for five minutes when she heard the rumble of the school bus, looked at her watch, groaned and dashed onto the porch in time to see a weary Jane dragging her bookbag across the street.

"What's the matter, sweetie?"

"I'm *tired.* My *throat* hurts."

Cat pressed her palm to Jane's forehead. It was warm and her thin face was flushed. Not Jane, too.

Jane threw her bookbag down in the center hall, shuffled into the living room. "They need two dozen cupcakes for Friday."

"Jane. You didn't volunteer me!"

"You're the only mom who's *home* all the time."

"Jillian Mattioli's mother is home."

"She makes stained glass in their *garage*."

"And I write articles in my office."

"Mommmm."

Which, freely translated, meant that crafting in stained glass was a valid endeavor and crafting in prose was not and therefore Cat was not exempt from producing twenty-four cupcakes for the fourth-grade Christmas party.

"Can I have some Seven-*Up?*"

"Wouldn't you rather have orange juice?"

"Orange juice has *things* in it."

Moreover, Cat discovered, it was gone. She had given the last to Mats that morning. In fact, there was little else to give Jane but Seven-Up and Cat added *Juice, no things* to her mental list as she poured out Jane's soda. She bussed it into the living room, found Jane sound asleep in a chair.

Cat slumped onto the carpet beside her and stroked her brown hair, dejectedly. Christmas. She hated it; and it wasn't a loss of spirituality or the materialism or the strained budget (well, maybe a little); it was that out-of-control feeling, that sense of losing one's bearings, so like the chilling sense of being cut adrift after Chris' murder, as though her anchor had been cut away and she was being drawn on the current of everyone else's expectations and demands and well-intentioned interference, the fear that she would ultimately flood, sink, vanish.

She took a sip of 7-Up, had a hard time getting it past the thickening in her throat. "You're not going to cry," she informed herself.

She heard the front door open, close. Ellice stood in the

archway, wearing the dark red coat Freddy had given her for her last birthday. She nodded toward Jane.

Cat wiped her eyes, hastily. "A fever," she explained. "Mats, too. I forgot to buy more Tylenol and—" her voice choked.

Ellice dropped her tote bag and sat on the floor beside Cat. "Honey, kids get sick at Christmas. It's in their job description."

"I've got these two articles going nowhere and I can't seem to get anything done and Jane signed me up to make two dozen cupcakes for Friday because I'm the only mom who doesn't *do* anything." Her laugh snagged and she began to sob.

Ellice put her arm around Cat's shoulder. "Honey, I'm with Victor. After Christmas, the two of you take off for some R and R."

"As in rancor and resentment."

"Well, whose fault is that? He was outta line Monday, you shoulda just blown your stack then and there, instead of stewing in it. God, you Sicilians and your grudges."

"We do hang on."

"Well, hang in. Give me ten minutes down time—Anouilh did not go over well—and I'll get dinner on the table, run out for the Tylenol after and you can hole up in your study. What's the second piece, anyway? Landis got you following up on that dead guy?"

Cat wiped her eyes. "Ellice...did Freddy ever mention an old friend of ours named Danny Furina?"

"Furina?" Ellice raked her fingers through her short hair. "Wait. Was he the one with the condoms and the frog?"

Cat knocked her forehead against the arm of the chair. "It doesn't matter what I do, does it? I win a *Pulitzer,* they'll call me up to the podium as the woman best known for having prophylactics crammed into her bio lab frog!"

"Now, now, there's gotta be worse claims to fame."

"Name one." The phone rang. Cat squirmed to her feet. "I'll take it in the kitchen. Go unwind."

Cat grabbed the receiver from the wall phone, stretched the cord to the stove so that she could check the soup.

"Mrs. Austen?"

"Yes."

"April Steinmetz? From *CopWatch?* I was wondering when we could schedule our get-together."

"I don't think I agreed to a get-together, did I?"

"Well, we didn't ink anything yet, but let me be up front. You're a principal in the scenario, that makes you hot. Plus the thing with you and the cop getting it on, gives us the romance angle, plus we got the shock jock angle and that makes it really hot. I mean, radio, you know, it's all of a sudden—"

"Hot." Cat stirred the soup.

"The KRZI crew's already signed on. The homicide cops are stonewalling, we were thinking maybe you could grease the wheels there, seeing as how you and the commander are—"

Ellice dashed into the doorway. "Cat, you gotta come hear this!"

Cat put her hand over the receiver. "I'm hot."

"That guy you were just talking about? Furina? They're talking about him on TV!"

Cat spoke into the phone. "Miss Steinmetz, I have an emergency here, I'll have to get back to you." Cat hung up and followed Ellice into the den.

The room was a homey retreat behind the staircase; the furniture had been taken from her childhood home when her mother moved to smaller quarters: simple overstuffed chairs, dark mahogany tables with scarred leather inlay, a pair of globe lamps, a TV. The TV was tuned to a special announcement on the local station. Roland Atkinson, his hair so glazed and immobile that viewers were convinced it was a toupee, spoke from the *NewsLine90* anchor desk. "...in the parking garage of the Sterling Phoenix Casino Hotel late last week. Furina, age thirty-eight, was a long-time Atlantic City resident. Although the medical examiner would not disclose the cause of death, sources have revealed that a search warrant for Furina's Ventnor Avenue office has been issued by the prosecutor's office, leading to the conclusion that Furina's death was connected to a matter under investigation. The county prosecutor has declined to comment, but our sources—''

''Sources! I'll kill Ritchie! I never confirmed Danny was the victim. Ritchie told me the cops ID'd him.''

''That guy you and Freddy knew from school? The Frogman? He's dead?''

''I can't believe Ritchie leaked this,'' Cat growled and stalked back to the kitchen, grabbed the phone, dialed.

''*South Jersey Magazine,* we're a shore bet for—''

''For the hottest in news and entertainment, I know. Cherry, it's Cat Austen. Is *he* there?''

''No. Wanna leave a message?''

''Did he go and feed that story to *NewsLineNinety?* I never said it was Danny Furina who was the John Doe. If this gets back to the cops that I'm the source on this—'' If it got back to her *brothers* that she was the source, Cat thought.

''Aw, Cat, Ritchie's got a million snitches out there, nobody's gonna think you're the one told him.''

''I don't appreciate being categorized as one of Ritchie's snitches.''

''You know what I mean. So what does this have to do with the tussle with Mrs. Amis?''

''What tussle with Mrs. Amis? I mean, she and I didn't exactly hit it off, but I wouldn't call it a—''

''I mean about the guy who tried to kill her.''

''What?''

Her name was Cherry Wein and she was wheelchair-bound. She moonlighted from her home as a manicurist, spent three mornings a week at the gym; nights, she worked her way through an online masters degree program and taught a self-defense class for the disabled in conjunction with the police department.

''After Ritchie talks to you yesterday, he tells me go back through the files, anything I can dig up on Amis. And it's mostly the Phoenix junk, the licensure, lotta PR stuff, and then I pull up a police report filed in Margate just last week. There wasn't much to it, so I called a gal in my PC users club who's a dispatcher downbeach, and she said the report was filed by Mrs. Amis. She claims she was attacked by a burglar at Ten Oh One Bay Landing Court. It's this humongous waterfront over in Margate?''

"Why does that address sound familiar?''

"'Cause it belongs to Mrs. Blaine Sterling."

"Are you kidding me?''

"No lie. This was early last week, maybe that's why Mrs. Sterling left the place and moved over to the Phoenix. She wasn't home, Mrs. Amis has her own key, lets herself in and this guy jumps her. She told the cops she fought him off, left him unconscious and split, called nine-one-one, at…wait a minute, I can't read my writing. Thirteen-thirty hours, that's what? One thirty in the p.m. The cops went to wherever Mrs. Amis was and got her to follow them back to the Bay Landing house, they check it out and the guy'd split.''

So that explained the bruise on her wrist, Cat concluded. Did it also explain the bodyguard? Had Mrs. Amis reason to believe that someone was out to get her?

"That's all I got from the dispatcher, but there may be something more on the department's computer. Want me to break into their system?''

FOURTEEN

VICTOR THREW HIS COAT on the rack beside his front door, checked the answering machine hoping for a message from Cat, found none, dumped a brown paper bag on the kitchen counter. He sifted through his mail with one hand as he yanked at the knot in his tie. A card from his sister Milly and her family, one from Mrs. DiLorenzo, even one from Jennie Fortunati ("You come to dinner Christmas Eve over Cat's.'')

Victor frowned, began to unpack the take-out from Bennie Song's, dug up the ivory-handled chopsticks Remy had brought him from San Francisco. No card from Remy. Without a man this Christmas, she would be immersed in self-pity, hating the season. He began with the Mongolian beef that set his palate ablaze. They knew how he liked it at Bennie Song's, whispered that it was probably the only fire in the somber lieutenant's life. They did not believe Suan's assertion that Lieutenant Cardenas sometimes lapsed into a sort of informality, could converse, could even smile like other cops Suan knew. Suan was the eldest of five, a deputy DA; her name, her tall, elongated figure had tagged her with the nickname "The Swan." Bennie and Jialing were baffled by their daughter's tallness, by the fact that the nice Chinese boy she had married stayed home tending to the children while Suan went to an office carrying a briefcase.

The fiery food worked on Victor, and his pessimism burned off like a dissipating fog. The Phoenix matter had been deposed by an attempted suicide at the high school, the girl obviously and recently post-partum, the infant discovered in a lavatory wastebin. A young woman, recently arrived from Guatemala for a family funeral was found dead in her rooming house, her carotid efficiently incised. He linked up with Raab at the woman's motel; Raab said that he'd cleared Stan to return to desk duty. Victor put Adane on the kid, Phil Long on the Guatemalan girl, because Phil was still working the hooker and the floater, and all three were starting to look too damned similar.

The fire settled into a steady pulse. Victor grabbed a seltzer from the refrigerator, picked up the receiver and was dialing Cat's number when he heard a sharp click, hollow and amplified by the cold: high heels on the wooden planks leading to his apartment. *Cat,* he thought, shoved the food aside and strode to the door, threw it open as the bell rang.

Fawn Sterling stood on the threshold.

Victor felt his pulse downshift. "Mrs. Sterling." Not a shade of bewilderment in his countenance, nor a trace of intensity in his inflection betrayed his surprise.

Fawn was wrapped in an ankle-length chinchilla, a scarf of violet silk over her hair. "May I come in, Lieutenant?"

"I'm not sure that would be a good idea."

"Donnie told me you'd been asking about Mr. Furina."

"A phone call would have sufficed, Mrs. Sterling."

"Must I tell you what I've come to say standing out here in the cold?"

Victor stepped back and allowed her to enter, glancing toward the street. He saw Mrs. Sterling's Jag parked behind his; no one was waiting for her. He hesitated only a second before he closed the door.

"Does Mr. Amis know you're here, Mrs. Sterling?"

"No." She tugged the scarf loose; her ashen tresses spilled over her shoulders, settling on the creamy chinchilla. "No one knows I'm here."

"Do you think that's wise?"

"Do you always do what you think is wise, Lieutenant?"

"Almost always."

"And would it be a lapse if you asked me to sit?"

"Certainly a lapse of courtesy. Please." He gestured toward the sofa in the small living room.

Fawn sat, allowed the fur to slip from her shoulders with an unconscious—or perhaps practiced, Victor reflected—sensuality. She wore a dress of dark jersey that coated her small form like a violet *glacé*. Amethyst earrings winked furtively from behind the loose, pale hair. "Lieutenant, will you sit? You make me uncomfortable standing there like that."

Victor hesitated. Cat had said something very similar when she had come to his office the day after the Dudek murder. Told him not to hover over her, that she knew enough about cops to recognize a posture calculated to intimidate. Mrs. Sterling didn't look intimidated.

He took a seat opposite her, the coffee table separating them. "What is it you would like to tell me about Mr. Furina?" he asked, his voice, his manner as coolly professional as if they had been in his office.

"I didn't know what I should do at first when Donnie told me about your call. And then, hearing the news that Mr. Furina was dead. I hadn't mentioned the matter to my husband, you see." Damsel in distress, with a *soupçon* of flirtation.

"You knew Mr. Furina, then?"

"Yes. I had hired him."

"Indeed." The two syllables betrayed no more than mild curiosity, and nothing at all of his conviction that this was an inappropriate setting for revelations concerning the dead PI. But there was nothing to be done about that now. "When did you engage his services?"

"Oh," she raked her fingers through her loose hair. "Last month. Shortly after I came down to Margate. I'd been in New York for the fall shows, planned to stay in Margate through the holidays."

"Alone?"

"Yes." There was a spark of amusement in her gray eyes.

"And why did you require the services of a private investigator?"

"I was being—I thought I was being—followed." One leg crossed over the other with a silken hiss.

"What made you think you were being followed?"

"I saw a man. In the city, something like that might have escaped me, but down here, in the off season, you see the same unfamiliar face again and again, you begin to get suspicious. At least, I did. I would run out for coffee, go to the post office, run over to CapriOH!, and there was this face. In the background, but there. After about a week or so, I called Mr. Furina."

"Why Furina? Surely, you could have gone to any one of the high profile agencies."

"I didn't want 'high profile,' Lieutenant. I wanted someone who would keep his mouth shut if he were paid enough and do as he was told."

Victor recalled what Linda Veach had said about Furina's mysterious client, the one who didn't have a file, a name. "Was there anything else to indicate you were being stalked, Mrs. Sterling? Hang-ups, anonymous letters, threats?"

"No."

"And you didn't mention any of this to your husband, until recently?"

"Why, Lieutenant, that wasn't a question. Not even the tiniest note of surprise. In fact, you haven't seemed surprised at anything I've said so far." The catlike gaze flicked over him like a tongue. "Either you've already been made aware of what I've told you, or you're quite past the point of surprise altogether."

He could not help feeling, though he was immune to its allure, a sexual aura that radiated from her like a shimmer of heat from sun-scorched earth. Victor could see how someone as susceptible as Freddy Fortunati would be easy prey. "I can still be surprised, Mrs. Sterling. Did you hire Furina without your husband's knowledge because you believed Mr. Sterling was associated with the man who was following you?"

"Well, I thought it was probable. I thought the man might have been hired to follow me."

"By your husband." *To catch you en flagrante delicto,* he added silently.

"Yes." There was a seductive lilt to her reply that answered the unspoken query as well as the spoken.

"And did Mr. Furina discover this man's identity?"

"No." The aura dissipated; something froze it out, though Victor could not decode the abrupt chill. "It seems the man disappeared. I never saw him after I hired Mr. Furina. A couple weeks went by, and Mr. Furina wasn't able to trace him, so I decided that perhaps I had been mistaken, or the man had just been some crank who got bored and started trailing after someone else. I dismissed Mr. Furina and never thought about it any more."

"Not even when Mrs. Amis was attacked in your home?"

"No. It never occurred to me that the two events were related. I know that sounds stupid."

But you're not a stupid woman, Mrs. Sterling, Victor observed silently. "You never considered that the stalking was a prelude to the attack?"

"No."

"But you moved into the penthouse."

"Well, the police said someone had broken into my home. It rattled me."

"Was your husband in Atlantic City when you moved to the penthouse?"

"Since the opening, he's been going up to the city on Friday, coming back Monday, sometimes early Tuesday."

"Forgive me, Mrs. Sterling, but if you believed your husband may have hired someone to follow you, I'm surprised you opted to move into the penthouse with him."

"Well, as I said, Blaine is only there half the week. Even under the same roof, I wasn't exactly 'with' him."

Victor rose, began to pace. "When was the last time you saw Mr. Furina, Mrs. Sterling?"

She plucked at the hem of her dress, letting it drop a couple inches above the knee. "When I dismissed him. That would have been...some time around Thanksgiving, I believe."

Victor's attention was not diverted by the display of flesh. "Never spoke to him after that?"

"As I said, Lieutenant, when he couldn't trace the man, I felt that I no longer required his services."

"Are you aware that Mrs. Amis identified the man in the lab photos as the one who attacked her, and a second party made the visual identification that this same man was Furina?"

A shudder passed over her, but to Victor's keen senses it seemed to be something other than shock. Artifice, perhaps. "I saw the news. I'm stunned, of course."

She didn't look stunned; irritated, perhaps. "So you can see why it would be so vital for the police to find out everything Mr. Furina was involved with at the time of his death."

"I know only what I've told you," she replied. Her eyes watered as she said it.

This one's good, Victor told himself. Real tears. And the story hung together, touched base with most of the available facts.

"Is there anything more you can think of that would help?"

"I don't think so." Vulnerable now, seeking aid and comfort. She rose, letting the silk slide over her small form.

Victor bent to retrieve the scarf that had fallen to the floor, handed it to her. She moved in close, her whole aspect suggesting desire, willingness.

"Thank you for the information, Mrs. Sterling. Please contact my office if you can think of anything else that might be helpful. In the meantime, I would advise you to discuss this with your attorney."

She threw her coat over her shoulders. "Yes. I suppose it was foolish to come here alone, without mentioning it to anyone." Final offer.

"I'll see you to your car." Declined. Still, his father would whirl in his grave if Victor had allowed a woman—even this one—to leave his house, walk into a dark street, unescorted. Victor realized that many of his father's standards of chivalry—most of them, in fact—were not for this world, but he could not quite shake off their influence.

He held the car door as she slipped into the seat, bundled the fur around her, gave one last glance.

"Good night, Mrs. Sterling."

She slammed the door, gunned the engine, made a daring arc on Delancy, swung right onto Atlantic and disappeared.

What the hell is her game? Victor wondered.

FIFTEEN

VICTOR ARRIVED AT his office early the next morning, began flipping through the stack of folders Adane had left on his desk, put in a call to Kurt Raab.

Raab skipped the amenities. "Okay, here's the deal. Rice is at his desk until the Reverend blows town. I don't think that'll be much longer, those SOBS roughed him up pretty good, especially that Shallett woman. Gave him a couple shots he won't forget in a hurry. Thank the Almighty he's not pressin' charges, I do not need to prosecute some taxpayer's churchgoin' grandma for assault and battery."

"Mrs. Sterling came to see me last night."

"She came to your office?"

"My home."

"What!"

Victor repeated the entire interview.

"Look, Victor, I don't like that. It doesn't look good. She pulls that again, you can't be alone with her, not without her attorney."

"Understood. And you're right, it doesn't look good, which makes me wonder exactly what she was after." *Except for the obvious,* he reflected. "Did you raise Furina's bank accounts?"

"Yeah. He put in twenty-five hundred mid-November, another two grand end of the month. Cash."

"The retainer and the kiss-off."

"If he really didn't come up with anything, forty-five's generous."

"Five thousand. The Veach girl said he gave her a five-hundred-dollar bonus."

"What about her, still a no-show?"

"Yes. I don't like it. I want her found."

"You don't really think she made off with the print card? Why would she do something like that?"

"Well, if I were in a philosophical mood, I would ask what motivates anyone to do anything?" Victor replied.

"And while we're on the subject of human psychology, the med center called, said the infant the kid tossed in the dumpster? Gonna make it. Patsy says can we adopt it. Jesus. The mother was fourteen years old. You wanna know how much I knew about sex when I was fourteen?"

Victor paused. "No, I don't think that I do."

Raab snorted. "The Murillo girl, I talked to the ME, he says it's lookin' too much like the floater. We finally got a name for that one, incidentally. Tamara Montgomery. Twenty. Put Long on both of 'em, but I don't want the Phoenix thing on a back burner. And, uh, I don't have to mention I'm sure it wasn't your people leaked Furina's ID to the press."

"That's correct, you don't."

"Keep Rice on a leash, okay?"

"Understood." Victor hung up and called in Adane and Long. Long, struggling with a stack of folders, bumped a chair up to Victor's desk with his knee. As he sat, Stan Rice strolled in, dropped a tissue-wrapped rose on Adane's lap, wedged a chair next to hers. "That's for the hand-hold, Jeannie. Hey, guess who calls me last night? Some production gal from *CopWatch*. Wants me to sign a release, they might wanna use me in a show they're doin' on the Dudek—"

"Sergeant."

"Huh?"

"First, we would like to welcome you back. You've been missed. Second, this television show can't be prevented from employing whatever's in the public domain, but I would consider a collaboration with them by anyone in this unit to be unprofessional, is that clear?"

"You never let us have any fun."

Victor unlocked the bottom drawer of his desk, removed Stan's service weapon and shield, shoved them across his desk. "I regret that fun isn't the order of the day as often as some of us would like."

The morning review belied him, however. True, the follow-up on the infant, the identification of the floater, the death of the Guatemalan girl, Estrella Murillo, were grim enough; but there was the Reverend Marlon's declaration that he would rise from his hospital bed to set himself down for justice at Lowell Jeffries' prelim; the Santa's helper who had robbed a bank at gunpoint, fled on inlines and was shot off his wheels by an armed guard; the guy in Ventnor who had clubbed his neighbor's yapping pit bulls, skinned the carcasses and fired up the outdoor grill.

Phil Long, balancing the folders on his lap, spoke first. "I already got the Montgomery kid, may as well take the Murillo girl, too, if the ME says they look to be the same."

Stan stood up. "Beached or not, I am not takin' the pit bulls—that does not belong in this department—I am not takin' the pit bulls."

Victor tugged at his mustache. "I've already referred it to animal welfare, Sergeant."

Stan sat.

"I got a call from the hospital, the Santa impersonator came through the surgery," Adane offered. "I can talk to the DA's office, but I don't believe we'll be involved. It's unlikely that charges will be brought against the guard."

"Not takin' the pit bulls…"

"Let's move on, shall we? First, I'm certain that no one from this unit is responsible for the leak to *NewsLineNinety* but the fact that they've gone public with an identification means that our unit and the DA's office are in for some media heat."

"Raab's probably on a freighter to Paraguay."

"Sergeant?"

"I said that Raab's great at keepin' the press at bay." Stan shifted in his seat, continued. "You know, this guy Furina? I met him once. Chris Austen's funeral. Mob scene…cops from all over the Delaware Valley. Jeez, it was awful for Cat. Anyway, he was there, seemed like a real hustler, total fruitcake."

The phone rang and Victor picked it up, thinking about what Stan had said. Cat. How long had it been since he had talked to her? A day? Two? Surely not longer. He listened for a moment, thanked the caller and hung up. "The hatchback's clean. No prints."

"Damn," muttered Long. "'Scuse me, Jeannie."

"Where are the search warrants?" Victor asked him.

Long groaned. "Judge Cooperthwaite's outta town and Judge Harkness was in court all day yesterday, doin' her gig and fillin' in for DiBartolo, who broke his leg on the ice, he's on painkillers, and Judge Johnson's wife went into labor, an' you are not gettin' me in that birthing suite."

"Check Harkness' schedule, she has to have three minutes to read and sign a warrant."

"Yeah, but do I have time for the pop quiz on the Fourth Amendment?" Long griped. All of the county cops avoided Judge Harkness when there was a warrant to be signed.

Victor shrugged, recounted his interview with Fawn Sterling. "Mrs. Sterling implied that the man following her may have been hired by her husband, that's why she didn't tell Sterling about Furina."

"You know," Stan ruminated, "how do we know this

stalker even existed? I mean, all we got is Mrs. Sterling's word for it, no one else saw him, right? Suppose it was Furina all along? Sterling hires him to whack the missus. She finds out what hubby's up to and hires the same PI, tells him she's bein' followed, but she's really tryin' to see what he's up to, maybe gets him to turn. And Furina, he's gettin' paid by both parties, so he plays both ends against the middle as long as he can. In the end, Sterling's pocketbook wins out, Furina sets up the hit, makes it look like a home invasion, only he screws up. It's the Amis woman walks in instead of the vic. They tussle, she knocks him out, he comes to, figures he blew it, manages to get outta there. What, Jeannie, what?''

"Nothing. I'm listening to you, Stanley. When do you get to the part about Mr. Furina making his way to the Phoenix, dressing himself in a stolen costume and dying?''

"I haven't worked that part out yet."

"It's not totally outta line, though," said Long.

Victor nodded for him to continue.

"I mean, the part about Sterling wantin' his wife outta the way. Like we talked about before. Look, Sterling's got money troubles. The hotels, they're Sterling Hotels, Inc., they're holdin' their own. Sterling Phoenix is a separate company. Got off to a rough start, and Sterling, he was maxing out even before he took it on. Last year''—he slipped a folder from the center of the stack on his lap, tossed it onto Victor's desk—''he did a lot of discreet debt consolidation, there was talk he was close to havin' to file.''

"Debt consolidation's no big deal," Stan said.

"It is on this scale. And it's not just the money. Sterling's King Midas, everything he touches turns profit, he's got his rep to consider. Now he was able to defer the first interest payment until January, on accountta they weren't up and running by Memorial Day, bondholders give him a break, but come January, he's got a whopper of a payment and the word is the revenue may not cover it. Sterling tried to fold the Phoenix into the hotel organization, the stockholders blocked that one, they don't wanna take on a dead elephant.''

"Isn't that a 'pink elephant'?" asked Stan.

"I believe it's 'white elephant,'" corrected Adane. "But I rather like 'dead elephant.'"

"Anyway, they're not gonna help him carry the freight and the Sterling name's not collateral the way it useta be. He's tried sellin' off the townhouses in Boca, the jet, the yacht—"

"Why doesn't he turn over the Phoenix? Isn't the first mortgage collateral on the bonds?" Victor asked.

Long frowned. "I guess he could, but he won't. It's like a whaddayacallit, thing for him making his comeback."

"Metaphor," Adane offered.

"Yeah. Like how he rises from the ashes with everyone writin' him off."

Victor recalled how Cat had said the same thing the night the body was discovered, how her hair had fallen over his face when he pulled her on top of him, how he could feel her laughter vibrating in her throat when he kissed her. "What's the interest payment come to?"

"Between twenty-five and forty. Million."

"You think he wants her outta the way so he can collect her insurance?" Stan asked.

"I think it's more complicated than that. I mean, she's got a couple policies, together they total about ten mil, and he's the beneficiary."

"Ten million won't keep the wolves from the door," Victor commented. "What else would he get?"

"I don't get all this high finance shi—stuff. 'Scuse me, Jeannie. Here's what I do get: Sterling and the missus, they hooked up when she was hungry and he was King Midas. She starts to reel in the big fish, she needs start-up cash for her yard goods and thread, whatever, and he starts her up. In return, he's like a silent partner. She sells a dress, he gets a check. Now, her setup's always been lean, she does the sketches, picks out the goods, jobs out the patterns and sewing and stuff to part-timers. Never had more than four, five full-timers on the payroll. Keep it small, you don't gotta pay benefits. Average dress goes for seventy thou; she's been doin' up to five mil a year, got some cash socked away 'cause she's been deferrin' her salary. I mean, they live off Sterling's bank account.''

"I'm still not seein' twenty-five to forty mil and all those future interest payments," Stan said.

"I'm gettin' to that. Couple months ago, she puts out her first line. Made a big splash and the wave brought a couple deals to the table. Licensing deals. You know, like they get to put the CapriOH! label on their handbags and undies and stuff, she gets a cut. I read this article in one of those fashion rags, said a deal like that, CapriOH! stood to make maybe a hundred mil in royalties. A year.''

Victor leaned forward, propped his elbows on his desk. "And you said he's a part-owner of her outfit?"

Long nodded. "She dies, CapriOH! goes to the surviving partner. Now, Sterling may not be much with a needle and thread, but so what? All he's gotta do is find himself a couple hungry designers like his wife was when he met her, pay them a salary, get a good business manager to handle the day-to-day, he rakes in the lion's share of the profits without havin' to put up with the lioness. I mean, you see some fancy label, you care who really designed it?" Long slipped another folder on Victor's desk. "Couple articles in there explain how it works.''

Victor studied the folder, thoughtfully.

"So, how 'bout this?" Stan proposed. "He sets Furina on the wife, Furina blows the hit, Sterling's afraid Furina might turn on him, he has him whacked.''

"And has the body deposited on the executive parking level of his own casino?" Victor challenged.

"How do I know? These're rich folks, Lieutenant, they're all used to gettin' away with murder and they're all a little nuts. Can't imagine what goes on in the head of a guy like that.''

"'There should be no combination of events for which the wit of man cannot conceive an explanation,''' Victor quoted.

"Wait, wait, I know that one," Long said. "*The Valley of Fear*. Sherlock Holmes," he told Adane and Rice. "It's the one where he said, 'Imagination is the mother of truth.'''

"Very good." Victor nodded, with a faint smile. "Okay, let's go ahead and draw names for the Christmas gifts, leave the rest of those files with me and push for the warrants. Adane? When you check out Furina's office, I want any notes, files, even the tape in the answering machine, so let me see the affidavit before you take it out. Check to see if the print lab's been out there. Long, have you had a chance to speak to the Adkins woman, the waitress?"

"I'm goin' over there this morning, Lieutenant."

"Adane, why don't you run over to Linda Veach's apartment, talk to the landlady. If she offers to let you have a look at the place, don't turn her down. I don't like this disappearing act of hers right after she identifies Furina."

"I can check out this kid, Lieutenant," Rice offered.

"You're at your desk, Rice."

"I'll steer clear of the Rev, scout's honor. Honest. Let me take the apartment, Jeannie can work the phones."

"You're beached, Rice."

"Yeah, but Jeannie's not—"

Long cleared his throat, loudly. Jean made a move to get up.

"Adane, sit down, please."

Jean sat.

Victor surveyed the trio. "I think I run a pretty flexible unit here, but the bottom line is this: I give the orders. I trust no one is implying that Adane can't hold her weight?"

Rice and Long exchanged uneasy glances.

Victor waited.

"Look," Long said. "Everyone here knows Jeannie's the brains of this outfit. I mean, she's the one got us on line, she's the one the paralegals call when they need help on the affidavits, she's the one knows how to find Captain Loeper when no one else knows where he's at, but basically, she's, you know, more like a..."

"No, I don't know."

"Well, for example, where's her shield?"

Victor looked at her. "Adane?"

Adane ran her finger along the crease in her navy slacks.

"I, um, it was an oversight, Lieutenant. I was placed here before I officially graduated from the Academy. We were quite short-handed then; there was a lot of transition. This was before your time, sir, and before Phil came on board. And I guess it got lost in the shuffle. I got my papers in the mail. And it didn't matter about the shield because, well, I've never been sent anywhere I needed it."

Victor stroked his chin. "Adane, I'm in charge here, so it's for me to apologize if you haven't been dealt with fairly…"

"Oh, but I have! It's just that—I guess being a cop never turns out the way you think it's going to. And we each ought to do what we do best."

"And we each need an opportunity to realize our best. As long as you have some ID, you shouldn't have a problem with Veach's landlady. There're a couple city detectives assigned to this, you can call one of them in if you like; I'll leave it up to your discretion."

"So whaddaya want me to do?" Stan asked.

"You seem to have a good working relationship with the ME's office. Ask if they wouldn't mind faxing us Furina's prints one more time. Make sure they get the right number."

"Gee, thanks."

"I think we'll have to contact Furina's mother in Florida, since the media leaked his ID. Don't make it an official notification, just ask her when she heard from him last."

"Then what?"

"You could check the CrimeStoppers tape, see if someone called in anything relevant."

"That I coulda done from the comfort of my bed, Lieutenant."

"Well, if that doesn't appeal to you," Victor lifted a scrap of notepaper from his desk, dangled it between two fingers, "and you're determined to get out of the office, there is this note from the county sheriff's department. Three of their deputies are out with the flu and they need a substitute to play Sergeant McBowser at the St. Agnes Primary School anti-drug assembly tomorrow afternoon."

Stan rose. "Say, Jeannie, what was that CrimeStopper's line

again?'' he asked, making tracks, nearly colliding with the
figure in the doorway.

Blaine Sterling.

SIXTEEN

VICTOR ROSE, dismissing his unit with a nod.

Sterling looked around; his glance took in the scarred linoleum floor, the battered desk, makeshift bookcases, as if
summing up the lair of an adversary. Victor processed the
glance; Sterling was implying that Cardenas was a small-town
cop, not a threat, but his coming to Major Crimes, unan-
nounced and unattended, betrayed him.

"Lieutenant, I hope I'm not inconveniencing you," Sterling
said.

"Not at all. Please sit down."

Sterling looked at the second-hand chair Adane had vacated,
sat after a moment's hesitation. "I'll get right to the point.
My aide informed me that you had spoken to her about the
incident that occurred at my wife's house last week."

"Yes."

"She also told me that you showed her those pictures, and
that she identified the man as the one who assaulted her. Now,
I hear on the news that this man is a private investigator named
Furina. Is that correct?" As he spoke, his glance moved from
Victor's implacable gaze, to the surroundings, back to the lieu-
tenant.

"Correct," Victor said. "You're familiar with the name?"

"As a matter of fact, I am." Sterling hesitated. "Lieutenant,
let me be frank. If the papers get hold of this, there could be
very unpleasant repercussions. I'm sure you understand."

"I understand very little at the moment, Mr. Sterling."

Sterling shifted; the bold fluorescent light exposed the scalp
beneath the careful arrangement of thinning hair. "To be per-

fectly honest, Lieutenant, it's my wife who knows this Furina person. She hired him.''

Victor's expression conveyed nothing.

"I've never been able to impress upon my wife the need for personal security. The rather free-spirited attitude she has about traveling on her own exposes her to injury, worse perhaps. It's been a cause of some dissension in our marriage." He said that last as though he were making a great concession to Victor, disclosing an intimate detail of his married life.

"I understand."

"But Fawn's a brave girl. Reckless. And yet, a little paranoid. Most fashion designers are, it goes with the territory. I admit, if she had told me she was being followed, I might have been inclined to write it off, but at the least, I would have insisted on a bodyguard."

"Your wife told you she was being followed?"

"Not until last night. I was in my room and I could hear her downstairs, arguing with her assistant. Agitated. I heard her utter the name Furina, I had heard the name on the news, and when she came upstairs, I asked her about it. She confessed that she had reason to believe she was being followed, some time last month, and that she had hired a local private investigator to look into it, this man Furina. This was all quite without my knowledge, you understand. If she had mentioned the matter to me at the time, I would have called in one of the better agencies."

"Was Mr. Furina able to help your wife?"

"Did he find out who was following her, you mean? She said he never did come up with anything, and after a couple weeks, she dismissed him. Do you know what I think, Lieutenant? I think the entire plot was staged by this man Furina."

"I don't follow."

"It seems Fawn had met this man some years ago. He knew who she was, perhaps heard that she was in the area. He staged some incident to convince her that she was in danger, then ingratiated himself to her, made his services available, put on a show of investigating this so-called stalking. Small-time private investigators, Lieutenant, they're not the most scrupulous of individuals." He looked at Victor for a sign of concurrence.

"It's plausible," Victor said, noncommittally.

"Naturally, he can't produce his stalker, and when Fawn terminates his employment, he stages an assault in her home to convince her she still needs his protection. Unfortunately, Mrs. Amis was a match for him. He couldn't have predicted that part of the scenario."

"And your wife disclosed all of this to you just last night?"

"Yes. I assure you, Lieutenant, if I had had any idea of this, I wouldn't have been so abrupt with you when you came to speak to Fawn last weekend."

"Mr. Sterling, I'm curious. You came down here alone..."

"Well, there's my driver—"

"I meant, you didn't bring your attorney."

"Lieutenant, when Fawn told me this incredible story and Mrs. Amis told me the nature of your interview, naturally I thought you would want the information. I'm sure you're anxious to close the file on this. I'm simply trying to fill in what details may be of help, as discreetly as possible."

Sterling citizen, Victor thought wryly. "Do your wife and Mrs. Amis know that you came down here?"

"My wife was in an interview; I left a message with her man, Finch. And of course, I had Mrs. Amis rearrange my morning."

Victor leaned back in his chair. Sterling's story didn't explain how Danny's body had wound up in the garage or how he had gotten into Mrs. Sterling's house. Abruptly, he asked, "Would Mrs. Sterling mind, do you think, if I had a look around her house?"

Sterling hesitated; he hadn't anticipated that question, which meant, Victor decided, it had been the right one to ask.

"Fawn's house in Margate? I believe she permitted the police officer to look around at the time of the attack."

"Then it's unlikely she would object if I had a look around myself."

Hesitation again, which contrasted sharply with the glibness that had preceded. *Perhaps he simply doesn't like yielding the*

upper hand. And perhaps he doesn't want me in that house.
Which made Victor all the more determined to check it out.

CAT AUSTEN SAT hunched on her bed, half listening to the
radio announcer run through a list of school closings due to
the ice storm that had swept up the Jersey coast, half scanning
the notes she had scribbled onto the last sheet of the last pad
of notepaper on her night stand. (*Buy notepads,* Cat added to
a growing list.) Cookie Amis attacked in Fawn Sterling's
house. Cherry routinely double-and triple-checked her facts,
so why didn't it make sense?

Cat would have given what was left of her paycheck (after
she got Mats' Citadel of the Deep out of layaway) to explore
Fawn's Margate neighborhood, answer the whys and hows and
whats jockeying for interpretation, investigation. But even
with Ellice free to look after Jane and Mats, Cat wasn't sure
the Maxima could handle the iced-over Longport Bridge, Margate's unsalted side streets. A glimpse at the uninviting streets
tempered frustrated curiosity with relief, however. She'd give
a lot to get a look at Fawn's lair, but she didn't want to trek
out in sub-freezing weather to do it.

But when Freddy called to check if the power lines were
down in Ocean City, if Cat needed anything, if he could give
her a hand, she decided that the Fates favored mettle over
complacency and gave in, asking Freddy if she could borrow
his Cherokee for the morning to do some legwork on a story.
Freddy arrived within the hour with her half-gallon of Five
Alive, liquid Tylenol, pack of notepads, plus a dozen doughnuts, a karate movie, two boxes of dark double fudge cake
mix and two cans of chocolate mint frosting. "I heard we gotta
bake a couple dozen cupcakes for school tomorrow," he
greeted Jane, who examined her tumbler of Five Alive for
"things."

"*Can* you make cupcakes?"

"You throw in the mix, the eggs, whatnot, beat it up, shove
it in the oven, what's the big deal? Who wants to lick the
bowl?"

No takers. Freddy's culinary incompetence was a blot on

the Fortunati name. Carlo joked that Freddy must have been adopted, no Italian could be so inept in the kitchen. Cat shuddered at the thought of what her kitchen would be like after he was let loose with cake batter and frosting mix. And Mats' dispirited gaze, following after her as she put on her jacket, muffler, gloves, gave her a twinge. Cat told herself that a morning together might thaw the coolness that was settling between Freddy and Ellice, dropped a blatant hint as Freddy helped her down the slippery porch steps.

"Damn it, the jeweler screwed up the ring size," he muttered.

"Ask her anyway."

"I can't ask her without a ring. Besides, with the kids around and all, I need for the timing to be right."

"If Mama and Pop waited for the timing to be right, I wouldn't even be here," Cat shot back. "*Ask* her."

Freddy only shrugged, handed over the keys, reminded Cat that he needed the car back by one-thirty so that he could report to the barracks on time. Cat maneuvered the Cherokee over the bridge, headed into Margate, wound in and out of narrow side streets for twenty minutes before she located Bay Landing Court. She idled for a few minutes, then retreated and drove to a broad intersection, parked in the lot of the city's recreation center and half-minced, half-skidded the three blocks back to Bay Landing.

The original site of the Caprio home had been at the end of a cul-de-sac, the rear backing up to the base of a long, narrow lagoon. In the first flush of success, Fawn had bought the adjacent homes, leveled all three structures and erected a small mansion of blanched siding and ornamental stonework, bordered front and sides by a four-foot stucco wall, a wrought-iron gate set into the front. Along Bay Landing Court, there were eight other residences, four on each side of the street, none as grand as Fawn's, and all shut up for the winter.

Cat wobbled down the sidewalk, grabbed the wrought-iron post to keep from falling. The gate was locked; an intercom button set into the wall was solidly iced in. The house was obviously unoccupied, secured. *You won't get in here with a bent coat hanger.*

Maybe not, but that didn't mean she shouldn't have a look around. Impulsively, Cat braced her gloved palms against the rounded top of the stucco wall, boosted herself up and slid over the slick surface, landing face down on the frosted lawn.

Well, wasn't that pleasant? Cat scrambled to her feet, shuddered as a trickle of icy slush slid under her collar toward her sternum. Gingerly, Cat began crossing the slippery yard toward the side of the house. A detached garage was connected to the house by a long, glassed-in corridor commonly called a breezeway. Shrubbery along the garage wall, swathed in burlap. Cat could hear the whisper of the bay behind the house, walked in that direction when she heard the faint hum of a car engine behind her. Someone was driving down Bay Landing.

Cat made a dash for it, dove between two muffled bushes, wriggled under one of the burlap coverings and pulled it down around her. She heard a slow, grating sound, wrought iron against frozen concrete. Someone was opening the driveway gate. A moment later the wall against her shoulder began to vibrate as the garage door opened.

Move! Her mind threw together a hasty scenario for flight, but her body took another route, scrambled around the corner, crouched and rolled under the garage door as it descended, and wound up huddled on the concrete floor beside the dripping tire of a dark van.

I'm dead, I'm dead, I'm dead.

She heard the driver's door open, heard quick steps move along the breezeway tile, heard the steps become fainter, heard silence.

Cat took a deep breath, crept along the side of the van, slowly raised her head to the passenger door window, eyes closed. Eyes open. The front seat of the van was empty; she could see through the driver's window to the door that opened to the breezeway, left ajar. Whoever it was had known how to get into the house and wasn't planning on hanging around long.

On the wall next to the door, Cat saw a button in the shape

of a doorbell, concluded that it operated the garage door and resolved to put it to use. What if the sound of the door was overheard? She would just make a run for it. But, since she was already there, and the passageway into the house was open, why not have a look around?

Why not have a look around? Just the other night, she and Ellice went halvsies on a Sara Lee cheesecake, and not one of those low-fat abominations either, turned on a woman-in-jep movie and when the heroine heard a crash in the back of her dark apartment and went to investigate, Cat and Ellice had shouted in unison, "Get out of the house, you—" Here, each employed a different epithet, though the sentiment was the same.

Okay, maybe she wouldn't look *all* around, just as far as the end of the breezeway. Cat tiptoed along the narrow corridor, emerged in a spacious kitchen, its broad bay window overlooking the front lawn. It was all terra-cotta and pale oak, a breakfast nook set against the front window, center island with a steel double sink, wooden lattice suspended overhead with crystal goblets hanging upside down.

Archways at either end of the room opened onto a wide passage. Tile became marble, apricot in hue with tributaries of green and black, slick as a coat of ice. It blossomed to a semicircle in front, reflected the six-tiered chandelier above the front entrance, reflected a pinpoint of red from the security panel beside the door. Across the corridor was a guest wing, bedrooms, a powder room and a full bath, small library. Cat backed up, followed the marble hallway in the opposite direction, approached twin staircases that formed an archway to a living room furnished in shades of cool mint with touches of peach and white, a wall of glass facing west; gauzy curtains turned the solarium beyond, the lap pool, Jacuzzi, white wicker furniture into an Impressionist painting, a still life of indulgence tempered with taste.

Cat stood against one of the banisters, listened. Whoever had entered the house had vanished; she couldn't hear a sound. Maybe it had just been the pool guy, or a cleaning service, she told herself, and decided she could improvise her way out of an encounter with either. So there was no reason that, since she had gone this far, she shouldn't just have a peek at the second floor.

Upstairs the rooms were even grander, more formal, and Cat realized that the house was an upside down, a common seashore design that allowed the owners to secure the prime views overlooking the waterfront. Here, brocade and plush predominated, midnight blue in the living and dining rooms; in the kitchen, it was reduced to an accent for the stark white. There was an exercise room off the kitchen and on the southeast corner, a workroom as large as the living room: oak floor; a row of dress forms; file cabinets; a pair of desks and computer terminals; fax machine; dozens of sketches carelessly pinned to the walls, scraps of fabric dangling from the corners; a half dozen plastic-covered bolts of fabric on the floor under the window sill.

A chill of discomfort ascended Cat's spine. There had been coded security panels on the garage wall next to the entrance, another beside the front door, probably other security measures. Maybe Fawn gave them to the cleaning people, but how had the person who attacked Mrs. Amis gotten in? And had Fawn packed her bags and headed for the Phoenix because she believed she was the intended victim?

And whose victim? Surely not Danny's.

Textbook sociopath, spent most of his life in the joint.

Falcone's echo caught her up on the threshold of the master bedroom. Textbook sociopath. Pritchard. Why would Danny have his friend Falcone check out this Pritchard right around the time Danny was also calling her, asking her if Fawn was looking Freddy's way for a shoulder to cry on? Cat crossed the room, her boots sinking deep into the midnight blue plush. She pushed aside the heavy drapes, peered down at the deck, saw no one checking out the pipes, the boatslip, the shrubbery. She let the drapes fall back into place, shutting out the last sliver of light in the dark room.

Textbook sociopath. Had he been the one who had attacked Mrs. Amis, killed Danny? Had he found his way into the house again? Was he somewhere inside?

Get out of the house, you—

A hand clapped over her mouth. Cat twisted violently, yanked her face free, tried to scream. Two hands shoved her onto the bed, covered her mouth once more.

SEVENTEEN

"BLAINE G. STERLING comes all the way out here just to tell you his wife knew Furina?" Stan scoffed. "Last night, his wife drops by your place? Don't they got working phones over the Phoenix?"

"I am not seein' it," Long concurred.

"You can't calculate the effect your disclosures are having on someone over the phone," Adane commented.

Victor gave her an appreciative nod. The phone rang and he answered it, handed it to Adane. "It's for you."

"You think he and the wife are each tryin' to sell you their version of what went down?" Long meditated. "Why? Unless he's tryin' to throw us off the track, keep us from findin' out what really went down."

"I got hold of Furina's mom down Delray Beach. I tell her one of Furina's cases overlapped with one of ours, we haven't been able to get in touch with him, has she heard from him lately? So she says"—Stan tugged his notebook out of his back pocket, flipped it open, read—"'Don't you lie to me, Sergeant, he's up to no good. That Danny, he's such a scamp, I don't know what to do about that boy. My husband, may he rest in peace, wanted more kids, but you have one kid like Danny, you get your tubes tied, Pope or no Pope.'"

Long stifled a chuckle.

"Did she say anything else?"

"Yeah, she said I had a nice voice and did I ever get down to Florida."

"I meant about Furina, Sergeant."

"She said he talked about flyin' down for Thanksgiving,

had a change of plans, called that day to say hi." He shoved his notebook back in his pocket.

Adane had been speaking quietly into the phone; a sudden jerk drew their attention to her. She was listening to the caller, her blue eyes round, eager. "No, no, I'll tell them. Thank you for your trouble."

"Anything wrong?" Victor asked as he took the receiver from her, hung it up. He had drawn her name in the Christmas pollyanna, was wondering what on earth he would buy her.

Her smooth complexion was pink with excitement and her expression uncharacteristically animated. "I—well, sir, I told you that when I went to Lemon Aides, I obtained the application form filled out by the man calling himself Allan Jones. It's understandable, of course, because Miss Veach positively identified the deceased as Mr. Furina."

"Furina was usin' an alias," Long interrupted.

"No. You see, I sent the form to the state police print lab and the report just came back. Mr. Furina's a private investigator, so his prints are on file. But the prints on the form don't belong to him, they belong to a parolee named Allan Pritchard. Age thirty-six. He served time for armed robbery as a juvenile and graduated to assault, burglary, weapons offenses. They were going to fax me, but some of the systems are down because of the weather. This man Pritchard disappeared on or about October thirty-first and there's a fugitive warrant out on him."

"Wait a minute, wait a minute!" Stan exploded. "The guy who rented the junker's this ex-con?"

"Yes."

"So who the hell is it on the slab, then? Furina, or this guy Pritchard?"

"Good question."

CAT DREW UP both knees, jabbed at her attacker's groin, made contact. The grip on her mouth eased. She rolled off the bed, grabbed an ankle with both hands and lurched to her feet, yanking her assailant off balance. Stumbling to one side, she scrambled for the door, felt a hand grip her calf, jerk her sideways. Cat fell toward the nightstand, snatched the phone and flung it toward the silhouette of a head, missed by inches.

He—it *was* a he—rose to his knees; Cat slammed her fist into the side of his face, heard a grunted exhalation. Two hands seized her waist and wrestled her to the carpet. She jerked her head forward, felt the carpet snatch an earring, took in a mouthful of throat encased in turtleneck, bit down hard. The weight rolled off her and she heard, "Dracula!" in a clearly recognizable voice.

"Oh my God, oh my God! Danny!" Cat scrambled across the room, yanked at the drapes. Pale winter sunlight relieved some of the darkness; the silhouette took on dimension.

"Cat? Alley Cat?"

He was lying on the carpet, panting. He wore a black turtleneck, jeans, sneakers. A lock of dark hair fell over eyes that were as rakish as ever.

Cat dropped onto the bed, clutched her side.

"I didn't hurt you, did I? 'Swhere you got shot?"

Cat wiped her eyes, concentrated on slowing her breathing. "Danny, what are you doing here? Don't you know you're supposed to be dead?"

"Don't sound so broken up about it." Danny slid onto the bed beside her. "Like Shakespeare said, 'reports of my death are greatly exaggerated.'"

"Mark Twain," she gasped. "Idiot."

"So who's got the time to read? Wanna tell me what you're doin' here?"

"Working. What about yourself?"

"Same. Workin' for who?"

"Whom. You first."

"Alley Cat, you wouldn't expect me to violate a client's right to privacy."

"I think you'd violate your grandmother's gravesite if the money was good and there was some fun in it."

Danny grinned, the lopsided grin that had snared nearly all those nice Catholic girls. "Can't all be goody-goody like those damned Keller kids or Stevie Delareto. How is the old gang? That priss Kevin Keller still sweet on you?"

Cat got to her feet, tucked in her shirt. "He's a deacon at St. Agnes. The gang's okay. How's Pritchard?"

Danny's smile leveled out. "Whom?"

"Who. As if you didn't know. And why do the cops think you're dead?"

"Cops are dumb, Cat."

"My husband was a cop. My brothers are cops."

"Exceptions prove the rule."

"They had to have someone ID that body, tell them it was you. I'm guessing it was Linda Veach."

"Great kid, Linny. Works cheap, does what she's told."

"Was she told to clean out your place and disappear? She did a great job there, didn't miss a postage stamp."

"What she missed, you can keep. Yeah, she's loyal, all right, sometimes a little too persistent."

Cat leaned against the headboard, crossed her arms over her chest. "You take off and you figure she's going to chalk it up to one of your quirks. But she starts calling everyone she can come up with who might know where you are. You get wind of it, get in touch with her, tell her to find out if the cops really hadn't ID'd the John Doe or whether they were just withholding the information. She actually told the cops it was you. Whose brainstorm was that?"

Danny's brows lifted wickedly.

"Forget I asked." Cat shook her head. "Mrs. Carlton Amis told the cops she thought she killed the guy. That's really what happened, isn't it? She did kill him in self-defense and that guy was Allan Pritchard."

Danny's gaze chilled. Cat shifted away from him involuntarily, slid one foot onto the floor. Don't be silly, she told herself, he wouldn't do anything to you, not crazy Danny Furina. Crazy...

"What was a guy like Pritchard doing around here? Does it have something to do with Fawn Sterling?"

"Now Cat, what would a lowlife like Pritchard want with the likes of Fawn Sterling?"

"You tell me. You called me asking about Freddy, if he was hooking up with Fawn. It wasn't Freddy, it was Pritchard dogging Fawn, wasn't it, and Pritchard who got in here and attacked Mrs. Amis and Pritchard's body you dumped in the Phoenix!''

"Everybody's gotta be somewhere.''

"Carlton Amis is going to be in for a shock when he finds out who attacked his wife.''

Danny's smugness evaporated. "Whaddaya mean? What's Amis got to do with Pritchard?''

So he hadn't figured that out yet, which meant she had a bargaining chip. "You first.''

Danny glared at her for a moment, then his gaze softened, surveyed her appreciatively. "You look good, Alley Cat. Still got the Fortunati mouth on you, though. Okay, I show you mine, you show me yours, but yours better be good.''

"It's good.''

"Back middle of November, I land the big one.''

"Sterling?''

"Her.''

"Fawn?''

Danny nodded. "She wants to hire me, but it's gotta be hush-hush, she don't come to the office, I don't open a file on her. She says things aren't goin' well between her and the King, she thinks he hired someone to take her out.''

"Take her out as in…''

Danny nodded, ran a thumbnail lazily across his throat.

"I can't see Blaine Sterling taking a risk like that. I mean, the first person the cops always look to is the spouse.''

"Me neither. I think she's a fruitcake. Then I think back to when I met her, when she and Fred were together. Smug, self-confident bitch is what I thought then, but now she's really spooked and she doesn't come across like a woman who spooks easy. So I figure I'll check it out. Tailin' her's a bitch. Runnin' up to New York, over to the hotel, out to get her hair done, up to Philly for her yard goods, but once she settles down Margate I made him. Give her credit, she's got a sharp eye, 'cause he was good. Pro, I could tell that right off.''

"And when you first saw him, it was from a distance and

the general build and hair color made you think it could have been Freddy."

"It crossed my mind. I mean, he was messed up when she dumped him. I borrow a zoom, snap a few, I can see it's not Fred. I send a couple shots up to a pal—"

"Mitch Falcone."

"Nice work, Alley Cat. You're turnin' pro yourself."

"Falcone ID'd Pritchard."

"An' I figure Pritchard's not after her autograph."

"So what makes you think Sterling hired him to eliminate Fawn? I mean, why not just divorce her?"

"*Che capisce?*"

"Or *cui bono.* You remember your Latin?"

"Not much."

"Who profits? Profits are very much on Sterling's mind right now, so it stands to reason that if he conspired to take her out, as you say, it's because it's more profitable than divorcing her."

"Damn, Cat, I oughtta have you come work for me."

"No, thanks."

"Well, you're on the right track. Sterling's livin' on loans. The Phoenix could turn things around, but he needs a transfusion now, and the banks are stallin'. And meanwhile, Fawn? You know fashion?"

Cat flicked open her battered jacket, nodded down at her plaid flannel shirt, washed-out jeans. "Not much."

"Yeah, well, she did everything right. None of that schlepping around Seventh Avenue, some third-string sketcher for some big label. She starts by skimming off the cream. Women who can pay fifty, seventy grand for a dress. Bagging the big ones first cuts out the advertising costs and gets you in bed with the serious lenders right off."

"I know that CapriOH! is small and select. I know I can't afford her clothes."

"Not yet. But couple months ago, she put out her first line. CapriOH!'s gearing up to go mass market. Got some licensing deals on the table. You only get those if the name's got juice, and the CapriOH! name is very, very. You know how licensing works? You agree to let 'em put your name on the neckties and the pillow cases and the leather goods and you sit back and collect the royalties. That's on top of the *haute haute*. We're talking megabucks."

"What's that got to do with Sterling? Other than the obvious Phoenix envy."

"They got together because Sterling saw a comer. He didn't just marry her, he backed her. He's a partner."

"I knew he put up some cash. I didn't know he was a partner."

"He is. A gamble back then, but it's payin' off now."

Cat thought for a moment. "So if CapriOH! is worth so much all of a sudden, and he needs money, why not just set a price for his half and sell it back to her?"

"Why go for a one-shot deal when you can have it all?"

"All of what? CapriOH! is Fawn and vice versa."

"CapriOH! is a name. I mean, there's still Chanel with no Chanel; Gloria Vanderbilt doesn't head up Gloria Vanderbilt. He doesn't need Fawn, he just needs her label."

"And—I'm only speculating here—this licensing thing isn't contingent upon Fawn..."

"Breathing," Danny concluded, grimly. "You buy a CapriOH! belt, you care if she personally drew the sketch an' picked the color?"

"What if he sues for divorce and gets community property? He'd hang on to half then, wouldn't he?"

"Maybe. Maybe half of the *haute*, because that's all CapriOH! is now. If she postpones the licensing agreements until after the split, forms a separate corporation, be awful hard for him to get his hands on that."

"So I'm guessing you have the world's oldest motive— profit—but you can't link Sterling to Pritchard."

Danny frowned, shook his head.

"So what happened with Pritchard?"

"Lemme take a breather, Cat."

"Sterling hires him to take her out. If he's such a pro, how come he made such a fatal error?"

Danny sighed. "That's the stumper. Like I said, Fawn hires

me, I make Pritchard, give her the file, his sheet, I find out
where he's holin' up, tell her I'm gonna call in a few markers
to see who's payin' his bills, she says no thanks, pays me
off.''

"You mean as soon as you confirm that she's not paranoid,
that she really is being stalked, you want to follow up, find
out who he's working for, she fired you?"

"You got it. Thanks for your time, goodbye PI. I tell her
this guy is a hard case, she shouldn't be stayin' in this place
alone, she should go somewhere more secure, the New York
place, the Phoenix, even. She says there's an alarm system,
she can look out for herself. I tell her, someone wants in, he's
gettin' in, someone wants to take you out, sooner or later,
you're gone. Remember that."

"This may seem like a silly question, but why didn't either
of you go to the police?"

"'Cause Fawn said no and Fawn was payin' the bills. She
says all she wanted to do was make sure she wasn't hallucinating. I'm thinking maybe she's gonna confront Sterling, ac-
cuse him of puttin' out a hit, figures maybe she throws out
Pritchard's name, Sterling'll come across with the quickie divorce, not make a grab for her cash."

"And not make allegations of adultery and so forth."

"Yup. Then a week ago Monday, I run out for a sandwich,
she calls my cellular, I gotta get over there right away. I make
it in four minutes flat, she's got the garage door open, waves
me in, drags me into the downstairs hallway and there he is.
Splat. She says she just walked in and found him like that. I
tell her we gotta call the cops, she goes off on me, says the
cops'll write it off as some botched B and E, they won't be
able to link the stiff to Sterling. I say, I'll tell them how she
was bein' tailed, she says how's that gonna prove it was
Sterling tried to take her out? She says a better plan is to hide
the stiff, tell Sterling there was a break-in. He's gonna think
Pritchard blew it, maybe got cold feet, he'll have to try an'
make contact, she can put them together. Now, she *says* she
walked in on the stiff, but I'm figurin' she's lyin', she really
killed him in self-defense, but so what? Her way, Sterling

thinks Pritchard's still alive, he's gotta get in touch, at least make a phone call to see why the deal fell through; it sorta makes sense to keep Sterling from findin' out Pritchard's whacked.''

"Well, 'Much madness is divinest sense,' I suppose, as Miss Dickinson said.''

"So we truss him up, get a blanket, roll him, stash him in the van, give the place a wipe down. Marble, you just gotta use a little warm water. The key's to seal the grout, remember that. We bag the trash, toss that in the van, we're gonna stash him until Sterling gets in that night thinkin' Pritchard did the job. Then we just gotta keep an eye on Sterling. We're workin' out the details when the doorbell rings. I hide in the van; Fawn says she'll get rid of whoever it is. So I'm sittin' in there with the stiff, twenty, twenty-five minutes, Fawn finally comes back and tells me it was the cops. Amis' wife was with them. Story is, she came by when Fawn was out, let herself in and Pritchard jumps her. *She's* the one took him out.''

"What was Mrs. Amis doing here?''

"Fawn'd asked her to run some papers over the Phoenix.''

"If Fawn was going out, why didn't she do it herself?''

"How should I know?''

"And why would Mrs. Carlton Amis bother with such a trivial errand, she must have some back office underlings of her own,'' Cat reflected.

"I'm thinkin' Sterling shoulda just hired his right-hand woman to take care of Fawn. The problem is, Fawn already went on to the cops how she walked in and everything was cool. They leave thinkin' the Amis woman's hyper an' the guy wasn't really hurt bad, he split before Fawn came in.''

"Fawn lied to the cops?''

"Yeah.''

"I'm not sure if I walked in and saw a man splattered in my hallway I'd have such presence of mind,'' Cat commented. "So at this point, I gather it was too late to modify the scenario, Pritchard being in your van and all.''

"Wait, it gets worse.''

"No, really?''

"I figure, whatever we do with the stiff, we're gonna have to tie up loose ends. So I cruise the neighborhood, lookin' for the junker I saw Pritchard tailin' her in, spot it over on Gladstone. He's got the rental contract in the glove compartment, used an alias, Jones, gave 'em the address on New Bedford, so I figure I better check the place out. So I borrow Fawn's car to run over there, on accountta I don't wanna be usin' the van, 'cause with a stiff in the back, I get carjacked, it could get, you know, awkward. So I get myself in his place, I'm checkin' it out, some gal starts poundin' on the door, yellin' 'Al, you in there, you sonofabitch? I know where you been, you wanna know who ratted you out, it was me.' I'm thinkin' she's gonna kick it in, but finally she takes off. Not much in the place except for the ten grand in the freezer. Always check the freezer for the good stuff, remember that."

"Freezer…good stuff…" Cat echoed, mesmerized.

"I'm thinkin' it's the down payment on the hit, 'cause a pro like Pritchard, he wouldn't do Fawn Sterling for under fifty and that's if the buyer don't want anything fancy and he don't have to handle disposal, you know what I mean?"

"I'm ashamed to say that I do."

"So I pocket the green, take back Fawn's car, tell her to get outta there, the Amis broad tells the boss how she got jumped, the cops thinkin' the guy's still at large, it's gonna look weird if Fawn hangs around. So Fawn's gettin' her gear together, and the phone rings. Guess who?"

"Sterling," Cat said immediately.

"I'm on the extension. He's shocked as hell to hear her voice, and she does this hysterical number, tells him how Mrs. Amis got jumped, the doer got away, she can't stay alone, she's moving into the Phoenix. Sterling's like, 'Oh my God, oh my God' and then he says how he'll try to get back to her as soon as he can but he thinks business is gonna keep him in town until maybe Wednesday but for God's sake, she should take care of herself. I mean to tell you Cat, it was Oscar Night. But now, we're kinda stuck with a stiff on our hands and we don't exactly have a game plan."

"Until one of you came up with the idea of dropping him in the Phoenix."

"Hey, I hearda worse plans."

"I haven't."

"Look, what's the diff? The guy's gonna be just as dead there as he was in the van."

"Well, you won't get an argument from me there."

"So, there's still the junker parked on Gladstone, so I gotta wait until it's dark to drive the stiff over there and get him into the hatchback—"

"Why?"

"So we'll be ready when it's time to make the drop."

"Why not just leave him in the van?" Cat could not believe she was discussing the particulars of human disposal in such a fashion.

"Cat," Danny explained, patiently. "You're dumpin' a stiff, you always use *his* car, remember that."

"Noted," Cat said, faintly.

"So, like it can't get any worse, I get him into the junker and all of a sudden, it *don't go!* So now I gotta go back to my place and get the cables from the Vega, 'cause this ain't exactly one for Triple A and I jump the hooper—"

"Hoopty."

"Huh?"

"Never mind."

"So I give it a jump, drive it over to Amherst, leave it runnin' while I run back to get the Vega off Gladstone, 'cause the street sweepers come in the morning, I don't wanna get ticketed. So I drive the van over to Amherst and by then the hatchback's petered out, so I gotta give it another jump, I get it goin', but it's low, so I hadda throw in a couple gallons, and gas, it's up to, what, one fifty? So I give Fawn a ring, tell her I'm drivin' the stiff over to the Phoenix, 'cause I figure I can just park him in the garage. So I drive the stiff over to the Phoenix, park at the top level, so the hatchback's outside. I gotta run back to move the Vega back to my place and bring the van over to the Phoenix, on accountta we might need a van. All this, plus I gotta keep a lid on Fawn, 'cause Sterling calls, says now he don't think he's comin' in 'til Friday, and she's ready to whack out. She decides we gotta get Pritchard outta his threads, so there's not any trace evidence could lead the cops back to her place. Me, I'm thinkin' she's been watchin' too much of your Court TV, but what the hell. So she tells me how they got these costumes comin' in Thursday, why don't we dress him up and leave him right where Sterling's limo'll drop him off. I am tellin' you, this is one wild broad. I figure, what the hell, it beats him fermenting in my van. Up top of the garage, cold weather, open air, anybody does get a whiff, they're gonna figure it's the usual seashore stink. Like when all those clams washed up last winter, remember? So what the hell. Anyway, Thursday night, she swipes the threads, Friday we get him into the suit. Me, I'd rather have a guy put up a fight than deal with your dead weight, not to mention your decomp, know what I mean?''

Cat felt her stomach do a slow rotation, nodded.

'''Member Trina Morosco, dad owned the funeral home? She gave me the guided tour once, showed me how they doll up the stiffs for the viewings. Anyway, now it's Friday night, we're makin' our move, out come the Amises, she's goin' off on him about something, we gotta hang back. Then Fawn says, we drop him too close to the door, one of the security guards might see him before Sterling pulls up, we better stash him in the elevator. I say what if someone pushes the button, door opens, Merry Christmas, know what I mean? She pulls out a batch of out-of-order signs she whipped up. Any wonder she's scoopin' the fashion world? This is a woman thinks on her feet. So, I do the inside doors, Fawn does the outside, we go back up, finally we make the drop. Then we gotta dump the hatchback, she follows me on accountta I'll need a ride back from the causeway. Get that done, we sit back, wait for the fireworks.''

"Except there were no fireworks, because I tripped over the body before Sterling arrived."

Danny flopped on the bed, frustrated. "Yeah, but still. You got a guy dead in a Santa suit, whaddaya gonna think?''

"I suppose I'd think someone had been trying to infiltrate the Phoenix for some illicit reason."

"Right. And you ID him and find out its some ex-con, you're gonna be all over the Phoenix, right? But the weekend goes by and the cops still don't have a positive. We're thinkin' maybe there's a chance Sterling will think Pritchard is still out there, get the sweats, try to give Pritchard a ring, see what happened to his ten G's. Maybe Mrs. A., smart cookie that she is, will figure the stiff's the one jumped her, she'll light a fire under whoever's investigatin'."

"And maybe Linda Veach asks the cops to help her locate her missing boss."

"I take off for a month, my own mother's gonna figure I just flipped out, I'll turn up. I'm gone not even a week and Linny's doin' the Nancy Drew."

"And now you hear the cops are looking for Danny Furina and you get Linda Veach to find out if the guy's been identified yet, send her to the morgue?"

"Look," Danny reasoned, "there's some snafu between the ME's office and the homicide cops, I figure I'll get some play time out of it. You know once Linny IDs the guy, the press is gonna get hold of it, I figure Sterling'll get shook up, figure the deal with Pritchard went south and go to whatever was plan B, 'cause gettin' rid of the missus, it's gotta be top priority."

"And has he? Arranged for another hit?"

Danny frowned. "Not so far as I can tell."

"Maybe Amis only had the one psycho in his pocket," Cat blurted, without thinking.

"What?"

Cat pushed her hair behind her ears, slid off the bed. "Carlton Amis knew Pritchard. When he was with Bevilacqua Macklin, he took on a manslaughter case *pro bono,* Pritchard was the defendant. He got him off."

"You mean to tell me Amis is owed by this nutcase?"

"Yes."

Danny smiled slyly. "Wait'll I let Fawnie in on that. That oughtta cool things off."

"Cool what things off?"

"She and Amis have been havin' a fling."

"So? Fawn is synonymous with fling."

"Yeah, but she finds out Amis was the go-between, she won't be feelin' so amorous."

"You think not? She may find it to be a turn-on."

Danny opened his mouth to reply when the phone rang. Cat gasped, looked at Danny. He sprang from the bed, his posture tense, calculating. On the fourth ring, he picked up the receiver, put it to his ear, listened, his eyes flicking toward Cat. At last he said, "What's your ETA?"

He hung up slowly, turned to Cat, a hint of the old roguishness in his expression. "Sorry, Alley Cat." He grinned, abruptly grabbed her face in his hands and kissed her on the lips, then sprinted for the door.

For a moment, Cat was so stunned by the dramatic shift in events that she sat motionless; then she shook herself and followed after Danny, who had cut through the kitchen to the garage. Cat ran along the breezeway, saw that the door to the garage was shut, the security panel light red.

Oh, no.

She didn't know the code. If she tried to open the door without punching it in, she'd trip the alarm. Could she take the chance that she'd make it back to her car before a police unit came down Bay Landing?

I'm going to kill Danny Furina. Right after I get myself out of this mess. Think. Okay, nobody can remember a code, they write it down somewhere. All I have to do is find it. All! Well, it has to be somewhere nearby. Cat backtracked to the kitchen, went through drawers, no luck, even checked the freezer, went to the hall and checked the library table, peeked behind the artwork, the closet, no luck, went into the guest bedrooms, the powder room. No luck. She was headed back to the kitchen when she stopped short.

Voices.

The winter air amplified them, two, more, accompanied by the scrape of shoes on the ice.

Oh, no.

One of the voices was Victor's. And then Cat heard the click of a key in the front door.

EIGHTEEN

FAWN WAS ON another line when Victor's call made it to the penthouse and Victor wondered if Sterling was putting her on the alert. Five minutes, ten minutes, and when she called back, the note of surprise in her voice rang false. She tried to plead off, alluding to the weather, her schedule. Victor suggested that she send Donnie or Mrs. Amis with the keys if it was inconvenient for her to come herself, politely reminded her that he would have no difficulty obtaining a warrant. Fawn capitulated; agreed to meet him at Bay Landing Court.

Victor arrived a few minutes before a sleek, black limousine coasted toward the curb. He heard a low, grating sound and saw the driveway gate open, realized someone in the limo must have activated the remote. Victor's eyes followed the movement of the gate, up the drive, saw the parallel tracks of a vehicle that had pulled into the garage recently, saw the random indentations of footprints on the iced-over lawn.

Fawn Sterling stepped from the limo, again wrapped in the chinchilla. This time, she wasn't alone; Carlton Amis emerged, took Fawn's elbow.

"You haven't been here already this morning, Mrs. Sterling?" Victor asked.

"No, of course not."

He pointed to the tracks, the footprints. "These marks are recent."

"Perhaps the cleaning service was scheduled. I'll have to check my book."

Amis spoke up. "Lieutenant, I know that Mr. Sterling came to see you today. I would appreciate it if you would suggest to Mr. Sterling that he have an attorney present before he makes a statement of any kind."

"Mr. Sterling came to see me voluntarily." His gaze shifted to Fawn; he thought he saw a slight shake of her head, a plea that he not tell Amis about their rendezvous.

The trio made their way toward the front door. Fawn punched in the code, waited for the light to go green and slipped her key into the lock. Victor allowed her to enter first.

"I'd like you to remain downstairs while I look over the house, Mrs. Sterling."

"Lieutenant, Mrs. Sterling has a workroom upstairs. I'm sure she would prefer that it not be disturbed."

"Understood. Where is the access to the garage?"

Fawn pointed toward the kitchen. Victor walked along the breezeway. "Is the code here the same as the front door?" he called.

"Yes," Fawn replied. "Six, six, six, one, four, three."

Victor punched in the code, waited for the click, opened the door. He saw the puddling tire tracks, the scrape of bootmarks, definitely one pair, perhaps two. Pritchard?

Fawn and Amis, seated at the kitchen table, had their heads together when Victor re-entered. "There was a car in your garage very recently," he told them. "I'd appreciate it if you gave your cleaning service a call, ask them if they were here this morning."

Fawn nodded.

"Mrs. Sterling, have you discussed with Mr. Amis what you revealed to your husband yesterday?"

"About this guy Furina?" Amis interjected.

"Yes." Victor continued to address Fawn. "Did you ever give Mr. Furina a key to this house?"

"Why would I?"

Not a "no," he observed. "Did you ever meet him here?"

"Once he asked to have a look around, check out the neighborhood, see what sort of security system I had."

"Did he have reservations about your security?"

"No."

"He wasn't apprehensive about the isolation? Didn't suggest you move out?"

"No." The gray eyes darted toward the tile floor.

Lie, Victor concluded. "Mrs. Amis was here because you had called her, asked her to come by and pick something up."

"Programs. I brought them down from the city."

"You arrived after the attack occurred, and pulled into the garage, correct?"

"Yes."

"Came in through the breezeway?"

"Yes."

"Did you notice anything amiss?"

"No."

"Mrs. Amis said she fled the scene in panic. Did you happen to notice whether or not the front door was ajar?"

Pause. A ripple of tension sent a slow undulation along the expanse of fur. "I, uh, I don't remember if I unlocked the door when I opened it for the police officer, or if it was unlocked."

Stalling, trying to figure out how much he knew. "You decided to vacate immediately?"

"Well…yes, I didn't feel very safe."

"Did you contact Mr. Furina?"

"Let me think…I may have tried to call him once before I left here, to let him know what had happened."

"What was his reaction?"

"I didn't reach him."

"And you didn't try again?"

"Lieutenant, the media reported that this Furina was the man whose body was found last week," Amis interjected. "So obviously Mrs. Sterling wasn't able to reach him."

"But Mrs. Sterling wasn't aware of that."

Amis pushed himself to his feet. "Look, Lieutenant, all this speculation's wasting our time. If you want a look around, maybe you'd better get to it."

Victor hesitated. He could continue fencing with her, but he knew he wouldn't get much further with Amis there. "I'll just take a look upstairs. That's where Mrs. Amis said the struggle took place."

He headed for the pair of staircases; Amis followed.

"Perhaps you should remain with Mrs. Sterling."

"I think it would be better if I witnessed the search."

Victor shrugged, cursed inwardly. "You're familiar with the floor plan?" he asked, as they mounted the stairs.

"Yes. It's an upside down. Living area and master suite face the water. Dining room, kitchen, exercise room, Fawn's office."

Victor said nothing, his eyes running along the sleek oak railing, unmarred, and the carpet was smooth. If a struggle had taken place here, no sign of it remained. Victor traveled the circuit, stopped in the kitchen, impulsively slipped his gloved finger under the handle of the refrigerator door, opened it. Empty. He slid open the meat drawer: tucked in the back was a plastic-wrapped package of gourmet ham. Victor checked the computerized sticker, dated ten days ago. Nothing else. Cleaned out recently, hastily.

Victor said nothing to Amis, who stood in the doorway, watching. He continued his tour, stopped at the master bedroom. Even in the near dark, he could see ruffling in the plush carpet where it had been crushed and trampled. A struggle? He ran his penlight over it; the light caught a spark of gold at his feet. He bent, retrieved an earring, a gold hoop with a flat circle and a tiny C engraved at the center.

"Mrs. Sterling seems to have lost an earring," Victor remarked, holding out the item for Amis to inspect.

Amis scrutinized it carefully. "This doesn't look like something Fawn would wear."

"Perhaps it's your wife's, Mr. Amis? Her name begins with a C."

"No, it's not Cookie's. I don't think she would wear anything this trivial. Maybe someone from the cleaning service lost it."

Victor shrugged, pocketed it. "I think I'm done here, there's really nothing more I need to see. Oh, but one thing more, while I have you here, Mr. Amis. Are you familiar with the name Pritchard? Allan Pritchard?"

Cat, hunched under the bed, pressed her fist to her open mouth, heard the prolonged silence, would have given a small fortune to see Amis' face.

VICTOR WATCHED Amis ease Fawn into the limo, watched the
vehicle glide down Bay Landing Court. Give him credit, he
had landed on his feet. After a pause, Amis had said, "Pritchard? You know, I know that name. A client of the firm some
time back? Give me a moment…Pritchard…Pritchard… I believe he was one of the *pro bono* cases I handled. Why do
you ask, Lieutenant?"

"His name came up during an investigation."

Amis didn't pursue it, didn't mention it to Fawn, though he
did hurry her out a shade too quickly.

Victor's car phone trilled as soon as he turned on the ignition. "Cardenas."

"Yo, Victor, it's Freddy Fortunati."

Victor felt a ripple of apprehension. "What's up?"

"You seen Cat today? The two of you have lunch or anything?"

"No, I haven't seen Cat since Monday. She went out?"

"Yeah. I called her this morning to see if her power was
on, if she needed anything. Kids got no school because of the
roads. She said she had something she needed to wrap up,
something about a story she's working on, asked to borrow
the Jeep. I said okay as long as she gets it back by one-thirty,
'cause I gotta work today. She's not back yet and she hasn't
called. I thought maybe she ran over to check on Ma, but I
don't wanna call there and get Ma worried if she hasn't heard
from Cat."

Victor checked his watch: 1:45. "No, don't call your
mother."

"I mean, I can make it in Cat's Maxima, she left the keys,
but you know how it is with me and Cat, I got this feeling."

Victor had the feeling, too. "Have you called the ERs?"

"Yeah. No accident reports but—wait, hold on."

Victor heard Mats in the background, heard Freddy say,
"No, it's not Mommy, hon…what game?…what kind of secret agents?… Victor, Mats is saying something about Cat
bein' out playing secret agents like they did the other day."

"Let me talk to him."

"Vi'tor, it's almos' Christmas."

"I know. You and Jane and Mom all ready?"

"I'm gettin' the Citadel of the Deep and two Swordfighting Samurai Sea Serpents if I be good. The Red Samurai and the Orange Samurai."

"I see. Mats, Uncle Freddy said you and Mom went somewhere the other day?"

"Uh-huh. You press the secret m'dallion and their heads flip around."

Victor thought for a moment. "On the samurai."

"Uh-huh."

"So where did you and Mom go?"

"It's a secret."

"I can keep a secret."

"To this place upstairs on a street."

"What was downstairs?"

"A kind of store with clothes. And there was a man and he was sewing and I didn't never see a man sewing before, did you?"

Upstairs from a tailor shop. Furina's office. "I have. So what was in this upstairs place?"

"Nothin'. A deks and a table and chairs and stuff."

"Anything like papers or letters?"

"Just the enblope in the mailbox Mom took."

Victor suppressed a groan. "And then did you leave?"

"Uh-huh. But first Mom talked on the phone and then we went to McDonald's and this fat man choked. Not Santa, this other fat man. And Santa gave him the Heimick remover and I got two lollipops, one for me and one for Jane."

"Okay, Mats, let me talk to Uncle Freddy again."

"You make sense of that?" Freddy asked.

Victor filled him in about Furina, Pritchard. Freddy listened in amazement. "Ma's already firin' up the rosary, prayin' for Danny's immortal soul and he might still be kickin', the jerk? Look, maybe I'll try *South Jersey*'s office. I know that guy owed Cat some back pay, maybe she ran over there to collect. I mean, the side roads are a mess, so she can't have gone far from the beaten path. Weather like this, how much trouble could she get in?"

CAT DECIDED she hadn't gotten in this much trouble since she was ten years old and she and Freddy had started walking to school with the new kid, Owen Johnson. Owen had broken his collarbone playing soccer and Cat was carrying his book-bag. Tony Colucci encountered them one day when Freddy had gone ahead with Danny Furina, said something that had concluded with "a nigger with his own personal slave, whaddaya know," whereupon Cat dropped Owen's bookbag and slammed her own bookbag into Tony's solar plexus and knocked him flat, which got her sent to the principal's office and dismissed with a note to her parents; Cat hung around the playground until school was out, then hid behind the holly bush at Richmond and Porter, waited for Tony to walk by, tackled him and pounded him with her small fists until his nose bled. Unfortunately, Mrs. Colucci came upon the ambush, pulled them apart, walked Cat home and told Mrs. Fortunati that her unruly tomboy ought to be locked up.

Cat was sent to bed without supper. Late that night, Carlo Fortunati, Sr., came home from the restaurant. Cat could hear her mother's voice expostulating in the kitchen below, then heard her father's heavy tread on the old stairs, saw his silhouette fill her doorframe, blocking the light from the hall. He came into the room and sat at the foot of her bed, his great form sinking deep into the thin mattress, and demanded an explanation. Cat choked back her fear and poured out the whole story. When she was done, her father asked, soberly, "Now Allegrezza, aren't you sorry?" pitching his voice to carry down to his wife.

"I'm sorry Mrs. Colucci came over before I could give him a black eye, too, since I was getting in trouble anyway."

There was a profound silence. Then an explosion of laughter filled the house. Crouched in a lower bunk beneath Joey, Freddy exhaled his relief.

Cat's father took her down to the kitchen and made her a sandwich, piling high the wafers of provolone, mortadella, prosciutto, ribbons of lettuce and red pepper. Cat could still close her eyes and taste that sandwich. "Allegrezza"—her father always addressed her by her Christian name—"the Colucci twins are two stupid sons of bitches. But you go and pound the"—he leaned close, whispered something that made her giggle—"out of every stupid son of a bitch you meet you're never gonna get anything done. I'll tell you what: next time you get mad enough to pound someone, you come home, write it down in a notebook. Write down everything you wanna do to Tony Colucci, some day you'll read it over, have a good laugh." Cat, attempting to latch her small mouth on the sandwich, wasn't sure about the laughter part, but the remainder of the idea intrigued her.

And now Tony was chronically unemployed and Owen was a judge and Cat still had those faded black and white composition books her father had bought, their pages filled with childish, rather melodramatic scribblings. She wished she had one now. She could write a column on Danny Furina.

Thank heavens Fawn had called the code aloud to Victor. Six, six, six, one, four, three. Cat slipped through the kitchen, the breezeway, punched in the code, heard the lock click and opened the door to the garage.

She pushed the button beside the door; the garage door began its rumbling ascent. When it reached the top, Cat pushed the button again and dashed under the door as it reversed, lowered. She rolled onto the slushy tracks left by Danny's van, got to her feet, hopped the wall, half-ran, half-skidded the precarious blocks to her car.

Hunched behind the steering wheel, she turned on the ignition, shoved the heat to high. Slush had trickled under her collar, her cuffs, her gloves. She pulled her gloves off and pressed her fingers to the vents. What had Danny been doing at Fawn's house? Was he still working for her? Had she found out the police were coming to check out the place and sent Danny there to tidy up any traces of their bizarre escapade?

And why had he revealed the conspiracy to Cat? Easy; he didn't trust Fawn. They might be allies, but he knew that if they got in trouble, she wouldn't hesitate to cut him loose, shift all the blame to him.

Where would he go now? *Where would you go?* Cat asked herself. To Pritchard's hideout, double-check to make sure that was clean, make sure Danny hadn't left any evidence of his search.

Atlantic Avenue had been badly salted. It took Cat twenty-five minutes to navigate the Cherokee to New Bedford; she rounded the corner, parked a half-block from J m's. Danny's van was nowhere in sight.

She got out, made her way onto the sidewalk. A solid wall lined half the block; only a couple doors, the change from siding to plaster to brick marking the division between buildings. Cat saw the door closest to Oriental Avenue was number Three Fifty-three, a dirty glass entry set into the brick wall. Cat pushed it in, stepped onto a square of linoleum with seams that puckered like open wounds. There were two metal mailboxes set into the wall. A strip of tape was affixed to the address slot on the one marked Apt. A: *E. Adkins* was written in blue ink. The tape over Apartment B had been ripped away. Cat tried the buzzers over the mailboxes, waited. No response.

Well, if Danny was inside checking out the place, he wasn't going to answer, was he? She pushed at the second glass door. Locked. She peered through, saw a dilapidated stair ascending to a second-floor landing, face-to-face apartment doors at the top.

Cat checked her watch: 2:20! Freddy! She backed out of the building, scurried around the corner to the coffee shop, praying the phone wasn't still out of order. It wasn't. Cat called home and got Ellice. "Tell Freddy I'm sorry, I lost track of the time."

"Freddy left, honey. He took your car. Where are you?"

"AC. Please tell me Freddy didn't call Mama or Carlo and throw a scare into them."

"He called Victor."

Cat winced. "Are the kids okay?"

"Jane's fever's up and down and Mats has a sore throat."

"I'll be home in an hour. Tell Mats I'm going to bring him some water ice."

Cat hung up, slumped on a stool at the counter, cursing herself for letting Danny Furina get away, for leaving the kids when they were sick, for wasting a precious pre-Christmas day running after blind leads. Lousy mother, worse reporter. Why was she knocking herself out like this, why not go back to the movie reviews and the concerts and the dance recitals? Had her life really been so bad the way it was before?

"You want some coffee or something?"

Cat glanced up at the shirtfront at eye level, read, WHAT IS OUT OF THE COMMON IS RATHER A GUIDE THAN A HINDRANCE.

"Conan Doyle," she said aloud.

"Huh?"

Cat looked up, saw the thin face, the buzzed hair, recognized the girl who had waited on them Friday night. She noted, too, that the eyes were still red-rimmed, bloodshot; the crying jag had apparently not abated. "It's from *A Study in Scarlet*."

"Is that a book or something?"

"Yes. Yes, I'll have some coffee."

The girl shoved a ceramic mug in front of Cat, poured in the last of the pot. Cat watched a trickle of grounds dribble onto the surface; her gaze drifted back to the shirt, the quote from Sherlock Holmes. Victor was a fan of Holmes. Of course, she wasn't going to think about Victor. She commanded herself to think of something else.

My boyfriend gimme this, made it up Yardville.

The boyfriend she was crying over.

But his name's not Milton, it's Al.

As in Allan Pritchard.

...some gal starts poundin' on the door, yellin' 'Al, you in there?'

Cat swallowed a mouthful of coffee. *Go slowly, now.* "So how's the boyfriend doing? Al, was it?"

The pale eyes narrowed to a squint, flicked around the room. "Look I already tol' that black cop this morning, Al ain't come back."

"Sorry. I'm not a cop. It's just that when I was in here last week, you mentioned your boyfriend Al had made you the T-shirt with the logo. I was wondering if he did that one, too. I like it." Cat steeled herself, took another casual sip of coffee.

"Yeah, he made it. Bastard." She disappeared behind the counter, emerged with a damp rag, began wiping down the counter vengefully.

"You guys split up?" Cat asked, sympathetically.

"Like I care, hookin' up with those bitches, thinks I don't know? Just try comin' around here get his ten G's back."

Despite the paucity of subject pronouns, Cat interpreted the girl's response to relate that Al had abandoned her for one or more other women and that, should he part company with them, he was not to expect that this girl would either take him back or return his ten—G's meant thousands—his ten thousand. Dollars.

But hadn't Danny found the ten thousand dollars in Pritchard's freezer, taken it? "At least you came out of it with ten thou— G's," Cat remarked.

"Yeah."

"Stashed it in his freezer, I gather."

"Hell no, in *my* freezer."

"You've got his ten thousand in your freezer?" Cat managed to convey her admiration of the girl's ingenuity.

"'Course you don't *keep* it there," she added, slyly. "Let him try to get his hands on it, he comes back. 'We're gonna be rollin' in it,'" she mimicked. "'Fifty grand on each end for a five minute job.' I figured why he didn't want me along after I heard him. Shackin' up with that bitch in his room, thinks I didn't know? So when he goes out on his big job an' don't want me along, I got Martita's car an' followed him over to that big house."

Big house? The Bay Landing house? Cat cleared her throat. "Did you, um, catch them in the act?"

"Hell no, I seen that bitch pull up in her Merc, I got so mad I split an' called the cops on them."

"The cops."

"Look, I figure whatever's goin' down, let the cops nail 'em. I call in a B and E, I was gonna go back and watch the fireworks, but I go past the same Merc, I figure I'll split, get the cash and wait for Al to call, 'Baby, come down make my bail.'"

"And he never called." Cat realized with a sickening jolt that the girl didn't know Al was dead.

"Jerk."

Another patron came in, took the stool beside Cat's. Cat shifted a bit in her stool, felt a thickening in her inner pocket press against an upper rib. The envelope she had taken from Danny's mailbox, stuffed in her pocket. She'd forgotten about it.

What she missed, you can keep.

Which meant that Danny had turned over possession of the envelope and its contents to her, didn't it? While the waitress tended to the new patron, Cat took a butter knife from the counter, opened the envelope, drew out a photocopy of a newspaper photo. The banner and the caption had been excised by the copier, but Cat recognized the cast of characters.

Blaine Sterling, two security guards at his back, the one who had been there the night the body had been found, Seltzer, and one who could have been his twin. Mrs. Amis on Sterling's right, her form partially blocked by the chauffeur in the foreground who was helping Fawn Sterling into a limo.

Fawn's bent posture sent a shower of blond hair over her face, concealing her expression. The others were regarding an autograph-seeker who had approached Sterling, notepad extended in one hand. Cat studied the supplicant's chiseled profile, dark wavy hair.

Puts our boy face to face with all parties involved.

Cat raised her hand to signal the waitress, eager to get her spin on the photo. The door opened and two patrol officers walked in, took the two stools at Cat's right. One of them recognized Cat, nodded. "How ya doin', Mrs. Austen?" he asked and then introduced his partner.

Cat nodded politely. She fished up a pen, wrote on the bottom corner of the picture, "Like to talk to you about this," added her name and phone number, passed it face-down to the girl, saying, "Take a look at this when you get a minute."

Cat put money for her coffee on the counter, rose, her knees shaking.

An' I figure Pritchard's not after her autograph.

The autograph hound had been Pritchard.

NINETEEN

THE FLOATER, Tamara Montgomery, had parents. The mother fingered her crucifix and wept quietly, the father answered Victor's grave questions in monosyllables with no display of anguish other than the hand that tightened over his wife's arm whenever he pronounced his daughter's name.

Laid out in the morgue, the girl looked like a character from a fairy tale, the hair a vibrant blue-black, the flesh milk white and unmarred except for the deep, sure gash under her left ear. "She was a good girl." The mother's voice was pleading, urgent, as if it was vital for Victor to understand that Tamara had been decent and loved. He watched them walk away, suddenly aware that they were only a year or two older than he. It was the grief, already working them over, that had aged the couple in his eyes.

Victor went straight home and called his mother, chatted about Milly and his nephews, about Remy ("What that girl needs is to settle down. When I was her age, I was already *una viuda*"), smiled sadly at his mother's exasperation with this wayward daughter who had reached age thirty-three without managing to get herself married and widowed. His mother talked a few more minutes about the virtues of settling down, reminded him he was expected for Christmas dinner, perhaps they might have company. Victor was too weary to rebuff his mother's matchmaking, said *"Buenas nochas, Mamí,"* with a weary smile, slipped into a reverie that mingled his father, Marisol, Chris Austen, all cut down in their prime. Here and gone.

The reverie shifted to Cat. He hadn't seen her since she had run out of his office Monday afternoon. Quarrels were for the young. Victor had not understood when his father had said it, but now he knew what it meant: quarrels were for people who still believed they were going to live forever.

He arrived on Cat's doorstep early Friday morning, rehearsing what he was going to say when she came to the door. But his knock was not answered by Cat or Ellice; instead, he was greeted by a petite, dark-haired woman with punkish bangs and three earrings in her right ear. She was wearing skin-tight jeans and a clingy angora sweater. Her oddly slanted eyes lit with recognition when they settled on him. "Hi, Lieutenant, what're you doing here so early? You remember me, right?"

And he did remember, remembered the little-girl voice, uptilted eyes, thought he hadn't given the figure the attention it merited when it had been camouflaged in scrubs. "Miss Wing," he said, and followed her through the foyer, threw his coat over an armchair in the living room, pushed a couple shopping bags inside the door. "Is Cat out running in this weather?" He eased the note of disapproval out of his voice. He'd made an early New Year's resolution: be supportive of whatever Cat did.

But Cat's friend replied, "Cat's still asleep. At least, I hope she is. She had a bad night."

Victor felt a chill ascend his ribs. "She sick?"

"No, it's the kids. They've got chicken pox."

Victor let his breath out slowly.

"Cat was out most of the day and when she got back the kids were feverish, wouldn't eat, and then Mats' temperature spiked to one oh four and the pediatrician had Cat take him to the ER while Ellice stayed here with Jane. I thought she was going to lose it, waiting around the ER, and poor little Matty was so uncomfortable. I got off at eleven and they still hadn't sent him home, so I hung around with Cat and this morning I called and told Ellice I'd come by and hold down the fort if she had to go to work. She's only got a half day today. And Freddy's out doing her grocery shopping. Thank God this is the last epidemic, though measles is making a comeback. I'm old enough to remember measles and German measles and mumps, what about you?"

"Old enough." He'd had mumps when he was ten; his sisters had charged the Inlet kids twenty-five cents apiece to have a look at him. "Can I go up?"

"Don't wake her."

Victor bounded lightly up the stairs. Cat's bedroom door was ajar; Victor peeked in, saw that the bed hadn't been slept in. He opened Jane's door quietly, saw Jane sleeping on her stomach, her pretty features lightly dotted with the rash, her long braid hanging over the side of the bed, the tip brushing the carpet.

He backed out and went to Mats' room. Mats was sitting upright in bed, whispering something to his loveworn plush bunny, a green plastic action figure grasped in one hand. At the foot of the bed, Cat lay in a heap, sleeping, a terry-cloth robe thrown over her legs.

"Vi'tor!" Mats whispered.

Victor put a finger to his lips, squatted down beside Mats' pillow.

"I got chicken pops!" Mats was clearly elated.

"I can see."

"Even on my butt." He lowered his voice, conspiratorially. "Jane, too." He giggled, amused at the notion of his sister being similarly afflicted.

"You feel like something to eat?"

"Mom brought me water ice."

"Let's not wake her." Victor eased Mats off the bed.

"She cried." Mats sat on the floor and pulled on a pair of fuzzy blue slippers. Victor helped him into a navy plush robe with a quilted collar, compared it to Cat's flannel nightgown, shabby robe, frowning. She spent the clothing budget on the kids. He thought of the gold-wrapped box from Bon Soie with satisfaction.

"She cried in the night, 'cause after we came home from the hospi'l and I went to bed, I woke up and she was sittin' on the bed cryin' in the dark. An' I told her I wasn't gonna die," he added, aggravated with his mother's sentimentality.

"Mothers worry."

"You know how to give piggybacks?"

Victor's mouth turned down, judiciously. "I think so. Put your arms around my neck."

Mats locked his arms around Victor's collar, his hands still clutching the plush rabbit, the action figure. Victor tiptoed out of the room.

"You're asposed to gallop."

"Ah, yes." Victor trotted down the stairs briskly enough to satisfy Mats, deposited him in the kitchen booth.

"How's my Matty?" Jackie Wing chirped. "Will you let Aunt Jackie take your temperature?"

Mats frowned. "Where?"

"Ear." Jackie produced the thermometer. "Hold still. I don't know how she does it," Jackie addressed Victor, "two kids and this place. I just have the one, and then only part-time and I still get frazzled."

"You have a son?"

"Robbie. He's Jane's age. That's where Cat and I met, in maternity. And then, I knew Annie Fortunati from work. You want some coffee? It's made."

"I'll get it." He took a mug from the drainboard. "Where's your son?"

"His father got custody." The pert face hardened with a veneer of contempt. Then she smiled, shrugged, checked the thermometer. "Well, we all make mistakes. Matty, I bet you'd like some water ice."

Mats nodded.

"Ninety-nine point three," she told Victor. "He'll be fine, but believe me, when your kids are under the weather, it drives you crazy."

"I can stay here, if you have to leave," Victor offered.

"You don't mind? Then maybe I will go; I want to finish up some shopping before I pick up Robbie at school. I have him for the weekend, and I had him for Hanukkah. There's Liquid Tylenol on the sink and Five Alive in the fridge."

Victor followed Jackie to the closet, helped her on with her coat.

"I heard there was some kind of break-in at the Sterling house over in Margate, you heard anything about that?" She laughed when Victor did not reply. "I get it, no comment. Anyway, I heard it from one of the nurses who's dating a cop. Tell Cat her mother called, she's coming over with dinner, so Cat's not to cook, and she said she'd straighten up the back room when she got here, so I think she's gonna move in. And she said not to worry, she's not driving, someone named Kevin is bringing her over."

Victor heard a shuffle on the stairs. Jane slumped down, rubbing her eyes.

"How're you feeling, honey?"

"Everything itches."

Victor gave Jane a wink that made her giggle.

"There were a bunch of phone messages, mostly family. And that Ritchie Landis. And some woman who didn't give her name, she said I should tell Cat she's the woman Cat gave the picture. I told them all to call back, I didn't want to wake Cat."

"Jane, you go in the kitchen with Mats, I'm going to walk Miss Wing to her car." Victor took Jackie's elbow, walked her down the porch steps, held her car door. Jackie flashed an engaging smile; Cat had said she played the field, yet her manner was fun-loving, an easy flirtation that was very different than Fawn Sterling's rapacity.

Victor walked back into the house, heard an animated, "Is *not!*" "Is *too!*" emerging from the kitchen.

Victor entered; his raised brows stopped them in mid-dispute, though Jane, unwilling to concede her point, hissed one final, "Is *not.*"

"What's going on here?"

Victor turned, saw Cat standing in the doorway, clutching the old robe around her. She looked at Victor, her face reddening. "Where's Jackie?"

"I'm her relief. If you don't mind. Are you all right, Cat?" Weariness had given her face a sweet vulnerability; his glance took in the faint violet crescents under her eyes, the pallor.

Cat gathered up her frayed pride. "I can manage."

"I don't doubt it. But I'd like to stay, at least until Freddy comes with the supply wagon."

Cat was about to protest, but sensed that Jane was listening a bit too earnestly, redirected her focus. "What was going on down here?" she asked her children.

"Jane says there ain't no Santa," Mats whimpered.

Cat slid into the booth, drew Mats beside her, kissed his hair. "You mean, 'there isn't.'"

"There *ain't?*"

"No, there is, but you should say 'there isn't.'" Too little sleep had eroded lucidity, sense.

"Why should I say there isn't if there is one? That's lyin'."

"Santa Claus is a *pigment* of the imagination," Jane declared, knowingly.

"Well, at one time, so were you, Miss Jane, and you're in living color now."

"Vi'tor," Mats appealed. "Is there Santa?"

"Would you feel better if you could talk to him, *hijo?*"

Mats nodded, wide-eyed.

Victor reached across the table for the wall phone, dialed. "Hello, Santa?" he greeted pointedly.

"Who the hell is this?"

"This is Lieutenant Victor Cardenas, *Santa,* and I have a young man here who has been told there's no Santa Claus—"

"Oh no, oh no, oh no, I am not doin' Santa Claus," Stan Rice sputtered.

"—who's home with the chicken pox, so I thought you'd like to say a few words to him."

"—not doin' Santa—"

"His name is Mats Austen."

"Matthew Christopher," Mats whispered, urgently.

"Aw, put him on."

Victor handed the receiver to Mats. "Are you the real Santa or one of those old people who pretends they're Santas when kids call up?"

"Ho ho HO!" Stan deepened his voice. "This is the real Santa."

"I got chicken pops. Jane, too."

"Ho, ho, HO! Bummer."

"I didn't make my bed yesterday or today."

"Neither did Santa."

"An' I only said the F-word 'cause Zack Libertini bet me a quarter." He sneaked a glance at his mother's face. Cat's brows were lowered, sternly.

"Did he pay up?"

"Uh-huh."

"'Cause Santa doesn't like it when a guy backs out on a deal. So what do you want for Christmas?"

"The Citadel of the Deep and two Swordfighting Samurai Sea Serpents."

"Sounds doable. You know you can press the secret medallion and their heads flip around?"

"Uh-huh."

"Is Mommy there?"

"Uh-huh."

"Let Santa talk to her, okay? And maybe you wanna ease up on that F-word business, it's not worth the trouble you could get into, unless this Zack is offering some serious cash, you know what I mean?"

"Uh-huh." Mats handed the receiver to Cat. "It *is* him!" he told Jane.

Jane gave her gullible brother a scathing look.

"Hello…Santa?" Cat said.

"Both kids down, huh? You okay? Need anything?"

"Everything's under control," Cat lied.

"Want me to do my bit for your girl?"

"You're not that good."

"Hey, you never gave yourself a chance to find out. Well, then, if it's all the same to you, I'll just hop back between the sheets with the ex-Mrs. Claus. Put the lieut back on."

Cat passed the phone to Victor, who saw the blush, gave her a quizzical look. "Phil told me he didn't know what he should do about that waitress over the coffee shop. Should he tell her Pritchard's dead?"

"Have Long pick her up. I want to have a talk with her. And get those nine-one-one tapes from Margate."

"You think she an' Pritchard were on the outs, she dropped the dime?"

Victor sensed Cat's attention as she peeled the lids from cups of frozen water ice, passed them to her children. "If she did, it means she knew where he was, even if she didn't know why. I'll be in later this morning."

Jane was commiserating into her water ice. "—they only let you have one party in fourth grade, and I'm *missing* it!"

"Look on the bright side," Cat teased. "You won't have to eat any of Uncle Freddy's cupcakes."

Jane poked at her water ice, unconsoled.

"Jane," Victor said, "there are two shopping bags in the front hall with a couple presents for you and Mats; I think it would be okay with your mother if you opened one each."

Jane brightened, made a dash for the hall, Mats at her heels.

Cat heard the rustling of paper, an excited squeal from Jane. "Kids," she muttered. "Their rebound amazes me. Last night I was thinking crazy stuff." Her voice choked for a moment. "You have no idea what goes through your head. Rhys syndrome and brain damage and seizures and how it was all my fault because I wasn't here." She propped her elbows on the table, cupped her face in shaking hands.

"You didn't give them chicken pox, Cat." Victor slid into the booth opposite her. "Did you?"

A glint of amusement brightened her gaze. "Of course not. But if I don't indulge in irrational guilt periodically I'll forget how it's done and all those years of Catholic indoctrination go right down the drain."

Victor smiled. "My sister Milly got acute appendicitis when she was ten. I went with my mother to the ER, they put Milly on a stretcher. Two people come in, a man and a woman, my mother grabs the guy, she's got a handful of his shirt in her fist, she's yelling, 'She's gonna be all right, *me entiendes? Me entiendes?*' and they pry her off the guy and sedate her and it's not until after the surgery she finds out the woman's the surgeon and the guy's a student nurse."

Cat smiled.

"A *makeup* kit!" emerged from the front hall.

"Victor, she's nine."

"Maybe she'll let you borrow it. You look pale, Cat."

"I didn't get much sleep."

"Well, you can take it easy today. Jackie said your mother called. It seems she's moving in."

"She's not driving in this ice—"

"No. Someone named Kevin is bringing her over. He's the one who works at St. Agnes with Dominic, right?"

"Kevin Keller. He's a deacon."

"Hm. Old boyfriend is what I heard."

"Friend. You know Mary Grace Keller, don't you?"

"Raab's office. She's an ADA."

"She's his sister. The Kellers were the only family on Richmond Avenue who had more kids than the Fortunatis. Nine kids." Cat ticked them off on her fingers. "Joe; Margaret Mary; Sean; Maureen and Kathleen, twins; Kevin; Mary Grace; Dierdre; Patrick. Paddy died when he was about Mats' age." She paused for a moment. "The rest of them fled the nest as soon as they could fly."

"Old friends seem to be popping up all over."

Cat thought about Danny. "You can say that again."

Victor slid one hand into his trouser pocket, drew out the gold earring he'd found on Fawn Sterling's carpet.

Cat's hand crept involuntarily toward her earlobe, her fingers pushing a strand of hair behind her ear.

"Well, at least you're not pale anymore."

Cat's mouth compressed resolutely. "Are you going to let on like you know something that you only suspect so that I'll assume you know everything about something you really don't know anything about and I'll spill my guts?"

Victor tugged at his mustache. "In eighteen years of police work, I have never coerced, entreated, duped or bullied anyone into spilling his or her guts."

"I know how cops think. You're wondering whether you ought to do the nice thing and give my earring back or the right thing and hold it for evidence."

"Evidence suggests a crime occurred."

"You'll never make me talk, copper."

"Mom, Uncle Freddy's here!"

Cat made a run for the front door. She shuddered as a

whoosh of icy air swept in with Freddy. Cat grabbed one of the four bags Freddy was carrying, Victor stepped forward to take another. "Cat, every week you haul groceries up these steps? You ought to build a dumb waiter."

"Dear. I have you."

"Hey. So how come you're up? Go back to bed, I'll hang around this morning."

"Mama's coming over."

Freddy lugged his bags into the kitchen, slung them on the counter. "You oughtta eat out more."

"Once my Christmas bills are paid, I'll be lucky to eat at all. How much do I owe you?"

"Forget about it."

"Freddy—"

"Fred, if you wouldn't mind hanging around, I'd like to take Cat out to breakfast."

"I don't want to leave the kids," Cat said.

"Hey, I can do kids. I see Jane hiding behind the tree putting on eye makeup."

Cat frowned at Victor. "I don't even own eye makeup."

"Go get changed," Victor said.

Cat stalked upstairs, took a quick shower. Well, if she had to sit through another interrogation, she wasn't going to give unless she got. What "her" had he told Stan to have picked up? Fawn? Earlene? She pulled on jeans, battered boots, a red turtleneck sweater, braided her damp hair behind her neck. As she descended the stairs, she heard a heavy tread on the porch, saw Freddy go to the door.

"Who here's got chicken pox?" Carlo's booming voice demanded. "Five dollars says no one here's got chicken pox!"

Mats shot into the hall, yanked up the shirt of his pajamas to expose his spotted tummy while Jane poked her head from behind the tree and asked, "Five dollars *each?*"

Carlo waved to Victor, began rummaging in his pockets. "What's that on your face?"

"*Eye* shadow, Uncle Carlo."

"You let her wear eye shadow?"

Cat heard a second tread on the stairs, muttered, "The

troops have landed. Just leave the door unlocked, Freddy, until all the Fortunatis are accounted for.''

Vinnie came in, stamping his shoes on the mat. "So the kids are sick, you don't call anyone?" he demanded of Cat, regarding Victor balefully. "You got the day off?"

"No."

"You look like hell," he told Cat as he gave her a rough kiss. "She look like hell or what?" His hands began rummaging in his pockets.

"Stop giving them money!" Cat demanded. "I'd like them to figure out how to earn it, eventually."

"Fine." Vinnie turned to Mats. "What's the capital of New Jersey?"

"Ocean City."

"Close enough," Vinnie slipped a bill into Mats' palm.

"Great. Corrupting their morals and their education."

"It's *Trenton!*" emerged from behind the tree.

Cat swept Mats into her arms. "Come on, baby, Uncle Freddy bought you Rice Krispie Treats cereal."

"Lorraine says do you want her to come by, give you a hand?"

N-O, Cat thought. "No, thanks," she said, sweetly. She seated Mats at the table, rooted through the mound of groceries for the cereal, looked in the cabinet for a bowl, found none, checked the dishwasher, which was full but hadn't been run, retrieved a mildly crusted bowl, washed it at the sink.

"I wanna pour it myself."

Cat poured a little milk in a paper cup, set it on the table, heard another ring at the front door, heard Jane cry, "Nonna! We got money!" with the calculated insinuation that her grandmother might want to match the take, heard an undercurrent of male voices. Someone asked, "Where's Cat?"

Jennie entered the kitchen; Freddy followed, carrying the three grocery bags his mother had brought with her. "Now you relax, I'm gonna take care of everything."

"Mama—"

"I had seven kids, they all had chicken pox."

Victor stepped forward to help her off with her coat. "I had just offered to take Cat out for breakfast,'' he said, and then framing his inducement in a manner that would make Jennie an ally, "Cat hasn't had anything to eat."

Bull's-eye. "Whaddaya mean, she didn't eat? You didn't have breakfast?" she demanded of Cat.

"Nice touch," Cat muttered.

Victor winked behind Jennie's back. "Don't those cupcakes need to be dropped off at Jane's school?" he asked innocently. "We could do that on the way."

The phone rang. In the living room, Carlo and Vinnie had launched into their rendition of "Dominic the Donkey." Cat rolled her eyes, picked up the receiver. "Hello?"

"You the lady was in Jim's yesterday?"

"I'm sorry?"

"Jim's? Coffee shop over Oriental? I called earlier, some gal said you were still in bed. You the one slipped me the photo yesterday? Austen?"

"Yes. Yes, that's me."

"This come from a newspaper or something? I wanna know when this was took, 'cause it's Al there with that guy Sterling and the same bitch I saw comin' outta his place."

"I beg your pardon?" Cat saw Victor watching her, closed her eyes, tried to call up the photo. Blaine Sterling in the center, Cookie Amis on his right, Fawn in the foreground, the two bodyguards. Pritchard. What did Earlene mean "Bitch comin' outta his place"? "That's Mrs. Amis," she said. "She's his secretary." Cat saw Victor cock an eyebrow. She bit her lip.

"Oh." Earlene sounded confused. "Wait, isn't Amis some kinda rich lawyer or somethin'? Isn't he the one come by tried to get Jim to sell out so's the Phoenix can build their garage onto our lot?"

"Yes, that's right," Cat replied, guardedly.

"They all livin' up in the casino?"

"No, the Amises live in Ocean City."

"What's up? You're talkin' like your phone's tapped or somethin'."

"It's just that I've got some people here. But I would like the opportunity to continue this discussion in person."

"Be straight with me, you a reporter or something?"

"Sort of."

"Yeah, well, discussion's gonna cost. Two bills."

Cat felt a thrust of panic, realized that the girl had said "bills" (i.e., hundreds), not "G's" (i.e., thousands). Though it may as well have been thousands, considering Cat's ravaged budget. Ritchie would just have to stake her, that was all there was to that.

"I'm kind of tied up right now. Can I get back to you?"

"Just make it soon, or I go to the highest bidder."

TWENTY

GET THROUGH BREAKFAST with Victor, figure out a way to pry two hundred dollars from Ritchie to bribe Earlene Adkins, smuggle in the Citadel of the Deep Freddy had redeemed from layaway and hidden in the downstairs apartment, clean house, clean the good silver that Aunt Cat had bought her as a wedding present, try on the dress Jackie had loaned her to wear to the Gambol.

Cat asked Victor to take her to the local coffeehouse, rather than the diner. The diner was a favorite breakfast spot for the local and county cops, while the coffeehouse was the preferred spot for readers and Cat felt that she needed the home café advantage. The coffeehouse produced scones, muffins, cinnamon buns, fresh orange juice and excellent cappuccino, which satisfied Cat's notion that the only true breakfast was the continental breakfast.

Victor ordered Cat's double cappuccino, assembled a plate of muffins and scones, ushered her to a small table in the corner. A few people were nursing lattes, reading; soft reggae drifted from a speaker mounted on the wall.

Vinnie had been right. Cat didn't look well. Not like hell,

of course, only careworn and much in need of some R and R. "Okay, let's have it," he began. "How did you get into Fawn Sterling's house?"

Cat prodded the foam on the cappuccino with her spoon. "No Miranda, no nothing?"

"I'm just asking—"

"—because it proves it can be done. Not without help, though."

"You had help?"

"I didn't break in, I sort of rolled in. Someone opened the garage door and I slipped in before it closed. That's not breaking and entering, is it?"

"Technically, it is. Trespassing, at the very least."

"Oh, technically." Cat sipped; the cappuccino produced a blissful smile, but her tone was withering.

"I'm expected to observe the technicalities."

"So you don't subscribe to actions that are morally justifiable but technically criminal?"

He grinned. "The DA doesn't allow our unit the same latitude as Conan Doyle did Holmes."

"Well, tell me this: If I'm sent up, can I still profit from a story on the Sterlings?"

"You haven't done anything to get yourself sent up, have you?"

"Not…intentionally."

"Just the unintentional B and E."

"Trespassing," Cat corrected. "That's a misdemeanor."

"I wasn't talking about Margate. I was talking about Furina's office, Secret Agent Austen."

Cat blinked. "Did Mats rat me out?"

"Adane's been in contact with a parole officer who's been in contact with a PI named Falcone. This Falcone called Furina's office a couple days ago, said he talked to Linda Veach. But Veach skipped. And yes, Mats did rat you out."

"That stinker."

"Furina's office was locked."

"Well, there's locked and then there's *locked*."

"*Dios me salve,*" Victor groaned.

"Do you want to hear this or not?"

Victor broke a cranberry muffin in two, gestured for her to continue.

"I called his office that morning and got his machine. But when I was in his office and the phone rang and kept on ringing, I realized someone must have been there in the interim. Cleaned it out, right down to the answering machine tape. And the place hadn't been sealed, so I knew it wasn't the police." Cat nibbled at a lemon pignoli scone. "I'll have to upgrade my opinion of Linda Veach, she's pretty efficient."

"How do you know it was Veach?"

Cat inhaled, braced herself. "Danny told me."

Victor dropped his muffin. "Furina? When the devil did you see Furina?"

"Who do you think I followed into Fawn's house?" She took a deep breath and recounted her confrontation with Danny. Victor's jaw tensed when she described Danny's ambush, recited mentally, *Be supportive. Damn it.*

"So you know he's not the John Doe. How did he get in?"

"She gave him access. He was working for her. He had the remote for the garage, a key, the security code."

But Fawn Sterling had told him Furina didn't have a key. No, she hadn't said that exactly, she had only said "Why would I?" when he'd asked if she had given Furina a key. "She said she dismissed him weeks ago."

Cat fortified herself with a gulp of cappuccino. "She helped him ditch the hoopty, if you understand my meaning."

"I do. According to Furina, of course."

Cat shook her head. "Friday night, when I was being shown the door? Amis came down from the penthouse, said Fawn had just gone out. And the car that followed the hatchback? Sportscar, manual transmission. I had six brothers, remember? No they're still together, but he doesn't trust her, especially not after I told him Falcone had made the connection between Pritchard and Amis. When I told Danny that, he looked like, I don't know…like he realized he was being manipulated."

"And Furina said he told Mrs. Sterling who was following her, where he was staying, how dangerous he was?"

"Yes, why? Did Fawn tell you something different?"

Victor frowned. She'd said Furina never turned up the identity of her stalker. "And the envelope?" he prompted.

Mats again. "This is the last time I work with a partner. Falcone had turned up a newspaper photo. Sterling, Fawn, Mrs. Amis, a couple bodyguards. And Pritchard. Coming up to Sterling like he's asking for an autograph. The caption had been cut away, but it looked recent."

Sounded familiar. Victor recalled the file Adane had assembled the day after the body had turned up. There had been a copy of a photo like that.

"And don't scowl and say *'Dios me salve'* because you know you're very glad to have the information."

"Elated. If they do send you up, put in a request for conjugal visits."

"Platonic visits."

"Well, one can dream, can't one?"

Dream. This had all started with a dream, really, an eerie impression of flight that still nagged at her; Danny had spotted Pritchard from a distance, wanted to know if it had been Freddy.

"So where did you go after you left Bay Landing?"

"AC, wound up in an interesting conversation with Pritchard's erstwhile girlfriend, a waitress named Earlene Adkins."

"You figured her into the picture, too?"

"I did. So how about a little *quid pro quo*, Lieutenant? You think Raab can charge Sterling with conspiracy?"

Victor shook his head, grimly. "Conspiracy to do what? Mrs. Sterling's suspicion that she was being followed and the word according to Furina, who has not only disappeared again, but who is, according to his nearest and dearest, a bona fide fruitcake."

Cat's gaze took on an introspective dreaminess. Victor watched her dark eyes flicker with a perceptive spark. "Yes, that's been his reputation. And why hire a bona fide fruitcake when you can have your pick of the best agencies and something as important as your personal safety is at stake?"

"Were they acquainted? I mean when she was with Fred."

Cat shook her head. "They'd met maybe once. But with Danny, once was enough. Enough for her to figure out he wasn't a by-the-book kind of guy. He was the guy you hang with if you've got something wild in mind, and pin the blame on if things go sour."

"Well, things went sour, all right. When the waitress heard someone in Pritchard's flat, that was Furina?"

"That's when he turned up the ten thousand in Pritchard's freezer. That's the going rate for a hit, you know, if you don't want anything fancy and the—do they still refer to it as the 'button'?—the button doesn't have to handle disposal," Cat said, knowingly.

"Ah. That would be your no-frills hit."

Cat worked on her scone, thoughtfully. "You know, Victor, if I wanted to get rid of someone, hire a hit man? I wouldn't cruise the underworld or post an ad in one of those mercenary magazines, I'd cozy up to someone who could give me the name of a certifiable pro. Someone like a social worker or a criminal attorney. Or a cop."

"Lovely thought." *Smart, too.*

"Don't pretend it hasn't occurred to you. Why else would you ask Amis if he was familiar with the name Pritchard?"

"How do you know that?"

She pushed a strand of hair behind her ear. "Lucky guess?"

"Cat."

"All right. I was sort of…under the…you know…bed."

Victor cleared his throat. "When I was in the room with Amis?"

"And for the record, my earrings are not trivial, they're tastefully understated, though I'm not surprised that anyone connected with that hideous casino would find them to be somewhat pedestrian."

"They're charming. Under Mrs. Sterling's bed? *Verdad?*"

"Mind your manners, Lieutenant. I haven't bought your Christmas present yet." Cat groaned, inwardly, added *Christmas present for Victor* to her list.

"Don't forget the cellophane."

"Cookie Amis must have nerves of steel."

"Why do you say that?"

"Well, in the photo, she's practically eye to eye with Pritchard. And Allan Pritchard was quite good-looking. *I* wouldn't have forgotten him right away. If I saw that same face moving in for the kill only weeks later, it would drive me to drink, and I don't mean Pepsi or cappuccino."

Toddies before noon, he thought.

Victor left her at her house, relieved that she wouldn't have the opportunity to follow up on her budding leads. The young man who had brought Jennie over in the St. Agnes van—Kevin Keller—was methodically de-icing Cat's porch steps. Carlo and Freddy were entertaining the kids with a makeshift puppet show. Jennie was presiding over a pot of ragu in the kitchen, chastising Marco for "arresting poor old ladies, what ails you?"

Marco, his wire-rims pushed onto his forehead, walked Victor to the door. "My sister okay?"

"She seems pretty resilient."

"Yeah, well, we're all combat-ready. Mom's on my case because of the SOBS. D'Esperance isn't pressin' charges, but I wish to hell he'd find himself another cause and split."

AND D'ESPERANCE MIGHT well have split had not Miss Liona Davis been dismissed the following afternoon from her position as a hostess at Tailfeathers, the Sterling Phoenix VIP lounge.

Liona's costume was dictated and unvarying: gold brocade vest under a pantsuit of green satin, the Phoenix crest embroidered on the lapel in gold thread. Green satin pumps, discreet jewelry, no dangling earrings, no charm bracelets, no piercing of any body part but the earlobes, and there, once only. Liona, in the mood for a change, spent her day off with a beautician who pulled apart the compact chignon and coaxed Liona's contentious tresses into a series of infinitesimal plaits that flared at the temple and curved under the chin in a simulated page. The results were so cunning and polished that it was not until one was within a few feet of Liona that one could see her new coiffure was a sculpture of diminutive braids.

This innovation was observed by the hospitality coordinator, who took it up with the assistant personnel supervisor, who mentioned it to the vice president in charge of hotel operations, who reported it to the office of Mr. Sterling's administrative assistant, who dispatched back down the chain that if the coif was indeed constructed of cornrows, Miss Davis was in violation of the hotel's Employee Dress and Grooming Code, Roman numeral three (hair), subsection B ("Ethnic" styling of).

Liona, who worked in a lounge where women tottered about in feathered skirts, sequined skullcaps, cinched waists and five-inch pumps, went into the ladies' room and took a good look at herself in the beveled glass mirror with the phoenixes etched onto the corners and decided, damn, she looked just fine. She declared that Roman numeral three, subsection B was clearly prejudicial toward minorities, and rather than waiting for the hotel's grievance committee to convene and hear her complaint, she tossed her plaited head and took her grievance to the Reverend Marlon d'Esperance.

VICTOR REALIZED, as Miss Adkins fidgeted in her chair, that she might have been pretty. There were good bones in the scrawny face, a kernel of refinement that hadn't been nurtured and so had withered. Family had failed her, education had failed her and now whatever hopes Pritchard had conjured in his quest for an ally had defected as well.

There was a knock on the door and Victor turned, saw Lauren Robinson slip into the room. "You're Miss Adkins' attorney?"

"I'm Jim's attorney. He called me on her behalf."

"Well, now I understand why the Sterling Phoenix hasn't made any headway taking over Jim's property."

She tossed her expensive briefcase on the table. "You know what you can do with your flattery, Lieutenant. Shall we?"

Victor offered her a chair.

Lauren Robinson was a striking woman. The skin was a

deep coffee brown, the brows straight and black over clear amber eyes. The voice was low and confident, but it could crackle with righteousness, though rarely. Generally, it was patient, droll. "Has Miss Adkins been charged with anything?"

"She could be charged with aiding and abetting a fugitive."

"And I could be related to the Queen of England."

"It wouldn't surprise me in the least."

"Be a hell of a shock to the Windsors. Let's get down to business, shall we? I still have Christmas shopping."

"What are you getting me?"

"A book. *Men Are From Mars, High Time We Sent 'Em Back.* Unless, of course, the charming Mrs. Austen has already bought it for you."

Earlene's pale eyes flickered to attention. "Hey, that the same Austen I talked to this morning?"

Lauren moved her chair a bit closer to Earlene's, laid her hand on the girl's arm. "Dear, the rule is that you don't speak unless I authorize it. I don't have to ask if my client's been Mirandized, do I?"

"She has." Victor leaned against the wall, his arms crossed over his chest. "Late October, a parolee named Allan Pritchard disappeared from his residence, didn't report for work, show up for his appointment with his parole officer. A week or so later, he sets himself up in Atlantic City using the alias Allan Jones. Leases a car, rents one of the flats above Jim's. Your client lives in the other one."

"You're not fascinating me yet, dear."

"Your client asked Jim to rent the place to Pritchard."

"Says who?"

Earlene opened her mouth to speak. Lauren tightened the grip on the girl's arm. "Let Mama do the talking. A man using an alias had a conversation with my client, she mentions a vacant apartment in her building."

"They had a relationship."

"You're still fishing."

"We have reason to believe Pritchard was summoned here for illegal purposes and that he made your client's acquaintance in order to secure an accomplice. I'm not saying your client had prior knowledge of the crime."

"Fine. Now I know what you have reason to believe and what you aren't saying. Now tell me what you know."

"I know that Miss Adkins befriended Pritchard. That he made promises to her and that she believes he ran out on her." He hesitated. "I know that he didn't run out on her."

Earlene half rose from her chair. "I knew it! He got picked up! I knew he messes with money, it's trouble!" She laughed, maliciously. "What, he wants me to make his bail? Tell him call his rich girlfriends, I ain't spendin' a dime to get him out."

Victor paused. "Counselor, would you step outside for a moment?" He opened the door.

Lauren shrugged, spoke a few words to Earlene and walked into the hallway. "Okay, what's goin' on?"

"We have reason to believe Pritchard came into town to harm Mrs. Blaine Sterling. He probably dropped into the coffee shop when he followed Mrs. Sterling to CapriOH!, strikes up a conversation with your client. He's looking for a place to hole up, she mentions the apartment. He gets close to her, figuring his plans may call for an accomplice who knows the area. If not her, it would have been someone like her."

Lauren looked past his shoulder toward the door. "None too bright and lookin' for love. Every ex-con's dream girl."

Victor nodded.

"Which means my client's dumb, Lieutenant. Not a crime, bein' dumb. Oughtta be maybe, but isn't."

"I'll concede that Pritchard was too smart to confide everything to her. But I need to know what she does know."

"And of course she won't be prosecuted."

"If it winds up in court, she'll testify."

"Victor."

"Raab's given his guarantee that she won't be prosecuted. If she testifies."

Lauren leveled her gaze at him. "There's something else, isn't there?"

Victor met her amber gaze. "He didn't run out on her. He's dead."

Lauren said nothing.

"You remember the John Doe turned up in the Phoenix parking garage?"

Lauren nodded. "The news said it was some flaky PI, Furina."

"No. It was Pritchard. Perhaps you would like to break the news to Miss Adkins, explain to her that he didn't run out on her."

"How'd he die?"

"It was an accident. He broke into Mrs. Blaine Sterling's home in Margate, attacked a friend of hers. She fought back, he suffered a fall, hit his head."

"Doesn't sound much smarter than she is," Lauren commented. "Okay, give me a couple minutes with her."

Victor paced for ten minutes, knocked. When he entered, Lauren was hovering over Earlene's chair. The girl's narrow shoulders heaved as she sobbed, wearily. Victor tugged a linen handkerchief from his pocket, pressed it into the girl's hand.

"Thanks. Been cussin' him for walkin' out on me, all the time, he's been dead, the bastard."

Victor held out a chair for Lauren. "Miss Adkins, how long have you known Allan Pritchard?"

"Tol' me his name was Jones, like you said. Figured he did time, he says yeah, he was up Yardville, but he's goin' straight, got a job with a big payoff, after that, he's gonna blow AC, head down Florida."

"Mr. Pritchard didn't disclose all of this at your first meeting?"

"No." She sniffled. "Guess it was November he first comes into Jim's. Early, 'cause we still had the Halloween stuff up. That neighborhood, Halloween, it's like a armed camp, but Jim, he still stocks up on the Hershey bars anyone comes in. Not the little ones, either, the two-ounce ones." She held her hands about six inches apart.

"And he began dropping in frequently?" Victor asked.

"Yeah. Came on to Martita at first, but she had a man, even

though he split about a week later 'cause he killed some old lady. By then, he's comin' around my shift, though. I usually work the four to midnight. Afterwards, we start to hang out. He's lookin' for a place, I told him about the apartment upstairs. Jim lets him rent it out by the week.''

''You saw him frequently during the month of November?''

''Mostly.''

''What sort of job was it, the one with the big payoff?''

''Dunno. He got this hoopty, rental. Useta park it in the casino lot, 'cause they don't charge the two bucks. I thought maybe he's workin' over there. Then, I find out all the time he's sayin', 'Baby, I do this one job, we're gonna head south, you an' me,' he's two-timin' me.''

''He was seeing another woman?''

''Yeah.''

''How did you find out?''

''Heard 'em. Eleven at night, they're goin' at it.''

Victor cleared his throat. ''Should you be called to testify, Miss Adkins, you will have to be more precise.''

''Al an' that broad are up in his room fu—''

''I think,'' Lauren intervened hastily, ''the lieutenant means he would like you to be more precise as to the date of the alleged encounter.''

''Look, there wa'n't no 'alleged' about it. I mean, I'm in the kitchen, the plaster's comin' off the ceiling. This is about three weeks after he shows up. I hear a door slam upstairs, I look out the front window, see her runnin' down New Bedford, long fur coat.''

''Did you see her face?''

''Nah.'' The pale cheeks blushed, shifted.

A lie. ''And afterward?''

''The next day, he's flashin' cash. Called it a down payment.''

''Ten grand.'' Victor recalled the amount Furina turned up.

''The only person I told about the money was—''

''Earlene,'' Lauren said, sternly.

''Down payment on what?'' Victor asked.

"I figure he was sellin' it. Like in that movie *Midnight Cowboy?*"

Victor stroked his chin. "That would hardly account for ten thousand dollars."

"I don't believe my client acknowledged whether she was aware of the specific amount, Victor dear."

Earlene sniffed scornfully. "Al had the equipment, I can vouch for that. He coulda got ten G's."

"And when was this encounter?"

"After Thanksgivin', I think. Right after, 'cause we still got creamed turkey over toast on the lunch special."

"Day of the week?"

"Saturday, maybe. Jim was fixin' to make the meatloaf."

"Which was," Victor studiously avoided Lauren's gaze, "Sunday's special."

"I think some of the plaster mighta fell in the gravy, but no one complained."

"Saturday," Victor calculated. "December first? Or more like December eighth?"

"More like the first."

"The next day, did you confront Pritchard?"

"Yeah. I says, is he two-timin' me, he says, 'No baby, it's just business, it's what's gonna get us outta this dump.' He could be real convincing, you know what I mean?" The question ended on a rasping sob; it had hit her that she was relegated to the dump once again unless chance sent another Al her way. "What the hell? What else I got goin' for me? Then he tells Jim he prob'ly won't be needin' the place past the fifteenth, even though he's all of a sudden got the cash to pay up through the month. Then one night, I think it was a Sunday, he's on the pay phone every fifteen minutes. I hear him say 'You sure she's gonna be there?' Then he says, 'One p.m., one a.m., it's all the same to me.' Next afternoon, he goes out, I say can I go along, he says it's business, I'll just be in the way, so I figure what I got to lose, I borrow Martita's car and follow him."

"Where did he go?"

"To some big place on the water. In Margate. One of those side streets, Bayfront or Bayview—"

"Bay Landing?"

"Yeah, that mightta been it."

"Where did he park?"

"Over on Gladstone. Like he don't want the car seen in the neighborhood."

Victor remembered what Cat had said, that Furina had found Pritchard's abandoned car on Gladstone.

"So I gotta park outta the way, too, 'cause that Bay Landing? Nobody lives there, all those places are shut up. So I see him go in the front door—"

"He entered the house by the front door?"

"Yeah."

"Like someone let him in or like he had a key?"

"Dunno. I was down the end of the block, I just seen him go up to the front door and after a second, he goes in. Then this fancy car comes down the street, this broad at the wheel. She pulls up to the curb, gets out, lets herself in the house and I got so mad, I went and called the cops."

"You called nine-one-one. Reported a break-in?"

"Yeah. I was hot. I don't even know if I tol' them the right street, everything around there's Bay this an' Bay that."

"And then what did you do?"

"I'm headin' down Atlantic and I pass this Merc, the one I seen parked at the big house, an' I'm gonna give the broad a piece of my mind, but I hadda get Martita's car back. So I just go home an' wait for Al to call me to bail him out, an' a little while later, I hear him come in, sounds like he's tossin' the place, I figure he's got the cops on his tail, I go knock, he don't answer, but I figure he can't hole up forever, right? So at four, I punch in, an' when I get off, he's not there."

"But you expected him to return?"

"Yeah."

"For the money he concealed in your apartment."

"Now, now," Lauren cautioned.

"We have information that Pritchard received twenty thousand dollars—"

"Twenty! I just got the ten—"

Lauren shot to her feet. "Interview's over. In case I don't see you, have a Merry Christmas, Lieutenant."

She seemed surprised that Victor didn't object, didn't move to detain them, even held the door as the two women passed into the corridor.

Long met Victor as he headed back to the unit. "I got the warrants. Johnson came through. Nothing like fatherhood to put you in a cooperative mood."

Victor nodded. "Get me a guest list for that holiday party over at the Phoenix. And tell Adane I want an APB on Furina."

He entered his office, picked up the phone, dialed Cat's number.

"Are you checking up on me?" she asked.

"Yes. How're the kids?"

"Napping."

"You do the same."

"With all this commotion around here?"

At least she wouldn't be able to give her brothers the slip. "Cat, Furina told you he found ten thousand in Pritchard's freezer."

"That's where you hide the good stuff."

"So it is. I just interviewed Earlene Adkins—"

"Oh?" Cat held her breath.

"—and I implied that Pritchard had held out on her, increased the amount of cash you said Furina turned up and she said she's also got ten grand from him."

"No kidding?"

"She also said she heard Pritchard with a woman in his apartment."

"Look, when I said I thought he was handsome, it was just an observation. It wasn't me. Honest."

"I'm relieved to know I can eliminate him from my competition."

Cat laughed, briefly. "Are you holding her?"

"No. But I do have a warrant to have the lab go over the

Bay Landing house. They're not going to turn up any more of your little trinkets, are they?''

"I don't think so.''

"Good. Incidentally, Miss Adkins said you two spoke.''

"Did she?''

"I don't want you communicating with her again, understood? She's a material witness and I wouldn't want you to interfere with a homicide investigation.''

"Any more than I already have, you mean.''

"You've been given fair warning, Cat.''

"'Fair and foul are near of kin,'" Cat quoted.

"You stay put this weekend, or I'll enlist your kin to see that you do.''

"Saturday *and* Sunday?''

"And all day.''

"Oh, all right.''

"Promise?''

"Cross my heart.''

Of course, sunset logged in around four-fifty these days and Sunday—the night of the Gambol—Ritchie wasn't coming by until nine, so technically, she'd be in all day, and technicalities were all that mattered to Major Crimes.

TWENTY-ONE

SUNDAY EVENING limousines clogged the *porte cochere* at the base of New Bedford and the Boardwalk. Gambolers were ushered through the hotel reception by elves in green satin coats, green-and-gold-striped bloomers. The plush, phoenixed corridor that skirted the east side of the casino floor was lined with twinkling runway lights. Marble columns were garlanded with green and gold tinsel. Suspended from the ceiling, fifteen feet above the floor, were chorus girls wrapped in diaphanous white, rigged with gilt wings, synching "Joy to the World" on faux trumpets. Buzzers, whistles, metallic jangling from the

casino floor gave the pious tableau a covetous undercurrent.
Cat, squirming in the snug silver sheath she had borrowed
from Jackie, groped for the small notebook in her handbag,
determined to record her five-hundred-dollar evening from
minute one.

She had nearly backed out. Family had been drifting in all
weekend, babying the kids, pestering her, whispering behind
her back how Cat was taking on too much, too fast. Worse,
Cat was reluctant to confide her recent discoveries to Ellice,
afraid that Fawn Sterling's name would nurture Ellice's suspicions that Freddy was still carrying a torch.

"What's the matter?" Jennie asked, when they had finally
gotten rid of the family. A buffet had materialized Sunday
afternoon; family swelled, then gradually departed to begin the
twenty-four-hour fast that preceded the Christmas Eve meal.

Cat picked up a dishcloth. "Nothing."

"You're not worried about Freddy an' Ellice."

Cat smiled. "What about you, Mama? She's not that nice,
Catholic Italian girl you and Pop were always angling for."

"Your father, may he rest in peace"—Jennie put down a
soapy plate to cross herself—"he asks my father for my hand,
don' laugh, an' my father, he says to me, 'You know, Vin-
cenza, he was born here.' Back then, your parents wanted you
to have someone from the old country. But your father was a
good man, and my mama and papa, they decided it's okay.
Then Carlo, he wants to marry Annie, and the Pescas, they're
not Sicilians, you know, they're Calabrese, an' your papa, he
wasn't real happy at first, but Annie and Nancy, they're good
girls. An' Lorraine, her grandmother was from someplace far
off—"

"She was Irish, mama," Cat smiled.

"—an' Sherrie, divorced, already with a girl of her own
and none of her people are one of us, whaddaya gonna do?
Freddy doesn't get married soon, people gonna think he's like
Mrs. Cicciolini's youngest, Louie?" Jennie shrugged. "Live
an' let live, and once in a while, you light a candle. So," she
shifted gears, abruptly, "you an' Victor have another fight, or
what?"

"What makes you think we had a fight at all?"

"People around here act like I don't know what's going on. I know what's going on."

Cat kissed her mother's bright auburn hair. "Maybe you should be the reporter, then."

"You do okay. Weren't you supposed to go someplace to-night?"

"Who told you that?"

"Jane said Jackie gave you a fancy dress."

"Was I that much of a snitch when I was nine?"

"Worse."

Cat rubbed a pot with a dishtowel. "I don't like to always be going out when the kids are under the weather."

"The kids are asleep. An' what am I, some old lady can't take care of my grandchildren?"

"Mama—"

"When the twins were little, I used to babysit two, three times a week, an' Lorraine, all the time with her aches and pains, always had me over there looking after the boys. And who did little Marco and Andrea stay with when Marco and Nancy went to Hawaii? You're the only one acts like I gotta sit in a rocking chair, watch television."

"Mama, I do not."

"You get dressed up, you go out, if Victor calls, I'll just tell him you been worked up getting ready for Christmas and you need your rest. That's not a lie," she added with a grin.

"Do you know absolutely everything?"

"God didn't make me a mama for nothing."

So Cat donned Jackie's dress, a silver drape that crossed over her breasts and fell to her ankles, drew her dark hair into a low chignon, added star-shaped rhinestone earrings and was ready when Ritchie and his parents arrived in a limousine shortly before nine.

She reddened and tugged up the too-low bodice when Ritchie gaped and said, "Jeezlouise, Austen, you put together real good," spoke politely to Ritchie's parents, who turned out to be a handsome, reserved, well-bred couple. They accompanied Cat and Ritchie as far as the escalator, where a guard stood checking invitations, decamped from their son's company as soon as they were passed through.

The Victorian Village was fabricated with false fronts laid over the shop entrances, wrought-iron gas lamps, staffed with carolers, pushcart vendors who offered hors d'oeuvres, waiters in Santa costumes bearing trays of champagne, half of the offerings its natural pale gold, the other half tinted green. Green-and-gold satin streamers had been fixed to the railing that surrounded the elliptical opening in the floor and were anchored to the chandelier, creating a striped awning that effectively obscured the partygoers from the *hoi polloi* milling among the slots twenty feet below.

The faux snow not only dusted the floor, but fell in a fine mist from above. Cat's silver pumps kicked up a cloud of it as she and Ritchie maneuvered into the receiving line assembled in front of a ceiling-high curtain that had been raised to separate the cocktail reception from the southern wing of the corridor that lead to the oceanfront ballrooms where the Gambolers would dine. Cat tucked her numbered invitation stub into her purse to free up her right hand, shook hands with the mayor and his wife, the committee chairwomen and their husbands, and the Amises.

Cookie Amis, her tall, limber figure tightly wrapped in green satin suspended by rhinestone straps, regarded Cat with cool amusement. "I see you've laid aside your woman-of-the-masses posture for the evening," she said, as she shook Cat's hand briefly and passed her along to Amis. He let his gaze slide over the silver gown with a brazenness that made Cat acutely conscious of how effectively the snug bodice had summoned forth cleavage. "What an unexpected pleasure," he murmured.

He passed Cat along to Fawn, who was vacillating tensely in green chiffon, a spray of gold erupting from one shoulder. The dark chiffon cast a hard, metallic light on her gray gaze. "Cat Austen. How long has it been?"

"Since what?"

Fawn's prominent jaw squared off. "Since we saw anything of each other."

"I think we've seen as much of each other as either of us wanted. I've been hearing about you, though. Seems like only yesterday your name came up. A mutual acquaintance of ours. Danny something or other."

Fawn jerked her hand away. "My husband, Blaine Sterling. Blaine, this is Mrs. Christopher Austen."

Clearly, it didn't register that she was the woman he had sent Amis to bribe the week before. He murmured her name, his watery blue eyes drifting on her to the next in line even before the last syllable of his greeting was uttered.

Cat and Ritchie moved away from the line. "Look, I wanna mingle awhile, okay?" Ritchie said. "How come half the receiving line's staring at you, Austen? Sterling's wife looks like she's gonna spit nails. There still hard feelings about the engagement? Hey, there's Deanna what's-her-name with that guy runs KRZI. I hear she signed with *CopWatch*. It gets the green light, she's gonna play herself. I hear she's gettin' ten grand. I'm gonna go say hi. Don't lose your stub, they're rafflin' off some great stuff after dinner."

Ritchie darted off. Cat looked around for a familiar face, mentally worked up descriptions of the ice sculptures quietly melting into shapeless configurations, the paté phoenixes reduced to brown mash, caviar glistening like obsidian beads on beds of slushy, shaved ice. She was a bit jarred when one of the waiters, dressed identically to the body in the garage, offered her a glass of green-tinted champagne. Perhaps they couldn't get a refund on the rentals, she thought, as she declined the concoction, but it seemed a bit bizarre and indecent to have waiters parading around in garb identical to Pritchard's corpse.

Cat continued to wander, got a glimpse of Fawn through a gap in the striped awning, having heated words with a tall, ponytailed man in a midnight-blue tux. She moved to get a better look at the pair, her pumps slipping on the soap-flake snow, saw Blaine Sterling, nowhere near his wife now, beginning his tour of the room, moving in sync with the photographer from Public Relations as he posed with the mayor, a state senator, the hospital administrator who would be presented with a check between dinner and dessert. A sextet of green-jacketed security guards fanned out in a fluid defense formation, ready to close ranks at Sterling's nod, should an untouchable attempt an unwelcome contact.

Cat's gaze moved on to the arrow of green satin in his wake, Cookie Amis, her arm linked through her husband's, the grip tightening when anyone—no, any woman, Cat amended—made a play for his attention.

Later, these tableaux would bear fruit; later, Cat would see how much of the private soul was revealed in this public display. Even now, she had the sense that she ought to record her impressions, was reaching for the notebook in her purse when the soles of her pumps slipped against an accumulation of "snow" and she stumbled against the railing. A hand caught her elbow and Cat was flanked by Kurt Raab and his wife, an attractive woman with a down-to-earth smile.

"Thought you were gonna pitch over the side," Raab greeted. "What're you doin' here, Mrs. A?"

"How'd the riffraff make the cut, you mean?" Cat teased.

Raab grinned. "You an' Patrice know each other?"

Cat and Patrice Raab nodded. "We spoke a while back when Mrs. Austen was working on her story about the Gambol. So is this business or pleasure?"

"Business. What about you, Mr. Raab?"

"None of your business. You ever heard the curiosity killed the cat thing?"

"'Some, that are mad if they behold a cat,'" she quoted, archly. "I have heard that."

"Merchant of Venice," Raab snorted. "Hey, don't look so surprised, every lawyer oughtta read it at least once. Senior year, I played Shylock, no kiddin'. I wasn't bad, either."

"Why didn't you go on the stage?"

"He did," Patrice replied.

Raab chuckled. "Go ahead, talk about me. I'm gonna go see if I can pry Carl away from the missus."

He walked off, assiduously avoiding the roving photographer. Patsy's gaze followed him to the Amises. "She ought to just get a leash," she murmured, then giggled. "So how's the article coming? Did Cookie take time to speak to you?"

Cat shrugged. "It's going to take time to make this sound—" she broke off, remembering that Patsy Raab was on some committee or other.

But Patsy only laughed. "Tasteful? That's going to tax even your journalistic talents, Mrs. Austen."

"Please, call me Cat. I guess I don't get out enough to know where elegance lets off and gaud begins."

"At the threshold. Did you see those poor girls strung up from the pillars down there? I don't even remember whose idea that was. And this silly snow—" she brushed her short dark waves with one hand, setting free a flurry of flakes. "I almost broke my neck. Oh dear, don't print that."

Cat gave her a scout's honor. "I think it was Mrs. Amis' inspiration."

"Well, what she lacks in discrimination, she makes up for in drive. They're talking about Amis as the next lieutenant governor. That's if he passes on the presidency of the Phoenix."

"And she's the woman behind the man?"

"She works at it. Works at not letting him or anyone else forget it, too."

"Really?"

Patsy nodded. "Married to one of the most prominent men in the state and right arm to one of the most well-known businessmen in the country and dead determined never to go back to being little Cornelia Schlafley from Nutley, New Jersey."

Cat thought about that for a moment. "'In Pride, in reas'ning pride our error lies. All quit their sphere and rush into the skies. Pride still is aiming at the blest abodes, Men would be angels, angels would be gods.' Pope. Alexander Pope."

Patsy smiled. She had a wide, generous mouth and an attractive forthrightness. She and Raab had been married for fifteen years. "I never quit my sphere. I'm Patsy Sniderman from Ventnor and you're a Fortunati from Atlantic City and your dad owned a restaurant and mine was a pharmacist and we're not in a hurry to forget it. If anything happened to Kurt, God forbid, I could make it on my own. Like you've been able to do. But Cookie…?''

"Aiming at the blest abode?" Cat jerked her chin upward toward the executive suite.

"More like standing guard over her blest abode, though I'm not sure Carlton Amis is an angel." She paused for a moment. "Some women want to be something, and some women just want to be Mrs. Something. You know what I mean. Oh, look, there's my poor angel skulking around like he's going to be nabbed for stealing the silver. He's afraid someone sneaked in a camcorder. You should have heard him say 'I stand for judgment: answer; shall I have it?' when he was Shylock. That's when I knew he was born for the law. I don't think he's figured out yet that justice is a lost cause. What on earth was I saying? Oh, the woman behind the man. I'm the woman my man hides behind. Excuse me?''

Cat nodded.

She continued to drift, circled the aperture until she came back to the ceiling-high divider, took a furtive glance over her shoulder and stepped behind the curtains, walked to the Phoenix Pavilion Ballroom and slipped inside.

She allowed her eyes to adjust to the semi-darkness, studied the tables arranged in clusters around the dance floor, saw a couple Santas fussing with the centerpieces, which were sculptures, some two-feet high, that were available for purchase.

Cat dug into her purse, checked her invitation stub. She was to be seated at table thirty-three. She took one of the programs lying on a dinner plate, bypassed the list of Phoenix Sponsors and Emerald Sponsors and Gold Sponsors to the list of artwork, saw TABLE 33: GODDESS OF THE MOON CONTEMPLATING HER ORBS: POLYHYDROSTONE, $4,500. *This I have to see,* Cat told herself and made her way to table thirty-three, confronted two feet of female voluptuousness. Cat tried to decide if she would prefer to be seated fore or aft, port or starboard; she was going to have a hard time managing her scallops of veal with hazelnut sauce and violets with any dignity while in the shadow of the Moon Goddess's prodigious orbs.

She heard a soft sound, an exhalation, a whisper of costly fabric emerging from one of the half-curtained recesses where dumbwaiters were located. Cat froze; she saw part of a black trouser leg, saw a slim, silken calf extend past it, saw a pant leg caressed by the heel of a green pump.

Cat smothered a gulp, slipped out of the room and hurried down the wide, dim corridor, holding her skirts shin high. She stopped at the divider, inhaled one-Mississippi, two-Mississippi, three-Mississippi and rejoined the reception where the cocktail hour was winding down.

"Mrs. Austen!"

Cat jumped. Cookie Amis stood at her shoulder. "Checking out the arrangements?"

"I, uh, wanted to get a look at the dining room, the place settings, before everyone began milling around."

"You didn't happen to see Carl, did you?"

"Mr. Amis? Not at all." *Only in part.*

Cookie frowned; the cobalt eyes had a fiery cast. "The paper wants a shot of the four of us with the mayor. First Fawn runs off, then Carl—" She scrutinized Cat. "Did you see her?"

"Well, a little while ago, I saw her talking to some guy with a blond ponytail." *Which wasn't a lie.*

"Oh. Back Office Donnie. I haven't seen him, either." Her expression relaxed a little.

"Well, it's not hard to get lost in this place," Cat commented, drawing away from Cookie. *Or to get in trouble, either.* She backed away, slipped into the recessed doorway of Bon Soie, drew out her notebook and began to write, covertly.

"Recording your impressions?"

Cat whirled, saw Carlton Amis at her elbow; he positioned himself at the entrance, cornering her in the small niche.

"Yes." She slipped the notebook into her bag.

"I've made a point of reading some of your work, Mrs. Austen. Quite…spirited. But with a certain detachment. The work of someone who doesn't reveal herself often."

"I thought attorneys appreciated discretion, Mr. Amis."

He shook his head. "What am I going to have to do to get you to call me Carl?"

Cat smiled, shrugged lamely.

"Maybe I can help. I've always been curious about the writing process. Would you like to see a program? Have you gotten a list of the door prizes?"

"Actually, I just treated myself to a peek at the dining room."

"Really? Just now?"

Cat felt the ripple of discomfort pass between them. *Gotcha*, she thought, wondered if she could maneuver past him without having to push him aside. "You know, maybe there is something you could do to help me."

"Anything."

"You could tell me about Allan Pritchard."

Amis' smile constricted, the petulant lips pursed in a mean little crescent. "A lawyer-client relationship that concluded long ago. I don't know what's become of him."

"I'm surprised he didn't make more of an impression. I mean, you were the only attorney who succeeded in getting him off the hook."

"Not for long."

"Then you did follow up on him."

Amis took a step nearer, his palm hovering above her bare shoulder as if to prevent her from fleeing. "You know, Mrs. Austen, a woman of your talents shouldn't be working for an insignificant publication like *South Jersey*." The hand settled on her shoulder. "I could do things for your career it would take you years to do for yourself."

Cat felt a ripple of revulsion. Long ago, she might have been cowed, or lured by this combination of power and seductiveness, but not now. She swatted his hand away, impatiently, tried to shove past him. Amis grasped her upper arms. "Who knows why Pritchard came to Atlantic City?" he hissed, leaning close. "This place attracts lowlifes. Who cares? He's gone." The grip tightened. "You get too nosy—"

Cat knuckled his sternum, driving a mother of pearl stud

into his breastbone. Amis started with the sudden pain, released his grip.

"Don't put your hands on me," Cat said, silently thanking Marco for teaching her the simple, yet effective maneuver. "And I would suggest that you get that lipstick off your collar before you meet up with your wife, Mr. Amis. I don't believe it's her shade."

Amis' eyes flickered for a moment, then he shrugged as if she were not worth his time, sauntered off.

Cat looked at her bare arms in the shop window's dim light. There were small reddening fingerprints on her flesh. As she stood rubbing at them, she heard a surge of voices, a current of indignation and a conflicting vocal tide that had the rhythm of a chant. Cat emerged from the recess and moved toward the guests collecting at the railing, pushing aside the green-and-gold streamers, peering down at the gaming floor below. Cat wedged between two men, saw a crowd had gathered below the mezzanine, Marlon d'Esperance at the epicenter, one corpulent arm circling a young woman. He was leading his followers in a chant, something about cornrows and racism and the Phoenix; Cat strained to hear what they were saying, was winnowed out by people pushing up to the railing. She stumbled and nearly fell on a patch of slick soapflake snow; a man turned to help her and then she heard the shriek, the timbre and tone striking a familiar chord. Cat was steadied in time to see a billow of green chiffon, a golden blur at the shoulder, falling into open space, plummeting to the floor like a falling phoenix.

It didn't rise. Cat stood transfixed as the cries of panic settled into a horrified silence. She was trying to push herself toward the railing when a wave of motion caught her eye. A slender man in a midnight-blue tuxedo—Donnie—leapt onto the railing, yanked a handful of the ribbons free and swung into space, the immense chandelier swaying under his weight, the crystal carillon showering over the chaos as he dropped to the floor.

The chandelier had snatched the smooth ponytail from his

head and Cat heard a voice scream "Danny!" Realized it was her own.

Danny knelt beside Fawn; the crowd parted and Cat could see that the reverend had broken the fall, lay silent and motionless beneath Fawn, her blond mane splayed across his massive breast, her white face in the crook of his shoulder.

This distinctly coital aspect of the tableau was not lost on one member of the crowd and Cat could hear, from somewhere on her right, Ritchie Landis bray "Jesus! Somebody get me a camera!"

TWENTY-TWO

RITCHIE'S CRY shook Cat out of her horror, shocked her brain into focus. A tidal wave of green jackets swept over the casino floor, a quartet blocked off the escalators to prevent the partygoers from rushing into—or fleeing—the chaos. Below, gamblers and gawkers were driven off by the DGE cops who rushed down from the fifth floor. Sterling, three-deep in bodyguards, was escorted to Fawn's side; the Amises and Raab were allowed to follow, everyone else was detained in the mezzanine.

Danny. His cover blown, he had fled the first wave of security, leapt onto a slot machine and bounded across the floor on top of them, disappeared in the vicinity of the Boardwalk exit.

Cat leaned against the railing, the green-and-gold streamers torn loose, dangling listlessly from the chandelier. The sea of security parted for the paramedics. Cat leaned forward, the crush of the crowd behind her shoving her against the railing. She felt the cold metal bar press against her hip bones through the thin fabric of her gown; the sensation triggered a thought and she looked at the rail gripped in her hands. She leaned forward a bit. Possible to fall off balance, especially with all this slippery stuff on the floor. Possible...but Fawn was shorter than she, the railing would have caught her at the waist. Fawn would have needed to boost herself up to be thrown off balance...or simply *be* thrown off balance. Cat probed her short-term memory, tried to recall who had been leaning at the rail, looking down at d'Esperance and his people. Everyone. And everyone had been distracted by the demonstration. How would one determine, from all of the pushing and shoving that had occurred, which swift, deliberate shove had sent Fawn over the side?

"Ma'am?" A green jacket was at her shoulder. Cat observed that the crowd had thinned out, was filing toward the ballrooms, shepherded by Sterling security and uniformed police.

"Yes?"

"The police are moving everyone into the ballroom."

"Police..." Cat echoed. She wondered whether any of her brothers were on duty.

"Yes, ma'am."

Cat began to move, looked around for Ritchie, his parents, the Raabs, saw none of them. No, Fawn hadn't been pushed. It had just been a horrible accident. And if Fawn and d'Esperance had been taken to the med center, that meant they hadn't died, and if it was an accident and they hadn't died, there would be no need to call in Major Crimes. Would there?

THERE WOULD. Amis and Sterling had been allowed to go to the hospital. Mrs. Amis remained behind, arranged for a divider to be set up in the ballroom in order to screen off an interrogation post for the detectives. She ordered sandwiches and coffee, had the waiters set up the dessert buffet, and enlisted security people to personally escort each guest to hotel room or car after questioning. Cat watched it all, undeceived. Mrs. Amis remained on the scene to observe the interrogation first hand and provided the escort so that the departing guests would be sequestered from the media, already circling.

Cat sat at a table with Ritchie's parents, who apologized profusely, as though they were personally responsible for her inconvenience. Ritchie himself had been the first one brought in for questioning, the first ushered out, and Cat realized she might have to arrange for her own ride home.

She felt a tap on her shoulder, looked up at a uniformed officer. "Mrs. Austen, they'll see you next." The man was mindful of the fact that she was a Fortunati.

Cat was escorted behind the screens; several tables had been arranged in a row, a collection of uniformed and plainclothes cops took statements; a handful of green jackets discreetly eavesdropped on the Q and A.

A woman in a voluminous gown rose; she drew away to reveal Victor standing next to a young woman—the one called Adane—who was writing something in her notebook. He lifted his eyes briefly; his expression was composed; only the interval that his eyes held hers, a moment too long, a shade too intensely, indicated that she would be lucky to get off with a tête-à-tête over cappucino.

The uniform deposited her at a table where Stan Rice stood scanning something on a clipboard. He looked down at Cat. "Honey, you okay?"

Cat shrugged. "I heard you were confined to quarters."

"I'm on a damn short leash as it is." He leaned down. "I woulda given a week's pay to see the Rev go splat. That's off the record."

"Noted. Actually, there wasn't much in the way of a splat. It was more like"—she swept her hands together—"whooof!"

"Well, these folks sure know how to throw a party."

"Oh, this is nothing. At Carlo and Annie's wedding, he and Marco and my great Uncle Condoloro from Messina spray-painted their posteriors a vivacious shade of indigo, dropped their drawers and sang 'Blue Moon' in Italian."

"Get out."

Cat smiled, gravely. "I have Polaroids. Of course, we stop short of tossing the hosts from the balconies."

"Tossin', huh? You sayin' someone helped her over the side?" His pen clicked; the faint sound signaled the transition from friend to cop.

"Well, there was this commotion below. Everyone ran to the rail, there was a lot of pushing and shoving, but .. "

"But?"

"Well, if the rail hits at your center of balance"—Cat tapped Stan's belt buckle lightly with her fingertips—"I suppose it would be possible to lose one's footing and tip over in all that crush."

"But a woman the size of Mrs. Sterling—she's small, I met her once—woman that size would have to be hoisted up. What's she weigh, you think? A hundred, maybe?"

Cat nodded.

"Clumsy way to put the Rev outta commission."

"But a very effective way of putting Fawn out of commission," Cat shot back.

"In front of a couple hundred people? Not smart."

"No? Well, you tell me how smart it is tomorrow when you look over several hundred statements and come up with a couple thousand versions of who was where and who saw what."

She saw Victor materialize at Stan's elbow, felt a flush rising from the décolleté to her cheeks.

"Thank you, Sergeant," Victor said, calmly.

"Hey, you want me to shove off, just say so."

Victor looked at him.

"Bon voyage." Stan shrugged, wandered over to Phil Long, who was interviewing two Santa Claus waiters.

"You look like Artemis in that dress."

Cat thought for a moment. "Goddess of the moon."

"I thought the goddess of the moon was going to stay in this weekend."

"All *day,*" she reminded him.

"Ah."

"Technicalities. I hear Major Crimes lives and breathes them."

He pulled a chair away from the table, his glance took in the sweep of silver, the wisp of hair that had come unpinned, curled under her chin, settled on the red marks on her upper arms. The line of his mouth hardened. "What happened there?"

"Nothing. It's nothing."

He sat, ran his fingers lightly over the marks. Cat didn't like his expression, leapt on the only subject she could think of that might divert him. "Danny. You know that he was here tonight?"

"Furina?"

"He was the back office boy. Donnie. His ponytail's probably still hooked on the chandelier."

Victor turned, strode over to a pair of uniforms and his unit, huddled with them for a brief, urgent conference, came back to Cat.

"He jumped over the balcony to get to her?"

Cat nodded. "And when the guards went after him, he ran out. They have to have some tape on it in Security, but it won't be much help." She thought for a minute. "You know, if Fawn told you she hadn't heard from Danny after she fired him, she was lying. And why lie, why keep him around? Not because she was in fear for her life. I mean if that was the case, I wouldn't depend on some flaky PI, I'd tell everyone around that there was someone out there trying to get rid of me."

"Well, there's an old saying that you should keep your friends close and your enemies closer." Victor drew something out of his breast pocket. "Have a look at this. Adane put together a file on the Sterlings the day after the body was discovered. Press coverage, photos, the book." He unfolded a piece of newspaper, laid it on the table in front of Cat. "This the same picture Falcone sent Furina?"

Cat saw the photo of the Sterlings, their entourage. BLAINE STERLING PAUSES FOR AUTOGRAPH FOLLOWING CAPRIOH!'S RUNWAY TRIUMPH. "That's it. Danny's friend said Pritchard was giving Sterling his résumé."

"By showing Sterling how easy it was to get close to Fawn?"

"Doesn't it strike you as being odd?"

"That Pritchard would take such a risk, you mean?"

Cat shook her head. "No. I suspect he would get a kick out of the risk. I meant it's odd that this is the only time he *did* manage to get close to her."

"While they were both breathing," Victor added, grimly.

TWENTY-THREE

CAT SURFACED from a mound of bedclothes, pushed her hair away from her face, squinted at the digital glow on the alarm clock: 11:50!

She rolled onto her back, inhaled the beginnings of tonight's dinner; rich tomato and pungent basil, sweet spices, garlic, honey, all mingled together, drifting up on a current of hushed female conversation. *I have to pull myself together, Cat told herself. It's Christmas Eve and—*

Mats burst into the room. "Mom, there's snakes in the refrigerator!" he screamed and threw himself on the bed.

Cat pulled him under the covers, pressed her hand to his forehead, examined the fading rash on his pale face and neck. "They're not snakes, sweetie, they're eels. Smoked eels. For dinner."

"They're yuck. They still got their eyes on."

"Mommy won't make you eat them, but don't tell Nonna her food's yuck, it'll hurt her feelings."

There was a light rap on the door and Ellice poked her head in, followed by Jane. Cat shifted, pulled herself into a sitting position, leaned against the headboard.

Ellice put a mug of coffee on Cat's night table, handed her a copy of the morning paper. FREAK FALL CANCELS GAMBOL; and in smaller type FAWN STERLING, MARLON D'ESPERANCE SERIOUSLY INJURED IN MISHAP. Mishap, Cat thought grimly as she ran her eyes over the story. Several witnesses placed the blame on d'Esperance's demonstration, which, it was disclosed, had resulted from the contested dismissal of a Phoenix employee. A sentence referred

to the police investigation, called it "routine," and that there
was no implication that the event was anything other than a
bizarre accident.

Ellice circled the bed, plugged in Cat's phone. "I took this
out so you could get some sleep. It's been ringing all morning.
I just got back from having my hair done." The sides were
rolled over her ears, fine curls threaded over her brow.

"I like it. Who's downstairs?"

"Annie, Nancy, Lorraine, Sherrie, some of the kids. Your
mom went to pick up the bread. Carlo came by, but they
chased him out."

"Did Victor call?"

"Not while I've been here. But Ritchie Landis has been
calling every half hour. Honey, if I knew that's what you
meant by the Party of the Year, I woulda kicked in the five
hundred." She paused. "Paper says she's still unconscious."

Cat nodded. "It was awful. Horrible. Freddy call?"

"No."

"Ellice—" Cat glanced toward Jane, who had picked the
silver gown off the floor, was holding it up to her chest, pos-
turing in front of her mother's mirror.

"Hey, it's okay. Oh, and get this. The woman who does
my hair said she did a gal a couple days ago, cornrows. The
girl goes back to work, works at the Phoenix, they tell her the
hair's some kind of violation of the dress code. She got suspended and went to d'Esperance."

"That's what the demonstration was about last night?"

"Uh-huh. Her name's Davis. Lanna—no, Liona. Oh, and
some woman's been calling for you, someone named Earlene."

"Earlene Adkins?"

Ellice shrugged. "I didn't pick up. Come down and get
some breakfast."

"Are they all fasting down there?"

"'Til sunset." Ellice glanced toward Jane, lowered her
voice. "Lorraine's going nuts around all that food. C'mon,
we'll make hoagies, it'll be fun."

"Ellice, that would be an absolutely bitchy thing to do. Give me ten minutes to make a call and get a shower."

Ellice shooed the kids out; Mats lagged at the door, asked his mother, "Do those snakes ever come alive?"

"Of course not."

"What if they did?"

Cat's eyes narrowed balefully. "If those snakes even think about coming alive and hurting my Mats, you just give a yell and I'll run downstairs as fast as a, a…"

"Fire engine!"

"…fire engine and I'll whack those snakes so hard they'll be as flat as, as…"

"'Tato chips!"

Cat grinned. "Four years old and already he has a way with a simile. That's my boy."

When they left her alone, Cat picked up the phone, dialed the medical center, tried to get a report on Fawn's condition, was diverted to the public relations administrator and stonewalled. She redialed and paged Jackie Wing.

Jackie's voice was hushed, breathless. "Honest to God, she went flying from the rafters?"

"Yes. She's in a private room, I guess."

"Suite. I tried to get assigned, but Sterling hand-picked his own rotation of nurses, plus security, plus there's some guy from the sheriff's office sitting outside the room. Sterling's been there all night, him and his lawyer, and the lawyer's wife came by early this morning."

"Fawn conscious?"

"Nope, stable, but she hasn't come to."

"What about d'Esperance?"

Jackie snorted. "You believe this guy? He comes to long enough to have me kicked off his rotation, says he'll only have minority nurses, thank you very much. I'm a Chinese Jew for crying out loud, how much more of a minority can you get?"

"I don't suppose I could be smuggled up to VIP?"

"No way, don't even try. Haven't you got enough to do, with dinner and all?"

"As usual, the Fortunatis invaded and took over. You and Robbie are coming, aren't you?"

"Yeah, I get off at three. It's real nice of you to have us over; I don't get to party with my son very often. Dwight's picking him up at eight Christmas morning, so I agreed to work. Frees up someone with family," she added, without a trace of self-pity. "Should I bring anything?"

"A sense of humor always helps." Cat hung up and dialed Jim's, asked for Earlene Adkins.

"She won't be in 'til four," said a pert female voice.

"Is she at home, do you know?"

"Beats me. Earlene's been weirded-out past couple days. I think she said she was goin' over Ocean City."

Not coming here! "Did she say why?"

"Nope. Come down for coffee and she's readin' the paper an' all of a sudden, she's outta here. Look, I gotta get back to work." She hung up.

Cat closed her eyes, saw the emerald and gold streak of Fawn's gown as she plummeted to the floor. Could it have been a freak accident? Or could someone have pushed her? But no one could have anticipated the Reverend's demonstration. It would have taken a fearless, or desperate, person to take advantage of such a diversion. Cat remembered something Victor had said about the Dudek shooting, that Jerry's murderer, spotting him isolated, had been able to take advantage of the opportunity and get away clean. How Detective Adane had called it a formidable combination of desperation and presence of mind. Cat thought about the Dudek business and its wretched conclusion and shuddered. Victor was right. She couldn't risk herself like that again. Cat tossed the paper under the bed and headed for the shower.

THE FORTUNATIS called it *La Vigil,* but there were as many names for the elaborate Christmas Eve meal as there were types of fish to be served. Little had yielded or varied from Cat's first Christmas; a day-long fast began at sunset on the twenty-third, the following day was given over to the preparation of food and the eating began at sunset Christmas Eve, often continuing until the family rose from the table to take themselves to midnight Mass.

Cat excused herself from both the fasting and the Mass. Chris' murder had shaken her faith in religion, her comfort in ritual, but she continued to participate in the dinner for the sake of the children, who needed some tradition to hold onto. Hosting holiday dinners was assigned according to rotation; Cat's turn had come up the Christmas after Chris's death. Sherrie had stepped in and taken over the burden, and now, with Sherrie seven months pregnant, Cat offered to reciprocate.

After the food was arranged, the women departed and Cat gave Mats his bath, checked his closets for resurrected snakes and put him down for a nap. Ellice took Jane into her room to French braid her hair and Cat settled into a tub of peach-scented bubbles. The aromas from the kitchen evoked memories of sweeter Christmases; Cat pondered whether it would ever return, that sense of wonder the season had once produced. She closed her eyes and actually drifted off for a few minutes, woke and took a cool shower, dressed in a clingy red jersey, put her hair up.

What the heck, just so it wouldn't be on her mind all through dinner, she tried Jim's again, this time got a gruff "Jim's!" from the proprietor himself. Cat asked for Earlene and was told, "She ain't come in yet, you wanna leave a message, or what?"

Cat hesitated. "My name is Mrs. Austen. I called earlier and was told she'd be in at four."

"Shoulda been. Gimme your number."

The doorbell rang. Cat hastily recited her number and set the matter aside as she ran to admit Joey, Sherrie and Meryl. Sherrie and Meryl were dressed in mother-and-daughter velvet jumpers, Sherrie's loose in the body, high in the hem. Vinnie and Lorraine came next with their three sons. Lorraine, in black knit, glared at Sherrie's short skirt while Vinnie demanded, "What the hell were you doing at the Phoenix last night, how the hell'd you get invited to that shindig?"

Then Dominic and Kevin Keller and Kevin's older sister

Margaret Mary, who was Sister Margaret Mary. Steve Delareto, Jackie Wing and Robbie, Carlo and Annie, alerting everyone that they were expecting phone calls from their son who was in the Air Force, their daughter who was spending the holidays in a Caribbean medical mission. Ellice descended, wearing a white wool knit and a troubled expression, for Freddy had not yet arrived.

Marco and Nancy with Marco, Jr., and Andrea, and the Misses Nixon from across the street. The ladies, daughters of one of the town's first police chiefs, were well-regarded in the law enforcement community; Marco had invited them to lecture on firearms maintenance at the Academy, and Cat still had one or two of the casseroles in her freezer that the ladies supplied daily when Cat was in the hospital. They had adored Chris.

Soon the room filled with overlapping conversations, greetings, laughter. The children poked at the presents under the tree, shook a few judiciously, while the adults inhaled the aromas from the kitchen, impatient to break their fast. Jennie presided over the stove, more than once chasing Carlo back into the living room, chiding him for complaining because Annie made him fast "Like one of the women!" he exploded, though everyone laughed and then laughed harder when Annie told Atlantic City's former chief of police not to be such a crybaby.

The phone and doorbell rang simultaneously, and Cat ran for the door, hoping it was Freddy. Victor entered, handing her a sheaf of red and white carnations, followed her into the hall. "What's wrong?"

"Nothing. Freddy's late. Where's Stan? You didn't make him work late, did you?"

"No."

"Hi, again." Jackie Wing wore a red satin blouse, snug black slacks. "You said you had someone for me, but all that Steve wants to talk about is you and the guy who came with Dominic, Kevin? Too, too serious."

Cat smiled. "He's coming."

"Matchmaking?" Victor whispered in her ear. "Can't you keep from meddling?"

Cat tossed her head and took the flowers into the kitchen, collided with Ellice, who was emerging with a tense expression. "What's the matter?"

"It was a guy named Majeske on the phone. The one who partnered with Freddy."

"Is Freddy okay?"

"Yeah. I mean, he isn't hurt or anything, but Majeske got a message that Freddy was running over to the hospital, and he asked someone to call here and say he'd be late for dinner."

"Which hospital?"

Ellice looked sadly resigned. "Cat, I don't need a blueprint. He was engaged to her, she needs someone right now—"

"Ellice, it's not like that!"

Ellice shook her head. "Look, I'm not gonna make a scene. I mean, I was the damsel in distress, too, when we met, some guys, that's what—"

"Ellice, this is my brother we're talking about—"

"Cat, we're ready to start serving," Nancy called from the kitchen.

"All right! Freddy is in love with you, Ellice. I know him. And I know there's a sensible reason he isn't here yet, and I know it has nothing to do with Fawn Sterling."

The doorbell rang. Ellice tensed, and Cat realized, with that one spasm, how much Ellice cared for Freddy. *If he's gone to see Fawn Sterling,* Cat told herself, *I'll kill him.* She wedged through the crush of nieces and nephews assembling at their card tables in the center hall, saw a red-garbed figure through the glass at the front entrance, standing on her doorstep. She yanked the door open and saw Santa on the threshold, two large, red-wrapped boxes at his feet.

"Ho, ho, ho," he panted.

"Stan?" Cat mouthed, staring.

"I got a present for a Cat Austen," Santa announced.

Carlo loomed up behind Cat. "I forgot about you, where you been?" he grumbled and tugged the boxes into the foyer.

Mats peeked around his mother's skirts. "Where's your reindeer?"

"Dinner break. You know the unions. Santa had to borrow that Camaro over there."

"You're not as big as I thought."

"Yeah, that's what Mrs. Claus tells me."

Cat heard Nancy's whoop of laughter, looked over her shoulder, made eye contact with Jackie and nodded toward Stan. Jackie came up beside Cat, looked him over. "So, you really a saint, Nick, or you like to party?"

"Just lemme get outta my gay apparel here so's no one gets the wrong idea. Hey, Lieutenant Cardenas over there? Guys, let Santa talk to the lieutenant for a minute, okay? And, you know, Merry Christmas and all that stuff."

Victor stepped onto the porch, pulled the door closed.

"Look, Long dropped in Jim's, the kid Adkins borrowed a friend's car, took off, hasn't come back."

"Call in the plates."

"Weird the way folks keep disappearing. Furina, we haven't turned him up yet, either. I'm gonna get outta these threads, be right in."

When Victor went inside, Cat was kneeling at the boxes, a mound of crumpled red foil surrounding her. He saw the top of a computer monitor protruding from a wad of Styrofoam popcorn. "It's got one of those modem things built in," Carlo was explaining. "And we sorta figured if you're gonna take the writing stuff seriously—Cat, don't cry—you're gonna need the whole setup, you can't make it with just a typewriter—Cat, don't cry—it was Freddy's idea, where the fu—where is he, the dumb— Mats, go get Mommy some Kleenex."

"I thought we were just doin' the pollyanna," Lorraine declared, looking as if she were calculating the cost of a home computer, dividing it by six.

"Which is not to say you got a green light to go turn up every stiff in the Delaware Valley," Vinnie added, told Cat his boys could help her get it hooked up because "all these damn kids do today is spend all their damn time in front of the damn computer."

Mats handed Cat a wad of Kleenex.

"Well, we gotta eat, or it's gonna get cold," Jennie declared. "Freddy, he can go hungry."

Victor saw the trace of concern in her dark eyes, knew that she was probably thinking about Chris, who had been late for dinner two and a half years before, and never came home. He followed her into the kitchen, spoke to her reassuringly, insisted on helping her buss plates into the dining room, was told, "You're company, you go sit down."

Stan popped in, neatly dressed in a three-piece suit, hung back a minute murmuring something to Jackie Wing while the others began a slow migration to the table. The kids stood around the table while Dominic said a blessing, then retreated to card tables in the hall, while Annie and Nancy took the first shift, bussed in soup plates, Nancy laughing, "Sit *down*, for heaven's sake, Victor. You're gonna drive us nuts standing like that!"

Annie slid a bowl in front of Victor. He looked down, critically, bent over Cat's chair (he could not bring himself to sit until all the ladies had taken their seats), said "Forgive me, but if biology serves, those appear to be gastropods."

Cat felt a shudder of desperate laughter. "*Lumache umido.* It's traditional."

"Are those really—"

"I'm *not eating snails!*" Jane declared from the hall.

Cat heard Ellice, on her left, mutter "Just when you think it can't get worse, the damn Sicilians are feeding you slugs." She felt the shudder rise to the surface; all the tension and chaos of the past few days emerged in peal after peal of hysterical laughter. After a moment, Ellice joined in; the two of them sat, their heads on each other's shoulders, shaking with uncontrolled mirth, tears soaking the red jersey and white wool.

"What the hell's the matter with you?" Vinnie demanded.

"They need to eat something," Carlo suggested. "They been drinking, or what?"

There was a knock on the door and a muffled, "Hey, lemme in!"

Cat lifted her head. "It's Freddy."

Ellice straightened her back, composed herself while Jane ran to the door. "We thought you weren't coming."

Freddy hurried into the dining room, out of breath. His hair was disheveled, his uniform crumpled, the tie pulled loose. "I'm sorry," he gasped. "I'm sorry, I got here as fast as I could."

"How's Mrs. Sterling doing?" Ellice asked, coolly.

"What? How should I know?"

"They called and told us you went to the hospital, Freddy," Cat said.

"And you guys thought I went to—" Freddy looked around the table, his eyes settling on Ellice. "Ellice, jeez, Ellice." He dropped into the empty chair beside her. "Ellice, I'm so sick of this tiptoin' around, waitin' for the right time. Let's just get married, okay?"

Lorraine's mouth opened, shut. The silence became strained.

"Where were you, Freddy?" Ellice asked.

"I was lookin' for a Big Mac."

"You stopped off for a Big Mac?"

Freddy laughed, wearily. "Here's the thing. I got twenty minutes left on my watch, I'm gonna pick up the ring, go change and come right over here. Then this guy hijacks a truck. BugsAway Exterminators. Giant cockroach painted on the side, givin' the Q sign. Hijacks it in Philly. He's on the Expressway, headin' into AC, he's gonna run up the ocean-front mall and jump."

"They have malls in Philadelphia."

"He's from AC, he's feelin' sentimental, wants to off himself down here. So I get the call. I pull up beside him, he's got a thirty-eight to his neck, one hand on the wheel. No hostages. So we got a two-man unit tailin' him, I'm ridin' shotgun, I got the window rolled down, I get him to roll down his window, he says he wants to die. What is it about Christmas? Anyway, I'm doin' all that 'Whaddaya wanna do that for? How 'bout I call your family? How 'bout we pull over an' have a chat' stuff, he says he don't wanna talk to anyone, I say what does he want, he says he wants a couple Big Macs and a shake, maybe some fries. So I say, fine, they got rest stops all along the way, all he's gotta do is pull over, it's my treat. So we call ahead to clear the place, he pulls over, still got the gun to his head.''

"Expressway, they got your Whopper, they don't got the Big Mac," Carlo informed him.

"I know!" Freddy cried. "And he wants the Mac. I tell him, what's wrong with your Whopper, you got your burgers, you got your lettuce, you got your sauce, but no, he wants the Mac, so off we go, all the way into AC until we find us some golden arches. Only—"

"It's Christmas Eve and they're all closed," Ellice concluded. There was a spark of amusement in her gaze; tenderness, too.

"Me, I like the Whopper," Carlo muttered, his hunger preoccupying him. "But that new deluxe over McDonald's, that's good, too."

"They're all closed," Freddy echoed Ellice's words. "So there we are sitting in the lot, four cop cars, guy in the bug truck, the gun right here"—Freddy poked his carotid—"I'm freezin' my keester, tryin' to talk some sense into the guy, maybe he'll settle for a hoagie from Wawa, no dice, so Joe Bogashefsky calls up the district manager and the guy comes over from a Christmas party at the Elks, he's got this reindeer rig on, he's late 'cause he got pulled over for speedin' and hadda explain the antlers, but he makes it and we fire up the grill, whip up a shake, the fries, they took a little time, but we get it together and the guy scarfs down the goodies, got the gun to his throat the whole time, last bite, he hands over the thirty-eight like nothing happened, commander decides the guy's gotta go over the med center for observation so the guy asks him will I go with him, on accountta by this time, we're pals, so I hang out 'til he gets checked in and sedated. And the thing is, talking to him, he's just your average Joe, nice guy who had a fight with his girl and flipped out. And as soon as they got him checked in, I run over pick up the ring and come straight here, I swear to God." He fumbled in his pants pocket for a small box, opened it. The ring was a small, simple marquise set in plain gold. "I can't wait for the right time, you're never gonna get a minute's peace in this family and that's no lie."

No one said a word. Carlo's fingers crept toward the bread basket; Annie slapped his hand.

Ellice took the ring. "Cat said there was sensible reason for your being late," she said as she slipped it on her finger. "And of course, I wouldn't want you to flip out and hijack someone's bug truck."

"Oh, don't get married until after the baby comes," Sherrie pleaded. "That way, I'll have my figure back and I can wear the green suit. You know, the one with the black piping on the lapels. Just that little bit of black wouldn't be bad luck, would it?"

"Well, I for one think this is great," Joey said. He was Freddy's immediate senior, closer to him than the others.

"You mean that?"

"Hell, yeah. It'll take some of the heat off me and Sherrie for not gettin' married in the church."

"You mean," Ellice inquired, "marrying out of the church is a lesser offense than marrying out of your race?"

"*Will* you marry in the church?" Kevin asked with such earnestness that Cat began to giggle.

"Actually," Ellice laid her hand over Freddy's, "I was thinking we'd ask the Reverend Marlon d'Esperance to perform the ceremony. I'll make all the arrangements and Freddy can show up the day of the wedding."

Stan laughed aloud. "You do that, I'm givin' away the bride."

"I'll take the pictures," Nancy volunteered, giggling.

"We were never so fortunate as to marry," said one of the Nixon ladies. "But our second cousin, Elinor, married a southern gentleman"—the latter a euphemism for black—"and it will be fifty years next June. Of course, he wasn't anything like that d'Esperance character. He had manners."

"Mama, let me bring out some pasta for the kids to start on. I want to propose a toast. To Freddy and Ellice—"

The phone rang. Victor had been contemplating the soup plate in front of him, felt a profound gratitude when Jane called from the kitchen, "Victor! It's for you!"

Victor excused himself, picked up in the kitchen. It was Adane. "Haven't you gone home yet?" he asked, wondered suddenly if she had somewhere to spend the holiday.

"I was just leaving, sir, when I got a call from an officer in Ocean City. It could be a minor incident, but considering the parties involved, I thought you would want to be informed."

"Where will you spend Christmas, Adane?"

"I'll be having dinner with my family, sir."

"Parents?" He was amazed at how little he knew about her.

"And my sisters. They're both younger."

"They cops, too?"

"Oh no, they're perfectly normal."

He smiled briefly, though she had been quite serious. "What's the problem?"

"Well, it seems a woman went over to the Amis house this evening and caused a disturbance. The police were called in. There will be a summons for disturbing the peace, most likely, but they don't want to hold her. She wasn't under the influence and she wasn't armed or violent."

"Was it that woman the Phoenix dismissed? Davis?"

"No, sir, it was Miss Adkins. Earlene Adkins, the waitress who was associated with Mr. Pritchard? I thought you might want to go over to the department and check it out for yourself before she has someone come pick her up."

CAT'S BROTHERS nodded in silent, coplike understanding when Victor announced that he would have to leave. He congratulated Freddy and Ellice, politely declined Jennie's offer to "wrap up some of the stew, you can warm it up at home," assured Stan that he was not needed. Cat walked him to the door. "Is it Fawn?" she inquired as they stood in the tiny foyer.

"No."

"But it's something to do with the case. Is it Danny? Have they found him?"

"It isn't Furina. Go back to your company. If I don't make it back tonight, I'll come by early tomorrow. I have something for you."

Cat felt dismay jab her diaphragm. She hadn't gotten anything for him. Then stubbornness eclipsed guilt. If he didn't trust her with whatever was calling him away, he didn't deserve a present.

When two hours passed and Victor had neither called nor returned, Cat considered coaxing Stan into finding out what had taken his boss away; but Stan was engaged in a serious flirtation with Jackie Wing, and Cat was soon preoccupied in serving the remainder of the seven courses, bussing coffee, promising the children they could have their pollyanna before dessert.

In the kitchen, assembling the cookie trays she had prepared to give her guests, Cat grabbed for the phone on the first ring.

"What the hell is going on, lady?"

Cat recognized Earlene Adkins' voice. "What?"

"I see the blond's picture in the paper this morning. She took a header at that fancy party over the Phoenix. *She's* the one who's Sterling's wife?"

"Yes," Cat said, baffled. It wasn't as if Fawn hadn't made enough magazine covers, but then again, Earlene had probably never heard of *WWD* or *Fortune,* and most likely picked up a newspaper only to check the winning lottery number.

"I thought the blond one was this Amis broad. I told you, in that picture with Al and that Sterling guy was the same woman was makin' it with Al an' you said it was Mrs. Amis."

"I thought you meant the woman standing next to Sterling," Cat replied. "*That* was Mrs. Amis. The blond getting into the car was Mrs. Sterling."

"So now she tells me. Don't make any difference though, 'cause I go over the Amis place—"

"You went to the Amises' house?"

"Yeah."

Cat gulped. "When?"

"Couple hours ago. An' that tall broad comes to the door, says *she's* Mrs. Amis, it hits me where I seen her before. She's the one drivin' the Merc, drove over to hook up with Al down Margate. I hand her that picture you gimme—"

"You showed her the photograph I gave you?"

"Yeah. An' I tell her she might have the cops thinkin' she did Al in self-defense, but I know she knocked him off. I bet Al was gonna go to her rich husband, tell him she was makin' it with an ex-con unless she came across with some cash, she whacks him 'cause she don't wanna pay. Well, she'll pay, all right."

Cat swallowed. Earlene saw Mrs. Amis drive up to Fawn's house the day of the attack and misinterpreted it. But why was she saying *Fawn* was "making it" with Al? "What makes you think Mrs. Sterling and Al were, you know…"

"'Cause I seen her leave his place. Even if I didn't see her close up, how many women you know can afford a coat like that? It was the real thing, 'cause Maritita's cousin fenced a couple dozen came offa shipment up JFK, was gonna gimme a deal on one, but can you see me wearin' a chinchilla? Calls the cops on me," Earlene grumbled.

"*Who* called the cops on you?"

"The Amis broad! Jee*zoo*, lady, can't you get anything straight?"

"When did Mrs. Amis call the cops on you?"

"Tonight. When I went to her place. Well, I'll give her a day or two to think it over, then I'll be goin' to the cops, tell them how she killed Al to keep him from tellin' her man she's gettin' some on the side. She doesn't know who she's dealin' with."

Cat peeked into the dining room. No one seemed to be monitoring her conversation. Annie was saying something to Ellice, smiling; maybe they wouldn't give Freddy a hard time, maybe…she saw Lorraine frowning, Vinnie scowling at his plate. Maybe not.

"Hey, you still there?"

"Yes, I'm still here. Listen, Earlene, I can't talk about this now, but I want you to promise me something: Don't go talk-

ing to anyone else, don't call anyone, don't do anything until
we talk. I'll try to come by tomorrow and fill you in on what
I think's been going on." *As soon as I can figure it out!*

"I know the score. An' you want what I got, it's gonna
cost."

*I'm going to have to hock my computer before I get it out
of the box,* Cat reflected. "Fine. But please be careful, Earlene.
You may be the one who doesn't know who you're dealing
with."

TWENTY-FOUR

CAT COULD NOT be persuaded to accompany the family to St.
Agnes for midnight Mass. She made the children her excuse,
but could not evade disappointment in the eyes of Kevin and
Sister Margaret Mary, and even Dominic's goodnight was distant.

Perhaps she should have gone. Even Ellice went along with
Freddy, and it might have been nice for the kids to see Dominic celebrate Mass. They never really understood what it was
their Uncle Dom did, not the way they understood cops.
Maybe next year, Cat told herself, as she helped Jane and Mats
set out a plate of cookies for Santa, got them ready for bed.
Then she dragged the Citadel of the Deep up from the apartment and for the next couple of hours was so absorbed in
hooking up turrets and catapults and drawbridges that she
stopped wondering if Victor might come back or if she should
call him and tell him about Earlene. Then, having filled stockings and unplugged the tree, Cat dragged herself to bed.

She fell swiftly into a paralyzing dream. She was running,
fleeing from something, something that threw a menacing chill
ahead of its course, immobilizing Cat as she tried to escape.

Shock threw her awake. Cat looked at the covers tossed
aside, tried to recall the eerie dream, felt only a residual sense
of dread. She shuffled to the window, pushed aside the drapes,

saw that it was still dark, heard the ocean's steady morning rhythm. She glanced at her clock. Five-forty. She tiptoed down the hall, checked on the kids, both sleeping soundly, slipped back into her bedroom and pulled on sweats, a thin all-weather jacket, running shoes. She crept downstairs, admired the arrangement of presents under the tree, hunted up gloves and a muffler, a wool hat. May as well run off a little of last night's dinner before they went Round Two at Carlo and Annie's that afternoon.

Cat filled the coffeepot, set it up and slipped out the back door, tucking her key into her glove.

The boardwalk was white with frost. Cat ascended the ramp, her shoes slipping a little on the planks, decided to chance it; there were already several pairs of tread marks on the glazed surface. The Santa Sprint had started a few minutes before and Cat could see the red and white blur of die-hards several blocks ahead.

The boards groaned and popped beneath her cautious trot. Pigeons bobbled out of her path, nestled in the doorways of boarded-up shops. The iridescent boards, the metal railing, glowed dull silver under the street lamps. Beyond, beach, surf, horizon were blue-black, indistinguishable.

Cat looked up and saw the cloud of red and white had reversed, was moving toward her. She jogged aside as the first few runners passed. Some had merely donned red running suits, red hats, others had gone all out, jogging along in padded jackets, white gloves, peaked caps, false beards muffling their faces, trailing over their shoulders. Cat didn't recognize any of them until a few called her by name or lifted false whiskers to reveal a familiar face.

She continued south for several more blocks, turned. The narrow pink horizon line began to split the sky away from the sea and as she ran north. The overhead lamps sensed daylight and extinguished themselves. Cat picked up her pace a little, anxious to get home before the children woke, felt the stitch in her side needling her, ignored it.

A latent Santa was closing on her left shoulder. Cat muttered "Morning," concentrated on regulating her breathing, willing the pain in her side to get lost. She realized the runner in the Santa suit was tracking her, and she slowed up, determined not to be nudged into a race.

Cat rubbed a trace of perspiration from her upper lip, moved toward the outer railing to let the other runner have a clear field, pass, heard the brisk tread closing the gap, riding her shoulder now. Cat moved aside again, slipping a bit on the frosted surface, regained her balance, realized that the other runner had moved in sync, dogging her.

The rest of the pack had gone ahead, disappeared around the curve at the narrow northern section of the boardwalk. Alone. You're alone. It's cold. A pale light, like mist, is rising off the shoreline. You can't hear anything except the whisper of the ocean and the sound of your own breathing. It's like a dream, and any minute the phone is going to ring and you'll wake up.

A powerful grip seized her left arm and shoved her against the railing. Cat felt herself lose footing on the slippery surface, fall against the cold metal, felt pain slam against her ribs; she grabbed the metal for support and looked up, saw the slender blade of a knife poised in her pursuer's hand, descend...

VICTOR DROVE TO Cat's house quite early. He had intended to leave the present on her doorstep, but there was a light on in the kitchen, so he walked around back and mounted the narrow stairs to the back door landing, knocked.

Jennie came to the door, wrapped in a pink quilted robe, waved him in. *"Buon' Natal."*

"Feliz Navidad. I just wanted to leave this for Cat." He handed her the gold-wrapped box from Bon Soie. "I have to run over to the office this morning, then I'm going into Vineland."

"You go to work, Cat goes out for a run, acting like it's just another day. Come, have some coffee." She went to tuck the box under the tree. "You get any dinner last night?"

Last night. Victor had arrived at the Ocean City department just as Lauren Robinson and a squat man with a bulldog face came to retrieve Earlene. The girl had been sullen, said noth-

ing. The Ocean City cops told Victor that Earlene had been
seen hanging around the Amises' neighborhood. Shortly before they left for the hospital to visit Fawn, Earlene showed
up at the door, demanded to see Mrs. Amis, became angry
when the maid tried to get rid of her. At last, Mrs. Amis came
to the door and words were exchanged, though Mrs. Amis had
said the woman was incoherent, and unknown to her.

Victor went to the Amis home and was informed by the
maid that Mr. and Mrs. Amis had not returned from the medical center. She said it looked like the girl had been trying to
show Mrs. Amis a photocopy of something; she believed that
Mrs. Amis had taken the paper from the girl, that the girl had
seemed very agitated.

Next, he trekked over to J m's and was surprised to see the
place bustling. A dark-haired waitress was shoving platters in
front of an assortment of weather-beaten patrons.

"Christmas Eve, Christmas day"…she explained to Victor,
her forearms covered with platters piled with mounds of something that appeared to be sliced turkey and something else not
entirely dissimilar to mashed potatoes…"anyone comes in,
Jim feeds 'em, no questions asked. They wanna leave a donation, fine, he gives it to the youth shelter. Earlene, she's
been actin' like she don't need the job, like she won the lottery
or something. Lucky the new girl took Earlene's shift today,
I'd be burned out. She'll work tomorrow, too, Earlene's too
high an' mighty to put in her time."

"Did Earlene tell you why she wanted to borrow your car?"

The girl shook her head. "But, like, she goes 'It's the last
time, I swear,' like as if she's gonna be able to get her own
wheels after tonight."

Victor thanked the girl, tried buzzing Earlene's apartment.
No answer. He drove down to the medical center, went up to
the VIP suite where Fawn Caprio-Sterling remained unconscious. Sterling had hired a private security guard to watch the
room; he and the sheriff's deputy stood facing each other
down.

The floor nurse told him that Sterling and the Amises were
in Mrs. Sterling's suite. Victor entered the room and saw Mr.

and Mrs. Amis sitting together on a little divan, flanked by flower baskets. "I never met that person in my life, Lieutenant," Cookie Amis told him. Victor turned to Amis then, said "You haven't given a statement regarding the incident at the party, yet. Can you tell me where you were when Mrs. Sterling fell?"

"I was—I believe I had been speaking to Mrs. Austen at the time. That's right, Mrs. Austen," he repeated.

"Really?" Victor recalled Cat's statement. She said she had been caught up in the pushing and shoving, hadn't mentioned Amis. He recalled the marks on Cat's arms. "Mrs. Austen said she wasn't with anyone in particular when the incident occurred."

"Well, when we heard Fawn cry out, everyone rushed in different directions, of course."

"Then you weren't with Mrs. Austen at the precise moment when Mrs. Sterling fell?"

"Lieutenant, you're out of line."

"I'm out of patience, Mr. Amis." There should be a quota, he decided, on the number of lies he should have to put up with in the course of an investigation. These people had exceeded their limit.

When he left the medical center, it was nearly eleven, too late to go back to Cat's. He headed home, woke early, drove to Cat's house and had coffee with her mother, told a lie of his own: yes, he'd eaten breakfast, he assured her, hoping that would thwart, or at least delay, her offer to heat him up some of that snail stew.

CAT GRIPPED the railing with both hands as she fell, swept her instep against the back of the other runner's heel, threw her assailant off balance. The runner stumbled, regained footing. Cat used the brief reprieve to push herself forward into a sprint. She heard his/her tread gaining rapidly, tried to assemble her thoughts. The face. She hadn't seen the face. From the bridge of the nose to the neck, it was swathed in a false beard, the fur-trimmed cap pulled low on the forehead, covering the brows. Who? She asked herself, who? The question emerged in little puffs of air as she panted, tried to accelerate on the slick planks. And had that been a steak knife? Last month, I get shot by a bullet ricocheting off a frying pan and now someone's trying to do me in with a steak knife. Cat felt a ripple of indignation. Assault with deadly cookware!

She felt a grip snatch the collar of her jacket, jerked her head forward, sidestepped, swung around the dogleg curve where the boards narrowed. How many more blocks to the ramp? Four? Five? And then a couple more blocks to her home. *I think I can, I think I can, oh God, I'm losing it!*

And then she heard the bells.

VICTOR HEARD THEM, too.

"Listen to those old ladies," Jennie sniffed. "They wake up the kids, I'll shoot them both."

Victor raised an eyebrow; Jennie explained. There were three year-round residents on Morningside Drive: Cat; the Ufflanders, who were so seldom seen that their existence had taken on the quality of myth; and the Nixon sisters. The latter greatly lamented that they had not been permitted to enter law enforcement; it had not been considered ladylike. But they were renowned markswomen nonetheless; Marco Fortunati had invited them to speak to his academy classes, and so it had fallen to him to visit the ladies and suggest that they discontinue their custom of firing off a couple rounds on Christmas dawn to celebrate the birth of the Prince of Peace. "Ladies," he said, diplomatically, "maybe it's time to think more along the lines of some jingle bells, whaddaya say?"

Bells.

"Ho, ho, ho!"

Victor looked out the front window, saw Carlo dressed in a Santa costume squeeze out of the driver's seat of Annie's Volvo.

"He's too early," Jennie fretted. "Victor, be a good boy, go out on the porch, tell him to shut up."

Victor stepped out onto the porch, saw a red Camaro pull

up and a smaller, more dapper Santa hop out, glare at his imposing counterpart. Victor shook his head, grinning.

A battered van, St. Agnes Roman Catholic Church painted on the side, pulled up behind the Camaro and a third Santa emerged from behind the wheel.

Victor began to descend the steps, wondered what was keeping Cat.

The largest Santa bellowed, "Is that you, Rice, you sonofabitch!"

"I don't gotta get the suit back 'til tomorrow, I thought the kids might get a kick out of it." He turned to the other Santa. "Dom, is that you?"

"I felt bad about laying a guilt trip on Cat for not coming to Mass last night." He adjusted the spectacles over his eyes. "She's had a rough couple weeks, I thought she could use a laugh. Anyway, it's my turn to do the Rescue Mission this year."

"Yeah, I do the pede wards," Carlo muttered, ashamed to be caught in a good deed. "So, all right, two of us gotta go, who's it gonna be? Yo, Victor!" he called across the street. "Which of us gets to play Santa, you be the judge!"

"I think I'll hold my score until I've seen the swimsuit competition."

Under Carlo's resounding laugh was a more ominous sound, one that spiked Victor's adrenaline.

"That sounds like someone screaming," Stan declared, lifting his cap and wig to uncover his ears.

Victor leaped down to the sidewalk; a figure in dark running attire rounded the curve of Morningside, a tall, fleet Santa in pursuit.

CAT LOOKED UP, saw three more Santas on her porch steps, thought she was hallucinating, felt her vision swim, her head go light, woozy.

Carlo let out a bellow, began lumbering down the street. The Santa froze, backpedaled nimbly, dashed toward Beach Road, headed north, a sharp silver object clutched in one hand.

Victor grabbed Cat as she fell, caught her by the waist and

eased her to the porch steps. "Put your head down," he ordered.

Cat yanked the knit cap off; her hair fell around her face as she rested her head on her knees. "He had a knife," she gasped, "He had a knife..."

"Dominic, go call it in. Annamarie—" Annie had rushed from the car "—help her inside. Rice, go after Carlo, hit the beach."

Stan took off after Carlo. Victor jumped in his car, drove along Beach Road, saw Carlo, and a good distance ahead, the runner. Without a break in stride, the latter made a smooth vault over the dunes and disappeared onto the sand. Victor heard a faint siren, drove ahead several blocks, got out of his car and crossed onto the sand, saw that he had undershot the mark. The runner was fifty yards to his left, Stan sprinting after, closing, Carlo nowhere to be seen. Victor saw Stan lunge. The runner spun and the two figures hit the sand together, but in an instant, one rose, ran on and it took a second for Victor to realize that it was Stan lying on the sand, not moving.

Victor raced toward Stan, his weapon drawn now, saw Carlo lumbering awkwardly on his right. The runner had disappeared around a curve in the beach. Hoping one of the patrol cars had been swift enough to cut off the runner, Victor reached Stan, who lay curled on one side, one hand clutching his ribs. A dark red stain was seeping between his fingers; his breath was labored, audible.

Victor pressed his palm over Stan's hand, shouted to Carlo, "He's down! Get the paramedics!"

Carlo spun on his heel, charged over the dunes.

Victor knelt beside Stan. "Don't move." He eased off the false beard, the hat, tugged at the fur-lined collar.

"Lieutenant..."

"Don't talk." Victor lifted Stan's palm. The incision had been swift, clean, the wound small, but that could be deceptive. Where the hell were the medics?

"Lieutenant..."

"Don't talk."

"Cat...?"

"She's okay."

"I'm gonna need..."

"Don't talk. That's an order. You'll get whatever you need."

"Really...cute...student...nurses..." Stan passed out.

Victor heard the sirens at last, an audible whine coming from the west. Later, he would learn that Carlo had snagged a guy as he opened the back door to let out the dog, charged into the house, grabbed the phone and called for an ambulance. His thunderous instructions were liberally punctuated with his favorite scatologies, which stunned the man's wife and two children, who later demanded to know why Santa was allowed to say the F-word, the S-words, the A-word, after he had told them not to.

Carlo stumbled back to the scene as the medics arrived, lifted Stan onto a stretcher. "You guys take him over to AC, I know one of the surgeons there. They're gonna make you pay for that costume, Rice, you dumb fuck," he muttered.

Victor helped the medics lift the stretcher over the dunes.

A patrol car pulled up in back of the ambulance. One of the uniforms met the stretcher, nodded to Victor. "Sorry, Lieutenant," he said, quietly. "Guy gave us the slip."

Victor shook his head. He looked past the ambulance to the arc of beach; already the stiff ocean breeze was sweeping away the shallow footprints.

Well, at least he wouldn't have to worry about Cat chasing after leads anymore. Now they were chasing after her.

TWENTY-FIVE

CAT URGED DOMINIC out of the Santa costume, asked Annie and her mother to get some coffee ready for the officers who would inevitably arrive. She pulled off her sweatshirt, ran her fingers through her damp hair, checked her reflection in the foyer mirror. The kids mustn't know that anything happened.

"It's Christmas!" Jane and Mats tumbled down the stairs and plummeted into the mound of gifts under the tree. *Not even a "Good morning,"* Cat thought, smiled ruefully. She sat on the floor beside them, admiring the Swordfighting Samurai Sea Urchins, the Citadel. "He knew everything I wanted," Mats marveled. "I didn't think he sounded so smart when I talked to him on the phone."

Cat smiled, then stiffened when she heard the knock on the door. Jennie admitted the two patrolmen, brought them into the kitchen. Cat exclaimed over the Barbie clothes, but Jane was not distracted. "What are the cops talking to Uncle Dom about?" she demanded.

"Let's start opening presents," Cat suggested.

Jane's eyes narrowed, but there was a stack of boxes tagged with her name. A dilemma. Jane opted for presents.

Cat slipped into the kitchen, asked Annie to sit with the kids, while she spoke to the police. Cat told them all that she could, realizing as they emerged that her explanation was disorganized, her voice was shaking. *Calm down and think!* "Five ten," she said, "maybe a little taller. Taller than I am." *Think.* "His face was covered completely, the hat was pulled down. I only saw this much." Cat made a narrow ellipse with her index fingers and thumbs, held it up to her eyes.

"Color of his eyes, ma'am?"

Cat blinked. "Blue. I think. Dark." *I think.*

"Are you a member of the Running Board?"

"Not really. I mean, I don't think they have an official membership, it's just a bunch of people who like to run. Sometimes they sponsor a mini-marathon."

"So where would we get a list of these people?"

Cat looked down at her hands. "I'm not very much help, am I?"

"It's okay, ma'am." Mindful that she was Chris Austen's widow, Carlo Fortunati's sister.

"Why aren't Carlo and the lieutenant and Sergeant Rice back yet?"

The officers looked at one another. One cleared his throat. "Sergeant Rice was injured; he's been taken to the hospital."

Cat listened quietly as they related what they knew. When she showed them to the door, Ellice and Annie were sitting with the kids. Dominic leaned over, whispered, "Why don't I run by the hospital?" Cat nodded, amazed that she felt so numb, so calm. She allowed the kids to help her open her presents, opening Victor's last, lifting the silken folds in her fingertips, feeling a fresh wave of guilt for not buying him anything.

She allowed the kids to empty their stockings while she fixed them breakfast, insisted Annie leave to get ready for the family dinner, asked if she and the kids could be excused. Then she went upstairs to take a shower and broke down.

Cat stood under the hot spray, her arms crossed over her chest as if she were trying to hold in the wracking sobs, her face pressed against the tiles. It took ten minutes for her to regain her composure.

There was a knock on the door. Cat pulled on a robe and opened it to admit Ellice. "You okay?"

"Stan got—"

"I know. Annie told me. Carlo just called, Stan's in surgery, he said it doesn't look too serious." Ellice put an arm around Cat. "You know, honey, you didn't have to go to such lengths to draw fire off Freddy and me."

Cat felt a ripple of laughter cut through her sobs. She sank onto the bed. "Some guy in a Santa suit tried to stab me with a steak knife." The laughter took over; there was a note of hysteria in it, but it was laughter all the same.

"You guys are all nuts around here."

"And look who's marrying into the family."

Ellice grinned. "C'mon, Freddy's downstairs, let's have some breakfast."

"I'm too keyed up to eat." The phone rang and Cat leapt on it, throwing herself across the bed. "Hello?"

"Keep it down, Alley Cat, and don't say my name if the cops are still there."

Cat inhaled. Danny. "Where are you?"

"Never mind. Cops still around?"

"No."

"What went down the north end this morning?"

"How do you know about that?"

"Never mind."

"Where are you?"

"Around. Look, I'm in a pay phone; I don't have Steve's number on me, it's unlisted. Track him down for me, will you? I need a lawyer."

"I don't doubt it."

"Tell him to meet me over Northfield. Tell him to get the DA over there, too." He paused. "Any word on how Fawn's doin'?"

Fawn. Cat hadn't given her a thought all morning. "No."

"Okay. Call Stevie. And you stay put, Alley Cat." He hung up.

"Should I have excused myself?" Ellice asked.

Cat looked at her. "It was Danny Furina. He wants me to call Steve Delareto and have him meet Danny at Major Crimes."

"Does that count as aiding and abetting?"

Cat lifted the receiver and began to dial. "No. He has the right to an attorney, doesn't he?" Cat got Steve's answering service, left a message for Steve to call her at home.

Ellice perched on the window seat, stared out the window, reflectively. "This guy Furina must be a real fruitcake."

"Certifiable."

"Only PI I ever met was the guy Ira hired to track me down."

Cat looked up. Ellice rarely talked about Ira, the brutal relationship that had driven her from a promising career into anonymity, left her emotionally and physically devastated. "What was he like?"

"Nondescript. Didn't look like Magnum or any of those guys on TV. You'd pass him on the street and never blink. Weird name, Rutger or Ragnar, something like that. He found me right after I moved into that room on Connecticut in AC."

"What happened?"

"You remember that place, what a dump it was." Ellice twisted the ring on her left hand. "I didn't have a dime. All I could do was tell him my side, told him he ratted me out to Ira, he may as well kill me. Told him if he had a shred of decency, he would throw Ira off the track. And he did. I never found out how he double-crossed Ira. Maybe he told him I made it out to my brother's in California, I don't know. I only know the heat cooled down and then I got sick, and then…" she smiled.

And then a chance meeting had brought her and Cat together.

"Ummm…double cross…" Cat murmured. Who else had said something like that lately? "Earlene." Cat answered her own question, aloud.

"Excuse me?"

Cat dialed Earlene's number. The phone rang, rang, rang, rang. Cat hung up. "Ellice," she said slowly, "If I needed to run into Atlantic City for about an hour, could you cover for me? Say I went over to check on Stan or something."

"Why is it I'm starting to feel like Ethel when Lucy says 'I've got an idea'?"

"One hour. And I'll drop in on Stan after I run my errand, so it won't be a lie. Tell the kids Uncle Stan had to go to the hospital and I went to visit him."

"Jane's gonna get nosy."

"Just play Barbies with her, she won't know I'm gone."

"I charge for playing Barbies. What do I say if Freddy or your mom asks where you are?"

Cat strode into her closet, hopped out, pulling on her old boots. "Plead ignorance."

"For some of us that's not so easy."

JOEY FORTUNATI found Victor and Carlo in the waiting room, Victor pacing, Carlo slumped on the couch, still dressed in his Santa garb. Joey had Meryl with him. "I was upstairs, heard about Stan," he greeted, but he was beaming.

Victor looked up. Upstairs? Maternity. "Sherrie?"

Joey flashed his killer smile. "Real Fortunati, impatient as hell. Figures seven months, he's done his time."

Carlo got to his feet, chuckling, gave his brother a hug, kissed his cheek. "Boy, huh? Whattaya gonna name him?"

Meryl looked up, her blond curls spiraling to her waist. "Giuseppe Giorgio," she said, primly. "But we're gonna call him Gio for short. Can I have some change for the vending machine, Daddy?"

Joey dug into his pockets for a handful of coins, handed them over. Victor watched her. "Daddy." With that wonderful resilience of children, Meryl had transferred her affection from her abusive father to Joey. Cat had said that Sherrie and Joey had been trying to have the father's parental rights terminated so that Joey could adopt her.

"Don't go far, honey. Uncle Marco's gonna come by and take you over Aunt Cat's."

Jackie Wing poked her head in. "Lieutenant, they'll be bringing Stan—Sergeant Rice—down in a minute. Don't worry, he's fine, it was just a scratch, really, but don't let on you know, I think he's planning to milk it a little."

She backed out, nearly colliding with Jean Adane, looking more flustered than Victor had ever seen her. Her fair complexion was flushed, her short hair windblown. Her coat hung open over a loose print dress. Phil Long was at her heels.

"Where's Stan? What happened?" Long demanded.

"He's coming out of the OR. He's okay." Victor related the incident, noticed that Joey was listening in; Joey and Rice had hung out together in Joey's bachelor days.

Victor's beeper went off. He wasn't surprised to see Kurt Raab's number on the read-out, he'd called Raab's service on the way to the hospital.

Victor found a pay phone in the hall, dialed.

"How's Rice?" Raab asked, immediately.

"He's fine, they're bringing him down now."

"Hurt in the line of duty may be just what he needs right now. Those SOBS hear about this, they're gonna run him for mayor. Listen, Victor, can you get away from there?"

"Adane and Long are here. What's up?"

"Furina's lawyer just called. Furina's coming in."

DANNY LOOKED none the worse for wear. He was lolling in a chair, staring down Steve Delareto across the interrogation cell when Victor and Raab walked in.

"I want my client read his rights," Delareto grumbled.

"I got the right to remain silent," Danny singsonged. "I got the right to my friend the counselor here. I got the right to stop this interview any time I want. Anything I say, you can hold against me in court, should it get that far, which I doubt. So what am I charged with?"

"Malicious mischief, interference with a homicide investigation, tampering with evidence—"

"Rinky dink."

"—conspiracy to commit a felony—"

Furina turned to Delareto. "You're not gonna let him get away with that one, are you?"

"Shut up, Danny," Delareto said.

Victor removed his jacket, hung it over the back of a chair. "Your client tell you about Allan Pritchard's death?"

"Danny, don't open your mouth," Delareto ordered. "Who's Allan Pritchard?"

"An ex-con who skipped parole, hid out in Atlantic City up in a flat across the street from the Phoenix. Your client spotted him stalking Mrs. Blaine Sterling. On Monday, December tenth, Pritchard broke into Mrs. Sterling's Margate home, presumably to attack her. Mrs. Carlton Amis happened to enter the house and Pritchard made a fatal mistake: he jumped her and she killed him in self-defense."

"Jesus."

"Now Mrs. Sterling sensed she was being followed, hired your client to find out who was after her. At the time of the attack, she was out of the house, walked in shortly after Mrs. Amis fled. When the police came by to investigate Mrs. Amis' allegation, Mrs. Sterling said she found no evidence of a violent attack in her home. But your client says she's lying, that she did find the body and persuaded him to help her conceal it, move it to another location."

"Wait a minute! You sayin' that guy Cat found in the Phoenix was this guy Pritchard?"

"That's right."

"What makes you think Danny moved the body?"

"He told Mrs. Austen he did."

Delareto turned on Furina. "What kinda jerk would—excuse me, I forgot who I'm talking to."

"Furthermore, your client instructed his secretary to misidentify the body in the morgue," Raab added.

"Says who?" Delareto demanded.

"Attaboy," Danny grinned.

"Shut up. Where's the secretary?"

Victor scowled. "She's disappeared."

"Well, you got one hell of a case."

Victor's scowl deepened. Delareto was right. With Linda Veach gone, there were only Danny's disclosures to Cat, heresay. He could back away from his version, Fawn could come to and deny it as well, or confirm the essentials but blame the entire escapade on Danny. He recalled what Cat had said, that Fawn had hired Danny because he could serve as the daring accomplice or the handy scapegoat, depending on the outcome of the conspiracy.

"And of course, you and Stevie here wouldn't want Cat dragged into this mess." Danny leaned back in his chair, threw his hands behind his head. "Still lands a mean punch, Alley Cat. Looks pretty good, too. Makes me wish I worked a little harder to get her in the sack. What about you, Stevie, ever get lucky?"

"Danny, I have to tell you shut up one more time, I'm walking."

Danny grinned, leaned across the table, yanked his turtleneck collar away from his throat. "Hey, get a look at this." He displayed the purpling teethmarks Cat's bite had left. "Some guys from the neighborhood woulda paid plenty—"

"I think it would be better if we eliminated Mrs. Austen's name from this discussion," Victor said, evenly.

"Yeah, yeah, or I'll wish I'd never been born."

"Oh no. You'll wish I'd never been born."

A chill settled over the room, though Victor's voice had been perfectly calm, his expression relaxed.

Raab cleared his throat. "Look, what I'm wondering is how come your client came outta the woodwork?"

Abruptly, Danny got serious. "'Cause I got played, and I don't like it. This ain't just a guy settin' up his rich wife for a hit."

"Why do you say that?"

"Uh-uh. Let's make a deal."

"What sort of deal?" Raab asked.

"You drop the charges; I keep my license. And you don't go after Linny. She's a good kid."

Raab thought for a moment. "I might be persuaded that Miss Veach, in her distress at your unscheduled disappearance, honestly mistook you for Pritchard."

"That's one."

Raab ran his hand over his balding pate. "Look, it's Christmas, I can't get anyone in here to ink a deal today."

Delareto hesitated. "Kurt, and don't ever tell anyone I said this, I'll deny it, you and the lieutenant here give me your word we got a deal, I'm okay with it. Tomorrow's soon enough for the paper."

Raab looked at Victor.

"It's not my call," Victor said.

Raab looked from Furina to Delareto, nodded.

"Like I said," Danny began, "I'm gettin' the feelin' Fawn's playin' me for a patsy—"

"Hold it right there," Delareto interrupted. "I will do this on Christmas, and against my better judgment I will do it without the paper, but we will not do the B movie dialogue."

"How 'bout 'she's playin' me'? Is that okay? When I first get the call, I see she's really shook up. Then, when I tell her something that oughtta shake her up, namely she's bein' stalked by a nutcase, he's set up camp in AC, she's like, 'Thanks for the information, Mr. Furina,' pays me off and that's that. I figure she's in, like, shock, it sinks in she'll gimme a call. But when she does call, it's just to haul his carcass off the Italian marble. She doesn't know he jumped the Amis woman, she thinks he had a fall, doesn't want the cops actin' like it's some botched B and E.''

"At least that's what she told you," Victor said.

"Yeah. And what she wants is to plant the guy so that it'll give Sterling the shakes, but things sorta got a little out of hand. And now here's where things start to get weird—''

"Start to!" Delareto cried. "You hang onto a stiff for four, five days, finally you stuff him in a Santa suit and drop him outside the executive suite and after that things *start to* get weird!''

"Okay, weir*der.* Who's side are you on, anyway? Fawn wants to move in the Phoenix, I say, okay, but I wanna stick by her, so she says okay, I can play houseboy. Then the lieut, here, calls asking about Danny Furina and Linda Veach an' I remember I forgot to fill Linny in. You think she'd be used to me by now. So I get a hold of her she tells me she saw Raab here walkin' outta the lieutenant's office with some gal cop, talking about how there was some delay in ID'in' Pritchard. So, I tell Linny, call up the lieutenant here, tell him she's been thinkin' maybe I'm the dead guy, maybe she should take a look. They got an ID, they'll tell her not to bother. But if there is some screw-up and she's already got 'em wondering if it could be me, they'll prob'ly ask her to give the stiff a once-over. The kid's got guts. Don't tell me I don't know how to pick 'em.''

"And the reason for having the deceased identified as you would be…?'' Raab's eyes darted around, nervously, as if he expected the *NewsLine90* crew to barge into the room.

"I wanted to turn it up a notch. Sterling's up the Big Apple wonderin' how the Bay Landing hit went sour, he can't stay there indefinitely, right? Comes the weekend, he's thinkin' is the dead guy Pritchard, is Pritchard still alive, is he holed up over Jim's, did he split with Sterling's ten grand? Throw some dead PI into the mix, he's thinkin', who the hell was Danny Furina, was I on to Pritchard, did Pritchard off me, is he still hangin' around waitin' to put the screws to Sterling? Sterling's bound to freak out, and me bein' the back office boy and all, I got myself a front seat.''

"And did he?" Victor asked. "Freak out?"

Danny shook his head in bewilderment. "*Fawn* does. She says I shoulda never had Linny go to the morgue without checking it out with her first. We had words, and that's when I started thinkin' there's somethin' about what went down she didn't let me in on."

Had words, Victor thought. Sterling had told him he had heard Furina's name mentioned in an argument between Fawn and "Donnie."

"And then I'm thinkin'," Danny continued, "that maybe the reason Sterling's so cool is because it wasn't him set up the hit. Then Cat tells me how Amis and Pritchard go back pre-Phoenix, and I'm thinkin' maybe it was *Amis* hired Pritchard. To take out Mrs. A."

"I've known Carl and Cookie Amis for years," Raab declared.

"Amis and Fawn been havin' a fling, you know that?"

Raab said nothing.

"He gets rid of Mrs. A., Fawn makes it look like Sterling was fixin' to get rid of her, kills two birds with one stone. Even if Sterling doesn't get charged with conspiracy, she can make sure things get real ugly unless he gives her a quickie divorce."

"It's getting thin, Furina," Victor said.

Danny shrugged. "By the Gambol, Sterling's stressed out, he wants Fawn gone, he sees his chance, he tosses her over the side. I shoulda been with her," Danny mused, soberly. "But she gave me the slip, and the next thing I know, the Rev's down below with his troops and Fawn takes a header. I figure my cover's blown, I split. Now, I got some time to think. I figure I'll keep an eye on Amis."

"Why?" Victor asked.

"Why not? It's Sterling or him, and I can't get to Sterling. I go in the Phoenix, I'll be spotted, so I stake out Amis. Over the marina on the causeway, you got sightlines straight across the bay to the north end of Ocean City. I set up camp on the marina, I'm there this morning with the zoom lens and around, what? Seven, maybe? I see him, Amis, come running up the beach in a Santa Claus suit, runs around the back of the house, lets himself in. I go back to my car, turn on the scanner, I hear an officer's down north end of Ocean City, they're looking for a runner in a Santa suit.''

"Why didn't you call it in right away?" Raab asked.

"I did, said I thought I saw the perp, the dispatcher told me they been gettin' false alarms on accountta there was some kinda race this morning, all the runners dressed up like Santa. So whaddamy gonna say? 'Not to worry, case closed, the perp's Carlton Amis'? I figure I'll go over check it out, so I head over the Longport Bridge, doesn't he drive right past me. So I can't do a three-pointer on the Longport, I gotta drive all the way into Ocean City, turn around at the toll booth, head back to AC. I figure he's headed for the med center, sure enough, I drive over, nearby lot, there's his car.''

"He was there with Sterling this morning." Victor had called up to the VIP floor while he waited for word on Stan.

"So, I figure I got enough to bargain with, I'll see if we can work out a deal. I don't have Steve's number. I get Cat to reach out touch and tell him I'm coming in.''

Delareto looked up. "You talked to Cat?"

"Yeah, why?" asked Danny.

"I got a message to call her place, she wasn't there," Steve said.

"What?" Victor said.

"She wasn't there. I talked to Ellice. She tried to stall me, I ask her straight out, is Cat there or not or do I have to call Carlo, she finally says Cat had to run out for an hour, everything was cool. Ellice gave me Danny's message.''

"Where did Cat go, did Ellice say?"

"No, just that she wouldn't be gone long."

She heard about Sherrie and drove her mother over to the hospital, Victor told himself. Or she went over to check on Stan. What if she ran into Amis at the med center? What if she did? No place safer than a hospital. Nothing could happen there.

CAT PARKED ON A lower level of the Phoenix, crossed Oriental, peered into the front window of J m's, was surprised to see the place crowded with patrons, saw two waitresses, one with dark curls, the other with a lank ponytail, bussing platters from the kitchen. No sign of Earlene.

She rounded the corner to New Bedford, entered Three Fifty-three. Her finger was poised to press the buzzer over mailbox A when she saw that the inner door was ajar, the bolt turned to prop it open.

Thump!

Cat had been ready to back out when she heard the sound, realized it hadn't come from Earlene's apartment but from the one across the landing, the one Pritchard had occupied.

Someone was inside Pritchard's apartment.

Cat slipped up the stairs. They were wood with rubber grids tacked to the center. One creaked and Cat pressed her lips together, mentally counted ten-Mississippi, stepped up to the landing. Pritchard's apartment door was closed; Cat could hear muffled sounds from within. The other door, Earlene's, was ajar. Cat took a deep breath and pushed at it with a gloved fingertip. She stepped over the threshold onto a two-by-two square of foyer. The odor of onions, roasting meat, and brown sugar percolated from the floor beneath her feet.

"Earlene?" Cat whispered. She stepped into the living room, saw sturdy industrial carpeting, a kitchenette to her right, cabinets of worn-out maple, a couple dishes in the sink, a mug of coffee on the divider between the living area and the kitchen. Cat lay her palm against the side of the mug, felt a faint warmth penetrate her glove. She remembered that Sherlock Holmes had calculated a passage of time by how far parsley had sunk into the butter on a warm day, wondered how long it took a cup of coffee to achieve room temperature in the middle of December.

The shade was drawn on the single window overlooking New Bedford. To the left was a low table with a small silver Christmas tree, cheap furniture in reasonably good condition, a couple paperbacks, yesterday's newspaper on a coffee table, the front page face up.

There was a door to the left, a bedroom. Cat approached,

stopped. An aroma teased her nostrils, underscoring the more dominant kitchen smells. Perfume, elegant, austere, something Earlene wouldn't have the refinement to purchase.

All that Cat had sensed she knew now; still, she didn't back away from the bedroom door because, of course, there was a chance, a slight chance that she might be wrong.

She wasn't. The mug of coffee, calmly set aside, the absence of disarray, hinted that the killer had not been entirely unexpected. The imprint of a fierce pressure on Earlene's throat, the mottled eyelids, the darkened lips opened in an *O* of outraged surprise suggested that the killing had been swift.

Cat squeezed her eyes shut. Inhaled J m's food and good perfume. Don't touch anything. *So we don't leave no fingerprints.* Cat squinted at the limp form flung aside so callously. Had she been left like that because the killer supposed no one would come looking for this hapless girl? Or because the killer planned to dispose of the body after...after what? *After he finished searching Pritchard's apartment!*

There was a pink princess phone by the bed. Cat lifted the receiver with two fingertips, her right index finger poised over the nine.

"Put it down, Mrs. Austen."

Not trusting to a steak knife any longer, nor to the scarf that had wrung the life from poor Earlene. Knowing that Cat Austen had figured it out and deciding that Cat's meddling had been endured quite long enough.

VICTOR AND RAAB were headed for the medical center when they were notified that Danny, consigned to Steve Delareto's guardianship, promptly gave him the slip.

"Shoulda slapped that jerk behind bars, Christmas or no Christmas," Raab grumbled. "Delareto's got an hour to turn him up, or I put out an APB. Look, Victor, I don't wanna go up there with uniforms, that'll just tip off the press. Let's the two of us go in alone, there's a deputy outside if we need backup."

Victor was still thinking about Cat. She wouldn't dare confront Amis herself, even if she had figured it out. Take care of Amis first; then he would have it out with her.

YOU'LL NEVER GET away with it. Cat had too much self-respect to actually come out with the words, but she couldn't deny they had sneaked toward her lips.

"The Santa suit," Cat said. "It was one from the Phoenix."

"And now it's in the laundry bin with the rest of them and tomorrow it'll be carted off to the dry cleaner's and back to the costume shop."

"What will you do with Earlene?"

"She was involved with a violent ex-con. Who knows what sort of associations he had? Drug deal gone bad, perhaps."

"Pas Glissant."

"I'm surprised you recognized it."

"Just because I can't afford two-hundred-dollars an ounce doesn't mean my olfactory nerves've atrophied."

Mrs. Amis nodded, jerked her chin sharply, backed out of the doorway, the gun's snub barrel level with Cat's breast.

Cat followed her across the threshold, thinking: *She's bigger, faster, more agile, more athletic, and armed. But, on the other hand, I'm...what?* Cat ran back through Marco's Self-Defense for Women class, couldn't come up with anything. *If you don't get shot (again) better sign up for a refresher course.*

Cookie Amis raised the window shade, unlatched the window, opened it.

"Well, I guess that'll take care of the scent," Cat said, "but cops can't afford *Pas Glissant* either, so I don't think they'd recognize the aroma. But they might be suspicious of an open window in thirty-degree weather."

"You walked in on this person's murder, there was a struggle, you were thrown out."

"Doesn't that get a bit old, tossing people from the upper story?" Cat couldn't believe she asked that.

"Consistence, Mrs. Austen, is the hallmark of an astute mind."

"Emerson said that foolish consistency was the hobgoblin of little minds," Cat remarked.

"And do you know what they say about curiosity?"

"I heard. Excuse my curiosity, but am I supposed to just jump?"

"Consider the alternative. You may survive a fall. You won't survive a bullet. This time."

Cat backed toward the window. It was high and narrow, the wide sill slathered with cracked paint. She glanced out over her shoulder. Maybe thirty feet to the ground. Fawn had survived such a fall. But she had fallen onto the Reverend Marlon, not the littered concrete walk of New Bedford.

"I'm not jumping," Cat said.

Mrs. Amis sighed, a sigh that said Cat's lack of cooperation was no more than an annoying detail.

Cat looked over her shoulder again. She saw a battered Vega swing onto New Bedford, a dark-haired form spring out. *Look up,* she cried, silently. Why hadn't she parked on New Bedford where someone would see her car? *Look up!* If he saw her at the window, he would know something was wrong, would call for help.

"I think you'd better come away from the window, Mrs. Austen."

WHEN VICTOR AND RAAB entered the VIP suite, they saw Blaine Sterling leaning against the shuttered window, Carlton Amis sitting in a chair by the bed. Amis rose.

"Carl, you wanna step outside a minute?" Raab asked.

Victor glanced at Fawn. She lay motionless, her pale hair spread on the pillow, a monitor beeping overhead.

"You have something to say to my client, you'd better say it with me here," Amis replied.

"You're the one I came to talk to."

Amis blinked. "So, talk."

"Maybe…" Raab hesitated. "Maybe you'd like to put in a call to Marty Bevilacqua."

Sterling turned, looked from Amis to Raab.

"You reading me my rights, Kurt?"

"Yeah. I am."

Amis squared his shoulders. "Consider them read."

"You wanna tell me where you were this morning?"

"Here."

"When'd you get here?"

Amis flashed the watch. "Early. Seven-thirty, eight. I wanted to see how Fawn was doing and I knew we wouldn't get by later. Cookie and I are having dinner with—" he named a state senator.

"Anyone see you come in at—what was it?"

"Seven-thirty." Amis shrugged. "Fawn's private nurse was coming on duty, she saw me. Go to the desk and ask."

Raab nodded toward Victor. Victor walked into the hall, saw a couple of nurses in flowered scrubs huddled at the station, approached and asked to speak to Mrs. Sterling's nurse. The younger of the two looked up, trying to make her appraisal of Victor subtle, failed.

"Were you on duty when Mr. Amis arrived this morning?"

"Yes, Lieutenant. I ran into him in the elevator. He waited in the hall with the guards while I spoke to the night nurse, took the patient's vitals. I believe he's been in there with Mr. Sterling ever since."

Victor thanked her, spoke to the sheriff's deputy, who confirmed the nurse's story, went back into the room and reported the information to Raab.

Raab was questioning Amis about houseguests.

"No one," Amis was saying. "The maid has the holiday off. No one's been home but Cookie and myself."

"I'll want to call Mrs. Amis to verify that."

Amis shrugged. "I'm sure she's been back for some time."

"I thought you said she was home?"

"Well, she went out for that run this morning. Her runner's group had one of those fun runs. Silly affair. The runners dress up like—"

"The Santa Sprint," Victor said. It was not a question.

"Yes. That's it."

CAT FORCED HERSELF to breathe slowly. She heard a swift, agile footstep on the stairs, the slight creak as it hit the middle

of the staircase; pause, then the ascent resumed almost noise-
lessly.

Cat felt the chill metal circle pressed to her carotid; Cookie
Amis stood with the gun to Cat's throat, nudged. Obediently,
Cat positioned herself in front of Cookie, facing the door.

Danny Furina stepped into the open doorway, his own
weapon angled low, his posture in a crouch.

"Well, well, Donnie," Cookie said, coldly. "You look so
much better as a brunette. Close the door."

Danny did say it: "You'll never get away with this."

Cat recalled Danny's affinity for B movies.

"This may work out even better. You were afraid little miss
blackmailer in there was going to expose your dealings with
Fawn, you took care of her, got into a fight with Mrs. Austen
here and shot her."

"Me shoot Cat? Nobody'd buy that. Besides, what happens
after that? I mean, I'm not the suicidal type."

"Well, we'll have to improvise. Let's start by having you
hand over your weapon. On the floor and kick it toward me."

Danny hesitated. Cookie shoved the barrel against Cat's
neck. Danny did as he was told.

Cat was thinking about Chris. Chris had been killed the day
before Easter. Easter would carry the pall of that tragedy forever. *It's Christmas, and I'm not going to die,* Cat told herself,
stubbornly. *I won't do that to the kids.*

Cookie was saying something to Danny; over the sound of
her own voice, she missed the crunch of tires on iced-over
asphalt, but Cat heard it; a car was rounding New Bedford,
stopping. Another. A third.

Cat's eyes flicked up, saw Danny's gaze dart toward hers,
signaling that he had heard it, too. "Or," Cat spoke up, playing for time, "you could shoot Danny first and make it look
like I thought he was an intruder and shot him and then, realizing I'd killed an old friend, I shoot myself."

"Hey," Danny interrupted. "I liked it better when you get
shot first. But that still doesn't take care of her stabbin' the
cop this morning, what's-his-name, Rice."

Cat blinked, played back the incident in her mind, saw the

cold blue eyes, the tall, agile form. The cold metal vacillated at her neck; Cookie was tightening her grip, readying herself. This time, she heard it first, the step on the stair.

Cat held her breath. The door across the hall opened, shut. The new tenant. Would he—or she—see that the apartment had been ransacked, call the police?

It happened a moment later, and this time none of them heard anything before the door exploded off the hinges. A uniformed cop was crouched against the door jamb, Victor on the threshold, both with weapons drawn.

Cookie gripped Cat's throat with her left hand, jammed the gun under Cat's chin with her right.

"Let her go," Victor said, stepped across the threshold.

"Gee, thanks a lot," Danny muttered.

"Shut up, Furina." Victor's tone was perfectly calm, almost conversational. "Mrs. Amis, what is it you want?"

"Nothing you have to offer, Lieutenant."

"Your husband's downstairs with the other officers. Would you like to talk to him?"

"I'm surprised he could pry himself away from Fawn's bed-side. Tell that one," she nodded to the uniform, "to get out. You come inside."

Victor glanced at the cop, jerked his head toward the stairs. The cop backed off.

Cat felt the nails, like talons, boring into her throat, the barrel of the gun no longer cold against her flesh.

"Move across the room, toward the window, Lieutenant. You, too, Donnie."

The two men made a cautious arc toward the window; Cookie pivoted, holding Cat in front of her, facing them, then she backed toward the door.

"Lay down your weapon, Lieutenant."

Victor shook his head, slowly.

"Oh dear, a stalemate. How many people are there in the street? And do be honest."

"Five uniforms. Two plainclothes. Your husband."

"You have communication?"

Victor opened his jacket to reveal the walkie-talkie at his waist.

"Tell them to get off New Bedford."

Victor's movements were methodical, his eyes riveted on Mrs. Amis. Then Cat. He communicated Mrs. Amis' order.

"I understand Mrs. Austen was shot last month," Cookie said, her voice eerily remote. "He missed. I won't. We're going down the stairs. Tell them I want Carl's car at the curb by the time I get down there."

Victor tensed. In the apartment, the situation could be controlled. In the street, shots could be fired into traffic, into the crowded coffee shop. He could signal Cat to take a dive, but Mrs. Amis might hit Furina before Victor was able to bring her down.

"You're not a stupid woman, Mrs. Amis. Think it through. How far could you get?"

Cookie was concentrating on Victor, on Danny; she did not hear the soft click of the door across the hall, but Cat did. *The other tenant,* Cat thought. *Soon, there will be more people in here than she's got bullets.*

Cookie released her grip on Cat's throat, held the gun in place while she reached back with her other hand, turned the knob, opened the door behind her, her eyes on Victor.

Cat heard the creak of the door, saw the flicker of alarm in Victor's eye and Mrs. Amis, sensing something amiss, relaxed her grip for a moment, and then came the explosion and the scream. Victor lunged, grabbed the gun hand that swung limply away from Cat's throat. Cat staggered, regained her footing and turned, saw the waitress in the doorway, the one with the ponytail; she looked about twelve.

Victor put Mrs. Amis in a chair, pressed her hand against the gaping wound where the bullet had exited above her clavicle, looked at the childish form in the doorway.

"Did I get the brachial nerve?" Linda Veach asked, wide-eyed. "I haven't been able to get out to the range, 'cause after I cleaned out Danny's office, he says I gotta keep a low profile, keep an eye on things around here."

"Linny, you did just great," Danny said.

TWENTY-SIX

CAT DIDN'T THINK about it. Didn't think about it when Cookie Amis was taken away, didn't think about it when Victor walked her down the stairs, didn't think about it when the plainclothes detective, Ballard, took her statement, didn't think about it when Vinnie appeared on the scene, yelled at her all the way to her car, followed her home and yelled all the way into the house. She didn't think about it when Jennie came to the door and told him to shut up, or when Ritchie called, called, called, called, or when Freddy and Ellice hovered or when Jennie warmed up some of last night's dinner and insisted that Cat eat.

Cat ate. She played Barbies with a zeal Jane had never seen her mother exhibit, then played Samurai Sea Serpents and volunteered to be all the bad guys so that Mats could be the Serpents, defeat the evil Lord Lionfish and take possession of the Citadel.

Victor came over late in the afternoon. Jennie answered his ring brandishing a wooden spoon, ready to ward off any of her sons who might take it into their heads to come by and pester Cat. He put Jennie at ease by promising to eat something, prayed she wouldn't resurrect those snails and sat on the floor beside Cat and Mats.

"How're you doing?"

"I'm okay."

"I suppose a reprimand would be disregarded."

"Utterly." Cat got to her feet. "You hungry?"

"Utterly."

Cat smiled down at him. "Come have something to eat. If you're eating, you won't be able to lecture. I have a theory I want to run by you and if I ask you something, I just want a straight 'yes' or 'no,' not a sermon and if you think there's something to it, I'd like to try it out again in front of a tougher audience.''

Victor ate the reheated linguine and listened to the scenario Cat fashioned from clues and suspicions, half-truths and hard data, filled in the blanks with a simple "yes" or "no," and when she was done, Victor was convinced she was the smartest woman he had ever met.

The next day he went to Raab. Raab listened, speechless, while Victor repeated Cat's theory, shook his head in disbelief. But when Victor was done, he picked up the phone and arranged the meet.

FAWN HAD RISEN to a state of intermittent consciousness, but was lying still, Sterling at her side, when Victor, Raab and Cat entered the room on the heels of Carlton Amis. His dashing exterior had thinned to a brittle shellac that threatened to crack when his wife was ushered in, her arm in a sling, a uniformed officer at her side.

Victor saw that her appearance caused Sterling's rigid countenance to oscillate with apprehension. The shudder was brief, quickly repressed, but it was enough to convince Victor that Cat's scenario was correct.

"I don't know what we're doing here," Sterling stated. "I'll have you know I'll be retaining Bevilacqua, Macklin, DeAngelo for Mrs. Amis' defense and—"

"I simply wanted all of you to hear a very interesting scenario that Mrs. Austen related yesterday," Raab interrupted. "Mrs. Austen's a rather talented writer. I think she may have a book in her."

Sterling stood in the far corner, near the head of Fawn's bed. Cookie was in a chair opposite him, Carlton Amis beside her. "What the hell does that have to do with us?" Sterling demanded.

There was a soft knock on the door to the suite; Victor opened it and ushered in Danny Furina and Linda Veach, pulled the only unoccupied chair away from the wall and offered it to the girl, who said, "Gee, thanks," agog at the sight of people she had only seen in newspapers, magazines.

"I think we're all here now. Mrs. Austen, why don't you tell us what you told the Lieutenant yesterday," Raab said.

Cat looked at her lap, twisted the thin gold band she wore on her right hand. "It begins a long time ago, really. Thirty years, maybe. Three college friends come together. One is the son of a hotel magnate, the other is a prominent attorney's daughter and the third is an ambitious but otherwise insignificant scholarship student. For the purposes of this discussion, we'll call them Blaine, Marlena and Cookie. Blaine's quite a catch, and Marlena lands him. He acquires the society wife, extracts the father's interest in an expanding enterprise and Cookie hangs on to her friendship with the pair, hoping to be carried into the upper strata on their coattails. Marlena charitably gets Cookie a job with her father's law firm, where, some time later, Cookie meets a law school graduate as ambitious as she, promotes his career and eventually marries him."

Cat paused; the silence in the room cowed her a little.

"Go on, Mrs. Austen," Raab murmured.

Cat pushed a strand of hair behind her ear and took a deep breath. "Eventually, Cookie is eclipsed by her young husband, as she had been eclipsed by her wealthy friends; reflected glory seems to be the best she'll ever be able to manage. Now, into this orbit, comes a star on the rise, young, talented, ambitious. Seductive. We'll call her Fawn. She lures Blaine away from his marriage and coaxes from him the money and connections she needs to get a jump start on her career as a designer. In return, she offers him the sort of celebrity that doesn't ordinarily brighten the corporate domain." Cat shrugged. "Doing well isn't enough for anyone anymore, is it? Everyone wants to be famous. Almost everyone," she added, casting an arch glance at Raab.

"Now, the end of Blaine's marriage to Marlena weakened the claim Cookie had on their sponsorship. Conflicting loyalties are tricky to manage and then there's the spectre that haunts the wife of every successful man: that one day, she'll be replaced by someone younger, sexier, richer. Whatever."

A visible shudder passed over Cookie's rigid posture; her eyes cast a hateful glance toward Fawn's still form.

"But it wasn't Cookie who was eclipsed. Not at first. It was Blaine. His new wife was a comet, rising at a time when his own star was on the wane. Her success was a reproach to his foundering empire and her affairs were becoming a nuisance. He's trying to hold off Chapter Eleven and she's weighing licensing offers that could multiply her income a thousand percent. For a company Blaine helped launch and which, should anything happen to his wife, might fall under his control. And what husband hasn't thought it when even less was at stake?" Cat speculated. "How much better he would be if his wife were out of the way."

Sterling spoke. "I'd watch myself, Mrs. Austen. You can't afford a libel suit."

"I didn't hear her say anything libelous," Raab said. "Anyone here hear anything libelous?"

"No," replied Victor.

"Not a peep," added Danny.

Linda Veach whispered something in Danny's ear.

"It means, like, if you smear someone's rep," he whispered back.

"Oh."

"Just a passing fancy at first," Cat continued. "But tally the royalties on all those CapriOH! bedsheets and handbags and accessories and the fancy becomes a hypothesis and the hypothesis becomes a plan. Of course, the priority is that the husband not be implicated, so he'll need a go-between. Who can he come up with who hates Fawn enough to do away with her? I imagine he considered his wife's ex-paramours, or perhaps their betrayed girlfriends and wives and then decided why risk trusting people you don't know when you can use someone you know very well? A primary rule of business is controlling the variables, right? I believe I read that in *King Midas*. Did you come up with that line, Mr. Sterling, or was it the ghostwriter?"

"Tell this bitch to make her point and get the hell out of here," Stering growled.

Victor's shoulders squared off as he spoke into the shocked silence. "Were you referring to Mrs. Austen?"

Cat saw Raab tense as though presented with a variable he had not anticipated. Unconsciously, he edged in front of Victor. "Keep going, Mrs. Austen."

"I've heard enough," Sterling snapped.

"I haven't." It was the first Amis spoke; his gaze darted from Cat to Sterling, his tongue running over his dry lips warily.

"I was just saying that you can control a situation better if you create it. Why conspire with some stranger who had been jilted for Fawn in the past, when you can set up someone you know, someone you've known for years, someone who is finally beginning to enjoy the perks of a successful, affluent marriage, and who would have a great deal to lose if the marriage were threatened?

"Why would Blaine hire Carl to handle his licensure? A talented criminal attorney, certainly, but with no special qualifications for the assignment. As a matter of fact, other than his aptitude for criminal defense, Carl's only other claim to fame has been as a flirt. The Casanova of Criminal Court. So Blaine hires the husband with the wandering eye, throws him into the company of the wife on the prowl and when the attraction takes root, brings Cookie into the Phoenix. What she doesn't observe or suspect, Blaine whispers in her ear, perhaps as a confidant expressing suspicions regarding their spouses. He stresses to Cookie the enormity of the loss if she were discarded for a younger woman, then speculates about how much better off they would be if Fawn were out of the way. Perhaps he even promises Cookie something material, a corporate presidency for her husband, perhaps even for herself." Cat looked at Danny who was nodding, ruefully, one hand over Linda Veach's.

"Now, where does one find an assassain? Well, a smart headhunter should be able to find anyone to fill any position, shouldn't he? Or she? Cookie thinks back to Bevilacqua Macklin's criminal defendants, and comes up with a promising sociopath named Allan Pritchard. Blaine bides his time, plays attentive husband, accompanies his wife to her showing, and gets caught in front of the lens when Pritchard rather arrogantly demonstrates to the woman who hired him how easily he can get close to the intended victim.

"Still, that slip might have passed unnoticed. A more serious oversight was underestimating Fawn. Remember, this is a woman who can spot a sequin out of place in twenty yards of chiffon. She spots Pritchard and needs someone to flush him out, someone who will do what he's told if the price is right, someone smart and not overly scrupulous. She remembers a local PI she'd met some years before, hires him to find out who's stalking her. The PI checks it out, finds out the guy's an ex-con holed up across the street from the Phoenix, suspects he's been contracted for a hit, a kidnapping, maybe. Yet, when he reports this to Fawn, expecting perhaps to be kept on the payroll as bodyguard, she dismisses him. The PI attributes her reaction to shock; she's scared, not thinking straight and he fully expects to hear from her in a day or two. But he doesn't. Because you see, Fawn didn't want to know *that* she was being followed—her own instincts told her as much. She wanted to know *who* was following her. How amazed Pritchard must have been when the very woman he was targeting showed up at his flat to find out what he was up to. Whether Pritchard tells her that Mrs. Amis was his contact is something we may never know. Fawn's counteroffer would probably have been the same in any case. She persuades Pritchard to adjust the scenario: instead of doing away with her, Pritchard will do away with her lover's wife, which should have the residual effect of throwing a scare into her husband."

Cookie's gasp was audible. Her head shook from side to side, her lips forming a soundless "No."

"The ex-con allows himself to be persuaded, as only Fawn can persuade, collects a second down-payment and he and Fawn set Cookie up. Now we have four accounts of the day Pritchard died: Fawn's, Cookie's, the PI's and Earlene Adkins'. And since they were all up to no good, we have to expect that they've all lied, so we have to look to those aspects of their stories that coincide and combine them with the facts we can verify to come up with a scenario. Start with Earlene

Adkins who saw a blond woman leaving Pritchard's flat and
sometime after she heard him on the phone saying he could
do 'something' at one p.m. Now was he talking to Fawn or
Cookie?'' Cat shrugged. ''Either way, that afternoon didn't go
as either woman planned because Fawn got Cookie to come
over to the house at one on some trumped-up errand, no doubt
in order to set her up. And Cookie's willingness to go over to
the house on the trivial errand suggests she had been lead to
believe she was going to walk in on the scene of Fawn's murder. Pretty good alibi, right? Anticipation's got her particularly
tense, particularly vigilant, and that's what saved her. Because
she was alert enough to fight off an attack and get out of the
house. Now, her story is that she ran to safety and called the
police, and Fawn's story—according to Danny—is that she
walked in and found Pritchard dead. Someone said that a lie
that's half true is the blackest of lies. Tennyson, I think. I
forget. Anyway, we have to forget what people said, and use
only what we know to develop a scenario that covers the available facts. That's what Sherlock Holmes would have done,''
she added, with a glance at Victor.

''Now, Cookie arrived around one and was attacked and
fled soon after, but doesn't call the police until nearly one
thirty. That was after an angry Earlene Adkins called in a
bogus B and E, flubbed on the address, probably because a
half dozen streets start with 'Bay' over there. Now, why is
there a delay before Cookie calls in the police? As panicked
as she is, she has to weigh the pros and cons, decides that
Pritchard can't be linked to her and at any rate, Fawn is bound
to walk in on the scene, call the police and tell them that
Cookie was there, so Cookie decides to call nine-one-one. And
what happens when the police go over to investigate? They
find Fawn inside the house, and no sign of a struggle. Danny's
version—that she had walked in on the corpse, called him in
a panic, and persuaded him to help her conceal the corpse in
order to throw a scare into her husband when he hears his plot
went sour—''

''Conceal the— What the hell!'' Amis shouted.

''Let Mrs. Austen finish,'' Raab ordered.

"I was saying that Danny's version wasn't based on what he'd seen, only on what Fawn told him. And, they may have been able to make off with the body and tidy up quickly enough, since Earlene's confusion over the street address, and Cookie's hesitation to call in the cops gave them some time to play with. But they'd have even more time if Fawn was in the house all along and called Danny immediately after Cookie ran out."

Danny ran his fingers through his dark curls.

Cat looked at him and nodded, gravely. "I think Fawn was there to let Pritchard in the house. To watch the fun, as it were, pay him off and play the unsuspecting homeowner who walks in on a murdered friend. But the deal goes bad and she's stuck with the corpse of the killer she paid to double-cross Blaine and Cookie, and doesn't know whether Pritchard's left something in his flat that could implicate her. She calls the only person she can trust—as much as Fawn trusts anyone—persuades the PI to conceal and move the body, convincing him that if they can figure out a way to throw a scare into Blaine, he'll reveal himself. But her motive is really simpler. She just needs to buy time to get inside Pritchard's apartment, make sure it's clean. It must have made her nervous when the PI insisted on checking the place out. He turned up ten thousand dollars, which may or may not have been her down payment. And because they couldn't exactly put the dead man back where they found him, they decided why not put him where his presence would throw a scare into the people who hired him as soon as Blaine came down from New York? But Blaine stalled and when they finally make the drop there's some sort of delay in identifying the deceased, one of those bureaucratic snafus that happen every once in a while.

"And then, there were four variables that couldn't be controlled. The first was the PI, who turned out to be more of a wild card than Fawn. When the police called Fawn's suite and asked her aide if he'd heard the names Furina or Linda Veach, he realized his secretary must have been looking for him; he got in touch with her and had her lie to the medical examiner."

"Is she great, or what?" Danny boasted.

"The second variable was the secretary who was willing to do whatever her boss asked, lie to the ME, make off with the lieutenant's set of prints, drop out of sight, no questions asked. The third variable was Earlene Adkins. She saw the photo of Pritchard with Fawn, Blaine, Cookie. She mistook one woman for the other at first, which led to the unpleasant scene at the Amises' Christmas Eve, but since her goal was to shakedown a wealthy woman it didn't really matter to her whether she blackmailed Blaine's wife, or his aide. Maybe she even figured out that Cookie, with her facility for throwing people from the second story, was the one who tried to kill Fawn. Poor Earlene. She should have realized a woman who could get the better of Pritchard was more than a match for her.

"Which brings us to the last variable. The curious Cat who discovers the connection between Amis and Pritchard and the waitress, which meant she was holding all the cards, even if she hadn't quite figured out the game. Not until it was too late for Earlene, and almost too late for Sergeant Rice."

Cat took a deep breath. "And that's it. Complex, I suppose, unless you see it in the light of what Blaine stood to gain and what Cookie stood to lose. I don't know if she actually planned to push Fawn over the railing at the Gambol, but suspecting that her husband and Fawn had slipped away for a private moment during the cocktail hour"—Cat would not have believed Amis capable of a blush, but he blushed at that—"and mingling with all those high rollers and their subsequent wives, I suppose she saw herself as the future ex-Mrs. Amis and took advantage of a fortunate diversion to get rid of her rival. Of course, there are people who believe that fortune is what we make it and I'd be curious to know who suggested that the suspended employee, Miss Davis, enlist the championship of Marlon d'Esperance."

Cookie Amis looked at Cat; there was little in her dark eyes other than hatred, but that little was surprise, perhaps appreciation.

Cat sighed. "And the irony is that Blaine has distanced himself very well from the conspiracy, and his wife chose a PI who will be the perfect fall guy if she needs one, and Carl simply comes off as a man who keeps his mouth more securely zipped than his trousers, so they'll all emerge from this relatively unscathed. The only one to take a fall will be little Cornelia Schlafley from Nutley, New Jersey.''

No one spoke. Cat forced herself to look at Cookie's face, saw that the appreciation had vanished; now there was only rage. At last, the silence was broken by Amis, whose tone was so human and tender that Cat felt her aversion go soft. ''It was nothing,'' he whispered, hoarsely, laying his hand on her uninjured shoulder. ''It meant nothing. I would never have left you, Cookie. I never loved anyone but you.''

''You're saying I did this for nothing?''

Cat shuddered. She knew now why she hadn't mixed much with other cops' wives, joined the auxiliaries, made them part of her social circle. She couldn't be Mrs. Someone Else, Mrs. State Trooper, Mrs. Doctor, Mrs. CEO—because if that's what she allowed herself to become, what would she be if he left? If he died? Mrs. Nobody.

Victor put a gentle hand on Mrs. Amis' elbow. ''The officer will see you back to your room, Mrs. Amis,'' he said. Raab held the door and the officer ushered Mrs. Amis out. She stared straight before her, never turning her gaze on her husband, Sterling, Fawn.

''Carl...this will be taken care of—'' Sterling began, his voice unsteady.

Amis turned his back on Sterling, faced Raab. ''What Cookie said just now, that'll never be admissible.''

Raab nodded, shrugged.

''What are we talking about, Kurt?''

''Cape May's office has the assault on Mrs. Austen and Sergeant Rice. I'm not involved in that. Conspiracy to commit. The Adkins girl, maybe murder two.''

''That can be beat,'' Amis said, more confidently. ''What if she testifies against—'' his eyes flicked toward Sterling. ''What can she do to help herself out?''

Cat saw Raab's Adam's apple rebound, knew he was envisioning the publicity. ''Maybe you'd better talk to Marty Bevilacqua,'' he suggested. ''Have him give me a call.''

"I can...I'm allowed to see her, right?"

"Of course, Carl. She's your wife."

Amis nodded, walked out of the room.

Sterling glanced nervously from Raab to Victor. Abruptly he darted out after Amis.

"Alley Cat," Danny exhaled, "I ever decide to take on a partner, you're it."

"You can't afford me," Cat replied.

"C'mon Linny, I'll pick you out a Christmas present." Danny put his arm around the girl, drew her out of the room.

"Mrs. A., you could write a book. Wait, I take that back, don't even consider it," Raab said.

"Fruitcake," Cat said.

"Huh?"

"For a title. *Fruitcake.* What do you think?"

Raab rolled his eyes. "Well, you do got your fruits and your nuts and some of that nasty bitter stuff you can't even tell is something you should be eating, you got a little spice—"

"And it all sticks together."

Raab shook his head. "Victor, lemme have a word with you in private, okay, and then you can take her home. *Fruitcake,* huh?" He nodded to Victor and the two of them stepped into the hall.

Cat shrugged on her coat, picked up her purse.

"Personally, I think it's exceedingly appropriate."

The voice was weak, but Fawn's gray cat's eyes shone with sly amusement before they closed once more.

TWENTY-SEVEN

CAT DECIDED to drop in on Stan, approached his door as a covey of giggling student nurses emerged. When Cat entered, he tried to modify his wicked grin, failed.

"Shameless," Cat greeted, giving him a kiss on the cheek.

"Annie says you've got no more than a scratch." She looked for a place to sit, saw the two available chairs piled high with decorated tins.

"Put 'em on the floor," Stan said. "They're my goodies, compliments of Seniors Organized on Behalf of Stanley." He nodded toward a balloon bouquet nestled against a corner of the ceiling. "Can you beat it? One week you're a racist, negligent cop, take one between the ribs, you're a knight in shining armor."

"In a Santa Claus costume, at least. You're certainly mine."

"Don't sweet talk me, I know where I stand. The lieutenant's one lucky sonofabitch."

"I do love you, Stanley," Cat replied with a grave smile. "If you had been seriously hurt, I think it would have broken my heart."

"Yeah, well anyone tries—breaking your heart, I mean?— he'll have to answer to me."

"And what about your heart? I wouldn't have fixed you up with Jackie if I knew you were resuming relations with the ex-Mrs. Claus."

"Judy? Oh, that's not on again. Truth is, she hated being married to a cop. Some women can't cut it. She'll always be there in a pinch, maybe if I left the department, we coulda made it work, but she didn't wanna be Mrs. Sergeant Rice, know what I mean?"

"Yes. I know exactly what you mean."

The door opened and Jackie Wing came in; Stan sat up, visibly brightening.

"It's just a blood pressure check, you don't have to go, Cat," Jackie said. "I heard you were up in the tower, I wanna hear all the dirt." She slipped the cuff around Stan's arm.

"I thought you were on private duty."

"Sterling brought in his own crew for her, and I got bumped from d'Esperance's roster, 'cause I failed the melanin count. Beth Easter's got him, says he hasn't shut up since he came to."

"He's all right, then?"

"He had some fractures and internal bleeding. He's still in

intensive care, needs another transfusion, they got a call out
for a couple pints of B-negative. Blood bank's always low this
time of year."

Stan sat up. "Oh, yeah?"

Jackie peeled the cuff off his arm, rolled it into a coil,
stuffed in into her pocket. "Uh-huh. Why?"

"Why? 'Cause I been stockpilin' the stuff. Every time the
blood bank pulls in, I make a deposit. A cop, I get hurt, I
wanna know there's gonna be a couple pints of Grade A Rice
on tap. I mean, Grade B. B-negative. Can you beat that? The
rev and I are the same blood type!"

Cat said it was Jackie's idea and Jackie blamed Stan and
Stan said he only mentioned his blood type and Cat actually
worked out the details and in the end all three blamed Frank
d'Allessandro because, three days after Christmas, he ran it
under the title "The Color of Life" and side-by-side photos
of Stan and d'Esperance. Cat's earnest prose, her sense of
mischief emerging only in those piquant modifiers that
d'Allessandro hadn't deleted, traced a unit of blood from
Stan's donation at a county blood bank reserve to the hospital
to its transfusion into the Reverend Marlon. Cat had even in-
corporated one of the Reverend's standard lines: "Can black
blood and white ever truly unite?" A reporter, who had been
hanging around trying to get at Sterling or Amis, came upon
the Reverend's covert escape, cried out the line as the man
was hustled into a waiting limo. The reverend pretended not
to hear, for once had absolutely nothing to say and it would
be a long time before he set himself down for *justice* in the
streets of Atlantic County again.

FOUR DAYS after Christmas.

The limo glided up to Cat's house. Cat, nestled on the couch
with a book, heard the slam of a door, craned her neck to look
out the window and saw Blaine Sterling step out of the vehicle, look up at her house with undisguised contempt.

"*Mom*. There's a *limou*sine outside!"

Cat tossed her book aside and got to her feet. "Jane, go
upstairs and help Nonna fold the laundry. Take Mats."

Jane eyed her mother suspiciously.

Cat crossed her arms over her chest and returned the stare and Jane stalked off. Cat hurried to the door and yanked it open, pulled her cardigan close as she watched Sterling mount the steps. She was surprised, when he reached the threshold, how little she had to elevate her gaze. He wasn't nearly as tall as he appeared in his photographs; she wondered why she hadn't noticed it at the Gambol.

"Mrs. Austen, we have to talk."

"Do we?"

"I think it would be to your benefit."

Cat hesitated, then shrugged. Freddy and Ellice were poking around in the apartment below, deciding what needed to be done to make it habitable. One cry from Cat would bring them both to her side. "Come in, then."

She offered to take his coat; he declined.

"I won't be long. That little tale of yours, Mrs. Austen. Quite an imagination you've got."

Cat passed under the archway to the living room, perched on the arm of one of the chairs. "You didn't come all this way to tell me you admire my imagination."

"No. What I came to tell you was that if one line of that story should make it into print, even disguised as fiction, it will be the last thing you write. You won't get so much as a twenty-five cent greeting card."

"You're out of touch, Mr. Sterling. A halfway decent greeting card goes for around a dollar seventy-five, plus tax. If you bought one for your wife, you'd know that. How is Fawn, by the way?"

"Coming around. Just as you should, Mrs. Austen."

"You don't scare me, Mr. Sterling. You sound like a common bully. I don't believe there's anything separating you from the likes of an Allan Pritchard but several million dollars."

"In that case, I ought to scare you. Just think of what havoc a man like Pritchard could wreak with several million dollars." He took a step closer to Cat. "You have children, don't you? A girl around nine and a little boy, right? Just you, the two children and their nanny, correct?"

Coming from him, it sounded like "Mammy;" Cat pressed her lips together to keep from laughing, nodded.

"Two old women across the street and a couple on the corner. Summer neighborhood, must be rather deserted this time of year."

"That's right."

"Now do you see why you should be taking me seriously?"

Cat paused for a moment. "Refresh my memory."

"An isolated neighborhood, let me tell you what you need. A nice, state-of-the-art alarm system."

"Like the one Fawn installed in Margate? But then, I don't imagine hers was state-of-the-art. One doesn't want anything terribly complicated, what with all the gentleman callers in and out. Awfully inconvenient to have the police raiding a tryst."

"But that's not a consideration for you, is it? So why don't I advance you the funds for installation, that way you could be more secure in your home. Would you say one hundred thousand dollars cash?"

"I never have occasion to say one hundred thousand dollars cash."

"Still, you would know what to do with it."

Cat tilted her chin. "Even if we're talking state-of-the-art, you'd have some change coming."

"Keep it. And I could throw in a job at the Phoenix. Something in the PR department, writing copy. Short hours. You would have plenty of time with your children."

"Really? I should think the PR department in particular would be working overtime. Sorry, not interested."

Sterling's pale eyes narrowed. "If you expect to make your fortune spreading your little tale around—"

Cat hadn't heard Freddy come in the back door, had to spring at him to keep him from grabbing Sterling by the throat.

"Freddy, stop it!" Cat cried. "He said *tale*, t-a-l-e. I can handle this, Freddy!"

"Did he threaten you?" Anger cast a frightening shade over

Freddy's placid countenance. "Get the hell out of my sister's house!"

Cat stood in front of Freddy, facing Sterling. "For your information, I wouldn't dream of peddling your sordid little escapade. So you can keep your hush money."

"Very smart, Mrs. Austen," Sterling sneered, with one eye on Freddy. "I'm sure you realize how preposterous your story would sound if you ever did try to publicize it."

"I gather you're not much of a reader, Mr. Sterling. Greed, jealousy, fear of rejection, those are universal themes."

Sterling shook his head. "No plot development. You'd need something like the climactic courtroom scene and Cookie won't make it that far. Even if Raab gets an indictment, Marty Bevilacqua gets before a jury and Pritchard and his little girl-friend are a couple of vicious blackmailers who threatened Cookie; she killed them in self-defense. You walked in, threatened to slander her, Cookie panicked. The cop in the Santa suit never identified himself, she thinks he's some lunatic assailant."

"The knife she was carrying?"

"A woman running alone? A lot of them carry weapons, and remember, Cookie had been attacked a couple weeks before."

"And it goes without saying that you and Fawn are both smart enough to cover your tracks, phone calls and bank records and so forth."

"Quite without saying."

Freddy directed one of Carlo's favorite expletives at Sterling. Cat elbowed him. "You may be right," she agreed. "And actually, I like your scenario better than mine. Because even if Mrs. Amis gets off, she and Amis will still know how they were manipulated, which may just strengthen the bond between them. You lose out on whatever profit you would have reaped from Fawn's untimely demise, so your only option now is to ingratiate yourself to the wife you wanted to kill, hoping she won't cut you out of the CapriOH! windfall. You may even succeed, because it'll occur to Fawn that Amis isn't going to marry her, and her recovery may put her out of circulation a while, so she just might reconsider the appeal of being Queen Midas. And if we have a mild winter, the Phoenix will start to crawl into the black, casinos always do. And if you're correct, and Mrs. Amis doesn't get convicted, you'll even have to take her back. How else could you contradict the DA's allegations? And the four of you will carry on as well as you can, with the only casualties being an ex-con and a little nobody. Still, I think I'd rather be dead than be a member of that uneasy quartet. How's that for an epilogue? Not really my sort of writing, I prefer something with a bit more heart, but there's a rather perverted irony that, God help me, I do find rather appealing.''

WHICH, WHEN IT ALL came to pass over the course of the next year, went off pretty much as Cat conjectured. Without a record of telephone or monetary transactions that would substantiate a conspiracy charge, and despite Furina's reluctant testimony and even more reluctant surrender of the ten thousand dollars he had taken from Pritchard's flat, the grand jury could not believe that Blaine G. Sterling, who had resuscitated the rotting Poseidon project and brought two thousand jobs to the area, would have any part in such a bizarre scheme. The financial motivations proved to be too complex, their gratitude for the Phoenix's economic boost too profound, even when Raab was permitted to introduce the sixty seconds of dialogue Cat had taped by covertly activating her answering machine recorder. He played it over to himself several times, chuckled whenever he got to the part where Cat said, "Really? I should think the PR department in particular would be working overtime."

"Do you read Sherlock Holmes?" she had asked him.

Raab scratched his head, shrugged. "I think the lieutenant's a fan."

"One of his most famous deductions was based on the curious incident of a dog barking in the night. A dog that was silent when one would assume he'd bark. You know how it is, sometimes you have to look at things that *do* happen from the perspective of when they *don't* happen. I don't think you'll have much luck tracing telephone calls between Sterling or Mrs. Amis and Pritchard, but it strikes me as unusual that Sterling would call his wife at her home the afternoon Pritchard was killed. I was just wondering how often Sterling bothered to call his wife all those other times she chose to hole up over Margate. Not many, I'll wager.''

Raab bumped into Victor a couple days after Cat turned over the tape, grabbed his sleeve and muttered, "You see Mrs. A., tell her Raab said, 'just that once.' You're one lucky bastard, Cardenas,'' walked on, leaving Victor looking after him, baffled.

FIVE DAYS after Christmas.

"OhmaGodohmaGodohmaGodohmaGod! Pleeeeeease! You got him on tape! Name your price!''

"Ritchie, what's the use? It probably won't be admissible.''

"So then whaddaya care if I hear it?''

"I have to give it to the DA.''

"A copy! Pleeeeease! Just run me off one copy!''

"Ritchie, there's no story here unless Mrs. Amis gets indicted, and I'm betting she won't.''

"Anything! Anything!''

"Oh, you can listen to it. But in return, I want an assignment. I need some money. I was thinking of doing a story on Jim's, the coffee shop? The way Sterling's trying to use eminent domain to get him out of his building. And I want it to be a cover story.''

"Jim'll fold. I hear he's low on funds. I mean, she'll give him a price break, but Lauren Robinson's still gonna wanna see some cold hard cash.''

"Oh, I think they'll come to terms.'' Pritchard had stashed one of his down payments in Earlene's freezer, but she had told Cat, "'Course you don't *keep* it there.'' And Cat decided there was no point in ten grand sitting around in some filthy evidence locker when it might be put to use, so she placed an anonymous call to Jim, suggested he defrost his freezer. "I have a feeling Jim's turned up a little cold hard cash.''

"But still, Austen, it's yesterday's news. Some old coot holdin' out against the big, bad casino operator."

"Maybe I could give it a fresh angle."

"I'll pass."

"Know what happens when you microwave an audiotape?"

"You're a witch, Austen."

"Bubble, bubble."

"How 'bout the story but not the cover?" Ritchie suggested.

"Come on, Ritchie, the world needs a little human drama between scandals. A gritty saga of the little man against the system. Another neighborhood landmark threatened with extermination. It was the best of times, it was the worst of times."

"Aaaaah, all right, already. But tone down the hyperbole and watch those clichés, they're a dime a dozen."

SIX DAYS after Christmas.

The Major Crimes unit finally got around to their pollyanna. Adane gave Long a year's subscription to *Glamour*, Long dropped off a copy of d'Esperance's autobiography, *Black As Black Can Be*, in Stan's hospital room, Stan sent Victor an IOU. Victor placed a small box among a vase of red flowers, left them on Adane's desk. She looked flustered, surprised, no doubt, that for once she wasn't the first one to clock in, opened the box gingerly, took out the detective's shield. Victor had taken it to a jeweler, who had buffed it to a vivid gold. She walked over to the window, held it up to the light. Victor watched, covertly, from his desk. The hell with Delareto and his twenty-nine five and his Monday holidays, he gloated, silently.

JANUARY SECOND.

"We'll never get this set up!" Cat's wail emerged from the closet.

"Come out here."

"I haven't got it on, yet. Victor, this is shameful. I really shouldn't accept it. Where would I wear something like this?

And from Bon Soie, it must have cost a fortune. Give up on the computer. We're going to have to call Nerds 'R' Us to get set up.''

Victor was kneeling at a long table Jennie had donated from her attic, attempting to hook up Cat's computer. ''Cat, people do this all the time. Look at the sort of people who work for Nerds 'R' Us.''

''I have. They're all intolerably young.'' She emerged from her walk-in closet wearing the peignoir from Bon Soie, the robe securely wrapped over the nightdress, closed high on her throat.

Victor leaned back against the wall, made a circling motion with his index finger.

Cat did a tentative supermodel turn.

''Let's see the rest of it.''

''No. It's practically transparent.''

''The mannekin in the window wasn't so coy.''

''Date her then.''

''I prefer my women with a pulse.''

''Really?'' Cat fingered the silk. ''Most men aren't so choosy.''

Mats toddled in, jumped onto Cat's bed. ''Jane says she won't play Sea Serpents unless I play Barbies first.''

''Have the Sea Serpents get captured and the Barbies can rescue them from the Citadel,'' Cat suggested.

''That won't work.''

''I don't know,'' Victor remarked. ''Those Barbies, they're pretty intimidating. If I were Lord Lionfish, I'd think twice before confronting them.''

''How come you're in your nightie in the day time? You got chicken pops, too?''

Cat smiled, ran her hand over his cheek, relieved that his rash was fading. Another crisis behind her. She picked up a manual from the bed. ''*Set up! Boot Up! Go!* Have you read any of this?''

''I'm winging it.''

Cat flipped through the book. '''State-of-the-art system. Cutting-edge engineering technology.' It says I shouldn't try to hook up immediately, but should take some time to familiarize myself with the new arrangement.''

''I like a system that promotes old-fashioned values.''

''Where's your power cable?''

''Madam, we've barely been introduced.''

Cat looked over the top of the book, sat on the bed. ''I'm supposed to find it and plug one end into the back of the unit and the other into the power source. Who writes this stuff?''

''I find it oddly erotic.''

''They recommend I use a surge protector.''

''Indeed?''

''And they strongly advise me not to power up until I check to make sure the surge protector is in place.''

''For safe cybersurfing.''

Cat threw the manual at him. Victor caught it in one hand, grinning. The phone rang; Cat leaned across the bed, reaching for the receiver on the night table.

''Mrs. Austen?''

''Yes?''

''This is Micki Cortez, we spoke before Christmas? Remember? You were doing a story on the party?''

Cat steeled herself, prepared to hear a proxy threat from one of Sterling's associates. ''That's right.''

''Well, Mrs. Austen, this is all rather bothersome because of the way the dinner ended, you know? But we took the money and we already advanced the funds to settle with the food and beverage people and the entertainment and so forth and well, the prizes were donated and the donors really would rather go ahead and take the tax break since it's the new year, rather than have the stuff back. So the committee got together and went ahead and got a notary and a witness and had the drawing.''

''I appreciate the call, Mrs. Cortez, but I think the story's fallen through. But if—''

''No, it isn't that, it's your ticket. It was one of the four from the Landis' reservation and none of them have that number. Two twenty-two? Do you know if that was the number on your stub? Because if you have it, you've won something.''

"Let me check." Cat pushed herself off the bed, rummaged in her closet. "It's one of the women from the Gambol committee, she says I might have won something." Cat pulled her silver handbag from a hook on the wall, unlatched it. The ticket was still inside. "Mats, hand the phone to Mommy."

Mats passed her the receiver. "I hope it's the sapphire earrings from Clevingers," Cat whispered.

Victor disappeared behind the table, busied himself with the wires.

"Yes," Cat said into the phone. "That's my number."

"How nice. You've won second prize, the one donated by Express Travel. Five days and four nights in San Juan. For two. We can send someone over with the packet, just have your ticket to show them, okay? Ten Forty-three Morningside in Ocean City, right?"

"Right," Cat said through clenched teeth, hung up. "Lieutenant, come out from behind that table."

Victor pulled himself to his feet, his expression a shade too innocent. "Yes?"

"That must have taken some doing."

He crossed the room, put an arm around her, kissed her right in front of Mats and whispered, "You'll never know."

MILWAUKEE WINTERS CAN BE MURDER
by Kathleen Anne Barrett

To my darling Billy, who brought me the joy
that enabled me to write

Acknowledgments

I wish to acknowledge and thank the following people: my parents, Dr. James M. Barrett and Mary P. Barrett; my brothers, James M. Barrett and Patrick S. Barrett; my sister, Mary Eileen Barrett; my husband, William E. Hoese, and my son, William J. Hoese, for their invaluable insights, encouragement and assistance; Nancy Fullam, Esq., for her unflagging loyalty and promotional assistance; Colleen Hartley, for the use of her elegant name; Jane Ristaino, for a means of escape; Patty Shannon at The Work Station, for her terrific typing; Dann P. Sullivan, for his always fertile ideas; Debra Wojtowski, for her great friendship and encouragement; and Donna Zahorik, for inspiring me to begin.

ONE

"BETH! What the heck happened?" Emily said as she rushed into my kitchen.

"I don't know a whole lot," I said. "We only talked for a few minutes. She just says Dave was lying on the floor with an empty pill bottle in his hand and there was a suicide note in the typewriter."

"But why would he kill himself?" Emily said. "It doesn't make any sense."

"Well...he may not have," I said.

"Huh?"

"He may not have killed himself. Janice is absolutely positive he was murdered."

Emily gaped at me and sat down, nearly missing the chair.

"I don't believe this," she said. "What makes her think Dave was murdered?"

"The suicide note, mostly. She says it's something he never would've written. She didn't tell me what it said but she says there's no way he could've written that note."

Emily squinched up her face.

"Well, she knows her own brother," I said.

"Yeah, maybe." Emily leaned back in her chair, folded her arms across her chest, pursed her lips, and stared at me. Great, I could just see what was coming next.

"Well, come on," she said. "How many people have you heard of who've been murdered with a bottle of pills?"

"Well, I don't know," I said. "No one, I guess. What does that have to do with it?"

"Well, what do you think, some guy just pried open his mouth and shoved the whole bottle of pills down his throat?" She gave me her favorite look, which I ought to be used to by now. Disdainful, superior, and *super* condescending. She'll never say she's superior, mind you. She'll never actually tell you you're stupid—but the *looks,* let me tell you. It's like you're the world's biggest idiot.

"I don't know," I said again. "Maybe somebody had a gun on him and forced him to do it."

"Oh, right. How likely is that?"

"Well, I don't know. Maybe the guy ground the pills up and put them in his beer or something."

Emily rolled her eyes. "Yeah, *right,*" she said. "It's a good thing you're not investigating his death."

I shrugged—very nonchalantly—picked up a pencil, and started doodling. When I looked up, Emily was watching me.

"What's going on?" she said.

"Nothing," I said, trying not to sound defensive. I made a long chain of ovals curled into a large "S." I looked up again. She was still watching me. I pursed my lips, put a stem on the "S," and turned it into a really weird flower.

"Janice says the police think it's a routine suicide, and they'll only do a routine investigation. She asked me to help her prove he was murdered, and I said I would."

Emily groaned. "Are you out of your mind? How could you let her talk you into something like that?"

"Well, what was I supposed to do, just tell her to forget it?"

"Yes!"

I rolled my eyes and looked away.

"What are you going to do," Emily said, "wrestle the guy to the ground when you catch him? You don't even weigh enough to donate blood, for Pete's sake. I mean, you're even smaller than my nine-year-old niece. You're not...my dog sat on you once and you couldn't even get up, do you remember that?"

I glared at her. "I was eleven years old when that happened."

"Yes. But you were the same size you are now."

I closed my eyes and took a deep breath. "Look," I said. "Let's just drop it, okay?"

"This has got to be the stupidest..."

I gave Emily the same you'd-better-shut-up look I like to give my brother—and it worked! I love it when that happens.

It wasn't quite three in the afternoon, but it was black as could be outside. The wind was screaming and throwing ice at my house. Milwaukee was having its third ice storm of the season and it was only December twentieth. Typical. Emily didn't want to drive home so she stayed over. We watched videos, ate some nachos, a bowl of popcorn, a small pizza, and about a dozen of the doughnuts I'd made that morning (no, not all at once). And we talked *ad nauseum* about Phil (Emily's husband) and all the guys we'd ever gone out with. We actually shared a few (no, not at the same time). At two a.m., I put Emily in one of my guest rooms and went to bed. The sound of a salt truck woke me at four, but I went right back to sleep.

MY NAME IS Beth Hartley, by the way. I'm forty-two years old, I live on the east side of Milwaukee, and I run my own business doing legal research and writing for other lawyers. We're like ghostwriters. (Actually, we *are* ghostwriters.) Lawyers who don't like writing briefs, or who don't have the time, hire us to do it and then put their own names on the finished product. No one ever knows, and everyone's happy. It's a fun way to make a living. I used to practice law myself, but I really hated it, so I quit when I was thirty-four and started the business. I brought my secretary, Janice Grezinski—she's the one whose brother died—with me, and a few years later I hired Emily Schaeffer (she's a lawyer, too). Emily and I have been friends since the fifth grade.

We work out of my house and we do all of our research at Marquette University or on Lexis. It's great. We do really well, I don't have anyone telling me what to do, and I can set my own hours. There's no back-stabbing and no competition. It's a really nice life.

I inherited my house from my Aunt Sarah, my father's brother's wife. I hope it doesn't sound like I'm bragging, but this house is really amazing. If you could dream up the perfect house, this would be it. It's on Newberry Boulevard, first of all, which is my favorite street in the whole city, and it's enormous. It has everything you could ever want. A real library, with sliding doors, seven bedrooms, four-and-a-half baths, three fireplaces, and the biggest kitchen you've ever seen.

The outside is really pretty—cream-colored brick with hunter green trim and a multicolored pastel slate roof. There's one of those covered carport things over the driveway which leads back to a four-car garage. I have a big yard, a small interior courtyard (I love that), a screened porch in the back, another second-story porch on the side, and a small third-story balcony. And everything is super fancy. The front door is solid walnut, recessed in a little alcove and surrounded by leaded glass and some kind of frilly gingerbread stuff.

The whole house has a sort of fairy-tale look to it. When I first moved in, Emily asked me what kind of architecture it is. I said, "How the heck should I know?" The only thing I can tell you is it's made of Cream City brick—a really pretty, light brick that's peculiar to Milwaukee. Most people assume the name has something to do with milk or beer foam, when they first hear about it, but it doesn't. It's just called that because of the color. (It comes from the sulphate of sulphur in the clay, whatever that means.) It always looks clean and cheery, and Milwaukee's well known for it, so it's kind of neat having a house made out of it.

It took me months to stop feeling like I had to dress up just to live here. I was embarrassed to put my beat-up old Honda in the garage. I felt like I should've had something more elegant, like a Mercedes or a Porsche (more like a Mercedes *and* a Porsche). I'm still not entirely used to it all and it's been more than five years now.

My whole family still lives in Milwaukee, which is nice. My dad's a retired lawyer and my mom stayed home to take care of us. They're in their late sixties now, but they're both in pretty good shape. My brother, Mike, is thirty-eight, unmarried, and runs his own business computerizing people's office records or something like that. My sister Ann is thirty-six. She's married to a guy named Don (a real weirdo, if you ask me), and has three kids (ten, seven, and five). She stays home to take care of them and does a great job, I think. I was married twice, but I don't want to talk about it.

AT NINE the next morning, Emily came in and woke me up.

"I'm going to Marquette," she said. "The roads are clear."

I squinted. "How do you know?"

"I had the radio on; I've been up since eight. I made you some coffee."

"Mmm, thanks," I said. "You coming back?"

"I don't know," she said. "It depends on how much I get done."

I lay in bed for a while and groaned, then finally got up and took a shower. I put on jeans and a sweatshirt and went downstairs. When I walked into the kitchen, I drew in my breath.

Sometime during the night, while I was sound asleep, my house had been transported by the ice storm to another galaxy, a magical world of shimmering, quivering glass. Through my bay window, I watched sun fairies play and dance, leaving sparkles and diamonds on every branch. My yard was a masterpiece of frozen perfection and light.

I poured myself some coffee, and before I had a chance to take a sip, my bell rang. I put the cup on the table and went to the door.

It was Janice. I put my hand out and touched her arm.

"Janice," I said. "Come in."

She didn't move. I had to draw her in and close the door.

"Let me have your coat," I said. "Come and have some coffee."

She shook her head, her eyes lowered to the floor. "I came to work," she said in a barely audible whisper.

"You don't have to work," I said. I touched her arm again, and tried to get her to look at me.

"I want to," she said.

I took a deep breath, not knowing what to say. "Okay," I said, for lack of anything better.

She walked toward the library.

"Janice?" I said. She turned around.

"Why don't you come in the kitchen for a while before you start? I have coffee, and I made doughnuts yesterday." I lifted an eyebrow and gave her a little smile.

She stood there for a moment, then smiled back. "Okay," she said.

I pulled out a chair for her, and got another mug and some plates from the cupboard. I poured her some coffee, took cream from the refrigerator, and set a plate with a half-dozen doughnuts in the middle of the table.

When I sat down and looked at her face, I almost started crying right then, but I managed to control myself for the time being. She looked so awful—so haggard and beaten up. Her skin sagged around her eyes and mouth, her color was pallid, almost gray, and she had dark patches under her eyes. She's only thirty-one, and she usually looks no more than maybe twenty-five. But that day she looked almost ancient. It was the look in her eyes that upset me the most. A sort of flat, lifeless stare, like she was tuning out her pain and the rest of the world along with it.

"How are you doing?" I said gently.

She made an attempt to smile and shrugged. Then her lip started to quiver and she put her hand against her mouth as a wash of tears spilled from her eyes. It caught me by surprise, and the tears I'd been holding back just poured out and wouldn't stop. My sister always says I make things worse for people when I do that. But at least I care, you know?

After we both calmed down a bit, Janice wiped her eyes and let out a sigh. She cradled the coffee cup in her hands and pressed the warm mug against her forehead.

I smiled. "You want a doughnut?" I said.

She looked at the plate I'd put in the center of the table and shook her head. "Maybe later," she said.

We sat in silence for several minutes, just looking out the window.

"I have to find out who did this to him, Beth," she said a little later. "I know he didn't kill himself, I just know it."

I put my hand on her arm and squeezed gently. "We will," I said. "I promise. We won't give up until we do."

She rested her eyes on my face for a few moments. "But how?" she said. "How are we going to do it?"

I wasn't really ready for that question. I hadn't actually thought about it yet.

"Uh...well," I said. "We could start by interviewing people, I guess. People he knew. See if anyone knew about anything weird going on in his life."

Janice's face brightened considerably.

"We could make a list of people we could talk to," I said.

"Okay," she said. "Let's do it."

"You mean you want to do it now?" I said, showing my surprise.

"Yes, I do," she said with an emphatic nod.

"Okay." I went into the library and got a legal pad from my desk.

I wrote *People We Need To Talk To* at the top of a page, and underlined it twice. I raised my eyebrows at Janice. "Any ideas?" I asked.

"Put down Jake Grossman," she said. "His roommate."

I wrote *1. Jake Grossman—roommate.* "I take it he wasn't there when you found him, huh?"

Janice shook her head. "No, and Mom's been trying to call him ever since but he never answers."

"So, as far as you know, he doesn't even know about it?"

"Oh, he probably does," she said. "The police would've told him by now. We gave them his name and everything."

"Do you know where he's from?" I asked.

"Cedarburg, I think."

"Okay, anyone else?"

"His girlfriend," Janice said. "Her name's Laura... something. I never actually met her, though."

Janice had a sort of injured look on her face. Or maybe it was annoyance.

"What's the matter?" I said.

"Oh, I don't know," she said. "I just had the impression he didn't want me to meet her."

"Hmm. Well, I'm sure you'll get to meet her now. Who else?"

"The doctor he worked for, I guess—Dr. Chapman. I think his first name's Anthony. His office is on Brady Street."

"I thought Dave didn't work during the school year."

"Well, this was a special case. It was only temporary and it was the same kind of work he wanted to do when he graduated."

"What was he planning to do?" I said.

"Put peoples' office records on computer and organize everything for them. He was going to start his own business."

"Hey, that's exactly what my brother Mike does. He has his own business, too. Weird—they would've been doing the same thing."

Janice didn't respond, but she looked like I'd flicked a little dart in her heart. There, I'd done it again. I had to go and open my big mouth. I hadn't thought about it before I said it, but it was like I was rubbing what Dave might've been right in her face. My brother Mike says I *never* think before I talk. I just jump right in and say everything that's on my mind. Which is why, he said once, I have very little to say on any subject. I won't tell you what I said back.

"What about his other friends?" I asked Janice, hoping to divert her attention from my insensitivity. "Did you ever meet any of them?"

"Just Jake," she said.

I tapped my pen on the table a few times, and scowled. "Can you think of anyone else?" I asked.

"Not really," she said.

"Well, what did he do with his free time? Did he have any hobbies or anything?"

"He was a wrestler," Janice said. "He was on the team at Marquette. He was always in some competition or meet or whatever they call it."

"Do you know who his coach was, or any of the guys he wrestled with?"

"No, sorry," she said, shaking her head. "I only went to watch him once. It was pretty gross."

I laughed. "Yeah, I know what you mean.

"What did he usually talk about when you saw him?" I said.

"His business, mostly. He'd been planning it for a long time. It was just about all he ever talked about lately."

"Was he going to do it alone?"

"Yes…well, he wasn't going to have any partners, but he was thinking of having some sort of investor for a while. But then the guy backed out."

"When did that happen?" I asked.

"I don't know, a long time ago. Like over a year, maybe?"

"Do you know who the guy was?"

Janice shook her head. "It was another student, I think, but I never knew his name."

"Okay." I gazed out the window and thought some more. This was harder than I'd expected it to be. I felt like I didn't know what to ask, or what to do with the answers once I got them. None of these people could possibly have anything to do with Dave's death, could they?

"Didn't you mention to me once that Dave saw a cardiologist?" I said. "What's his name?"

"Uh...shoot, I can't remember. The empty bottle of pills was Dave's heart medication. I'll have to ask Mom what the doctor's name is."

"How's she doing, by the way?"

Janice's face said "Don't ask," but she answered anyway. "Who knows?" she said. "It's hard to tell with Mom. If you ask me, she's either in complete shock or she's crazy or something. You'd never even know anything had happened to her."

"What do you mean?" I said with a frown.

"She acts just like normal. She doesn't even talk about it, she doesn't cry, and she doesn't act upset. She just cleans the house all day long and then goes to work just like usual. It's like she doesn't even care."

I gave Janice a sympathetic smile. "Maybe she really is in shock," I said. "Maybe this is the only way she can cope with it all. It might be too painful for her to acknowledge it right now. You know what I mean?"

Janice hesitated a moment. "Well, maybe," she said, a little grudgingly.

I had a sudden thought. "Does your mom know we're doing this?" I said.

"Yeah, don't worry, she doesn't care. She didn't even say anything when I told her."

"Do you think she'd mind talking to me?"

Janice gave me a rather sharp glance, and lowered her eyes. "Well, I don't know; you'd better let me ask her first."

"Okay," I said, a little confused by her reaction.

Now what? Friends, hobbies. School! "How was he doing in school?" I said.

Janice smiled. "He always got straight As," she said. "All his life."

"Wow. Must be nice, huh?"

"Yeah, right," Janice said.

"So tell me about Jake," I said. "How'd he end up living with Dave? Was he a computer major too?"

"No, he wasn't a computer major. He doesn't even know how to use one," she said with a derisive laugh. "I think he's in Soc, or something like that."

I considered reminding her that I don't know how to use a computer, either, but I decided against it—too embarrassing to mention.

"Where'd Dave meet him then?" I said.

"He was living with someone else," she said, "but the guy moved out so he put an ad in the paper and Jake answered it."

"Do you like him?"

"Who, Jake? Oh, sure. He's nice."

"Did he and Dave get along all right?"

"Yeah, I guess," Janice said, frowning. "Why? You don't think he did it, do you?" She seemed shocked that I would even consider such a possibility.

"No, it's not that," I said. "I'm just trying to find out as much as I can about anyone who knew him, that's all." I was trying to fight it, but I felt a little resentful that I was having to defend myself for asking questions I thought I needed to ask. After all, Janice was the one who'd begged me to do this in the first place.

That's when I remembered the suicide note.

"Oh, tell me about the suicide note," I said. "Why are you so sure Dave didn't write it?"

"Because it doesn't make any sense," she said. "It says he was taking his own life because he couldn't pay his debts, and because he couldn't face prosecution for the bomb scares. But he doesn't have any debts, and they weren't going to prosecute him for the bomb scares."

I was totally confused. "Bomb scares?" I said. "What are you talking about? What bomb scares?"

Janice blushed a deep pink. "Remember all those bomb threats they had at Marquette during finals last week?"

"Yeah?"

She took a deep breath and let it out. "Dave was the one who called them in."

I stared at her in disbelief. "What? Why in the world would he do that?" I said.

"I don't know," Janice said, lowering her eyes and her voice. "He wouldn't tell me. But he did tell me they weren't going to prosecute him," she added. "He knew that for sure. We were talking about it the night before he died."

"Wow, I see what you mean. What about the debts? Are you sure about that, too?"

"Well, yeah. The only debt he would've had was his school loan, but he wouldn't even have to be paying that yet."

"I thought you were paying his tuition."

"Well, I was paying for the rest," she said. "Whatever the loan didn't take care of."

I nodded, thinking hard. Maybe Janice was right. It wouldn't make any sense for Dave to have written that suicide note. Maybe it really was written by someone else. Well, in that case, I already knew what I was going to do next.

TWO

JUST THEN, Mrs. Gunther walked in. What perfect timing. She could keep Janice company while I did what I had to do. Mrs. Gunther is my housekeeper, and I love her. As far as I'm concerned, she's a part of my family. In fact, my whole family knows her. She worked for my Aunt Sarah since I was a little kid and I kept her on after Aunt Sarah died. My aunt had Mrs. Gunther in every Monday, Wednesday, and Friday for twenty-five years, and now, so do I. With a house this big, it takes her the whole three days just to get through all the rooms.

I really like having her here. We can talk about almost anything, and we've helped each other through some pretty unhappy times. She's a widow, fifty-five years old, and she lives in the same neighborhood she's lived in all her life (only a few miles from me). Her sister Erma lives three blocks away from her. Erma's not too well off financially, but she refuses to move in with Mrs. Gunther. She won't even accept any money from her. She says she doesn't want to be a burden to anybody.

Aunt Sarah left Mrs. Gunther quite a lot of money but Mr. Gunther got very sick soon after that so they went through it pretty quickly. He had to be put in a nursing home and their insurance didn't cover it. She still has the life insurance from him, and a good income from me, though, so she lives pretty comfortably—which makes her feel all the worse about Erma.

She was wearing a blue flowered dress that day with a pink scarf holding back her hair. She makes all her own clothes and wears flowered cotton dresses all year-round. It's like looking at a big flower garden in the middle of winter.

When Mrs. Gunther spotted Janice, who had her back to her, she gave me a quizzical look.

I answered with a little shrug, and a sad face.

Mrs. Gunther walked over to the table and sat in the chair next to Janice's. Janice turned, took one look at Mrs. Gunther, and started sobbing. I was a bit surprised, but maybe it was a good thing, I thought. It would do her good to get it all out.

"You go right ahead and cry, honey," Mrs. Gunther said. "You just cry as long and as hard as you want to." She folded Janice in her arms and rocked her gently, back and forth, like a little baby. That made me start crying again, and I quickly left the room.

I went into the library, closed the doors, and sat down at my desk. I closed my eyes for a while and just sat, listening to myself breathe. This whole thing was so emotionally draining. I got up, opened the drapes, and sat down again. The sun reflected off the ice on the trees, creating a curious mottled pattern on the books lining the walls. There must be a thousand of them. I tried counting them once but I got tired and quit.

I leaned back in my chair.

What in the world happened to Dave?

And why in the world did he make those bomb threats? It wasn't just a few, either. The paper said it was almost twenty over a period of three days. Really weird.

He'd always gotten straight As, Janice said. Until now, maybe? He was flunking out for the first time in his life and he couldn't handle it, so he…what? Made a desperate attempt to postpone his exams by making a bunch of bomb threats? Somehow, that didn't seem likely. And even if it were true, how would it tie in with his death?

Well, time to get to work, I decided. I got the number for the computer sciences building at Marquette, and dialed the main office. A woman with a sort of trembly voice answered.

"Hi," I said. "My name is…Janice. Janice Grezinski. My

little brother, Dave, was a computer sciences major at Marquette."

"Oh," she said. "Yes." I could tell by the sound of her voice that she'd recognized the name.

"He died last week, though," I said in a sad voice.

"Oh, yes, dear, I know," she said. "Please accept my condolences."

"Thank you," I said. "I know this is probably an unusual request and I don't want to put you to any trouble..."

"It's no trouble at all, dear. How may I help you?" she said.

"Well, I'd really like to talk to Dave's teachers," I said, "but I don't know who they are. I don't suppose you'd have a record of that."

"I'm sure I can get that information for you," she said. "Why don't you give me your number, dear, and I'll call you right back."

"Thank you," I said, after I'd recited the number.

"It's no trouble at all, dear."

"Oh, his wrestling coach," I said as she was about to hang up. "I'd really like to talk to his wrestling coach. Wrestling meant so much to Davy."

"Well...all right, dear," she said. "I'll do my best."

I turned off my answering machine and waited. Ten minutes later, I had the names and office numbers of all of his teachers and the name and home phone number of his wrestling coach. I couldn't believe it.

I sat back in my chair and grinned. Ha. This was fun.

Okay, next step. Go to Marquette and talk to his teachers.

I walked back toward the kitchen and Janice was heading for the library with two doughnuts in her hands.

"Feel any better?" I said.

She nodded and smiled. She really did look better. Most of the tension had left her face.

"I was thinking of going to Marquette to talk to some of Dave's teachers to see if I can find anything out about this bomb threat business. You want to come with me?" I said.

Janice hesitated for a moment. "No, I can't," she said.

"That's okay," I said with a smile. "I didn't really think you'd want to but I wanted to make sure. I'll talk to you when I get back. You going to be all right?"

"Yeah," she said. "Thanks." She gestured with one of the doughnuts. "Next time, leave the calories out, okay?"

I laughed. "I'll try. Just eat the holes."

She smiled and I watched her as she walked into the library. Janice is always worrying about her weight. She's really cute, though, and she's not overweight at all. So what if she's not model-thin. Who wants to look like a stick, anyway, right?

THE SUN WAS BRIGHT, the sky blue and cloudless. The roads were clear, but every tree and bush, even some of the cars, were covered with a thick layer of ice. It looked like something out of a science-fiction movie.

Marquette University is located in downtown Milwaukee between Eleventh and maybe Twentieth streets, about a mile down from the start of the shopping district. It doesn't have a sprawling, wooded campus like you see in most of those college brochures, although there's a really nice tree in front of the language building. The building's pretty neat, too. It's all white, with oblong octagonal things all over it. It looks kind of like a honeycomb with windows. I mean that as a compliment.

I hope you don't get the wrong idea. I really do love Marquette. I spent a lot of years there and I'm very attached to it. It's a Jesuit university with just about every major you could possibly want. People come from all over the world to go there, which is kind of neat. And the campus does look a lot better than it used to. They've put up some attractive new buildings recently, with some pretty decent landscaping, too.

I found a parking space near the bursar's office, which is kitty-corner from the law school on Eleventh and Wisconsin. Three of Dave's teachers had offices in the Cudahy Math and Computer Science building, one in Lalumière (the language building), and one in Wehr Life Sciences. The closest was computer sciences.

Cudahy Math and Computer Science is one of the positive, relatively new additions to the campus. I absolutely love the lobby. It has a high atrium with two staircases going up in different directions at one of the entrances, and a single staircase at the other. A huge seal of the university is inlaid in the marble floor. (That's my favorite part.)

A lot of intelligent-looking computer types were milling about. For all they knew, I was one of them. I mean, you can't detect computer illiteracy at a glance—or can you? I tried the offices for all three of Dave's computer teachers, but they were all gone for the semester. Darn. I left, trying to look like I had bits and bytes on my mind, and headed for Lalumière.

Lalumière is less than a block away, right across from the old student union. Dave was taking French I from a Dr. Jardin, and, voilà, she was there. Dr. Françoise Jardin had finely sculpted features, honey-blond hair worn in a French twist (why wasn't I surprised?), and brilliant green eyes. She was thin, and petite, and wore a pale pink knit dress with a print scarf in a deep shade of rose around her neck. She was so delicate, and elegant, and beautiful, I couldn't believe it. I tried my best not to stare. I told her who I was and explained why I was there.

"I'm sorry," she said, "but I did not know Monsieur Grezinski." She gave the Polish surname a mellifluous French lilt. I smiled at that and she gave me a puzzled look.

We talked for a few minutes. It seems she didn't require attendance (although she took it) and Dave only showed up for the exams. Her final was not disrupted by a bomb threat, and she really couldn't tell me anything about the incident that I didn't already know. Oh, well. Four strikes out of four, so far.

My final stop was Wehr Life Sciences. Dave was also taking Biology I. Languages and science must have been his least favorite subjects so he saved them for the end. I know what that's like. I did the same thing with speech and history. Yuck.

I took the long way and cut through the chemistry building for old times' sake, entering the biology building through the back door. Dr. Higgins' office was on the second floor, room 207. The door was closed but I could hear someone tapping away on a manual typewriter. It was the only sign of life I'd detected in the building.

I knocked on the door and someone said, "Enter." I opened the door and went in.

Dr. Higgins was about forty-five years old, with very little hair and hazel eyes. He looked at me and smiled in an easy, laid-back way and said, "Can I help you?" in a voice to match. I liked him.

I was just about to answer when I spotted his tropical fish

tank at the back of the room. I drew in my breath and just stared. It was a vision. Vibrant blues and yellows, oranges and reds, moved gracefully through clear, filtered water and slowly swaying sea plants.

"Beautiful, aren't they," he said after a moment.

"Oh, they're gorgeous," I said. "I could watch them for hours."

He laughed. "I've done that myself, on occasion."

I introduced myself, and told him my reason for being there.

He arched his eyebrows and sat up straight. "How would you like a Coke?" he said.

"Sure," I said with a laugh.

"Have a seat," he said. "I'll be right back."

After he left, I went back to the fish tank to take a closer look. There's something about fish, especially ones as beautiful as those, that calms me down. I can actually feel my body relax as I'm watching them.

On the wall to the left of the tank were two drawings, obviously composed by a child. They looked like circles with little lines and dots in them.

"Admiring my daughter's artwork, I see," Dr. Higgins said from behind me. I turned and grinned.

"Do you mind my asking what they are?" I said with a look of apology.

"Actinosphaeria and paramecia. Invertebrate protozoa."

I smiled and looked impressed. I only drew houses and stick men when I was a child. Maybe a cat every once in a while.

"My daughter, Kelly, wanted me to teach her some biology so I told her that actinosphaeria eat paramecia. I even brought her down to the lab and showed her some specimens under the microscope, but she didn't like seeing one eat the other so she drew them in separate petri dishes. The one on the left's the paramecia, in case you're interested," he said with a lopsided smile.

Dr. Higgins handed me a Coke and I sat down in the pale green molded plastic chair in front of his desk. He sat in his own chair behind it.

He rested his eyes on my face for a few moments, and nodded. "So, how can I help you?" he said. "I'm afraid I didn't know Mr. Grezinski personally. I have a rather large class—seven hundred and fifty this semester."

"Wow," I said. "Do you take attendance?"

He laughed. "No, not anymore. It wasn't worth the trouble. Now I just tell them if they don't attend the lectures they'll probably flunk, and they usually show up."

"Yeah, I guess I would, too."

"What sort of information are you looking for?" he asked.

"I'm trying to find out why Dave made all those bomb threats," I said. "I think it might be related to his murder somehow because they were mentioned in the suicide note. His sister, Janice, says he's gotten straight As all his life, though, so why would he interrupt his exams that way?"

Dr. Higgins took a swig of Coke and set down the bottle with a tap. He raised his index finger. "Two points," he said. "One, none of the disrupted exams were postponed long enough to do him any good even if he had planned it to get more study time. And two, he didn't make any of the threats during his own exams, anyway. Every one of them was made during an exam in a course he wasn't taking."

"Huh, how strange," I said with a frown.

Dr. Higgins raised his eyebrows and nodded. "He caused a heck of a lot of damage, though."

"What do you mean, damage?"

"This is just a for-instance," he said, raising his index finger again. "We had a Ph.D. candidate, working on an experiment in one of the labs—the subject of his thesis—and they vacated the building. He refused to leave. They had to carry him out." Dr. Higgins shook his head. "The experiment was ruined. He dropped out of the Ph.D. program and had to be hospitalized for depression."

"Oh, my gosh," I said. "That's awful. But why couldn't he just rerun the experiment?"

Dr. Higgins let out a big sigh. "Well, it wasn't that simple," he said. "The material required for the experiment is particularly difficult to obtain, and it's used up in the process. To start over would have set him back, who knows how long. He'd already been working on the degree for five years because of some earlier problems and I guess this was the last straw for him. His heart just went out of it."

"When was he hospitalized for depression?" I asked.

"The day before yesterday. Why?"

I shrugged. "I'm just curious," I said. "Would you mind telling me his name?"

Dr. Higgins shot me a quick look of annoyance. "I'm sorry, I can't do that," he said. "He's already suffered quite enough. I can assure you, Ms. Hartley, you're barking up the wrong tree with that one."

"Okay," I said with a sigh. I was already running out of ideas. "Do you know anything at all about Dave?" I said.

Dr. Higgins shook his head. "Only what I read in the *Tribune* about the bomb threats," he said.

"Do you have any theories about why he did it?" I asked.

"I'm sorry," Dr. Higgins said. "I wish I could help you. As far as I know, he never revealed his reasons."

"Well, thanks, Dr. Higgins," I said, and stood up to leave.

"Oh, do you know how he got caught?" I suddenly remembered to ask.

Dr. Higgins snorted a laugh. "He was making one of his calls from a pay phone in one of the dorms," he said. "Another student overheard him and turned him in."

I rolled my eyes. "Well, thanks, again," I said. "You've been a big help." I offered Dr. Higgins my hand.

"Glad I could be of service," he said. "Feel free to call me if you have any more questions." We exchanged numbers, and I asked him to do the same if something else occurred to him.

WELL, AT LEAST I was getting somewhere. I didn't know much yet, but it was better than nothing. There was something very strange about that prank of his. It just had to tie in somehow. I was disappointed that Dr. Higgins hadn't even met Dave, though. What I really needed was to talk to someone who knew him well. His *mother*—she was the one I'd talk to next. It turned out to be a good plan, too. I picked up some pretty useful tidbits of information from her, later that night.

It was just a little before noon when I left Dr. Higgins's office, and I was starving. I stopped at McDonald's, got Janice a Big Mac, a regular hamburger for myself, and a fish sandwich for Mrs. Gunther. The ice was beginning to melt and the otherworldly look was dripping away. I went through the drive-thru along with about two dozen others, and didn't get home until almost one.

I poked my head in the library when I came in. Janice was hard at work, typing even faster than her usual eighty words per minute. Boy, I wish I could do that. The best I've ever managed is about thirty words per minute, and that's with a whole ton of mistakes. When I first started my business, I had Janice typing on my old electric typewriter, but then the "G" broke so I splurged and got the computer. Just try writing an appellate brief sometime without using any words with the letter "G" in them.

"McDonald's delivery," I said in a singsong voice.

Janice turned around and grinned. "Hey, great," she said. "Thanks."

I found Mrs. Gunther upstairs and we all sat down at the kitchen table. I suddenly remembered Emily with a twinge of guilt. "Emily didn't come back, did she?" I said.

Mrs. Gunther put on a snooty face and said, "No, Ms. Schaeffer has not graced us with her presence."

Janice and I looked at each other and laughed.

"How's Erma doing?" I said to Mrs. Gunther.

"She's feeling a little better," Mrs. Gunther said. "She has her monthly checkup next week, so we'll see."

"What's wrong with her?" Janice said.

Mrs. Gunther threw up her arms. "Honey, what isn't wrong with her? She's got arthritis so bad she can hardly dress herself, she's got fifty pounds too much, she's got high blood pressure, she's diabetic, and now they think it's her thyroid."

"Good grief," Janice said.

We kept up the same sort of chitchat for a good half-hour, and then went back to work. When Janice and I reached the library, I told her about my conversation with Dr. Higgins.

"Do you have any idea at all why he'd do that for classes he wasn't even taking?" I asked.

She looked at me with a mixture of anxiety and confusion. "I really don't," she said.

We worked in relative silence for the rest of the afternoon. At four, Janice started packing up. I looked over at her and smiled.

"I want to go see Mom before she takes off for work," she said. "Do you mind?"

I shook my head and smiled, then had a sudden thought. "Do you think she'd mind if I came to the restaurant and talked to her tonight?" I said.

Janice wrinkled her brow. "Let me ask her and I'll call you," she said. "Is it okay if I let you know about tomorrow, too?"

"Sure," I said. "I only want you working if you want to do it. As far as I'm concerned, you can have all the time you need. I mean that."

She gave me an appreciative smile. "Thanks," she said.

After Janice left, I ate a banana and a mango and made myself a cup of tea. Mrs. Gunther was gone, too, so I brought my work into the kitchen and continued writing there.

I actually do quite a lot of work in my kitchen. It's one of my favorite rooms in the house. I'm not nuts about the wallpaper—it's a sort of dingy green with teapots and big spoons all over it—but I like everything else. The table's big, over six feet long, so I have lots of room to spread out. It's made of farmhouse pine, with a really nice finish, and there are two china cabinets to match. It's the kitchen of my dreams, except for the wallpaper, of course.

I was working on a brief that I'd promised to a client by Christmas Eve, and I was about two-thirds of the way through. I arranged all my stuff on the table and got to it.

At five-thirty, the phone rang.

"Hi, it's me," Janice said. "Mom says stop by any time but if you come around ten she'll be able to talk better. It's pretty dead by then."

"Great. Thanks," I said. "Did you decide about tomorrow?"

"Yeah," Janice said. "I think I'll spend the day with Mom, if you don't mind."

"I was hoping you'd say that," I said.

I told Janice I'd see her tomorrow night at the wake, and hung up. I made arrangements then for a temporary typist for the next day, and went back to the brief. At seven-thirty, I was through. I called Emily and asked if she could come a little early the next day, so she'd be in the house while the temp was here. I had some research to do, and it had to be done tomorrow. She said she would.

Good. That was taken care of. I NordicTracked for twenty minutes, showered and changed, and went to work on another brief. This one was due several days after Christmas. I worked for another hour, put everything away, and called the weather.

Ten above. Hey, downright balmy. You think I'm kidding, don't you? I'm telling you, these Milwaukee winters are absolute murder. Between December and March, anything above zero is sheer heaven. It's not as bad as it sounds, though. There's plenty to do here to make the months go by. It's actually kind of fun. We have ice-and snow-sculpting events every year, and there's always cross-country skiing or outdoor ice skating at quite a few of the public parks (we have a lot of parks). You can go downhill skiing, too, at the nearby slopes (manmade, of course, but who really cares?). Or, if you're a real outdoors wimp, you can skate inside at the Pettit National Ice Center. I've watched Olympic trials and World Cup speed skating there, too. You can even watch the athletes practice. It's pretty cool (yes, in more ways than one).

My favorite winter sport is cross-country skiing, though—gliding through the woods at Whitnall Park after a huge snowstorm, when everything is still pure white and glistening in the sun. It's especially beautiful when the creek is still flowing. The running water melts the snow that fell on top of it and you see this gurgling, sparkling stream poking through the mounds of surrounding snow. It's such a gorgeous sight, and so peaceful, too. You really have to see it to appreciate it. It makes you feel like you've been let in on a special secret of nature. Well, no winter fun and frolics for me that night, though. I had a murder to solve.

MARGE, JANICE'S MOM, is a waitress at a truck stop right off of I-94, about halfway to Racine. She started working there about twenty years ago, right after Janice's father abandoned them. In all that time, she's never filed for divorce. Janice says Marge is still hoping he'll come back. Now, why would she want him? That's what I'd like to know. Janice was ten when he left, but Dave wasn't even old enough to remember him. He actually showed up once, about three years ago, and then took off again the next day. Janice and Dave didn't even have a chance to see him. What a jerk. Wouldn't it be something if he showed up at the funeral?

The ice and snow that had melted during the day was frozen solid now, forming jagged ruts where tires had moved through the slush. The sand crews were out but the roads were still treacherous. I took my time, even though I'd be late, and got there at a quarter after ten. The parking lot was empty with the exception of two semis, both of which were unoccupied but still running.

This restaurant isn't much to look at, I'm afraid. The outside is nothing but a big white box with a neon sign saying eat, only most of the "E" is missing so it looks more like at. I don't think the restaurant even has a name.

The interior is decorated in a manner consistent with the exterior. White Formica-topped booths and tables, white chairs with chrome legs, plain white counter with white stools, and nothing on the walls. They're white, too. So is Marge's uniform. So are the menus. Boy, is it boring.

The only customers in the place were two guys sitting in a booth in a far corner. They looked at me when I came in. One said something to the other and they both laughed uproariously. Ha, ha.

Marge smiled when she saw me. "Ignore them," she said.

I gave her a halfhearted smile.

"Cup of tea with lemon?" she said.

I nodded and took a seat at the counter. Marge set the tea in front of me, and handed me a paper napkin from the dispenser.

"I was worried about you, Beth. You shouldn't be out there in this weather. That road's like a skating rink."

"Yeah, I know," I said. "I probably wouldn't have come if I'd known how bad it was going to be."

Marge looked at me for a few moments. "How does Janice seem to you?" she said.

I shrugged with one shoulder. "Okay, I guess. She wanted to work today and I think it helped a little."

Marge nodded.

I took a sip of tea, purposely stalling. I'd driven all the way out there to talk to her and now I was hesitating. It seemed ridiculous. Here it was only a few days after her son's death and I was planning to bombard her with questions about his life. She knew why I'd come, though, so I could hardly get out of it.

"Would you mind if I ask you some questions about Dave?" I said in a tentative voice.

Marge shook her head. "No, that's fine with me," she said. "Just start right in."

I took a deep breath. "Okay," I said. "Just let me know when you want me to stop."

Marge gave me a faint smile and nodded.

"Janice said you were trying to reach his roommate. Did you have any luck?" I said.

"No, I didn't," Marge said. "Seems awfully strange to me. You'd think he'd have called me, just to express his condolences if nothing else."

"Well, I'm sure we'll see him tomorrow night," I said.

Marge shrugged, and made a face like she didn't care.

"Did you ever meet him?" I said.

"Oh, yes. I met him all right."

"What did you think of him?"

Marge raised her eyebrows. "To tell you the truth, he's not quite polite enough to suit me. But I suppose none of them are nowadays. That boy's never said two words to me, in all the time I've known him. Of course, I wasn't over there at the apartment all that often, now that I think of it. Not very polite, though. I'll have to say it. He really isn't very polite."

I tried to keep from smiling. Marge likes to make sure you get the point, whenever she has one.

"Did he seem like he got along with Dave?" I asked.

"Well, now, I really couldn't say much about that, although there was a time Dave was talking about moving to another place. When I asked him why, he just said he wanted more space. But that place was plenty big enough for the two of them. I had a feeling it was something else, but he never said."

"So he never complained to you about Jake?"

"Well, no, but it wasn't his way, you know. He wouldn't have said; even if there was something, he just wouldn't have said."

I nodded, wondering if I should ask her to clarify that. I decided not to bother.

Marge peered into my cup. "How about a refill?" she asked.

"Sure, thanks," I said.

She filled the cup with hot water and put another tea bag and two lemon wedges on the saucer.

She looked tired. Marge is forty-eight, I think, but she looks quite a bit older. She has the same cute face as Janice, though. Same bright brown eyes, tiny nose, and sort of a little kid's smile.

"Did you ever meet Dave's girlfriend?" I asked.

She frowned.

"Laura?" I said.

Marge made the equivalent of a shrug with her mouth. "No, I can't say that I have," she said. "This is the first I ever heard of her."

"Well, it probably wasn't very serious," I said. "Did you ever meet any of his girlfriends?"

"Oh, sure," she said. "He'd bring a girl home every now and again."

"How about his other friends? Guys, I mean. Did he have any he hung around with from your neighborhood?"

Marge pursed her lips. "Well, there was John Stachowski," she said. "But they moved away about ten years ago."

I smiled. Just then, one of the men in the booth belched so loudly it made me jump. Marge yelled over to them to keep the noise down and we both laughed.

"You sure it doesn't bother you, my asking you all these questions?" I said.

She gave me a weak smile. "No, Beth, it's just fine, really. I know you're just trying to help. I'm grateful for anything you can do. Just ask away."

"Okay," I said. "How often did you see Dave during the school year?"

She shrugged. "Twice a month, maybe three times. He'd come Sundays for dinner or Saturdays sometimes he'd help around the house. There's a lot I can't do myself and I can't afford to hire anyone. He wasn't a stranger, that's for sure."

"Did he come any less often recently?" I said.

Marge thought for a few moments before she responded. "Well, come to think of it, I guess he did. I'd be expecting him and he'd call and say he couldn't make it. He always said it was schoolwork, though. He was a good student, I'll give him that."

"Did he seem any different to you lately? Did he act strange in any way?"

"No, no stranger than usual," she said. "He always was a bit odd, though. I used to say if I didn't know better I'd think he was somebody else's."

I laughed and took a sip of tea. "What did he usually talk about when you saw him?" I said a few moments later.

Marge let out a deep sigh, and shook her head. "Whatever crazy scheme he had going at the time," she said. "He had a lot of big plans, that one, just like his father. Jerry was sure he'd be a millionaire by the time he was thirty, can you believe that? He didn't know what to do with himself when he didn't make it. I always worried Dave would end up the same way. He was smart as a whip, but he could come up with the most fool-minded, harebrained ideas. You'd think he didn't have an ounce of sense in his head. He wasted more money trying to make money than anybody I ever knew—even his father."

I raised my eyebrows, and wrote *greedy, super intelligent, but very poor judgment?* on my notepad, making sure Marge didn't see it.

Just then, the guys in the booth got up to leave. Oh, darn. They walked by and the tall one looked me over, tried his best to memorize all my parts, and winked. Oh, yuck.

Marge asked me if I wanted another cup of tea and I said yes but I needed to go to the bathroom first. I'd been waiting for half an hour because I didn't want to have to walk past the dashing duo in the back. It was already past eleven and I wanted to get going pretty soon. I only had a few more questions in mind, anyway. If I thought of anything else I could always ask her later. When I came back, we chatted about the weather while I drank my tea.

"You have any more questions, Beth?" Marge said when I'd finished. She really was making it easy for me, which was nice.

"Just a few," I said with an apologetic smile.

She waited.

"Did he ask you for any money recently?"

Marge smiled with satisfaction. "Nope," she said. "He never once asked me for any money."

I was afraid to ask the next question, but I really wanted to know.

"What did his apartment look like on Saturday?" I said. "Did it look like someone had broken in, or like they'd been looking for something or anything like that?"

Marge took a deep breath and blew it out. "I don't know," she said. "Everything looked normal as far as I remember, but to tell you the truth, Beth, a cyclone could've gone through that place and I mightn't have noticed it. I just wasn't thinking about that."

I nodded, feeling stupid for asking in the first place. I got up and put on my coat.

"Oh, I almost forgot," I said. "Could you give me the name of his cardiologist?"

She wrinkled her brow.

"I want to ask him how Dave might have been given the overdose."

Marge winced slightly, and sighed. She scribbled the cardiologist's name on a napkin and handed it to me. "I'll ask him to talk to you," she said. "I don't think he'll give you any trouble."

"Thanks, Marge," I said, and squeezed her hand.

"Thank you, Beth. Will we see you tomorrow?"

I nodded.

I WAS TIRED, despite all the tea. As soon as I got home, I put the car in the garage and went to bed. There was a message on my machine but I didn't even bother to listen to it.

THREE

THE NEXT DAY was Tuesday, December twenty-second, the day of the wake. I wasn't looking forward to that, although I'll have to admit I was looking forward to meeting Jake and Laura. Who would know more about his everyday life than his roommate and his girlfriend? I expected I'd learn a lot from them, assuming they were willing to talk to me.

I got up at seven so I'd have time to eat breakfast before the temp arrived, and I put on a pot of coffee for Emily, who showed up at eight-fifteen.

She looked kind of tired, but just as beautiful as ever. You should see her, she really is gorgeous. She's five-seven, without an ounce of fat on her body. Her eyes are probably her best feature, although it's hard to choose. They're sort of an amber hazel—almost gold, like a cat's—and she has really dark lashes and eyebrows. Her hair's dark brown, too. It's all one length and comes to about the top of her shoulders and it's that really shiny, glossy kind of hair that picks up and reflects every light. And her skin is flawless. It's funny, though. I don't think she's even aware of what she looks like. She's never given any indication of it. Either that or she just takes it for granted.

She took a mug from the cupboard, poured herself some coffee, and plopped down on a chair, her legs extended halfway across the room. Sometimes I wonder what it'd be like to be so tall. Where do you put all those appendages? Don't they just get in the way?

"Late night?" I said with a tentative smile.

She rolled her eyes and shook her head.

"You guys ought to argue during the daytime," I said. "At least you'd get some sleep."

She pressed her lips together and hesitated a moment before responding. "We do that, too," she said with a slight quaver in her voice.

I gave her a sympathetic look, but said nothing. I really don't know what to say when she gets that way. Usually, I just listen when she's in the mood to talk, and she knows I care. I don't know what else to do. I can't come up with any solutions. In the male-female relationship department, I'm at a total loss. No matter how many I have, I never seem to learn a thing. It's more like I'm just perfecting my mistakes.

"You want to talk about it?" I said.

Emily pressed her lips together again and shook her head. "Not now," she said.

I got up, poured myself a cup of coffee, and sat down again. "Where's the temp?" I said. "She was supposed to be here at eight-thirty."

"You can go if you want," Emily said. "I'll take care of her when she gets here."

"Okay," I said. "Thanks."

I really did want to get going. I had to get the research done and it would take me a while, but I didn't want to be late for the wake. Not only was it important to Janice and Marge, but I didn't want to miss Laura or Jake. As it turned out, the night proved to be rather revealing, but not in a way I'd expected.

I went into the library to check my messages before I left and to leave instructions for the typist. My message light was blinking. I reversed the tape and played it back.

"Oh, great," I said. "The temp's not coming until ten."

"Want me to slap her around when she gets here?" Emily said.

I laughed. "No, thanks," I said. "I'll do it myself when I get home."

I wrote out the instructions, told Emily to help herself to anything edible she could find (same for the temp if she ever worked up an appetite), and headed for Marquette.

The sky was overcast, gray, dingy, and depressing. The roads had been salted, so driving wasn't a problem, but the temperature had dropped to twenty below with a windchill of negative forty. Lovely.

The closest parking space I could find was three blocks from the law library. I grabbed my briefcase, wrapped my scarf around my face, pulled my hat down to my eyebrows, and ran, making sure to sidestep any slick-looking ice patches. By the time I reached the building, my chest felt like someone had plunged two knives in my lungs, my hands and feet were throbbing with pain, and I had ice on my eyelashes. Gosh, I love winter. It's so exhilarating.

I went downstairs for a cup of hot tea to warm myself up. There's a lunchroom in the law school basement across the hall from the student lockers, with soda, coffee, and junk food machines in a little alcove. I peeked in the lunchroom but no one was there. I bought a cup of tea for a quarter and took it upstairs, hoping I could sneak it in.

I signed in, tea unnoticed (it's amazing how you retain certain skills even after years of nonuse), and went down to the Wisconsin Room. The place was full of students, which I hadn't expected, but then I remembered it was the second week of law school exams. (I had one on Christmas Eve, one year.) I found a small spot at the end of one of the tables, sat down, and went right to work.

At one, I was hungry, so I headed for the lunchroom again. I wasn't really in the mood for junk food but I wasn't about to walk anywhere in that cold. I settled for a package of cheese crackers with peanut butter and another cup of tea.

This time the lunchroom was packed. It was a weird feeling not knowing anyone. I felt kind of lonely and envious. I had actually liked law school—a lot. I like school generally. If somebody had been willing to pay me to do it I think I would have gone on forever. Oh, well. The crackers were gone and I was still hungry. I had an ice cream sandwich and another cup of tea, and went back upstairs.

By three o'clock, I'd finished my research. I didn't have to be at the wake until seven so I had just enough time to squeeze in a little Christmas shopping. Except for the sweater I'd knitted for my dad, I hadn't even started.

MILWAUKEE'S DOWNTOWN shopping district was converted to an indoor mall in the early eighties. The mall is on Wisconsin Avenue but they named it the Grand Avenue Mall because Wisconsin Avenue was called Grand Avenue way back when. It's three blocks long, starting with Marshall Field's on Plankinton (which is the equivalent of First Street and immediately west of the Milwaukee River) and ending at Boston Store on Fourth.

It's pretty neat. They attached the old Plankinton Arcade, which was built in the early nineteen-hundreds, to the already freestanding department stores, and filled in the gaps with new retail space. I like the Plankinton Arcade part the best (it's right behind where Big Boy's used to be). It looks like a European marketplace.

The mall was built as a part of a larger plan to revitalize the downtown area. They also cleaned up the Milwaukee River and built condos along the edge. Each one comes with its own marina slip. The Third Ward (otherwise known as the warehouse district) was dramatically refurbished. They even turned some of the old warehouses into apartments. And some of the new skyscrapers are fantastic (like the 100 East Building on Wisconsin Avenue, for instance).

I parked in the mall parking structure, went in at the second level, and headed for Marshall Field's. I always go there first. It used to be Gimbel's, which was my favorite store, but they went out of business. I stopped at one of the carts and bought honey and glycerine soaps and moisturizers for Emily, Janice, and Marge, and Mrs. Gunther and her sister, Erma. I bought gardenia for my mom and my sister, Ann.

I still wanted something else for my mother and my sister. I looked through every department at Marshall Field's and finally found something for my mom near the cosmetics—a little comb in a cloisonné case and a matching compact. She loves that sort of thing. I went to the scarf department next, and bought a brown paisley silk scarf for Mom and a powder-blue silk for Ann.

I went out of the mall, then, and ran across the bridge to Schwartz's Bookshop (my favorite bookstore, considered by many to be the best in the city—it has four branches now) to pick up some books my dad had requested.

Time to go home. I still had two more days before Christmas Eve and I didn't want to finish my shopping all at once. It's one of my favorite parts of the holiday. I went back to the mall, bought a fancy chocolate cake with mocha buttercream frosting, finely chopped walnuts, and chocolate shavings (now how could I pass that up?), and went home.

It was five o'clock. I NordicTracked for twenty minutes, took a shower, dried my hair, and put on a little makeup. Then I searched through my closet. I do own a black dress, but if I'd worn it there'd have been two people at the wake who looked dead. Who am I to steal the limelight? I settled on navy blue instead. I'd still look a little pale, but at least I'd look alive.

I went downstairs, made myself some coleslaw, drank a glass of skim milk, and had a banana. After ingesting all those nutrients I figured I was entitled to a piece of cake. I made a cup of tea to go with it and then had to get going.

The air was still frigid, but the wind had died down considerably. I took I-94 to Hawley Road and then drove down Sixtieth to Lincoln Avenue. Schaff Funeral Home is on the northeast corner of Sixtieth and Lincoln, in the city of West Allis, kitty-corner from St. Rita's Church, where the funeral would be held the next day. When I'm not there for a funeral or a wake, I'm usually glad for an excuse to be in West Allis. I grew up there, and still enjoy going back, just for old times' sake. We moved to Wauwatosa when I was twelve and I liked it there a lot, but I always missed West Allis. I used to fall asleep at night to the sound of a factory (we had a million of them back then), and every morning, around two a.m., I'd hear a train rumble by. It was so darned quiet in Wauwatosa. I couldn't sleep.

It was ten to seven when I arrived at the funeral home, and the lot was overflowing. I found the room for David Grezinski, walked in, and took my time about signing the guest register. I already had a sick feeling in my stomach. I really hate this sort of thing. The room was full, with everyone speaking in hushed tones and milling about with somber looks on their faces. It was so depressing.

I looked around for Janice and Marge and finally spotted them on the other side of the room. The casket was off to the far right but I averted my eyes, not wanting to look at him. I'd never seen Dave alive, and I wasn't ready yet to see him dead.

When I approached, Marge was talking to a man in a gray suit, who held both her hands as they spoke. Janice was clutching the hand of a woman who stood next to her. The woman appeared to be in her mid-fifties, with brown hair streaked with gray, and a plump, matronly sort of physique. She wore a purple crepe shirtdress with a big brooch on one side.

"Beth," Janice said, and she reached for my hand. Her face was blotchy and her eyes swollen. I gave her a big hug and smiled a hello to Marge and the other woman. Janice introduced the woman as her Aunt Mary and told her I was her best friend. When she said that, I started to cry. I don't know why, I just couldn't help it.

"Why don't you two girls sit down," her Aunt Mary said, "and I'll see if I can rustle you up some coffee."

I smiled. "Thanks," I said. "That would be great."

Another man was talking to Marge then, so I walked with Janice to some folding chairs that were lined up against the walls. Aunt Mary came back a few minutes later with two black coffees in Styrofoam cups.

The heat of the coffee was comforting, and we sat and sipped it for a while, without talking. I looked over at Marge. The man she'd been talking to was gone and had been replaced by a couple about Marge's age. The woman hugged and kissed Marge and the man squeezed her hand. There were two older women talking to Aunt Mary.

"How's your mom doing?" I said.

"I don't know," Janice said with a sigh. "Not too good, I guess. I think it's finally starting to sink in."

I nodded and looked over at Marge again. She was talking to someone else now and her face had the same look I'd seen when I came in. Like all the life had gone out of her, if you'll excuse the expression.

I started checking out the guests, playing a little game with myself. Does she look like an Ethel or a Blanche? What does he do for a living? Does that woman have homicidal tendencies? Is that guy a closet killer?

A group of students stood off to one side. Every one of them looked ill at ease. I wondered if Jake or Laura were among them, but I didn't want to leave Janice right then to find out.

"Is your Aunt Mary your mom's sister?" I asked.

Janice smiled. "Yeah, she's my favorite aunt."

I smiled, too. "She seems really nice," I said.

Our coffee was gone and we just sat there for a while, surveying the crowd. Then Janice let out a big sigh. "Maybe I should go help Mom," she said. But she didn't budge.

"Come on," I said. "I'll go with you."

We stood with Marge for another thirty minutes, while neighbors and friends, some students, Emily and Phil, Mrs. Gunther, and even one of Dave's grade school teachers came over and offered their condolences. I'd asked Janice earlier to point out Jake when she saw him, but she never did. The next forty minutes were spent in organized prayer and a short eulogy, and then it was over.

On their way out, guests lined up to sprinkle holy water on the body and offer a personal prayer. I waited until they were gone, and then forced myself to kneel before the casket as everyone else had done.

I really don't like looking at dead people. It makes me shudder. I keep thinking I see them breathing. I'd never even seen Dave before. I stared at him for as long as I could stand it, trying to memorize his face, trying to imagine what he looked like alive.

I said goodbye, then, to Marge, Janice, and Aunt Mary. Before I left, I looked over the guest list.

No Jake Grossman. And no Laura.

Now that was very strange. It didn't look like Dave's father had shown up either. I wondered if he knew, or if he'd even care. I noticed Dave's cardiologist and his employer had been there, though, and I thought that was nice.

I glanced back as I was about to walk out the door. Marge stood where she had been all evening, but her eyes were focused now on the casket across the room. Janice was holding her by the arm, trying to coax her over to her boy, but Marge was pulling back, shaking her head. I turned away and burst into tears.

AT NINE FIFTY-FIVE, I put the car away and hung up my coat. I sat for a long time at the kitchen table with the lights out, and looked out the window. There was nothing out there but inky darkness. No stars and no moon. Even the wind was gone.

I AWOKE far earlier than I'd intended the next morning, and lay in bed for quite a while, just thinking. It was the day of the funeral. Jake and Laura would *have* to show up for that. At six-thirty, I got up, showered, and dressed. This time, I put on one of the suits I used to wear to court—they work equally well for funerals. I had time enough for a banana and a glass of orange juice, and I made a cup of instant coffee to drink in the car.

The weather really wasn't too bad. It was sunny, and quite cold, but there was very little wind. I took the same route I'd taken the night before and arrived at the church a few minutes before eight.

It had been years since I'd been inside St. Rita's, and it revived a lot of memories. The building is very modern in design, with the roof slanting in all different directions, and enormous stained-glass windows everywhere. It looks the most beautiful when the light filters through, as it did that day. I was married in that church once—the first time. My second husband's funeral was held there. He died three years after we were married. That was ten years ago, December fifteenth.

The service seemed to last forever. As is the custom at masses for the dead, the priest wore black and there wasn't any singing. The altar boys carried incense, swinging the censers above the casket. I tried my best not to listen to the eulogy, willing myself not to cry, but it didn't work. By the time it was over, I felt like I'd eaten hot embers for breakfast instead of fruit.

The burial was worse. I saw Marge cry for the first time, great gulping sobs that shook her whole body. Even Emily had tears in her eyes. After that, we had the traditional after-funeral get-together at Aunt Mary's house, everyone drinking and eating, laughing and joking, talking about everything but Dave and his death. You know, some of the best parties I've been to were after funerals. Now, why is that?

Aunt Mary lives in West Allis, on Fifty-fourth Street, just off of Lincoln Avenue—very close, I realized later, to where Jeffrey Dahmer's grandmother lived until shortly after he was apprehended. Can you imagine? What a hideous thought. Janice could have played with a serial killer when she went to visit her aunt.

Aunt Mary's house is quite common for the area—slate siding, a front porch with steps, stained-oak woodwork throughout, including built-in china cabinets in the dining room, bookcases in the living room, and a pair of stained-glass piano windows. It's a lot like the house I grew up in, except we didn't have the woodwork.

Aunt Mary had a buffet laid out on the dining room table, with hot ham and rolls, two kinds of potato salad, raw beef and onions (this is something Milwaukeeans actually eat, on purpose, and consider some sort of delicacy), coffee, and three kinds of cake. There was also some kind of casserole with potato chips on top, and another made with hot dogs and macaroni and cheese. Yum.

I wasn't hungry just then, so I went to the other table, which was loaded with beer and liquor being served by a neighbor named Sam. I asked for white wine, and he gave me a full twelve ounces in a plastic cup—a little more than I had in mind, but what the heck. It made me shudder every time I took a sip but I was grateful for the numbing effect that went with it.

I looked around the room, feeling slightly uncomfortable, not really knowing what to do with myself. I've always been shy, especially in crowds of people I've never met (even in crowds of people I know, for that matter). I caught sight of Janice and Marge, but both were on the living room couch with an elderly woman between them. The woman must have been ninety years old, so frail she looked like she'd simply blow away in a strong wind. I wandered around, looking for Emily and Phil, but I didn't see them. I knew Mrs. Gunther wasn't there. She'd gone back to the house to get a start on her cleaning.

Laura and Jake! I'd forgotten all about them. I could talk to Laura and Jake. I had no intention of actually discussing the murder right then, but I could introduce myself, give them my number, and ask them to call me. I searched carefully through the entire group, but I couldn't even find anyone who looked under thirty.

Could they both have missed his funeral *and* the wake? It didn't make sense. They had to have been there. They'd probably just neglected to sign the guest register. I knew that neither Janice nor Marge would know Laura, but they'd both recognize Jake. Maybe Janice had just forgotten to mention it. I'd have to ask both of them if they'd seen him.

I'd finished my wine, and it was doing horrible things to my stomach. I felt like I had a little rodent in there, gnawing away at my insides, trying to get out. I know that sounds gross, but that's exactly what it felt like. I decided to have a ham sandwich. At least it would give the varmint something else to chew on.

I was putting some ham on a roll when I heard someone call my name. "Yes?" I said as I turned around.

I recognized the man from the funeral home. I'd seen him talking to Marge but we hadn't been introduced. He was fifty, maybe fifty-five, with coarse straight hair a mixture of charcoal and lighter gray, small, dark-brown eyes, very close together, and bushy gray eyebrows almost meeting in the center. His nose was large, somewhat swollen and discolored, and his physique was sort of squishy. He was tall but carried himself like someone who wished he were shorter—unusual in a man, I thought. He had a drink in his hand, something like brandy or Scotch on the rocks, and a thin layer of sweat covered his brow and upper lip. Not my type. How about yours?

"Ms. Hartley?" he said, extending a clammy hand. "I'm Dr. King, Dave's cardiologist."

I was surprised, and I think I showed it. I know it's stupid, but I still expect doctors to look healthy. Nurses, too. Half the nurses I know, and a good many of the doctors, actually smoke cigarettes. What's the matter with these people?

"Oh, hello," I said. "I'm very glad to meet you."

"I understand you want to talk to me about Dave," he said.

"Yes, if you don't mind."

"I've already discussed it with his mother," he said. "I'd be happy to oblige. If you'll call my office first thing Monday morning I'll instruct my nurse to set aside some time for you. Just let her know how much you'll need."

"Thank you," I said, and shook his hand again. "I'm sure half an hour will be plenty."

"Very good, then. I'll look forward to seeing you."

I spotted Janice walking toward me after he left, and I grinned. "Hey, that was Dr. King, Dave's cardiologist," I said. "I'm going to talk to him on Monday."

Janice smiled slightly but said nothing.

"How are you doing?" I said.

"Okay," she said. "I'm so glad it's over, though, you know?"

I nodded, trying to smile with more certainty than I felt. In my experience, it's a whole lot worse *after* the funeral. When everyone's gone home, and you're all alone in the house, that's when you really start to feel the separation. Some of the most difficult times occur months later, when something happens and your first impulse is to share it with the person, and then you realize you'd momentarily forgotten he was dead. That's an awful feeling. I really think those are the worst moments of all.

"Hey, I want to ask you something," I said. "Did you see Jake at either the wake or the funeral?"

Janice gave me a sharp look and wrinkled her brow. "No, I didn't," she said. "But I suppose I could have missed him."

I didn't think so, but I didn't say it. If he had been there, why hadn't he said something to Janice and Marge?

"How about Laura?" I said. "Did she come up and introduce herself?"

"No," Janice said, looking a little perplexed. "Hold on a minute, I'll ask Mom."

Janice came back a few minutes later and said Marge hadn't spoken with either of them, either, and hadn't seen Jake.

I stared off into space for a while, running the information through my head. Both his roommate and his girlfriend failed to show up for his funeral. One would have been weird enough, but both of them? What did they do, run off together? I had a sudden vision of Jake and Laura in some island paradise, lounging in the sun and sipping drinks from coconut shells with little umbrellas poking out. Jake was wearing a Hawaiian shirt and one of those big straw hats with the frayed edges. Laura was in a bikini and she looked fabulous. Well, I'd like to see how good she looks when she's forty-two.

"What are you thinking about?" Janice said, and I gave a little jump.

"Oh, nothing," I said. "I was just wondering where Jake and Laura are."

The look on Janice's face said she didn't really care.

Almost everyone was gone now, including the old woman. I stayed a while longer, said my goodbyes, and went home. I had some phone calls to make. I wouldn't be able to track down Laura just yet but I had a good idea how to find Jake.

FOUR

IT WAS ALMOST TWO when I got home. I changed into jeans and a sweatshirt, made myself a cup of tea, and sat at the kitchen table. I had work to do and I knew I should be doing it, but Jake and Laura were really bugging me. After I finished my tea, I picked up the kitchen phone, dialed information, and asked for the number for Jake or Jacob Grossman in Cedarburg, thinking Jake might've been named after his father. No such luck.

"How about J. Grossman?" I said.

"No, ma'am, I'm sorry."

"Okay," I said. "Can you just give me all the Grossmans you have?"

There were seven in all, and I started dialing. The fourth number was the one I was looking for.

A woman answered, identifying herself as Ann Grossman. After learning she was Jake's mother, I introduced myself and told her about Dave's death.

She didn't say anything.

"Mrs. Grossman?" I said.

"I'm sorry," she said, sounding distracted. "I already knew about that. The police were here looking for Jake."

I wasn't sure how to phrase the next question, so I settled for "Did he turn up yet?", and immediately regretted it.

"I...uh, no," she said. "But..."

"When was the last time you talked to him?" I said.

She hesitated for a moment. "Can I ask what your involvement is in all this?" she said in a snippy voice.

"I'm sorry," I said. "I guess I should have explained that to you. I'm a friend of Dave's sister, Janice, and she believes Dave was murdered. She asked me to help her find out what happened to him and I was just hoping Jake would know something. We'd expected to see him at the funeral but he wasn't there."

I could hear her catch her breath and then she was silent.

"Mrs. Grossman?" I said.

"The police said it was a suicide," she said in a voice that sounded almost frantic.

"Well, it was made to look like a suicide," I said, feeling a little confused by her reaction. "The police may very well believe it. Mrs. Grossman, did you know Dave?"

"No," she said. "I'm sorry, I have to go now. I have to find Jake." And she hung up—just like that.

I thought about it for a few minutes and decided to call her back. From the way she'd sounded, I figured she must be worried that something had also happened to Jake, now that she knew Dave might have been murdered.

She answered on the first ring.

"Mrs. Grossman, please don't hang up. It's me again."

She made a sound indicating annoyance but stayed on the line. I asked her if she'd agree to let me come to see her so I could help her come up with a way to find Jake. She hesitated, but said okay. After getting directions, I grabbed my jacket and purse and ran out the door.

CEDARBURG'S ABOUT twenty miles north of Milwaukee and it would take me at least thirty minutes to get there, maybe another ten to find her house. I'd been to Cedarburg many times, but the address she gave me was unfamiliar.

The traffic on I-43 was reasonably light, and the sky at least partly sunny. It was a long time since I'd driven that way. My Aunt Sarah and I used to shop there all the time but I hadn't been back since her death. I guess I was afraid it would revive too many memories.

Cedarburg's a beautiful little place with a quaint downtown and a lot of antique shops. Aunt Sarah and I picked up quite a few gems on those shopping trips, mostly walnut and mahogany. She left the furnishings as well as the house to me. The pieces we bought together are my favorites.

Mrs. Grossman's directions were surprisingly good, given her state of mind when she gave them to me. The house was at the end of a cul-de-sac lined with ash and maple trees. The lots were big, probably half an acre or more, and the houses were large and ostentatious—a lot of those French country manor things that look so out of place in a subdivision. No sidewalks, either. And enormous front yards no one ever uses. Personally, I'd rather have my land in the back and on the sides, and have sidewalks so I don't have to walk in the street.

The Grossman residence was an imposing beige Tudor with dark brown trim and a deep red door. A brick walkway led from the street to the front steps, which were constructed of the same brown and beige brick. To the right of the doorway, three large oaks were arranged in a conversational grouping for trees.

The Christmas decorations were simple but elegant, large wreaths with gold bows and tiny white lights.

I lifted the brass door knocker and rapped twice. The wind was starting to pick up again and the sky was overcast now, with some pretty ominous-looking clouds in the distance. I pulled my collar up and jumped up and down a few times to keep warm. I was on the "up" side of a jump when she opened the door. I smiled and her brows lifted just a teensy bit.

Mrs. Grossman wasn't far from what I'd expected in terms of appearance. She looked to be in her late forties, maybe early fifties. Very thin, about five-six or -seven. She was dressed in beige tailored slacks (linen, I think) and a perfectly coordinated sweater. Gold earrings, gold bangle bracelet, gold rings on each hand. Her hair was blond with carefully placed streaks, worn short in a style I've seen on a hundred women her age. They were blonds, too, come to think of it. Maybe that's part of the style.

Her nails looked professionally done, painted a deep shade of rose. Her features were regular but not remarkable. Thin lips, average nose, blue eyes. The only thing wrong with the picture she presented was her makeup. What little she was wearing was smudged and on the wrong parts of her face.

She glanced nervously over my head, peered outside, and pulled me in and shut the door before I'd even identified myself.

"I'm Beth Hartley," I said, smiling again.

She looked a little startled, and for a moment I thought she'd mistaken me for somebody else. "Yes...I mean...I'm sorry," she said, shaking her head. "You'll have to forgive me. I don't know where my head is. Please come in. May I call you Beth?"

"Oh, sure," I said.

"Please call me Ann."

She led me through a foyer tiled in large black and white squares like a big chessboard. I've always wanted a floor like that. If you got enough people together you could play chess on it just like in *Alice in Wonderland*. Wouldn't that be fun? The woodwork and staircase (off to the right and straight ahead) were painted a gleaming white, the walls papered in a gold-and-white fleur-de-lis print. The entryway to the living room was on the left.

The woodwork there was also white, the carpet a deep shade

of gold. Two white brocade couches were arranged in the center of the room, facing each other, with a large square oak table between them. Matching wing chairs, upholstered in a white, gold, and green stripe, faced the fireplace on the wall opposite the doorway. The artwork was of a modern sort, and some of it looked original. To my left, in front of the window, was a gorgeous Steinway grand piano. (I've wanted one of those since I was five, but I've always felt I didn't play well enough to deserve one.)

Mrs. Grossman offered me a seat on one of the couches and sat down herself on the other.

"I love your piano," I said. "Do you play?"

She looked surprised, as if she'd forgotten it was there. "Oh, no," she said. "None of us can really play."

I nodded.

"I'm sorry," she said. "Would you like coffee? Or soda? I have Diet Coke and Fresca."

I smiled, not really wanting anything but afraid I'd offend her if I turned it down. "Coffee would be great," I said.

She smiled, looking almost grateful, and said she'd be right back. She returned a few minutes later with a tray, holding two mugs of coffee, a pitcher of what looked like skim milk, artificial sweetener, and a plate of oatmeal cookies.

"These are fat-free," she said in a conspiratorial voice, "but they're really good."

I grinned and took one, wondering why in the world she felt she needed to diet. She had no excess fat anywhere on her body, from what I could see.

She gave me a sheepish smile, as if she'd read my mind. "I lost forty-three pounds in the last year and I'm terrified I'll gain it back," she said. "Divorce," she added with a rueful look. "Got myself a new hairdo, too." She moved her head around so I could inspect it.

"Well, I'm sorry about the divorce," I said, "but you look great. You really do. And the hairdo's perfect on you."

"Thanks," she said with a wide grin. "I appreciate your coming all the way out here. I'm sorry if I seemed rude on the phone."

"No, you didn't," I said. "That was my fault. I should've explained myself before I started firing questions at you."

"Do you have any experience at this sort of thing? Are you a private investigator?"

"No," I said, laughing. "I have no experience at all. But Janice is convinced the police will never pursue a murder theory so she begged me to help her and I just couldn't say no. She seemed so desperate."

She nodded. "I understand."

"You know, I realize you're worried something might've happened to Jake," I said, "but I don't think there's any reason to believe that's true."

Mrs. Grossman pressed her lips together and tears suddenly filled her eyes. "I'm sorry," she said, and took a tissue from her pocket.

"That's all right," I said. "I'm not sure how to say this without upsetting you even more, but I think if Jake had been killed, too, he'd have been found with Dave. It seems so unlikely that he'd be killed somewhere else or that they'd move his body but not Dave's. You know what I mean?"

She looked at me, tears still in her eyes, but there was a smile poking through. "You really think so?" she said, sniffling.

"Yes, I really do."

Mrs. Grossman took a deep breath and closed her eyes, then let it out and leaned her head back against the couch. "I can't see why he wouldn't have gone to the funeral, though," she said. "Where would he go for so long a time? He must not know about it. I'm sure he would've been there if he did."

I nodded, giving her a look that feigned agreement.

"When was the last time you talked to him?" I said.

"Thanksgiving. He was here for the day and went back to his apartment the day after."

"And you haven't talked to him since?"

"No," she said, shaking her head. "But that isn't unusual. I often don't hear from him for weeks at a time. He has his own life. You know how it is."

"I hate to ask this, but do you know if he talks to his father?"

"No," she said. "George hasn't spent a moment of time with Jake since the divorce. Of course, he never spent any time with him before the divorce, so I suppose that shouldn't surprise me."

I gave her a sympathetic smile, not really knowing how to

respond to that. "How about friends?" I said. "Does he have anyone in the neighborhood he usually sees?"

"There's Bob Sheridan down the street."

"Do you know if he talked to him at Thanksgiving?"

Mrs. Grossman sat up a bit straighter. "Yes," she said. "He did. He went over to the house before he left on Friday. He must've been there an hour or more."

I raised my eyebrows and gave her a little smile. "It might be worth calling him," I said.

"Yes, just a minute, I'll get the number." Mrs. Grossman left the room, returned with an address book opened to the number, and handed it to me. "Here it is," she said.

"Do you want me to call him?"

She gave me a plaintive look with a little sheepishness mixed in. "Would you?" she said.

"Sure. Where's your phone?"

She led me through a dining room with an enormous pale oak table that probably could have seated twelve comfortably, and a matching sideboard and china cabinet. The carpet was the same deep gold as in the living room, the walls papered in a gold, green, and white stripe pattern that looked a lot like the wing chairs in front of the fireplace. The drapes were green brocade with balled fringe. The table was set for eight, with china, silver, a full set of crystal, and cloth napkins.

"Are you expecting company tonight?" I asked, afraid I'd interrupted her preparations.

"Oh, no," Mrs. Grossman said. "I always keep it set."

I followed her into the next room, which looked like a small den. The floors were hardwood, with a deep red Oriental rug on top. Bookcases covered three of the walls and an oak rolltop desk was pushed against the fourth. The phone was on the desk.

I punched in the number and a woman answered on the fifth ring. I gave her my name, told her I was a friend of Jake, and asked for Bob. When she said she'd get him, I smiled at Mrs. Grossman and nodded.

A minute went by. Two minutes. When Bob finally picked up the phone he sounded as if I'd roused him out of bed.

"Hullo?" he said.

"Bob?"

"Yeah, this is Bob. Who's this?"

I introduced myself and said Jake's mother and I were look-ing for Jake, but I didn't explain why.

"Uh...well, what do you want him for?" he said.

I decided I'd better give Bob the whole story if I wanted to get any information out of him. I told him how Dave had died, that we suspected he'd been murdered, that Jake hadn't been at the funeral, that his mother didn't know where he was, that she was worried something had happened to him in addition to Dave, and that we desperately needed his help in locating Jake.

He was wide awake now, listening to every word, interrupt-ing me at appropriate junctures with phrases such as "Are you putting me on?" and "Whoa, this is some heavy stuff, man." I kept smirking, and Mrs. Grossman was giving me funny looks.

"Do you have any idea where he is?" I said when I'd fin-ished.

Now he was silent.

"Please," I said. "This is really important. He's not in any trouble, if that's what you're worried about."

Bob hesitated for a moment and then I heard him sigh. "He said something about hitting Green Bay before he went home."

"Green Bay?" I said. "Why was he going there?"

Mrs. Grossman wrinkled her brow at me and I shrugged.

"He went to play blackjack," Bob said. "There's a casino there. It's legal, you know."

"I know," I said. "But why didn't he just go to the Mil-waukee casino?"

"I don't know," Bob said. "Maybe he was tired of it. What difference does it make?"

"It doesn't," I said, starting to feel defensive. "I was just asking. Did he tell you how long he was going to be in Green Bay?"

"No, but he wouldn't have stayed this long. That was right after Thanksgiving."

"You haven't talked to him since then?"

"Nope," Bob said.

"You wouldn't have any idea where else he might've gone, would you?"

"Sorry," he said. "It's not my week to watch him." Boy, do I hate it when people say that.

"Okay," I said. "Well, thanks, Bob. If you do hear from him, would you let his mom know?"

"Sure thing," Bob said. Yeah, I just bet he would.

I looked at Mrs. Grossman after I hung up. "Well, he says Jake went to Green Bay to some casino to play blackjack but that was right after Thanksgiving. He has no idea where he is now."

Mrs. Grossman shook her head. "He must be mistaken," she said. "Jake doesn't play blackjack."

I shrugged. "Maybe it was his first time."

Mrs. Grossman looked at me with a combination of worry and irritation.

We walked back to the living room and sat down. "Well," I said. "Maybe we should try to think of someone else he might've talked to."

She didn't say anything.

"Does Jake have a job?" I said.

"No. I don't want him working during school. His grades suffer too much."

"Is there anyone else you can think of?"

Mrs. Grossman just shook her head and stared off into space.

"We probably ought to tell the police about Green Bay," I said.

She took a deep breath and pursed her lips.

"It might help them find him," I said. "I can do it for you if you want."

She looked up then and gazed at me for a few moments. "No, I'll do it," she said.

I gave Mrs. Grossman my phone number and asked her to please call me if she heard anything from Jake. She said she would. I said goodbye, told her not to worry too much, and left.

I thought about Jake all the way home. Maybe he had a gambling habit and took off for a casino every chance he got. He could be one of those guys who hangs out for days, not even bothering to take a shower. Maybe he really hadn't heard about Dave's death.

I considered calling the police myself, when I got home, but I didn't really want them knowing what I was doing—about my investigating and all. I decided to call Emily instead.

"Hi, what's up?" I said.

"Not much, how about you?"

"I went to see Dave's roommate's mom in Cedarburg. He never showed up at the funeral."

"That's weird," Emily said.

"Yeah, I know."

"What'd his mom say?"

"She hasn't even talked to him since Thanksgiving, but some guy he hangs around with says he goes to Green Bay to play blackjack."

"Ooh, a little gambling action, huh? Maybe that's where he is now."

"Yeah, that's what I was thinking. Want to drive up there and see if we can find him?"

"What, are you nuts?" Emily said. "Let the police find him. I can't believe you're actually going through with this, anyway. It's really stupid, you know. You could get yourself in a lot of trouble."

"I'm not going to get in any trouble," I said. "All I did was talk to some woman about her kid. What's the big deal?"

"Well, what if the killer finds out you're doing this, then what?"

"Just drop it, okay? What are you doing now?"

"Nothing, why?"

"Want to go to the Downtown Club?"

Emily hesitated. "Tell you what," she said. "I'll meet you in the whirlpool."

I laughed. "Okay, great. What time?"

"Half an hour?"

"Great. I'll see you there."

I ran upstairs, got my swimming suit and workout clothes, drank a glass of orange juice, and got in the car. The Downtown Club is on Van Buren and Juneau so it only takes about ten minutes to get there.

I signed in, put on my workout clothes, and went to the weight room. I jumped rope for fifteen minutes, used a couple of machines, and decided to quit. There wasn't anyone else in the room. I usually dislike exercising in front of other people (especially men!) but it felt kind of eerie being there all alone.

I went back to the locker room and changed into my bathing

suit, then peeked around the door to the pool room before I went in. Good. No men. I hate walking past men in my bathing suit.

Emily was in the whirlpool with her eyes closed and her head laid back against the edge. Two young women were in the sauna and an older woman, about fifty-five or sixty, was in the pool, swimming slow laps. Other than that, we had the place to ourselves.

"Hi," I said.

Emily opened her eyes. "Nice suit," she said with a smirk.

"What's wrong with it?" I said in a defensive voice.

"You look like Gidget," she said, and closed her eyes again.

I made a face she didn't see but kept my mouth shut. I'm such a wimp when it comes to stuff like that. I can always think of the perfect comeback two hours later but when someone says something to me (especially Emily), I just stand there like a dummy.

"Did you go to the house after the funeral?" Emily said when I got in the pool.

"Yeah, it was pretty nice. Dave's girlfriend never showed up either, by the way. Isn't that bizarre?"

"Yeah, it really is. You know, I was thinking," Emily said. "Remember Brian McHenry from grade school?"

"Ha. Brian McHenry. You bet I remember him. Why?"

"He's a homicide detective with the Milwaukee Police Department."

"You're kidding," I said. "How do you know that?"

Emily shrugged. "He went to the police academy with my brother. And," she said, the corners of her mouth turning up just slightly, "I went out with him for a while."

"You went out with him?" I said. "You're kidding. You never told me that. When'd you go out with him?"

"Right before law school, during the summer."

"I can't believe you never told me that. How'd you end up going out with him?"

"Steve and Lynn. They were having him over to dinner all the time when he got divorced and they sort of set me up with him—without telling me ahead of time."

"I'd kill my brother if he ever did that to me."

"Yeah, I almost did," Emily said.

"Well, what was he like? What does he look like now?"

"Really good," Emily said. "He's six-two and he has a really great build. You can tell he works out. And he looks...I don't know, really good. He has nice hair and he wears wire-rims. Dresses nicely, too."

I grinned, trying to conjure up an image of our class nerd looking really good when he grew up. He was the smartest kid in our class. He wore glasses with black plastic frames and he wasn't one of the guys the girls drooled over, but I'd always found him appealing. I think it was his intelligence. And he was really nice, too. Kind and considerate.

"How long did you go out with him?" I said.

"Just a couple of months."

"Why'd you stop seeing him?"

"He went back to his wife."

"Ah."

"They were going to try to work things out," Emily said. "It was so stupid. If they were going to work things out, why didn't they do it when they were married?"

I sighed. "So what happened? Did they get married again?"

"No, she took off again."

"Did you go out with him after that?"

"I'd already met Phil by then. I guess I always did have lousy timing."

I frowned at her. "You mean you wish you'd gone back to Brian instead?"

Emily shrugged and made a face that said, "Who knows? Who cares?"

"Phil really loves you, you know. Frankly, the guy worships you. That's not easy to find."

Emily didn't say anything. She didn't open her eyes, either, but I could see her clenching her jaw. In a few moments, she stood up and got out of the whirlpool.

"I'm going for a swim," she said.

I watched her do thirty laps at a pace at least twice that of the poor woman in the lane next to her. Then she got out and wanted to go home.

"Why'd you bring up Brian McHenry?" I asked her when we were getting dressed. "What'd you want to say about him?"

"I just thought you could talk to him about the case, see if he'd tell you anything."

"Hey, that's a thought," I said, "although he probably wouldn't give me any information. It'd be worth a try, though."

"You want to go get something to eat?" I said then.

"No, I'd better not," Emily said. "Phil will be home pretty soon, and I haven't cooked for a while. I was planning to make roast beef and I already took it out of the freezer."

"Okay. Say 'hi' for me."

"Will do. Talk to you later."

I got in my car and sat. I didn't want to go home. I decided to go Christmas shopping again. Tomorrow was Christmas Eve and I wasn't anywhere near through with my gift buying. I took I-94 west, then US-45, and got off on Mayfair Road.

The Mayfair Mall is in Wauwatosa, and it's about what you'd expect. Classy stores, tony decor. It used to have an ice-skating rink in the center, but it's gone now. In its place, during the holidays, is the largest Christmas tree I've ever seen indoors. It's decorated in the best of taste, too. Nothing but little white lights, big red balls, and silver bows. It looks *really* good if you're nearsighted and you don't have your glasses on.

I had a lot of trouble finding a place to park, and was almost ready to turn back, when someone pulled out of a space very near my usual entrance. I parked, ran in, and then slowed down, taking my time to wander around. I can spend hours in a mall, especially near Christmas.

I found gifts for my father and brother and another for my sister, Ann. I went through my mental list. I'd taken care of everyone but my sister's kids, and I could take care of that tomorrow. Well, okay. Then I was done.

It was snowing when I left—big, fat flakes, my favorite kind. I opened my mouth and ate a few. I know you're not supposed to do that but it hasn't killed me yet. My grandmother taught me that important lesson (the flakes fall through polluted air, you know) along with many others. Always wear a hair net when you go out-of-doors (it was never "outside," always "out-of-doors"). Never sit next to a man on a bus. Never chew with your mouth open (I agree with that one), and never wear patent leather shoes with a dress. There were others, but I can't remember them right now. If I do think of any, though, I'll be sure to let you know.

There was already a good two inches on the ground and it was really coming down. The salt, sand, and plowing crews were doing their best but the highway was pretty slick. Most of us slowed down to a creep, but the occasional moron (that's an alternate spelling for "man") would whip by at the posted speed.

When I got home an hour later, I put the car in the garage and went in through the back door so I could take my wet clothes off in the mudroom. (The back door opens to the mudroom, which is right off the kitchen.) On the other side of the mudroom is another door, which opens to the basement. I think it's really handy, but my Aunt Sarah thought it was inconvenient. She actually had my Uncle Bill build a clothes chute from the kitchen to the top of the basement stairs, just so she wouldn't have to go through the mudroom to put her laundry downstairs. It's just a square hole in the wall, with doors on both sides. I never use it myself because I don't like having clothes on my basement steps.

I made myself a cup of tea, and looked through the refrigerator for something to eat. I didn't have much, which isn't unusual since I hate to go grocery shopping. I decided on a frozen pizza. I brought some work into the kitchen and wrote while I waited for the pizza to bake. The flakes were falling even faster now, full and fluffy. I smiled and watched, feeling safe and warm inside my house. I ate my supper, took a cup of hot chocolate into the library (I love hot chocolate when it's snowing), and read for about an hour. At ten, I went upstairs, read a little longer, and turned out the light.

Snuggled under my covers, I thought snowy thoughts and dreamt snowy dreams. White-capped mountain peaks and frosted evergreens. Silent, dark forests, the soft secret sound of snow falling in the night, and breezes whispering to the trees.

I WOKE UP with a smile on my face. It was Christmas Eve. I didn't know it then, but that was the day I would learn what had happened to Jake.

FIVE

As soon as I opened my eyes, I ran to the window to see how much snow we'd gotten.

A lot. A whole lot. Like a couple of feet? Good grief.

I have a neighbor boy on a sort of retainer to shovel my walk, front and back, whenever it needs it. He was out in front of my house, just getting started. I opened the window wide enough to stick my head out and got a blast of cold air and snow in the face.

"Hey, Peter. Merry Christmas," I yelled.

Peter stopped shoveling and looked up with a grin. "Hey, how're ya doin'?" he said.

"Great. Come around back when you're through. I have something for you."

He grinned, knowing what it was—a big fat Christmas bonus I give him every year.

The whole neighborhood was full of people shoveling, most with snowblowers rather than shovels, though. I guess I should break down and buy one so Peter won't have to work so hard. I think he enjoys it, though. (Yeah, right, who am I kidding?) The street was already plowed, leaving three-foot banks along each side. I love that. Sometimes I still walk across them when I'm pretty sure nobody's looking.

I made the bed, showered and dressed, and went down to the kitchen. Snow always makes me hungry, and I was starving. I turned on my kitchen radio, made a pot of tea, and baked some blueberry muffins. I wasn't due at my parents' house until noon and it was only nine so I had plenty of time. I had a bit of shopping to do before I went but I didn't think it would take too long.

At ten-fifteen, Peter knocked at the door and I asked him in for a cup of hot chocolate and some muffins. He was thrilled. He looked like a big icicle, poor kid. He's sixteen, a junior in high school, and I love talking to him. He dripped snow all over my kitchen floor, and me, but I didn't care.

At ten-forty-five, I loaded my presents in the car and headed for the expressway. I couldn't wait to get to my parents' house—partly because it was Christmas Eve, of course, but also because I had something I wanted to ask my brother, Mike, about Dave. I'd have to wait until I got a chance to talk to him alone, though. And I'd have to wait for everything, until after I got my shopping done.

I took 894 to Seventy-sixth Street and stopped at Barnes & Noble on my way to the toy store. I buy a lot of books there, even though it's way across town, because I really like the store. It's enormous, the staff is very helpful, and they have a great coffee shop.

Seventy-sixth Street is one of those commercial strips with movie theaters, shopping malls, and every fast-food restaurant in existence. Barnes & Noble is a relatively recent addition. The traffic is often heavy, but today it was heavier than usual. I hadn't expected so many people to be out on Christmas Eve, especially with all the snow.

The parking lot was plowed, the snow pushed over to one end forming a mountain at least ten feet high (we used to make snow forts out of those when we were kids). The bookstore was crowded but I was kind of glad. It was more festive that way. I looked around for a while, found some books for Ann's kids, and a couple of mysteries for myself. I stood in a long line, which moved very quickly, paid for the books, and brought them back to the coffee shop.

I love that café. I could sit there for hours. It has a player piano and it was playing jazz renditions of Christmas carols when I came in. I found a table, ordered coffee with cream, and sat down.

An older couple (maybe mid-to late sixties) was sitting at the table next to mine. The woman had wavy silver hair and she was wearing the most beautiful seafoam-green sweater with a plaid wool skirt, long wool stockings, and short boots. The man had a beard, wore wide-wale corduroy pants, an old cardigan with leather patches on the elbows, and a wool, herringbone-checked hat that looked sort of like a tam with a visor. He was reading a newspaper and she was eating cake. Every once in a while, she'd give him a bite. Every so often, he'd read something to her from the paper. They looked so companionable. I think I'd like to be married at that age, but it'd have to be to the right sort of person. Someone whose company I enjoy. Someone who appreciates my good qualities. My first husband saw all my best qualities as faults. Now, how's that for building your self-esteem?

A few tables over, two college-age kids were playing Scrabble (with a game supplied by the café) and drinking some kind of fancy coffee with that funny milk on top. I hate that stuff. The coffee's always too strong and the milk feels weird. I like regular old-fashioned coffee with regular old-fashioned cream (although whipped cream is awfully good). Ann says I'm just not hip. Oh, well. Her husband, Don, is. He always orders a "double cap." I'm pretty sure that means double cappuccino, but I've never had the nerve to ask. I guess I'd know if I were hip, huh? Heck, if I were hip, I wouldn't even care. I'd just order the stuff, drink it, and pretend I liked it even if it made me gag.

Don smokes a pipe, too, with some expensive tobacco he never shuts up about. You should see this guy. He's about five-ten, maybe thirty pounds overweight, light brown hair, and a really scraggly beard. He wears a tweed sportcoat and jeans all the time, even in summer, and he says things like, "It's very sort of..." and "One finds that..." Talk about things that make you gag.

I sipped my coffee and read the back covers of my mysteries. After a second cup, I decided I'd better get going. I still had the kids' toys to buy and I had to pick up a mincemeat pie I'd ordered from Baker's Square for my dad. How anyone can eat a pie made of suet is beyond me, but Dad loves it so I get him one every year.

The toy store I was so sure was close by was no longer there. Luckily, Southridge Shopping Center is just down the street so I went there to Kay-Bee Toys. I found a purportedly safe chemistry set for ten-year-old Don, a set of K'NEX for seven-year-old Kristin, and Tinkertoys for five-year-old Katy. It's so much easier now that they're older. I have the hardest time finding toys for toddlers. It's that ubiquitous "not suitable for children under three" that causes all the problems.

Baker's Square is also on Seventy-sixth Street, on the same side of the street as Southridge. I picked up the animal fat pie, put it in the trunk, and drove down Seventy-sixth to Bluemound, then took Bluemound to Eighty-fourth. My parents' house is on Eighty-fourth Street, a few blocks north of Bluemound. I drove slowly through the neighborhood so I could look at the decorations.

Most of the houses were decorated, but everything was pretty subdued. Tiny white lights. Wreaths with bows. An occasional crèche. Nothing like West Allis, where, in at least one neighborhood, they put on an extravaganza you wouldn't believe.

My mom has something different each year and she makes everything herself. This time it was wreaths of ferns and pinecones with red apples and big red plaid bows. The best on the block, as always. The street is lined with mature deciduous trees, mostly maples and oaks, and all the houses are different. Ours is red brick with dark green shutters (the real thing with wrought-iron hinges) and a dark red door. In the summer, my mother's pink roses form an arch over the door and she has pale pink gardenias in every window box. Blossoming beauty everywhere. I always mean to try something like it at my own house but I've never made the time.

I parked behind Don's Range Rover, gathered up all my stuff, and went inside. The house opens to a foyer with a big hall tree and a small table for mail and keys and such things. The living room has stuccoed walls, painted off-white. The couch and the love seat are a plum-and-cream plaid. There are two wing chairs in a plum-and-navy print on a braided wool rug a few feet from the fireplace. The wood furniture is walnut, bought at secondhand shops or estate sales and refinished by my mom. There's an antique desk against one wall, a large chest against another, and a gateleg table to the left of the love seat. Above and on each side of the fireplace, from floor to ceiling, are bookshelves constructed by my grandfather.

A fire was burning in the fireplace and Dad was using it to roast chestnuts and pop corn for the kids. I gave him a big hug and kiss, and moved the kids a little farther from the fire. I love the ambience of a crackling fire but it does make me nervous. I settled the kids on the rug with the corn my dad had already popped, and went to the kitchen to find my mom.

She was there, with Ann, making cornflake cookies (sounds weird but they're great). The kitchen is small, but nice and homey. The floor is reddish-brown ceramic tile and the wall behind the oven is the same red brick as the outside of the house. The other walls are off-white (stucco again) with a chair rail and oak paneling beneath it. The cabinets are oak, too, and so are the table and chairs. And there's a walk-in pantry.

I kissed Mom and Ann and poured myself a cup of coffee.

"Where's Donny Dear?" I said to Ann.

She shot me a look. "Do you have to call him that?" she said.

"Sorry, I thought it was a term of endearment," I said. She wasn't fooled. I could tell. Oh, well. That's what she gets for marrying him, I guess.

"He's in the library," she said grudgingly.

"How's Janice holding up?" my mom asked.

"Oh, that is so awful what happened to her brother," Ann said. "I just can't believe it."

"Yeah, I know," I said. I told them how I thought both Janice and Marge were faring and that Janice believed Dave had been murdered. I left out the part about her asking me to help her find the killer.

"Oh, my Lord," my mom said.

"Oh, that is so horrible," Ann said.

I agreed, again, and tried to change the subject, but just then Mike walked in and wanted to know what was so horrible. I told him the story then, and added a few details about Dave's career plans, since he'd intended to start a business so much like Mike's. I finally succeeded in changing the subject after that by asking Ann about the kids. We talked about Don, Jr.'s basketball and soccer prowess for the next half-hour, and the murder was forgotten.

The rest of the evening was our typical Christmas Eve. Lasagna, mostoccioli, Italian sausage, and meatballs for supper, a ride after dinner to look at the lights, and then home to open presents Santa Claus conveniently left while we were out.

We put the kids to bed at eight, and played games until almost midnight. When Mike went to the basement to replenish the soda between Risk and Monopoly, I offered to help.

"Let me ask you something," I said when we were out of

everyone else's earshot. "If somebody wanted to break into a computer at Marquette to change their grades or something like that, would they need to do it in any particular building or could they just do it from any computer?"

He looked at me with puzzlement and surprise. "What do you want to know that for?" he said.

I told Mike about the bomb scares. "I was just wondering if Dave could've been using them as a ruse to get access to a computer."

"No. He wouldn't have to do that," Mike said. "If anyone could get in those files and change their grades—which they almost certainly couldn't, by the way—they could do it from home if they had a modem."

"Why couldn't they get in?" I said.

"It's encrypted and encoded to death. It'd be almost impossible to figure it out. Some engineering students got in years ago and after that they made it pretty much burglar-proof."

I sighed. "Okay, thanks," I said.

"What are you so interested in that for?" Mike said.

"I don't know," I said with a shrug. "He was Janice's brother, that's all."

THE DRIVE HOME was peaceful. Everything was quiet and the sky was full of stars. I put the car away, wished Orion a Merry Christmas, and went inside.

I went into the library to see if I had any messages. There was one. It was Ann Grossman. Jake had been found. He'd come home for Christmas.

Hallelujah, I thought as I scrunched under the covers. Ann Grossman's child was safe.

I SLEPT UNTIL TEN and then hurried to get dressed. I'd promised my mom I'd be back before noon so I could help with the Christmas Day meal, but I had to call Ann Grossman first. It was a little early, so I had a banana and some toast and made myself a cup of tea. I sorted through Christmas cards until a quarter to eleven and then made the call.

"Ann? This is Beth Hartley," I said when she picked up the phone.

"Beth. Thank you for calling. I wanted you to know Jake is all right and to thank you for all your help," she said. She was so excited and so happy it brought tears to my eyes.

"You're very welcome," I said. "Did the police find him?"

"No," she said. "He just came home. He came home because it was Christmas." From the sound of her voice, it was the best Christmas present she'd ever received.

"I'm so glad," I said. "I know how worried you were."

"Yes, I was," she said. "And thank you again, Beth. Merry Christmas to you and all your family."

When I thanked her and wished her the same, she was about to hang up.

"Ann?" I said. "Would you mind if I talked to Jake for a few minutes?"

She hesitated and then said, "No. No, of course not. I'll go get him. He's already talked to the police, by the way."

A few minutes later, she returned and said Jake would be right down. When he finally picked up the phone he sounded a little nervous.

"Jake?" I said. "My name is Beth Hartley and I'm a good friend of Dave's sister, Janice."

"Yeah, I know Janice," he said.

"Well, she's asked me to help her prove Dave was murdered and I was hoping you could help me."

"The police are working on that," Jake said.

"I know," I said, "but Janice is afraid they won't take it seriously enough or they'll just abandon it too soon or something."

"Yeah, so what do you want from me?" he said. "I already told everything I know to the police."

"Would you mind telling me, too?"

He grunted in annoyance.

"I know it seems like a waste of time," I said, "but you'll be doing Janice a big favor."

He sighed loudly. "Yeah, okay," he said grudgingly. "But not on the phone. Can you come to my place tomorrow?"

"Sure. What time?"

"Eleven?"

"That'd be great," I said. "Thanks, Jake."

I called Janice next, but there was no answer. I tried Marge and didn't get an answer there, either.

I went to my parents' house, spent the rest of the day eating Christmas cookies and trying to fix broken toys, and was back home by ten. I was still tired from the night before. I made myself a cup of chamomile tea and went up to bed.

THE NEXT DAY WAS Saturday, December twenty-sixth. I awoke at nine and took my time getting dressed. It had snowed lightly during the night and everything was dusted with a clean white powder. I made apple muffins for breakfast and ate three along with two cups of tea. I called Janice at ten and asked if she wanted to go with me to talk to Jake, but she said no. She didn't want to go into the apartment again. Not just yet, anyway.

"How was your Christmas?" I asked in a cautious voice.

Janice let out a big sigh. "It was miserable," she said. "But we went to Aunt Mary's both days. We always have Christmas at home, so that made it easier."

"Well, that's good," I said. "I'm glad you had somewhere else to go."

Janice sighed again. "We don't know what to do with the presents we bought him," she said, her voice breaking.

"Oh, my gosh," I said. "I know just what you mean."

"What did you do with Eric's?"

"I kept them," I said. "But I put them in a box in the attic where I don't have to see them unless I want to."

Janice didn't say anything for a few moments, but I could hear her sniffling. "Yeah," she said after a bit. "That's a good idea."

"What are you planning to do today?"

"I don't know. Go over to Mom's, I guess." She sounded so hopeless and lost it brought tears to my eyes.

"Are you going to be all right?" I said.

"Yeah, I guess. Will you call me when you get back?"

"Sure," I said.

JAKE'S APARTMENT is on the east side, just off of Brady, in the old Italian ward. At one time, the neighborhood was populated almost exclusively by Italian-Americans. A lot of them are still there. In the sixties and early seventies, the area became a hippie hangout. Drug paraphernalia shops and other counterculture establishments moved in, and some of the residents moved out. Nearly all of that's gone now. You'd hardly know they'd been there.

Jake's building is a light salmon brick in an art deco style. I found the button for the apartment to the left of the mailboxes and rang. A few moments later, the door clicked and I walked in.

The lobby was sprawling, with brocade-curtained floor-to-ceiling windows, a checkerboard-tiled floor in tan and beige, and a winding staircase with a painted railing and steps covered with worn Oriental carpeting.

I took the stairs to the third floor. Jake's number was 314. The door to the apartment next to Jake's was wide open, and another, farther down the hall, was slightly ajar. The one next door appeared to be inhabited by a woman, probably elderly, if I could judge by the furnishings. I knocked on Jake's door.

"It's open," I heard.

A young man was standing about eight feet from the doorway, packing items into a box. The box was on a coffee table in front of the couch. He was about five-nine or -ten, of normal weight except for a slight paunch. His black hair was long, about two inches over his ears, and he looked like he was starting a beard. He wore a brown one-pocket T-shirt over faded blue jeans. The jeans had holes all over them.

"You Beth?" he said, not bothering to look up.

"Yes," I said. "I assume you're Jake?"

He didn't respond so I took that as a yes. He went right on with his packing.

The room was large and square, the floor bare wood with most of the varnish peeled off. The couch was to my right, a drab olive green, partially covered by an orange, red, and blue afghan. Across from the couch was a stereo, a CD player, two speakers, a TV, and a VCR. The wall directly across from the door was all windows, but the only view was of a brick wall from the building next door. The plants hanging in the window were yellow and wilted.

"Are you moving?" I asked.

"Yep," he answered, and went right on with what he was

doing. He still hadn't taken a peek at me. If he was trying to make me feel uncomfortable, he was doing a darn good job of it.

"I asked Janice if she wanted to come with me," I said, "but she didn't want to see the apartment again. She was the one who found Dave, you know."

Jake tightened his jaw, but said nothing. He'd been packing things in a careful way up to that point, but now he started flinging things, one after the other, into the open box. He just took whatever was closest and pitched it in. When something shattered, he threw the next three items in with particular force, punctuated each time by what I soon learned was his expletive of choice.

He dropped himself onto the couch, and stared out the window with his teeth clenched.

"Would you like me to help you with that?" I said.

"No. Forget it," he muttered.

I sat down on the other end of the couch.

"Nice view," I said.

He turned his head, stared at me in disbelief, and laughed. He shook his head a few times, a smile still on his face.

"Do you want me to come back some other time?" I said.

"No, forget it," he said. "I'm sorry, you want a beer or something?"

"No, thanks," I said, stifling a laugh.

Jake sighed, then sighed again. "So, what'd you want to ask me?" he said.

"Well, quite a few things," I said. I didn't want to start off with anything too personal for fear of scaring him away so I decided to ask about Laura first.

"Do you know Dave's girlfriend, Laura?" I said.

He snorted. "Yeah, I know Laura. Why?"

"She wasn't at the funeral."

Jake gave me a sudden look but didn't say anything.

"Do you know where she's from?" I said.

"Boston," Jake said in a sort of mock-elitist voice. I had to force myself not to smile.

"Do you have any idea why she wouldn't have gone to the funeral?"

He shrugged. "Maybe she doesn't know he's dead. She went

home Thursday night. Dave drove her to the airport. Or,'' he added with a smirk, ''maybe she does know and Daddy wouldn't let her come.''

I frowned. ''You mean Laura's father didn't like Dave?''

''Let's just say Senator Big Shot VanderHayden thought his precious daughter could do better. Bunch of lousy snobs.''

''Hmm,'' I said, pursing my lips. ''Do you know where I could reach her?''

Jake got up, pulled an address book from beneath a pile of mail on top of the stereo, and handed it to me. I found the address and phone number and copied it onto the back of a credit card receipt I had in my pocket.

''How long was Dave going out with her?'' I said.

''Couple of years, at least.''

''Was her father aware that he was still seeing her?''

Jake looked at me without answering, but his face said, ''How should I know?''

''You don't know?'' I said.

He rolled his eyes. ''No, I don't know. Okay?''

''What made you come back?'' I asked carefully.

Jake looked at me, turned away, and shrugged. ''It was Christmas,'' he said. ''I didn't want my mom to be alone.''

I smiled. ''That was nice of you; she was really worried.''

No response.

''Why weren't you at the funeral? Where were you?'' I said.

Jake glared at me. ''I was in Green Bay, playing blackjack, okay? It's not a crime, you know.''

''So you didn't know about Dave until you got home?''

Jake stared out the window for a few moments, got up from the couch, and put an empty box on the coffee table. He started packing again, but this time in a very careful, measured manner.

''Did you know about Dave's death before you left?'' I said again.

''I already explained all this to the cops,'' he said slowly. ''Why don't you just leave it to them and stay out of it? You could end up like Dave.''

I watched him intently for a few moments, trying to gauge his meaning, but he didn't vary his movements or his expression.

''Why do you say that?'' I asked.

Jake stopped what he was doing and looked up at me. He closed his eyes and let out a deep breath.

"Look," he said as he opened them again. "I found him, okay? I found his body long before Janice did and I just freaked and took off." Jake's voice had a slight quaver. He looked away quickly and busied himself with his packing again.

I wrinkled my brow. "When did you find him?" I said.

"Friday night, around one o'clock, when I came back from the bars."

"Did you see anything that looked out of the ordinary?"

Jake looked at me like I had my head screwed on backward.

"I mean other than Dave," I said. "Did it look like someone had broken in, like they'd been searching for something? Anything like that?"

He frowned and thought for a while. "I don't think so," he said. "I didn't notice anything looking unusual."

"Nothing was wrong with the door lock or anything?"

"No, it was fine," Jake said. "I let myself in with my key and it worked just like it always does."

"No papers or anything strewn around the apartment? No drawers emptied on the beds? Nothing like that?"

Jake shook his head. "No, nothing. I would've noticed it."

"Why did you run when you saw the body, instead of calling the police?"

No answer, just an uncomprehending stare.

"I mean, didn't you think it was a suicide when you saw his body?"

"No, I didn't think it was a suicide," Jake said. "There's no way he would've killed himself. I was pretty sure I knew who did it, too, and I wasn't going to hang around so they could get me, too."

"You think you know who did it?" I said, my eyes opening wide. "Who? Who do you think did it?"

"I already told this to the police," Jake said.

"Well, tell me, too," I said. "Please, Jake."

Jake gave me a jaded look. "You really shouldn't be messin' around with these guys," he said. "You're just going to get yourself hurt."

I clenched my teeth and tried to remain calm. "Jake," I said.

"Please. Just tell me. I'm not going to do anything stupid. Trust me."

Jake gave me one of those Oh-gosh-I-guess-I'll-have-to-humor-you looks. He was really starting to get on my nerves.

"It had to be the guys he borrowed money from," he said. "Those guys don't mess around when you don't pay them back."

I stared at him with my mouth open. "You're not saying he borrowed money from loan sharks, are you?" There was no way I was going to believe that one.

"All I know is, Dave told me he borrowed two thousand bucks off some guys and he was supposed to pay them back in a week. They must've been loan sharks. Who else lends money like that?"

"Jake," I said, growing exasperated, "it could've been anybody. Who's going to kill somebody for a measly two thousand bucks? Do you even know for sure Dave didn't pay them back?"

"Yeah, I know he didn't pay them back. He told me he didn't. He thought he was going to double it in a week but instead he lost it."

"How'd he lose it?" I said.

"Playing blackjack."

"Dave was a gambler, too?"

Jake rolled his eyes. "Dave was a blackjack *expert,* man. He had a method worked out that was practically foolproof."

"Well, if it was so foolproof," I said, "why'd he lose all the money?"

Jake sneered at me. "It just had a few bugs in it, that's all. He was still perfecting it."

I put my head in my hands.

"So maybe it wasn't the loan sharks," Jake said. "Maybe it was the guys from the casinos. They don't take too kindly to people who win a lot of money, you know, and they're all run by the mob." Jake adopted a tough-guy stance and gave me a look like he'd been around, and I hadn't.

I screwed up my face. "Jake, they're run by American Indians," I said. "Didn't you ever notice that?"

Jake stared off into space. "Oh, yeah," he said after a few moments.

"Do you have any Advil?" I said.

"No, why?"

"Never mind," I said. "Forget it. Did Dave ever talk to you about those bomb scares?"

"No," Jake said. "I don't know anything about that."

"What about his other friends? Do you know any of them?"

Jake shrugged. "I met a few of them. There's some guys he wrestled with—Scott Chapman, I think, and Dick Burghoff."

I wrote the names on the same credit card receipt I'd written Laura's name and number on.

I gazed out the window at the brick wall, trying to think of something else to ask him, but nothing came to mind.

"Jake, would you mind if I hang around for a while and look through Dave's things? I want a chance to check everything out before you move. When are you leaving?"

"End of January," Jake said, "if I can find another place. You can stay and look around if you want to, but I'm taking off, so lock the door when you're done."

"Okay," I said. "Thanks."

SIX

JAKE SHOWED ME to Dave's room and left a few minutes later, for which I was thankful. It'd be a lot easier to snoop without him peering over my shoulder.

The first thing that struck me about the room was the mess. Jake said nothing seemed out of place. If that were true, Dave was an absolute slob. The bed was unmade, and clothes were strewn everywhere. A dresser drawer was on the floor, the contents dumped out and scattered. The closet door was open. Clothes were pulled from hangers and left in a heap on the floor. A box, formerly full of odds and ends—notebooks, an old calculator, paperbacks—was overturned and emptied on top of the clothes.

The room was small and square, painted a dirty bluish-gray,

with one small window. The nightstand next to the bed was oak, the varnish peeling away, and it was piled high with paperbacks and magazines. I looked through them but found nothing of interest. Most of the magazines were computer-oriented; the paperbacks were science fiction. There weren't any drawers.

An armchair was on the other side of the bed, covered with an old chenille bedspread. A pile of books and papers was on the seat and I sorted through them, too. Nothing. Just textbooks and school assignments.

The three-tier bookcase lining the window wall was one of those homemade things constructed of unfinished plywood and bricks. The top shelf held half a dozen wrestling trophies, the bottom two, a variety of textbooks, dictionaries, and other reference texts. There were also three large stacks of Dick Tracy comic books, a volume of Shakespeare's plays, books on astronomy, computer languages, computer games, computer viruses, and computer hacks, and several on blackjack, sheepshead, and chess. Good grief.

What looked like an old school desk was pushed against another wall, with a computer and a bunch of papers on top. The drawers were open, the contents still inside, but somewhat messed up. The top side drawer contained several boxes of computer disks, the other two, computer printouts. The center drawer was locked.

Behind the desk, on the wall, was a bulletin board. Pushpins held snapshots, news clippings, various handwritten notes, and some postcards. Two of the snapshots were of a young woman, probably in her early twenties, with long, unstyled, medium-brown hair parted in the middle and pushed behind her ears. In both pictures, she wore jeans with holes in the knees and an oversized T-shirt. There was a relatively recent picture of Janice and Marge, sitting on Marge's front porch. They had their arms around each other and happy smiles on their faces. Another showed a much younger Marge with a tall, good-looking man, a young girl, and a small baby.

There were three news clippings. One had something to do with the validity of SAT scores reported by colleges and universities, another was about Medicaid fraud, and the third about a proposed shopping center to which East Side residents were objecting. The handwritten notes were just reminders of test dates and wrestling practices.

There were two postcards. One was a picture of the Eiffel Tower and the other a French bakery with small tables and chairs outside, next to the sidewalk. I removed both from the bulletin board so I could read what was written on the back. The card with the Eiffel Tower was undated and I couldn't make out the postmark. It read:

Dear Dave,

I'm having a great time but I sure wish you were here with me. Maybe someday we can do this together. Dad's being a jerk, as usual. Can't wait to see you.

Love,
Laura

The other had a postmark from last April, and read:

Dear Dave,

I ate breakfast here this morning. Hope you like me chubby. I miss you. I really love you and can't wait to see you on Tuesday.

Love,
Laura

Interesting stuff, but nothing in the way of a clue as far as I could see. I put the cards back where I'd found them, sat on the bed, and looked around the room.

Where was the typewriter?

I was sure Janice had said the suicide note was in the typewriter. There was no typewriter in Dave's room and I didn't remember seeing one in the living room. I went back to the living room, looked everywhere there, and in the dining room. No typewriter.

I passed by Jake's room on the way back to Dave's, turned around, and went back. The door was closed. Hmm. I was pretty sure Jake wasn't coming back. What harm could it do to take just a teensy little peek? I opened the door—and gasped.

There was an outline of a body on the rug and a typewriter on the desk. Well, I guess I know a clue when I see one.

I went back to Dave's room, sat down at the desk, and started to sort through the papers on top. There was nothing there but school assignments, old tests, and class notes. Well, that was about it for Dave's room. I went back to Jake's.

This time I went in and closed the door behind me. Jake's room was larger than Dave's and a little more cheery. Instead of dreary gray-blue, it was painted a clean, bright yellow. And there were colorful posters all over the walls. The carpeting was bright blue.

His bed was unmade, too, and covered with folded clothes, belts, and socks. There was a highboy chest with five drawers. I opened them one by one. Three were empty. The other two contained sweaters and underwear.

An old orange crate was next to the bed, with a lamp and a few books on top. Five more orange crates were under the window, turned on their sides and used as bookcases. The only other thing in the room was the desk. This one was gray metal with two side drawers and another in the middle. The side drawers held tests, school assignments, and class notes; the middle one, pens, paper clips, and the like. There was nothing on top of the desk but the typewriter and a page-a-day calendar. I flipped through the calendar. No entries.

The typewriter was an electric, fairly new, with no paper. I checked the ribbon to see if it was the type that retains an impression of everything that was typed, but it wasn't. I saw that on *Columbo* once—that's how he caught the killer. Oh, well.

I went back to Dave's room and sat down at the desk again. I suddenly remembered the center drawer. (I'll tell you, the next time one of my friends asks me to help her find a murderer, I'm going to be a lot more organized about it.)

I needed to find the key. I hadn't noticed one in any of the drawers, but there was a wooden jewelry box on top of the dresser. I got up and opened it. It appeared to be filled with nothing but change but underneath I found a key.

I went back to the desk. Darn. Wrong key. Out of sheer frustration, I gave the drawer a couple of hard shakes—and it opened!

The drawer was lined with brown paper and was empty except for a high school diploma. I took the diploma out and looked at it, checking to see if there was anything hidden inside. Nope. I put it back, but when I did, the brown paper moved and so did the piece of plywood to which it was attached. On the left upper edge, I could see what looked like a catalog or magazine poking out from underneath. I opened the drawer as far as I could, lifted the plywood, and removed it. It wasn't a catalog. It was a calendar. Inside the calendar was a bankbook. Underneath it were a computer printout and a letter.

The letter was from Laura. I started to open it and then put it back. It was probably just a personal love letter. I shouldn't be reading that kind of thing, should I? Oh, what the heck. I took it back out of the drawer. I had the letter out of the envelope when my conscience got the better of me again, and I put it back. It'd still be there, if I ever decided it might be important.

I opened the calendar instead, and paged through it. There were no entries at all for January. In February, he'd had a dentist appointment and gotten his hair cut. Good for him. On March seventeenth, he'd penned in *Party! Party! Party!* Nothing in April. May was blank, except for May twelfth—*Last day of classes!!* In June, he'd had an appointment with Dr. King. Then nothing for July all the way through October. In November, he'd circled Thanksgiving Day. In December, he'd circled the first and third Saturdays, and written *8:00* on the first Friday and *9:00* on the third. He had another appointment with Dr. King for the twenty-third. That was it. It didn't mean a darn thing to me, but I copied the entries on a blank sheet of paper and put the calendar back with the letter.

The bankbook was next. Now this was a little more interesting. His balance was relatively stable through September, and then, on October ninth, he made a withdrawal of five hundred dollars. He deposited twelve hundred on October twelfth. On October sixteenth he withdrew fifteen hundred, then deposited two thousand on the nineteenth. November sixth, he withdrew two thousand; November thirteenth, another five hundred. November twentieth he withdrew three hundred and November twenty-third, he deposited eight-fifty. There was nothing then until December fifth. On that date, he made a deposit of ten thousand dollars. On December eleventh, he withdrew eight thousand. That was the last transaction. I copied everything and put the book where I'd found it.

Now for the computer printout. Fat chance I was going to understand that. I opened it and let it trail to the floor. The thing was enormous, pages and pages of names, numbers, and dates. There were three columns. After every name was a number, meaning I didn't know what, and a date. There were no column headings so I couldn't tell what the numbers meant, although most of them were the same. The oddest thing was that every name, with its accompanying number and date, was recorded twice, one right after the other. It made no sense to me but I decided to take it with me since there was no way I could copy all the information.

I replaced the plywood and the diploma, made sure nothing was sticking out, and closed the drawer.

I looked at my watch. It was almost one-thirty. Mike ought to be up by now, even on a Saturday. I went to the living room and dialed his number. No answer. I tried my parents' house.

"Yes, he's here," my mom said. "Why? Is anything wrong?"

"No, Mom. I just want to ask him a computer question."

"Are you sure?" she said.

"Yes, Mom," I answered patiently. "I'm sure."

When Mike came to the phone I told him not to let on where I was and what I was doing and then I gave him a quick explanation.

"Now. Can you tell me how to work a computer over the phone?" I said.

"Well, it depends on what you mean," he said. "What do you want to do?"

"Well, first, how do you turn it on?"

I heard him grunt in disgust. "You're kidding, right?"

"No, Mike, I'm not kidding. You know I don't know anything about computers. That's why I'm calling you."

He sighed loudly. "It has an on/off switch," he said in his most condescending voice. "Just find it and turn it on. Look in the back, if you don't see one in front."

"Okay," I said, trying not to let my anger show. "Hold on." I ran into Dave's room, found the switch, and turned it on.

It made a familiar computer-type noise, so I grabbed one of the computer disks and went back to the phone.

"Okay, I'm back. Now, listen. He has a whole bunch of these little computer disks. Can you tell me how to put them in the computer and look at them?"

"Get a pencil and paper," Mike said with a groan. After he told me what to do, I hung up and got to work.

The first disk (excuse me, diskette) had some sort of school project on it. The one after that looked like a compilation of all his grades, from every course, through all four years of college. Every last one was an A. Now why would he need a record of that? Maybe he just liked looking at all those As.

The next two were course outlines. The one after that was a record of his medical bills, and the next, a record of his monthly expenses. I put those two aside. There were three more course outlines, several school projects and papers, and about ten I didn't understand at all.

I called Mike back.

"How do I print something out?" I said.

He sighed loudly, again, and gave me step-by-step instructions in a voice you might use to explain sharing to a two-year-old. What a jerk.

I printed out the medical bills and the monthly expenses, put everything back where I'd found it (with the exception of the printout I was "borrowing"), and left for home. It was time to call Laura VanderHayden.

WHEN I GOT HOME it was almost three. I called Janice right away, and then Laura. A woman, whom I judged to be a housekeeper, picked up on the third ring.

"VanderHayden residence," she said. She was using an extremely formal voice, sort of butler-like, and it had an annoying nasal quality.

"Miss VanderHayden is not home at present," she said when I asked for Laura. I left a message asking Laura to call me as soon as she could, and said only that it concerned Dave Grezinski. When she asked me to spell "Grezinski" she pronounced it like it was a dirty word she'd never heard before.

I went to the refrigerator and opened it. No juice, no fruit, no vegetables, no eggs, no milk. No nothing. I had to go to the store. I exhaled loudly, put on my coat, and got in the car. I was a little reluctant to leave the house again, in case Laura should call, but Sendik's is only a few blocks away, on Oakland. If I really worked at it, I could make it back in no time at all.

For a grocery store, Sendik's is pretty neat. I actually went to law school with a guy who met his wife there. They have all kinds of little gourmet things and their produce section is wonderful. I picked up a loaf of French bread, some fresh onion rolls, cheddar and pepper jack cheeses, the makings for a salad, some mangoes, kiwis, apples, and bananas. I added some skim milk, two kinds of juice, a carton of eggs, threw in a package of store-made beef-and-onion pastry things that looked really good, and I was done. I got through the checkout line, put the groceries in the car, and was back home within half an hour of the time I'd left.

As soon as I got in the door, I checked my messages. There was one, but it was from a client. I put the groceries away, returned the call to my client, and then made myself a cup of tea and a sandwich of pepper jack cheese on an onion roll with lots of mustard. I gathered all my "evidence" together and sat at the kitchen table sorting through it as I ate. I made a list of things I'd found out and questions I had, using a sort of stream-of-consciousness method, just writing down whatever came to mind. I read it over twice after I'd finished, but it didn't trigger any great flashes of brilliance, so I put it away.

I was restless. It was Saturday, I didn't feel like working, but I wanted to get something accomplished. If only I had a suspect, I could stake out his house. Or follow him in my car. Well, I didn't have one, so I decided to do some laundry instead. I left my list et al. on the kitchen table, went upstairs, collected a basketful of dirty clothes, and brought it down to the basement. I have two rooms down there. The one farthest from the steps has a washer and dryer, furnace, fuse boxes, and all that sort of thing. The one right at the bottom of the stairs is carpeted and furnished, with a couch, three big easy chairs, a TV, and a pool table. There's a play area for the kids with a big box of toys my Aunt Sarah had kept for us to play with when we were small. And there's a nice little powder room and a shower. I put the laundry in, started the cycle, and went back up.

On my way back to the second floor for another load, I took my "Dave" file to the library to put in my desk. My message light was on—it was Laura VanderHayden! She must have called when I was downstairs. I couldn't believe it. I called her right back. A maid-type answered again, but this time it was a different voice. Ms. VanderHayden has stepped out, I was told, and might she take a message? I asked her to please tell Ms. VanderHayden that Ms. Hartley was returning her call. So much for that.

I went upstairs, put as much laundry as I could fit into the basket, went back down to the basement, and sorted, while I tried to imagine what Laura VanderHayden's life was like. I had visions of maids and butlers and other assorted domestics bustling about, cleaning and shining, dusting and waxing, doing all the laundry and putting everything away. Dinners were served at a mile-long table with candles and silver and crystal and everyone in formal dress. When Miss VanderHayden "stepped out" she was transported in a gleaming Rolls Royce by a uniformed chauffeur, who took her wherever she wanted to go and waited for her in the car until she was through.

The chauffeur.

James? Or Charles, maybe. Tall, dark, and handsome. Young. Virile. Forbidden. Now, who can resist forbidden? Laura has an affair with Chuck the chauffeur, gets bored, breaks it off, goes back to Dave, and Chuck kills him in a fit of envy. Well, things like that do happen, you know.

After the laundry, I did some knitting and reading, had the beef-and-onion pastries for supper (they were good), read some more, and went to bed. Laura didn't return my call that night.

THE NEXT DAY was Sunday, December twenty-seventh—the day I met Mrs. Robinson. I called Janice just to see how she was doing. I told her I wanted to show her the computer printout to see if it meant anything to her. She said she'd be in to work the next morning and she'd do it then.

I called Emily next, but she wasn't home. I was caught up enough with my work that I didn't need to do anything, and I was still feeling restless. I went to the library and got out the "Dave" file, and looked through everything I had. Still no ideas. I made a list of the people I hadn't talked to: Dr. King, Dave's wrestling coach, Scott Chapman, Dick Burghoff, Laura, Laura's father, Dave's employer.

Who else might know something? I had a sudden thought. I could question the people in Dave's apartment building. One of the doors was ajar when I went to see Jake, the one right next door, wide open. Maybe someone had seen or heard something that night, or some other time.

I called Jake to tell him what I was doing and he said he'd buzz me in when I got there. I grabbed a notebook and a pen and I was gone.

The sky was completely overcast, not a hint of sun. I hadn't called the weather but I could tell the temperature was well below zero. The snow near the sides of the streets was black now, which added a lot to the overall effect of the day. Darn depressing.

Jake let me in and I went straight to the third floor, figuring the people there were the only ones likely to have witnessed anything. I knocked on Jake's door first, and told him I had some more questions for him but I'd have to do it some other time since I'd forgotten to bring along the computer printout.

"Call anytime," he said.

The door to the apartment next door was wide open again and I could hear someone moving about inside, probably in the kitchen from the sound of things. I knocked several times, and pretty loudly, but there was no response.

"Hello," I called out, and knocked again.

The kitchen noises stopped and I could hear someone walking—shuffling, actually—toward the doorway. It took close to a minute before she came into view. She was elderly, as I had guessed, probably in her eighties, maybe even nineties. She was tall, but hunched over so badly she had to raise her head to look at me. Snow-white hair, very sparse, soft and wavy. Brown eyes, but a lighter shade of brown than I think I've ever seen.

Her hands were knotted and twisted, covered with veins and brown spots. Her face was like a crumpled piece of paper, but probably as soft as silk, I thought.

"Hang on," she said with a smile and a wobbly voice. "I'm not as spry as I was in my youth."

She made walking a few yards look like running a marathon, but she was so good-natured about it I couldn't help smiling.

When she reached me, she raised her head and squinted. "Do I know you, dear?" she said.

I smiled. "No, you don't," I said. "I'm sorry to cause you so much trouble. I was hoping I could ask you a few questions about something that happened in the apartment next door the Friday before Christmas."

"Oh, dear me, yes. That poor boy."

She was starting to totter so I suggested we sit down. She gave me a grateful smile.

"That might be a good idea," she said. "I've been on my feet for quite some time and I could do with a rest. Would you mind helping me to my chair?"

"Sure," I said, and guided her by the elbow to a chair near the couch. It was a plush armchair, upholstered in a faded green fabric with tiny pink roses in the foreground, a crocheted doily hanging over the back. When she was seated and comfortable, I sat on the couch directly across from her.

"Are you the boy's family?" she asked.

"No, but I'm a very close friend of his sister."

"May I offer you some tea, dear?" she said.

"Oh, no, thank you," I said. "If you'd like something, I'd be happy to get it for you, though." I hated to think of her walking all the way back to the kitchen.

"No, thank you," she said. "I've already had mine. But you're very kind to offer."

"My name is Beth Hartley, by the way. I'm sorry, I forgot to introduce myself."

"Don't apologize, my dear. When you get to be my age, some days you'll forget your own name. But today I remember. I'm May Robinson," she said with a warm smile.

"I'm glad to meet you," I said.

She looked at me curiously then. "Are you married?"

I laughed. "No, I'm not. I was, but my second husband died ten years ago."

"Oh, dear. I'm very sorry. Do you work?"

I told her about my business and she seemed utterly fascinated. "My stars," she said. "My stars. Well, good for you. I like to see you young women making your own way in the world. Not many of us did that in my day. If I had to do it all over again I think I'd do things differently."

I smiled. "What would you do?" I said.

She looked at me with a twinkle in her eye. "I'd be a doctor," she said. "I'd go to college and become a doctor."

"That's what I'm planning to do in my next life," I said with a laugh.

"Maybe I'll wait for you," she said. "We'll do it together."

"It's a date," I said, grinning.

"Now, my dear. Let's get down to business. What did you want to ask me?"

"Well, I noticed that your door was open the other day when I was here, and today, too. Did you have it open last Friday night, by any chance?"

"I generally keep it open until I retire at ten," Mrs. Robinson said. "I can't recall specifically, but I imagine I kept it open until ten that night as I usually do."

"Do you remember hearing or seeing anything unusual?"

She considered that for a few moments. "On that Friday. No. I can't say that I do. Of course, I don't remember well, as I told you."

"Do you remember seeing anyone come or go? Anyone walk by your door?"

She frowned. "I remember seeing a delivery boy with a pizza box walk by a while back. But I can't be sure what day that was."

"Did you ever hear any arguing next door?" I said.

"Well, yes, I did. Although I couldn't make out what was being said. I don't hear so well, either. Warranty's run out on all my parts," she said with a chuckle.

I laughed. "Do you remember when it was that you heard the argument?"

Mrs. Robinson slowly shook her head, something which seemed to take some effort on her part. "Could've been anytime," she said. "I'm sorry I can't remember better. I'm afraid I'm not much help to you."

"You're a big help," I said.

She gave me an appreciative grin, then wrinkled her brow.

"My neighbor friend told me the boy committed suicide," she said. "What is it you're trying to find out, if you don't mind my prying?"

"Oh, no, of course not," I said. "I'm trying to find out if it was actually a murder. His sister, Janice, is sure it was and I really think so, too, at this point."

"Oh, my stars," she said. "Oh, my stars. Well, now I understand. Oh, my."

"You know, I'm a little concerned about your keeping your door open," I said, "especially if it was open when the murderer was here. It might be a lot safer for you if you kept it closed."

Worry lines formed on her face. "Oh, dear," she said. "Maybe you're right. I do like having it open, though. It makes me feel less lonely."

"Do you have any family?" I asked.

"I have a daughter, Marie, but she lives in Florida now. She comes to visit a few times a year, but that leaves a lot of time in between." Mrs. Robinson looked up at me. "I wish you'd come to visit me again," she said. "I enjoy your company."

"I'd love to," I said, fighting against the lump I felt in my throat. "If you'd like, I'll come to see you every week until you get sick and tired of me and throw me out."

"Oh, my dear girl," she said. "You're an angel if there ever was one. I'll so look forward to that every week. We'll choose a special day, any one you like."

I grinned and thought for a moment. "How about Sundays? Would you like that?"

"Splendid," she said. "Splendid. Sundays. I can hardly wait. What day is this?"

"Sunday," I said, smiling. "See, we've started already. I'll give you a card with my name and number and you call me if you need something in the meantime, okay? You have a phone, don't you?"

"Yes. Right on my dressing table next to the bed. I'll give you my phone number, too. We'll be just like two girlfriends, won't we?"

"Yes, we will," I said, and gave her a hug. "I'll call you on Saturday and we'll decide on a time. In the meanwhile, will you promise me to keep your door closed, at least until this man is caught?''

"I'll lock up right after you leave," she said.

I helped her to the door. "Who is the neighbor friend who told you it was a suicide?" I said after I stepped outside.

"Mrs. Markham in 309. Just tell her May sent you," Mrs. Robinson said with a kind smile. "I'll look so forward to seeing you, my dear."

"I will, too," I said, and gave her another hug. When she closed her door, I had to wipe a few tears from my eyes.

I HADN'T TAKEN any notes while I talked to Mrs. Robinson, so I stood in the hall and wrote down everything she'd told me, so I wouldn't forget. Then I knocked on number 309. Mrs. Markham was younger, probably no more than sixty. She was tall, maybe five-five, about thirty pounds overweight. Her hair was a dark, coarse gray, worn short and close to her head. She wore bright green sweatpants, a matching sweatshirt, and hot pink feathery house slippers. She greeted me with a big smile.

"Well, now. What can I do for you?" she said, giving me a look like I was a little girl.

I told her who I was, said that Mrs. Robinson had sent me, and explained what I wanted.

"Come on in," she said. "I'd be glad to talk to you. Just sit yourself down; I have something on the stove." She hurried out of the room at a sort of modified jogging pace, her slippers flapping against her feet as she went.

She came back in a minute, looking a little winded. She sat down in a blue vinyl recliner across from the couch on which I was sitting. The couch was upholstered in blue vinyl, too. The whole room was weird. The floor was bare, hardwood like Jake's, although the finish was in better shape. The throw rugs she'd scattered about were all different, some red, two green, one a bright orange. At least two of them were meant for a bathroom. The walls were the same off-white stucco as in the other apartments, but hers were decorated with mirrors—five in all, each a different size. She didn't have any plants. Thank goodness.

"How's May doing today?" she asked when she'd caught her breath.

"Fine," I said, smiling. "She's really very nice."

"Yes, she is," Mrs. Markham said. "She has no one in town so I try to look in on her whenever I can."

I told her I'd talked May into closing her door.

"I've been telling her that for years," she said. "You must've put some kind of spell on her to get her to do that."

"Well, I'm afraid I probably just frightened her," I said. "But I am worried she may have had her door open when whoever did this showed up. If he noticed it, he might think she knows something."

Mrs. Markham took a deep breath and let it out. "Oh, Lord," she said.

"He was killed on Friday, but they didn't discover the body until Saturday," I said. "Do you remember seeing or hearing anything unusual either Friday or Saturday?"

"I remember Saturday real well," she said. "There was an awful lot of commotion when they found him, police coming in and out and all. I believe I saw his sister and his mama. The young one was crying her eyes out, pretty near hysterical with grief. I believe his mama was just in shock. Didn't even know what to do with herself, poor thing. It's a horrible business."

I sighed and nodded. "Can you remember anything at all about Friday?"

She put a look on her face to show she was thinking hard. "I think I saw one of the boys who live there," she said. "Not the one who was killed. The other one."

"Do you remember what time that was?"

She thought for a moment, and nodded her head. "Yes. It was right before the program I always watch on Friday nights. A few minutes before eight."

"Was he coming or going?" I said.

"Coming. Walked right by me and didn't say a word, same as always."

"May said she heard arguing coming from their apartment sometime or another. Did you ever hear anything like that?"

"I heard one of them screaming at someone," she said. "On the telephone, I assumed, since I only heard the one voice. But that was way back, probably over a month ago."

"Do you know which one it was?"

Mrs. Markham shook her head. "No, I wouldn't know which one unless I'd seen him."

"Could you hear what was said?"

She raised her eyebrows. "He was telling someone to mind his own blankety-blank business and to stay out of his life." Mrs. Markham's face said, *I'm sure I don't have to fill in the blanks, do I?*

"Is that all you heard?" I said.

"I was just walking by, coming back from the supermarket. I didn't hear anything else and frankly I didn't want to. Those boys ought to have their mouths washed out with soap."

I laughed. "Would you do me a favor?" I said. "I'll leave you my number and if you think of anything at all, would you call me?"

"I sure will," she said. "I'm sorry I couldn't be more help."

"That's quite all right," I said. "I really appreciate your talking to me."

I CHECKED MY WATCH when I was back in the hallway. It was almost noon. I was getting tired and hungry but it was Sunday and the most likely time to find people home, I figured. I made a few notes regarding my conversation with Mrs. Markham, and knocked on number 310, the door I'd seen ajar when I first visited Jake. There was no one at home. I made a note on my pad to come back another day.

Next, I tried the door on the other side of Jake's. A young guy answered, late twenties, with shoulder-length, dark blond hair, a scruffy beard, and bloodshot eyes. Six feet tall, maybe a hundred and thirty pounds, no muscle at all. He wore dirty jeans and a wrinkled T-shirt frayed around the neck.

"Can I help you?" he said, in a genuinely polite and friendly voice. It took me by surprise and I'm afraid it showed.

I grinned at him and he grinned back. I told him the whole story and he asked me to come in. His name was Gordon Kohn.

Gordon offered me a seat on his couch, which was worn, actually threadbare, but clean and neat like everything else in his apartment. He had the same layout as Jake, but he had more furniture and there was a more permanent look to the place, as if he intended to stay a while. The walls were covered with pictures, all prints framed inexpensively, but they were nice. A couple of Monets, a Utrillo (which I love), and some Renoirs (which I also love). He had bookshelves (real ones), a stereo, a TV, and a dining room table and chairs.

I told him how nice I thought it looked and admired his pictures. He flashed me a shy but very pleased grin. "Thanks," he said. "I like it, too. I hope you'll excuse my appearance. I just got home from work and I haven't had a chance to clean up."

"What do you do?" I said.

"I work at a garden center," he said. "I'm planning to open one of my own someday." He looked so proud, it made me smile.

"That's great," I said.

"Can I offer you something?" he said. "A Coke or some coffee?"

I smiled. "A Coke would be great. I'm dying of thirst."

"I'll be right back," he said. "Just make yourself at home."

He came back with two Cokes and two glasses, handed one of each to me, and sat down.

"Do you know Dave and Jake at all?" I asked.

Gordon shrugged. "Not really," he said. "I say hello when I see them but that's about it. I'm not home much anyway."

"Were you home the Friday night before Christmas? They found Dave on Saturday but he was killed sometime Friday night."

"I was home until around seven, but then I took my girlfriend to a movie and didn't get back until about one."

"Did you see or hear anything before you left or after you came home?"

Gordon shrugged. "Nothing unusual," he said. "I saw one of them coming home from somewhere. The one with the dark hair."

"That's Jake," I said. "Dave was blond. Did he say anything to you?"

"He said 'hi' like he always does."

"Did he look strange in any way?"

Gordon laughed. "He looked a little drunk, but other than that he seemed normal enough."

"Have you ever heard anything weird going on next door? Any arguing, or anything like that?"

He shook his head. "No, I really haven't," he said. "But like I said, I'm not home much. I work a lot of hours and then I try to spend as much time as I can with my girlfriend. Fiancée, I should say, as of Christmas." He grinned, and turned a light shade of pink.

"Congratulations," I said. "She's very lucky."

"Naw, I'm the lucky one," Gordon said.

I shook my head, still smiling. The building appeared to be filled with such warm, genuine people, but there'd been a murder in their midst. For some reason, that made it seem all the more gruesome.

Gordon asked me what I did, and we talked about that for a while. I gave him one of my cards as I was leaving, and asked him to call me if he thought of anything he hadn't told me. He said he would.

I tried three more apartments after that, the ones nearest to Jake's, but no one answered. I thought of stopping by Jake's then, but I was too hungry to put off eating any longer. I decided to call him from home instead. I really wanted to talk to him about the stuff I'd found in the apartment. It's a good thing I did, too. He picked right up on something I hadn't even noticed.

SEVEN

IT WAS AFTER FOUR when I got home. I made myself a salad and an omelette with onions and sweet peppers and paged through my notes while I ate. I reread my stream-of-consciousness list and made from it a new list of things I needed to ask Jake. As soon as I'd finished eating, I called him.

"Yeah," he said.

"Jake, it's Beth," I said. "Are you busy? I just wanted to ask you a few questions."

I heard him sigh. "Shoot," he said.

"Did Dave gamble a lot?"

"Depends on what you mean by a lot," Jake said.

"Well, how often did he do it, let's put it that way?"

"For a while he was going every weekend. Depended on what else he had going, you know?"

"Do you have any idea how much money he made or lost?"

"Sometimes a lot, sometimes not so much."

I let out a deep breath. "Could you give me some idea how much you're talking about?" I said.

"I...oh, I don't know. It varied. Sometimes he'd win real big and sometimes he'd lose everything. Depends on the night."

"What's real big?" I said. "Can you give me some numbers?"

"Couple of thousand, I guess."

"Did he ever win as much as ten thousand dollars?"

Jake laughed. "No way," he said. "I would've heard about that one."

"How about losses?" I said. "Did he ever lose more than five thousand?"

"No," Jake said, starting to sound impatient. "I told you, the most he ever lost was a couple of thousand. Far as I know, anyway."

"Do you know if he ever borrowed as much as ten thousand dollars from anyone?"

"Not that I know of. What's the big deal about the ten thousand dollars?"

"Oh, he made a deposit in that amount to his savings account on December fifth," I said.

"Sorry, can't tell you nothin' about it," Jake said. "It's news to me."

"Okay, that's fine," I said. "You're doing great. Okay, I also found a calendar in his desk and he had the dates December fifth and December nineteenth circled, and then he wrote 'eight o'clock' on December fourth and 'nine o'clock' on December eighteenth. Both of those were Fridays. Does any of that mean anything to you?"

"Well, wasn't he killed on December eighteenth?"

I slapped myself on the forehead. "Oh, of course," I said. "That's right. How could I forget that?"

I suddenly thought of something I hadn't asked Jake before. "Did you see Dave at all that day?" I said.

"Yeah, I saw him in the morning before I took off."

"Did you see him before you went out that night?"

"No, he wasn't home then," Jake said.

"Do you remember what time you left?"

Jake hesitated a few moments. "It was probably around eight-thirty," he said. "I was meeting someone at nine so I would've had to leave around then."

"Okay, so he could've had someone at the apartment at nine and you wouldn't have seen him, right?"

"Yeah, that's right. You think it was the killer?" He sounded incredulous and excited at the same time.

"Could be," I said. "Did Dave know what time you were going out?"

Jake thought for a while. "Yeah. I think he asked me that morning what I was doing later."

"Okay," I said. "Two more questions. Do you have the phone numbers for Scott Chapman and Dick Burghoff?"

"Hold on, I'll look in the address book."

"Got 'em," he said when he returned to the phone. He gave me both numbers, and their addresses, too.

"Great," I said. "Thanks."

"Anything else I can do you for?"

I laughed. "Not right now, thanks. But I do want to show you that computer printout I told you about and see if it means anything to you. Maybe sometime this week?"

"Sounds good to me. Just let me know."

"Okay. Thanks, Jake."

"No problem," he said. I could've sworn he was beginning to like me.

It was almost five. I hadn't exercised in a couple of days so I NordicTracked for my usual twenty minutes plus another ten. Then I made myself a bowl of popcorn with butter and salt and watched videos for the rest of the night. I checked my messages before I went up. None. Laura VanderHayden hadn't returned my last call. Was she avoiding me, or what?

THE NEXT DAY was Monday, December twenty-eighth. Dave's cardiologist had asked me to call his office first thing that morning so I did just that. I got up at seven, showered and dressed, ate breakfast, and dialed his office at eight. Too early. His service said no one would be there before nine.

Both Emily and Janice showed up around eight-thirty, within five minutes of each other, and Mrs. Gunther at ten to nine. We sat in the kitchen and chatted for a while, and then everyone went to work. I told Janice and Emily I'd be in after I made a few phone calls.

I dialed Dr. King's office again, and this time a receptionist picked up. She was expecting me, just as he'd promised.

"The doctor will see you at five-thirty tomorrow evening, if that is convenient," she said crisply.

"That would be great," I said, and hung up with a smile.

I tried Scott Chapman next. There was something about his name that seemed familiar but I couldn't quite place it. It'd been bugging me ever since Jake had mentioned him.

"Hello," said a groggy voice.

"Is this Scott Chapman?" I said.

"Yeah, this is Scott," he said.

"I'm sorry if I woke you," I said. "I guess I forget everyone doesn't have to get up as early as I do."

I could hear him yawn. "Oh, that's okay. No problem. What time is it, anyway?"

"About nine-fifteen."

"Boy, you *do* get up early."

I laughed. "I'm sorry. My name is Beth Hartley. I understand you were a pretty good friend of Dave Grezinski."

"Oh, yeah," Scott said, sounding sad. "I was."

"I'm a friend of his sister and she believes he was murdered. She asked me to help her prove it. That's why I'm calling. I was hoping you might be able to help me."

"How?" Scott asked.

"Just talk to me, tell me what you knew about his life, what he was like, that sort of thing."

"Sure," he said. "I can do that. I had a lot of trouble believing he did it myself. I just can't see it. What did you have in mind?"

"I don't know. Could I buy you lunch?"

"Sure," he said.

"Are you free today?"

"I have to be somewhere at three, but I'm free before that."

"Do you like Mexican?" I said.

"Love it," Scott said. "Have you ever been to La Casita?"

"Yeah, like about a million times. Meet you there, say twelve-thirty?"

"I'll be there with bells on," he said. (I've never understood what that means.)

"Hey, how will I know who you are?" he said then.

"Oh, right. Well, I'm five feet tall, normal weight, light brown shoulder-length hair, sort of blue-green eyes—but they change color so just ignore that."

He laughed. "Okay. Well, if I get there first, just look for the exceedingly handsome guy with the awesome body and piercing black eyes."

"Gee, I can hardly wait," I said, laughing.

I called Laura VanderHayden next. Not home. Wonderful. I left a message with the maid.

I worked until twelve-ten, ran upstairs, threw on my olive green corduroy slacks and one of the sweaters I made (it's a light plum Icelandic type with an olive green and ivory design), pulled my hair back with a burgundy bow-clip, and left for La Casita. That day, the sky was a deep blue, sun glistening everywhere. The kind of day that makes you feel glad to be you. The restaurant's on Farwell, very close to where I live. The food is fantastic, the atmosphere uplifting. I love the sound of Mexican music and the ethnic decor. I try to imagine I'm in Cancun or Puerto Vallarta whenever I'm there.

I arrived about ten minutes early but had to park a few blocks down, on a side street, which required several trips around the block until I found a space (all the streets are one-way). Scott hadn't arrived yet, according to the woman who showed me to my table. I ordered a strawberry seltzer and waited, enjoying the escape.

Several minutes later, a young man about six feet tall, maybe a little less, with wavy black hair, dark eyes, and gleaming white teeth, walked in, spoke to the hostess, and was directed to my table. He flashed me a truly disarming grin and held out his hand.

"I'm Scott Chapman," he said.

"Hi, I'm Beth." That's all I said. I was tongue-tied. He really was exceedingly handsome. He really did have an awesome body. And his eyes—wow. Too bad he was at least twenty years too young for me.

"Sorry I'm late," he said. "I got a phone call right when I was about to leave."

"That's okay," I said. The waitress came to the table just then, took Scott's drink order, and left.

"So how did you know Dave?" he asked, eyeing me with undisguised curiosity.

"I'm a good friend of his sister," I said. "She was my secretary when I worked for a law firm and I took her with me when I started my own business. I never actually met Dave."

He asked me about my business then, so we talked about that until the waitress returned with his drink and took our lunch order.

"How did you meet Dave?" I asked Scott when the waitress left.

"We were on the wrestling team together at Marquette," he said.

"Were you in any classes with him?"

"No," Scott said. "I'm premed and he was a computer sciences major. We didn't have any classes in common."

"Did you ever meet his roommate, Jake Grossman?"

"I met him once when I was over at Dave's place."

"How about any of his other friends?"

Scott shrugged. "Not really," he said. "Except for Dick Burghoff. He's the only other guy from the wrestling team he really hung around with."

I nodded.

"So you really think he was murdered?" Scott asked.

"Well, it sure looks that way. There are a lot of things that wouldn't make sense if it was a suicide, and Janice and Jake both say he'd never kill himself. How do you feel about that?"

"The same way," Scott said. "It just doesn't fit. He had plans. I'm talking big plans. A business, getting married, the whole bit. He just had too much going for him. The guy was brilliant at what he did. Just ask my dad. Dave was working for him for less than a week and already my dad was saying he was some kind of a genius.''

The light bulb went on, and I slapped my forehead with the heel of my hand. "That's why your name sounded so familiar to me," I said. "You're the son of the doctor Dave worked for.''

"Yes, that's right," Scott said. "I guess I just assumed you knew that. I was the one who introduced them. Dad had been talking for almost a year about hiring someone to put all of his records on computer so I told him about Dave because that was the kind of business he was planning to start. He did a great job for my dad. He just raved about him.''

"I know this is kind of a personal question," I said, "but do you happen to know how much your dad paid him?''

Scott's eyebrows went up almost imperceptibly and he remained silent.

"Actually, what I'm really interested in knowing is whether it could have been as much as ten thousand dollars. I have a good reason for asking.''

Scott looked incredulous. "It couldn't have been that much," he said. "He only worked for him a couple of months, part-time, and he wasn't even finished with the job.''

"Did Dave ever talk to you about his gambling?" I asked.

Scott wrinkled his brow. "Gambling?" he said. "What kind of gambling?''

"Blackjack?''

He shook his head, the frown still on his face.

"Did he ever mention anything about the bomb scares?''

Scott exhaled sharply. "No, he never mentioned it," he said. "That whole thing was really bizarre. I can't believe he'd pull something like that.''

"Did he ever say anything to you about owing money?''

Scott shrugged, and shook his head. "No, not really," he said. "I mean, he said he was glad for the work from my dad because he could always use the extra cash but it was nothing like he was in desperate need for it.''

I nodded. The waitress returned with our food and we busied ourselves with that for a few minutes.

"Did he ever give you the impression that something was

going on with him? Something that worried him or bothered him in any way?" I said a little later.

"Not that I noticed," Scott said. "I didn't really see him that much, though. Not lately, anyway. He was using a lot of his free time to work for my dad."

"So, you're premed, huh?"

Scott nodded and attempted a humble smile.

"Are you planning to practice with your dad when you get out of medical school?"

"I hope so," he said. "He could really use the help. He must work eighty, ninety hours a week since his partner died last year."

"What kind of practice does he have?"

"Family, general practice."

I smiled. "Well, that's great," I said. "I wish you luck."

"Thanks," he said.

"Didn't you say Dave was planning to get married?"

"Yeah, he had some girl he'd been seeing for a couple of years. I met her once. She was pretty cool."

"Was her name Laura?"

"Yeah, Laura Vanheusen or something like that."

"VanderHayden," I said.

"Yeah, that's it. They were going to get married right after graduation."

"Did Dave ever say anything to you about her dad objecting to them getting married?"

Scott laughed. "Yeah, the guy was a real jerk, I guess. I think they were going to just elope and tell everyone after the fact so it'd be too late to stop them."

"You never met her father, did you?"

He frowned. "No, I think he lives in Boston."

"Yeah, he does. I just thought he might've come to visit Laura."

"Well, not that I know of," Scott said with a shrug.

"Can you think of anything else that might help?" I said. "Anything I haven't thought of?"

"Not right off," he said. "If I do, I'll let you know, though."

I smiled. "Okay, that'd be great," I said. I took one of my cards from my wallet and handed it to him.

We'd finished eating and it was a little past one-thirty. "Would you like coffee or anything?" I asked.

"No, thanks," Scott said. "I'd better get going, anyway."

"Well, I really appreciate your coming and talking to me. You've been a big help."

"Happy to be of service," he said with a charming grin.

Scott waited for me while I paid the bill, and we walked out together.

"You should talk to my dad," he said. "He might be able to tell you something."

"I was planning to," I said. "Maybe I'll call him when I get home." Little did I know then how much I was going to enjoy *that* conversation.

"Tell him I said 'hi,'" Scott said with a smile.

"Okay, I will."

We were parked in different directions so I said goodbye, thanked him again, and took my time walking to my car. The day was beautiful, unusual for winter, and it was actually pleasant being outside.

When I got to the car, I decided to stop at The WoolWorks before I went home. That's my favorite yarn store, also on Farwell. I parked on Kane, walked a block down, and spent a leisurely thirty minutes looking through knitting patterns and choosing some yarn.

I drove home along Lincoln Memorial Drive, enjoying the lake view. The water close to shore was frozen, waves caught in mid-air, but the sun sparkled off the surface and made me think of spring.

WHEN I GOT HOME, Janice was in the kitchen, eating her lunch.

"Hey, did you ever meet Scott Chapman?" I asked.

"I don't think so," she said, frowning. "Who's he?"

"One of Dave's wrestling buddies. I just had lunch with him. He's the son of the Dr. Chapman Dave was working for."

"Oh, yeah, that's right. That's how Dave got the job. What did he say?"

"Well…he said Dave and Laura were planning to get married right after graduation."

Janice gaped at me. "He never even told me that. He never

even let me meet her.'' She turned away from me with a wounded look.

"I'm sorry,'' I said. "I think the only reason they were keeping it a secret was because of her father. He wasn't too keen on the idea.''

Janice's response was a cross between a sneer and a wince.

"Scott also said his dad absolutely raved about Dave's work. Said he was some kind of a genius.''

Now I got a happy smile, a proud big-sister look flashing across her face.

"He's a nice kid, too. I can see why Dave liked him.''

She smiled again, gratitude erasing most of her anger.

"I think I'm going to call his dad today,'' I said. "I want to see if I can arrange to see him, although it looks like he's so busy he may never have time.''

Janice nodded. "Dave said he had a lot of patients.''

"Oh, I just remembered something,'' I said. "I wanted to show you that stuff I found in Dave's apartment.''

I went to the library, retrieved my file, and showed Janice everything I had. None of it meant anything to her, although she wondered where Dave had gotten all that money.

When Janice went back to the library, I put in a call to Dr. Chapman's office. I left my name and number with his receptionist and asked that he call me regarding Dave Grezinski if he had the chance.

I worked until Janice and Emily left at five o'clock, then brought my brief into the kitchen and worked some more. My phone rang at seven-thirty.

It was Dr. Chapman. I couldn't believe it.

"I'm sorry I took so long to get back to you,'' he said. "I've been pretty backed up here.''

"Oh, don't apologize,'' I said. "I know how busy you must be. I'm grateful to you for taking the time to call me at all.''

He laughed. "That's quite all right,'' he said. "Now what can I do for you?''

He had a soft, easy voice, the sort that makes you feel you've known someone forever. If he looks anything like his son, I thought, I'm going to be in big trouble.

"I was hoping to talk to you about Dave Grezinski,'' I said.

"If you can spare any time at all, I promise I'll try to keep it short."

"I'll make the time," he said. "I understand from my son, Scott, that you suspect he's been murdered?"

"Yes, that's right. His sister Janice asked me to help her prove it, so I'm looking for any information that might help."

"Have you had dinner yet?" he said.

"Uh...no, I haven't. I've been working."

He laughed, a soft, easy laugh, just like his voice. "Then we're two of a kind," he said. "I'll tell you what. I just saw my last patient for the day and I was about to get a bite to eat. How about if I take you to dinner and we can talk then? I usually eat alone, and I'd love the company."

"Sure, that'd be nice," I said. "Shall I meet you somewhere?"

"Let's make it Karl Ratzsch's. I feel like splurging."

"Hey, that'd be great."

"Would eight-fifteen be all right?"

"Perfect," I said. "I'll see you then."

EIGHT

EIGHT-FIFTEEN. I had forty minutes, twenty of them traveling time. I ran upstairs, showered quickly, keeping my hair dry, washed my face, reapplied my makeup, and threw on a pale gray knit dress I never need to iron. Stockings, medium-height heels (I can't stand the high ones), earrings, my hair in a French twist. Done. It was ten to eight. I ran downstairs, threw on my coat, and was gone.

It was dark now, and a little colder, but the wind was barely perceptible. The air smelled like snow. I took Farwell to Ogden, and Jackson to Mason. The whole drive there I had the feeling I was going on a date. Just like a teenager—the same nervous anticipation, the old shyness resurfacing like one of those incurable viruses. It was ridiculous.

Karl Ratzsch's, on Mason Street, is a family-owned German restaurant known all over the country for its excellence in food, wine, and service. I've eaten there quite often, and enjoyed it every time. The decor is, well, sort of German, like you'd expect. Lots of steins, leaded-glass windows, antiques, hand-painted murals, and assorted ethnic paraphernalia. There's always a crowd, night or day, and often a bit of a wait, but it's well worth it, believe me.

I availed myself of the valet parking so I wouldn't have to trudge through any snow or slush in my inadequate shoes, gave my name to the maitre d', and was directed to a gentleman in the bar, seated on a barstool with his back to me.

I went in and tapped him on the shoulder.

"Dr. Chapman?" I said.

He turned around, and gave me an engaging smile. I just about passed out, he was so gorgeous.

"Tony," he said, standing up and holding out his hand. "And I hope you're Beth." He had the same confident manner as his son—flirtatious, with no hint of shyness or self-doubt.

I laughed (and blushed, but fortunately the bar was so dark he couldn't see). "Yes, I am," I said, shaking his hand.

He had dark, wavy hair peppered with gray, a little thin on top but really attractive. Dark brows and lashes, dark eyes, and gleaming white teeth. He was tall, about six feet, athletically built—narrow hips, muscular legs, flat stomach, broad shoulders. He was wearing black jeans, a blue chambray shirt, and a blue tweed sportcoat. He looked an awful lot like Scott, only twenty-five years better, if you know what I mean.

He offered me his seat, which I declined, ordered me a champagne cocktail at my request, then turned around and looked at me.

"So," he said with a seductive smile, "do you always look this good on just a few minutes' notice?"

He was giving me an openly appraising look, but there was nothing leering about it, just frank appreciation. A little unnerving, but I loved it.

I shook my head and grinned.

Conversation was difficult because the bar was pretty noisy, but we managed to make small talk for fifteen minutes until we were shown to a table.

"Have you ever regretted leaving your firm?" he asked after the waiter had taken our drink order.

I smiled and shook my head. "No, I never have. I love what I do and I'm really happy being on my own. My hours are flexible if I want them to be, I'm my own boss, and I have control of my own life now. I don't think I could ever go back to the way things were before."

He gave me an approving look. "I know exactly what you mean," he said. "My father was a doctor, too. Cosmetic surgery. He'd always intended for me to take over his practice when he retired, join up with him right out of med school." He shook his head. "I just couldn't do it. I couldn't see spending my life that way. It wasn't me. It wasn't what I had in mind when I went to medical school. I may not have the income I might've had, but I'm doing something I really feel matters. So many of my patients are indigent, helpless. Some are even homeless. When I go home at night, I feel like I've accomplished something. I don't think I could've said that if I'd followed my dad's path."

I smiled at him and nodded. "Well, I think your son wants very much to follow your path," I said. "He told me he hopes to practice with you someday."

"He did?" Tony said, a flush of pleasure sweeping across his face.

"Yes, he did," I said with a grin. "He went on and on about how wonderful and dedicated you are and how badly you need his help. He says you had a partner who died?"

Tony winced. A mixture of pain and regret flickered in his eyes.

"Yes," he said. "Art Freeman. He was a good man, a fine physician. Died of a heart attack at the age of forty-nine. He was cross-country skiing. They found his body frozen in the snow the next day. It was horrible. He had a wife and four children at home."

He looked genuinely distressed at the memory, and I was sorry I'd brought it up. I didn't say anything. I didn't know what to say.

The waiter returned then and asked for our order. When he left, Tony looked at me with a serious face. "You said you wanted to talk to me about Dave. I haven't let you do that. I apologize.''

"That's all right," I said. "Believe me, I've been enjoying every minute of our conversation."

He nodded graciously and smiled. "So have I," he said. "But now, please, what did you want to ask me?"

"Well, I'm not sure exactly. I'm trying to find out what was going on in his life before he died. So far, I've learned some pretty strange things but none of it makes any sense to me."

Tony wrinkled his brow. "Like what, for instance, if you don't mind my asking?"

"Well, the bomb scares, for one. Did you know about that?"

He raised his brows. "Yes," he said. "Scott told me about that." He shook his head, a wry smile on his face. "Dave was far too intelligent to be doing something as reckless and stupid as that. I'll admit I was a little wild myself when I was that age, but I never pulled a stunt like that, not even close."

"He was also doing a lot of gambling, apparently."

Tony looked surprised, then laughed and shook his head. "Boy, did I misjudge him," he said.

"Now, I do have a question for you," I said, "but you don't have to answer this if you don't want to. I found a bankbook of his and it shows he deposited ten thousand dollars at the beginning of December, and I'm trying to find out where it came from. Did you pay him that much for the work he did for you, by any chance?"

Tony laughed. "I don't mean to laugh," he said. "But no. I paid him well, even more than he asked, but it was nowhere near that much. He only spent a total of maybe sixty hours on the project and he hadn't even completed it when he died."

"Had you paid him anything yet?"

"Yes. I paid him every week," Tony said. "I know what it's like being a college kid with no money coming in. I didn't think it'd be fair to make him wait until the end."

I nodded, and let out a long sigh.

"Maybe he won the money gambling," Tony said. "It might be as simple as that."

"Yeah, that's probably what it was," I said, although deep down I wasn't convinced.

"Did he ever talk to you about his personal life?" I asked.

"No, we didn't talk much about anything but what I hired him to do. That alone took more time than I'd anticipated, because I had a hard time describing what I wanted. I don't know the first thing about computers, unfortunately. I wanted to learn the basics and then have all my records put on a system so I could retrieve them at will. I thought it'd be a simple matter for him to set that up, but apparently I was mistaken."

"How far did he get before he died?"

"I'm not even sure of that," Tony said with an embarrassed look. "I'm probably going to have to hire someone just to figure that out."

"Boy, that's too bad," I said. "Well, my brother does that sort of thing, so if you don't find anyone else, just let me know. I'm sure he could help you."

"Thanks," Tony said. "I'll keep that in mind."

"Did Dave ever receive any phone calls while he was at your office?" I asked.

Tony frowned, shaking his head. "Not that I know of," he said. "I was usually in with a patient, though, and he was there at night a few times after I'd already left. I just don't know."

"Did anyone come to see him?"

"Not that I'm aware of."

"How about his behavior?" I said. "Did he ever act strange, or out of the ordinary?

"I don't think so," Tony said. "But I wouldn't have had much of an opportunity to observe any change in his behavior. We didn't communicate much after the first few times. He usually came in and did his work and then left. I was either busy with a patient or at home."

I nodded, feeling a bit discouraged.

"Hey, it sounds like you're on the right track," Tony said. "At least you're coming up with questions. The answers will fall into place sooner or later."

I smiled appreciatively. "I hope so," I said.

He gave me a look of concern then. "I hope you're being careful," he said. "If he was murdered, there's someone out there with very little to lose. He may not balk at adding one more notch to his belt if he thinks you're getting too close to the truth."

"Well, thanks for worrying about me," I said with a smile, "but I'll be fine. Really."

Tony looked doubtful, and a little anxious, which I found kind of touching.

"Oh, I just thought of something else," I said. "Did you know anything about his medical condition?"

"What do you mean?" he said. "What medical condition?"

"His heart condition. The one he was taking the medication for."

"No, I wasn't aware he had a heart problem. It was an overdose that killed him, wasn't it?"

I nodded.

Tony shook his head. "Sorry," he said. "I can't help you there. He never mentioned it, and I don't know what heart medicine he was taking, if any. Did the police make any determination on that?"

"I have no idea," I said. "I've never even talked to them. As far as I know, they still think it's a suicide."

"Why are you so sure it wasn't a suicide?" Tony asked.

"A feeling, more than anything," I said. "And a lot of things just don't look right. For one thing, the suicide note didn't make any sense. It said he didn't want to face prosecution for the bomb scares, but they weren't going to prosecute him and he knew that."

Tony looked at me with interest. "I see," he said. "That does raise a few questions, doesn't it?"

The waiter approached, and asked if we'd like coffee or dessert. We ordered coffee, and took our time about leaving. I'd exhausted my mental list of questions and was tired of talking about it anyway. We spent the remainder of our time discussing my family and his, his divorce, mine. The usual sort of chitchat you engage in with someone you've just met.

When we walked outside, it was snowing lightly, soft flakes illuminated in the shafts of light beneath the street lamps. I'd enjoyed his company so much I didn't want to go home.

We ordered my car first. When he shook my hand as we were saying goodbye, he held on to it and looked into my eyes.

"It's been quite a while since I've relaxed like this," he said. "Thank you."

I smiled, and blushed, saved again by the lighting. "I enjoyed it, too," I said.

Tony gave the roof of my car a tap as I drove off.

Darn. Darn. Darn, I thought. This is all I need. Another man messing up my life. Well, I'd solve that problem. I just wouldn't think about him. At all.

WHEN I WOKE UP the next morning, it was still snowing. I turned on the radio and listened as I made my bed. Only three inches overnight and maybe another inch expected. Big deal. I took a shower, put on jeans and a sweater, and then looked out the window for Peter. Nowhere to be seen. Of course, it was only seven o'clock. What did I expect?

I went downstairs and made myself some Bisquick biscuits and a little pot of hot chocolate. Mmm. Snow food. This was the day I was to see Dr. King, and find out how Dave was most probably administered the overdose. But for now, I had work to do. I had a brief to get out that day and Emily had one due the next, so we'd all be busy, particularly Janice, poor thing. On days like this I feel guilty about not calling in a temp to help her, but what good would it do? I only have one computer. We try to anticipate overloads and I tend to get all my work done early, with several days to spare, but sometimes it just fails to work out the way I've planned. With all the investigating I'd been doing, I hadn't been keeping up with my regular schedule. Ordinarily, a brief due today would've been done last week, but this time I had a good third yet to be written. I didn't expect anyone until eight-thirty so I brought my file into the kitchen and worked while I ate.

The snow was still falling when I looked up an hour later, the flakes slightly larger than before. In case you haven't noticed, I love snow. I wasn't too fond of having to traipse through it when I was all dressed up and going into an office, but now that I'm on my own with nowhere I have to go, I thrive on it. I can just sit at my window and watch it fall.

Janice and Emily arrived at eight-thirty sharp, as promised, and went right to work. At twelve-thirty, we took a break, and lunched on cold chicken legs, a vegetable-pasta salad, and leftover biscuits.

At three, my brief was done and ready to go. I left the two of them working on Emily's and drove downtown to drop it off. Such door-to-door service isn't usually required, but this was an exception. The streets were clear, and it was no longer snowing, the air already turning colder as it so often does after a snow. I was back by four, leaving me about half an hour before I had to take off again to see Dr. King.

"Laura VanderHayden called while you were gone," Janice said. "She left a message on the machine."

"You have got to be kidding," I said. "I have been trying to get hold of her for days and every time I call, she's not there. Then I go out for a few minutes, and she calls while I'm gone. I can't believe this."

Janice and Emily stared at me, not saying a word.

"She said she'd be home all night," Janice said, the corners of her mouth turning up ever so slightly. "If you call her now I'm sure you'll catch her."

"Great," I said. I grabbed my "Dave" file, took it to the kitchen, found Laura's number, and dialed.

"VanderHayden residence," said a maidly voice.

I asked for Laura. She said she'd get her. A few minutes later, Laura answered the phone.

"This is Laura," she said.

"Laura, this is Beth Hartley," I said.

"Oh, I'm so glad you finally got me," she said in a barely audible voice. "I've been out of town for a few days. I'm sorry I wasn't able to get back to you sooner."

"That's okay," I said. "Are you free to talk?" Something about her voice told me she wasn't.

"Not on the phone," she said. "I really want to talk to you but it'll have to wait until I get back to Milwaukee."

"When are you coming back?" I said.

"Not until Saturday. I'm sorry. There's no way I can get away before then."

"What time are you getting in?"

"My flight is due to arrive a little before two," Laura said. "I could come and see you right after I get there if you want."

"That'd be great," I said. "Do you want me to pick you up at the airport?"

"Uh...sure," she said. "I guess I hadn't thought about how I was going to get home."

We exchanged descriptions, agreeing to meet at the gate, and hung up. I'll have to admit, I was more than a little intrigued. She'd have to know something the others didn't. Of all the people in Dave's life, her connection to him was the most intimate.

I went upstairs, put on a burgundy corduroy skirt, matching opaque stockings, and a burgundy tweed fisherman sweater I made last year. There. Good enough for Dr. King. I told Janice and Emily to lock up if they left before I got back, and headed for the expressway.

Dr. King's office is on Oklahoma Avenue, right off of Sixtieth. I arrived a little before five-thirty, but the receptionist asked me to wait.

"Doctor is in with a patient. We were a little slow today. He had several emergencies this morning." She said this as if she took all emergencies in stride. Towering infernos, sudden deaths, losses of life and limb. She'd seen them all.

I sat in an orange molded plastic chair, one of many lined up against the waiting room wall. The walls were painted a sort of apricot color, accented with startling orange and fuschia chevrons that looked almost like they were darting from wall to wall. It was unsettling to look at. Probably even worse if you were sick.

I picked up a magazine from the table next to my chair, trying to avert my eyes. *Cosmopolitan*. I put it back. I picked up *Newsweek* next, and was in the middle of an article about Unified Europe, when she called my name.

"Doctor will see you now. It's the third door to your left," she said, pointing to the hallway beyond her cubicle.

Dr. King's door was open and he sat at his desk, making notes in a file. When he heard me approach, he looked up, smiled, and stood to shake my hand. His hand was sweaty, just as it had been the other day.

"Miss Hartley," he said. "It's good to see you. Please, have a seat. I'll be with you in a few moments."

I sat in one of the twin upholstered armchairs in front of his desk, and waited while he completed his notations. His office was nicely furnished, and decorated with taste, in sharp contrast to the waiting room. His desk was walnut, highly polished, his chair a luxurious black leather. The chair in which I sat, and the one next to it, were covered with an expensive-looking fabric the color of burgundy wine. The walls were gold, the rug an Oriental in varying shades of red, one of which matched the chairs perfectly. It was lovely. It didn't suit him at all.

He put his pen down on his desk with emphasis, closed the file the same way, and said, "There. Now what can I do for you?" He folded his hands and placed them in front of him on his desk. I guess I had his attention, huh?

I smiled, a little awkwardly, not really knowing what to make of him. He had a phoniness about him I didn't like. I always have trouble dealing with people like that. I don't know how to make conversation with them. I'm not sure how to respond to their comments.

"Well, I'd like to ask you a few questions about Dave's cause of death," I said. "I know you're busy. I promise to keep it short."

He waved at me dismissively, flashing me a disingenuous grin. "Don't give it a moment's thought," he said, looking at his watch. "My time is at your disposal. Now then, what can I tell you?"

"Can you tell me what kind of medication Dave was on and why he was taking it?" I said. I hoped he wouldn't cite doctor-patient confidentiality. After all, the patient was dead. He didn't care. Neither did his mom.

"Dave was taking a form of digitalis called digitoxin," Dr. King said. He pronounced the medical terms slowly and distinctly, in case I was too stupid to get it, I guess. Nice of him. Very thoughtful.

"Why was he taking the digitoxin?" I asked, enunciating the word in the same way he had. He lifted one brow just a teensy bit.

"Dave suffered recurrent episodes of rheumatic fever as a child which caused some damage to his heart. The digitoxin was part of the treatment for the damage."

"Was he using any other medications that you're aware of?" I asked.

"No, he was not," he said.

"Is there any way, that you can think of, that Dave could

have been tricked into taking an overdose? Rather than being forced to do it, I mean."

Dr. King frowned. "What leads you to believe he was tricked?" he asked.

I shrugged. "Well, as far as I can tell, there wasn't any evidence of a struggle. Or forced entry, either. And it looks like he might have been planning to meet with the person who killed him."

Dr. King pursed his lips, and gave it some thought. "Well," he said, stroking his chin, drawing the whole thing out for effect. "How could he be induced to take the overdose without his knowing it?"

He tapped his upper lip with the index finger of his right hand, several times in succession, and nodded his head. "I suppose it could be done in any one of several different ways," he said. "The drug comes in two forms, tablet and liquid, and can be administered orally, intramuscularly, or intravenously." He defined both "intramuscular" and "intravenous" for me. What a guy.

"An injection, of course, he'd be aware of, but once it was given, a fait accompli. That's a French phrase meaning..."

"I know," I said. "How else?"

"It could be added to his food or to a beverage, as a liquid or a powder," he said. "Of course, the ingestion of food could have an impact on the absorption time, but it could be done." Dr. King nodded his head several times. "Yes, it could be done."

"How much would it take to kill him?" I asked.

"Well, that would vary with the individual, of course, depending upon body weight, medical condition, and use of other substances, but it wouldn't take much. Digitoxin is an extremely toxic drug. In Dave's case, it might require very little indeed."

"Why is that?" I said, frowning.

"Dave was a wrestler," he said. "He took it a bit too seriously, like many of these boys, and used laxatives to keep his weight down. Both his low weight and the laxative abuse would increase the risk of toxicity."

"So he could've been given a lethal dose in food or drink and not even have noticed it?"

"It's entirely possible," Dr. King said.

I nodded. "Okay," I said. "Thank you, Dr. King. That's all I wanted to know."

I stood and offered him my hand. He leaned forward from his chair, without actually rising to his feet, and took it.

"I hope I've been helpful," he said, looking as if he were sure he'd just provided me with case-cracking information.

"You have," I said with a smile. "Thank you very much for your time."

He got up then and walked me to the door.

"Feel free to call if you have any more questions," he said. I assured him that I would.

It was very cold when I left, and a brisk wind made it all the worse. I ran to my car, cranked up the heater, and sat in the lot until everything warmed up.

When I got home, I changed into sweatpants and a sweatshirt, made myself some pasta fajioli, and added some notes to my "Dave" file regarding my meeting with Dr. King. I did the same for Scott and Tony.

I went to the library after supper, curled up in my favorite chair, and read for a few hours. I did a little knitting for maybe half an hour, and went up to bed. Tony kept intruding upon my thoughts, but I pushed him away. Little good that did, he called the next day.

NINE

IT WAS WEDNESDAY, December thirtieth, a pretty uneventful day, all in all. Unlike the Wednesday after that, which I'm sure I'll never forget. Mrs. Gunther showed up early, whipped through the house like a madwoman, and was gone by two o'clock. She had to take Erma to her doctor's appointment.

Emily got her brief out, I sent Janice home early for a well-deserved rest, and Em and I got a head start on projects due in the next two weeks.

Then Tony called. My heart went flippety-flop and I patted myself on the chest.

"Hi," he said in a soft, almost caressing, voice. "How are you?"

"I'm fine," I said. "How are you?"

"Great. Listen, I only have a minute, but I have a question to ask you. I know this is disgustingly short notice, but are you doing anything New Year's Eve?"

"No," I said. "To tell you the truth, I usually stay home. I don't like the crowds."

"Neither do I," he said. "How would you like to have dinner with me, at my place? I'm a pretty fair cook, and I promise to be on my best behavior."

I took a deep breath. Oh, what the heck. "I'd love to," I said. "What time did you have in mind?"

"How about if I pick you up at eight?"

"Great," I said. "I'll look forward to it."

"So will I," he said.

I gave him directions to my house and hung up. This was not good. I was supposed to be forgetting all about this guy.

Emily left at six and I worked straight through until seven, had a bite to eat, and worked some more. Then I worked some more and went to bed.

THE NEXT DAY WAS Thursday, December thirty-first. I'd promised Janice and Emily short days but I got up early myself to make up for some of my lost time. They both arrived at eight-thirty, one right after the other, and left at three. When they were gone, I decided to knock off, too.

I had loads of time before Tony would be here and I was restless. I got out the "Dave" file and paged through every bit of it, making notes as I went.

I was stumped. I knew what killed him, and probably knew how it had been done. Chances were, it was someone he knew, someone he trusted enough to let in his apartment. And he might have arranged to meet him there, actually invited him over for some specific purpose.

But what?

He'd written 9:00 on his calendar, and hidden the calendar

under a drawer. And the bankbook. Maybe he owed someone ten thousand dollars and meant to pay it back that night. Jake said he'd borrowed two thousand from "some guys" and hadn't paid them back. Maybe he'd borrowed more than Jake was aware of. But even if that were true, why would they kill him? If he paid up, they'd have no reason to complain. If he didn't, killing him wasn't going to get them anywhere.

And then there was the computer printout. I decided to call Jake and read some of it to him over the phone.

I dialed. Five rings, no answer. I was just about to hang up when I heard a breathless hello.

"Jake?"

"Yeah, who is this?"

"It's Beth," I said. "Are you all right?"

"Yeah, I just ran up the stairs. What's up?"

"Remember that computer printout I told you about? If I read some of it to you over the phone could you tell me if it means anything to you?"

"Sure," he said, "but make it quick. I gotta go."

"Okay," I said, and read him a few lines, after describing the format and telling him that each line was printed twice.

"Greek to me," he said. "Talk to you later." And he hung up.

I went through the list I'd made of people I intended to interview. I still hadn't talked to Dick Burghoff, but he'd probably be off to some party like Jake apparently was. I could try his wrestling coach, though.

I rooted through my notes for the number I'd gotten from the woman in the Computer Sciences office and dialed. A woman answered and I asked for Mr. Hodges.

"You just missed him," she said in a good-natured voice. "I just sent him to the store with a list. I can have him call you when he gets back."

"That'd be great," I said. I gave her my name and number and asked her to tell him I wanted to talk to him about Dave Grezinski. She said she would.

I sat for a while, thinking, then decided to try Dick Burghoff anyway. At the very least I could leave him a message. I dialed the number, and a young woman answered, almost in the middle of the first ring. I was immediately assaulted by raucous rock music and the sounds of a party in motion.

"Happy New Year!" she screamed into the phone. I yanked the receiver from my ear in a reflexive motion, and cautiously put it back.

"Is Dick Burghoff there?" I said in a loud voice.

"Hang on," she yelled.

Five minutes passed and nobody came to the phone. I hung up.

I went upstairs and looked through my closet, trying to decide what to wear that night. I didn't want to get too dressed up since I was only going to Tony's house, but I didn't want to underdo it, either. Oh, decisions, decisions.

I rejected the dresses, one by one, and settled on a navy velvet slacks and vest outfit I usually wear sometime during the holidays with an ivory organza blouse. I didn't need to press it so I just laid it out on the bed and went back downstairs.

I was making myself a cup of tea when Coach Hodges returned my call.

"Thank you for calling me back so soon," I said. I told him the whole story, including what I'd learned from Dr. King about the laxatives.

"Were you aware that he was using laxatives?" I said.

Coach Hodges hesitated briefly, before responding in a defensive tone. "None of my boys use that stuff," he said. "I strongly discourage it. It's unhealthy. There's no need for that."

I smiled, wondering how many of the others were doing the same thing as Dave.

"Did you know Dave very well?" I asked. "On a personal level?"

"There was a time I tried to get to know all my boys," he said. "Used to have 'em over to the house after meets, took 'em out after practice. None of 'em are interested anymore."

"That's too bad," I said, feeling sorry for him. "So you really didn't know anything about Dave's personal life?"

"Naw. Met his girl, once. Made a nice couple, I thought."

"Do you know if he hung around with any of the other wrestlers, other than Scott Chapman and Dick Burghoff?"

"Not that I ever saw," he said. "He did seem pretty tight with those two, though."

"Did you ever get the impression that anything was bothering him? Lately, I mean?"

He considered that for a moment. "Well, I'm not sure I'd say that," he said. "But he did mouth off more, seemed cockier somehow. They often do right around graduation, though. Probably nothing more than that."

"Well, thank you very much for talking to me, Mr. Hodges. If you think of anything else, would you call and let me know?"

"I sure will, little lady. Goodbye now."

I smiled when I hung up. He seemed like a nice man.

It was still early, so I NordicTracked for thirty minutes to dissipate some of my nervousness, had a piece of fruit, and read for a while.

At six-thirty, I showered and took my time getting ready to go. I hadn't realized how really anxious I was until then. I must have done my hair ten different ways before I was satisfied, my makeup three times. It was ridiculous.

I try so hard not to get attached to men, but it always happens when I least expect it. It's like they're waiting to ambush me, catching me off guard before I have time to put up my defenses. There was something about Tony I really liked, though. Okay, there was a lot about him I really liked. He was sensitive, caring, incredibly good-looking, divorced, uninvolved, charming in the most attractive way, and incredibly good-looking. Oh, I guess I mentioned that already.

On the other hand, he was involved with his work to the point of obsession, something he admitted played a major part in the demise of his marriage. He also avoided intimacy and commitment, he told me, fearing it wouldn't work out again, just like the first time. In that sense, we had a lot in common. I guess life's the only trip you go on where you're guaranteed *not* to lose your baggage, huh?

Tony arrived at eight, right on time (see, he's punctual, too), wearing dress slacks, a gorgeous cardigan sweater with a white Izod shirt, and a subtle after-shave that sent shivers up my body (the good kind).

"Hey, you look fantastic," he said, with his slow, lazy smile. "You really do."

"Thanks," I said, grinning. "So do you." It was so awfully corny.

"Great house," he said when I asked him inside. "The furniture is magnificent. Do you mind if I look around?" he said with a shy smile.

"No, not at all," I said. "Come on, I'll give you the full tour."

"I hope you don't mind my curiosity," he said as I showed him through the house, "but I collect antiques myself and you have some really fine pieces here."

"Oh, thanks," I said. I told him about Aunt Sarah, and how we'd shopped for many of them together.

We left then, drove no more than half a mile, and pulled up in front of an absolutely gorgeous house with a slate roof and a turret on one side.

"What're we doing here?" I said.

Tony looked at me and grinned, and then turned off the ignition.

"You mean you live here?" I said.

He laughed. "I sure do," he said. "I couldn't believe it when you gave me your address. Come on. Now I can give you my tour."

The house was enormous, mansion-like in its proportions, and one I'd always admired from the outside. The interior was even better. There was a foyer with an inner door of leaded glass. The tile there and in the hallway beyond was the same black and ivory checkerboard sort I'd seen at Mrs. Grossman's, but Tony's was a lot less modern. The woodwork was dark, polished to a high gloss. Brass fixtures were everywhere.

The windows in the dining room and the living room were leaded glass. The dining room itself had dark wood paneling beneath a chair rail, fixtures and a chandelier beyond compare, several pieces of original art, and an awesome Oriental rug. The furniture was antique, as he'd promised. An eclectic assortment with more good taste, character, and charm than I think I've ever seen.

The turret had a winding staircase, with doors to the second and third floors. There were five bedrooms and four baths, each one unique, impeccably furnished and decorated. My own house seemed modest in comparison. I was speechless.

Tony laughed. "Well, what do you think?" he said.

I stared at him. "It's incredible," I said. "I've never seen anything like it. I absolutely love it."

He gave me a proud smile. "I hoped you would," he said. "Come on. I'll fix you a drink."

We went to the living room, where he settled me on the couch, and put a log on the fire he already had going. "What's your pleasure?" he said. "I have Scotch, champagne, wine, sherry, vermouth, whatever you like."

"How about champagne?" I said.

"Coming right up." He disappeared into the kitchen and returned a few minutes later with a bottle of Dom Perignon and two champagne flutes. He filled both glasses, handed one to me, and raised his in a toast.

"To a happy new year, and many more," he said.

"Happy New Year," I said.

"I hope you're hungry," he said. "I probably made too much food but I sometimes get carried away."

"I'm always hungry," I said with a laugh. "Don't worry about a thing."

He put his glass down on the table in front of the couch and touched my knee with his right hand.

"Sit tight, then. I'll be right back."

He disappeared into the kitchen again, and returned several minutes later with a small tray of appetizers. Crab meat in little puff pastries, shrimp in a buttery garlic sauce, and assorted cheeses and smoked fish on flatbread and toast points. It was wonderful.

"Did you make these yourself?" I asked, unable to hide my amazement.

His cheeks tinted slightly and he shrugged. "It's a hobby of mine. I've always enjoyed cooking."

"Well, it shows," I said. "You're really good at it."

He smiled appreciatively and a little shyly, which made me like him all the more. Men. Such sneaky little devils, aren't they?

"How's your investigation going?" he asked. "Have you made any progress?"

I gave him a rueful smile. "No, not a bit," I said. "I talked to his cardiologist, though. That was kind of interesting."

"Who is he?" Tony asked.

"Thomas King. His office is in West Allis, on Sixtieth and Oklahoma."

He frowned for a moment, then shook his head. "No. Don't think I know him," he said. "What did he have to say?"

"He said Dave was taking digitoxin because he had rheumatic fever a lot when he was a kid."

Tony arched his eyebrows. "I didn't know that," he said. "So the cause of death was an overdose of digitoxin?"

I nodded. "He said it could've been put in his food or something he was drinking and he probably wouldn't even notice it."

"Interesting," Tony said.

"He also said it wouldn't take very much because Dave used laxatives to get his weight down for wrestling and that would make the digitoxin more toxic for some reason."

"Yes, that's true," Tony said, nodding. "I wasn't aware of his laxative abuse, either." He shook his head and exhaled sharply. "I guess I wasn't aware of a lot of things." He gave me a look tinged with pain and guilt.

"You can't blame yourself for that," I said. "You barely knew him. You only just met him a couple of months ago and you were busy with your practice almost every moment he was there."

Tony smiled appreciatively. "I know," he said. "I just can't help wishing I could have done something."

"Yeah, I know what you mean," I said. "I feel the same way and I never even met him."

TONY'S DINNER WAS salmon with a rich white sauce, new potatoes with butter and parsley, and fresh asparagus with hollandaise sauce. We had white wine, so good it didn't make me shudder, a chocolate mousse for dessert, then coffee and cognac by the fire.

He had candles on the table and he spent a lot of time watching me. His smile was subtly seductive, his come-on barely perceptible, but undeniably there. He asked me a lot of questions about myself and my family, and he listened intently as I talked. He'd move his eyes slowly across my face, paying particular attention to my eyes and mouth. His look was almost palpable.

At midnight, he kissed my hand and made me a toast I may never forget. We sat near the fire, listened to music, and talked some more, and at two, he drove me home.

He walked me to the door, and when I turned to say good night, he cupped the side of my face in his hand, and gently brushed my lips with his thumb.

"Good night, Beth," he said softly. And then he left. I could have killed him!

I hung up my coat, and walked into the library in a daze to check my messages.

I had one.

The voice was muffled and gravelly but the words were unmistakable:

"Mind your own business or you'll die."

I GOT INTO BED and turned out the lights, but I couldn't close my eyes. I stared in the direction of my bedroom door, which I'd closed, trying to adjust my eyes to the darkness so I could see the doorknob. I heard the furnace go on and then another noise and then my heart was beating so loudly I couldn't hear anything else. I took the telephone from the nightstand and put it under the covers with me. I had to go to the bathroom but I was afraid to get up. I was still wide awake when the sun started to rise, but I must have dozed off some time later. I didn't wake up again until eleven o'clock.

IT WAS New Year's Day, a Friday, and I was expected at my parents' house. I was thoroughly grateful for that. I couldn't wait to get out of the house. I showered as quickly as I could, threw on some clothes, and headed straight for Wauwatosa without eating breakfast. I could do that at Mom's. I'd missed the brunch which she had planned for ten, and I had no idea how I was going to explain myself. My head hurt and I felt sick to my stomach. This private-eyeing was getting to be more than I'd bargained for.

I wanted to tell someone about it, just to calm myself down, but who could I tell? If I talked to Emily, she'd just say "I told you so." If I told Janice, she'd be scared out of her wits. Maybe I could talk to my dad. Or maybe not. I'd have to think about that. Boy, did I wish I'd called Brian McHenry when Emily had suggested it. Monday, first thing, I was going to do it.

"Sorry I'm late," I said to my mom when I walked into the kitchen.

She gave me a perplexed look. "Didn't you get my message?"

"What message?" I said.

"We're not eating until twelve. Ann and Don couldn't make it until then."

"Oh. Well, where are they?" I said. "It's quarter after twelve."

Mom looked at the clock, and tightened her jaw. "I'm putting this food on the table in five minutes," she said. "I could use some help." She was more than a little peeved, but it wasn't at me. Ha. Don and Ann to the rescue again.

We laid everything out, called Mike and my dad in from the den, and started eating. It was great. Bacon, sausage links, fried potatoes, scrambled eggs with onions and peppers, toast, blueberry muffins, coffee cake, and caramel-pecan buns. Don and Ann showed up at twelve-thirty, which wasn't too bad, and Mom was calmed down before the meal was over. No one even noticed I was a perfect wreck.

"What'd you end up getting off of that computer?" Mike asked me later when we were alone in the kitchen.

"Oh, nothing much," I said in a nonchalant voice. "The only files I printed were his monthly expenses and his medical bills. The rest of the stuff was just school projects and outlines or whatever."

Mike gave me a strange look. "What do you want with all that stuff anyway?" he said.

I shrugged, ready to give him some sort of fabricated response. Then I sighed and decided to just tell him the truth (except for the part about the threatening phone call, that is). He already knew something was up, anyway.

"You have to promise not to tell anyone," I said.

"Fine," he said. "Just tell me what's going on."

"All right," I said. "Remember when I told you Janice thought her brother had been murdered?"

"Yeah, so?" Mike said. He had a look on his face like he almost knew what was coming.

"Well," I said. "She asked me to help her prove it."

Mike gaped at me, a really annoying look on his face. "You're crazy!" he said.

"All I'm doing is trying to find out what was going on with him before he died. What's the big deal?"

"Don't you know how dangerous that could be?"

"I'm not going to do anything stupid," I said. "If I figure out who did it I'll just go to the police."

Mike looked somewhat relieved, but not entirely convinced.

"You might be able to help me, you know."

"I don't think so," he said. "I usually leave that sort of thing to the police."

"Just let me ask you one question, okay? It's about a computer printout I found in his desk."

Mike rolled his eyes and kept quiet. I took that as a yes.

"I'm just trying to figure out what it is," I said. "It's about a mile long and it has no title or anything. Maybe there never was one or maybe he just cut it off, I don't know. It actually looks like the top part was torn off."

Mike gave me a bored, and slightly impatient, look.

"It has three columns," I said. "None of them have headings, but the first one's a bunch of names, the second one has dates, and the third one's just numbers but they look like they could be dollar amounts. No dollar signs, though, so I'm not sure. Most of the numbers are the same. And then every name, date, and number is printed twice, one line right after the other. The dates go from January all the way through the end of November. Now, do you have any idea what it could be?"

He laughed. "How the heck should I know?" he said. "It could be anything. He could've retrieved data from some sort of records and just recorded it in that fashion. Maybe he was organizing it differently. Were the names in alphabetical order?"

"No, they were all over the place," I said. "But the dates were in order."

"Hmm. Well, I don't know. He was obviously organizing data of some sort and he was doing it by date. But you can see that for yourself."

"Why would he print every line twice like that?" I said.

"That I don't know. I don't know what purpose it'd serve. Unless he found it that way to begin with."

I frowned. "What do you mean?"

"Maybe the original source had everything entered twice."

I gave him an annoyed look. "Well, why would that be?"

"I don't know," Mike said. "You asked me what I thought and I'm telling you. I told you I don't know. I'm just trying to come up with possible explanations. What makes you think it's significant in the first place?"

"He hid it in a false bottom he made in his desk drawer."

Mike's eyes bugged out and he stared at me. "Are you serious?"

"Yeah. He also hid a calendar and a bankbook in the same place. The calendar had 'nine o'clock' written in for the night he died."

"Wow," Mike said.

"See what I mean? I think he hid that stuff for a reason, so the printout has to mean something."

"Yeah," he said. "Let me take a look at it sometime. Maybe something'll register if I see it."

"Okay," I said. "You want to do it tonight?"

He squinted. "How about tomorrow?"

"Fine," I said. "What time?"

"I don't know. I'll call you when I get up."

"Oh, I just remembered," I said. "His girlfriend's coming tomorrow. I'm picking her up at the airport at two so it'll either have to be in the morning or later in the afternoon after she leaves."

"I'll call you when I get up," he said.

"Okay. Oh, I just thought of something else," I said. "Dave was working for someone, putting all his business records on a computer, but he never finished it and he didn't teach the guy how to use it, either. Is it possible to just go in and look at something like that and figure out what he was doing?"

Mike wrinkled his brow. "You mean could I figure out the system and finish it for him?"

"Yeah."

He shrugged. "I'd have to see it, but sure, probably. Unless there was no indication of what he was doing."

"Well, I told the guy about you when he said he'd probably have to hire someone to finish it and he said he'd let me know."

"Fine. Whatever. Just have him give me a call."

"Okay," I said. "Now don't forget. Don't tell anyone about this. Promise?"

Mike rolled his eyes again. "Don't worry about it," he said. "I'll call you tomorrow." And he walked out of the room.

The rest of the day was pretty enjoyable. The guys watched football all day, the kids hardly even fought, and Ann and I got along reasonably well. Something had to be wrong, but I wasn't going to complain. We had another meal at five—baked ham, twice-baked potatoes, some green bean dish my sister always makes with onion rings on top, and cranberry-apple cake for dessert. Ann and Don went home at seven, Mike at eight. At nine, I finally got up the nerve and left, too, still fearful of going back in my house.

I put the car away, unlocked the door with my heart pounding in my throat, and ran through the house turning on all the lights. The sheer size of the place had been unsettling when I'd first moved in. So many rooms, and so much space. I'd keep imagining I heard someone in another part of the house. It'd taken months to get over that, and now it was back, bigger and stronger than ever. The worst part is the basement; I'm always wondering if someone is down there. The only comfort is in knowing they can't enter through a basement window. They're too narrow for anyone but a small child to fit through.

Should I go down there, or not? If I did, I'd probably faint from fright. If I didn't, I wouldn't sleep all night. I decided to take my chances and get it over with.

I put my hand on the mudroom door, yanked it open, and switched on the light. Empty. Now I had to go through the same thing with the basement door. I put my ear to the door first, and listened. Nothing—at least I was pretty sure I heard nothing. I put my hand on the knob, my heart beating wildly. I turned the knob slowly, and pulled the door open. No one at the top of the stairs. I turned on the basement light. I tiptoed down the stairs, pausing at every step to listen. No one, nothing.

I turned the lights on at the bottom of the stairs and whipped my head around the corner. There was no one in the room, unless they were in the powder room or the shower. I started toward the shower and changed my mind. I'd do the shower and the powder room last. I went to the doorway between the two main rooms, reached my hand around the corner, and switched on the lights.

This room wasn't as easy to search. There are a lot of corners to peek around because of the way the place is configured. I approached the furnace, took a deep breath, and quickly looked behind it. I did the same with the other hidden spots. Nothing. No one there. Okay. The only places left to look were the shower and powder room.

I went back to the first room, hesitated more than a few moments, and threw back the shower curtain. It was empty. Now for the powder room. I held my breath, put my hand on the knob, turned it slowly, yanked the door open—and screamed! My own reflection had just scared me half to death. I'd always dreaded the day that would happen but I didn't think I'd be so young.

I turned out the lights, made sure every door was bolted, and went up to bed. I lay there for a good half-hour, my heart still beating like a drum, and tried to come up with a way to get this over with so I could feel safe again. I couldn't think of a thing.

TEN

WHEN I WOKE UP the next day, there was frost on my windows, delicate little portraits of fairies and mountains and lace. It was twenty below zero with a windchill of negative thirty. I had some shredded wheat and a mango for breakfast, made a pot of tea, and read through some cases Em had copied for me at the law library.

Mike called at eleven and said he couldn't make it before I went to the airport. Maybe later in the afternoon. He'd let me know.

I worked straight through until one, had a bowl of soup, and left to pick up Laura. I got there with ten minutes to spare, parked, and checked the monitor to see if her flight was on time. It was ten minutes late. Not too bad.

I walked to the Northwest terminal, found a seat at the gate, and watched the people go by. I never get bored in an airport. I just look at the people and try to guess where they're going and where they're from. The good-looking ones are all from Milwaukee, of course.

The plane pulled in fifteen minutes late. A young woman with long brown hair, brown eyes, no makeup, wearing jeans with holes in the knees and boots that looked like a construction worker's, walked off alone carrying a knapsack and a down jacket over her shoulder. She was about Emily's height and weight, and she fit the description Laura had given me. She also looked an awful lot like the woman in the pictures I'd seen on Dave's bulletin board. She looked around as if she were searching for someone, and rested her gaze on me. I got up and walked toward her.

"Are you Laura?" I asked.

"Yes," she said, smiling. "Are you Beth?"

I nodded. "I'm sorry you had to wait," she said. "We took off late."

"That's all right," I said. "Do you have any luggage?"

"Yeah, about a thousand bags. I got a new set for Christmas and I filled them with all the other stuff I got. My dad really went berserk this year. I think he was trying to make up for Dave."

I smiled. "Well, it's nice to know he cares," I said.

She gave me a look like I was the most naïve person in the world.

We spent almost forty minutes retrieving her luggage, piled it all on a rent-a-cart, and tried to pull it to the parking lot. We'd get it about two feet and something would fall off. After the third such mishap, I told her to wait where she was, went back and got a second cart, and put half on that.

We loaded everything in the car, which wasn't easy, paid more money to get out than I thought I should have to, and headed downtown.

"You know, maybe I should just take you home first, at least to drop off your luggage," I said. "In fact, if you want, we could talk there, although, in that case, we'd have to stop at my house first. I want to ask you about something I found in Dave's apartment and I don't have it with me.''

Laura hesitated. "No, that's too much trouble," she said. "Let's just go to your place. I don't mind leaving the stuff in the car, if you wouldn't mind taking me home later."

"Oh, no, of course not," I said. "I was planning to do that."

"This is a great street," Laura said as I unlocked my front door. "I've never been here before."

"Thanks," I said with a grin. "It's my favorite in the whole city. My Aunt Sarah left the house to me. Sometimes I feel like I'm living in a fairy tale."

She gave me a funny look.

"Wow!" she said when she walked through the foyer. "This is so cool."

I could see by her face that she was sincerely impressed, which amazed me no end. Wasn't she the one with the maids and the butlers, chauffeurs, and ladies-in-waiting?

"I love your antiques," she said. "Gosh, you have the greatest taste."

I laughed. "Thanks," I said. She made no attempt to disguise her enthusiasm, just walked right in and started checking things out. I liked her. I'd been expecting snobbery, maybe cashmere and pearls, I don't know.

"Do you have time for a tour?" I said.

"Sure," she said. "How many rooms do you have?"

I opened my mouth, and shut it again. "I don't know," I said. "I never counted them. Seven bedrooms and four-and-a-half baths, but I don't know how many altogether."

I took her through the whole house and watched her inspect my furnishings as if she were appraising them for an insurance policy.

"I love antiques," she told me. "My mom collects them, too. She usually waits till I'm home to go hunting 'cause I have a fit if she goes without me. We hit all the auctions and estate sales. Are you into that?"

"Actually, I've never even been to an auction," I said. "I

used to go to estate sales with my mom and my aunt, some-times, but we usually just shopped in antique stores.''

She nodded.

"I always felt weird at estate sales,'' I said. "Like I was intruding on someone's privacy or something.''

Laura wrinkled her brow. "Yeah, I kind of know what you mean,'' she said. "I just never thought of it like that.''

"Are you hungry?'' I said when we'd completed the circuit.

She hesitated, then shrugged. "Yeah, I could eat something. All they had on the plane was some really gross powdered egg thing.''

I winced. "You should fly Midwestern next time. Their food is great.''

She looked skeptical.

"I'm serious,'' I said. "I actually look forward to it.''

We went into the kitchen where I offered Laura a seat and gave her several choices for lunch. She opted for a cheese sand-wich and a Coke, so I made the same for both of us.

"Have you lived in Boston all your life?'' I asked her as I was making the sandwiches.

"Yeah, it's pretty cool. You ever been there?''

"Twice,'' I said. "I love it. It's a great city. I actually went on one of my honeymoons there.''

She frowned. "You went on more than one honeymoon?''

"Well, only one with each husband,'' I said.

She raised her eyebrows.

"Are you planning to move back after you graduate?'' I asked.

She hesitated, a touch of sadness flickering across her face. "Yeah, I guess I will now,'' she said.

I finished the sandwiches and we made small talk while we ate, primarily because I was stalling, feeling unsure how to open the topic. I really hated to bring up Dave's death—even worse, his life—forcing her to relive all the horror and pain she must have experienced in the last few weeks. Fortunately, she eased me into it herself.

"What was that thing you wanted to show me?'' she said when we'd finished eating.

"Oh, just a minute,'' I said. "I'll go get it.''

I went to the library, retrieved my whole "Dave" file, and came back.

"I found this in his desk, hidden under a drawer," I said, handing her the printout. "No one seems to have any idea what it is. Does it mean anything to you?"

She looked at it, leafing through a half-dozen pages, and wrinkled her brow. "I've never seen it before," she said. "Maybe it was for school."

I raised my eyebrows and made a face. "Well, we'll probably never know." I put it away.

Then I showed her the calendar notations. "Do you have any idea what he was doing at nine o'clock that night?"

She shook her head. "No, I don't think he said. He took me to the airport on Thursday and I talked to him on the phone after I got home but I don't remember him saying anything about Friday."

I nodded. "Okay," I said. I showed her the bankbook transactions next. She didn't even react.

"Did you know he had this much money?" I said.

"I don't know, I guess."

"Do you know where he might have gotten it?"

"He could've gotten it lots of places. Gambling, work, whatever. He did lots of things for people for money."

I frowned. "Like what?" I said.

Laura sighed. "Well, I suppose you know about the bomb scares."

I stared at her with wide eyes. "Are you telling me someone actually paid him to do that?"

"Yeah," she said with a shrug. "Some guy offered him five hundred bucks to do it so he did."

"Do you know who the guy was?" I asked.

She shook her head. "Just some guy he met at the bars."

"Did Dave tell you why the guy wanted him to do it?"

"The guy never told *Dave*," Laura said. "It was kind of stupid, really. I don't think he should've done it."

I shook my head. This was too much. "Do you know if the guy ever paid him?" I said.

"I don't know. Probably."

I wrinkled my brow, something suddenly occurring to me.

"Why would some guy he'd never even met before ask him to do something like that? It doesn't make sense."

"He was a friend of someone who knew Dave and the guy told him Dave would do anything for money, which was true."

"I just can't believe this," I said.

Laura shrugged, again. None of what she was telling me seemed to strike her as unusual. It was as if she thought this was all normal, everyday stuff.

"Do you know if he borrowed money from anyone?" I asked.

"I don't see why he'd have to borrow money," she said. "He obviously had enough of his own." She looked at me as if I were a bit obtuse.

I'd made a list of things I wanted to ask her, so I took it out and looked at it, checking off the things I'd already covered.

"Do you want anything else to drink?" I said. "Another Coke or coffee or anything?"

"I'll have another Coke," she said. "Thanks."

I went to the refrigerator, and refilled both our glasses. "You want anything else to eat?" I said. "I have cookies, or ice cream?"

She smiled. "No, this is fine," she said. "Thanks."

I looked at her for a few moments. "I almost hate to ask this," I said, "but why weren't you at the funeral?"

She colored slightly, and lowered her eyes. "My dad wouldn't let me," she said through clenched teeth.

"Jake said your dad wasn't too happy about your seeing Dave," I said.

"That's putting it mildly," Laura said. "My dad hated Dave. He didn't want me to have anything to do with him. He never even gave him a chance. He just wrote him off the minute he saw him."

"When did he meet him?"

"Thanksgiving. I brought him home with me so he could meet my family. I gave him this big buildup like they were really great, you know? And my dad just treated him like dirt. I thought I was going to die. I was never so embarrassed in my life."

I gave her a sympathetic look. "Why did your dad dislike him so much?"

Laura shook her head, and her eyes filled with tears. "I don't know," she said. "He just hated him right away. You could just see it. He's such a jerk, you wouldn't believe."

She was sniffling, and wiping the tears from her cheeks with the back of her hand. I got up and found her some tissues.

"I'm sorry," she said after she'd blown her nose and dried her face.

"You don't have to be sorry," I said. "I think you have some pretty good reasons to cry."

She laughed and sobbed at the same time, and blew her nose again.

"Did your dad know you were still seeing Dave?" I said.

Laura shook her head. "No, I told him I broke up with him. He threatened to cause Dave a lot of trouble if I didn't."

I frowned. "What kind of trouble?"

Laura gave me a jaded look. "Who knows?" she said. "There's no end to what my dad can think up to ruin people's lives. He's a politician."

I started to smile, but caught myself.

"How'd you find out about Dave's death?" I asked.

"A friend of mine called me. She read about it in the paper."

"Have the police talked to you yet?"

"Yeah," she said. "I'm supposed to go down there later. They want to talk to me in person."

I nodded. "Well, tell them everything you told me," I said. "The more they know, the easier it'll be for them to find this guy." She didn't respond, just stared out the window.

"What were you going to do about getting married?" I said a few moments later.

"Do it behind my dad's back," Laura said. "Ignore him. I hate him. He said he'd disinherit me if I married Dave but I didn't care. I don't want his lousy money."

"Are you the only child?" I asked.

She nodded. "Yeah. I suppose that's why he's so protective. That's what Dave said, anyway."

"How about your mom? What did she think about it?"

Laura snorted. "My mom doesn't think, she just does whatever my dad tells her. All he has to do is look at her and she's trembling in her boots. Sometimes I just want to tell her to wise up and get a life."

I smiled weakly, not really knowing what to say.

"Did you know any of his friends?" I said. "Besides Jake and Scott Chapman and Dick Burghoff?"

She shook her head. "Not really, not that I could name."

I nodded. I looked over my list of questions, again. I'd covered everything on it, and I really couldn't think of anything else to add. "Would you like anything else to drink?" I said.

"No," she said without energy. "Would you mind taking me home now? I'm really tired and I still have to go to the police station."

I smiled. "Sure," I said. "Come on."

I drove Laura home, helped her carry her luggage inside, exchanged phone numbers with her, and left. It was five o'clock. Mike hadn't called and I just remembered I'd promised to call Mrs. Robinson about our visit the next day. I was really looking forward to that. Maybe I could cook something and bring it along.

I DIALED Mrs. Robinson's number as soon as I hung up my coat. I let it ring for quite a while, knowing it might take her some time to get to it. She answered on the tenth ring, sounding quite out of breath.

"Hello?" she said.

"Mrs. Robinson, this is Beth Hartley," I said. "Do you remember me from last Sunday?"

"Oh, Beth," she said in a delighted voice. "Oh, my dear. I should say I do. How are you getting along?"

"I'm fine," I said. "How are you? Are you keeping your door locked?"

"Yes, I am," she said. "I kept my promise."

"It's only until the killer's caught," I said. "I'm sure it'll be all right to keep it open again after that."

"Oh, I hope so," she said. "Now, then, are you calling about our visit tomorrow?"

"Yes, I am," I said. "I was thinking maybe I could cook something for us and bring it over. Would you like that?"

"That would be lovely," she said.

"What's your favorite thing to eat?" I said.

She laughed. "Well, now, I don't know. Let me give that

some thought. My favorite thing to eat. Hmm. Let me see.'' True to her word, she did give it some thought, for almost three minutes.

"Pork chops,'' she said decisively. ''Pork chops and corn.''

"Pork chops and corn it is,'' I said. ''What time would you like me to come over?''

"Oh, my. Anytime,'' she said. ''I don't have any plans but to see you.''

"Well, what time do you usually eat supper?'' I asked.

"Oh, five or thereabouts.''

"Okay,'' I said, ''then how about if I get there at four? That'll give us time to talk before dinner and I can heat everything up in your oven. How's that?''

"That's super,'' she said. Super. I couldn't believe it. She was so cute.

I hung up, and decided to call Mike. It was after six and I hadn't heard from him. He was home, but on his way out, and he apologized for not getting back to me.

"How about tomorrow?'' he said.

"That'll be fine as long as it's in the morning,'' I said. ''I have to do some cooking and baking in the afternoon and be somewhere by four.''

"Okay,'' he said. ''That's fine. I'll call you.''

I rolled my eyes. ''Okay. Talk to you tomorrow,'' I said.

I spent the rest of the night knitting and reading, and went to bed at ten o'clock.

I WOKE UP AT nine the next morning, made myself an omelette and some toast for breakfast, and went grocery shopping to get the things I needed for my dinner with Mrs. Robinson. I decided to make biscuits to go with the pork chops and corn, and an apple pie for dessert. I found everything I needed, including cinnamon ice cream to go with the pie.

Mike hadn't called by the time I got home, so I made the pie and baked the pork chops in gravy. The biscuits I'd make at the last minute. The corn I could heat at her house.

Mike called at eleven-thirty.

"Sorry,'' he said, sounding flustered. ''Is it too late for me to stop by?''

"No," I said. "I already did most of what I had to do, so it's fine."

"Good," he said. "How about if I swing by in a few minutes? I can't stay long, though. I have to be somewhere."

"That's okay," I said. "It won't take very long."

I hung up, made a pot of tea, and poured myself a cup. Mike was here ten minutes later (he lives only a few miles away) and I handed him the printout. He paged through it quickly, but carefully, his eyes darting across the page as he read line after line. After about five minutes of that he put it down.

I raised my brows. "Well?" I said.

"It could be a record of office billings of some kind. Medical possibly. Didn't you say he was working for a doctor?"

I frowned. "Well, yeah, but…"

He shrugged. "Find the guy and ask him."

I nodded, and stared out the window. "Yeah, I guess I could do that."

"I have to get going," Mike said. "Is that all you wanted to show me?"

"Yeah, that's it," I said.

"Okay. Catch you later," he said. And he was gone.

I was disturbed. I didn't like this. I didn't want to think that Tony figured in this at all, even tangentially. I sat at the table, nervously doodling in the margins of the printout, drinking cup after cup of tea. I was going to be a complete wreck until I found out, I decided, so I called him.

"Hi, it's Beth," I said when he picked up the phone.

"Well, hey, what a pleasant surprise," Tony said. "I was just thinking about you."

I smiled, a wash of desire and anxiety colliding to form a knot in the pit of my stomach.

"I have to ask you something," I said, just to get it over with.

"Sure," he said. "What's up?"

"I found a computer printout in Dave's apartment and I showed it to my brother Mike and he says he thinks it might be some sort of medical billing record. It's just a bunch of names and dates and numbers that look like they could be dollar amounts. If I read some of them to you do you think you'd be able to tell if it was something he might've been doing for you?"

"I don't know," Tony said with a laugh. "We can give it a try."

I read about ten names with the corresponding dates and numbers and then he stopped me.

"I don't recognize any of those names," he said. "And the numbers wouldn't be right. I'm sure it wasn't anything he was doing for me."

I let out an enormous sigh. "Thanks," I said. "That's all I wanted to know."

He laughed. "Sorry I couldn't help you."

"Don't be sorry," I said. "I just had to ask."

"I had a great time Thursday night," he said.

"So did I," I said. "You're a great cook."

"I hope that wasn't all you enjoyed," he said with a mock-wounded tone.

I laughed. "No, believe me, it wasn't."

"Well," he said, "I hate to cut this short, but I'm due at Scott's in ten minutes and I'm already running late. Can I call you later in the week?"

"Sure," I said with a grin.

I PULLED UP in front of the apartment building at ten minutes to four, and carried everything up to Mrs. Robinson's in two trips. The second time up, I ran into Gordon Kohn in the hall.

"Oh, hi," I said. "How are you?"

He took a moment, then a flash of recognition crossed his face.

"Beth, right?"

I nodded.

"I'm fine, how're you?" he said. "Are you making any progress on the case?"

I shrugged, giving him a sheepish smile. "A little," I said. "I'm getting there, but it's pretty slow going."

He grinned, put a key in his door, and unlocked it. "Hang in there," he said. He walked into his apartment and closed the door.

"I CAN HARDLY wait to eat this scrumptious dinner," Mrs. Robinson said, giving me a hug. "I can see you've gone to quite a bit of trouble on my account."

"It wasn't any trouble at all," I said with a smile. "I enjoyed making it and I'm going to enjoy eating it with you even more."

She grinned happily, clearly delighted to have me there. I felt a surge of emotion, almost to the point of tears. I'd become so fond of her in so short a time, I could barely believe it.

"Now sit down on the sofa with me and tell me all about your week," she said. She patted the seat right beside her and I took it obediently. "How is your investigation progressing?" she asked in a conspiratorial voice.

I smiled. "Not very well, I'm afraid. I've found out a lot more but I still can't figure out who did it. It could be so many people."

"Well, I have faith in you, my dear. If anyone can crack this case, you can."

I grinned and squeezed her arm. We talked for another forty minutes about this and that, and then I got up to take care of the dinner. I'd already put the pork chops in the oven on low. I raised the temperature, put the corn on, and set the table. Fifteen minutes later, dinner was ready, the biscuits nice and hot, and the pork chops heated through but still tender and moist because of the gravy. I'll have to admit, the meal was really good. Mrs. Robinson thought so, too.

"My dear, these are the tastiest pork chops I've ever eaten," she said. "And the *biscuits*. They're heavenly."

I grinned, feeling quite proud of myself.

"Have you seen Mrs. Markham lately?" I asked her.

"Yes," Mrs. Robinson said. "She stopped by today, as a matter of fact. She told me she had a nice chat with you last week."

I smiled. "She was nice," I said. "I talked to her for quite a while. I also went to see Gordon Kohn in apartment 316."

"Oh, yes, he came to see me the other day. Just wanted to look in on me to see how I was doing, he said. Now wasn't that thoughtful of him?"

I hesitated before I smiled. "Yes, it was," I said.

When we'd finished dinner, I put the pie in the oven to warm, and made a pot of tea. Mrs. Robinson made an even greater fuss over the dessert than she had the dinner. I'll tell you, if everyone was that appreciative, I'd cook for people all the time.

I stayed for another hour, and then she looked tired, so I decided it was time to leave. I packed everything up, gave her a big hug and kiss, happily accepted several minutes more of praise and gratitude, and promised I'd call her next week.

After she bolted herself in, I considered knocking on the doors of the tenants I'd been unable to talk to the week before, but decided against it. They'd probably be a lot more receptive if I didn't bother them on a Sunday night. It was time I went home anyway. I'd spend a leisurely hour reading, get to bed a little early, and call Brian McHenry as soon as I got up.

ELEVEN

I CALLED the police administration building first thing Monday morning, before Janice, Emily, and Mrs. Gunther arrived, and left a message for Brian McHenry.

Janice showed up early, at twenty to nine, so I took advantage of the time to tell her about the latest developments.

"Somebody *paid* him to do that?" she screeched. "Who?"

"She doesn't know," I said. "Just some guy he met through someone else."

Janice's face turned a bright pink and she looked away, shaking her head in disbelief.

"They really were planning to get married, by the way, but it was because of Laura's father that they were keeping it a secret. For some reason, he was totally against it. He didn't want her seeing him at all."

"Who does he think he is?" Janice said.

"I don't know," I said. "Some hotshot senator from Boston. Probably used to getting his own way, you know?"

Janice turned down her mouth in disgust.

Emily came in then, poured herself a cup of coffee, and sat

down at the table. Mrs. Gunther arrived a few minutes later, took one look at us sitting in the kitchen and scampered toward the library.

"I'm going to vacuum that room while I have the chance," she said over her shoulder.

I gave Mrs. Gunther the time she needed, then the three of us got down to work. At eleven-thirty, Brian McHenry returned my call. I took it in the kitchen, so I could talk freely, and brought my "Dave" file with me.

"Hey, is this the same Beth Hartley I pined away for through eight long years of grade school?" he said.

I laughed. "This is the first I ever heard of that."

"Well, I was shy back then," Brian said.

"You know how it is." I laughed again, mostly out of nervousness. I was feeling a little uneasy and strange, talking to someone whose voice I hadn't heard for thirty years, whose face I hadn't seen since the eighth grade.

"How did you know where to find me?" he asked.

"Emily Schaeffer," I said. "She suggested I call you."

Brian hesitated a moment. "How is Emily?" he said in an odd voice.

I told him she was fine, happily married, and even more happily working for me.

"That's great," he said. "Say hello for me."

"I will."

"So, what can I do for you?" he said. "I have a feeling this isn't just a social call."

I took a deep breath and let it out. "No, it isn't," I said. "I called you because Emily told me you were a homicide detective and I'm kind of involved in a homicide right now."

"Is that right?" he said in a cautious voice.

"Well, I'm not involved exactly. I'm just investigating it."

"You're investigating a homicide," Brian said flatly. "Maybe you'd better tell me about it."

So I did. I told him about Dave, Janice asking me to help, a skeletal outline of what I'd done so far, and the message I'd found on my answering machine.

"Hold on," he said. He cupped his hand over the phone and yelled something to someone, but I couldn't make out what.

"Tell me what the message was, exactly," he said.

" 'Mind your own business or you'll die.' That was it."

"Man, woman?"

"Man," I said. "At least I think it was a man. The voice was kind of weird."

"How so?"

"I don't know. Kind of muffled. And funny. Like he was trying to disguise it."

"Did it sound familiar?" Brian said.

"No, I don't think so."

"Okay. You saved it, didn't you?"

I didn't say anything.

"You did save it, didn't you?"

"I meant to but I erased it by mistake. I'm sorry," I said.

I heard Brian groan. "All right," he said. "Don't worry about it. Okay. This isn't my case. It belongs to a guy named Bruce Cousins. What I ought to do is have you come down and talk to him directly, but I'd rather talk to you myself. How about going to lunch with me? Are you free?"

"Sure," I said. "When and where?"

"Where are you now?"

I told him.

He thought for a moment. "I'm at Seventh and State so how about meeting me at the Pfister?" he said. "In the coffee shop?"

"That'd be fine," I said. "What time?"

"Twelve-thirty?"

"Okay. See you then."

"Beth?" Brian said as I was about to hang up.

"Yes?"

"Meet me in the lobby. It'll be easier to find each other that way."

"Okay," I said. "I'll see you in an hour."

I hung up with a grin. I couldn't wait. This was somebody I hadn't seen in thirty years. *Thirty* years. For some reason, I found that absolutely amazing.

What in the world should I wear?

I ran upstairs, pulled a half-dozen skirts from my closet, stared at them, and went back for more. I tried on two dresses, three skirts with about a hundred different combinations of sweaters and blouses, and a turquoise tweed wool jumper. I decided on the jumper with a light gray sweater underneath, threw it on, fixed my makeup (twice), redid my hair (three times), and finally rushed out the door, leaving a huge pile of clothes on the bed.

The Pfister Hotel is on Wisconsin Avenue, a few blocks east of the river. I absolutely love it. It's the oldest hotel in the city, and it has three restaurants, all very nice (especially the English Room which, quite honestly, is superb). The coffee shop is the most casual, although it's a little fancier than it used to be. The food is really good now, but I kind of miss the old place.

I was there a little early so I sat on one of the lobby chairs and watched the people go by. The lobby is just gorgeous. It has a marble staircase with two bronze lions at the bottom. It's such an elegant, sort of old-fashioned place. Someday I'm going to rent a room there and stay for a few days, just for fun.

I didn't recognize Brian at all when he walked over. He was very tall, well-built, with wire-rimmed glasses, light brown, slightly wavy hair, cut short in a traditional man's style. He was wearing a suit, gray tweed, with a white shirt and striped tie, wing tips, and a trench coat. He looked great. I couldn't believe it was him.

"Beth Hartley?" he said when he approached.

"Brian?" I said, showing my surprise.

"Wow, you haven't changed at all. You look exactly the same," he said.

I wrinkled up my face. "Brian, that's impossible."

"Well, okay," he said with a sheepish grin. "Not exactly. But I knew it was you. I recognized you as soon as I saw you."

I laughed, and stood up.

"You're still the same height," he said.

"Thanks a lot, Brian. I guess I can't say the same for you, though."

"Tell me about it," he said with a laugh. "I shot up six inches my first year of high school."

"Good grief," I said. "Could you feel it?"

"No," he said, eyeing me curiously. "Are you hungry?"

"Always am," I said.

He was staring at me. "You look great," he said. "Really great."

"Thanks," I said, blushing. "So do you." Boy, this was awkward. I was glad I had a murder to talk about.

"So," Brian said after we'd ordered, "what have you been doing all these years?"

I told him about law school, the firm, my business. How I happened to hire Emily. My house. My marriages. All that sort of thing. He told me about his divorce (no kids either), his career, his lack of a social life. We talked for over an hour, just about personal things, but then he got serious.

"I want to talk about the Grezinski case," he said.

I took a breath, feeling like I'd just been called to the principal's office.

"I want you to start at the beginning, tell me everything you know, everything you've done, people you've talked to, et cetera, et cetera. Okay?"

"Okay," I said.

"Start with how you got involved to begin with." He leaned back in the booth, stretched his right arm across the back, and waited.

"Well," I said, "his sister Janice is my secretary and we're pretty close. I've known her for over ten years. She was the one who found his body. Well, she wasn't the only one, but I'll get to that later."

Brian raised one eyebrow but remained silent.

"She was supposed to go out to breakfast with him on the day after he died but he never showed up so she went over to his apartment and she found him. He was lying on the floor with an empty pill bottle in his hands and there was a suicide note in the typewriter. It wasn't his room or his typewriter, by the way—it was Jake's, which is weird in itself."

Brian sat forward. "Wait a minute. Who's Jake?"

"Dave's roommate. He's the other one who found the body."

Brian pulled a pad and a pen from his pocket. "Give me his full name," he said.

I did.

"Address, phone number?"

I did. "He's already talked to the police," I said.

"When did he find the body?"

"Friday night," I said. "But you're getting me off track now. I'll get to that."

The corners of Brian's mouth turned up a little and he leaned back again.

"Anyway," I said. "He's lying on the floor with this pill bottle which is a prescription for the heart medication he took, digitoxin, and there's a note in the typewriter. Only the note didn't make any sense, according to Janice."

"How so?" Brian said.

"Well, first of all, it said he couldn't pay his debts and Janice didn't think he had any debts, although it looks like she might've been wrong about that. But the other thing was, it said he didn't want to face prosecution for those bomb scares they had at Marquette during finals. He was the one who did that. But they weren't going to prosecute him and he knew that so he couldn't have written the note. You see what I mean?"

Brian took off his glasses and rubbed his eyes. "I think so. Go on."

"So she asked me to help her prove he was murdered."

"And you said yes, just like that."

"Yes, I did."

He stared at me for almost a minute, with a really strange look on his face. I was getting ready to strangle him.

"What did you do then?" he said finally.

I told Brian a sort of truncated version of everything that had transpired so far. He seemed particularly interested in Jake and Laura.

"Neither one of them showed up at the funeral?" he said.

"No, but Laura's dad wouldn't let her go. He didn't want her to have anything to do with Dave and I guess it applied even after he was dead."

Brian made a few notes. I was trying to see what he was writing, but he was shielding it from my view. You know, I'll have to admit, that really annoyed me.

"Do you know any more about that?" he asked. "Did her father ever make any threats?"

"Well, he sort of threatened Dave through Laura, I guess. He told her he'd make Dave's life miserable or something like that if she didn't stop seeing him."

He made another note, also shielded from my view. "Okay, what about Jake?" he asked. "What was his story?"

I told him everything Jake had told me, and added that Jake had neglected to mention that Dave had been found in his room. He wrote all that down, too.

"Okay. You searched the apartment," Brian said, sounding as if he were trying to control his temper. "You left the pass-book and calendar there but you took the printout?"

"Right."

"Where is it now?"

"The printout?" I said. "It's at my house."

"All right. We'll pick up the calendar and the passbook from the apartment and I'll send somebody by your house to get the printout."

Darn. I'd have to hurry up and copy it before they got there.

"Anything else?" he said.

I thought for a few moments, and slowly shook my head. "Not that I can think of," I said.

Brian sighed, sat forward with his elbows on the table, and rested his chin on his hands. "What is your impression so far?" he said.

I raised my eyebrows. "You mean about who did it?"

"Yes. Who do you think did it? Who do you think couldn't have done it?"

"Well, I don't know," I said. "I don't think Jake did it, even though he looks suspicious. Jake thinks it's the guys who lent Dave money."

Brian frowned. "Is there any evidence at all that these guys even exist?"

"Well, no, I guess not," I said. "Jake's the only one who seems to know anything about that."

"So you don't have any good suspects, huh, Sherlock?"

I gave him a cross between a scowl and a sneer. "Well, from what I can see," I said, "neither do you."

"Touché," Brian replied.

"So who's this Cousins guy?" I asked.

"He's a new detective," Brian said. "This is his first case."

"Oh, great," I said. I rolled my eyes and shook my head.

Brian pursed his lips, and looked like he was counting to ten. Then he leaned forward and gave me an intense look. "Beth,

I want you to listen to me," he said. "I want you to stay out of this. This is not Nancy Drew. This is real life. It's dangerous. You could get hurt. You could get killed."

I sighed. I sort of appreciated the concern, although I could've done without the Nancy Drew comment. I didn't say anything for several moments.

"I can't stay out of it," I said finally. "I promised Janice and I can't let her down. It means too much to her and she's counting on me."

Brian's face turned red and I could see him tighten his jaw. "You have no business messing around in a police investigation," he said. "You're going to louse things up. You could end up destroying evidence."

"Well, so far," I said, "it looks like I found evidence the police never even noticed."

Brian shifted his position abruptly and took a few deep breaths. If I'd touched him, he probably would've felt like a piece of granite.

"Brian," I said in a not-unfriendly voice, "I don't want you to be upset with me. I don't want to fight with you about this. But just try to understand, I'm just doing a favor for a good friend. I promise I'll be careful. As soon as I even think I know who it is, I'll call you. I won't even go near him. I won't do anything on my own. I never intended to."

His face softened some as I talked, and the red tint disappeared from his cheeks. He sighed, and gave me a caring smile. "I'm sorry," he said. "I didn't mean to get so hot. I'm just worried about you. I don't think you know what you're getting into."

I shrugged and smiled back.

He reached across the table and took my hand and held it in both of his. "I want you to promise me something," he said. "I want you to keep in touch with me every step of the way. Every time you talk to someone or think of something else I want you to call me. Will you do that?"

I hesitated. "Sure," I said, a bit reluctantly. "I promise."

Brian looked as if he were about to let go of my hand, but he suddenly raised it and pressed it against his lips. He turned a light shade of pink and let it drop.

"Sorry," he said. "I don't know why I did that."

I laughed. "It's all right," I said. "I didn't mind."

He gave me a shy smile. "Let's get out of here," he said. "I have to get back to work."

AS SOON AS I got home, I pulled the printout from my file and started copying it.

"What are you doing?" Emily said.

"I'm copying the computer printout I found in Dave's room. I just had lunch with Brian McHenry and he says I have to give it to him."

Emily colored slightly and bent over her work. Janice gave me a quizzical look. I raised an eyebrow and shrugged.

It must have taken me a good forty minutes to copy the darn thing. I folded it up, placed it in a folder I marked "Brian McHenry", and put the copy in my file.

I didn't feel like working. I had Dave on my mind. "I'll be in the other room if you need me," I said. I picked up the file and went to the kitchen.

I looked through everything I had, and made a "to do" list:

—*call Dick Burghoff*
—*interview other tenants*
—*call Mr. VanderHayden?*

I picked up the phone and dialed Dick Burghoff's number.

"Hello?" someone said.

"Could I speak to Dick Burghoff, please?" I said.

"This is Dick."

"Hi. I'm Beth Hartley," I said, and told him why I was calling.

"I'll tell you one thing," he said. "I never believed Dave killed himself. He had no reason. And he wasn't like that, anyway. Nothing bothered him. He didn't let things get to him."

"It seems like everyone who knew him feels the same way," I said. "Did he talk to you about what was going on in his life, other than wrestling?"

"Sure, some," Dick said.

"Do you know if he was in any kind of trouble?"

A slight hesitation. "Like what?" he asked.

"Anything," I said. "Did he ever say anything about owing anyone a lot of money, for instance?"

"No, he never said anything like that," Dick said. "But he did seem a little low on funds sometimes. He borrowed money from me a couple of times, but it was just a few bucks."

"Did he seem like he was worried about money?"

"Are you kidding? The guy never worried about anything. He just figured everything would work out somehow and it usually did, for him. Last time I lent him a twenty he said he was going to have a thousand of 'em in another week. He probably would have, too, if he hadn't died."

I frowned. "When did he say that?" I said. "Do you remember?"

"Yeah, it was the Friday before he died."

"Did he tell you where he was going to get all that money?"

"No, he never said. Look," Dick said, "he might not have been serious anyway. He was always talking like that. Like he thought he was going to be the next Donald Trump or somebody. He was just that kind of guy."

"Okay. Is there anything else that you can think of?" I asked. "Anything that was bothering him? Anyone angry at him for anything?"

Dick thought for a few moments. "No," he said. "I'm sorry, I really can't."

"If you do think of something, would you give me a call?"

"Sure thing," he said, and I gave him my number.

"Oh, I almost forgot," I said. "Do you know if he used anything to get his weight down for wrestling?"

No answer.

I told him why I was asking.

"Oh, wow," Dick said under his breath. "Yeah, he used them. Everybody does. It gets your weight down real quick. 'Course, it goes right back up again but all you need it for is when you weigh in."

"Do you think anyone else knew he was taking them?"

"Heck, yeah," he said with a laugh. "Anyone on the team would've known. Heck, Coach probably even knows."

I sighed. "Okay, thanks, Dick. You've been a big help."

"No problem," he said.

I WENT BACK TO the library and got to work. Mrs. Gunther poked her head in an hour later and said a policeman was at the door. Emily and Janice exchanged looks, and raised their eyebrows at me.

"He's just here to pick up the printout," I said with a laugh. I grabbed the file and went to the door, had a nice chat with the guy, turned over the evidence, and went back to work. I was still slightly peeved. That was my own personal evidence that I found with my own ingenuity and I didn't feel like giving it up. I knew I was being totally unreasonable, but that's how I felt.

Brian McHenry called me a couple of hours later.

"Hey, didn't they teach you in law school you're not supposed to doodle on the evidence?" he said.

"Oh, no!" I said, turning bright red. "I'm sorry. I wasn't thinking about it when I did that. Does it really matter?"

He laughed. "Don't worry about it," he said. "You behaving yourself?"

"Yes, I'm behaving myself," I said, making no effort to hide my irritation. "I just talked to another one of Dave's friends, though. A guy named Dick Burghoff."

"Beth…never mind. What'd the guy say?"

I told him.

"Spell his name for me."

I did.

"Number?"

I gave it to him and he sighed. "Were you planning to call me and tell me this or did I just luck out by calling you?"

"I was going to call you," I said. "I just hadn't gotten around to it yet."

"Okay," Brian said. "I have to go. Talk to you later. And be careful," he added quickly.

"I will," I said. "I promise."

THE NEXT DAY was Tuesday, January fifth. I worked hard, all day, and Emily stayed late because Phil was out of town for the next week. At six, seven Boston time, I decided to call Mr. VanderHayden. I left Emily in the library and took my "Dave" file to the kitchen.

I dialed the number, praying the Senator was home in Boston rather than off legislating in Washington, D.C. A maid answered.

"Whom shall I say is calling?" she said when I asked for the Senator.

"My name is Beth Hartley," I said. "I'm a friend of the family of Dave Grezinski, that's G-r-e-z-i-n-s-k-i, and I'd like to talk to Senator VanderHayden about his death."

It was a good five minutes before he came to the phone, something I suspected he did intentionally. Intimidation? Putting me in my place? Stalling so he could come up with a good story?

"This is Senator VanderHayden," he said. His voice was deep and resonant, like a bass singer's. Beautiful, really. A voice like that must command a lot of attention.

"Senator VanderHayden, my name is Beth Hartley," I said. "I'm a close friend of Dave Grezinski's sister and I'm helping her investigate his possible murder."

"And how does that concern me?" he said. His tone was cold and unfeeling, but I detected a hint of caution.

"I understand you didn't want Dave seeing your daughter, Laura," I said.

No response.

"Is that true?" I said.

I heard him sigh. "Frankly, my dear young woman, I fail to see how that concerns you. Nor do I see how that relates to the young man's death."

"Well…I'm not sure if it relates, either," I said. "But I'm looking for people who might have had a motive to kill him."

"I see," he said, after hesitating a few moments. "My dear young lady, the mere fact that I did not want my daughter dating the boy is hardly a motive for murder. I found him wholly unsuitable, but I certainly had no reason to take his life. Your suggestion is utterly absurd, and quite frankly, slanderous. I can assure you, young lady, that if you profess your views to anyone else, I will turn the matter over to my attorneys."

"I never said you did it, Mr. VanderHayden. I never even expressed the opinion that you did it, and an opinion wouldn't even be slanderous anyway. Besides that, you're a public figure so you don't have a chance. You'd be wasting your attorney's time.'' I knew I was being childish, but he really ticked me off.

I heard him take a deep breath and let it out. ''Do not call me again,'' he said, and hung up.

What a jerk! This time I did call Brian right away, but he wasn't there so I left a message for him to call me.

I went back to the library, still working to control my anger.

''You want to go out for a pizza?'' I said to Emily.

She raised her head, and gave me a puzzled look. ''Sure,'' she said. ''What's the matter with you?''

''Oh, nothing,'' I said. ''I just talked to a real jerk. Senator VanderHayden from Boston, Massachusetts.'' I was using the same sort of voice Jake had used when he'd first told me about him and I smiled at myself when I realized it.

''You want to go to Balistreri's?'' I said. ''You won't have so far to go home, then. We can take both cars.''

''Sure,'' she said, and packed up her stuff.

Balistreri's is in Wauwatosa, on Sixty-eighth and Wells. They don't take reservations, so you usually have to wait, but it's really worth it. The pizza's the best I've ever had. Really thin crust. It's just perfect. I'm never satisfied with anyone else's pizza anymore.

I followed Emily there so we arrived at the same time, but we had to park a block apart. The wait was short and we got a table in the back room near the window. We ordered a large pizza with about a hundred toppings and a pitcher of Coke.

''So, how was Brian McHenry?'' she asked, without looking up. She seemed uncharacteristically absorbed in rearranging her silverware, seeing how many permutations she could come up with.

''He's fine,'' I said. ''Really nice. It was pretty weird seeing him after all these years, though. I never would've recognized him.''

She looked up then, smiling. ''Yeah, I felt the same way when I saw him. He got so tall, for one thing.''

I laughed. ''Yeah, he said he grew six inches in one year. He turned out pretty good-looking, too.''

She nodded, and gazed across the room at the other customers. ''Did he say anything about me?'' she asked, her eyes still roving the room.

"He asked how you were. He seemed glad that you were happily married."

Emily gave me a strange look, a mixture of annoyance and confusion.

"Well, you didn't want me to tell him you're having problems, did you?" I said.

She let out a deep sigh. "No, I guess not," she said. "I don't know."

"You're still hung up on him, aren't you?"

Emily's face got a little red and her eyes looked kind of glassy. "No...yes," she said. "No. No, I'm not. What's the point, anyway? It's too late now. He's all yours, if that's what you're after."

"I wasn't even thinking about that," I said. "I guess he would be kind of nice to go out with but I wasn't thinking about it, and if it would bother you I wouldn't do it."

She shook her head, still averting her eyes. "It wouldn't bother me," she said quietly. "Go ahead if you want to. He'd be perfect for you, actually." She looked at me then. "I think he'd be just your type."

I smiled. "Really?" I said. "Why?"

She shrugged. "He's genuine," she said. "Real. Like you. And he's really nice, not just to people who are close to him but to everyone. He's just what you need. You're two of a kind, really."

I had to fight against the lump I felt in my throat. I took a deep breath and smiled, then leaned forward.

"Well, you know something," I said. "You may not realize it, but I think Phil is perfect for you. And I think you love him as much as he loves you. You just fight it, he doesn't. He doesn't have your history. You're so afraid of losing someone that you put up barriers. You create obstacles to keep the relationship from getting anywhere in the first place. You'd rather not have it at all than have it and lose it."

Emily burst into tears. Oh, great, I did it again.

"Oh, Em, I'm sorry," I said. She put her hand to her head and shielded her face, hoping to keep other people from seeing her. It didn't work. At least three tables of customers were staring at us.

"I'm sorry," she said in a few minutes. "I know you're right, that's all. I just wish I knew what to do about it."

"Well, don't ask me. I have the same problem."

She started laughing then, and *everyone* was looking at us. "We're hopeless, you know that?" she said.

I gave her a tell-me-about-it look. "Let's get out of here," I said.

ALL THE WAY HOME, I thought about Senator VanderHayden and the conversation I'd had with him. The guy was such a jerk, and he really made me kind of nervous. I told myself I was being silly, though. He was halfway across the country, in Boston. What could I possibly have to worry about?

TWELVE

IT WAS ALMOST ten when I got home. The air was bitterly cold, the sky a mass of swiftly moving clouds ranging in hue from dirty gray to ugly black. Broken branches were flying about and one of my next-door neighbor's trash cans had blown over. I put the car in the garage, took a cup of tea and a book up to bed, read for about an hour, and turned off the light.

The next day was Wednesday, January sixth. It was snowing lightly when I woke up but the forecast was ten inches. I went downstairs to make breakfast and discovered I had a bit of grocery shopping to do. I'd have to do it early, too, before the snow got too deep. I scrounged around for something to eat, waited for Janice, Emily, and Mrs. Gunther to arrive, and told them I'd be back in about an hour, that I had some errands to run.

I loaded up on food, and restocked my liquor supply with some Scotch, tequila, a quart of vodka, and some Jim Beam whiskey (I don't actually drink any of that stuff but it's good to have for guests). The snow was coming down fast now, big flakes that were so close together they nearly formed a sheet.

Peter was out shoveling, poor kid, barely able to keep ahead of the fall. I told him not to bother. He could come back tomorrow after it'd stopped. He flashed me a grateful grin, scooped up some snow, and made a snowball, which he playfully threatened to throw at my head.

"Never throw snowballs at the people who pay you," I said.

I hung my wet clothes in the mudroom, set the liquor on the kitchen table, and put the rest of the groceries away.

I was just about to go into the library when the phone rang. It was Jake.

"Some cops were here last night," he said. "They took that calendar and savings book out of Dave's desk."

"Oh, yeah," I said. "I forgot they were going to do that. I should've warned you. Sorry."

"That's okay," he said. "I sort of freaked when I opened the door, though."

I laughed. "I'll bet," I said. "So how've you been? You getting your packing done?"

"Yeah, pretty much. I'm still trying to find another place, though. I might be stuck here another month."

"Are you looking for one with a roommate?" I asked.

"Yeah," Jake said. "I really can't afford it by myself. Why? You know someone?"

"No, but if I hear of anyone I'll let you know."

"Thanks," he said. "So, how's it going with you? You getting any leads yet?"

"No, not really. I found out he was expecting to make a lot of money about the time he died, though. Did he say anything to you about that?"

"Naw," Jake said. "He didn't say anything like that."

"Okay, well, thanks, Jake. I'll talk to you soon. I'll let you know if I figure anything out."

"Okay, catch you later," he said. "Let me know if I can help."

"I will," I said with a smile. He'd warmed up a lot since I'd first met him and I was really beginning to like him.

I worked the rest of the day, sent everyone home at three because of the snow, and Tony called at five-thirty.

"Hi," he said softly, sending my heart aflutter. "You snowed in over there?"

I laughed. "I sure am," I said.

"Me, too," he said. "Luckily, most of my patients canceled so I got home before it was too late. I got stranded at the office once last year."

"Wonderful," I said.

"You doing anything Friday night?" Tony asked.

"Nope," I said. "What'd you have in mind?"

"A little dinner? Maybe Fox & Hounds if the weather's not too bad?"

"I'd love it," I said. "That's one of my favorite restaurants." Fox & Hounds is a great German restaurant in the Kettle Moraine, near Holy Hill.

"Mine, too," he said. "I'll tell you what. I'll call you early Friday, when we know what the weather's going to be like and if it's too bad for Holy Hill we'll go somewhere in town."

"Okay, great," I said. "I'll talk to you on Friday."

I made myself a cup of tea after we hung up, and sat at the kitchen table watching the snow. Its pace had picked up considerably, which excited me no end. Ever since I can remember, I've been mesmerized by snowstorms, elated at the thought of being snowed in, all cozy and warm inside while great mounds of white stuff enveloped my house.

When I was little, my father told me stories of growing up in northern Wisconsin, where the snow was so deep it sometimes covered the windows. Once, my dad said, it was so high he was able to climb to the top of the drift and just step onto the roof. I wonder now if he was telling me the truth. He once told my brother that Fritos were made from pigskin.

I went into the library and knit for a couple of hours, made myself some dinner, and decided to finish my laundry. I went upstairs, piled at least three loads' worth into a basket, brought it down to the basement, turned on the radio, and started sorting. Ooh, Rachmaninoff's second piano concerto was on. I put the first load in, cranked up the radio, and listened to the whole thing before I went back up the stairs.

I couldn't get the basement door open.

I pushed on it with all my strength, trying several times, but it wouldn't budge. And then I saw the smoke. Little wisps at first, then great curling clouds. It was coming under my basement door and there was no way out. The windows were too small. Mere slits no grown human being could ever fit through. My house was on fire! I started to panic. I was coughing and the smoke was burning my eyes. I looked around frantically for a way out, but there was no escape.

The clothes chute! I could go through the clothes chute! I'd crawled through once as a kid. I could do it again. I pulled on the door. It wouldn't open. I yanked on it as hard as I could, but it still wouldn't move. I ran downstairs, grabbed a screwdriver, and came back up. I pried around the edges, trying to loosen it up. I put the screwdriver down, and tried again. It opened! I put my palm on the other door. It was hot. My kitchen was on fire! I'd be escaping into the fire rather than out. I panicked again. What the heck was I going to do? If I stayed down here, I'd surely die. I had no choice. I had to get out. I pushed on the second door. It was stuck too. I ran down the stairs, again, and got a hammer. I ran back up, and banged on the door as hard as I could, hitting it around the edges. It seemed like hours went by, but finally it opened, heat and smoke blasting me in the face. It was hideously hot, but the fire was still some distance away from the chute. I decided to go for it.

It wasn't until that moment that I considered the size of the opening.

The chute couldn't be more than fifteen inches wide, maybe sixteen at the most. I tried to get through, but the fit was too snug. Now what was I going to do? All I needed was a little more room, just a little. The smoke was so dense I could hardly breathe. The heat was almost unbearable. I pulled my shirt over my face, coughing and crying, my mind racing for something to do.

I had it! I took off all my clothes and tried again. It was *still* too tight—darn! I ran downstairs, grabbed a bottle of laundry detergent, and ran back up. I greased myself from neck to toes, wiped my hands on my clothes, and tried again. This time, I got my shoulders through. I was halfway there, now for the hips. I could've sworn they were the same width as my shoulders. But they wouldn't go through. I was stuck.

I felt faint and sick to my stomach. The heat and smoke were suffocating me. There wasn't any air to breathe and I was weaker by the minute. I knew I'd die if I didn't get out. I had to try one more time. I grabbed the outside door and pulled with every ounce of strength I could muster. The last thing I remember is making it through, screaming with pain, and then everything went blank.

WHEN I CAME TO, I was in the back of an ambulance, wrapped in blankets, with All-Purpose Cheer smeared all over my body. The fire department was there, as well as the police, and my next-door neighbor, Marie, who'd reported seeing the smoke. I was taken to the hospital, given all kinds of tests and treatments, and released at one the next day. I called Marie (to save alarming anyone who didn't already know), begged her to bring me some clothes, and went home in her car. When she pulled up in front of my house, I started to cry. I couldn't see any of the damage from the front, but the place was swarming with people, investigating who knows what and invading whatever privacy I had left. All I wanted was to be alone, in my own bed, with no one to bother me.

Brian was standing in my living room when I walked in. The look on his face was so tender I just ran into his arms and sobbed into his chest. He stroked my hair, kissed the top of my head, then walked me over to the couch and sat down beside me with his arm around my shoulders.

"How're you feeling?" he said in a gentle voice.

"Awful," I said, and started to cry again. Every inch of my body hurt. My shoulders and hips were bruised and scraped. My head felt like the housing for a kettledrum. I hadn't even seen my face and I was afraid to look.

"Emily and your secretary were here"

"Oh, no!" I said. "Janice and Emily. I forgot all about them."

"It's okay," Brian said. "I told them what happened and said you'd call them when you felt up to it."

"Thanks," I said. "Janice is Dave's sister, you know."

Brian nodded. "She told me. She's blaming herself for what happened."

I looked at Brian and frowned. "What do you mean?" I said. "Why would she blame herself for this?"

Brian gave me a puzzled look. "I assumed you knew," he said. "Someone deliberately set the fire."

I closed my eyes and took a deep breath. "I guess I really did know," I said. "I just didn't want to believe it."

Brian sighed, and took my fingers in his. "I hope you're going to stop all of this now," he said. "You could've been killed last night. Whoever did this *meant* to kill you." He gave me the most pleading look and waited for my response.

I didn't know what to say. I couldn't quit. He should've known that. On the other hand, what was left for me to do?

"I don't know what else I would've done anyway," I said. "I've already talked to everyone I can think of who might know something." (Of course, if someone or something else came to mind, I'd surely pursue it. But I didn't have to tell Brian that.)

Brian let out a big sigh, and smiled. "Thank you," he said.

"Oh, I just remembered," I said. "I talked to Laura VanderHayden's father. I forgot to tell you about that." I winced. "Sorry."

Brian shook his head as if to say *Forget it.* "What did he say?"

I told Brian everything, including Mr. VanderHayden's threat to call his attorneys.

"Where's your phone?"

"In the ki...in the library," I said. "I'll show you."

"No," he said quickly. "Don't get up. Just tell me where it is."

He came back a few minutes later, and sat down again.

"How long have these guys been here?" I asked.

"Since early this morning. They'll be here a while yet."

"Darn," I said.

Brian put his hand on my knee. "Hold on," he said. "I'll see if I can find out how long they're going to be."

He came out less than a minute later, with another man, who was carrying four clear plastic bags tied with string.

"Ma'am," the man said. "My name is John Clancy. I'm an arson investigator." He showed me the bags, and asked if I recognized the contents.

I frowned, and nodded in confusion. "That's the liquor I bought yesterday."

"Were they empty before the fire, ma'am?"

"No," I said. "They were full. I never opened them."

He nodded, and addressed Brian. "Looks like the accelerant," he said. He looked at me again. "We detected alcohol with a chromatograph, on your kitchen table and in front of the basement door. Whoever started this fire, ma'am, used your alcohol to fuel it. That and the newspapers you had piled up in your mudroom. Do you remember where the alcohol was before the fire?"

"I left it on the kitchen table," I said, and started to cry. Brian gave the investigator a silent signal and he left us alone.

He sat me down on the couch again and put his arm around my shoulders. When I stopped crying, he asked me if I felt up to telling him what I could remember.

"Can it wait?" I said. "I already went through the whole thing for the police who came to the hospital. I don't want to have to think about it again right now."

"Sure," Brian said. "It can wait. These guys will probably be here another hour or so. I'll stay with you until they leave if you want me to."

"Thanks," I said, and rested my head against his arm.

"Hey, remember John Schroeder?" Brian said. "The one who was a new kid in fifth grade and then he left the next year? The one who was always brushing his teeth in the bathroom after lunch?"

I laughed (which hurt, by the way). "Yeah, I think so," I said. "Why?"

"He's a dentist now."

I laughed even harder then, which hurt even more. Brian went on like that, telling me anecdotes about our former classmates, none of whom I'd seen or heard of in all those years, until everyone was gone. When the last of them left, Brian stood up.

"I have to go," he said. "You ought to try to get some sleep and put it out of your mind. I'll call you tomorrow."

I got up, too, and gave him a big hug. He hugged me back and we stood there for several minutes, neither of us wanting to break away first. He finally did, gave me a kiss on the top of my head, and said goodbye.

As I walked upstairs, I heard the phone ring but I let it go. I couldn't wait to get into bed. There's nothing like being in your own bed, all snuggled under the covers, to make the goblins go away. I took a painkiller, pulled my quilt over my head, and fell fast asleep.

The smoke was blacker and thicker this time, and the flames were out of control. I was naked again and I was frantic. I crawled through the hot metal maze, searching for a way out, but every opening was a doorway of flames. Fiery tendrils reached deep into the chute, snatching and grasping, scorching my flesh. I screamed, shrinking back, and they only reached farther.

I sat upright in bed, drenched in sweat, trembling all over, and I started to cry. I stayed in that position, wide awake, for the rest of the night.

The next day I did nothing but sleep, not even bothering to eat. Janice called, said she'd warned Mrs. Gunther not to come, and asked if I needed anything. She was beside herself with guilt and I didn't have the energy to make her feel better. Emily called, then Tony, whom I'd completely forgotten about. He was shocked when I told him what had happened, offered to come over to do anything he could, but I said no. He gave me a rain check on our dinner date and asked me to call him when I felt up to it. Brian called, asked how I was doing, and promised to call again the next day.

I woke up Saturday morning, feeling like I could eat a seven-course meal. The last nourishment I'd had was on Thursday morning before I left the hospital, and *it* was awful.

I called Emily. "How would you like to meet me at Ma Fischer's?" I said. "I don't have a kitchen anymore and I'm starving to death."

"I'll be right there," she said.

I took a quick shower, wincing every time I touched myself, and looked in the mirror for the first time since I'd come home. The sides of my body were black and purple, abrasions stretching from the pelvic bone halfway down my thighs. My face was a mess, with a large violet lump on my forehead, and something that looked like a blistering sunburn across one of my cheeks. I drew in my breath, tears stinging my eyes.

I didn't have any liquid makeup to cover it because I never wear the stupid stuff. I tried powder instead but it actually looked worse. I washed it off and left it the way it was. I put on baggy sweats to minimize the friction, and went.

I got there before Emily and took a booth as far away from the door as I could get. Ma Fischer's is an old, home-style place on Farwell, just south of North Avenue, open twenty-four hours a day. We used to go there for breakfast a lot, after a night on the town. I ordered coffee, and was sipping it with my head down when Emily came in.

When I lifted my head, she gasped and actually got tears in her eyes.

She sat down and gingerly touched my arm. "Are you all right?" she said, her voice breaking.

I smiled weakly. "Yeah, I guess," I said. "It could've been a lot worse."

"I don't know how you could be so stupid," Emily said.

I closed my eyes. "Please, Emily," I said, tears welling up. "Give me a break, at least for today."

"I'm sorry," she said, and sounded like she meant it. She even looked guilty. Maybe near brushes with death would be good for her, as long as they were mine.

We had omelettes and sausage, drank over a pot of coffee between us, and even had dessert. We walked to the corner and browsed through the Oriental Drugstore for a while, and then decided to go to Emily's. We stopped on the way to drop off my car, and drove to her place in hers. I stayed the rest of the day, and night, and for the first time since it happened, I got a really good night's sleep. I remembered to call Mrs. Robinson while I was there, told her I'd been hurt, but not how badly, and we decided to postpone our visit until the next week. I reminded her, again, to keep her door closed and locked. It's a good thing I did, because she had forgotten. She had to go and shut it while we were still on the phone.

Emily brought me home early Sunday morning, and came in with me. I hadn't seen my kitchen yet and didn't want to experience it alone. We went in the front door, crossed through the living room into the dining room, and gasped, both at the same time.

The dining room was untouched, except for some water damage, but the kitchen was a total disaster. The whole room was a sooty, sodden mess. The curtains were gone, the linoleum blistered and buckled, the wallpaper blackened and seared. In the center of my kitchen table was a shiny black scar, with a succession of black marks extending from it in a pattern that looked like alligator skin.

I stepped gingerly through the room, with Emily behind me, went into the mudroom, and stared, openmouthed, at the basement door. A large "V" was burned into its surface and the floor beneath it was black and blistered. The mudroom itself was destroyed, the wallpaper burned off, wooden coat hooks gone, the small chest, where I'd kept hats and scarves, completely ruined. The memory of the fire and the fear that went with it came back in a rush. I wondered if I'd ever have the nerve to go down those basement stairs again. I shut the door, walked out of the kitchen to the living room, and sank down on the couch.

"Good grief, what a mess," Emily said. "Did the insurance company come out yet?"

I nodded with my eyes closed.

"What's the damage estimate?"

"I don't know yet," I said. "And I don't care, as long as they pay it." I shook my head. "I'm glad my Aunt Sarah isn't here to see this."

"Yeah, I know what you mean," Emily said. "Well, look at it this way. At least you can finally get rid of that hideous wallpaper."

I opened my eyes and laughed. "Hey, you're right," I said. "You know, I actually had a nightmare about that wallpaper once? The spoons were chasing me all over the house and they had big hands and feet and really mean, ugly faces."

"Pretty spooky," Emily said. "When was that?"

"When I was seven or eight, I think."

She laughed. "Well, now you can redecorate the whole kitchen, furniture and all, and it won't cost you a cent."

"Yeah," I said, grinning. "I can buy an Ethan Allen table and china cabinet and maybe get ceramic tile this time. I've always wanted ceramic tile."

"You'd better curb your enthusiasm a bit or they'll think you torched the place yourself."

"Yeah, right."

"Well, are you going to be okay?" Emily said.

I nodded.

"Okay, I'm going to get going but I'll call you later. Maybe we can go out to dinner somewhere."

"Great," I said. "I guess I'll be eating out for quite a while, huh?"

"Hey, live it up," Emily said. "I'll talk to you later."

I WENT TO the library, sat at my desk, and took out my "Dave" file. I hadn't even opened it when I heard someone banging on my door.

It was Jake.

"I found something," he said breathlessly. "I found something in the apartment."

I pulled him in and closed the door.

"What the heck happened to you?" he said when he saw my face. He frowned, and wrinkled his nose. "Do you smell smoke?"

"Someone set fire to my house," I said.

Jake took a step back and whipped his head around, looking frantically about the room.

"Not now, Jake. Wednesday. That's where this came from," I said, pointing to my face.

"Oh," he said, looking relieved. "Do they know who did it?"

"No," I said, "but my guess is it's the same person who killed Dave."

"Holy cow," Jake said, his eyes bugging out. He sat down on the couch with his mouth open.

"I'd offer you something to drink," I said, "but the fire was set in my kitchen so I don't have anything."

"Oh, no problem," he said.

"So, what did you find?" I said. He'd been holding a business-sized envelope in his hands, fingering it nervously and bending it around the edges.

"This," he said, thrusting it toward me. "I found it under Dave's mattress when I took the sheets off."

I frowned. "Why'd you take the sheets off?"

"Because they were mine," he said, clearly annoyed.

I removed the letter from the envelope and unfolded it. There was only one page. No letterhead. Just plain, white, heavy bond. No date on the letter. Illegible postmark on the envelope. It was to Dave, from Laura's father. A check was enclosed, the letter said, to be cashed in exchange for Dave's agreement to stop seeing Laura. There was no reference to the amount of the check, and the check was no longer in the envelope.

"It has to be him," Jake said when I'd finished reading it. "He must've found out Dave was still seeing her and he killed him because he cashed his lousy check." Jake's jaw and both fists were clenched. "Senator Lowlife," he said.

"Jake," I said. "Do you know Dave cashed the check?"

He gave me a look like my head was ten feet thick. "Of course he cashed it," he said. "It's not in the envelope."

"He could've sent it back," I said. "He could've torn it up. Maybe he put it somewhere else."

"Oh," Jake said, looking dejected.

"This is still a very important piece of evidence no matter what he did with the check," I said.

Jake's face brightened up and he gave me a wistful smile.

"I think you should take this to the police," I said. "I'll go with you if you want."

He nodded, grinning. "Cool," he said. "Let's do it."

I called Brian at home. "Jake Grossman found something in the apartment I think you'll be interested in," I told him, winking at Jake. Jake grinned like a little kid.

"I'll be right over," Brian said.

A half-hour later, Brian was in my living room, removing the letter from its envelope, holding it at the very tip of one corner. Jake and I exchanged a look.

"How'd you happen to find this?" Brian asked Jake when he'd returned the letter to the envelope.

Jake explained, got thoroughly interrogated, and explained some more. I was getting really ticked off at Brian for giving him such a hard time. The poor kid was just trying to help.

EMILY CALLED later that evening and we went out to dinner, this time to T. G. I. Friday's. The bump on my head had gone down a lot and I'd bought some liquid makeup to cover the scrapes and bruises. If the lighting was right, I looked almost human.

"Jake Grossman came over today," I told her. "He found a letter to Dave from Laura's dad. The guy actually bribed him to stay away from his daughter, can you believe that?"

"You're kidding!" Emily said. "How much?"

"I don't know," I said. "The check was gone and it didn't say how much in the letter."

"You mean the little creep cashed it?"

"Who knows?" I said. "He could've sent it back, for all I know."

"Yeah, that's true," Emily said. "What about this Jake guy, though? Don't you ever wonder about him? I mean, he finds the body, right? He doesn't tell the cops, he takes off for days, doesn't even show up for the funeral, and the body's found in his room with a note on his typewriter."

I sighed. "Yeah, I know what it looks like," I said, "but I still don't think he did it."

"Why not?" Emily said.

"I don't know. Just a gut feeling, I guess. I really like him. He's so funny, he gets all these really crazy ideas about who did it, and he was so excited about finding that letter, like he thought he was going to solve the case and become famous or something."

Emily gave me a skeptical look. "How do you know it's not just an act?" she said.

"Well, I don't know for sure," I said. "I just don't think he did it, that's all."

"Okay, okay," Emily said. "I'm just trying to help. But don't you think it..."

I shot her a warning look.

"Just one more thing and then I'll shut up," she said.

I waited.

"Don't you think it's strange that the note was typed on a typewriter instead of a computer? Dave's supposed to be this computer wizard, right? And the note's supposed to be written by him, so why's it written on a typewriter?" She sat back with a smug look on her face.

I frowned. "I just figured the killer was in a hurry and a

typewriter was faster. He wouldn't have to print it out, for instance."

"Yeah...or maybe the killer doesn't know how to use a computer."

My eyebrows shot up.

"Does Jake know how to use one?" Emily said.

I groaned. "No, but neither do I. Neither do you. Where does that get us?"

"It's better than nothing," she said. "Of all the people you talked to, which ones do you know of who don't know how to use a computer?"

I thought for a moment. "I don't know," I said. "I didn't ask anyone that. I know Jake and Tony don't but I didn't ask Laura, or Laura's father, or Dr. King, or Dave's friends, or..."

"Okay, you made your point."

"Brian thinks the guy could've been after something I have in the house, or something he thinks I have."

"Why does he think that?" Emily said.

"Because of the fire, I guess. Maybe he thought the fire would destroy whatever it was."

Emily shrugged.

"The thing is, he used the liquor I left on the kitchen table to start the fire, which makes it look like he might not have intended to set a fire and maybe just got the idea on the spur of the moment."

"Hmm, good point," Emily said. "What were you doing in the basement?"

"Laundry. I was only down there about fifteen or twenty minutes but I had the radio on so I didn't hear anyone come in."

"So there's no way this person could've known you'd be down there when he decided to come over, right?"

"Right," I said. "Yeah, so he decides to come over planning to do who knows what and hears me in the basement and gets the idea to set the fire and lock me in."

Emily shuddered. "How did he get in to begin with?" she said.

"I don't know. It had to be through the back door. The front was deadbolted. There wasn't any damage to the back door, though, but he could've picked the lock, I guess. Or maybe I just forgot to lock it. I do that sometimes."

"Why don't you get a deadbolt for the back door?" Emily said.

"I never thought I needed it. The lock worked fine. Besides, I hate having to use a key to unlock it from the inside. They always put that kind in when there's a window in the door and I don't think it's safe. What if there's a fire or something and you can't get out because you don't have the key?"

Emily gave me an exasperated look. "Do you really feel safe with it the way it is?" she said.

"No," I said with a sigh. "I guess you're right. I'd better get one."

Boy, was that a mistake.

THIRTEEN

THE NEXT DAY was Monday, January eleventh. Janice, Emily, and Mrs. Gunther showed up, and we all worked a regular day, except we had to go out to lunch and Mrs. Gunther didn't have to clean the kitchen.

I had a locksmith come over and install a deadbolt in the back door, the kind that requires a key to get out—the kind I don't like—but I did feel a lot better when he was through. He convinced me a bolt that didn't need a key would be a waste of time because an intruder could just break the glass, reach in, and undo it. I guess they know what they're doing. I had him put a new one on the front door, too.

"If you don't mind my saying so, ma'am, you ought to get a security system installed. They're priced reasonable nowadays and they're well worth the trouble," he said.

I gave the man a weak smile. "You're probably right," I said. "Maybe I need one of those, too."

As soon as he left, I made some calls, priced a few systems, and arranged to have someone come out the following week. I'd turn the place into a fortress before I was through.

Emily went back out again, right after lunch, and returned almost two hours later with a cooler, a small automatic coffee-maker, coffee, filters, non-dairy creamer, disposable plates, cups, and utensils, napkins, trash bags, cereal, tea bags, instant soup, crackers, Jiffy Pop popcorn, and a hotplate! The cooler was full of ice, soda, fruit, and cheese.

My lip trembled and tears filled my eyes. "Thank you," I said, and hugged her until she pushed me away.

"Cut it out. You're getting me all wet," she said with a laugh.

Later, after everyone went home, I called Jake. "You want to help me investigate?" I said.

"Sure," he said with undisguised excitement. "What do you want me to do?"

I told him about the tenants I still wanted to question. "I'd do it myself," I said, "but I don't want to run into Mrs. Robinson. I don't want her to see me until my face looks a little better, you know what I mean?"

"Yeah, you do look pretty gruesome," Jake said. "What do you want me to ask them?"

I gave him a list of questions. "Let me know what they say, okay?"

I hung up, had myself a picnic supper of cheese and crackers, fruit and tea, and ate in the dining room with my back to the kitchen. Twenty minutes later, Jake called me back.

"Okay," he said. "The only one who was home was Mrs. Seinfeld, but she says she didn't hear anything. She was home all night but she had her TV on real loud 'cause she's hard of hearing. She also told me Mrs. Duncan's in Florida and she left before it happened, so she wouldn't know anything anyway. I don't know about the others."

"Okay," I said. "Thanks, Jake."

"What do you want me to do next?" he said.

I laughed. "That's it for now, unless one of the other ones comes home. But I'll let you know if I think of anything else."

"Okay," he said. "I'll keep on it."

I called Laura next. I wanted to find out if she knew about

her father's offer to Dave. I found her at home but she was on her way out.

"I have something I really need to talk to you about," I said. "Are you free at all tonight?"

"No, I'm not," she said. "I have to work. That's where I'm going now. How about tomorrow?"

"Okay. What—"

"Wait, I have an idea," she said. "You could come see me at the mall and talk to me during my break. I could meet you at the food court."

"Great," I said. "Which mall?"

"Grand Avenue. My break's at seven-thirty. I could meet you, like in front of Chick-Fil-A? I only get a half-hour so I'll have to eat while we talk if that's okay."

"Sure," I said. "I'll see you then."

I retouched my makeup and winced at the sight of myself, wishing I'd thought to warn Laura about my appearance. I was still wearing sweats, since nothing else was comfortable. In short, I looked horrible.

I left at seven, parked in the mall lot, and went in at the second level as I usually do. I was a few minutes early so I bought a cup of tea and sat at a table in our agreed location.

"Oh, Beth, what happened? Were you in an accident?" Laura said when she saw me. She looked genuinely shocked, and frightened.

"Someone locked me in my basement and set fire to my house," I said. "I got hurt trying to escape."

"Oh, no," Laura said. She put both hands over her mouth. "Oh, no," she said again.

"It's not as bad as it looks," I said. "I'm all right."

"But you could've been killed," she said.

I raised my eyebrows. "I think that was the idea."

She flinched.

"Why don't you get something to eat?" I said with a smile.

"Okay," she said with uncertainty. "Do you want anything?"

"No, thanks," I said.

Laura returned a few minutes later with some breaded chicken, french fries shaped like little waffles, and a lemonade.

"So what's up?" she said after she'd taken a few bites.

I took a deep breath. "Jake Grossman found a letter to Dave from your dad," I said.

She stopped chewing for a moment and stared at me. "What kind of letter?" she said as she resumed eating.

I hesitated, not knowing how she'd take it. "He asked Dave to stop seeing you and he offered him money to do it."

The look on her face was a mixture of pain, and maybe confusion, and I don't know what.

"I'm sorry," I said. "I wasn't sure if you knew."

She didn't respond, just lowered her eyes and shredded a napkin.

"Dave never mentioned it to you?"

Laura slowly shook her head.

"I called your dad the other day," I said.

She looked up, and waited for me to continue.

"I don't think he liked me."

Laura burst out laughing. "I'm sorry," she said. "I didn't mean to laugh but it sounded so funny."

I smiled. "When did your father first tell you to stop seeing Dave?" I said.

"Thanksgiving," she said. "Right after he met him."

"There was supposed to be a check with the letter but it wasn't there when Jake found it."

Laura frowned. "You mean you think he cashed it?" she said.

"I doubt it," I said, not really believing what I was saying. "He probably just tore it up or sent it back."

Laura looked grateful and relieved. She glanced at her watch then. "Uh-oh," she said. "I have to go. I'm sorry. Was that all you wanted to tell me?"

I nodded. "Yeah, that was it," I said. "I hope I didn't upset you too much."

She shook her head. "It's not your fault," she said, and walked away.

I went home, made some notes about our conversation, and looked through my file. When I came to the bankbook notations I suddenly remembered something. I called Jake.

"Jake, I do have something else for you to do," I said.

"Sure. What?"

"There's a letter from Laura to Dave in the false bottom of that center drawer. The police didn't take it, did they?"

"I don't think so," Jake said. "Hold on, I'll check.

"Got it," he said a few minutes later. "What do you want me to do with it?"

"I hate to ask," I said, "but could you bring it over here?"

"Sure, no problem. I'll be right there."

"DID YOU READ IT?" I asked when he handed me the letter.

Jake looked a little embarrassed. "Yeah, I read it," he said. "Pretty heavy stuff."

I raised my eyebrows and removed the letter from the envelope. This one was five pages long, handwritten on both sides. There was no date on the letter but the postmark was December fifth. It had been mailed from Milwaukee.

The "heavy stuff" to which Jake referred were Laura's repeated declarations of love for Dave ("I love you more than anything in the world," "I just know we're destined to be together," and "I don't know what I'd ever do without you," to quote a few), some surprisingly detailed references to their love life (you don't really want to hear those, do you?), and complaints about Dave's refusal to verbalize his feelings. Apparently Dave was one of those wonderfully circumspect guys who says "I love you" once and then expects you to feel you don't need to hear it again. I hate that. I'd love to see how men would react if we gave them what they wanted only once.

The portion of the letter that interested me the most was at the top of the last page:

> I told my dad there was no way I was ever going to stop seeing you. He knows I know about the check, too. You should have seen his face when I told him what you said. He is such a complete jerk. I told him if he ever tried anything like that again he'd be the one I'd never see again.

"Why would she lie to me?" I said, thinking out loud.

"Who?" Jake said.

"Laura. When I told her about the letter from her dad she acted like she didn't know anything about it."

Jake shrugged. "Maybe she forgot."

Yeah, or maybe she was protecting her father. But why? Talk about misplaced loyalty.

I sighed. "Well, it looks like we have another letter to show Brian McHenry," I said. "But it'll have to wait until tomorrow."

TUESDAY, January twelfth. I called Brian, first thing, but he wasn't there so I left a message asking that he return my call. We worked all day, Em and Janice went home at five, and the phone rang at six o'clock.

"Sorry I didn't get back to you sooner," Brian said. "How are you feeling?"

"A lot better," I said. "My bruises keep changing color, though. It's pretty weird."

He laughed. "I'll bet," he said. "You're staying out of trouble, I hope."

"Yes, I am," I said in a mock-obedient voice. "But I do have another piece of information for you." I told him about Laura's letter.

"Okay," he said. "I was just about to leave here. Why don't I stop by and pick it up on my way home?"

"Okay. I'll see you in a little while," I said.

BRIAN WAS HERE in twenty minutes. He didn't say much, just asked for the letter and left. I had the feeling he was angry with me, but I couldn't be sure. I felt kind of hurt, though, and that sort of annoyed me.

I had another cheese, crackers, and fruit dinner, and sat at the dining room table paging through my file.

What if Brian was right? What if I did have something the killer wanted? Or maybe he just thought I had it. In any case, whatever it was he wanted, it probably contained the answer, or a really strong clue to the answer. Otherwise, why would he want it? Now how's that for brilliant deductive reasoning?

So, what did I have?

My own notes. That couldn't be it. Dave's monthly expenses. I read through them twice, then a third time. There was nothing the least bit unusual about them. His medical expenses? Cardiologist, dermatologist, podiatrist, dentist. Sickly kid, but big deal.

The information I'd copied from the bankbook. Now there was a possibility. Maybe the killer had given Dave money, and didn't want any evidence of the deposit lying around. I don't know; that didn't sound too plausible. Maybe Dave and the killer had some sort of illegal business going together and the killer thought the bankbook would give that away. No, stupid idea. I put the bankbook aside.

I picked up my list of the calendar entries. He did have a notation about something happening at nine o'clock on the day he was murdered, and we knew he was killed around that time. But why would the killer want the calendar? Because it was evidence of an arranged meeting? Possibly. That would show Dave knew the killer. The notation was only for the time, without any mention of a name, though. But I suppose the killer wouldn't necessarily know that. I put the calendar aside, too.

What about the letters to Dave, from Laura and her dad? What if it were Laura's dad, and he suspected I had his letter? Laura knew about it and she was protecting him. She must think he did it.

I dialed her number.

"Laura? This is Beth Hartley," I said when she answered the phone.

"Hi," she said. "What's up?" She sounded wary to me, but I could've been imagining it.

"I found a letter from you to Dave, in his apartment," I said. "In it, you make reference to the money your dad offered to pay Dave to stop seeing you."

Silence.

"Laura?" I said.

"Yeah?"

"Well, why didn't you tell me you knew about it?"

"I don't know," she said. "What's the difference?"

"Do you suspect your dad did it?" I said.

"Did what?" Laura said.

"Killed Dave," I said. "Do you think your dad killed Dave? Is that why you didn't tell me?"

Silence again.

"Laura, if you do," I said, "I think you're making a big mistake protecting him. Dave was someone you really loved, and your father knew that."

She started to cry then. "I have to go," she said, and hung up.

Darn. I went back to my file.

The only thing I had left to consider was the copy of the computer printout I'd found in Dave's desk. I'd never actually read through the whole thing—I hadn't seen any point and it was too long. I started to page through it then, reading every name, date, and number, hoping to trigger something. I must have gone through ten pages before I saw it.

Erma Shemanski. Mrs. Gunther's sister.

What the heck was Erma Shemanski's name doing in the computer printout?

I kept going. Eight pages later, I found it again. By the time I'd gone through the entire document, I'd picked up eleven Erma Shemanskis (twenty-two if you count the fact that every entry was printed twice). Each one was the same, except for the date. There was one duplicate entry for every month from January through November.

I sat there for a long time just thinking. Then I picked up the phone and called Mrs. Gunther. The question I asked her was whether the particular dates and numbers had any significance for her. The answer I got sent a chill through my body that caused my teeth to chatter.

I called Jake next.

"Jake, it's Beth. Do me a favor," I said. My voice was shaking so badly I could hardly talk.

"What's the matter? Are you all right?" he said.

"Look on Dave's bulletin board," I said. "I think there's an article on there about Medicaid fraud."

"Okay, hold on."

"Got it," he said.

"Read it to me."

"That's enough," I said, my voice breaking. "Hang on to that. Please, don't lose it."

"But what's"

"I'll talk to you later," I said.

I started to cry, then hyperventilate. It couldn't be true. It just couldn't be him. I decided to call him.

"Well, hi, how are you?" he said in that sweet, soft voice. My heart was pounding so hard I was afraid he'd hear it over the phone.

"Oh, fine," I said. "I just felt like talking to you."

"I always feel like talking to you," he said. "Are you feeling better?"

"Yes, I am."

"Good. What are you doing?"

"Oh, nothing really," I said. "I understand you know a friend of mine. Erma Shemanski."

"Who?"

"She's one of your patients," I said. "You see her once a month."

"Is that right? I have a lot of patients. I really can't keep them all straight."

"I suppose not," I said. "That's why you hired Dave, wasn't it?"

A short hesitation. "That's right," he said. "It is. Well, what are you doing tonight?"

"Working," I said quickly. "I have a brief to write."

"How about tomorrow night? Would you like to have dinner?"

"Can I let you know tomorrow?" I said. "I might be up all night."

"Sure," he said. "Well, I won't keep you then. I'll talk to you tomorrow."

As soon as I hung up, I called Brian.

"Brian, it's Beth. I think I know who did it." I was crying and I had to stop talking to calm down.

"Take it easy," Brian said. "I'll be right over."

"Wait..."

"Just hang on till I get there," he said.

I hung up the phone, went into the living room, and started pacing. I was shaking so badly my muscles hurt. I had to calm down before I drove myself crazy.

I put on Bach's first piano concerto and my headphones,

wrapped myself in a blanket, and lay down on the couch. Music like that can cure almost anything, even a broken heart. At the end of the first movement, I sat up, took off the headphones, and almost jumped a foot.

Tony was standing in my living room, no more than ten feet away.

"Tony!" I said. "How'd you get in here?"

He gave me a slow, smug smile and just stared for a few moments. "Same window I came through last time," he said.

"Window?" I said.

"I unlocked it when you gave me a tour of your lovely home. It's come in pretty handy."

Tears welled up and spilled from my eyes. "You set fire to my house?"

Tony shrugged. "It seemed like a good idea at the time."

I started to tremble, and pulled the blanket around my shoulders.

"Cold?" Tony said.

I nodded, sniffling.

He sat in a chair on the other side of the room, his face almost hidden by the shadows.

"You killed Dave, didn't you?" I said.

No answer.

"And you tried to kill me, too."

Still no answer.

"You left that message for me, didn't you? Why, Tony?" I said as I started to sob. "You're a doctor, you're supposed to save lives. I thought you cared about people. How could you do something like that?"

He just sat there, perfectly still, and watched me cry.

"And you've been cheating your patients," I said. "I thought they meant so much to you. You seemed so dedicated, so…"

"You stupid little fool," he said. "You just don't get it, do you? Can't you see I'm doing this for my patients?"

"First you overcharge them and then you kill someone? You call that helping your patients?" I said.

"My patients don't pay a cent for my services. You ought to know that. The government pays for everything. They're the ones I'm double-billing, not my patients. It's their own blasted fault for undercompensating to begin with. I only get what's rightfully mine. Without overbilling, I wouldn't be able to treat these people at all. They're indigent. Helpless. It's impossible to treat them for what Medicaid pays. Someone has to take care of them. I can't allow some—'' He broke off, and sat forward in the chair, clutching the arms with both hands.

"What about your partner, Tony? Did he find out, too? Did you kill him, too?"

Tony didn't answer at first, just took a few deep breaths. "That one was regrettable," he finally said. "He, of all people, should have understood."

"Oh, Tony," I said, sobbing. "How could you?"

His face was no longer hidden in the shadows, and I could see him glaring at me, seething with loathing and anger. I probably should have kept my mouth shut, but I felt like I had nothing to lose at that point.

"You met Dave at his apartment at nine o'clock the night you killed him, didn't you?" I said.

No response.

"Was he blackmailing you? Is that why you killed him?"

Still no response.

"You paid him ten thousand dollars, didn't you?"

Tony grabbed the chair arms and yanked on them as if he were trying to pull them off.

"Shut up, you little idiot," he said. "Yes, I paid him ten thousand dollars, but he wasn't satisfied with that. He wanted more, and more. That greedy kid would've milked me for the rest of my life."

"And all this was so you could double-bill your patients?" I said. "Talk about greed. You're the greedy one!" I was screaming at him now, my fear overcome by my anger.

"What do you expect me to do, work for nothing?" he said. "Is that what you expect?" Now he was screaming, his voice growing louder with every word. "You self-righteous little…" He stood up and started moving toward me.

I shook my head and tried to say "No," but it wouldn't come out.

He was coming for me, but he was taking his time about it, so certain he was that I'd never get away. "You do realize, don't you," he said in the calm, soft voice I'd found so seductive only hours before, "that your own life is worth far less than the lives of all those others? It's their lives I'll be saving by taking yours.''

He continued moving slowly in my direction and withdrew a syringe from his pocket. My heart leaped into my throat and I shrank back against the couch, almost paralyzed by fear. As I moved, my hand touched the headphones. I held on, having no other weapon, and waited until he was about two feet away. I flung the headphones at his face—and missed—but he ducked to avoid them, which gave me just enough time to dive over the side of the couch. I ran through the dining room and the kitchen, and then I remembered.

I didn't have the back door key!

I ran into the mudroom, down into the basement, through the first room, and into the second. Then I shut off the power.

I heard him coming down the steps. I had to find someplace to hide, but there was nothing there. A few little corners he'd have to peek around, but they'd never do for more than a few minutes. There were no windows and no furniture, just the furnace, a sink, and the washer and dryer. I lifted myself up, climbed into the dryer, and silently shut the door.

Moments later, Tony was in the room with me.

He was talking, softly calling my name, getting closer and closer all the time. Then he ran right into the dryer and banged on it with his fists.

''Come out, Beth!'' he screamed. ''Let's get this over with.''

He was rushing around now, bumping into things, and cursing in a venomous voice.

And then I heard something else.

''Freeze!'' Brian yelled.

I heard scuffling, and then a little while later, silence. I didn't move, for many minutes, until I heard Brian calling my name. I pushed open the door, and shielded my eyes from the beam of his flashlight. He lifted me out, not saying a word, and carried me upstairs.

''It's all over now; you're safe,'' he whispered. ''It's all over.''

He held me for a long time. I could feel his warm breath on my neck and his lips on my hair.

''Where's Tony?'' I said a bit later.

"Outside, in a patrol car," Brian said. "I called for backup when I went for the flashlight. What happened to your power?"

"I turned it off," I said.

"You're going to need a new back door, by the way. I had to shoot the lock to get in."

I opened my mouth to say something, and shut it again.

He held me closer. "You did a darn good job, sweetheart. You ought to win a medal for this."

I laughed, and then started to cry.

"What's wrong?" he said gently.

"I don't know," I said through my tears. "I'm just relieved, I guess."

EPILOGUE

THREE WEEKS LATER, my injuries had almost disappeared. My kitchen was looking a lot better, too. All the rubble had been cleared away, and the linoleum and old wallpaper were removed. And they'd started laying the ceramic tile. It's so cool. A really pretty terra-cotta color that blends perfectly with the wallpaper I picked out. (It's a cream background with a tiny flower print—no big spoons, nothing scary.) I ordered an eight-foot farmhouse pine table and chairs from Ethan Allen, a china cabinet with a hutch top to match, and a jelly cupboard. I can't wait till it gets here, it's so gorgeous. They're making the curtains, too—a really cute café style. The fabric's just like the wallpaper only the colors are the opposite—the background's in terra-cotta and the flowers are in cream.

I'm still upset about Tony. I feel like there's something wrong with me, that I could've been attracted to someone like that. I've always felt I made poor choices when it came to men, but this is entering a whole new arena. The worst part is that I actually catch myself missing him—not the guy I know he is, of course, but the one I thought he was. It's almost like the Tony I liked, died.

Janice hasn't gotten over it, of course, but she's starting to feel it less, and that makes her feel guilty. I know just what she means—you do feel guilty when that happens. But I honestly think that's a built-in survival mechanism. You can't tolerate feeling that much pain, so you protect yourself emotionally, and you do it without thinking. I told her (and I really believe this) that it's the fact that she cares so *much* that makes her withdraw from it. If it didn't mean so much to her she wouldn't need to do that.

Emily and Phil aren't getting along any better than they ever have. I don't know what to say about that. I saw Brian a few times. He came over to see how I was doing, and he took me to lunch, and dinner, once. I feel like I really like him, but I'm fighting it. I don't know why I can't learn to take my own advice.

I see Mrs. Robinson every Sunday and it's become my favorite part of the week. For now, I cook our suppers in her kitchen, which works out just fine. She's keeping her door open again, which really seems to make her happy—although she says she's a lot less lonely than she used to be.

Jake already moved out. He found a place, with a roommate, and grabbed for it for fear of not finding another one. I really miss that kid. He gave me his new number, though, so I think I'll call him sometime and maybe take him to lunch.

Laura is doing okay. She's having a hard time being at Marquette without Dave, but she only has one semester left and she's gone. She *did* suspect her dad, she told me, and she was trying to protect him, although she doesn't know why. She says she really hated him, but he was still her dad. She feels so guilty now for having suspected him that she calls him all the time, just to talk. Funny, huh? I still think he's a jerk.

Both Emily and Brian said they hoped I learned my lesson, and won't even *think* of investigating a murder again. I don't know. Horrible as it was, I don't think I've ever felt so exhilarated, you know? I'm the one who solved it. Not the police, *me*. I don't think I could hold myself back if another one came my way. Besides, Brian said I did a darn good job of it. I take that as encouragement. Wouldn't you?

A PERFECT TIME FOR MURDER
by Fred Hunter

IT HAD BEEN SNOWING steadily for almost seven hours. A thick, constant shower of white muffled sound like a heavy blanket and severely limited visibility. By evening, all but the most stalwart or foolhardy had been driven indoors by the blizzard and frigid temperatures, leaving the city of Chicago virtually silent except for the hiss of snow.

Lynn Francis stood at the front window of Emily Charters's house. She had worked as Emily's housecleaner in the two years since the elderly woman's bypass surgery, and they'd become very close. Lynn held back the curtain and peered out into the night. The street lamps illuminated small halos of falling snow. Most of the cars had been parked for hours and were so thoroughly coated, they appeared as irregularly shaped mounds along the curb. Smoke rose from every chimney on the block.

Inside Emily's small wood-frame house a fire burned in the grate of the redbrick fireplace in the living room, and in the far corner stood a seven-foot-tall blue spruce, neatly trimmed with antique glass ornaments and dotted with multicolored miniature lights. Beneath the tree were several boxes of different shapes and sizes wrapped in shiny gold paper and tied with silver ribbon.

"All this snow on top of what we had yesterday," said Lynn, still gazing out the window. "Unbelievable. I thought it couldn't snow if it was really cold."

"I believe that's an old wives' tale." Emily sat in an armchair by the fireplace. Her emerald-green dress was tied loosely at the waist with a gold belt, and her voluminous gray hair had been woven into a large bun and pinned at the back of her head. She closed a well-thumbed copy of *A Christmas Carol* and laid it on the table beside her chair, then folded her hands in her lap.

Lynn let the curtain fall back across the window, her hand lingering on the edge of the fabric. It was her second Christmas since the death of her longtime partner, and she'd expected it to be a little easier this time. Instead, she was finding it more difficult. She sighed deeply, then crossed the room and took the seat opposite Emily by the fire.

"It's really nice of you to have me for the holidays."

"Nonsense, I wouldn't think of you being alone at Christmas." Emily paused for a moment and regarded the young woman. "By the way, I don't know if I remembered to tell you, but you did a beautiful job with the tree."

Lynn smiled weakly. "I'm glad you like it. I haven't done one since Maggie died."

"I know, my dear."

Lynn ran her fingers through her tawny hair. "The storm is pretty bad. I don't know if your detective friend is going to make it."

Emily's eyes twinkled at the mention of Ransom, who had become a sort of adoptive grandson to her. "Jeremy? Nothing will stop him from getting here. Except, perhaps, a murder."

"His own or somebody else's?"

Emily laughed. "Yesterday he was assigned a very difficult case, which he'd hoped to have cleared up by tonight. He told me about it last night. I told him what I believed to be true, but I'm not sure..." Her voice trailed off uncertainly.

"I find it hard to believe you would've steered him wrong. What was it all about?"

Emily pursed her lips. "I don't know that this is the time for this kind of story."

"Christmas Eve by the fire?" Lynn said, halfheartedly attempting to buoy her own spirits. "It's a perfect time for murder."

Emily adjusted herself in her chair and cleared her throat in a gentle, ladylike manner.

"Well, Jeremy and his partner, Gerald White, were called to the home of Edward and Loreen Swenson, who live about three blocks from here. The Swensons are a respectable, middle-aged couple with two grown children, a house and the mortgage that goes with it, the very type of people one would expect to go through life pleasantly affecting those around them, if never making a particularly important mark in the world. The sort to whom nothing extraordinary would ever happen. And yet, their world was turned on its ear yesterday when they returned from dining out to find their home broken into, and a dead body lying beneath their Christmas tree."

"What?" Lynn exclaimed. In her preoccupied state, she hadn't been giving Emily her full attention, but she couldn't help having her interest piqued by this pronouncement.

"That wasn't the most extraordinary part of it. The Swensons live at 2021 Fairdale. When Jeremy and Detective White arrived on the scene, they were glad that a squad car marked the location they were seeking, since there were no numbers on the house and the ones painted on the curb had been covered with snow. Of course, they would've found it easily enough anyway, since the house next door, 2019, had lighted numbers clearly displayed. As they went up the walk they were greeted by two uniformed officers."

"WHO'S THE VICTIM?" Detective White asked.

"You're not going to believe this one," one of the officers replied. Without another word of explanation, he led the detectives into the house and introduced them to the Swensons.

"Who is he?" Jeremy asked, motioning toward the body.

Mr. Swenson, a gray and rather flabby man, shook his head mutely, and his wife stared at Jeremy with wide, teary eyes. "We don't know!" she said. "We've never seen him before!"

"YOU'RE KIDDING!" Lynn exclaimed, once again interrupting the flow of Emily's recital.

"It's quite true. Of course, Jeremy found it difficult to believe at first, but no amount of questioning could shake the Swensons—any more than they'd already been shaken by the event, I should say. They steadfastly insisted that they'd never seen the young man before, and had no idea who he could be. And yet, there he was, dead beneath their Christmas tree. The back of his skull had been bashed in, and the casual way that he lay sprawled on the floor made it look as if he belonged there. If you can understand what I mean, he looked as if, perhaps, he was in his own home and had been surprised by a burglar. At least, that was Jeremy's impression.

"As I said, Jeremy was disinclined to believe the Swensons at first, but he is a very good judge of character and felt that their state of total bewilderment was genuine. The men from the crime lab arrived to do their work, and Jeremy asked the Swensons to check around the rest of the house to see if anything had been taken. He reasoned that it was possible the young man had been there to rob the place—perhaps with a confederate—and that they'd had a falling-out and one had been killed, and the other had fled the scene." Emily stopped and smiled. "Far-fetched, perhaps, but it would have explained the body. The Swensons reported that nothing had been stolen.

"After the police photographer had taken pictures of the body as it was found, Jeremy and Detective White rolled it over. Once on his back, the fatal wound hidden from view, the young man looked quite at peace, almost as if asleep. Except for one thing—his right hand was formed into a fist, though not tightly. Jeremy carefully uncurled the fingers and found, embedded in the palm, a small piece of glass, slightly curved and about half an inch wide. It was painted a light yellow-green and had a thick coating of something that looked like sugar."

"A Christmas ornament?" Lynn offered.

"Exactly," said Emily. "But nothing like it could be found on the tree, nor was there any sign of the rest of it anywhere.

"Jeremy asked the police photographer to take some Polaroid shots of the victim's face to show around the neighborhood in hopes of discovering his identity. As it turned out, it didn't take them long. When they showed the photo to the Watsons, a couple living in the house directly across the street, the boy was instantly identified."

MRS. WATSON'S EYES widened to saucers when she looked at the picture. "That's our nephew...Neil Carter.... What's this all about?''

"I'm afraid he's dead, ma'am," said Jeremy.

She raised the back of her hand to her mouth and began to cry. Mr. Watson put his arm around her shoulders. Jeremy and Detective White went with them into their living room, where they all sat down.

"But how...what happened?" Mrs. Watson asked when she had recovered herself enough to speak.

"That's what we're trying to find out," said Jeremy. "His body was found in the home of the Swensons across the street."

Both of the Watsons stared dumbly at the detectives.

"What?" the husband said at last. "That's impossible!"

Jeremy was, of course, at a loss. "Why is that?"

"Because he flew to Minneapolis this afternoon!"

"Are you sure?" Jeremy said after a pause.

Mr. Watson nodded. "We drove him to the airport ourselves, just after noon. He was going home for the holidays. Neil is from Minneapolis. He was accepted at Central Midwestern University—the one down by the lakefront—starting this year. He has a scholarship that covers his classes and books, but not housing. Since we live here, and we never had kids of our own, we told his parents he could live with us while he went to school. But...today...he was going home for Christmas." Mr. Watson stopped and his jaw fell open. He turned to his wife. "My God, honey, what're we going to tell his parents?"

This produced a fresh flood of tears from Mrs. Watson. Jeremy assured them he would take care of it, then he asked, "Did you actually see your nephew board the plane?"

"No," Mr. Watson admitted somewhat guiltily. "We just dropped him off. It's the day before Christmas Eve, you know. It was a madhouse out there."

"It was the way Neil wanted it," Mrs. Watson said. "He said it would be crazy to wait with him."

Jeremy thought for a moment, then said, "Can you tell me if Neil knew the Swensons?"

"No," Mr. Watson said, shaking his head with total bafflement. "*We* don't even know the Swensons!"

"So you have no idea why he might've been in their house?"

"No."

EMILY PAUSED IN HER STORY and clucked her tongue. "So terrible nowadays, isn't it? Nobody knows their neighbors anymore. When I was a girl, we knew everyone who lived on our street. Neighbors watched out for one another."

"Emily…" Lynn said with a smile.

"Oh, yes. Sorry, dear. Where was I?"

"They didn't know the Swensons."

"Oh, yes." Emily shifted in her seat. "The next thing for the detectives to do was notify the poor boy's parents, which Jeremy took upon himself. He spoke with Mr. Carter, Neil's father, by phone. Carter was understandably devastated by the news, and it was quite some time before he was lucid enough to answer questions.

AFTER SOME PRELIMINARIES, Jeremy said, "Mr. Carter, there's one thing I'm curious about. Weren't you concerned when your son didn't arrive home today?"

There was a long pause, then Carter said, "What?"

"He was supposed to catch a plane just after twelve this afternoon. His body was discovered here at about eight o'clock. Obviously he wasn't on the plane. Weren't you concerned?"

"There must be some mistake," Carter said. "Neil wasn't coming home until Christmas Day."

"You're sure of that?"

"Of course! We don't have a lot of money. Neil was going to fly home on Christmas Day because it's cheaper." The father stopped, a catch in his throat. "To save a few dollars… If he *had* come home today, he might still be alive."

Jeremy did what he could to placate him, then said, "Do you know anything about his friends? Was he close to anyone at school?"

"I don't know a lot about them. You know how kids are. But he did tell us he was dating this girl. I think her name was Alice. Just a minute." Carter put his hand over the mouthpiece and Jeremy could hear the muffled sounds of him speaking to someone else. Then the hand was removed. "Yes. It was Alice. Alice Baker. He was pretty excited about it."

Jeremy asked if Carter knew where she lived, and Carter told him he thought she was in the university's dorms.

"What do you think?" Detective White asked once Jeremy was off the phone.

"Well, Neil told his aunt and uncle that he was flying home today, even going so far as to have them drive him out to the airport to bolster the illusion. And his parents weren't expecting him until Christmas. I have a feeling that Neil wanted to disappear for a couple of days without anyone knowing where he was."

"He could've just been planning to surprise his parents by coming home early. Christmas is a time for surprises."

"Hmm." Jeremy's imagination was spurred by this. He smiled enigmatically at his partner. "I think you might be right. But maybe his girlfriend will know what he was planning."

"JEREMY CALLED the Watsons on his cellular phone to find out which airline Neil was supposedly using, then called the airline, identified himself and had them look for the reservation. Neil's reservation had been for Christmas Day."

"So he wasn't planning to surprise his parents," Lynn said.

The old woman smiled at her. "No, he wasn't. It took the detectives about half an hour to get to the university, which is on Lake Shore Drive just south of Chicago Avenue. It's a very old and musty building, all gray stone and huge cornices, built during a more elegant time, and stately in its own way.

"Jeremy waited in the car while his partner went in and asked the location of the residences. When he came back, he reported that the 'Halls of Residence'—as the information clerk had called it—was the apartment building on the opposite corner.

"They stopped at the manager's office on their way in. Jeremy described her as an unnaturally blond and rather bulky woman named Elizabeth Dougherty."

"WE'RE HERE TO SEE Alice Baker," Jeremy said. "Is she still here or has she left for the holidays?"

Ms. Dougherty eyed them suspiciously. "And you are…?"

"Detectives Ransom and White," he replied, showing her his badge.

"Oh, my Lord!" she exclaimed. "What's happened? Has Alice…?"

"We just need to talk to her," Jeremy said. "Someone she knows has been murdered. Perhaps you were familiar with him? His name is Neil Carter."

"There's nobody by that name living here."

"We understood that he was dating Miss Baker. Maybe you've seen him?" He described Neil to her.

"I may have seen someone like that with her, but I don't know who she's dating." Ms. Dougherty added with some hesitation, "I've seen her with other people."

"Many other people?"

The woman's face flushed. "I'm not a housemother. I can't keep track of who's seeing who."

Jeremy raised an eyebrow at this. "Ms. Dougherty, I don't know whether you mean to or not, but you're leaving a very bad impression of Ms. Baker."

The woman sighed. "It's the first semester for these kids, their first year here. For a lot of them it's also their first time away from home and family. It's just natural for some of them to be…feeling their way. If you want to see Alice, her room is 204 on the second floor." With this she flipped open a magazine that had been lying on her desk and gave it her full attention.

The detectives left Ms. Dougherty without another word and took the stairs to the second floor. As they rounded the corner, they found a young man and woman having a hushed conference halfway down the hall.

"A HUSHED CONFERENCE?" asked Lynn.

"Well, that's the way it appeared to Jeremy. They were speaking in low tones despite the fact that with the holidays the dorms were all but deserted."

THE YOUNG WOMAN WHEELED as they approached.

"Excuse me, are you Alice Baker?" Jeremy asked.

"Yes?" she replied crisply.

Jeremy introduced himself and Detective White, then said, "We have some distressing news for you. Your boyfriend has been found dead."

"What?" the girl said loudly. Jeremy was rather shocked that she had almost laughed. She glanced over her shoulder at the young man. "This is my boyfriend, Detective Ransom. John Cameron. He looks fine to me."

"Oh, I'm sorry," said Jeremy. "I was referring to Neil Carter."

Alice's face went blank. "Neil? Neil's dead? That's awful!"

"So you did know him?"

"Sure I did. I've gone out with him. I suppose that's why you thought he was my boyfriend. Who told you that, anyhow? That old busybody Dougherty?"

"Neil's father," Jeremy replied flatly. "So you broke up with him? When was that?"

She glanced at her current flame again. "I said I dated him, not that we were going together or anything like that. It's not like we were exclusive. That's just…just…archaic."

Jeremy got the impression that she was trying very hard to appear modern, but didn't really have the talent for it, which often happens when a young person tries to put on sophistication.

"When did you last see him?" Jeremy asked.

Alice knit her brows for a long moment. "I think it was yesterday…or maybe the day before. Just in the hallway. It's hard to remember. Everything's been so crazy with finals and the end of term and everybody getting ready to go home."

All the way through this exchange, John Cameron had stood

behind Alice staring wide-eyed at the detectives, his mouth slightly open.

Jeremy directed himself to the young man. "Did you know Neil Carter?"

"Me? No. N-not really," he stammered. "I know who he is, I mean, but I didn't *know* him."

"What happened to Neil?" Alice asked.

"His body was found earlier this evening out by the home of his aunt and uncle. Have you ever been out there?"

There was a beat before she answered, and Jeremy thought just maybe she was wondering whether or not, under the present circumstances, it was better to say that she had or she hadn't. "Yes, I have," she said at last. "Why?"

"I was just curious," Jeremy replied with a slight smile.

"Well...well, I wish I could help you, but I don't know anything about it. And I've really got to get packed."

"You're going home for Christmas, then?"

"Of course. Doesn't everybody?"

"The roads are very bad. You'll have to be careful."

"I'm flying," Alice replied. "Back to Cincinnati. Tomorrow."

"How about you, young man?" Jeremy said amiably. "Are you going, as well?"

John stared at him blankly. "No, I'm going to my folks's house."

Alice Baker shot the boy a very annoyed glance.

"No, I meant are you driving?" Jeremy said with a raised eyebrow.

"Huh? Yeah. I live downstate."

"Hmm. Well, be careful. Thank you very much for your help."

Alice and John looked at him warily for a moment, as if they thought perhaps this abrupt dismissal was suspect. Alice then opened the door in front of which they'd been standing as John went down the hall to his own room. As Alice closed the door, Jeremy caught the glint of the lights from a small tabletop Christmas tree.

The detectives went to the end of the hall where an exit

sign was posted. They opened the door beneath it and found an enclosed emergency staircase that led down to a loading dock discreetly hidden at the back of the building.

"You were awfully interested in how they were getting home," Detective White said.

"Yes. I wanted to know whether or not either of them had a car. And if they knew where Neil lived."

"Why?"

Jeremy sighed. "Because Neil Carter's body had to get out to his neighborhood somehow."

Detective White was surprised by this. "Why would they kill him? Isn't it just as likely that he was killed where he was?"

"In a stranger's house across the street from where he was staying?"

"I know, it doesn't make any sense. But neither does the idea that those two kids killed him and put him in the Swensons' house."

"I know," said Jeremy. "None of it makes any sense."

EMILY STOPPED and folded her hands in her lap.

"Well, go on," Lynn prompted.

Emily looked over at her with a twinkle in her eye. "But I can't, you see. I don't know the end of the story."

"You don't?" Lynn exclaimed with dismay.

"That was the state of things as Jeremy described them to me last night when he stopped by to tell me he might be late tonight."

"He told you all of that?" Lynn asked with a skeptical smile.

Emily's cheeks turned a delicate pink. "Well, I may have added a little detail. After all, the story's in the telling. The facts remain as facts."

"But...but you said you told him something—that you hoped you hadn't steered him wrong. What could you have made out of such little information?"

Emily sighed and looked at the fire, which was still burning brightly. "I told him to look for someone from a very small town. And one other thing…"

"What?"

Emily turned to her. "Pears."

"Pears!" Lynn laughed with disbelief.

Before Emily could explain, they heard someone come up the stairs and onto the front porch.

"That will be Jeremy," Emily said, her face brightening affectionately.

They heard him stamp his feet several times, presumably to remove some snow, as Lynn went to get the door. She found Ransom standing on the welcome mat brushing the frosting of snow from his hair and the shoulders of his overcoat. He had a shopping bag in his right hand.

"We thought you might not make it," said Lynn.

"*We* did?" he replied with a coy smile.

"Well, I did. Emily was sure you'd come."

She took his coat and hung it on a peg on the rack by the door. He proffered the shopping bag. "These are for under the tree."

"Okay," she said, taking it from him and leading him into the living room.

Emily quickly looked him over once they'd said their hellos. "You must be frozen! Sit by the fire and let us get you some tea."

"Oh, no, you don't!" Lynn said as she placed the last of the packages from his bag under the tree. "He doesn't get any comfort until he tells us the end of the story!"

"What story?" asked Ransom, taking a seat beside Emily.

"About Neil Carter. Emily was telling me about it. What finally happened?"

"Oh, that." He turned to Emily. "You were right, of course. We went back to the university's Halls of Residence first thing. We stopped by the manager's office and asked Ms. Dougherty where John Cameron was from. We already knew Alice Baker was from Cincinnati, and I doubted if she'd lie about something so easy to check. As it turned out, Cameron is from Smithville, a very small town in downstate Illinois."

"Yes," said Emily, "when he said he was from downstate, I thought he might be the one. And is this his first time in Chicago?"

Ransom nodded. "It's his first time outside of Smithville."

"You two want to fill me in on it?" said Lynn.

"Certainly," said Ransom. "We went up to Alice's room and knocked on the door. She didn't look pleased to see us, to say the least. In fact, she looked frightened. I asked her if we could come in, and she hesitated for quite a while before deciding to admit us. I believe she thought it would look worse if she didn't. The first thing I did was glance over her Christmas tree. You were right about that, too."

"About what?" Lynn asked.

Ransom turned to her. "She had several pieces of glass fruit on her tree, all coated with this stuff that's supposed to make them look glazed, or covered with dew, or whatever. Anyway, there were a couple of pears."

Lynn looked at Emily. "You said those were important. Why?"

"The piece of glass that was found in Neil Carter's hand. When Jeremy described the color—yellow-green—and the coating, I thought that's what it might be. And so often people will have more than one of the same ornament on their tree, especially when it's something like fruit."

Ransom continued. "Also, on the tree skirt there were some tiny bits of a broken ornament. Small, but large enough to tell it was from the same type that was in the boy's hand. I pointed out to Ms. Baker that it looked like she'd broken one of her ornaments.

"She folded her arms across her chest and asked me what it was all about.

"I had already decided to take a chance. I told her that we knew her friend John Cameron was the one who disposed of Neil Carter's body, but we wanted to know which of them killed him.

"Her face went deadly white, and she wanted to know what we were talking about. What made us think John did that.

"I told her it was because he put the body in the wrong

house. Neil's body wasn't found in the home of his aunt and uncle, it was found in the house across the street.

"Ms. Baker's face quickly went from white to bright red. 'That idiot!' she exclaimed without thinking. Of course, after that the whole thing was up.''

"What?" said Lynn, her mouth hanging open. "What happened?"

"It was as we thought, Emily. She simply couldn't pull off anything sophisticated. Once she realized she'd been tripped up, the whole story came out of her." Ransom paused and smiled. "Gerald was right about Christmas being a time for surprises. He thought that Neil had told his parents he wasn't coming home until Christmas Day because he'd planned to surprise them by arriving early. But the surprise was really for his girlfriend. At least, that much I think we can surmise. He'd planned to surprise her and spend those two days alone with her. Unfortunately, the surprise was on him. He walked in to find her—'' he glanced at Emily ''—in flagrante delicto with John Cameron.''

"Oh, dear," Emily said primly.

"Remember, Neil didn't live at the dorm, so he didn't have any idea she was fooling around. According to Alice, Neil was 'like a wild man' when he saw them, and he attacked Cameron. In the ensuing struggle, Neil was thrown back against a sharp corner on her dresser and died.''

"And as he fell," Emily offered, "he grabbed at the tree and caught the ornament.''

"Exactly."

"Then it was self-defense," said Lynn.

Ransom sighed. "Perhaps. But he must've been pushed with a lot of force to hit his head hard enough to kill him. Now, Alice and Cameron are really only kids. They panicked, and decided that the best thing to do was put Neil's body in his own house and let him be found there. You remember I said that the way he was found he looked almost as if he'd surprised a burglar and been killed? That's exactly how they thought it would look. The dorm was practically deserted, so it wasn't very hard to sneak him down the back staircase and put him in the trunk of Cameron's car at the loading dock.''

"But didn't they realize how strange it would look for the body to be found at his aunt and uncle's house if he was supposed to have left town?" asked Lynn.

Ransom shook his head. "You have to remember, Neil didn't have time to tell them why he was there. He just walked in and the fight began. They assumed that since he was still in town, that meant he was still staying with his aunt and uncle."

"I see," said Lynn. "But wait a minute! How did the body end up in the wrong house?"

Emily smiled. "That's where the business of being from a small town comes in. You probably wouldn't know this, since you're from Chicago, but not all places have their buildings numbered the way we do, odds on one side of the street, evens on the other. In some small towns, the buildings are numbered consecutively, up one side of the street and down the other."

"The Swensons' house didn't have a number on it, and the ones painted on the curb were covered with snow," Ransom reminded her.

Emily clucked her tongue. "So foolish. It can make a house very hard to identify in an emergency."

"Well, I don't think many people anticipate an emergency quite like this one," Ransom said wryly. "Anyway, the house to the left, 2019, had lighted numbers on it. Alice had told Cameron that Neil lived at 2020 Fairdale. Since he was new to the city and was in a panic, he thought that that was *next door* to 2019, rather than across the street."

Emily nodded. "Which is how the poor Swensons ended up finding a stranger's body beneath their tree."

"Oh, my God!" said Lynn. "What an awful way to begin the holiday!"

"Yes," Ransom agreed. Then he added with a sly smile at Emily, "And hardly an appropriate story to be telling on Christmas Eve."

Lynn laughed. "Emily was just trying to distract my mind."

Ransom raised an eyebrow. "Did it work?"

"Of course it did. Just like all of Emily's plans!"

The lady in question sat with her hands folded delicately in her lap. Her eyes glimmered at her two friends. "Now, how about some tea?"

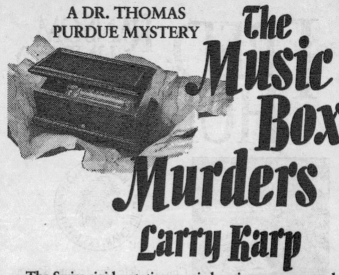
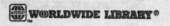

Riding in her husband's Piper Arrow, Grace Beckmann and her family make a refueling stop at a small, isolated airstrip. When they find James Delacroix, whom they had met on the outward bound journey, sprawled across his new Cadillac with a bullet hole through the heart, the Beckmanns know they are looking at murder.

Putting her sleuthing skills to work, Grace discovers that any number of people could have wanted Delacroix dead. Soon Grace uncovers some bizarre coincidences, uncanny associations, shocking revelations and lost treasure—which add up to secrets that a ruthless killer intends to make sure Grace Beckmann takes to her grave.

DEATH
FLIES ON
FINAL

A GRACE BECKMANN MYSTERY

*Available November 2000
at your favorite retail outlet.*

JACKIE LEWIN

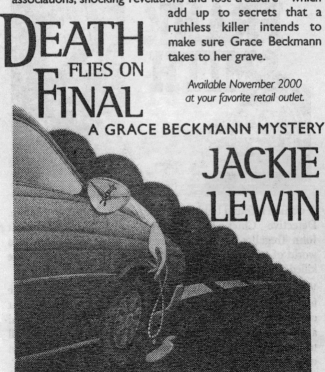

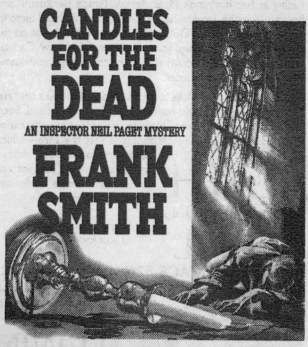

CANDLES FOR THE DEAD

AN INSPECTOR NEIL PAGET MYSTERY

FRANK SMITH

A woman is found bludgeoned to death in St. Justin's Church. Detective Chief Inspector Neil Paget and Sergeant John Tregalles probe Beth Smallwood's life and discover a world of tragedy, violence and ugly secrets. Who could have killed her in such a brutal fashion?

Was it the son she was ready to turn over to the police? The fellow employee who'd lost his promotion to Beth? Paget cleverly uncovers the missing pieces as he confronts the third anniversary of his wife's death and the demons that still torment him. With Tregalles by his side, the duo close in on an unexpected killer.

Available October 2000 at your favorite retail outlet.

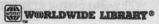

A NEW YORK TIMES NOTABLE BOOK

LAURA VAN WORMER
EXPOSÉ

Sally Harrington abandoned the rush of working for an L.A. magazine to return home to Connecticut to work on the local paper. But when a chance encounter leads to a high-profile assignment, Sally's life is about to change again.

But not the way she thought.... Her plum assignment isn't what it seems, one of the men in her life just might have a secret agenda and her father's accidental death might have been murder....

"A master at romantic suspense."
—*New York Times Book Review*

On sale November 2000 wherever paperbacks are sold!

MIRA®

NORDIC NIGHTS

AN ALIX THORSSEN MYSTERY

Lise McClendon

The wealthy resort town of Jackson Hole, Wyoming, is knee-deep in ice and snow, but winter is a thriving season for gallery owner Alix Thorssen. Glasius Dokken's talent as an artist makes him a Swedish national treasure, and thanks to Alix, he's brought his Viking murals for the annual Nordic Nights Festival. Unfortunately, murder steals the show.

When the artist is found dead, Alix's own stepfather, Hank, is jailed as the prime suspect. Soon, Alix is unraveling a complex web of greed, deception and misplaced loyalty in the frigid, icy landscapes, which are at once surreal and deadly.

Available October 2000
at your favorite retail outlet.

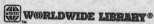

WORLDWIDE LIBRARY®

WLM364